# Mu On Tiki Island

## A Detective Bill Riggins

## Noir Paranormal Mystery

## In The Florida Keys

## by Christopher "Tiki Chris" Pinto

(author of Murder Behind The Closet Door)

---

THIRD PRINTING, MARCH, 2015

---

# STARDUST MYSTERIES PUBLISHING

Fort Lauderdale, Florida

www.StarDustMysteries.com

©2012 Christopher Pinto

All Rights Reserved

# A SPECIAL THANKS...

To **Marina the Fire Eating Mermaid**
for making a splash on the cover!
(Find her flipping around Fort Lauderdale at the Wreck
Bar, or online at www.MeduSirena.com)

To **Tracey Kurilla of Fort Lauderdale**
for that fantabulous shot of the
stormy sky on the cover.

To **Bob Ho of Tiki Hana** for the
Tiki on the spine (find him at www.TikiHana.com)

To **Everett Peacock** and **Will Viharo** for their
help; two excellent writers who deserve a lot more
attention (*look 'em up, Google those guys, too much to
list here!*)

To **Mickey Spillane** for creating Mike Hammer;

And to my old friends Mr. Walker, Mr. Daniels,
and my new pal Sailor Jerry.
(They are to blame for any typos)

I thank you all, and sincerely
hope you enjoy reading this as much
as I enjoyed writing it.

www.StarDustMysteries.com

# THIS BOOK

is dedicated to:

My Mother, who taught me how to write;

My Father, who taught me how to be creative;

To my wife Colleen, always helpful & beautiful too;

To Molly, who was my muse (and appears as a ghost);

To all the Tiki lovers of the world –

This is for you;

To all the Mid-Century

Pop Culture lovers and Rat Packers of the world –

It's for you too;

And to the people who lost their lives

in the Great Atlantic Hurricane.

*You can never be forgotten.*

TIKI ISLAND

# This book is a work of noir-style fiction.

If I did it right, you should feel like you're digging a tome from somewhere in the late 1940s to late '50s. The tone, style and feel of the story and writing should swing you back in time to the days before home computers and iPhones, back when Chevy sold more cars than anyone on the planet and everything was shaped like a jet plane, spaceship, flying saucer or boomerang...When dames were dames and a quarter could get you a ham sandwich and a coffee from a guy who knew your name, and Tiki Bars were the place to go to get away from it all. So here's a few suggestions to help get you in that retro, kool, jazzy mid-century mood...

## COCKtaiLS tO SIP:

Recipes for these traditional South Florida/Tiki Bar drinks can be found at www.TikiLoungeTalk.com...just click on the Tiki Drinks page.

The (original) Mai Tai
Zombie
Cuba Libre
Mojito
Navy Grog
Molokai Mike
Banana Banshee
Melinda Lindy
Suffering Bastard
Singapore Sling
Dolce de Leche
Tahitian Rum Punch
Scorpion Bowl

## MUSIC tO REaD BY:

Here's a list of era-appropriate, Tiki Bar-approved albums to play on the hi-fi while digging this volume of lore:

Martin Denny - Exotica, Quiet Village
Arthur Lyman - Taboo, The Legend of Pele
Les Baxter - Space Escapade, Ritual of the Savage
Frank Sinatra - In the Wee Small Hours, Come Fly With Me
Henry Mancini - The Peter Gunn Soundtrack
Elvis Presley - Blue Hawaii Soundtrack
Miles Davis - Birth of the Cool...

And pretty much anything else by these swingin' cats, as long as the tracks were laid down before December 31, 1959. Dig? Groovy. Hit it.

*Bitter brine upon our tongues, the brackish water fills our lungs.*
*With darkened woes our life lines slip, our bodies bare, our organs rip.*
*And while we die, the others live. Our fate to those we soon shall give.*
*Wrought with the storm, your last night's breath,*
*We carry you now to your wretched death.*

*— Unknown*

# FORWARD

One of the worst storms to ever make landfall on the eastern seaboard of the United States smashed into the upper Florida Keys on Monday, September 2nd, 1935. Dubbed "The Labor Day" Hurricane, this category-five beast bored down on the marshy islands with two hundred mile-per-hour winds and a fury unmatched in modern history. At noon, when it was evident the storm would cause deadly destruction, a call for an evacuation train was dispatched from Miami. But due to the poor weather, poor communications and poor planning by city officials, the train didn't make it to Islamorada until well after 8:00 p.m. – at the absolute height of the storm.

When the evacuation train backed into Islamorada, the hurricane was in full force. Winds blew cars off the roads and were strong enough to spear signposts

through the trunks of palm trees. Immense waves crashed against the islands, flooding the causeway, crushing houses and stripping trees. Giant stretches of land were ripped away in minutes. At 8:30 p.m., while the rescue train attempted to save hundreds of WPA workers trapped on Matecumbe Key, a storm surge – a black, deadly wall of water over twenty feet high - raced across the causeway with the force of millions of tons of deadly pressure and toppled the rescue train, drowning the helpless victims trapped inside the railcars or carrying them out into the open sea. When the skies cleared and the waves subsided, no less than four hundred souls were dead or lost. By most accounts, over eight hundred people lost their lives in what was soon to be called "The Storm of the Century."

In the days following the tragedy, bloated corpses washed up on beaches by the dozen; islands and sandbars as far north as Florida City and as far south as Key West were littered with bodies and debris. In the intense sub-tropical heat of the late Florida summer bodies became completely unrecognizable, bloating with gases and bursting in the hot sun. The horrible sight of decay and abominable stench became so unbearable the government ordered the corpses cremated immediately before proper identification could be made.

Racing against the intense Florida heat, volunteers worked hard to collect the corpses, inter them in pine boxes, and cremate them for mass burial. Within a few days over three hundred bodies had been burned and the ashes buried in a mass grave on Islamorada; others were buried on the beaches or islands where they were found. Countless more simply washed out to sea, consumed by sharks and crabs, never to be seen again.

The destruction caused by the Storm of the Century included almost every building from Key Largo to Bahia Honda. The sea wall washed out entire sections of train tracks and bridgework of the Florida East Coast Overseas Railway, the main link from the mainland to Key West. FEC, which was already in financial distress due to the Great Depression, agreed to sell the crippled railway to the United States Government, and through Roosevelt's Work Progress Administration the Overseas Railway was rebuilt as the Overseas Highway, a two-lane modern roadway for automobile traffic built on the trestles of the existing railroad bridges and paved over the rail bed's causeways. It opened in 1938, and with it came a new kind of tourism. – Motoring. Along with it motor inns, gas stations, roadside diners and juice stands grew prosperous, born from the wreckage of the storm. By the 1950s the Keys had become a favorite spot for tourists traveling down the east coast from New York, Philadelphia and Washington, D.C.

Driving down US 1 all the way from Manhattan, a guy with a fast car and enough clams for gas and grub could make it down to the southern-most point of the 48 States in about three days. Once there, fresh air and sunshine could do wonders for a city boy sick of the grime, sick of the crime, sick of the politics and junkies and all the trash in between. Take a few days, they told me; take two weeks if you need it, kid. And you *do* need it. That last job I pulled really put the heat on me, even though the Captain was the one who told me to do it. Sure, he *told* me, under wraps of course with plenty of plausible deniability. And I sure as hell wasn't going to rat him out to the top brass, so a little two-week paid vacation in the land of palm trees and sunshine was all right by me. Little did I know that Florida sunshine would make me a chump, twice. First, with a crime. Second, with a dame, of course. Two dames, actually. Looking back, I wish I'd never laid eyes on either of those dames, or Key West, or that crazy little Island my buddy (ex-bud, that is, but that's another story) turned me on to, back in late October of 1956.

# CHAPTER ONE

Late October, 1956

Damned dreary. Typical for this time of year, I guess. These were my thoughts as I stepped out into the cold October morning, the gray clouds bunched up tight over my head, keeping the sun from making its half-baked attempt at burning through. It was damp too, that kind of bone-chilling dampness that you don't expect until late November but sneaks up on you like a snake before the kiddies have a chance to pick out a Halloween costume. It seemed like just yesterday it was a nice, crisp Jersey fall, with rainless skies and a temperate breeze that made you feel alive. But that was gone now, too soon; Old Man Winter came home from vacation early this year and blew his icy breath across the City before the trees had a chance to finish changing colors.

It was days like this I wished I'd stayed at my apartment in the city, where I could catch a cab out my front door and spend a limited amount of time outside. But sometimes sentimentality got the best of me, and I just felt like I needed to spend some time in the house I grew up in. With my parents both gone I hardly stayed there anymore. I guess this week things were worse than usual, and I just needed to get out of the city for a night.

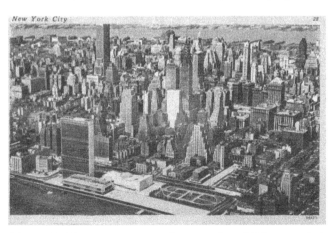

I walked fast down the two blocks to the ferry, my trench coat's collar flipped up, my gray fedora pulled down tight, my hands stuffed in my pockets. Always cautious, I made sure my right hand slipped through the custom-sewn hole in my coat pocket and rested on the butt of my snub-nosed .38, the Detective Special I kept on my belt. I got caught with my pants down once before. Never again.

I made it down to the docks in plenty of time to catch the boat. As I walked up to the gate, the wind whipped up off the Hudson and froze me further than it already had.

"Mornin' Officer Riggins," said the kid taking tokens. He was way too happy for a day like this.

"Hello Darrin."

"Beautiful day, ya?" he said with annoying cheer. I swear I would have belted him, if he didn't tower over me like a building.

"You're crazy, kid. It's cold enough to freeze the balls of a brass monkey." Wacky kid wasn't even wearing an overcoat, just his uniform.

"Ah, well for me this is just right. I was born and raised over in Norway, ya know. This is like summer for me."

"That's nice Darrin," I said glumly, and flipped him the token. "You can have it. In fact, you can take my share of the cold too."

Darrin smiled and gave a little laugh. "You betcha, sure Officer. Have a happy day, ok?"

"Ya," I said and got on the boat.

Inside the cabin the temperature was a good thirty degrees warmer than outside. At first it hit me like a furnace, but once I got a cup of hot joe and newspaper from the vendor, I realized it was just right to keep my coat and hat on. I sat on a bench between a laborer and an old woman, and started to read the rag.

Fires. Murders. A suicide, two armed robberies and a mugging. Two car accidents on Broadway. Politicians battling it out for next month's election. Our Mayor, who was doing a decent job, had run his two terms and was on his way out. He endorsed the democrat, a young guy named Tolaski who was American born of Polish immigrants. He was determined to clean up the slums, get people back to work. His plan was to broaden social programs and create more government jobs, getting some money into the hands of the poor. His opponent, a 53-year-old die-hard republican named Burke was on the warpath to eliminate crime from the city by giving the police more power and money, and by helping small and large businesses to grow, thus creating jobs and cleaning up the slums. They were both full of malarkey and I knew it as fact. Tolaski had a back-end agenda: He hated the cops, distrusted them. His plan was to expose abusive techniques used to fight crime – basically giving the criminals more rights, and taking away our power to protect. Sure, we went a little far sometimes, but the days of rubber hoses and beatings with chains were gone with Prohibition. That was the stuff my old man did on the force. These days we used more...subtle...techniques.

Burke, on the other hand, while big on supporting the cops, was as corrupt a man as they come. My old man knew; he knew him personally when he had to deal with him ten years back. At the age of seventeen, Burke's son came home from the Big War minus an arm, and used his other arm to get shot up with opium to escape the realities of his screwed up life. My old man nabbed him, and tried to get him to come clean on who his supplier was. He threw him in the clink, and not an hour later he got a visit from Burke.

"Lay off my son," he said, "Or I can make things very difficult for you. I have a lot of pull in high places, cop."

"I can't do that, I don't care who you are. Your kid is a junkie."

"I can have your badge in fifteen minutes, you hard-headed moron. Don't believe me, try me."

My old man had his morals but he was no fool. He had a family to feed, and the only thing he knew was how to be was a cop. It made him sick, but he had to play along.

"I don't have to do a damned thing you say, Burke. But I can't disobey a direct order from a superior. Talk to your people in high places. The order will come down to me and I'll have to lay off. No problems. But I'll tell you this: If I don't help your kid, you better, or he'll be dead from that garbage in a year."

Burke nodded to my old man, a gesture of superiority and thanks rolled up in one, and left. An hour later he got the call; he was off the case and was to leave the Burke kid alone. That was the end of it for him. Six months later Burke's kid came out of a rehabilitation hospital clean, and took up a job as vice president in Daddy's construction company. At least one good thing came out of it, my old man always said.

Now Burke was making a bid for Mayor. That meant only one thing. He had a scheme, and I didn't like the idea of that, not one bit.

At eight-thirty a.m. the ferry left the Weehawken dock and started making its way across the water to the Big Apple. And here I was, my mind wandering all over the place from the weather to politics to my old man. Where the hell was my concentration? I had more important things to turn over in my head than events long over. Then I realized I hadn't had a cigarette yet. That's what I needed, a stick to help me get my thoughts organized, to focus on what I needed to get done today. I slipped the deck of Camels out of my pocket and shook one out. The guy next to me took a quick look over, the lady on the other side stared straight ahead. I offered a smoke to the guy. He accepted. To the lady I said, "Would you like a cigarette, m'am?"

"Oh, my no, I don't smoke."

"Mind if I do?" She looked at me sort of surprised, sort of like I was crazy.

"No young man, not at all. Thank you for asking." She went back to staring. I guess politeness was getting so rare these days people were shocked when they saw it.

I shook a butt out of the pack and lit it with my Zippo. The first drag went down smooth, and already I could feel my cold, cloudy head clearing up. Between the coffee and the cigarette, I was awake and alert. In fifteen minutes I'd be in Manhattan, sitting in the back of a Checker with a cabbie named Fast Freddie. In a half hour, I'd be sitting at my desk in the Vice Squad office of Precinct #10.

I stepped off the boat and onto the cement dock. The wind gave me a left hook that nearly took my fedora with it, but I managed to grab it just in time. At the end of the block sat the row of cabs, some old enough to have shuttled around Hoover, a few new and sparkling yellow. At the end sat a brand new custom job, a '56 Checker Marathon painted jet black with red wheels, white checks and a black oilcloth interior. Hand painted on the back fender was a red-headed pinup sitting on a tire, with the lettering *"Fast Freddie"* in pink underneath. The engine came to life as I climbed in the back seat.

"Nice weather we're having, huh Riggins?" Fast Freddie said from the drivers seat.

"When did you become a comedian?"

"When the wind blew my brassier off." She turned around and looked at me with her baby blues, her hair redder than that of the pin-up painting. "Usual place?"

"Where else?"

She gave me a wink and pulled out into traffic.

"What's the word on the street, Freddie?" I said, lighting up another Camel.

"Nothing going down since dark. Couple'a cats on the East side tried to get a date with me, but I turned them down."

"Whatdya' do that for?"

"I told 'em I was waitin' for you," she laughed.

I laughed too. "Keep waiting doll, you're too nice a chick to get mixed up with a mug like me. Anything new from the boys in blue?"

"Yeah, one bit…they got a lead on that pusher you've been tailing. Might be able to pick him up today. You ready for a long one?"

I sighed, heavy. "I guess I'd better be." I wasn't.

Fast Freddie pulled the cab up in front of the station at four minutes to nine. I gave her a wink and a smile and jumped out. No need to pay or tip; I paid her a flat fee once a week and she took me wherever I needed to go. No point in driving a car in the city was my motto; it would take me an extra forty-five minutes to drive in every day, and the gas, tolls and parking came out to a ten spot a month more than I was paying Freddie. No thanks, kids.

The precinct looked down harshly on me as I began jumping the steps. In the gray morning the gray building looked even grayer than usual, almost ghostly. The wind gusted and I shuddered. I felt it in my bones…this was going to be a bad day.

Once at my desk my spirits were lifted, at least a little. Four of the guys had already gotten in and were either typing away on the Smith-Coronas or jabbering on the horn. Coffee was already made, and someone brought in a box of sweet rolls. I settled into my desk, one of those sturdy hardwood types with a nice new ink blotter and a green metal lamp, courtesy of the taxpayers. It was situated about halfway back in a room of twelve desks, all vice detectives. At the far end behind frosted glass sat the Captain's office, nicotine-stained blinds drawn. Hats and overcoats hung from the coat trees at each end of the room. All the office needed was a fresh coat of paint to hide the years of nicotine and grime and it wouldn't be half bad, I thought. Funny that I should be so cheerful all of a sudden, knowing damned well the minute they brought in the pusher it was going to be all down hill on a handcart.

Like they read my mind, two uniforms busted in through the office doors with a rather annoyed man handcuffed behind his back. He was rattling off something about a phone call and a lawyer and police brutality when they shoved him into the chair next to my desk.

"Mornin' boys, I see you brought me a present."

"Good morning, Detective," answered the older cop with a gruff voice. "Yeah, Christmas is come early for ya this year. You take him from here?"

"I got him," I said, and thanked the officers. They left without another word. The guy in the chair started rapping again, and when he didn't stop talking after I asked him nicely, I pulled the billy club out of my desk and smacked it on the edge of his chair, making him jump like a scared kid.

"Cut the comedy, yo yo. You'll get your phone call soon enough." Finally, he was quiet. I took a form out of my desk drawer and fed it through the typewriter.

"Name?"

"Screw you copper."

"Name?"

"Up yours."

"Now look, we both know your name isn't Up, is it Mr. Yours?"

"Now who's the comedian?" he replied with an oily sneer. He was right, enough playing.

"Listen, Johnny," I said to him, and he seemed surprised I knew his name. "Johnny, there's two things that can happen here today. You can play nice, answer my questions, and eventually leave here with all your teeth still in your mouth. Or, you can be a smart ass, and leave here with your teeth in your pocket. Really, makes no difference to me, but it would be faster if you just answer the questions."

"You know my name, why you askin' me?"

"Protocall. Now, Name?"

"Johnny Princeton."

"Good. Address?" I asked as I banged out his name on the keys.

"Four-thirteen West Eighty-third."

"Supplier?"

"Hey, wait a minute," he said, annoyed, "What is this? You can't ask me questions like that! I want my phone call! Who's in charge here?"

Almost as he said it, Captain Waters appeared behind me.

"I am punk. What's your beef?"

"I want my phone call, flatfoot," said the man in the steel cufflinks.

The Captain made no change of expression, except for the most minute twitch in his left eye. "Detective Riggins, why don't you show the gentleman to the interrogation area, then please see me before proceeding." With that, Captain Waters gracefully walked back to his office and shut the door.

"Interrogation room? What about my phone call?" Princeton whined.

"Phones are down. We forgot to pay the bill. Let's go."

I yanked him up by the arm and took him through the back door, down the stairs to Interrogation Room B, the one where the walls were so thick, you couldn't hear a thing coming from inside. I locked him in and made my way back to the Captain's office. I had a sick feeling I knew what he was going to say. At the same time, a little bit of a thrill ran through me. Maybe I was the sick one.

"You've been tailing Princeton for six months. Got anything on him worth our time?" the Captain asked as I entered the office. His overheads were out; the only light came from a dim desk lamp with a brown-stained shade.

"I know he's supplying half the Village with H. Sells reefer to high school kids. At least one junkie died from his stuff."

"Which one?"

It was hard for me to say it. "Toots Freeman. The horn player." It hurt to say because he was a damned good bugle boy, dead at twenty-three with a needle in his arm.

"Got anything that can stick?"

"Not really. Witnesses won't talk. They're too scared. Uniforms caught him making a drop this morning. We can get him on possession, but not much else."

"So why all the bother?" The Captain asked. He already knew the answer; he just wanted to hear it come from my jaw.

"He's not as small potatoes as he would lead us to believe. He's got connections – big connections. If we get him to talk, we can go after the big guys." You know, the usual.

"He won't talk. He's smart enough to know you can't pin anything on him. There's only one way to get a little prick like that to squeal."

"I thought you'd say that, Captain. He's already in B."

"Take LaRue with you. And try to keep him quiet."

I nodded and turned to leave.

"Oh, and Riggins?"

"Yes sir?"

"Don't go too far this time. Got it?"

"How far should I go, Captain?"

"Keep him alive."

"Got it."

Ten minutes later my hands were starting to ache from bashing Princeton's face in with my fists. LaRue played the good cop well; he gave Princeton ice for his face, water and a towel. Then I'd smack the water out of his hands, wrap the towel around his neck and pull it until he almost choked out. I didn't particularly like this detail; in fact I'd only had to do it twice before, once on a juiced-up punk that was going around carving up old ladies with a switchblade, the other time on a middle-aged man who had a thing for thirteen- year old girls, even if they didn't have a thing for him. This time was a little different; Princeton hadn't *directly* hurt anyone. Then I thought about high school kids getting their hands on reefer before they were old enough to make an intelligent choice about it, getting strung along for a good time, until a couple of years later when he'd turn them on to opium, or hash, or heroin. Then I thought about the last couple of weeks, a rough couple of weeks, with three junkies dead, two OD'd and one who jumped off his roof thinking he could fly. My right fist smashed his nose dead-on; blood gushed from the broken mass and he cried.

"Tell us who your supplier is, or so help me God I'll take your head off!" I screamed at him through his sobs.

"I can't, I ca…can't, they'll kill me."

"*I'll* kill you if you don't talk soon."

"You…you *can't* kill me, you're the *cops*, man! You ain't supposed to…" Before he could finish I grabbed the billy off the floor, and swung it hard, aiming right for his face. He screamed; LaRue jumped to his feet ready to stop me, knowing the blow could crush his facial bones and pierce his brain. But I had no intention of killing Princeton. I stopped just short of his face.

"Don't tempt me, punk. I've done it before. I'll lay you out and put a blade in your hand, make it look like the uniforms missed it when they frisked ya. Don't believe me?" I raised the club.

"I believe you!" He screamed, and blood shot out of his mouth.

LaRue stepped in. "Johnny, just tell us who your man is. If you want, we can set you up somewhere where no one will find you. We can help you get a job, live a respectable life. Get away from all this junk. Just give us the name."

"Copper," he said, weeping, "I believe *him* more that he'll kill me than I believe you'll give me a new name and a job. So can it, ok? The guy's name is DeFalco. Lenny DeFalco. He works for the…"

"We know who he works for," came a voice from behind. Funny thing, when you're in the moment, when your adrenaline is pumping and you're focused on one goal, it's hard to hear a door open. I turned around and saw Captain Waters, a very sad look on his face, standing next to none other than Mayoral candidate Tolaski. Oh, guess I forgot to mention it…he was an Assistant District Attorney.

Damn.

An hour later I was sitting in the Captain's office, alone, listening to some non-descript big band blaring out the Jersey Bounce way too fast and way too loud. Generally the Captain didn't like anyone touching his radio, but the soup I was in now was so thick and so hot I honestly believe I could have jumped up and down on the damned thing and not made things any worse. I smoked as I sat, the minutes ticking by; when I smoked through a half a deck of Camels, the Captain walked in and shut the door.

"Well, fine pickle we're in this morning," was all he said as he sat in his over-stuffed red leather chair, the kind of chair reserved for Captains and Mayors and guys like that. "Fine pickle."

"What's this 'we' stuff?" I said somewhat belligerently. I didn't care much for niceties at the moment. He knew and I knew the score – the D.A. saw *me* beat the guy to a pulp. Not the Captain. All Waters had to say was the obvious: he didn't condone brutality, and had no idea I was going to turn the creep into a punching bag.

"What I mean, Detective," he said rather snottily, "Is that the D.A. is pissed to boiling. He's on a rampage against our use of force. The dumbass believes he can fight crime in this city by turning the cops into a bunch of well-wishing choir boys, and he could very easily use this little incident as an example."

"No shit," was all I said, not regretting the curse.

"No, none at all." The Captain paused; he was deep in thought now, a million miles away, his eyes fixed on a point in space far behind me. I lit another Camel and sat back.

"Detective," he started, slowly, "You've been on the force for, in one capacity or another, more than ten years. Your father was a damned good cop for almost thirty. You're one of the youngest men to make Detective in the history of New York, and your record, though flawed, speaks for itself." He paused, I waited. "What you did to Princeton may not have been official police business, but I gave the order. I'm a part of this as much as you are, and I won't let a good man like you get pummeled by that arrogant Tolaski so he can get votes. If you go down, I'm coming with you."

That took me by surprise. I knew the Captain was a man of honor, of his word, even if he too were flawed, but I never expected him to stand on principal to the point of his own ruin. I wasn't sure what to say. I thought about it, carefully.

"Captain, how much trouble can Tolaski make for us? I mean, really, what can he do? Charges? Dismissal? Smear story in the paper?"

"He can do all of that. But he won't. I've cut a deal."

A deal? I thought. What was going on here…since when did Captain Waters start dealing with politicians?

"I don't understand, Captain," was all I managed to say.

"It's a new world, Will," he answered; he always called me 'Will' when he was deadly serious. He'd called me Will when I was a kid, before I started going by Riggins. He called me Will when he told me my old man had been killed by a junkie. "It's a new world, with new rules. Men like Tolaski are using tactics in place of brute force. He'll turn this little incident into a crusade to get votes, to give him more power so he can enact his own form of corruption. He'll funnel money earmarked for fighting crime into welfare and urban renewal projects…of which he'll get some hefty kickbacks, on the taxpayer's nickel. But the wonderful thing about this new world, my boy, is that anyone can play." An evil, scary grin stretched across his aged face, giving him the countenance of some demonic cartoon. I didn't recognize him at all in that instance. And I was sure as hell glad he was on my side. Then it clicked.

"You have something on him, don't you. You have dirt on the D.A." I said, soft and cool.

"Not something. Many things. He's a dirty man, Will, like all the rest of the politicians. For starters, he has a mistress in the Village. He's got ties to union bosses, many of them with connections to the mob, of course. And he's got a secret little corporation, under an alias, that supplies office paper to three of the top construction companies in the city. Funny, how a ream of typewriter paper can cost $450, isn't it?"

"The kickbacks," I said, not surprised one bit.

"That's right. The kickbacks." The Captain got up from his chair, walked across the room and poured himself a coffee from his private pot. He took a long sip, then poured a second cup and returned to his desk. Without a word he produced a bottle of Dewar's White Label from his desk, poured a shot into each of the cups, and handed one to me.

Normally I wouldn't use Dewar's for anything except to strip the varnish off my wood floors, but at the moment I didn't really care if he were handing me Sterno with an olive. "Thanks, I could certainly use it right now."

"It's not to calm you down, kiddo, it's a celebratory drink. To the system," he said, raising his cup, "May it always work to our advantage." We clinked and drank. He let out a heavy sigh, and spoke again, a little more quickly this time. "Tolaski will keep his mouth shut. None of this will ever be brought up again. In return, we promise to *minimize* our use of force, except in extreme circumstances. To placate his mainly false sense of morality, he insisted you get at least a suspension without pay. It was at that point I mentioned the name of his mistress in the Village, and the final outcome was that you get to take a two-week vacation, paid, in order to help relieve the stress of working so hard for so long. Acceptable?"

Acceptable? It was freaking fantastic.

"What about the case? What about Princeton?"

"Don't worry about Princeton. He talked. We'll follow up the leads. By the time you get back, we should be ready to move, with you back at the helm."

"What about Princeton's safety? LaRue promised him we'd protect him."

"Do you *want* him to have protection?" Funny thing was, I did. I had always believed that people could change, if they really wanted to. If they weren't too far gone.

"He at least deserves a shot at a new life. We owe him that much, I think."

The Captain looked at me strangely, as if he never considered me to have any compassion for the dregs. "I'll make the arrangements. But he gets one chance only."

"That's all he deserves, that's all he gets. Now what about LaRue?"

"I was wondering when you would ask. He's in the clear. He'll be taking over the investigation in your absence."

"Good," I said, "I feel better already."

For once I wasn't being sarcastic.

An official memo went out to the boys who needed to know: I was taking a two week vacation, effective tomorrow, a little R&R to alleviate the stress this case had brought down on me (citing how close it was to the case that inevitably killed my old man.) The boys in Vice shook my hand, wished me well and told me to hurry up and get back so we could kick some keesters; LaRue went over the case files with me and told me not to worry, he'd have everything nice and neat for me when I got back. A swell bunch, those guys. Not one of them offered to take me out for a drink.

I called Fast Freddie and told her to meet me in front of the station at two-thirty. No point in sitting around here all day, I figured. The black cab pulled up in front of me at 2:29:50 on the dot.

"You're early," I said as I climbed in the back.

"By what, ten seconds?" she shot back. The chick was uncanny. "What's the score, Riggins? You never need to hitch in the middle of the bright. You always use a squad car to do your daytime snooping. So what gives?"

"I got into a little trouble, nothing big, but I get to take a two-week vacation courtesy of the state, starting now."

She turned around, a look of surprise and worry on her face. Damn, what a beautiful face. Shame it was always pointing away from me. "You got sent up? Suspended?"

"Not exactly," I said. She didn't need to know the details. "Two weeks with pay, officially a vacation to relieve stress." Dirty thoughts of Freddie relieving some stress entered my mind, and I shook them off quick. She didn't say anything, kept looking at me, wanting more info. I had to give her something, so I said, "Crooked politician caught me putting the chops to a pusher, and tried to make a big deal out of it. Captain Waters saved my ass. Now I get to take it easy for a while. No big deal, really. Everything is cool as a cucumber."

"I'm hip," she said back, turned around and pulled the Checker out into traffic, the custom Continental engine and twin pipes roaring like a hot rod. "So since you're on leave, how about some tunes?" Before I could answer she had the radio turned up, with Chuck Berry rockin' it up through the dashboard speaker.

"Don't you even want to know where I'm heading?" I said above the twang of the guitar.

"Jerry's Bar and Grill, and I'm buying," she said, and hit the gas harder. That was all right with me.

We sat at the bar at Jerry's, far from the TV so we didn't have to hear the noise. Jerry, the owner/bartender, had been a pretty good friend of mine now for about two years, ever since I moved into the building across from the bar. And I don't just mean bartender-customer buddies; we went to ball games together, hung out watching the tube and even went on a couple of double dates. I still had to pay for my drinks though, so having Freddie pay the tab (and therefore getting back some of my hard-earned money I forked over to her every week) sounded like a nice way to start my vacation.

"Hey Riggins, hello Freddie," he said with his typical half smile, half tough-guy look. "The usuals?"

"Too early for the hard stuff, Jerry," Freddie said, "Just a beer for me. In a glass, if you don't mind."

"I don't. How about you, Riggins? Hair of the dog?"

"Yeah, set me up with my buddy Jack and a beer chaser. I'm on vacation."

"Vacation?" he asked fast, as if I'd never taken one before. Well, come to think of it, it had been a while.

"Yep, two weeks with nothing to do but enjoy the good life."

"Some guys have all the luck," he said, and poured the drinks. We toasted, we drank. Fast Freddie told me about some of the mods she made to the cab, including cop tires and a beefed up suspension. Jerry talked about football like he always did. I didn't say much. The events of the day were swirling around in my head like water in a drain. Images of Princeton's pale white face marked with purple bruises popped up. Snapshots of the Captain's evil grin bearing down on me replaced them. The Captain backed me up, the vacation was official, and I knew what the cap knew about Tolaski so I was safe, but somehow I couldn't shake the feeling I was being set up for a fall.

"Crazy," I said out loud.

Freddie and Jerry stared at me; apparently they were in the middle of a conversation of which I had heard none.

"It's only crazy if you believe all the hype," Jerry said. Good, a nice generic statement to weasel out with.

"I suppose you're right," I returned.

"Of course I'm right! Just think of the kids," he continued. More generic I-don't-know-what. I nodded and finished off my second Jack. Slowly, with the help of the alcohol, I let the images in my mind wander off and got back into the conversation. A few more customers came in, calling away Jerry's attention, leaving Freddie and me alone to talk. She started.

"So what's your plan? Are you hanging around the burg or taking off?"

"No idea, I hadn't even thought of it yet. I guess I'll just hang around and see what turns up."

"You're nuts. I've known you for three years, and you've never taken a real vacation. Why not live it up a little? Go to the mountains or something."

"The mountains are colder than here."

"Then go to Florida, the weather's perfect down there this time of year. I know, I used to go all the time, at least twice a year."

"What stopped you?"

"Ha, well a bad breakup, that's what. It's no fun for a chick like me to go down there alone. A young looker like you on the other hand, you'd have a ball, Riggins. Plenty of sun, plenty of booze and plenty of dames looking to have some fun before heading back to Smalltown, Idaho." She finished her beer and looked at me for a response. The two double Jack Daniels I had must have been clouding my mind, for suddenly a trip to the tropics sounded kinda kool. I'd never been to Florida, never even seen a palm tree in person, except for the ones at the Tiki Bar at the Plaza. And I did like the Tiki Bar down at the Plaza, so what the hell?

"Maybe I will, doll. Maybe I will. You gonna drive me?"

"Can't, Riggins. Girl's gotta make a living, and you can't afford to pay me for two weeks straight."

"Good point." Jerry walked back up just then, and threw in his two cents.

"Did I hear you kids rapping about Florida?"

"Yeah," I said, "Thinking about it."

"If you want to go to the Keys, I can give you the hook up," he said, with a bigger smile than usual. "My brother runs a little resort down there. A little private island off of Key West. Neat place, the whole joint is made up to look like a Hawaiian village. I'll bet you dimes to donuts he can get you a room for free, if he's not booked up."

"Free? Free is great. That clinches it, if you can get me the free room, I'm all in." It *had* to have been the booze doing the talking for me now. Had to be.

Fast Freddie stood up and said, "Well there you go, Riggins! What could be better than a mostly free vacation? You deserve it. You've been working your tail off without a break." She leaned over and gave me a big hug and a kiss on the cheek, and said more quietly, "Have a great time down there, hun. Really live it up. I'll be here when you get back, with the engine warmed up." Damn, that chick was already warming up my engine. Again, the booze talking. "Later Jerry," she said, and slid out the front door.

Jerry watched her wiggle as she left; even after the door shut he stared in her direction, as if he were imagining her still there. After a few seconds he shook it off and started wiping down the bar.

"Man, that chick is a real looker," he said, not looking at me. "So, are you two an item or what?"

"Huh? *Her?* Hell no, we're just friends."

"Really, just friends, not like, eh 'bosom buddies' or something like that," he said, smiling again. "I mean, I see you two hangin' around togedder for years, right?"

"Ha, yeah, sure. I wish. But no, nothing like that."

"But you want her, don't you."

"Who wouldn't, she's as hot as hell. But no, no dice in that game."

"So you're sure, 'cuz I was kinda thinking of asking her out, you know, if you two don't have anything in the works or nothin'."

At that I had to laugh, not that I didn't think Jerry could land a dame as smokin' as Freddie, but because I knew the score.

"Whatya laughin' at, wise ass?"

"Nothing, Jerry, it's not you…it's just that you're barking up the wrong tree."

"You don't think I'd have a shot at her?"

Nope. Not in a million years.

"Sorry Jerry. I'm going to have to say no, I don't."

"Why not? You think she's out of my class?"

Still laughing I said, "No Jerry. Because her cab's an automatic."

"Huh? I don't follow you."

"I mean you don't have a shot because Freddie doesn't drive stick, are you hip?"

The smile left Jerry's face and was replaced by a twisted sort of scowl.

"That's a damned shame for the male sex," he said, "a damned, rotten shame."

Jerry called his brother down in the Keys and made all the arrangements for my stay. It was Friday, and the joint was booked up through Monday, so I got me a room starting Monday night with an open-ended stay. I thanked Jerry and headed back out into the cold, across the street to my building.

The wind bit me hard as I crossed over, turning my face into an ice cube. A thousand pin-pricks of cold pain stabbed at my cheeks and nose, and as I opened the front door to my apartment building, I realized I was absolutely thrilled that in a couple of days I'd be in the land of palm trees and sunshine. And warm weather.

The elevator ride up to the twelfth floor seemed to take longer than usual. I couldn't wait to get home, to pack, to call for train tickets; it seemed all of a sudden this vacation seemed real, and it seemed like a hell of a good idea to go. I was actually looking *forward* to this time off, and couldn't wait to get started.

When I got inside my apartment, the first thing I did was go to the closet to grab a suitcase. It was then I realized just how long it'd been since I took a vacation.

"I ain't got a suitcase," I said out loud. "Ain't that somthin'."

A few minutes later I was back out in the cold, walking down to the Bank. I withdrew three hundred clams for the trip, and made my way down to the Five and Ten on the corner. There I picked up a nice new suitcase, plus a matching hanging suit bag and a tin of Oreos to take on the ride down. I thought a minute, and decided to grab a pair of boat shoes, swimming trunks and a new pair of sunglasses. Man, was I a tourist or what?

I threw all the junk in the big suitcase and headed home. It was only a block, but that bitter, early winter cold made if feel like a mile. Sure, I knew the temperature would go back into the forties and fifties by next week, but at *twenty-eight* degrees today, all I could think of was sipping a Mai Tai under that palm tree.

I was back home by four-thirty. I tossed Miles Davis' Birth of the Cool on the hi-fi and started making calls. The first call was to Union Station, to get a train ticket to Key West. Then I'd call Shirley, the girl who cleaned the apartment once a week to let her know I was taking off. Next I'd call Fast Freddie and let her know what time to get me for the train. Last, I'd call Jerry, and thank him one last time for the room. All set.

The first call was a disaster.

"Sorry sir, but we don't have a train that goes to Key West."

"What are you talking about? What about the Overseas Railway? I swear I remember hearing about it when I was a kid."

"Yes sir, sorry to say the Overseas Railway was destroyed in a storm, back in 1935."

"1935*?*" How could I have missed that?

"Yes sir. It's the Overseas Highway now; you can take a train to Miami, rent a car and drive down to the Keys, or fly."

"Well, OK, I guess. How long is the train ride?"

"About thirty hours, sir, from here to the last stop in Florida."

"Ok, and how much is it?"

"Eleven-fifty sir, one way."

I made the reservation to pick up the ticket Saturday morning, then got the operator back on the phone. A few clicks and whirs later I was connected to Miami Beach information in Florida. After just a few minutes I was able to get the number of a dealership that rented cars, and ordered a convertible to meet me at the Miami station Sunday evening. The train wouldn't pull into Miami until after five on Sunday, and it was a four to five hour drive to Key West, so I called and made a reservation for Sunday night at the new Fontainebleau in Miami Beach. Sure it was pricey, but I was staying at an island resort for free. What the hell, I could splurge a little.

I phoned Freddie and told her to pick me up at eight-thirty a.m. She said no sweat, and as she hung up I heard a couple of girls giggling in the background.

Damn, was I jealous.

It was still early, only a little after six when the phone calls and preparations were done. I was all packed, ready to go. I was getting hungry and realized if I had anything in the fridge, it would have to go. There wasn't much – some bacon, a few eggs, pint of milk, and a couple of apples. I decided to finish off the eggs and bacon in the morning, ate an apple, and took the other one with me when I walked back over to Jerry's.

The north wind came ripping around the block on two wheels, screeching like a banshee. I swear it almost took my head off.

"Frigggggin' freezin' out there!" I said to Jerry as I came busting through the door. The bar was in full swing now, the dinner crowd filling seats and booths, the two waitresses that worked the night shift slipping easily between tables carrying giant trays of drinks and chow. I pulled up to the bar at my usual spot, blowing warm air on my hands.

"I didn't think I'd see you for two weeks," said Jerry, already pouring the double Bourbon.

"I got hungry," I said back, "And since I'm on vacation, how about one of your famous plank steaks, medium rare with a side of fries."

"You're the boss, Riggins. I'll pick out a good one for you myself."

For some reason, and I still don't know why, that was one of the best steaks I ever downed in my life. Maybe it was because I really, really was on vacation. Maybe it was the addition of about six ounces of whisky that accompanied it. Maybe it was that the prettier of the two waitresses, Diane, brought it to me with a wink. Whatever it was, that steak made me feel like a million bucks. By this time tomorrow I'd be on my way to Miami. By this time Monday, I'd be in paradise.

"You digging the steak, Riggins?" Jerry asked.

"It's tops, Jerry, one of the best I ever had."

"Secret recipe. We started putting a little steak sauce on them while cooking. Ya know, to cover up the taste of the cheap meat."

Yeah, well ok, maybe that was all it was after all.

At eight o'clock the little jazz quartet started playing in the far corner. When I started coming to Jerry's three years ago, they played standards, usually with an easy, swingy style. Now they were into the Modern Jazz movement, *progressive* jazz, playing more sophisticated numbers; occasionally they'd even throw in some bop or Latin styles, at least until Jerry would give them the fisheye. Then they'd count off something smooth and mid-tempo like 'As Time Goes By' or 'Once in a While' with a West Coast feel. They were a bunch of krazy beatnik jazzers, but they needed the bread and knew how to please the guy who was signing the paychecks.

Tonight they added a fifth element to the quartet, a vibraphone which gave the little combo a kool depth. The bells blended in nicely with the piano, base, drums and saxophone that made the core of the group. They started off with a medium-tempo version of At Last, with the vibes and piano taking the lead and the saxman falling back. The sax came in on the bridge, really decorating the melody. The guy's fingers moved so fast you couldn't see them. If a butterfly made music, that's what it would have sounded like.

I was enjoying the riffs so intently that I didn't even hear Jerry call my name.

"Riggins, Riggins!"

"Huh? What?"

"Phone."

"Phone? Who is it?"

"Guy named LaRue."

This can't be good, I thought. "Can I take it in your office? It's work."

"Sure," he said, pushed a button on the phone and hung up the receiver. "Line two."

"Thanks." I slid off the bar stool, steadied myself against the Jack, and eased my way back to the office. "LaRue? It's Riggins."

"Sorry to bother you on your vacation, Riggins, but we have a problem." My heart sank. Everything was set to go on my trip. A call from the squad could only mean something was about to screw it up. "Let me have it."

"Almost the minute we released Princeton to the hospital, someone tried to ice him."

"Damn. Did he make it?"

"He got lucky. The bullet brushed by his leg. No lasting damage. Riggins, I think he's really had enough. He kept yammering about living in the country, working as a carpenter, building things. I think he really can go legit."

"Everyone deserves one chance," I said, meaning it.

"That is, if he lasts long enough to get out of the city. We need to keep him here for a few days, a week maybe. Someplace safe. Any ideas?"

I don't know what came over me. Maybe it was guilt for rearranging the guy's face just to get a name that might not amount to anything anyway. Maybe it was the booze. The booze was doing a lot of my talking lately, and I didn't like it. Whatever the cause, I said, "You can stash him at my place. I'm leaving tomorrow in the A.M."

"That's perfect. I'll bring him by in about an hour."

"What? No, not tonight! Bring him around tomorrow."

"Where's he supposed to stay tonight?"

"You and your wife have an extra room, ain't ya?"

"Cut the comedy, Riggins, Eileen would never let a pusher stay in our house overnight."

"Then lock him up. He can't stay here tonight, sorry kid. Bring him around tomorrow. There's an extra key in my desk drawer. And if anything's missing when I get back, you're paying for it." I hung up before he got a chance to answer. I was already on my vacation, and nothing was going to interrupt it. No police work for two weeks, period. Captain's orders.

I walked back out to the lounge and re-established myself at the bar. The combo was swinging Shiny Stockings, and Jerry had another double Bourbon on deck.

"Everything kosher?" he asked, lighting my smoke.

"It will be tomorrow," I said, and sat back to enjoy the show.

At around midnight the band took a break and the sax player took a stool next to mine.

"Eve'nin Riggins," he said in his low, gravely voice. "Diggin' the riffs? Or just shootin' the breeze?"

"Hey Rillo," I said offering a smoke. He took it. Rillo was what the downtowners called a 'high yellow'…a light skinned black man with blondish hair. Call him that to his face and he had a nice eight inch Stiletto blade that he'd show you up close and personal. He wasn't a big guy, thin and only about five foot seven, but you didn't want to get on his bad side. A cool cat, Rillo was, as long as you didn't cross him or insult his music.

"Yeah I came in to get some chow and take in the tunes. Sounding tops tonight kid, I'm diggin' the bells player."

"He's a ringer, a classical cat from the N-Y Phillo. Thought a Vibraphone would make a nice edition to the gig. He needed to stretch his legs a little, wanted in for a few ticks. Cat ain't bust, he can swing."

"I'm hip. Drink?"

"Sure man," he said, then turned to Jerry and said, "Razorback, black on a sling, light, uptight and outta site" then lit his stick with a high-flame Zippo.

Now I can usually talk jive with the best of these guys, but they were coming up with new stuff so fast it was hard to keep up. I was still stuck on saying things like "all reet" from my younger days. This time I was stumped.

"Razorback, black on a sling?"

"Yeah man, you don't dig?"

"Not without a shovel. Give."

"Man, you the detective. You can't figure that fine piece of hip prose out?"

I thought a minute. It didn't come to me. "I've been liquored up since five o'clock. Just lay it on me."

Rillo laughed and took a drag. He blew the smoke out slow. It seemed to disappear, blend in with his brown tweed suit and nicotine-yellowed tie. "Razorback…sharp, right? Sharp like a knife. Or a saw. A saw that cuts. Or like a shark that bites."

It hit me. This guy was a little crazy, but there was a certain logic to his prose. "Cut..shark…Cutty Sark."

"Bones," he said. Bones meant 'right'. He continued, "black, bleak, bland."

"Plain, neat," I said.

"Bones again, baby. Now, on a sling…"

"Wait," I said, "I got it. On a sling, light, uptight and outta sight…you want it in a tall, highball glass. A single shot, not a double, and you want the bartender to give you the second shot when no one's looking because if the bandleader catches you getting too drunk, you're in the can. Am I green?"

"Give that man a cigar," he smiled, and drank down the tall glass with the single shot of Cutty Sark that magically appeared on the bar in front of him.

"Man, you've got a word or phrase for everything, don't you."

"Dig it," he said, meaning yes. Then he asked again, "So you diggin' the tones tonight? Cuz we're throwing around the deal of letting the bells man slip in."

"You cats were really smokin'," I said, and for some reason a vision of some cartoon cats smoking cigarettes came into my head. "Got a real West Coast vibe going, adds some ice to the set. I'd go with it."

"Cool," he said, and downed his second, sneakily-poured Scotch. He tipped his imaginary hat and went back to the bandstand. A real cool customer, that Rillo. He left a pack of matches on the bar; written inside was the name & address of a small-time pusher I'd been looking for. Shame I was on vacation; it wasn't easy to get jazz musicians to squeal on drug dealers. Plus it cost me two shots of booze. I put it in my pocket anyway. I could always follow up when I got back.

A half-hour later I stumbled back across the frozen tundra to my apartment, barely able to keep my lids from slamming shut. That's just the way I wanted it too. I had a good seven hours of sleep ahead of me, enough to get me revved up for the trip. I put the chain on the door, turned out the lights, and fell into bed.

At two-thirty my head started pounding, over and over again. It wouldn't stop. I put the pillow over my ears but no dice, the hard pounding kept up. Soon it was accompanied by the muffled sound of my name in the dark. As the deep alcohol sleep slipped away, I realized the pounding was a knock on the door.

I got up, said a nasty word and made my way to the living room. The pounding continued.

"Knock it the hell off or I'll shoot you through the door," I yelled at the top of my lungs.

The muffled voice came back, "Riggins, it's LaRue. More trouble."

Dammit.

I opened the door and found LaRue standing there holding up Princeton. He'd been worked over, again.

"What the hell happened now?"

"This happened to him in the clink. We've got a bad cop on the payroll."

"Son of a bitch," I said quietly and helped him into the apartment. I snapped on the table lamp, and we settled Princeton down onto the couch. "Any idea who?"

"Yeah, we know exactly who. Now this guy's *really* important. I couldn't chance taking him to my home."

"You know if anyone followed you"

"Ninety-nine percent sure only the two uniforms that came with me. I hand picked them, I know they're trustworthy."

"You better hope so. I was dead asleep, you know. I gotta get up early to catch a train."

"You were dead asleep. He was almost dead."

Princeton was half unconscious when we laid him on the sofa. He woke up for minute and saw me through his swollen eyes, and started screaming.

"No, no, calm down, I'm not going to hurt you, ya fat head. That's finished, we're going to protect you now, we're going to help." I know he didn't believe me but he at least stopped yelling. His eyes were filled with terror. I actually felt sorry for him. Then I thought of the kids on reefer. His reefer. I didn't feel sorry any more, but I still felt pity.

"You, you son of a whore, you busted me up pretty good, now you say you're going to *protect* me? Up yours!" he said through swelled lips, shaking, wincing, fearful that my fist would come crashing down on his face again. He wasn't being arrogant this time, he was being honest. He honestly thought I was going to *kill* him.

I thought about those kids, and that horn player. Believe me, I thought about it.

"Johnny," LaRue said in a soft voice, "Detective Riggins was following orders. He has nothing against you personally. Our orders have changed. We're to make sure you stay alive now, unharmed. So far we've screwed up, but Riggins is willing to let you stay here until we can get you a new identity, and find you a place in another state where you can start over." Princeton seemed to be buying LaRue's spiel.

"Why him, why here?" he asked, still terrified.

"The safest place I could think of was here. You weren't safe in the jail, so this is it. There are two uniformed officers outside – one at the door, one downstairs in the lobby. Riggins and I will both stay here with you tonight. If anyone tries to get to you, they're dead. Ok?"

"I guess it'll gotta be. Just make sure this big ape doesn't take out his grudges on me again, ok?"

"I'm not gonna touch you, dummy," I said. "I'm on vacation."

I woke up before the alarm went off at seven, coaxed out of sleep by the sound and smell of bacon frying in a pan. My first thought was to grab the .45 off the nightstand and let loose, but as I reached for it I remembered that LaRue and that crumb-bum Princeton were shacking up in my living room.

"That's my bacon, ya jerk," I said to Princeton through bleary eyes and a foggy brain.

"No kidding, I'm making it for you. Sort of a thank you for letting me land here last night. And for not icing me."

"I don't buy it. You put rat poison in it or something."

"Nope, just bacon and eggs. See?" He proved his point by breaking off a piece of bacon and eating it. "All swell."

"Is there coffee?" I groaned.

"In the pot."

"Where's LaRue?" I asked, looking around.

"I killed him in his sleep," Princeton said, mockingly. Then real fast he said, "He's in the can." Good thing he said it fast.

"You look like hell," I said, "There's a steak in the icebox. It's a cheap one so thaw it out and put it on your eyeball, it'll help the swelling."

"The cop giveth the black eye, the cop taketh away. Why you being nice to me now, Riggins? Because I squealed? Because I exposed a dirty cop?"

"No Princeton. To me you're still a piece of garbage who pushes dope on kids. But if I'm gonna keep my sanity, I gotta believe people can change. Maybe even you. You get one chance. If you make it, good for you. If you go back to being a degenerate drug pusher…well, let's just say the next time I see you I won't use my fists." The smile left his face and even through the swelling and bruises I could see he was serious.

"I want out, Riggins. Seriously, I ain't kidding. I want to change things up. So help me God, I'm sick of the rackets. I ain't gettin' nowhere fast. You know what happens to young guys like me? They turn into old guys like me, and then dead guys like me. I started pushing to get a little cash flow going. Put some lettuce in my pocket. I promised myself I'd stay away from kids, ya know, keep it among the junkies, I mean, who cares about those freaks, right? Then I wanted more. Rocks on my fingers. A big, fancy Cadillac car. Broads. The best of everything. So I started pushing harder. I turned my head when peddlers would turn around and sell sticks to kids, broads, anybody. I started pushing H. Opium. Anything I could get my hands on to get more respect, more luxury. Well, I didn't get it. Sure, I got money, but I can't flash my cash because the minute I do the cops will know a punk like me had to be doing something bad, right? I know how you found me," he said, cracking the eggs into the bacon grease.

"You do? Lay it on me."

"It was the car. That big red convertible of mine drew way too much attention. You or one of your boys got wise that I had a car I shouldn't have been able to afford, and that was the end of that. Am I right?"

"You are," I said. It was, in fact, that '55 Caddy ragtop that originally got my attention.

"Bingo. Well, I'm done with it. I've got a few bucks, and I want out. I like building things. Maybe furniture. Or maybe houses, I dunno. I know I ain't too sharp in the brains department but I think I can handle a saw."

"Believe it or not kid, I think you can do it. I think if you really want to you can. That's the only reason I'm letting you stay here, in my own joint. Just don't let me find anything missing - "

He cut me off, raising his hand in a pretty gutsy way for a guy who just got the juice beat out of him. "I'm not a thief. A pusher, yea. A pimp, sometimes. A scumbag, probably. I ran numbers when I was a kid and delivered a few packages, but I never, never steal. That's not my gig."

"I didn't ask for a confession."

"It's a matter of pride. I don't take what ain't mine."

I could have gone a few rounds with Princeton on why that statement was a load of horse manure, but LaRue came out of the john just then, poking his head into the kitchen.

"What's going on?"

"The kid's making me breakfast."

"Is there rat poison or something in it?"

I was showered, shaved and in my nice suit when the clock turned eight twenty-eight. I knew Fast Freddie would be waiting, so I said my goodbyes, threw on my hat and coat, grabbed my bag and headed out. The fact that by tomorrow night I could go two weeks without the coat made me smile.

Fast Freddie lived up to her name, weaving through mid-town rush hour traffic like a bee through a daisy patch. She made it to the station about ten minutes before the train was scheduled to leave.

"Have a great time down there, Riggins. When you get to Key West, make sure you hit Sloppy Joe's."

"What the hell is Sloppy Joe's?"

"Whatdya think it is? It's a bar, goofy!"

"Of course," I said, and slid out of the cab.

The interstate train was nice. I didn't have a cabin, just a reclining chair in the observation car. I figured I'd spend most of my time in the lounge car anyway, and didn't want to waste the extra three clams for a room. The iron horse pulled out on time at eight fifty-five, and I was on my way.

Most of the ride proved uneventful. I did some reading (since I was going to Key West, I figured I'd bring Hemmingway's The Old Man and the Sea along), had a nice fried chicken lunch in the dining car, had an interesting conversation with a traveling salesman who was going to meet with a big client in Miami to seal the deal on two-thousand pillow cases, and spent a good amount of time just staring out the window, watching the eastern states fly by, thinking about work, and trying *not* to think about work.

At five I made my way back to the dining car and ordered the Yankee Pot Roast. It wasn't as good as the chicken lunch, but it was still good. Afterwards I retired to the lounge car. At the far end a squeeze-box artist was quietly playing Peg O' My Heart. I picked out a nice padded seat and settled in with a Jack and ginger.

Seven drinks later, the clock hit ten after ten. The alcohol now made the music sound weird and the broad next to me seem interesting. She'd been sitting next to me forever, yammering on about her sister in Palm Beach, as if I cared. She couldn't be a day under forty, and I wondered why I hadn't the luck to get stuck next to the pretty brunette sitting across from me, or the two blonde model types that were chatting it up at the bar. Lucky me. The good thing was, by the time they brought me my eighth drink, I no longer cared about the broad, her sister, Princeton, or anything else for that matter.

Then I heard something a little odd, and had to ask the question. I slurred, but tried my best to sound coherent. "Excuse me m'am, but did I hear you correctly?" I said through a cloud of smoke.

"Yes, I'm sure you did," she said, "I've got a cabin. If you'd like to stay there…with me…tonight."

"M'am, surely I'm misinterpreting your meaning," I said shakily, not sounding anywhere near as polite or intelligent as I thought I would, "I mean no disrespect, but I am, in ff…in fact, twenty-eight years old," I continued, hoping she'd get the point and leave. Older dames were always putting the moves on me. I was only twenty-eight, but I looked and acted a lot older, so I've been told.

"How old do you think I am?" she asked, kindly, not as though she were hurt.

"I couldn't say, m'am, but I am qu—quite sure you are considerably older than me. Uh, than I."

She blew the cloud of smoke away and moved a little closer. "Are you sure about that?"

Apparently, either I was much drunker than I'd first thought, or somewhere down the line the older woman got up and the brunette took her place. "Really, I'm only twenty-four."

See, now that clinched it; twenty-four year-old dolls didn't go around hitting hard on drunk guys on trains. I must have been hallucinating. Then she said, "Do you have cash?" and all at once I knew the score.

It never occurred to me a prostitute could work a train. Then, through the alcohol haze it hit me…the two model types at the bar were now separated and talking with men. The brunette was talking me up even though I was clearly drunk as a skunk. At the far end of the car near the squeeze-box player was another blonde, talking to a man twice her age. How long had this racket been going on, I wondered? Who was behind it? Was it the rail company, providing a customer service? Or did an industrious pimp figure out a way to make a few easy bucks where the cops would never think to look? All I knew was, I was three sheets to the wind, disgusted, off-duty and ready for sleep.

"You…you're a *prostitute?*" I finally said, perhaps a little more loudly than I meant to.

"Shhh, yes, of course, what did you think? Do you have the cash or not?" she asked impatiently. Call me old fashioned, but it sickened me to see these girls make a living this way. High-class call girls or lowbrow streetwalkers, made no difference to me. A hooker's a hooker. It wasn't so much the moral thing, as it was how the girls were taken advantage of. Most of them were in it because they were at the end of their luck or strung out and needed the money for dope. The pimps made all the dough while they did all the work, and when they got too old or too worn out they were tossed out on the streets to die. But I wasn't in any mood or any position to throw the book at these kids tonight.

"Listen sister, it's your lucky night," I said, rising. I fell against the train's window and steadied myself, ready to leave.

"So you've got the cash?"

"Nope."

"Then how is it my lucky night?"

I looked at her and smiled. "Because I'm on vacation."

I woke up around nine the next morning, splayed out in my reclining seat with no idea how I got there. I sort of remembered something about hookers in the lounge car, but wasn't sure if it was real or just a dream. I instinctively went for my wallet – it was untouched. Then I double-checked the .32 caliber Berretta I had stashed in the ankle holster – safe and sound. Maybe it was a dream. I'd check it out again, in two weeks.

The train had made great time in twenty-four hours. Now looking out the window I could see rows of palm plants, giant green fans with spiky centers, plus large, plush bushes with oversized leaves that looked like green plates. An occasional palm tree would stick out, and at crossings the countryside was flat, vast, and distinctly southern. At around eleven a.m. we began passing orange groves, and I knew we had entered the great state of Florida.

A breakfast buffet was being served in the dining car, and I spent the next two hours chowing down and reading, until finally I took up a spot in the observation car on the east side of the train, enjoying the countryside and occasional stretch of beach. The train made short stops in Daytona Beach, Palm Beach, and Fort Lauderdale. Finally at around six p.m. Sunday evening, we pulled into the station at Miami Beach.

The weather was warm with a nice breeze. I grabbed my bags and headed down the platform, my winter coat zipped up in the suit bag. Right at the curb sat a beautiful, brand new bright blue 1957 Chevrolet Bel Air convertible, top down and ready to go. A young man in a uniform leaned up against the side; when I walked up he came to attention.

"Mr. Reegins?" he asked with a thick Spanish accent.

"That's me."

"Your car," he said, rolling his 'R's, and opened the driver's door. "Please, let me take your bags. I put them in dee trunk, perhaps with your hat too, no?"

"Si," I said, and he smiled. I got directions to the hotel, and a few minutes later I was roaring down Collins Avenue, heading to the Fontainebleau.

The hotel was pure class all the way. Marble, brass, palm plants, the whole Florida works. A string quartet played classical tunes in the lobby. To the left, the lobby bar featured a small jazz combo with a sultry female singer. I valeted the car and had a bell hop bring my bags to the room; it was on the fifth floor and had a great view of the beach. I tipped the hop a buck and he lit up.

"Anything you need sir, just call the front desk and ask for Andy. Seriously, anything."

"Anything?" I asked, the suspicious cop part of me awakening.

"Sure, anything. Special cigars, show tickets, champagne, you name it, call and ask for me. I'll get it from the concierge and bring it up personally."

Ok, that wasn't *anything*. The kid seemed all right.

"I'll do that," I said, and he left smiling.

I stood out on the veranda in the seventy-four degree evening. A cool tropical breeze came up from the beach and brought the slightest hint of suntan oil with it. It was amazing, I thought, that a few hundred miles could mean the difference between icy cold gloom and sunny paradise. Almost made me want to give up my life in the city, get a job down here as a P.I. or something. Maybe join the Miami vice squad or something crazy like that. Eat coconuts and drink Mai Tais all day. Something like that. Then reality snapped back in, and I sat down at the phone to make a few calls.

First I called my apartment. LaRue answered on the third ring.

"Everything kosher?"

"Yeah, all's quiet on the western front. Where are you?"

"Miami. Fontainebleau."

"Well ain't we fancy-assed."

"I rented a big blue convertible too, a V8."

"Maybe I oughta beat the tar out of some kid, get me a nice vacation."

"You should try it," I said. In the background I heard a faint voice say, "Not me!"

"Everything's money here, Riggins. Don't worry a bit."

"I'm not. Just checking one last time before I become unreachable. There's no phone service on the island I'm staying at. Only radio," I lied.

"No sweat. You have a good time. Ciao."

"Later kid." He hung up, and so did I. Next I called Fast Freddie, but didn't get an answer. I called Jerry, but he was in the thick of a Sunday night crowd and couldn't talk. No worries, I'd get Fast Freddie later and make sure she had a plan to check on my house in Weehawken a couple of times a week.

Since I was only in town for a night, I didn't bother to unpack. What I wanted was to see the town, maybe take a walk on the beach, possibly take in a floorshow somewhere. I made my way down to the lobby, and into the men's store where I picked up an uncharacteristic floral shirt, a nice Hawaiian job with sailboats and tropical flowers on a black background. I also splurged on a really nice Panama hat. Hey, when in Rome…

They let me change into the shirt there and had my old shirt laundered and sent up to the room. Class joint, I thought. I wandered out into the warm evening as it was just getting dark, and found my way down to A-1-A. The beach was pretty, small waves hit the shore and sparkled in the waning light. Jazz and Rock 'n' Roll seeped out of nightclub doorways, South American and Cuban music could be heard in the distance. I heard the distinctive sound of a big band bellowing out of one of the large hotels, and found that Harry James' orchestra was playing. I slipped in and had a seat at the bar and enjoyed the music.

The house drink was a Cuba Libre, and again I figured when in Rome… I liked the taste of the dark rum they used, and thought to myself hey, maybe I should add a fifth of this stuff to the home bar. After the second drink, I was convinced.

James was soaring away with Cirribiribean when I spotted a very pretty chick sitting alone at the other end of the bar. I figured what the hell, and sat down beside her.

"Big Harry James fan?" I asked casually. She looked at me, knowing where this was going.

"Yes, matter of fact I follow him all over the country."

"No kidding," I said. This was good, I wanted to see where it led.

"Nope, every show, every state."

"You must really dig the trumpet," I said, leading her on.

"Not really. I'm more of a saxophone kind of gal," she said, holding up her left hand and pointing to her wedding ring.

"I'm hip," I said. "Tell your husband I love his work." She smiled, and I went back to my original perch. Just my luck, again.

Andy was at my room's door bright and early at nine a.m., just like I asked. He brought the bags down and had the valet bring the car around at nine-thirty, just as I was finishing up the Continental Breakfast. I tipped him three bills and thought he'd have a heart attack. Apparently tipping in Florida was really, really rare, and really, really appreciated.

The morning was bright as hell, cloudless and already in the seventies. I stowed the Panama under the seat so it wouldn't blow away, rolled down the four windows and hit the electric switch to let down the top. It was weird; I'd never ridden in a convertible with an electric top before. It was like the roof was being peeled off by a giant can opener.

A minute later I was motorvating down US Highway Number One with a full tank of gas and smile on my face.

## Late August, 1935

Over one hundred guests had been invited to the island for the Great Party of Labor Day Weekend. By Friday the caterers had been hired, the tents set up, the bars fully stocked; hundreds of pounds of cubed ice had been brought in and stored in anticipation of three days of drinking and carousing on Eliot & Vivian Hawthorn's private island. But the plans were as useless as the booze without bodies to drink it. A storm was ripping towards the upper keys, gaining strength as it twisted its way through the Atlantic.

It was already being called "The Storm of the Century", with ships reporting gusts in excess of one hundred and fifty miles per hour. No one was sure yet where it would make landfall, but most experts agreed it would slam into the Florida Keys sometime in the next seventy-two hours. Whether it would hit Key West and spare the island or miss the lower Keys completely and hit the middle and upper keys head-on remained to be seen, but the guests weren't taking any chances. Most hadn't bothered to come to the island, fearing they would be stranded as the only means off would be by boat. The few who showed up early left by Friday evening, planning to head to the mainland for safety, far north of the Keys. Only Eliot and Vivian stayed, along with Eliot's close friend Gregor; he had a forty-foot boat with plenty of space to store valuables, and agreed to help Hawthorn pack and remove family photos, heirlooms, clothes and art in anticipation of the island's probable flooding.

Hoping for the best, Eliot Hawthorn insisted on staying on-island until the authorities were absolutely certain of the storm's progress. To be safe, he booked passage for three on the Monday morning train from Matecumbe Key, the fastest and most practical means to get to Homestead and their mainland home in Miami Beach. Leaving too early would leave the island wide open for thieves to rummage the house. Leaving too late, however, could mean death for him, his wife and his best friend. But he was in charge, he always was and always would be; his friend and wife looked to him for leadership as they always had, not because he was a great leader but because he signed the checks. Eliot had been born rich, had made it through the Great Depression getting even richer, and made lots of friends by spreading his green around. He knew it, knew that was how he was able to land such a beautiful, well-bred yet impoverished wife, knew how he was able to keep friends like Gregor who counted on him for loans when times were tough. He was a somewhat shy and quiet man, Eliot Hawthorn, but he let his money do the talking and that helped him get people around him. And he needed people around him for some oddball reason, because loneliness for Hawthorn was a fate worse than hell...or death by storm.

Saturday came and went; the skies were mostly clear but now darkness could be seen on the eastern horizon. The wind picked up slightly and the waves of the Gulf began to pitch a little more sharply than usual. Being on the Gulf side of the Keys and buffered by the larger Keys to the east, Eliot hoped beyond reason that the storm would not affect his private little island too badly. But he knew this was a bum hope. If the storm hit the middle Keys with one hundred and fifty mile an hour blasts, it was a sure bet there wouldn't be anything left of his mansion...or the island itself, possibly…when it was all over.

Other than a quick stop in a little town called Florida City (the last town before getting on the Overseas Highway) to top off the gas and use the facilities, I was able to make great time on a straight run all the way down to the end of the world. I must admit, it was a little spooky traversing those narrow, two-lane bridges, especially the one dubbed "The Seven Mile Bridge" that seemed to just go on and on over the water with no end in sight. But it was a pleasant drive, with the beautiful, clear-blue Gulf of Mexico on the right and the majestic Atlantic Ocean on the left. Little roadside stands advertising fresh catch of the day, coconuts and oranges dotted the highway. A few signs for resort hotels peaked out from the foliage, and when I got near Key West I was greeted by a string of signs welcoming tourists to the Southernmost Point of the United States. Once I crossed the last bridge onto the Key, just for fun I drove all the way down to the end of US 1 to Mile Marker 0.

"So this is the end of the U.S.A.," I said to the beachhead. "Hmmph. Smaller than I imagined."

Following the directions Jerry gave me, I motored the Chevy to a marina on the Gulf side of the island. I parked the car and followed the ramp to a little shack with sponges, cork and fishnets hanging off of it like cobwebs. Inside, an old man in shorts and a polo shirt looked up.

"My name is Riggins. Pal named Jerry should have called ahead for a boat to..uh.." I looked at the name of the resort for the first time. *Tiki Island?* " I said to myself, then to him, "Yeah, Tiki Island, the Resort."

"Yep, it's a resort," he said, his accent half southern, half pirate. "Only place 'round here goes by the name of Tiki Island, I suppose,"

"Yeah, so what time does the boat leave?"

"Well, Mr. Riggins, that depends on what time you want to go. The big boat leaves the dock at eight a.m., three p.m. and six p.m., but the small boat is for custom charters, at an extra price, of course."

"Well it's already after three, so I guess I'll take the six. I want to check out the Key a little first, anyway."

"Suit yourself."

"Say, uh, when I go to Tiki Island, can I leave the jalopy here?"

"Sure can. Fifty cents a day, and I'll even keep a keen eye on her."

"Sounds great," I said. Yeah, great…nickel and dime me to death already.

I took the car down to Duval Street, the main drag in town. Even for a Sunday evening it was crowded; throngs of people of all kinds moved up and down the sidewalks, hopping from bar to bar, or heading to the beaches. Most of the women were wearing light sundresses over swimsuits, and the men were in either tank tops and shorts or Hawaiian shirts. But in addition to the tourists, there were some pretty strange locals mingling with the crowds. A man in a pink tuxedo shirt had a dog, with a cat sitting on the dog's back and a mouse sitting on the cat's head. A sidewalk musician, a sax player, with a bouquet of tropical flowers sticking out of the bell of the horn. An old woman wearing about fifty necklaces of varying styles. Another guy with a real peg leg, walking back and forth in front of a seafood joint, talking like a pirate...and he wasn't on the payroll.

Funny enough, I didn't feel out of place with my little sailboats and Panama hat.

I parked in front of a men's clothing store, and proceeded to pick out a half-dozen more shirts, plus two pairs of white and two pairs of beige linen pants. I never wore linen before, but the Key West heat was already turning my black wool slacks into water bags. They let me change into the white pants in the fitting room, so I threw the rest in the trunk and took a walk down Duval.

It wasn't anything like I expected. I was figuring on a sleepy beach town with a hotel or two, something like in *Key Largo* but without the storm. Instead, it was a bustling city, though on a really, really small scale. The buildings were as old as the hills, mostly made of wood or stucco. The stores and bars were open air, half outside and half inside. On the corner was a giant bar with the name "Sloppy Joe's" painted across the front. That's the place Fast Freddie clued me into, so I went there.

A Rock-a-billie band was playing up on the bandstand, cranking out Elvis and Bill Haley tunes. I asked the bartender for a Cuba Libre, and he looked at me funny. "One rum and coke coming up," he said. I guess they ain't as fancy in Key West as they are in Miami. They apparently aren't too keen on mixing Cuba Libres either. The light rum he used was oily and not nearly as good as the dark stuff. When I ordered again, it was a double Jack on the rocks. He smiled with a "that's more like it" kind of grin.

I wasted a half hour there, listening to the band. Just as I was getting ready to leave a local character sat down beside me and started rapping. I wasn't in a hurry, so I rapped back.

"My name ees Fernando," he said with an educated accent, "I'm from Cuba, (he pronounced it "Koo-bah") but live here now. You're not from here, are you...lemme guess, New York Ceety?"

"Close enough, what gave me away?"

"Ah, the black shoes, señor." Yep, that would do it. White pants, tropical shirt, black leather cop shoes.

"You have a good eye."

"Thank you, señor. For years I called the horse races in Havana. I had to have an eye for the detail, no?"

"I'm sure you did." The friendly banter went on for a while; I thought he was going to try to weasel a drink out of me, which I would have gladly bought him, but he didn't. Just conversation, a friendly guy looking to shoot the sugar with someone new and interesting, I guess.

"Where are you staying, señor?" he asked, sipping a rum and soda with a piece of mint sticking out of it.

"A place called Tiki Island, heard of it?"

He got a strange look on his face, and backed up an inch or two. "Oh, señor," he said with a touch of dark drama, "I know the place, she ees haunted, they say."

I laughed. Loudly. "Haunted? Oh come on, it's just a hotel."

"Sí, a hotel but where many strange things happen. They say the ghost of a young woman comes to people in the night and *jumps into their beds!*" he said, jumping at me as he raised his voice. It gave me a good jump, and got a great laugh out of the crowd around the bar.

"Ha ha, you goofball, almost made me spill my drink."

"Aye, I'm sorry señor, but seriously, I've heard some strange things about that place. And I think it is fascinating, too. So, you come back to Sloppy Joe and find me, after you stay, you tell me if you see anything strange, no?"

"Sure I will," I laughed, "But don't hold your breath. I've never seen a ghost and I don't believe I ever will."

"Aye we'll see, señor, we'll see."

At quarter to six I parked the Chevy at the marina, raised the top, rolled up the windows and grabbed my bags out of the back. A rather large boat, probably a fifty-five footer, sat next to the dock with a gangplank leading to the open back. "Tiki Island Express" was painted in bamboo-style lettering across the side of the bow, and the cabin was festooned with thatch, Tiki masks and palm fronds. On the back deck two bamboo Tiki torches burned, their crimson flames dancing in the evening breeze.

I handed the car keys and a five dollar bill to the old man in the shack. "This should cover the first week on the parking, and then some. It's rented so please don't let anything happen to it."

"My pleasure, Mr. Riggins," the man said, and locked the keys in the desk. I almost hated leaving the car there; it was a beauty, had a great ride. Without doubt it was the nicest car I ever drove.

I hopped on the boat and found there were already several people seated inside and out, waiting to shove off. A man came down from the bridge and took my bags.

"Sir, do you have sneakers? Or boating shoes?"

"Yeah, in the bag," I said.

"Would you mind changing into them please? We don't allow black-soled shoes on-deck."

"No problem," I said. How was *I* to know? The last time I was on a boat was at Kiddieland in Wildwood.

### Sunday, August 30, 1935

Sunday was as calm and non-threatening as Saturday had been, with the exception of that evil, eerie darkness lingering in the east and an occasional gust of wind blowing through the tops of the palms. There was no doubt now; the weather service issued a hurricane warning for all of the Florida Keys, yet it was still not clear where the eye would make landfall. All indications were that it would hit the upper Keys or possibly even the tip of the Florida peninsula, but no one could be sure. After speaking with his wife and Gregor, Eliot decided to change their train reservations to take them to Key West where they could ride out the storm in safety. Gregor would leave Sunday evening with his boat and meet them in Key West. Neither he nor Vivian questioned Eliot's judgment; neither dared to ask why they didn't all leave together by boat, why they didn't head north to Miami or Lauderdale. He had a plan, and they would stick to it. After all, it was his island, his boats (yes, even Gregor's boat was actually bought by Eliot) and his money. He knew how to best protect it.

Sunday afternoon drudged by. At around two o'clock, Gregor prepared his boat for the one-hour voyage to the southern-most key. He would leave the dock by three; by five, the vessel would be safely moored at Hawthorn's private slip in Key West.

I stood on the back deck of the The Tiki Island Express and soaked in the atmosphere while getting soaked from the evening's humidity. The boat was a beaut, all teak wood with brass fittings and chrome railings. The whole back was open but a cabin area took up nearly two thirds of the middle deck. Inside the cabin were padded benches along each side with a long bar in the center. A young, tan-skinned girl in a sarong served the drinks. She had long dark hair, the kind you only see in the tropics, and wore a tropical flower above one ear. Nice. And this was just the ride over.

I ordered a Jack and coke but she didn't have any Jack. "Only rum drinks are served on the cruise, Mr. Riggins. But don't worry, there's a full bar on the Island."

"That's good to hear." Wow, she knew my name. There's a neat trick.

"Would you like to try a Mojito?"

"What's a Mosquito?"

"A Mojito. It's a rum and mint drink."

"I wouldn't have it any other way," I snarked, and she smiled. I took a sip; it wasn't half bad, so I stuck with those for a while.

As the boat shoved off, the first mate introduced himself (a young kid named Roger from the Bahamas), and proceeded to give some info on the local flavor. He had a nice demeanor, and his sing-song island accent helped make the time go by.

"Aloha, ladies and gentleman, and welcome to our little boat. We are traveling due north-east of Key West, at approximated twenty-tree knots. The seas are calm and de weather clear, so we should reach Tiki Island, our destination in a little over an hour."

An hour? Holy cats, I thought the place was closer than that. Better easy up on the booze, buddy boy. Might not make it to the shore in one piece, I thought to myself.

"Tiki Island is approximately twenty miles from Key West. However, we are only a few miles from, and in hawk's eye view of Sugarloaf Key, incase anyone needs to get to the main islands quickly for any reason. But you will probably not, as Tiki Island has *every* accommodation you could want for, from exquisite cuisine to fabulous tropical drinks, from music and dancing to quiet, torch-lit beaches."

Now the kid sounded like he was reciting the guidebook.

"We have our own power generating station, and due to de magic of technological advance, an undersea cable has been laid in order to give you de telephone usage in every room."

"What if we don't *want* a telephone," I asked, seriously. That got a good laugh from the crowd, and the kid.

"Ha ha! Well that too, sir can be arranged, Mr. Riggins." Another one who knew me by name. I wondered how they got everyone memorized so fast. Either that, or he remembered me from my shoes. People seem to notice shoes a lot down here. Maybe it's because hardly any of the locals seem to wear any.

The mate continued, "Here on de boat, we have cocktails, appetizers and, if necessary, medication to keep you from feeling the sea," he said smiling. "Once on Tiki Island, you will have your choice of any beverage available to the free world, and some only available behind the Iron Curtain!" Another chuckle from the crowd. "And twenty-four hour room service with some of the finest foods on

Earth. Our five-star chefs pride themselves on every dish, whether it is a twenty-ounce Porterhouse steak or a simple hot dog." More chuckling.

He continued on, pointing out different Keys along the way, talking about the fishing and the boat rentals, etc. etc. During his little talk the hostess in the sarong brought around a tray of little cheese puff things and chicken satay, and freshened the drinks. I asked her her name, she said it was Dawn. I asked her if she stayed on the Island when she wasn't in the boat, she said yes. She smiled and winked, and walked away. I wondered how many dozens of times a week she said that to men who asked the same questions.

The mate wrapped up his speech with a reminder that tips were graciously accepted by all crew, and joined the Captain on the flying bridge. He was actually pretty entertaining, and when he was done his spiel the boat ride was almost half over.

I sat back and took the time to scope out the people around me. Like they say, once a cop, always a cop, even on vacation. There were a baker's dozen of tourists on the boat besides me. All couples, and one girl sitting alone, looking out at the passing waves. Four of the couples were young, my age or younger. At least one of them seemed to be on a honeymoon, as they were joined at the face for most of the trip. One couple was middle-aged and obviously well-to-do - too obviously. You know the type. The last couple were retired, at least I hoped they were. In their sixties at least.

The boat hit a couple of waves that made it rock enough for me to nearly spill my drink, and I noticed the middle-aged man start to turn a little pale; in another minute his skin was as doughy as a bowl of milk, and he excused himself to the rear deck, where he leaned over the side. His wife, looking put-out, got up and found Dawn, apparently to get her squeeze a few sea-sickness pills.

I looked at my watch. It was almost seven which meant the boat would be pulling up to Tiki Island soon. I started to get a little fidgety…I wanted to get this vacation going, I was getting hungry, and I wanted another drink, although I didn't want to push my luck over-boozing while still on the ocean.

I looked around again; the four younger couples had grouped up and were talking about Jerry Lee Lewis and Gene Vincent. The middle-aged man recovered and was back with his wife, conversing with the older couple about stocks and trading and some other BS that he shouldn't have been talking about on vacation. His wife looked annoyed. I had a feeling she always looked that way.

That left me and the solo chick the only two not making friends. I knew *my* excuse – I was so wrapped up in *watching* that I didn't get in on anything. Not wanting to interrupt the intelligent conversations spread around me, I got up and moved over next to the dame.

"Hello there," I said nice and friendly-like. "Looks like you and I are the only ones left out in the cold."

She turned from her gaze and looked straight into my eyes. Hers were blue. Mine were taken by surprise. I had only seen her from ten feet away before. Now, right next to her, I could see she had the face of an angel, draped in a blonde mane that looked fantastic even in the salty wind; she couldn't have been more than twenty-five, and was a true beauty, the kind of girl you see on the silver screen or parading down some runway at a fashion show. But there was something in her eyes, a sadness maybe, or just the look of experience, too much experience in too short a life. She was striking.

She smiled.

I melted like a stick of butter in the sun.

"I suppose we are," she said back with a lilting southern accent. Her voice matched her looks perfectly. Angelic.

I got my act together fast and smiled back. "I'm William, William Riggins." William? Where the hell did that come from? Ha, it's like I was trying to impress her with my name or some crazy thing. "My friends call me Riggins."

She extended a hand. "Jessica. My friends call me Jessica," she said, smiling more. That smile wiped the sadness right out.

"Are you meeting someone on the Island?" I asked, hoping to hell the answer was no.

"No," she said, and I was relieved beyond belief. "I'm…just going to get some rest, to de-stress."

"Well how do ya like that?" I chirped, smiling like a dumb schoolboy. "Me too." I was raked.

"I really needed some alone time," she said, and my heart sank like a lead slug. "I've done some work for the management. They let me stay a few days for free, now and then."

The similarities were piling up, but that line about being alone threw me. I didn't know if it was a brush-off or just the truth. "No kidding, I'm staying rent-free too. Friend of a friend owed me a favor. What kind of work do you do?"

"I'm a hostess," she said. She didn't elaborate. She replied fast, almost too fast; almost in a way that made me think that wasn't what she did. It sounded rehearsed. When you're a detective for a few years you pick up on these little things.

"I'm in the insurance business. Don't worry," I joked, "Claims investigation, not sales." I had my lie down pat too. I learned a long time ago never to tell anyone I was a cop, unless it was cop business.

The wind gusted up as the sun sunk its last light into the west. The twilight was beautiful. In a sky of cobalt blue a billion stars started twinkling above, more than I'd ever seen in my city life. The Tiki Torches, by some crazy Tiki magic were still lit, and their flickering light played on Jessica's face like shadowy ghosts and lit her eyes with dancing phantoms. I didn't even notice when the boat's motor powered down and the rig slowed down to a crawl.

"Looks like we're here," Jessica said breaking the spell. My back was to the Island so I had no way of knowing – when I turned around and saw the sight, I nearly flipped.

*Tiki Island.*

Wow, and what a sight it was.

Jerry wasn't kidding. The whole front of the Island looked like a scene from South Pacific. The beachhead was lit by giant fires and Tiki torches, illuminating two-story high, hand-carved Tiki idols. Palm trees crisscrossed behind, perfectly placed to show-off the perfect setting while sneak-peaking the resort through the fronds. Hand-built catamarans were parked up on the beach. A giant arbor of bamboo and thatch made up the centerpiece to the entrance, and arced across the top read in bamboo lettering, "Welcome to Tiki Island. Mahalos!"

I whistled a long one. "Holy flamingoes, this joint's crazy!" I said to Jessica.

She seemed indifferent. "It's a swell place."

As we drifted closer I could see the large dock that extended out about one hundred feet from the beach. The dock too was lit with torches, and several women in grass skirts waited there. The sounds of drums came lilting up from the shore; as the boat docked I realized the drums were part of a band playing Hawaiian music on the beach.

The boat stopped and the mate directed us to the gangplank. We got up; Jessica started to leave ahead of me, and I caught her gently by the arm just in time.

"Jessica, if it's ok, I'd like to see you on the Island. Maybe drinks later on? I know you said you wanted to be alone but - "

"I don't want to be *that* alone," she said coyly, that smile coming through again, lighting up the night like the Fourth of July. "I'll be around. Maybe the Tiki Bar on the beach, around ten."

"I'm hip," I said, feeling like that schoolboy again.

Once on the dock I was greeted by more girls who looked like Dawn; they placed real flower lies over my head, and said something like Aloha-lala wala waheenee or something or other, smiling the whole time. The mate and Dawn brought the bags to the dock, and porters took them from there.

One of the porters, possibly a Jamaican, came up to me and said, "Welcome Mr. Reeggins, we have been eagerly expecting you. If you would come this way, please." I didn't get it...I seemed to be getting the VIP treatment, which for someone who was staying free seemed an awful lot.

The porter lead me through the arbor, and once through I got my first real look at the Resort, silhouetted against the deepening dark blue sky.

It was amazing.

Everywhere I looked, breathtakingly beautiful tropical flowers and plants bloomed up out of the sand and coral rock, orange and red and blue and yellow splashes contrasting against giant green ferns and palms. Tikis rose from the ground like the proud Gods they were, some towering over fifty feet tall, looking eerily alive in the light of the dancing flames. But the hotel itself...now that was something for the slideshow. The main building was huge; at least six stories high and nearly a football field long, it was a bamboo and thatch masterpiece of epic Polynesian magnitude. The giant A-frame structure bowed in the middle and the thatched roof came to an exaggerated point jutting out thirty feet beyond the front of the building like the prow of a ship. The entire front façade was covered in a woven reed-type of material, trimmed in dark bamboo and decorated tastefully with carved Tiki masks and live plants. Every inch of wood was carved with ancient island symbols and graphics. Two giant, round, black cast-iron bowls sat at the entrance to the steps, held up by stanchions of coral rock lit with orange flames that shot up five feet high into the night. With some carefully-hidden colored spotlights the torches seemed to be the only illumination against the front of the building, giving the whole works a dark, mystical atmosphere that had me believing I was actually somewhere on a mysterious island in the Pacific, not on a Florida island a few miles from the U.S. mainland. For the first time in a very long time, I was speechless.

A pink and gray flagstone path led the way to the entrance, and we arrived there a few minutes ahead of the others from the boat. People were milling around, sitting on benches, walking paths that led through mystical gardens and around to the other beaches. The Hawaiian music was louder now but not too loud; a mellow melody was sliding gently from a lap-steel, with strumming guitars coming in behind it just right. I recognized the tune as "Beyond the Reef."

The porter directed me up the limestone and teak steps to the front entrance where two towering, mahogany doors stood between us and the lobby. Those suckers had to weigh-in at around four-hundred pounds apiece. Toothy Tiki gods were hand carved into the wood, smiling down on me from ten feet above as we entered the cavern.

Once inside, I was even more amazed.

I was standing in the middle of a great hall, at least sixty feet high at the roof's giant wooden backbone. Along each side ran two floors of balconies railed with mahogany; these held the rooms that flanked the two long sides of the hut. Everything was bamboo, teak, mahogany, ebony, rattan or thatch. The inside of the roof was covered in woven thatch, as were the undersides of the balconies. The front desk was a mile long stretch of carved ebony and teak with mother-of-pearl inlays. Giant sailfish, turtles and other sea creatures decorated the walls, and lamps made from blowfish and stretched hides hung down from the ceilings. Giant chandeliers of carved wood and colored glass hung from the roof's keel-like center beam. Every inch of the place had a pattern, a mask or a fish on it. The floor was natural-looking red and grey slate flagstone, and the forward lobby sported bamboo furniture that would make a witch doctor drool. I was so busy taking in the crazy sights that I didn't even notice the swingin' brunette standing right in front of me.

## Monday, Labor Day, 1935

It was unfathomable. Just yesterday the skies were blue and crystal clear, the waters tranquil as a summer pond. "The calm before the storm" in every sense of the phrase. Now the wind howled ruthlessly through the palms, bending them and toying with them like matchsticks on a vent. The ocean crashed into the beach with the force of an invading army; already giant chunks of sand had been washed away into the gulf and flood waters were slipping dangerously close to the garden. The sky, constantly in motion, turned a muddy gray with an unearthly orange glow behind it.

Time was running out.

The storm had set its course for the upper keys, and Hawthorn Island was going to get the brunt of the south end of the hurricane where the winds were strongest, and deadliest.

Eliot Hawthorne had made all the necessary preparations to leave the island. Valuables were packed, hurricane shutters secured, lawn furniture sunk in the Olympic-sized pool and the boat made ready for the choppy trip to Sugarloaf Key; From there he and his wife would take the Overseas Railway to Key West where they could ride out the storm.

But all his preparations and all his plans had backfired. A call placed to the Florida East Coast Railroad confirmed his fear: No trains to Key West today, Labor Day Monday, due to the oncoming storm. Only an evacuation train from Islamorada would run, and it would run back up to Homestead in the north.

"We'll have to make a run for Islamorada," he said to the very frightened woman as he helped her onto the boat. "I'm sure our yacht will cut through the rough waters without hesitation, but it will be a bit bumpy, I'm afraid."

"We should have gone back to Key West," she replied, shaking.

"I told you that's no good," Eliot screamed above the rising wind and the roar of the Gulf. "Waters are too open, we can capsize. Too late for that. We'll stick close to the islands and make it up to Islamorada in less than two hours, tops."

"Let's just get this over with," she said, this time more disgusted than afraid, and slipped into the cabin. Eliot took a last look at his home, his mansion. A last look at everything, knowing very well it would probably be the last time he ever saw it again. He untied the rope from the stern, started the engines, and ran them up to full power heading towards Matecumbe Key.

1956

"Mr. Riggins?" came a sweet but strong voice from somewhere just below my line of sight. I looked down from the hypnotic effects of the ceiling; when my eyes got eye level, a luscious dame with the biggest brown eyes I'd ever seen was staring into mine, her hand extended in the customary manor for which one might shake. The smile on her face could make a glacier melt.

"Huh?" I said with the eloquence of a moose, "Oh, uh yeah, hi there. Riggins, that's me." I really was a sap for the pretty ones.

"Welcome to Tiki Island, Mr. Riggins. We've heard a lot about you, and are honored to have you as our guest."

Honored? I thought.

"Oh, well yes, thank you, it's a pleasure to finally be here."

Man was I cooked. This doll was all curves, in all the right places. High, proud cheekbones that looked a little out of place under her sundrenched face gave her a look of beauty that was unexpected and damned welcome. Her Hawaiian print dress was both sexy and professional, considering the casual surroundings. It strained against the swell of her breasts, spreading just enough to give a tantalizing tease of tan cleavage. Luscious, plump lips. Dark, flowing hair. Pins that would make Ginger Rogers green. And those eyes. Damn those eyes.

"I'm Melinda Hawthorn, Entertainment Director," she said, and I could barely detect the slightest Spanish accent.

"My pleasure, Melinda. Do you work for Rutger Bachman?" Bachman was Jerry's brother, the guy who set me up.

"Hmm, not exactly," she answered, trying her damnedest to stay professional. "You see, my father owns the resort. Mr. Bachman is our General Manager, but I don't report to him. It's more the other way around, if you know what I mean," she said, still smiling, but with just a hint of annoyance.

As if I cared I said, "Sure, sure. Say, is he around? I guess he was supposed to set me up with a room and all."

"Mr. Bachman is off-island tonight. His only day off is Monday and he usually spends it in Key West. But I've got everything in order for you, Mr. Riggins."

"Call me Bill." For some reason I didn't want this doll to just call me Riggins. Kinda funny.

"That wouldn't be very professional of me."

"This joint's as casual as it gets, kiddo. Call me Bill, and I'll call you Melinda, if that's ok." She blushed just a little, and laughed. Her smiles and laughs were probably phony, but she put them over so well I couldn't tell.

"Ok then, Bill. Anyway I've got our best suite all ready for you, plus a welcome basket of fresh fruits and champagne is waiting for you in your room. All of your meals and drinks are strictly on the house. All you're responsible for on this trip is tips. And believe me, if you tip well, our staff will bend over backwards for you."

"Meals and drinks? Say, he didn't mention that. Listen, it's swell enough you kids are springing for the room, I don't want to take advantage of the situation…"

"Don't be ridiculous, Mr. Riggins…"

"Bill," I interrupted.

"Bill…It's not everyday we get a hero such as yourself staying with us."

It was all I could do not to let the surprise show on my face. A hero? What kind of cacka-mamie story did Jerry lay on these kats? Not to seem off-base, I played along.

"Oh, uh, so you heard about that, huh?"

"Well yes, of course, Mr. Bachman's brother told us everything."

"Did he? All of it?"

"Well, yes, all about the murder, and how you found the killer and how you almost single-handedly brought him in. Quite remarkable."

Ah, so that was it. Since I was a Vice cop it was easy to nail this one down. I helped the homicide boys bust a guy named MacGreery. He was wanted for beating up a thirteen year-old girl and leaving her for dead. Only she lived long enough to say who did it. Trouble was they couldn't find the bum. Turned out he was a reefer hound. Just so happened one of my informants knew a guy who knew the guy who was his connection. I leaned on the guy a little and got an address. Then I handed it over to homicide, and they nabbed him while he was in the middle of chowing-down on some hash and eggs. I went along for the ride, but that was it. Jerry must have talked me up to his brother so they'd give me the full treatment. Not bad, that Jerry. After all, it wasn't a lie, it just wasn't exactly the truth. I'd swing it back to center, just to clear my conscious, but I'd still take the free grub and booze.

"I didn't exactly do it all myself you know, the homicide boys had a lot to do with it too."

"Well, they aren't our guests, and you are. So from here on in, anything you want, you just ask. And I do mean anything."

Seems I'd heard that before somewhere in the great state of Florida. Such accommodating folks here in the south. I wondered what she'd say if I asked for a half dozen hookers, a box of bananas and cello player to meet me in my room in twenty minutes. Then again, no I didn't.

"There is one thing you can do for me," I said with a sort of worried look, "I'd really prefer no one here know who I am or what I did. In fact, I don't really want anyone to know I'm a cop at all, if you catch my drift."

She thought for only a second before answering. "Oh, of course, I understand you want your privacy. Of course we sometimes know celebrities love the attention, but in your case I can see you just want to relax, have a quiet time, am I right?"

Yeah, exactly, except for the hookers and the cellist.

"Yeah, exactly. I just sorta want to blend in. If anyone asks, I'm in the insurance biz, claims investigator."

"Not a problem Mr. – Bill."

"Thanks doll," I said, and gave her the smile back. Maybe I'm imagining things, but I could swear she dropped the professional bit for just a second, and came through as all woman. Her eyes seemed just a little wider, her stance a little more relaxed, her smile just a little more coy than before. Then in a flash she was back to business as usual.

"I'll show you to your suite now if you like, your bags are already there."

"Sounds fine," I said, and she led me to an automatic lift on the south side of the hut.

A moment later we were in the biggest hotel room I'd ever seen in my life. It was a good thirty feet wide and twenty deep, with lava rock walls and bamboo wood floors. It faced south, with floor-to-ceiling picture windows looking out over the ocean and Keys. A sunken hot tub and a Tiki bar graced the left end of the room; a sunken, circular living room with bamboo furniture and a TV/Hi-Fi combo dominated the right. Behind the living room an arched doorway led to the bedroom with a king-sized bed and bath that belonged in a magazine. The bar was stocked with every top-shelf booze available, from twelve-year-old Scotch to imported Russian vodka to Jamaican rum. A fish tank was set into the wall, filled with exotic tropical fish lazily swimming around just to drum up some atmosphere.

I let out a long whistle. "This place must rake in the clams. You sure I'm staying here?"

She laughed again, that not-quite-professional laugh that made her seem more interested than she probably was. "It's all yours, compliments of the house. Aloha, Bill. If you need anything, just ring me up, my extension is on the phone. Enjoy your stay. Mahalos!" she said, and turned to walk out.

"Say, wait a minute," I said, and she stopped short, almost as if she knew I'd try to make her stay. "What you just said, what exactly does that mean?"

"Mahalos?"

"Yeah, I saw it on the sign up front too. Never heard it before."

"It's Hawaiian. There's no literal translation for it, it pretty much means I wish you the best, thank you, you're a swell guy, good luck, may you have a happy and healthy life…you get the picture."

"Yeah, I suppose I do."

"It's a very important word to the Hawaiians. It's not to be taken lightly. We take it very seriously."

"We – you're Hawaiian?"

"Half Hawaiian and half Mexican."

"That explains that slight accent," I said with a smile.

"Very perceptive of you, detective. Aren't you going to ask about my name?"

"Hawthorn's not a common Hawaiian tribal name?"

Another laugh, definitely a real one this time.

"No. My father passed away when I was very young. When I was five years old, my mother remarried. She married Eliot Hawthorn, who is the owner of this island."

"I see, then it's your stepfather who owns the joint."

"He's the only father I've ever known. But surely you don't want to hear my family history."

"No, no I'm interested, this is a fascinating place. I'd love to hear the story of how you got here." I paused, then "How *it* got here."

"It's a long story."

"Why don't I mix us a few cocktails at my little Tiki Bar over there while you give me the history of Tiki Island."

She smiled. I got all warm inside and got that crazy school-kid feeling again.

"I guess a little history lesson can't hurt. At least that way it will be job related. Giving historical tours is part of what I do here."

"Sounds cozy. Lay it on me."

"Do you know how to fix a Mojito?" she asked.

"Not really. Do you use a monkey wrench or a hammer?"

"I better fix the drinks," she said with another little laugh. I was beginning to really dig those little laughs.

We moved over to the thatch and rattan bar, and Melinda got to work building the drinks. It was like being on a movie set, all that bamboo, the mood lighting, the hand-carved Tiki masks staring at me from the wall. I sat on the bamboo stool and lit a Camel. She talked, I listened intently. That sing-song voice of hers was so melodic, so sweet, with that near-perfect diction peppered with a pinch of Spanish accent, she could've been telling me the history of lock-washers for all I cared; I'd still have listened intently.

"Eliot came to California in just over twenty years ago, devastated after the loss of his wife."

"Loss? What happened?"

"She was swept out to see in the Great Atlantic Hurricane of 1935."

## Monday, Labor Day, 1935

The rains came hard, slashing at the boat and filling the stern. It was as if God turned on the faucet the minute they left the dock. Visibility was so low Eliot was afraid he'd run aground one of the sandbars or smaller islands, but he didn't dare pull back on the throttles. The twin diesels were pushing the craft through the two-foot swells at well over twenty knots, and he knew he'd have to maintain that speed to survive the journey to Islamorada. There, he would dock the boat at the public dock, take whatever they could carry and to the devil with the rest of the junk. As far as he was concerned, his home would be washed away to the sea, and his old life with it. Tomorrow when storm was long-passed and the seas receded, his new life would then begin.

Inside the cabin, the ghostly-pale woman in the yellow sundress and pearl necklace hung onto the rail with both hands, trying desperately not to be sick. Although she grew up in the Keys and had been on a million boats, she'd never experienced such a horrifying ordeal. Waves were crashing over the sides of the yacht, and although it was at least fifty feet long it was still being tossed about like a cork in a tub. A cork in a tub of gin, she thought, and wished she had some gin now. Then the thought of drinking gin and being tossed around like that made her stomach churn, and the sickness came. She didn't care; she actually felt a little better after that. But the horrible feeling of being so close to doom was overwhelming, and no matter how hard she tried, she just couldn't shake it.

Two hours later the boat pulled up at the public dock on Islamorada. Eliot lashed it to the cleat and climbed to the dock, a wet and sickly woman following. Together they ran up to the shore and across the street to the train station. The winds were already strong enough to push them off balance, and twice Eliot had to keep his frail companion from sailing away.

The station was crowded to the hilt, far over occupancy. Mostly men from the public works department, employees of the WPA, Roosevelt's 'New Deal' Work Progress Administration. It was they who helped build the islands, the bridges, the railroad. Now they were waiting for that same railroad to take them to safety over the very bridges they built and maintained.

"Passage for two, and if you've got room for luggage we've got plenty," Eliot shouted over the clamor to the man behind the ticket window. "One for me, and one for my wife, Vivian. I'm Eliot Hawthorn," he added, as if his name meant anything to the man.

"We've got room for people and one bag you can carry yourself, no more."

Apparently, his name meant nothing in the face of an oncoming hurricane.

"That's fine. How much are tickets?" he asked, pulling his wallet from his drenched jacket.

"No fee today, mister. This is an evacuation, not a vacation."

"Ok, ok. Just let me know when the train is leaving."

"Leaving?" the man said disgustedly, "It ain't even got here yet. Wired Homestead yesterday we needed a train here pronto. The dumb suckers didn't have one ready! Had to bring it down from all the way from Palm Beach to Miami. Just left Miami this morning, and with this weather...aw, hell, sure as hell ain't gonna be here before five, maybe six o'clock!"

"Six o'clock!" Eliot screamed, mortified. But then he calmed down, and remembered all his planning, and back-up planning, and realized it was not the end of the line. "You realize the storm will likely be on full-throttle by six," he said mournfully.

"Yessir," the man said, his face showing fear thick and real. His eye twitched just a little. "Yessir, we are well aware of that." With that he turned and left the ticket window.

"Come on," he said to his wife, and pulled her out of the station and back into the rain and wind.

"What gives?" she exclaimed as the wind nearly pulled the door off the hinges. "What are you doing?"

"Plan B," Eliot responded, not stopping to explain. In another minute they were back on the boat, heading North.

The big brass star-shaped clock on the wall sang to the tune of nine-fifteen when Melinda came up for air. Not that I minded; her voice was as beautiful as her face, and I could have sat there all night just listening. Well, listening for part of the night anyway. Other things had already crept into my mind, and by the time she told me about her stepfather at the train station, I had undressed her with my eyes right down to a bikini and a flower lei. What she didn't know wouldn't hurt her.

Another problem that I had was that while this woman was captivating, she was an employee of the resort and was no doubt just trying to make a VIP guest happy. To what extent she'd make me happy was questionable. I had the distinct feeling the doll would stop short just when things were getting good.

On the other hand, I had a standing date with the pretty blonde from the boat ride, and although that seemed like a millions years ago, she too had been strangely captivating to the point of illicit fantasy. As much as I wanted to see where I could get with Melisa, or Marimba or whatever her name was I still wanted to meet up with Jessica.

At a break in her tale, I took the opportunity to try to speed things up.

"So they jumped back in the boat and headed for the mainland. Is that when his old lady bit it?"

"Pretty much," she said. Good, I thought. Nice, quick ending.

"Eliot motored the boat at full power up along the Keys, hoping to make it to Florida City where he could take a car up to Miami. But he never made it. A six-foot sea wall tossed his boat into the air like a toy. When it came back down, Vivian was gone. Eliot doesn't remember much after that, except he ran aground in the swamps just below Florida City, and remained stuck there until the storm passed. When it was all over the police found him in the cabin, unconscious. His wife's remains were never recovered."

"Tough job," I said, finishing my drink.

"Very. He lost his wife, and much more. The island was completely wiped out in the storm. His entire home was reduced to a pile of wood and seaweed. His best friend Gregor was also lost at sea, his boat found washed up on a sandbar five miles out. And of course, there was the tragedy of the storm itself."

"What exactly happened? I heard the train tracks got washed out in the storm."

"Not just the tracks, Bill. That train left late…much too late. It was taken-out by a forty-foot tsunami. Over three hundred people were onboard that train. None survived. In all, the official total was four hundred and eight souls lost in the storm. But people who lived here knew that estimate was very low."

It was a sad tale, all right. Sad and depressing. After all, that was less than twenty years ago, and signs of the storm were still evident along the Overseas Highway.

"That's real terrible, what happened. Probably could have been prevented with some better planning. Damn shame."

"Most certainly. And now that we know how to prepare, it will never happen again. Now, even if a storm is three days out, the county evacuates the Keys. No playing around anymore."

"At least something good came of it."

"Yes, at least something," she answered with a far-off look. She held it a second then shook it off. "Anyway, after that Eliot was devastated. He never went back to the Island. He moved as far away as he could, California, and ordered his workers to remove and destroy every bit that remained of his house. When the Island was cleared, he ordered four feet of topsoil to spread across then entire surface, and brought in dozens of plants and trees to repopulate it with vegetation. His plan was to leave it as a sanctuary, a monument to his late wife who loved the palms and tropical flowers. Then he met my mother, and they married and we lived in California…but not long after he heard the Overseas Railway was becoming the Overseas Highway. And a spark was lit inside him. An idea popped into his mind, and he began drawing up plans for what would become Tiki Island as you know it today."

She shot me that award-winning grin again, the one that made me melt, but now that I had Jessica on my mind the effect didn't seem as intense. *Still there,* but not as intense.

"An incredible story," I said, and lit up a smoke. "You know it's almost nine-thirty?"

She turned and looked at the clock, and let out a tiny shriek. I guess she didn't.

"Oh, my! My my, I shouldn't have stayed so long. I've got a luau in a half hour! Please excuse me Mr. Rig…Bill, It's been wonderful speaking with you. Maybe tomorrow we could get together again?" she said as she left. She didn't wait for a reply.

By nine-forty I was freshly shaved and showered. There was a nice selection of platters for the Hi-Fi, so I cued up an Arthur Lyman album (hey, when in Rome…) and sat out on the deck watching the lights from the lower Keys flicker in the night. I wasn't sure if it was Key West I was seeing, but it sure felt like it. I had learned to make a pretty decent Mojito from watching Melinda, and built one for myself before heading out to meet Jessica on the beach. Above in the night sky little stars twinkled like they did in songs, and an occasional shooting star streaked across the heavens just for fun. Below, dancing Tiki torches lit the beach and gardens, casting a soft yellow glow over the east side of the Island. It was down there, at the Tiki Bar by the beach, where the lovely Jessica would be waiting. Paradise.

At ten minutes after ten I left my room, saying so-long to the goldfish and rum. I motored the self-service elevator down to the lobby, exited out through the massive front doors of the Resort and took the eastern path, winding around to the beach bar.

At the bar were lots of hot babes, slick beauties in bikinis even though it was after ten. Turns out there was a salt water pool behind the bar, and twenty-four hour swimming was encouraged. A group of older men sat together at a wicker table. A few couples, including two I recognized from the boat, sat around looking starry-eyed and enjoying the romance. Seated at the bar were several people. None of them were Jessica.

I pulled up to the bar and asked the bartender for a Mojito. She smiled and built it just right, adding a mint sprig and a little tropical flower as garnish. I asked if she'd seen a blonde who may have asked for me. She didn't.

At ten-thirty I was about to give it up as a bad job (after all, she did say *maybe*) and go find Melinda when I heard a sweet, lilting voice behind me.

"Sorry to keep y'all waiting, Billy. I had to put my face on."

When I turned around, that same rush I got on the boat hit me again, and my mind whispered, *"Melinda who?"*

## September, 1935

Eliot was alone.

His wife was gone, and there was no bringing her back.

What was done was done; the storm had taken her body out to see, mangled it, deformed it, bloated it beyond recognition so that if it did wash up, no one would ever know it was she. Only a handful of people he'd seen at the train station had survived the onslaught, among them the ticket taker, the last person to see the woman together with him, alive.

They said hundreds had drowned, horribly. Hundreds more were injured. Every building on the upper keys was either washed out to sea or destroyed beyond repair. Hawthorn Island itself – being essentially limestone – remained intact, but his home – the family mansion which had stood for nearly forty years had been reduced to rubble. According to his workers, no bodies had washed up on the island, and they would be able to remove the debris, fill in the holes and cover it over with trees and plants to remain that way forever. End of story.

Later he was told that Gregor's boat was recovered from a sandbar, but Gregor was never found.

His wife and his best friend, gone without a trace.

He sighed, and strained to hold back the bitterness and tears that pressed against his eyes. His trembling hand held a picture of the trio, taken last summer on the island. He on the left, his wife in the middle, Gregor on the right. It wasn't a very good picture, he thought; at the last minute something had gotten Vivian's attention, and she'd looked over to the right, smiling at something off-camera. She never liked the photo, thought it made her look aloof, she'd said. But it was the only one taken that day, a very special day to Eliot. That was almost exactly a year ago in late August of 1934. She always said there would be plenty of time for plenty more pictures. She was never so wrong.

It was at that moment Eliot decided to leave Florida, possibly for good. He wired ahead to his lawyers and told them to secure a suitable temporary home for him in San Diego, something by the sea. No matter what, he loved the sea and wanted to be near it always. He arranged passage on a cross-country train, and by October of 1935 Eliot had extricated himself from Florida and took up residence in San Francisco, California. His old life was over. His new life was about to begin.

"I was about to go look for greener pastures," I said with a flirty smile. That was me, Mr. Smooth, playing all the angles. "You walked up just in time."

She sat next to me and leaned in close. "You'd have waited all night for me."

"Would I?"

"Natch, sugar. I know; men have done it before." There was a playful, yet truthful tone in her voice, that angel voice tinged with southern charm.

"Oh, so you're the game-playing type," I said. "Great."

"Don't worry, William, I won't play any games with you. You wouldn't take it too well, and I have a feeling I'd be the one losing out."

Without even asking, the bartender slid Jessica a tall drink in a ceramic blue glass shaped like one of those Tiki poles I saw out front. It had so much fruit on it I thought it might fall over, but it held up.

"Here's to a winning season," I said, and clinked her drink. She drank from the straw, pursing her ruby lips in a way that could make a dead man come to life. All I could think about was sinking my lips deep into hers, kissing her wildly, making love to her in the sand of that crazy beach. Man was my mind on a single track or what? I don't know why I was thinking these things, about Melinda, about Jessica, even about the chick waitress on the boat ride. I mean sure, I liked the company of dames, and took a few around the block whenever I could. But it seemed like since I got to Florida all I could think about was getting in bed with a doll, or several dolls, or *hell all* the dolls. Must be something in the water. Or maybe the rum.

"What are you drinking?" she asked, and it tossed me because I thought she was reading my mind or something.

"Oh, eh, a Mojito. Just had one on the boat ride over for the first time. Not bad. Generally I'm a Bourbon man, but I can get used to these rum concoctions."

"You should try one of these," she answered, and turned the straw around to face me. "It's a lot stronger than it looks."

"What is it?" I asked, then took a sip as she answered. The little paper umbrella almost went up my nose. She laughed.

"It's called a Mai Tai. It's the Island's signature drink. Supposedly the owner learned the recipe from the guy who invented it, and even pays the man a license fee for using it."

"No kidding? What's in it?"

"Rum. And more rum. And a bunch of other stuff. Not bad, huh?"

"Best drink I've had in Florida, so far," I said, and I wasn't kidding. I was hooked.

Three Mai Tai cocktails later we were sitting in the sand, facing the ocean. We'd found a secluded little spot away from the bar, away from the lights. Now it was just the two of us, the ocean and the stars. There was no moon at all.

We riffed for a while on this and that, the weather, the usual stuff. I lied about my job as an insurance investigator. She lied about working as hostess and cigarette girl. She told me what it was like to grow up and live in Key West, I told her what it was like to live and work in New York City. I told her about the new blue Chevy and promised to take her for a ride; she laughed and asked if that was an innuendo and we both laughed together. It was right then the booze got the better of me and gave me that false courage that only comes from a high blood-alcohol level.

"Jessica, what's your last name?" I asked, and she answered, "Rutledge, why?"

With one smooth move I leaned over and kissed her, slowly and softly at first, then a little harder until I had to come up for air. She didn't resist.

"Because I like to know the name of the girl I'm kissing, that's why," I oozed with corny charm. She said nothing; she just looked into my eyes with a half-wonderful, half-frightened look. I leaned over and kissed her again, and she took my kisses and returned them with hungry lips, lips full of passion and lust and pent-up desire. We kissed for what seemed like hours, although surely it was only minutes. The fire lessened slightly, and we took the opportunity to get our heads together, to plan the next move. She was silent. I figured I'd go for broke.

"I, eh…Listen, Jessica, I know we just met, but I…well what I'm saying is they gave me the biggest room in the hotel, the Kona Kai Suite, and there's a full bar up there and a Hi-Fi, and so I was thinking, maybe if you'd like you could eh…come up?" There I go again, Mr. Smooth. I was never too sure of things like this. Ask that to the right dame and you're in for a hell of a night. Ask it to the wrong dame and you could get your puss slapped, or worse, no second date. Then again not asking at all got you nowhere.

She didn't answer right away, as if she were contemplating the situation and how it would play out. I could tell from her eyes this wasn't the first time she'd been asked to go to town. I could tell from her smile, she'd gone slumming a few times. When the silence lasted too long, I said, "Or we could just stay…"

"I'd love to," she interrupted, and raised herself up from the sand. "Just let's make one thing clear. I'm just coming up for a few drinks and a few laughs. I'm not that easy, OK? So don't get any ideas."

Sure she wasn't. "That's fine, Jessica. I'll even leave the door unlocked."

Two drinks and a half an hour later she joined me in the king-sized bamboo bed.

Jessica was gone when I awoke at nine in the morning. It had been a hell of night; a few drinks, a few laughs and then some. Frankly I hadn't met a doll like her in my entire life. It wasn't just that the sex was great, there was something about the way she did it, the way she *performed*, almost as if she were showing off skills she'd learned in some French women's training camp or some crazy thing. She did things most other women wouldn't even consider, wouldn't even have ever *heard* about, and certainly wouldn't do willingly. From the way she slipped her sundress off her shoulders to the way her back arched and her whole body shuddered, there was an air of superiority to other women in her manner that made me want to take her again and again. Now she was gone, like a faded dream; all that was left were the blurry memories of her face close to mine, her soft body pressed against me, her hair brushing against my chest. Damned good memories, if you ask me.

It took me a minute to find the phone. It was actually built into the headboard, which was mahogany and ebony, hand-carved with tropical flowers and Tiki guys like everything else in this crazy place. The handset was hand-caved too, and blended in with the rest of the décor. A little door flipped down to expose the rotary and a list of numbers to call for services. I dialed #3 for room service, ordered up a breakfast fit for a king (I remembered all the food and booze was on the house) and hung up. I yawned and stretched like a bear, the memories of Jessica still lingering.

Twenty minutes later I was sitting out on the lanai (in Jersey it would be called a porch, in the City a balcony. In Florida it was a lanai), drinking fresh-squeezed Florida orange juice and eating poached eggs with salmon and grits. Never had a grit before; wasn't sure why a southern dish would be served in a Hawaiian resort but what the hell, they weren't bad. I finished it off with an excellent cup of java; supposedly the beans were grown on the side of a volcano on one of the Hawaiian Islands.

"I sure could get used to this," I said to no one as I looked out over the lower Keys. A little wisp of wind came up, and I could almost swear I heard, *"Don't"*, faintly on the wind. Just my imagination, or fate reminding me that in less than two weeks I'd be back in the dark, dingy office at the station, breathing in too much cigarette smoke instead of the mild scent of tropical flowers, dealing with the dregs of society instead of pretty dolls and interesting island characters.

I lit the first Camel of the day and my mind drifted.

Maybe a transfer, I thought. Maybe I could get a job with the local sheriff's office, or hell, start my own private investigating agency in Miami. I could buy one of those new blue Chevys with the rag top and the Powerglide transmission. Trade in my cop shoes for a pair of boat shoes, and live next to the beach where the temperature never dipped below sixty. And maybe we'd land on the moon next year and find out it really *is* made of green cheese, and the Ruskies would realize communism was for boneheads and would beg America to teach them democracy, while handing over all their atom bombs for us to bury in the desert. Yeah, all that might happen, but it wouldn't, of course. In a couple of days I'd be back on the iron horse heading home, heading back to the City with all its crime and all its grime, and all its wonderful art and theater and food, with its crazy people and its fantastic people and cool jazz and hot rock 'n' roll and all that goes with it. And I'd complain about the cold but I'd like my coat and gray Stetson fedora, and wearing ties and watching sophisticated women walk in black leather boots and silk stockings with the seam up the back. Florida was nice, but the north had its advantages, too.

I realized I hadn't even unpacked yet. If I was going to be here for another eight days or so, I might as well settle in nice and cozy, I figured. First I unzipped the suit bag and hung the two suits in the closet. They were wrinkled as hell, and I'd have to get them pressed before wearing them. Wasn't sure if I'd actually need to wear them though; even though they were summer-weight, they still seemed out of place here on Tiki Island. Next I unpacked the big suitcase. At the bottom of the suitcase was my .45 automatic, the Colt 1911A I carried in the shoulder holster for work. Next to it was the snub-nosed .38 detective special, the Smith & Wesson issued by the department that went in the fast-draw hip holster on my belt. It was small-framed enough to conceal easily under these flowy Hawaiian shirts, so I loaded it up, slipped it into the holster and clipped it to my belt. The .32 Beretta was there too; being ever so careful I checked the clip, made sure there was a round chambered and slipped it into my nightstand. The .45 would stay in the suitcase. I hadn't had a heater on my side since I got on the train to Miami. I felt better now, more like my old self. Once a cop, always a cop.

At a little after ten-thirty it occurred to me I had nothing to do. I wasn't about to stay in the room all day, but I had no idea what this little island offered as far as daytime activities. From the lanai I could hear the faint call of Bingo, but I really had no interest in it. I was thinking more along the lines of something on the water…boating, maybe even taking a crack at fishing. I found the phone in the living room…another hidden job, built to look like a coconut sitting on the table in the center of the sunken, circular sofa. I dialed #7, and a familiar sweet voice answered.

"Hey kid, it's Bill. So what's there to do on this little piece of paradise?" I asked. Her voice lit up with real excitement as she ran down the short list. She really did love her job. Melinda told me to meet her in the lobby bar in fifteen minutes, and she'd help me plan some fun stuff to do. As I hung up, all I could think of was seeing her beautiful face again. Man, was I gone. Then the memory of Jessica floated by, and I was gone way out, so far out I almost didn't make it back in. Two smokin' chicks, taking up all my thoughts. Not one thought about work. This was certainly turning out to be a great vacation.

In the lobby bar (a separate room made up to look like a sunken ship) Melinda did not disappoint. She stood near a giant fish tank built into the wall, holding a clipboard and smiling that smile again. A single, yellow flower held back long, dark hair behind her right ear. She wore a red and blue flowered dress, similar to the one she wore last night but considerably tighter and just a smidge more revealing. This number featured a plunging neckline that made my legs wobble, and a slit up the right side that almost made it illegal. She was barefoot.

"Hello Melinda," I said, full of unusual friendliness.

"Good morning Bill. Did you sleep well?"

I damned near blushed. "I had a great night," I said and left it at that.

"Let's have a seat, and we'll see what we can arrange for you to do today." She directed us to a table next to the fish tank.

Melinda showed me some brochures, very colorful and full of valuable information on such important topics as sport fishing, sail boating and snorkeling. It was hard to concentrate on the brochures of course, as she held them at about the same level as the plunge in her neckline. My one-track mind was full steam ahead.

I had just about settled on a little afternoon fishing trip when a mermaid came up and knocked on the glass.

"What the hell!" I said, and jumped out of my skin. In the giant tank were two women dressed in mermaid get-ups, complete with fishy tails, swimming around among the fish and coral. I could tell the one who knocked on the glass was laughing at my jump.

"Lelani and Kaliki, they're our mermaids," Melinda told me with pride. "They sometimes swim in the tank, sometimes in the pool. Occasionally they even swim in the ocean, but we have to be careful they don't try to swim away to their underwater city," she said jokingly.

"Underwater city, huh? And where might that be?"

"Spring Hill," she answered, and laughed that special little laugh again. I couldn't stand it.

"I've been a mermaid myself," she said a little playfully.

"Really? You swim in the tank?"

"I used to a lot growing up...even have my own tailfins. See those fish?" she asked pointing at the tank, "I know everyone of them by name."

"Come to think of it, I think I'll take the fishing trip," I said with a grin.

"Nice," she answered with a smirk. "Sure, go hook all my aquatic friends."

"Hey, you said the best fishing in the world is off the Florida Keys."

"I can't deny it Bill, I did say that. Just try not to reel in any blondes."

I know she said it jokingly but there was something behind it. Maybe...aw, what the hell, can't hurt to try...

"So that'll get me back by what, five?"

"Yes, around then."

"Good. Just in time for you to join me for dinner." There, I said it. She continued to smile, her eyes giant brown moons gazing at me. She hesitated.

"Normally I'm not supposed to dine with the clientele," she said slowly.

"You spent an hour locked in my room last night," I said coolly.

"In your case, Mr. Riggins," she said with that smile getting brighter, "being that you are a *VIP*, I'm sure the management can make an exception."

"Groovy. Eight o'clock work for you?"

"That's perfect. Mr. Bachman is back on duty today, so technically my responsibilities end at six. Not that it would matter."

"What do you mean?"

"Daddy owns the Island, remember?" she laughed, and said goodbye. She offered her hand, very businesslike, and I shook it. It was soft and luxurious, and that single touch made my soul scream for more. Then she was gone. I turned and looked at the mermaids. They were smiling at me. They knew. Smart fish.

## 1935

The weeks went by, then the months, falling away like too little sand in an hourglass, counting away the days since that wretched storm. Eliot had taken a moderate hacienda in San Francisco, a four-bedroom brick and stucco house overlooking the bay. The Miami and Key West properties had been sold, as well as the St. Augustine summer house and the Tampa townhome. All that remained of his life in Florida was the Island; by now it had been bulldozed and replanted with coconut trees and ferns, tropical flowers and palm plants of all kinds. And that's how it would stay, he thought, a memorial to those who died in the storm, never to be inhabited by people again.

It had been eight months since the storm when he met Marietta. She and her daughter had moved into the villa across from him, and stopped by one sunny June afternoon to introduce themselves. Marietta had been recently widowed, her husband's life taken by a steam shovel accident while building a pier. Eliot fell for her almost instantly, her and her beautiful five year old daughter. He invited them in for coffee; later he invited Marietta to a show. Within two months they were married...not quite a year from the date of the storm. Marietta and her daughter Melinda moved into the hacienda with Eliot just after the wedding in late August, 1936. As the nightmares of the Storm of the Century faded, Eliot once again found happiness.

I found fishing to be nice, if not a little dull at times. There were six other people on the forty-foot boat with me: the Captain, the first mate and four other tourists. None of us five knew anything about fish, fishing or boats, which made it a comically interesting day. The Captain, Captain Steve, was pretty patient with us as was his first mate Raul. They taught us how to hook the bait, taught us how to reel 'em in. We didn't reel much in though; in fact, only one of us five caught anything, a skinny kid that I recognized from the boat ride in. He hooked a forty-pound bass, and with the help of Raul got it into the boat. We all cheered, had a beer (all they brought on the boat was beer and pretzels) and headed back. Captain Steve told us he'd arrange to have the fish cleaned and cooked on the applewood fire pit for tonight's luau, with Jim (the kid) as the guest of honor. Perfect, I thought, a great story for dinner with Melinda.

A short ride back got us to the dock on Tiki Island.

Things had changed since we left.

Something happened.

There was a boat docked there with the word SHERIFF painted in big white letters across the back. Dozens of people were crowded on the north end of the Island, down by the gardens. Police were turning people away, and erecting barrier tape with signs that read "Crime Scene, Do Not Cross." My heart sank down into the pit of my stomach.

How? What? It seemed unthinkable that crime could find its way here, to this paradise, so far detached from the rest of the world. Maybe a little back-room gambling, possibly even some high-class call girl action, but this was no broken-up card game.

I knew what a scene like this meant.

It meant murder.

Damn.

I walked up to the crowd, not wanting to look too curious, and tried to see what was going on. As luck would have it Melinda was standing off to the side, speaking with one of the officers. She caught my eye; her face lit up and she called me over. I obeyed.

"Bill," she said, and that was all, as if she didn't know what to say next.

"What happened Melinda?"

She didn't answer. "Bill, this is Deputy Curtis, Deputy, this is Bill Riggins."

The deputy answered politely in a very deep tone. "Hello Mr. Riggins. Ms. Hawthorn tells me you're a detective from New York."

"Yes," I said with a slightly annoyed tone, looking at Melinda, "I'm on vacation."

"Well sir, when you have a moment, I'd like to introduce y'all to Sheriff Jackson. I'd hate to bother you on your vacation but something's come up, and I think he's gonna want to talk to you about it, if you don't mind sir."

"Not at all." Whatever it was, I really didn't want to get involved with it. But now that my pal Melinda had let the cat out of the bag, I guess I was stuck. "Do you mind if I have a word with Ms. Hawthorn, Deputy Curtis?"

"Sure 'nuff," he answered, "I'll go let the Sheriff know you've done arrived." He walked off past the crowd, through the crime scene tape and out of view.

"Ok sugar, spill it," I said to Melinda. Suddenly my cop demeanor was back.

"They found a skeleton buried in the garden," she said flatly. "The landscapers were digging up a section to put in two new totems and some plants, and hit the bones about four feet down. We called the Sheriff immediately."

A skeleton? That's all? Thank the lord, I thought. Even if it was criminal, it was old. "That's it, huh? Nobody murdered today?"

"No, thankfully. But it's extremely unnerving to find an unmarked grave in the middle of our beautiful gardens. We conduct *wedding* ceremonies there, for heavens sake."

"Listen, Melinda, those bones could have been there for years, maybe a century. How long did you say this place has been here?"

"The resort was built in 1937, 38. Before that, the Hawthorn mansion sat here, in basically the same layout as the main hall. I don't know what was here before that."

"Then it seems to me," I said while lighting a Camel. It was my last one. "That those bones have been here since at least before the resort was built, right? Pretty unlikely that someone would have planted them there while the place has been in operation twenty-four-seven, three-sixty-five."

The relief was apparent on her face. She let out a sigh that told me yeah, you're right, why didn't I think of that. I moved a little closer and put my hand on her arm. Her skin was warm, warm as copper on a hot day and the same tone. I gave her a little squeeze and she flashed that smile that I'd come to know so well.

"You're right, of course," she said, "I should have realized that. That garden's been undisturbed as long as I can remember. The body must be at least twenty years old, probably more."

"Probably. For all we know it could have been a native from a hundred years ago. I saw something in Key West about Indians living here, and tribes having wars with each other all the time."

"That's true," she said looking over at the gravesite. "After all, that's where Key West gets its name."

"I don't follow you."

She leaned in close. My hand was still on her arm. "When the Spaniards first landed in the Florida Keys, a major war between the native tribes who inhabited the islands had just ended. The beaches…in fact the entire island was covered in the bones of the dead, as one entire tribe had been wiped out and left to rot in the sun. The Conquistadores named the island *"Cayo Hueso"*, Spanish for 'Bone Island'. Through poor pronunciation by pirates and English sailors, Cayo Hueso became Key West, so the story goes."

"No kidding?" I said. "So the whole damned island of Key West is basically one big graveyard, huh?"

"Pretty much."

"Huh, crazy." I went for a stick. I was dry. "Say, is there someplace I can get a pack of smokes around here?"

"I'll have some sent to your room. Camels, right?"

"Yeah."

"And they sell them in the gift shop too. Here comes the Sheriff," she said, and I casually dropped my hand from her arm.

Sheriff Jackson was a big man. I'm six-two, and this man towered over me. He was broad too, a chest like a locomotive and a stomach like a rain barrel. He wore one of those cowboy-looking hats you'd expect to see on a southern Sheriff, a light beige one that matched the color of his uniform. On his hip slung low was a six-shooter about the size of a cannon. An antique .44, I'd guess.

Melinda introduced us.

"Pleasure," he said in a husky, breathless voice, the 'sure' in pleasure sounding more like 'shuh'. "Ms. Hawthorn tells me you're a detective with the New York City police. Hate to impose, but maybe you'd like to take a look at the scene and render your opinion. We haven't got a forensics analyst here; we have to wire up to Tallahassee and have a man sent down. Could be a few days. I'd like some experienced eyes before the rain washes everything away."

I must say, after seeing how southern lawmen had been portrayed in movies and TV, I was a little surprised he was asking for my help.

"I don't mind at all," I said, "Although forensics isn't really my gig. I'm on the vice squad, so I don't know how much help I can be."

"Any help would be help, Detective. Sho' would appreciate it." He motioned over for us to follow him through the crime tape. Melinda stayed behind. She hadn't seen the bones yet, and the last thing she wanted was to see something that would change her perception of paradise. I didn't blame her.

The Sheriff and I walked through the crowd and over to the grave. The gardeners had dug down into the soft, dark topsoil by hand, exposing the entire skeleton.

"There she is," Jackson said as he wiped his face down with a handkerchief.

"What makes you think it's a she?" I asked, curious.

"Found remnants of a lady's shoe…look down by the left foot."

I saw it, a dark mass of rotted leather and a two-inch heel. Definitely a woman's shoe. I shot my peepers over the rest of her. Remnants of rotted material clung to the bones like dead sails on a ghost ship.

I said, "Looks like a little of what's left of a brazier and a dress, too. Looks old."

"Yeah," he said, "probably from the thuhrties, I think. My wife used to wear 'em like that back during the war, when they was hard to come by." He knelt down and looked closer into the hole. The late afternoon sun was moving across the sky, casting angular shadows over everything including the grave. "Light's gonna be gone soon. You see anything else here that might help?"

I knelt down beside him and peered into the rectangular hole. It was almost as if they intentionally dug a grave there, pretty spooky. I wasn't new to finding bodies, but I usually found them in alleyways or in the trunks of cars. I looked over the remains, noticing the bits of clothing still clinging to the bones. The body had been laid out flat, intentionally, not a hasty burial where the body was thrown in a ditch, indicating it was more likely done with plenty of time, not a rushed murder. I relayed this to the Sheriff.

"I thought the same. Looks more like a proper burial than a cover-up. Notice anything else?"

"The skull," I said as I moved my position closer to the head, "Has been caved in. Could be from years of being underground. Or it could be from a club or other weapon."

"Yeah, I thought that too. Anyway to tell without moving it?" he asked.

"Is there any way I can get down there without disturbing the scene? If I can, I could look for sharp edges on the bones. If it caved in from the weight, the bones would be flattened more than broken. If someone crushed her face with a lead pipe or a baseball bat, the breaks would probably be jagged. Not exact science but it might give us an idea of what you're dealing with, Sheriff."

Jackson thought a minute. He wiped his face again, then took off his hat and wiped down his mostly bald head. Without the hat I could guess his age was around fifty-five, maybe older. He whistled over to the Deputy, and asked him to get a good flashlight, some rope, something called "the rig" and a pair of coveralls from the boat.

"We have a way to get you down there. I've got some coveralls you can wear so you don't get your fancy duds all muddied up. We've got a harness we used to pull people out of the swamps. We can use it in reverse to lower you down there. If your idea of the bones being jagged works out, I'll section off this area and call Tallahassee right away."

"Sounds like a plan," I said, and added, "You wouldn't mind if I have a drink while you set it up, do you? I am still on vacation after all."

Jackson laughed and shifted his weight to the right. "Go right ahead, Detective.

This'll take about twenty minutes to get together. Just come on back at five-thuhrty, we'll be ready."

"Groovy," I said, and walked back to where Melinda was waiting.

"How bad is it?" She asked, a little shake in her voice.

"I need a drink, come on and I'll tell you."

We made our way back to the Shipwreck bar in the lobby. No mermaids this time. I ordered a double bourbon on the rocks for me and a Mojito for Melinda. Somehow a fruity tropical cocktail just didn't seem right just now. Maybe later, but not now. I told Melinda what we saw, and what we were about to do.

"Do you think it was," she paused, then dropped her eyes. "Do you think someone was murdered, Bill?"

"Honestly, no. Not by the way the body was neatly buried, and so deep – four feet down. No one commits a murder then buries the body four feet down. It's too much trouble."

"Not if you have all the time in the world. Remember, this Island was uninhabited from late in thirty-five until construction began on the resort in 1937. If someone wanted to hide a body, this would be the perfect place for it."

"True," I said, and downed half my drink in a single belt. "But even still, why bury her so deep, if no one was around to find the body? They could have just as easily covered her over in a shallow grave."

"Maybe they did," she said, looking into my eyes. "Remember what I told you about Eliot planting over the Island with palms and plants? He instructed the workers to…"

"Lay down four feet of topsoil," I finished. Her eyes widened, as did mine. "Sharp thinking , dollface. You might just have something there."

"Actually, I hope not. It would be one thing if there were an old cemetery or something here that Eliot never told me about. But if someone were murdered here and the body hidden on the grounds, I don't think Eliot would ever get over that. He hardly comes out of his room now as it is."

"Wait a minute," I said, realizing what she was saying. "You're telling me that Eliot Hawthorn is here, on the Island?"

"Why yes, of course. We came here in 1938 to open the resort. We've lived here ever since. He used to run the Island until my mother passed away back in 1950. Since then, he's slowly become a recluse. He hardly leaves his room now, sometimes only to walk the grounds for a short time."

"I thought you said he left the Island for good?"

"That was his plan. Things changed when he heard they were rebuilding the Overseas Railway into the Overseas Highway."

## 1936

It was just a small blurb on the bottom of page two of the San Francisco Chronicle. Beginning in late 1936 the U.S. Government and the State of Florida would be turning the now defunct Key West Extension of the Florida East Coast Railroad into a passenger car highway, a two-lane stretch that would make use of the existing bridges and causeways once used for railbeds. The project was planned to be completed in less than two years, and the state hoped it would help drive automobile-based tourism to the central and lower Keys.

Immediately Eliot's mind started grinding its gears. Already bored of living the quaint family life, he yearned for the parties, the boating and the fun of the Keys. The memory of his lost wife and the events of Labor Day Monday, 1935 faded with each day, and he found himself ready to regain his rightful place as the premier socialite of Monroe County.

He just wasn't sure how the hell to do it.

Then one evening while driving through Oakland, he and his wife Marietta discovered a restaurant with a strange theme. The outside looked like something out of the Hawaiian Islands, with oil-burning torches and mystic voodoo masks (or so they thought). The inside was festooned with fishnets, floats and various sealife on mounted plaques. Palms and tropical flowers accentuated bamboo furniture and rattan wallpaper, and the bar was made of a dark carved wood, decorated with more masks and palm trees. Eliot had stumbled upon an establishment that went by the name of Trader Vic's, and his outlook would never be quite the same.

They stayed for dinner and spoke to the proprietor; they stayed for drinks and watched a live show of Polynesian dancers performing with lit torches to exotic jungle drums. They sampled original drinks with such outrageous names as Zombies, Scorpion Bowl and Samoan Fogcutter, and were floored by the signature drink, a rum concoction known as the Mai Tai. Eliot was hooked; right there he made a deal with the owner to pay him royalties to use the recipes and décor ideas, and made plans to open his own version of the Tiki-themed restaurant in the Florida Keys.

At first he planned to buy some property along the highway on Marathon Key, the unofficial half-way point between Florida City and Key West. Then he remembered the Island, with its beautiful beaches and lush landscape. He remembered the Island's secrets too, but decided to let those secrets fade into history just like the memory of his lost wife Vivian. He contacted an engineering firm, an architect, a master chef and a hotel industry supplier and put his new plan into action.

As the plans took shape, Eliot and Marietta's excitement grew, and it rubbed off on their six year-old daughter, Melinda. She was old enough to know what was happening, that they would be moving to an exciting new home with their own private beach and boats and music and laughter every day. Before the blueprints were even drawn up, Eliot had bestowed upon Melinda the title of Entertainment Director, in charge of making sure the guests were always well fed, well entertained and always smiling. She took her new title so seriously that by the time she was fourteen it was evident that she would indeed take over as Entertainment Director in the near future.

Together Eliot and Marietta oversaw every aspect of the new resort. The idea started out as a restaurant and bar that could only be reached by boat; by the time construction started it had turned into a sixty-room luxury hotel with several lounges, restaurants, outdoor dining, beach games, boat rentals, a giant salt water pool in the shape of a lagoon and a ballroom with dancing and Polynesian shows, all themed with the Tiki culture that was becoming so popular across America. The décor would be mostly Hawaiian, the food a combination of Asian, American and Caribbean, and the drinks exotic. A special area of the top floor would be sectioned off for Eliot and his family to live in, and Melinda would be schooled on the Island…in fact, Eliot would erect a school house on the east shore, where twenty children from Sugarloaf Key would come daily by boat to attend classes. It was run by one of the best school teachers in the state, and by the time the children reached ninth grade they were not only reading and solving math problems on a twelfth grade level, they could rig a sailboat, operate a motor boat, spearfish and were experts at Hawaiian culture and the hospitality industry.

Melinda even learned to speak Hawaiian, partly from her mother and partly from a tutor.

On October first, 1938, Eliot, Marietta and Melinda arrived at the west dock (the front entrance) to their recently finished resort. They christened it "Tiki Island," and officially opened for business at noon. In anticipation of the opening, tourists from all over the country booked the minimum two-week stay...and from opening day until the onset of World War Two, the resort remained booked at full capacity at least four months ahead.

Eliot was finally happy again.

He ignored the Island's secrets. Soon, he forgot all about them.

But not for long.

"Then in 1950 my mother was diagnosed with a failing heart. She was only forty-five when she passed away. Eliot was torn apart, he really loved my mother. Without her, he didn't seem to want to go on. I tried to become closer to him, and for a while I did, but I'm afraid his mind started to...slip."

Melinda finished off her Mojito and ordered another. I said no to a second Bourbon, as I was expected to do some police work in a few minutes. Ugh.

"What do you mean, started to slip?"

"Well," she said hesitantly, as if she'd realized she said too much. "He started...*seeing* things, mostly at night."

"Things? What things?"

The second cocktail arrived, and she used the interruption to try to change the subject. But I pressed her...curiosity had me by the neck.

"Ghosts," she said softly, "Ghosts from the past. Ghost of his first wife, mostly. He only told me once, after he'd been drinking quite a bit. He saw Vivian's ghost, and that of another woman, who he never called by name."

"That doesn't surprise me much. The shock of losing his second wife at a young age was enough to trigger some hallucinations. Seems textbook psychiatry to me," I said, trying to calm her. Tears were beginning to form in the corners of her eyes. She dabbed them with the cocktail napkin and took a long pull on her drink. Then she continued with that hushed tone that gave my spine a chill, and not in a good way.

"The funny thing is, it turns out he's not the only one who's seen ghosts on this island. Some guests have seen them too. And the staff. And even myself...I've seen a woman walk through a wall on the second floor." She paused and sipped her drink. Her eyes didn't come up to meet mine. "But it may have only been a trick of the light, right? The low lighting in here can certainly be misleading sometimes, don't you think?" she asked, as if needing reassurance, needing it bad.

"Sure," I said, because it was what she needed to hear.

"But now, now we have a skeleton of...of a *woman*, here on the grounds, in the garden. And so I don't know what to think." She was visibly holding back the tears now.

"Listen doll," I said; I put my hand over hers on the table and gave it a little squeeze. She looked up at me, her big brown eyes glistening wetly in the glow of the table candle, pleading for answers. "Listen, it's probable that women was part of an old burial ground or something, laid down long before Hawthorn even built his first home here. And as for ghosts…I don't believe in anything I can't feel or see, and I ain't never felt or seen no ghost, so as far as I'm concerned it is just a trick of the light or tormented man's hallucinations. So don't sweat it, OK? I'm sure we'll find a reasonable, natural answer to why there's a woman buried in the garden. So just hang in there kid, all right?"

The smile broke through, and she thanked me. I would have kissed her right there, I'm sure of it, if the Deputy hadn't come in to get me. Damn my luck, timing is always just a little bit off.

"We're ready, sir," Curtis said. I winked at Melinda and said so long, and left with the Deputy.

It was already getting dark when they lowered me into the hole. I had a powerful spotlight in one hand, a foot-long stick with a sharpened end in the other. High tech stuff.

"Can you see her skull clearly yet, Riggins?" asked Sheriff Jackson.

"Yeah, I've got a good angle here," I yelled back, and shined the light on the caved-in face of the skull. The black topsoil contrasted so well against the yellow bones that it was easy to see details. Tiny pieces of gold glittered in the area of the mouth; gold fillings no doubt. The cloth that clung to the bones was much easier to see now…red or pink broadcloth, remnants of a belt around the torso, and even the criss-cross pattern of a bra could be made out. I reached down with the stick and moved part of the bone away from the soil, just enough to see the edges. My heart missed a beat. My fears were met.

"Well, whatdya see?" came the voice from above.

"The edges are pretty jagged, Sheriff," I yelled up, "Can't be 100%, but if I had to guess I'd say this young lady had her face bashed in with something like a lead pipe, or a brick."

They pulled me up. Vacation over.

I'd been looking forward to my date with Melinda, but after having a skeleton dug up in her back yard I didn't think she'd be up to it. She agreed though, said she needed to eat anyway and the company would be nice. She was still strictly professional though, and I began to think my infatuation with this heavenly chick was a one-way street.

We met in the main restaurant, a little room they called The Hukilau, at nine. She had changed into a white, billowy sleeveless dress with white sandals and a white flower in her hair. It was the first time I'd seen her wear something without a floral print.

"You look very elegant in white," I said as I pulled the chair out for her.

"Thank you. Here in the Tropics, we don't really follow the rules of 'no white after Labor Day.' Seems somewhat silly when the temperature is in the eighties, don't you think?"

"Very silly indeed," I replied, happy that she was taking things light.

Everything she did was in slow motion, deliberate. She slid into the chair with the grace of a leopard, leaning over just enough to give me an eyeful. I wasn't sure if it was intentional, but it sure got my attention. Then she slipped a cigarette from out of her purse and slowly brought it up to those ruby reds, those lips that were a roaring fire begging to be doused. I almost forgot to light her up, I was so taken.

"So what's good in this joint?" I said foolishly while lighting her stick. "They serve burgers and fries here or what?" Yeah, real smooth, that was me. Mr. Smoothy. At least it got a chuckle.

She slowly took the cigarette from her mouth and handed it to me.

"It's for you, Bill. I don't smoke."

"Thanks doll," I said, kind of in a trance.

"Burgers and fries are only on the kiddie menu. For us, I'd suggest something a little more…exotic. I think the roasted mahi for me; for you, I'd bet you'd enjoy one of our eighteen-ounce filet mignons fire-roasted over applewood, and flanked with barbecued jumbo shrimp and jumbo lump crabmeat."

"They have a lot of cattle in Hawaii, do they?" I snarked.

"Only on Maui," she joked back. She laughed, not as lovely as before; it was tinged with a little sorrow and worry, but it was a nice laugh.

"The food we serve is actually not specific to the Pacific, so to speak. It's an eclectic combination of Asian, Latin, American, Caribbean and Polynesian cuisines, fused together to create something different, something…exotic."

"You sound like you memorized that off the sales brochure," I joked.

"I not only memorized it," she answered, "I wrote it!" The laughs came easier now, and it looked like dinner wasn't going to be an awkward drag after all.

We ordered and drank cocktails while waiting for the courses, talking about inconsequential things like Florida's sunshine and Weehawken's snow. The conversation drifted from the weather in the Keys to the hotels in Miami to the blue Chevy that I rented (a car I realized I really liked a lot, more than I probably should have). I smoked through a half a deck of Camels and drank a second round of drinks before the main course came, and the talk stayed light. She never mentioned skeletons or murders or Eliot's ghosts or anything that would put the brakes on an otherwise great evening.

She ordered Bananas Foster for dessert, and the waiter made a production of it tableside, setting it aflame before serving it up.

"You kids don't miss a beat, do you? Even pour rum on the bananas."

"The guests love it, especially when we set fire to it. We have several flaming dishes, and even a few flaming drinks. Care to try one?" she asked in that excited, still-at-work tone. I had other ideas.

"No thanks, I think I'll stick to the Mai Tais. Listen, what do you say you and I take a stroll along the beach? I hear the evenings are very beautiful down here in the Keys." I was laying on the charm a little thick, thanks to the rum. I tell ya, I could drink Bourbon all night and not feel it. But throw a couple ounces of pirate juice down my throat and watch out, sister.

"I can't," she said, taking me a little by surprise. "I have to spend some time with Eliot. He's been a wreck since he found out about the…you know."

"I do know. I didn't want to bring it up because I didn't want to spoil a great evening. But since you did…"

"I really don't want to talk about it Bill. It's very…disturbing. I may need to have a doctor come for Eliot."

"That bad, huh?"

"Yes, that bad." She looked down at her drink. It was empty. She slowly spun the glass in her hand, making little wet rings on the table. I waited. "He thinks…" she said and stopped abruptly, then looked up at me with those Bambi eyes. "He thinks it's his first wife. He thinks her body washed up here on the Island, and was somehow buried here after the storm."

"Well, what makes him think that?"

"He says he sees her. Now he hasn't told this to me directly, mind you. He talks…in his sleep. And sometimes I listen to him. He's said over and over that he sees his dead wife, Vivian, in his room, walking the gardens. And now he thinks her ghost is here, because her body is here."

"Melinda," I said as kindly as I could, "You have to understand, if he thinks he's seeing dead people, he's delusional. There's no such thing as ghosts."

"Are you so sure, detective?" she asked with a sort of odd tone.

"Like I said before, if I can't see it or handcuff it, I don't believe in it. I've seen plenty of people hallucinate over the years. The mind can be a powerful movie projector when it wants to be."

She leaned forward and looked into my eyes. I felt like she was using x-ray vision to burn right through me. It was a kookie feeling, and not a good one.

"What if I told you I saw her too?" she said, dead serious. Well I wasn't about to call her nuts, or a liar. I'd have to play this cool.

"I'd say tell me more." That was a smart move.

"Three times," she said, leaning back. "The first time when we first moved here. I was just a child, but I remember it clearly. I was in the garden, very near where the…body…was dug up today. I heard something behind me and turned to see what it was. I saw a misty, translucent form in the shape of a woman, hovering over the flower beds. She was wearing a large hat, so it seemed, and was looking down at me. Then she just disappeared. This was in the middle of the afternoon mind you, not at night when I was half asleep. At the time, I thought I was seeing things. Overactive imagination. Then I saw her again, when I was nineteen."

"What happened that time?"

"Almost exactly the same thing. Same place, except this time I noticed movement out of the corner of my eye. When I turned, I saw the shadowy figure moving away through the garden trail. I followed, but found nothing."

"Not a trick of the light?" I asked. I *had* to ask.

"No, I don't believe it was. If light did tricks like that, I should have seen it more often."

"Good point. What about the third time?"

"I don't think you'll believe me," she said, signaling the waiter for another drink.

"Lay it on me. I have no reason to doubt you." I didn't, really.

"Last night, in Eliot's room. I walked in to say good night. He was sitting straight upright in his bed, staring at the far wall, a pale, painful look on his face. He was trying to say something, I think maybe 'Go' or 'Gone'. He frightened me. I thought there was actually someone else in the room with him. I looked over to the wall, and for only a second…less than a second…" The drinks came and she took a long pull, trying hard to keep her cool. It wasn't working. She started to tremble just a little. "I saw that billowy image, that *trick of the light*. It was floating at the foot of Eliot's bed, arms spread wide, and I could see it clearly…" again she took a slug, and choked back tears and fright. "It was a woman. Her face was vague, her eyes…just dark, vacant ovals…And she looked…*angry*." That was too much for her. She turned away, then covered her face with her napkin. Before I could say a word she jumped up and made a run for the ladies' room. All I could do was wait, and let her words roll over in my mind.

Ghosts. She thought she was seeing ghosts. What the hell was that all about? With all the death I'd seen, from the battlefields of Korea to the streets of the City, I'd never seen, heard or even suspected I'd seen a ghost. Phantoms were fairytales made up to scare kids, not a thing more. But this doll had seen *something*. I was sure of it. Maybe not a ghost, but something, and it was scaring her silly because the timing was rotten, and a twenty-plus year-old corpse was sitting in her flower bed.

I finished my drink before she came back. She was well composed and looked great, as professional as a princess and twice as beautiful.

"You OK, kid?"

"Yes, I am now. Just needed a moment. I'm sorry I can't stay with you much longer, Bill. I really do need to stay with Eliot tonight. I'm afraid for him. I'm afraid this may drive him over the edge."

"But listen," I said, "What exactly is it that you think is going on here? I mean, do you think he's seeing things, or do you believe there's really something haunting Tiki Island?" I tried to sound sincere, not come off like a jerk. The rum wasn't making things easy for me.

"I don't know what to think," she answered calmly. "Maybe there is something here. Maybe that woman's ghost was trying to tell us she was buried here, although I can't imagine why. Maybe it is...no, that's impossible."

"Impossible that his first wife's body washed up here, or that her ghost is running around the place?"

"Both, I'd imagine. After all, she was lost in the upper Keys, in the sawgrass just south of the Florida mainland. It would be highly unlikely that her body would have come down this way. It's over one hundred miles," she added, taking another long sip of her cocktail. "I think that woman can be anyone. But it does raise a good point," she said, giving me a minute to think about it.

I said, "It could be anyone...anyone who drowned in that storm twenty years ago. The workers your father hired to clear the Island probably found her, and since there were so many bodies and no place to put them, they set her down nicely where she now lays, and poured the topsoil right over her, giving her an instant grave."

"Yeah, that would make sense, wouldn't it Bill?" Melinda finished off her Mai Tai and signed the check. Everything on the house. I had a feeling I was gonna earn it, and then some.

"I really must be going, Bill. It's after ten and Eliot shouldn't be alone." We got up and I walked her out to the lobby elevator.

"Can I see you again tomorrow?" I asked, and it was obvious to her now that I wanted more than a history lesson, more than just company. I wanted a date, and I made it plain and clear.

"I don't know, possibly. Tomorrow is going to be a busy day for me; it's Wednesday, and there are a lot of things going on. I'll let you know."

Disappointing. "Ok, kid. Good night," I said, and leaned in to give her a good night kiss. At first I thought she would pull away, she seemed hesitant. Then suddenly she surrendered; her lips met mine in a hungry passion fueled by the hot tropical night, and she gave herself to me completely, if only for a few, exciting seconds. Then she pulled away, and the look in her big browns was one of passion mixed with fear, and pain. I'm not sure what was going on behind those peepers just then, but she said the three words no man ever wants to hear.

"Sorry. I...I can't."

She pulled away, got into the elevator and went up and out of the moment, following me through the glass with those dark, sad eyes.

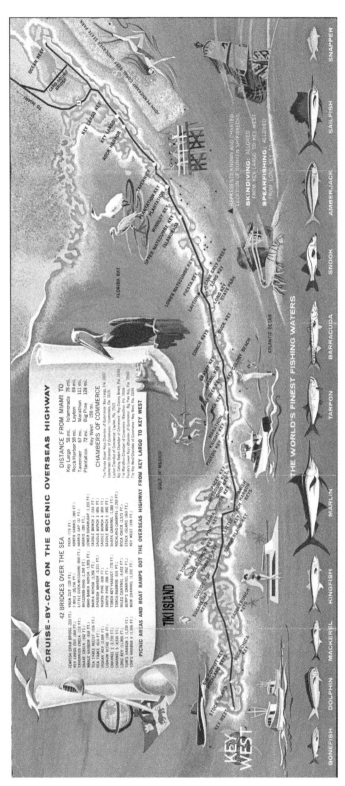

# CHAPTER TWO

Key West Florida, Tuesday, October 23, 1956

The white linen stuck to her like wet glue. Little drops of sweat slid down her cheeks and onto her nightgown, giving her a rained-on look. Blonde hair seemed almost chestnut as it matted itself against the soaked pillow and the side of her face.

The open window and the electric fan did almost nothing to quell the late October heat of the Key West flat. By five a.m. Jessica Rutledge had given up on sleep, given up on even getting any rest. The humid heat, the noise from the street below, the sounds from the next apartment, the slimy sweat and the incessant hum of the fan all worked together in a terrific effort to make her thoroughly miserable. They did a bang-up job.

On nights like this a few drinks (or something a little stronger) was usually enough to get her off to la la land. But tonight was different. She had a lot on her mind, and her brain raced with the events of the last few days. She had gone to Tiki Island to get away from…from her *life*, as it were, to take a few days to get cleaned up and rested and back on her feet so she could come back home with a little better outlook, a little better chance of survival. But it hadn't turned out that way. Jessica didn't get any rest, she didn't get cleaned up and she certainly didn't get away from it all. In fact, she had invited it in, on her own terms, and she thought that might give her a little feeling of control over her own life. Instead it made her sad. Sad that she had no control at all. Sad that she could have one night and one day of happiness sandwiched in between a dozen months of loneliness and hardships. Sad that she was stuck hiding on this little two-by-four island they called Key West. Sad she couldn't get away, no matter how much dough she saved or how many favors she gave; she was trapped in the Keys, in her life, and the only way out was to marry a millionaire or be carried out in a pine box.

Jessica stood up and peeled the wet linen off her body. For a second a cool whiff of air brushed her naked body, and she was relieved. But another second later the sub-tropic humidity closed in on her like a sauna to the point of nearly choking her. She had enough. Jessica struggled a thin, two-piece swimsuit over her sticky skin, grabbed a towel, and headed downstairs.

Her flat was on Duval Street, just above one of the busiest bars near the west end. Automobiles ran down the road even at this late hour, filled with drunken pirates and teenagers on a spree. The bars closed at four, but locals knew they could stay as long as they wanted, as long as they were friendly with the owners. Her place was noisy, but it was cheap.

She slipped out the backdoor of her building and headed straight for the beach a few blocks away. Surprisingly she didn't encounter any late night (or early morning) walkers along the route, and made it to the beach in a few minutes. It was dark but lights from the town and a few stars made walking along the shore easy. She found a nice spot as far away from the houses and hotels as possible, laid out the blanket near the surf, and stretched out.

It was a good ten degrees cooler by the surf, and the muffled sounds of the small waves running ashore were actually soothing to Jessica, a hell of a lot more soothing than the sounds of electricity and drinking and muffled sex back at her flat. She closed her eyes. The breeze gently brushed her body, her face. The waves purred. Her mind slowed down, and she finally began to drift.

Faded images of the man she met at the resort slowly floated over her mind. In her half-sleep, memories of sleeping with him became dreams, realistic dreams that carried her back to the bamboo suite at Tiki Island, dreams of him softly caressing her body as she slid over him, taking him, giving him everything she had. She smiled in her half-sleep, and was happy for a few precious minutes.

Then something went wrong. The dream changed; the man was gone, the sea had become wild. Giant waves crashed over the shore, ripping sand and coral away as they receded. The wind howled through her head like a hurricane, scrambling her brain and ripping through her eyes. A tidal wave loomed up in front of her, and as she gaped in horror at the twenty-foot wall of black water she tried to scream. Nothing came out. The wave crashed down on her with a hideous roar…

Jessica bolted straight up on her towel. The ocean was calm as ever, the night humid but cool. The first essence of sunlight began to glow in the east. In front of her stood a woman, tall, thin. She was in the surf, but the waves didn't splash around her ankles. Jessica strained in the dim light to see the woman more clearly, but the more she concentrated, the less focused the woman became. Then she began to move towards Jessica, walking out of the surf and onto the shore. Her feet made no impressions in the wet sand.

As she grew closer, Jessica realized she could see the surf beyond the woman…behind her…through her. Her eyes opened wide with terror as the transparent apparition came ever closer, revealing a swollen, bloated face devoid of eyes; black sockets dripped with salt water and seaweed, small crabs crawled out of the open mouth down the neck. It stretched out its arms in a sad soul-wrenching manner and reached for Jessica.

Jessica screamed.

The apparition dispersed, leaving her alone on the shore.

Shaking with fright, Jessica ran back to her apartment, forgetting the towel.

This wasn't the first time she'd seen this apparition. She'd seen it before, years ago, months ago, weeks ago, then again days ago in her room. She ran to Tiki Island to get away from it and still saw it there, looming over the bed after Jessica awoke from her night with Bill Riggins. Now it was before her, in front of her doorway.

It was following her.

"Leave me alone, please!" she screamed and the image disappeared.

Once inside the apartment, she did the only thing she knew how to do to make the visions go away.

It was only a little after ten-thirty when I nodded goodbye to Melinda through the glass elevator. Sure it was a long day, but I wasn't ready to hit the sack just yet. After all, I was on vacation, skeleton or not.

I decided to try Jessica's room. I didn't have the number so I made my way over to the front desk and rang the bell. The man behind the carved-wood counter looked like he might have carved it himself.

"Can you tell me the room number of Miss Jessica Rutledge?" I asked, lighting up a smoke.

The man nodded and flipped through a small card catalog, pulled out a card and said, "I am sorry, suh, but Mees Rutledge checked out thees morning."

"I see." I said, "Thanks just the same," and walked out into the night.

To my right were the gardens with the bones. I'd had enough of that for one day, so I ventured left. I was a little disappointed that Jessica had taken off without even saying a word, but I tried not to mull over it. This was a resort. Things like that happened at resorts. No big deal.

I followed the path around to the south side of the Island. Tiki torches lit up the beach and the little cabana bar. I ordered a Mai Tai and continued down to the beach. About halfway down a ring of people were enjoying some acoustic guitar and islandy singing. I kept going. A little farther down two hula girls and an old Hawaiian man were telling stories of Tiki magic and Island lore to a group of people sitting around on split logs. I stopped for a minute and watched. I caught something about the Goddess Kapu, something about Pele and a volcano. After a few minutes, I kept walking.

Soon I found myself at the back end of the Island. The beach was shorter here, only a few feet between the grass and the water. There were no Tiki torches here, only a few small incandescent lamps burning. They lit up a little road that wound back to the main building. This was the back of the house, the place where they brought in food, booze and other supplies. A small barge was docked at a wharf near the road, loaded with what appeared to be empty crates. 'Hawthorn Enterprises' was painted in big block letters on the side of the barge.

I kept moving, walking past the wharf and the road, hooking back along the beach to the north side of the resort.

This end of the beach was a little darker, and much less inhabited. The only light here came from the windows of the rooms in the north wing, the cheaper, smaller rooms added on long after the original building had been in business. The wing still looked like it belonged, still covered with rattan and Tiki masks and all, but it had a decidedly *less expensive* look about it. This is where the college kids and families stayed, just far enough away from the VIPs…like me. This was also where those same college kids were hiding out in the dark, apparently. At least three times I heard rustling and girlish giggling coming from behind a stack of palm plants and ferns. Crazy kids.

I passed the back of the Island and headed west along the north beach. The dark night was slowly being replaced by the yellow glow of Tiki torches once again. About half way up the beach I came across the outdoor bandstand where a quartet was playing Hawaiian songs led by a steel guitar. They really knew how to play it up at this place, I thought. A handful of people were slow-dancing to the music, while a few dozen more sat at bamboo tables and sipped drinks with lots of fruit and little umbrellas in them. At this point my Mai Tai was bye-bye, so I decided to order another. I sat at the bar and another pretty, Polynesian bartendress threw a bunch of crazy stuff together in a glass and slid it my way. Before I could take a sip, I had company.

"Mighty hot night, even for these parts," came the voice of Sheriff Jackson from my right.

"Well hello Sheriff. Surprised to see you here so late."

"Well, my business took so long to finish up I thought I'd just spend the night here, get a little rest before tomorrow. The wife don't mind, she rather enjoys the peace and quiet of my not snorin' in her ear, I imagine." He laughed and I did too.

"Find out anything new about the body?" I asked, interested.

"Nothing, no. Won't know a thing until the government man comes down from Tallahassee with the proper tools for forensics. I got my ideas, though."

"Oh? Care to share them?"

"Well," he said, and as he spoke he rolled a cigarette the old fashioned way, "Strictly off the books, I think she was a victim of a crime from way before this resort was built. I think she may have been murdered and buried in a shallow grave, then when those boys came in after the storm and added a few feet of topsoil to the Island, she got buried deeper." He lit the cigarette with a match and took a long pull. "I think maybe she was a victim of one Mr. Hawthorn's wild parties, back in his day."

That was a new one. No one had said anything about Hawthorn having wild parties. Then again I'd heard most of his story from his stepdaughter. "What kind of wild parties, Sheriff?"

"Oh, the usual. Rich folk gatherin' around the Island with lots of illegal booze back durin' prohibition. They used to bring it right up from Cuba, cases of the stuff on their yachts. A few bucks paid-off the local law at the time and the liquor flowed freely. Hawthorn bought hooch by the boatload and stored it in his mansion, and gave it out like candy at his parties. From what I hear back in the Twenties they done a lot more than that, too…reefer, cocaine, opium, you name it. They'd get all high and have themselves a grand ole time, and more times than not it'd end up in a roomful of naked folks sinnin' like there was no tomorrow."

"Sounds fun," I said jokingly. He didn't laugh.

"Well sure, fun for the men. But after every one of those parties there were a half-dozen or so young girls who left a little older and wiser, if you catch my meaning. And a few of them didn't have any good time at all. A few of them wound up in the hospital up in Islamorada."

"That wild, huh?"

"Yessuh, that wild. At least two or three girls every season would wind up getting themselves impregnated, and Hawthorn would pay big to shut them up…either enough for them to move off and start a life somewhere new, or to…well, you know…"

"Terminate?" I said, softly. I could see this man was very uncomfortable talking about such things, and I wondered why he was sharing with me so freely. I blamed it on the booze.

"Yessuh. He paid a doctor to do it, illegally of course. But he got away with it because big money talks big, and Hawthorn liked to get his way."

"What about his wife? What did she have to say about all this?"

"Ha! She was just as bad as he was. She was a showgirl in New York City when they met."

"Well, those New York showgirls do usually have a wild streak," I said. I knew from experience.

"In any case, tomorrow I'm gonna search through the old files for missin' persons and things of that nature. Y'all are welcome to come and help, if you'd like."

"Thanks for the invite Sheriff, but I've already got plans mapped out for tomorrow," I said, then added, "You know, you sure are being nice to me. I thought southern lawmen didn't like us Yankee boys much. I kind of expected you to say something like, 'stay outta my way, Yankee' or something like that. What gives?"

He laughed an honest, hearty laugh and finished his beer. Then he slapped me on the back and said, "I like you, Detective. You're a straight shooter like me. Sure, some of us southerners have a bad reputation for distrusting outsiders. And ya'll are gonna meet a lot of people like that here. But not me. I'm a Sheriff, and that makes me responsible for a lot of things around my county, from tippin' drunks into the lockup to chasin' down speeders to dealin' with murderers and pirates. And if I can get some help from a big city boy who might know a thing or two more about investigating a murder than I've ever had to know, then I'd be a fool to turn him away, don't you think?"

I took a long sip of the Mai Tai and said, "Well in that case Sheriff, anything I can do to help I'd be happy to, even though I'm on vacation. Except tomorrow. I've got an important thing I've got to do tomorrow."

"Well thank you son, I'm sure I'll be dialin' ya up in the next few days. In the mean time y'all have yourself a great evening. I'm gonna retire now to my room."

He left, and walked back toward the cheap rooms. I stayed and ordered another drink while the band played 'Beyond the Blue Horizon" with an island flair.

Two hours and four Mai Tai Cocktails later I stumbled up the beach toward the front of the resort. I tried to figure out how to maneuver around the garden so I wouldn't come near the skeleton, but the twelve ounces of rum I'd consumed made that an impossibility. I found myself walking straight towards the grave.

A few people walked past me in both directions, foggy-looking through my rum-induced haze. Brother, I could drink anyone under the table with Scotch or Bourbon, but that rum really did a job on me.

Up ahead the grave loomed on my right. It was roped off, but if someone weren't careful they could fall right in. As I got closer I moved to the left as far from it as I could.

Sitting on the bench next to the open grave was a young woman. She was in the shadows and I could hardly make out her silhouette, but she was there, leaning back and looking up the path away from me. As I approached she turned to face me. I nearly toppled over backwards. Her face was a hideous blur with black, eyeless sockets staring straight at me. I fell back against a palm tree and heard a voice say "You all right, mister?" The voice came from my left; I turned to see who it was – a young man, very large and muscular, probably a porter, I thought – and when I turned back to the girl she was gone.

"My eyes are ply..playin' tricks," I managed to say. "You work here?"

"Yes sir, I do. Can I help you in anyway?"

"Sure, if you don't mind buddy, I think I've hadda…a few too many…of those

My-thingies," I couldn't remember the name just then. "If you can help me back to my room there's a fin in it for ya."

"Of course Mr. Riggins," he said, and put my arm over his shoulder. "Come now, we go back to your suite. Is your friend coming to?"

"What friend?" I said, verily confused.

"The young woman that was sitting on the bench…I thought you were talking to her."

"You saw her too?"

"Why of course, she right over…Oh, I suppose she has left. Never you mind then, come, I help you."

My head was spinning like a top. Maybe I wasn't seeing things. I couldn't tell.

"Say, bud, did you get a load of her looker?"

"What, sir?"

"Her face, did you see her...face?"

"Ah, no sir. It was very dark, I just saw her shadowy figure there on the bench, then she was gone."

"Yeah, gone. Well…never mind, just throw me in my bed, k?"

"Yes sir."

Somehow he managed to get me up to my room, and I either gave him a fiver or a fifty, still not sure which. I flopped down in the bed and in a few minutes I was zonked out like a little kid at midnight. Crazy dreams bugged me all night. Dreams where Princeton was digging a grave for a woman with a brick embedded in her face. Dreams of giant waves washing over the Island, pulling me out to see. In one dream was Jessica, the pretty blonde who gave me the grand treatment last night and disappeared.

I awoke around eight fifteen with the rum still swirling around in my head. The soft crash of small waves against the beach came up on the morning breeze and filled my room. It was Wednesday morning, and I had plans.

By ten I was on the boat back to Key West. The Island was great, but my curiosity had kicked in and I'd gone into detective mode. While Jackson was snooping through old files, I planned to spread some questions around town, get to know the locals a little and see what they had to say about Hawthorn and his sexy parties. I was also excited by the prospect of motoring around in that blue Chevy ragtop…and about finding a pretty blonde who lived at the southernmost point of the United States.

The Tiki Express docked. I got my keys from the same old man I gave them to, jumped in the Chevy, pushed the button to take down the electric top and was on my way.

If I learned anything about the Florida Keys it was that the locals did one of three activities: They fished, swam, or drank. At this hour of the morning it was a sure bet the people I were looking for would be in the bar. So I headed down Duval Street and parked in front of Sloppy Joe's. Not surprisingly, I found my old friend Fernando sitting at the bar.

"Señor!" he shouted as I walked into the bar. "Ees only two days, the ghosts already chase you away?" he laughed, and patted the barstool next to him. He was wearing all white today, linen pants, baggy button-down shirt open at the collar down to his sternum. A bleach-white short-brimmed panama hat with a purple band sat above his tanned face.

"Not a ghost my friend, but an actual skeleton," I said quietly so no one else would hear. Publicity like that, Tiki Island didn't need. I palmed a twenty and shook Fernando's hand. "Shhh," I said leaning in, "Uno secreto."

"Aye," he said quietly. He took the bill without even looking at it. "For twenty anything ees a secret."

I ordered a cup of java. The bartender told me they had the grill going so I also ordered up a couple of eggs over easy and some toast. Just for the hell of it I offered to buy Fernando his breakfast too.

"Ah, thank you no, Señor. Ees no good with the rum this time of morning. I wait for the lunch, later. Now what ees this about the es-skeleton, huh?"

I gave him the quick rundown, leaving out the part about getting chummy with Melinda. Then I asked him about Hawthorn.

"Aye, Señor Hawthorn ees a very famous man around here. Even when I was a young boy in Cuba, I hear tales of his parties and wealth. He brought his yacht to Havana many times, and would pick up dee women...you know, the ladies of the night, to bring back. He would also pick up the rum and sometimes the cocaine or the opium. That man, he throw one hell of a party, no?"

"Sí," I said, thinking that if I were a vice cop in 1935 I'd have run him in and made it stick. The drugs and booze weren't so bad, if there were no kids around. But bringing in hookers from the slums of Cuba...

"You ever hear any stories about anyone getting killed, or disappearing from one of his parties?"

"Ah, no, I don't think so. Many people hurt...they get too much drink in them, they fall off the boats, or off the balconies and crack a bone or something, but I don't remember any keeled. Then again, Señor, I only live in the US for ten years. If you want to really know about him in the olden days, you must drive up to the Islamorada, and talk to the workers who built the roads. They were here when he had his parties, they were the ones who clean up dee Island after the Big Storm."

"Islamorada, huh?"

"Sí, you go, and you find a little bar next to the dock on the Gulf side. The bar, she named 'Coco's'. You ask for Henri, he is the owner. Nice man. For twenty dollores, he even nicer."

"Thanks pal. Just one more thing," I said while finishing the last of my eggs and java. "I'm looking for a girl. A blonde, about twenty five, name is Jessica. Rutledge, I think. Supposed to live here on the Key."

Fernando's expression changed from his usual smile to something of curiosity mixed with fright. I don't know what was going on in his head, but he was being careful. Too careful.

"Aye, Jessica. Why you look for here, huh?"

"I met her on the Island. Thought maybe she could answer some questions."

"Questions," he said quietly, as if pondering it over before answering. "Aye, questions. About the Hawthorn, no?"

"That's right."

He hesitated just long enough to make me suspicious something wasn't right. Then he said, "She lives above that bar across the street. I don't know dee number. She usually sleeps all dee day, and works dee nights, you know?"

I didn't know. Anything.

"Across the street. Thanks, I'll check it out." I tipped my Panama hat and Fernando nodded, a sort of strange look still stuck on his face.

It only cost two bucks to get Jessica's flat number from the super. Well, he wasn't exactly a super...he owned the bar and collected the rents, that was about it. Same difference. For two dollars this guy would have beat his own grandmother with a busted beer bottle till she gave up her knitting needles. You know, that type.

I walked up a hot, rickety stairway to the second floor. There were only four apartments there; only one had a big "B" painted on the door. I knocked. No answer. I called her name softly, then a little louder. Nothing. I knocked one last time and gave up. She was either out or out of it; either way she wasn't doing me any good.

I made my way back to the bar and got the super. He was chatty all of a sudden, probably expecting more scratch. I laid a fin on the bar and asked for a ginger ale on ice. He poured it, took the fiver and kept the change.

"Looking for info on a guy named Hawthorn. Know him?"

"Sure, everybody knows him, or knows of him. What's the angle?"

"Not sure yet. Keep it under your hat. I hear he threw some crazy shindigs back in the day."

The super/bartender wiped the sweat off his meaty face with a bar rag. "Yeah, that's right. He was a real swinger back in his youth. Big society things, with a twist...since no one was around to judge the people at the parties, they could pretty much do what they wanted."

"Yeah," I said, "Like if you were *at* the party, that meant you were just as guilty of the craziness as anyone, right? So no one would squeal if something went bad."

"Natch."

"How bad did it get?"

"Pretty bad. I worked there, years ago, long before it became the Tiki bar. Back in the late twenties, during prohibition."

"No kidding?" I said, "You don't look so old."

"Well thanks pal, it's the Florida water, and the climate. I'm fifty-six." He didn't look a day over forty. "Anyways this guy Hawthorn and his old lady would swing that place like there was no tomorrow. Booze, broads, dope, gambling, you name it."

"I heard all this before. I want to know specifics."

"Like whats all?" he said so eloquently.

"Like rapes. Beatings...even, murder."

The guy sunk back a little, his fat rear smacking up against the back counter. "Nah, I don't hear nothin' like that. Rumors, yeah. People love to make rumors. But nothin' like that went on when I was there. Sure, there were hookers, and sometimes things got a little rough with a drunk, but Eliot had bouncers the size of Reo Speedwagons that took care of things fast."

"So no beat-up dames, no...accidents?"

The guy looked a little nervous. More sweat, more wiping.

"No I said. Look pal, I think you drank up your fin worth of pop. Why don't you go for a swim or something, it'll do you good," he said, obviously trying to get rid of me. I knew I was licked; this poor schmuck was hiding something, and I was never going to get it out of him without laying on a fat pounding. Maybe not even then.

"OK, Mack, thanks for the info. And if you see Miss Rutledge, tell her Riggins was here asking for her.

"Sure thing pal," he said, and didn't take his eyes off me until I was out the door.

I was two for two. I popped into two more bars and a lunch joint and asked the same questions. I got the same answers, and the same curious sort of cut-and-run attitude as the first two guys. Everybody loved to reminisce about Eliot Hawthorn's wild parties, but as soon as you mentioned anything to do with murder they all clammed up. Coincidence? Don't believe it.

I was walking down Duval in front of an old church pondering these thoughts when a heavy, black pain nailed me in the back of the skull and the lights went out.

She escaped. Even the noise from the street and the afternoon crowds in the bar couldn't take her away from that blackness, that warm, comfortable feeling of being shut inside a coffin with just enough air to live. This was the end result; it was breezy, wonderful, filled with hope and the happiness that can only come from her one true friend. Then the happiness turned to exhaustion, and finally the dark wall of sleep slipped over her mind. It was a half-sleep though; while her body rested her mind still clung to gray thoughts, good thoughts, happy, content thoughts mixed with dark memories. Her future stretched out before her like a long bridge, long like the Overseas Highway's Seven Mile Bridge, long and high and on top of the world. And in that half-sleep she knew her life had meaning, had purpose. And she would not only survive, but *live*, and live well.

At eleven in the morning the darkness enveloped her mind completely, and she slid into full and complete sleep. Even the hard knocking at the door couldn't rouse her. It wasn't until after four that she awoke, and found him collapsed against her apartment door.

The voices were fuzzy and blue, like after a night of too much hundred-proof whisky. Although they were just whispers, every sound thundered through my head as if Thor himself were trying to beat his way out through my temples. Then a little light came in, and that hurt more. A grainy voice said something like "Let him have it again," and a cold, wet sensation closed out the light. A second later my eyes were half open and the light came in bright and heavy. The pounding in my head stayed steady. I tried to move and couldn't.

"You, wake it up boy, I ain't got all day," came a less fuzzy voice through the cloud of white light. It was a southern voice, an unfamiliar voice. It smelled.

"Give it to him agin," the southern, unfamiliar voice repeated, and this time I recognized the splash of cold water over my face. It snapped me out of the fog and the light began to focus.

"You awake boy? Say somthin' if you are," said the voice. Now it was attached to a fat man in tan shirt and cowboy-looking hat. His face was still a blur.

"I'm awaifff" I tried to say. Whoever bopped me on the skull did a great job.

"Well wake som'more. You got some things to answer to."

"Where..am I? Wah's going on?" I managed to croak out. I should have shut up. A big, meaty open hand came across my face, just enough to sting. "Hey, what the hell?"

"You asked enough questions boy. Now you gonna do some answerin'"

"Go ahead and ask, I ain't got nothing to hide, pal. I'm on vacation."

The fat man grunted in a sort of oinkish laugh. "Vacation, huh? So what's a New York City detective doin' snoopin' around other people's affairs all the way down in Key West Flori-day? Answer me that one, boy."

So he had my wallet. He knew my name then, where I was from. I didn't understand the cowboy hat. My brain was fuzzy and my head still pounding, hard. Then it occurred to me. He was a lawman. One of those Gaddamned redneck types I read about in interstate reports and dime novels. He no doubt hated strangers, hated black folks and hated Yankees.

"Doing a favor for Sheriff Jackson," I said. It was the only thing I could think of.

"Jackson? Well you listen here, dee-tective. Jackson don't mean shit in my town, and neither does no Yankee badge. I'm Chief of Po-lice Roberts, Key West. This is my town, and I don't appreciate no gat-damned Yorky boy askin' disparagin' questions about one of our most auspicious citizens, y'all here?"

Great, I though, this guy was more of a caricature than a real person. But I guess they had to get the stereotype from somewhere. I guess they used this guy to cast the mould.

"OK, Chief Roberts. This is your town and I respect that," I said not meaning a damned word of it. I was just buying some time.

"Now that's more like it, boy. Why don't you tell me what all this is about." He pulled up another chair, giving me plenty of time to survey the room. It was old, dark and damp, wood-planked on all sides. Large wooden barrels and stacks of burlap bags lined the wall. The space around a narrow wooden door and a closed window let in the only light in the room. It was a little cooler in here than it had been outside.

I was tied to a wooden armchair with medium-sized rope. My wrists were tied to the arms, my ankles to the front legs. An amateur job for sure. The chair was old and rickety.

"Well go on," he said.

"Did you hear about the skeleton found on Tiki Island?"

"No, I did not. What skeleton?"

"The gardeners dug up a twenty-year old skeleton in the garden. No one knows who it is. Sheriff Jackson found out I was on the Island on vacation and asked me to help with his investigation. Looks like it's probably just a body that washed up during the storm back in Thirty-five, but he didn't want to leave any loose ends. He asked if I wanted to help him get some information, so that's what I'm doing."

"Why you askin' about Mr. Hawthorn?"

"Why do you care?" I asked, fully expecting the fat hand that came across my mouth. I was ready for it though, and made it look a lot worse than it was.

"You stick to answers, boy, I's askin' the questions. Now, spill it all."

"One of the locals mentioned Hawthorn had some wild parties back in the Thirties. I was just asking how wild they were, in case maybe a hooker went missing or something. Doubt anyone would care now, but it would make the Sheriff feel better to know what the story was, that's all. It's been more than twenty years. Even if Hawthorn himself knocked off some doll and buried her on his island, there's no way it could be proven."

"That's right, there's no way. So there's no point in stirrin' up any trouble, is there?" he asked, and seemed to relax just a little. That was all I needed.

"Nope, none at all."

There's a definite advantage to being young and from the city. At twenty-eight years old I'd had my fill of bad situations, and learned the hard way how to get out of them. One of the youngest detectives on the force, ever, but the mind of man twice my age they told me. A lethal combination. Experience mixed with the strength and the balls of youth. I tilted the chair forward on the balls of my feet and rammed the top of the chairback into the fat man's face with as much force as I could muster. Blood burst from his ruined nose as he screamed in pain. I spun around on one foot, and planted the back leg of the chair square against his shin and ran it down to his foot. More screams. Then I heaved myself up, jumped as far high as I could and came down sideways on the chair legs. The legs folded up under me, and I was able to get up and smash the back into Roberts again. This time he saw it coming and put up his hands, but I was too fast for him. The wood split his lips wide open and more blood came.

I rammed the chair against the wall and on the third time it broke apart, freeing my hands. Roberts lay on the floor, gasping for air. I was in no mood to be merciful.

"Ok, you fat, lousy red-neck two-bit excuse for a cop," I said, and nailed him the gut with the end of my boat shoe. Good thing I hit the soft flab; I'd forgotten I wasn't wearing my cop shoes, and a swing like that to the ribs would have cracked a toe. I kneeled down next to him. "This," I said as I drove my fist into his already bloody nose, "Is for whacking me in the head with a sap. This," I said, punching his chest, "is for the two slaps, and this," I said as I took his own six-shooter out his holster and held it to his face, "is for being a jerk-off who thinks he can get away with anything he wants."

He screamed, he yelled No! at the top of his fat lungs. Then he wet his pants. He honestly believed I was going to shoot him. Good.

"You're under arrest for assaulting a police officer. You have the right to remain silent, and if I were you, I would."

"You…you can't arrest me, you're a New York City cop!"

"And at the moment I'm assisting the Sheriff of Monroe County. And if you think that doesn't mean shit, you're as stupid as you look and sound."

He considered that. He whimpered.

"What do you want, Riggins?" He knew I had him. Even if I couldn't arrest him, he was too stupid to bring a witness along to say I had resisted arrest or something like that.

"I want you to lay the hell off. You don't want me asking questions around town, fine, I'll back off. But you find someone I can talk to who has the answers and who will shut up about it. Otherwise I get my boys back in the city to start digging up dirt on your stupid ass, and I have a feeling it's gonna come up dirty, dig?"

"Yeah, yeah, sure Riggins, sure. Whatever you want. Fuck, I don't need that shitstorm comin' down on me."

"Then we have an understanding?"

"Yeah. Y'all just shut up about Hawthorn around town, all right? Then you and me, we can be great pals, right? No more tearin' each other apart. I'm gettin' too old for this shit," he said, and I believed him.

I helped him up, and gave him his gun back, sans bullets. He holstered it and sat on a crate. I found another and sat down.

"Why did you go after me like that, Roberts? What the hell's so important it's worth all this?"

"Mr. Hawthorn," he said breathlessly, "Is a great man. He's done a lot to make this town and all the Keys a better place to live. His cash rebuilt a lot of broken houses after that big storm, and helped to get the roads paved, and the drainage system put in. And he never asks for a cent. Sure, he had some wild parties way back. He was young and rich and that was his business. And yeah, he ran rum and hookers up from Cuba, and once in a while he even brought in some cocaine, or hash. But that was a long time ago. That all stopped after Vivian died."

"Vivian Hawthorn?"

"Yeah, of course."

"Funny you should call her Vivian, and him Mr. Hawthorn," I said.

"Well," Roberts said, then paused for a long breath. "I'm almost fifty years old, Riggins. Twenty years ago or so, when I was around your age, I was a deputy sheriff here. It was my job to make sure those rum and whore boats got into the docks down there safely, and that the liquor and ladies made it to Hawthorn Island without any trouble. I worked through Vivian. I knew her for years. She was a wonderful woman, a saint, and she was like a sister to me. I got myself invited to some of those parties and let me tell you, they were as fun and as crazy as you've heard."

He swallowed hard. I wondered if "sister" was the correct term for the relationship, but decided not to push it. He was still the law here and could still make trouble for me.

"So who are you protecting? Hawthorn, or Vivian's memory?"

"Both, boy, 'cuz when you slander Mr. Hawthorn, you slander her good name too. I can tell y'all this…There ain't never been a girl killed or even hurt bad for the five years I helped run liquor to that Island. I'da known. Those girls he brought in from Cuba, they may have been whores but they were high-class merchandise, and he paid top bucks for 'em. If anything ever happened to one of those girls, those Cuban boys woulda come up here and slit throats from Key West to Matecumbe Key. Everything was worked out real nice, and everybody got along or stayed out of the way."

"Just like with you and me," I said.

"Yeah, exactly like that. Come on boy, let's get outta this hole. I'll turn your direction to a man who can fill you in on the details." We got up and left. He never knew I had the .38 on my ankle the whole time.

After I left Roberts I crawled into a little side-street bar and grill, and took a seat way in the back of a covered outdoor patio dining area. Live chickens roamed the patio. Electric ceiling fans cooled the air just enough to be pleasant. I ordered a Jack and Ginger from a Latino fella, and asked him for some aspirin too. He came back a minute later with four aspirins, the drink, an extra glass of ice and a towel.

"You no look so good, friend. You can wash up in the back eef you want."

"Thanks pal, I think I'll take you up on that offer." I took the aspirins and two big gulps of the booze, and followed him back through the kitchen. On the way back I asked him for a grilled cheese sandwich and chips, and re-took my roost at the back of the patio. The ice was already melting.

While I waited for the sandwich I looked over the card Roberts gave me. The name and address was written in the scrawl of a man who had seen too many rough nights and bloody days.

"Captain Reams, Tours and Charters, Sunset Docks, Islamorada, Florida" the card read. Roberts said he'd be out all day, and to try him in the evening. Figures, I thought.

The sandwich came and I tipped the boy an extra fin to let me sleep off the head-pounding. He obliged and said he'd wake me up at four. I finished the sandwich in six big bites, downed it with the last of the drink and sat back in the chair, my panama resting over my eyes. I didn't even realize I fell asleep so fast, because what seemed like a minute later the boy was waking me, the ice was water, the sun was hanging low in the sky and my Bulova told me it was four o'clock. I was still pretty exhausted but managed to pull myself up to Jessica's door. I knocked. Still no answer, so I sat on the floor. That fast, I fell asleep again, right there next to the door.

"Bill? Bill??" she said as she shook me hard. I woke up, and the head-pounding started again though a lot duller than before. "Bill! What the hell happened to you?"

I looked up and there was Jessica, wearing nothing but a filmy nightgown, her blonde hair pinned up. She was beautiful.

"Hiya doll, been lookin' for ya," I said as I got to my feet. "Tried knocking but got no answer. Figured I'd wait up here 'til you came home. Guess I fell asleep."

"I was home," she said, "I was just sleeping…I took a valium before I hit the hay, and when I do that even the roosters can't wake me up."

I got to my feet. "Can I come in?" I asked pleasantly.

"Um, sure…just a sec," she said, and closed the door in my face. Noises of a few things being thrown around, drawers being shut, and the door opened again. "It's not very big I'm afraid, just a place to lay my head. But I do have an icebox with some pop. Would you like one?"

"Sure," I said, and she gave me a cold bottle of Coke. It hit the spot. "So what are you doing here in Key West, Bill? Taking in the sights or did you just miss me?" She took a long pull of her soda, and pressed the cool bottle against her cheeks. The filmy negligee left very little to the imagination. There's no describing that sight, so I won't even bother trying.

"Little of both. Actually I have to make a run up to Islamorada, and I could use some company. Thought maybe you'd join me. I have a convertible."

"Ooh, nice, she said, "But I'm supposed to work tonight."

"What time?"

"Eleven."

"Can we make it up there and back by then?"

"We might but it would be pushing it."

"Then call out sick. If you need the dough, I'll spot you a day's pay. I'm loaded, since I don't have to pay for anything at the Island."

"I don't know Billy, not so sure an insurance investigator can afford me."

"Try me, What do you make as a hostess, fifteen, twenty dollars a night?"

"Try a buck-fifty," she said, and got a sort of strange look in her eye.

"A buck-fifty?" I repeated, and almost choked on the Coke. "Where do you hostess at, the Ritz?"

"No," she laughed, "I just know how to bring in the tips."

"Tips? Wait a minute, what kind of hostesses are we talking about here?"

"The kind that look pretty, and have nice conversations with rich men to make them have a fun time. Usually at golf clubs, country clubs, and sometimes even at parties over on Tiki Island."

Of course she was lying, but I didn't know that at the time. I was barely listening to what she was saying. It was hard to listen with nothing between us but a thin layer of see-through silk.

"And they give you money for being pretty?"

"Sure," she answered, "And for making good conversation, of course."

I had no reason to doubt her, so I continued on.

"Well look, if you can swing it, I'd really like the company on the drive. If you want, you can stay with me...at the uh...you know, at the suite."

She gave a little giggle, and took another drink of her Coke. She lifted the bottle high, which lifted her breasts high too. It was all I could do not to jump her right there.

"Sure," she said, "Monday night was fun. I don't get to have fun like that much. And I could use a nice drive too. I haven't been in an open car in a long time. Just give me a minute to change."

"Ok then, should I wait outside?"

She slipped off the nightgown exposing her fully-nude self to me. "Don't be silly, Billy. There's nothing here you haven't seen already." She turned and slid into a sundress and sandals. I downed my Coke in one long gulp, wishing it was spiked with Bourbon.

The late afternoon sun was drifting down into the west, but at four-thirty it was still bright as could be. By now in the city, the sun would be almost gone, hidden by the tall buildings then hidden by the horizon. The days were longer here, somehow. Like perpetual summer.

We motored down the Overseas Highway in the ragtop Chevy with the top down and radio on. I had it set to a Rock 'n' Roll station, and Jessica didn't seem to mind. She sat in the passenger seat wearing a pair of big, pink, cat-eyes sunglass and an oversized yellow straw hat the flapped in the breeze (don't ask me how the hell she kept it from flying off, just a dame thing, I guess), and bopped along with most of the tunes that came over the noise box.

The temperature dropped a good five degrees as we started over one of the smaller bridges near Bahia Honda.

"So this used to be all train tracks, huh?" I asked.

"Before my time," she yelled over the wind and the radio. "I don't remember it at all."

"Were you born in Key West?"

"Born and raised. I never went north of Key Largo until I was eighteen."

"What happened when you were eighteen?" I asked, just making conversation. She looked away, over the Atlantic. I looked straight ahead at the long stretch of flat bridge.

"I met a boy," she finally said, "He lived in Miami and invited me to come up to South Beach. Said he liked me and he'd help me get a place and a job there." Jessica looked back out at the ocean again, away from me.

"So how did you wind up back here?"

"Things didn't work out," she said quietly, and I knew not to push it any farther.

An hour later we were pulling into Islamorada. I wouldn't have time to follow up the lead Fernando gave me, so I headed for the address Roberts scribbled down. I found a sign for Sunset Dock and turned off a little side road paved with clamshells. It led back to the Gulf side of the island, to a little set of weather-worn gray docks with a shingle-clad shanty at the shoreline. The shanty was small, only about thirty feet wide and fifteen deep, and was covered with rusting metal signs adverting everything from Nikkle Pop to Shell Oil. Various oars, barrels, fishnets, old fishing rods and coils of rope completed the decor. The words "Bait and Tackle" were painted in a semi-circle of faded white letters on the single, large-pane window, a window so dirty you could barely see the yellowed curtains behind it. A wooden sign nailed to the door read "Sunset Docks, Cap't Reams, Proprietor."

"Are you sure you got the right place, Billy? This joint's a far cry from Tiki Island."

"This is it. I'm not here to rent a boat. I'm here to get a story."

Jessica didn't ask any further questions, which sort of surprised me. We headed up to the dock and over to the shanty. A small garvey boat was docked behind the little bait and tackle shop. It was the same color gray as the dock and the shop. Next to the building, however, sat a forty-foot fishing trawler with a net crane and a big sign that read 'Charters'. I saw movement behind the sign.

"Hello? Captain Reams?"

A man, rough around the edges and dressed in green rubber overalls came out from the cabin of the boat.

"Aye, that'd be me," he said, not sounding like an islander at all, but more like a cross between a New Englander and a pirate. "Charter's done fer today, closin' up shop til mornin'."

"I'm not here for a charter," I yelled back.

"I reckon I could open up the shop for ye, ifin' it's bait or fish line or the like yer needin'." He walked up the gang plank to the dock, and met me in front of the store.

Captain Reams was not a young man, and not a particularly handsome man either. The years of salt and wind had eroded his face like so many chasms on a mountainside, but his eyes were bright and alive. He couldn't have been more than five-foot six, but he seemed much bigger.

"My name is Bill Riggins, I'm an investigator from New York, down here on vacation, and have offered to help Sheriff Jackson with an investigation. I was asking some questions around Key West when the Police Chief, man named Roberts decided he didn't like that idea too much." Jessica let out a little gasp but took it back quick. Seemed she wasn't too kool when it came to mentioning the cops. Good thing I hadn't told her I was one, I guess.

"Oh yeah, Roberts. Nasty man he is, but not too rough when you get to know him. He send you here, son?"

"Yeah, he said you might have some answers for me."

"Well, I'd imagine that would greatly depend on the questions. Come on inside, I've got cold beer and I could use one. You too missy," he said to Jessica, "Or I've got pop if you ain't old enough to imbibe," he said with a wink.

Jessica flushed a little. I said, "Sorry, I've forgotten my manners. This is

Jessica, a friend."

The old man took her hand and shook it gently. "You look a might familiar, Miss Jessica. Have we met? Possibly on Key West?" She looked over at me sort of jerkily, then looked down.

"No sir, I'm sure I would have remembered you," she answered sort of timidly. Little gears were clicking away in my head. I ignored them. I said,

"I think we'll both take you up on the beers Captain," and he led us inside the shop.

Once inside, the aroma of fish and seawater assaulted me like a slap in the face with a wet mackerel. It was fairly dark, and every inch of every wall was covered in shelves stacked with fishing gear, or hooks with hanging fishing gear. The exposed rafters were draped with giant fishing nets, and cork and glass floats hung from every available nail. Sets of oars, probably not used for decades, criss-crossed above the front window. The back of the shop had no windows, only a door leading out to the dock with the garvey. The floor was just like the dock except covered in crates and barrels, probably filled with more fishing gear and bait.

A refrigerated tank stood by the wall. Captain Reams retrieved three Pabst Blue Ribbon bottles from it, and as he did I could see packages marked "Squid", "Eel" and the strangely vague "Baitfish". He directed us to sit at a table (actually a giant wooden cable spool that was doubling as a table) and we pulled up a couple crates and sat.

"So how is ole Lem," Reams started.

"Lem?" I asked?

"Roberts. We call 'eem Lemon Head, Lem for short. You know, on account he has lemons for brains."

I laughed, and so did Jessica...a lot more than she should have, maybe.

"That's great! Well, 'ole Lem' has a busted nose and a couple of loose teeth at the moment, Captain."

Reams looked square at me, rocking slightly back and forth on the chair. He was still wearing his weathered, grayish-white Captain's hat. He tilted it back off his face, and lit up a pipe. "Messed with the wrong man, did he, ole Lem?"

"That he did Captain."

"Don't you trust 'eem son. He's a sneaky sort. Lawman or not, iffin' he don't take a liking to ye, he can make things pretty hard for ye."

"I'll keep my peepers open, but I ain't too worried. I can make things hard for guys like him too," I said, and lit two Camels. I handed one to Jessica. Her hand had the slightest tremble in it when she took it.

"So what was it the Chief thought I could oblige you with, Mr. Riggins? Islamorada is a long way from Key West, and I ain't been down that way in nigh-on fifteen years, I'd imagine."

On a feeling, I looked over at Jessica. Her usually calm, cool demeanor was slipping. Her eyes were a little wider than they should have been, but I didn't really notice. A gear clicked. I ignored it.

"I'd like some information on Mr. Eliot Hawthorn," I finally said. I got no reaction.

"I never knew the man personally."

"Roberts seemed to think you might know something that could help me."

"Well, son, maybe that's why we call him ole Lemon Head."

He had me there. But that wasn't it. This old salt wasn't the talking kind. You had to ask the right questions to get what you wanted out of him.

"You ever work for Hawthorn?"

"That I did," he said, and took a puff on the pipe. The scent of cherry pipe tobacco filled the air, overpowering the odor of the bait.

"When?"

"Twenty-seven through Thirty-six, I'd imagine. I was an officer in the Navy, put in my time during the Big War...the first one. Then, after it was over, I was diagnosed with a TB. I lived through it, as you can plain see, but my career in the Navy was over. I wandered down here one winter when the fish weren't bitin' up in Maine, and ended up stayin'. I bounced from job to job, fishery to fishery, boat to boat until Eliot Hawthorn found me workin' on a trawler. He needed someone to build and oversee his docks for him out a Hawthorn Island, and said he didn't want to pay a rich firm when he could give the money to some folk who really needed it. So he made me the man in charge of his docks, and eventually his boats, and I ran the docks and boats until the Great Hurricane washed it all away back in thirty-five."

"I though you said you never met him."

"I said never personally. On a business basis, I know him well."

What a kook this guy was.

"You ever been to any of his parties?"

Reams shook his head, "Nah, nah. Hawthorn was a nice man, a generous man. But he knew where the line divided friends from employees, and stuck to it. The only ones on the payroll that got invited to parties were the few who helped him uh…import…stuff."

"Like booze and hookers from Cuba," I said. I noticed Jessica, who had been very quiet, shot a very faint look of surprise. Click, click.

"Yes, son, like booze and…ladies of the evening, from Cuba."

"Ok, well did you ever hear of anyone getting roughed up at those parties…bad I mean, like a rape, or possibly a murder?"

Another laugh from the old man; this time he slapped his knee so hard I thought his bones would crack. "Murder? Rape? No sir, not on Eliot's Island. Miss Vivian would never have put up with such things. Remember, they were high society. Least the fact is that Eliot Hawthorn was. Vivian was a showgirl from up north, I believe. But she could be very lady-like. She'd never have forgiven anyone who committed such a crime at her home. She'd not hide it, either. If there was a murder back then and either Hawthorn knew about it, they would have had the murderer strung up by the nearest palm. Funny thing to ask a man, Mr. Riggins. Why, may I ask?"

It occurred to me just then that I hadn't told any of this to Jessica yet. I planned to tell her about it on the ride down, but it slipped my mind somehow. Now I had to lay it all out for both of them. No sweat, I guess.

"Well, Captain, and I meant to tell you this on the ride down Jessica but just didn't get the chance…"

Jessica tensed up, noticeably.

"Yesterday a skeleton was found on Hawthorn's Island, in the garden. It was buried down about four feet, and appears to be a woman. Also seemed to be she was buried there purposefully, not just thrown in a shallow grave."

Jessica's tenseness relaxed but was replaced by an expression of shock and a little horror. Reams just looked at me.

"Now I know why Lem sent you down to see me," he said, taking another puff of his pipe.

"Why's that?" I asked, not catching his drift.

"Well, he likely thinks I might have been the one to burry her, I'd imagine."

The early years of Tiki Island were some of the best of Eliot's life. For the first time, Eliot Hawthorn was not just squandering his days sipping gin, playing golf and enjoying the luxuries of the rich. He was working, something he thought he'd never want to do. Eliot ran the day-to-day operations of the resort, along with a general manager and several assistants, of course. Marietta worked too; as Food & Beverage Manager she was in charge of all the resort's restaurants, bars and snack shacks. Melinda, of course, was the unofficial Entertainment Director, a good-will ambassador who often greeted the guests at the dock wearing a traditional Hawaiian Hula skirt and lies. She learned to dance several authentic Hulas before she was ten, and performed once a week in the main dining room with the seasoned professionals. She was so enamored with the idea of being in charge of the Island's entertainment at such a young age, that Eliot even went as far as to change the real Entertainment Director's title to Showroom & Special Events Manager.

Then in December of 1941 the war came to America. Suddenly people were cancelling vacations, and soon Tiki Island was losing employees to the draft. The sounds of fighter planes on training missions from Fort Lauderdale filled the afternoon skies, and fuel for the water taxies became difficult to find, even for a wealthy man like Eliot Hawthorn. Several hurricanes, no where near as strong as the Great Atlantic Hurricane of Thirty-Five but destructive nonetheless damaged areas of the Island and the hotel. With less than half the money coming in and the mounting costs to repair damage and operate the resort on war-time rations, Tiki Island went into the red for the first time.

And of course, there was the war itself. America was at war with the Japanese, and the war was being fought in the Pacific on the shores of the islands that Tiki Island had embraced. Now when people thought of Hawaii, instead of thinking of pretty Hula girls and luaus, they thought of Pearl Harbor. When they saw a palm tree on the news, it often had a wounded soldier leaning against it. Eliot and Marietta feared their Island getaway would be seen in a very bad light, an insult to the men who fought and died in the Pacific.

But that wasn't the worst of it.

Eliot had started seeing things.

From the day they landed on the Island in 1938, he had a strange, foreboding feeling that had him looking over his shoulder and keeping nightlights on in every room. The feeling was weak at first, but it was there. But soon after they opened the resort Eliot saw the first apparition, nothing more than a white, wispy cloud hovering over the garden but something that definitely didn't belong there. It didn't look like anything in particular, but Eliot could *feel* it was a presence; he somehow knew it wasn't just fog, but something that once had a soul.

1942 saw the toughest, slowest year for the Island yet. And for the first time Eliot and Marietta seriously considered closing down the resort.

"But you can't!" protested young Melinda. She was only twelve years old but had become so wise, especially where the Island was concerned that when she spoke, her mother and stepfather listened.

"It's no use, sugarplum," Eliot said, "We can't even get pre-mix for the boats. No boats, no people. No people, no Tiki Island."

"Is that the only thing keeping us from operating?" she asked, already knowing the answer.

"Of course not. There's the economy. And the fact that we can't get most of the supplies we need to cook a proper dinner for our guests. And of course, there's those damned airplanes going by every day."

Melinda sat down at the carved mahogany table with her mother and Eliot. She was wearing a floral sundress and had a tropical lily holding her hair back on one side, as she often did. She thought only a moment before speaking, and chose her words very carefully.

"Mother, Eliot, as Entertainment Director of this Resort, I would like to tender my suggestions for its improvement."

Eliot and Marietta smiled; they didn't laugh because they knew this wasn't a joke, but they smiled because of the enormity of the sentence coming from such a small, young girl.

"Oh would you now?" Eliot said. "Go on then, we are listening."

"Our first concern is the boats. No gas, no boats. Well it seems to me our native ancestors got along fine without gas-powered motorboats for a very long time. So I suggest we moth-ball the motorboats for the duration of the war, buy several smaller sail & oar-powered launches and hire boys too young to get drafted to operate them. After the war we can sell the boats, or keep them to use as rentals for guests."

Eliot stared in amazement. Being someone who always had things handed to him on a silver platter, it never even occurred to him that there could be alternatives to the problems at hand. He was ready to give up; Melinda was just getting started.

"I like that idea. It even gives the Island a little more authenticity, if less convenience," he said smiling. "Ok, so we have a way to get people to the Island. What about the cost? The war has still put a dent in a lot of people's pockets."

"And it's making others quite rich," Melinda said. "So many business that are getting government contracts for the war effort…right down to the housewives who are taking jobs to help while their men are in action. Those are the people we advertise to. And we offer them special war-time rates. So what if we cut our prices a little? It's not like we need the money. We just want the resort to flourish. As long as we don't lose money, we're golden."

Marietta joined in the conversation then with, "I think that's actually a splendid idea. It's true there are many who are doing well. If our past customers can no longer come to us, we simply appeal to new customers."

"That could work," Eliot agreed. "Ok, so let's say we get enough people to operate the Island at two-thirds capacity. We've got rowboats to get them here. Now they're here. Now what? What do we feed them?"

"Mother, as Food and Beverage Manager that should be a no-brainer for you," Melinda said. Marietta simply shrugged.

"We modify the menu to include more local fare. More fish, more lobster, more beef, more citrus. Anything difficult to acquire, we save for nightly specials. We'll have to challenge the head chef to make some changes not only in the menu, but how things are cooked, what with the rations on butter and all. Gosh, we can really do anything we want and tell people it's from some obscure island in the South Pacific! Who's going to know the difference?"

Eliot considered. He held his stubbled chin in his hand, and rubbed it as he thought. "Ok, kiddo. Assuming all that is true, and we can pull it off…we still have the stigma of the war in the Pacific to deal with. How do we keep people from equating Tiki masks and palm trees with the war?"

"We don't," Melinda said without hesitation. "We exploit it. We scream it to the world, 'This is what life in the Pacific is all about! This is what our men are fighting for! Experience the culture, the magic of Hawaii and Tahiti and see for yourself why we're sacrificing so much to save it and its people!' In fact, Eliot, we could go one further…we could sell war bonds, and anyone who books a stay with us and buys war bonds, we could match it…say, up to ten dollars per person…to help the war effort!"

Eliot was floored. Sell war bonds? Rowboats? Fish? Where was this child coming up with such things? Was she really only twelve? "I've got to hand it to you sugarplum, you've got something there. All that just might work."

"You really think so Eliot?" asked Marietta, not doubtfully but hopefully.

"I do. Tomorrow we start looking for a place to stow the motorboats and buy some sail launches. Marietta, you talk to Chef Kumo first thing in the morning about a new menu."

"What 'bout me?" Melinda asked, hoping to be taken seriously, and to finally be given a real, adult task to undertake. "I'm sure I could be of help. Really."

Eliot said, "Sugarplum, you're smart as hell, but you're still only twelve. I'm not sure you could –"

"Put me in charge of the war bonds!" Melinda blurted out before Eliot could finish. "I already know who to call to get things set up. I'll call the War Department tomorrow. And get it all set. It'll be a snap! Oh, and I can help with the advertising too."

"Advertising?" Eliot asked, now actually laughing.

"Natch. I can write all about how wonderful we are for the new brochure. Then we can hand it over to an agency so they can tweak it up and make it look pretty. I can do that. I know I can!"

"I don't know, writing copy for a brochure takes a lot of experience…"

"Oh, let me try at least! Please Eliot! Please Mother! I know I can do it, it's a cinch!"

"Oh, let her try Eliot, what harm can there be?"

"You're right Marietta. OK then sugarplum, you set up the bond sales, and begin writing about how wonderful Tiki Island is, and we'll go from there. Fair enough?"

"All reet!" Melinda screamed, sounding more like her age now. She was smiling from ear to ear, really.

"Good. Just make sure when you write the brochure, you don't put in things like 'cinch' and 'all reet', ok?

"That's a plenty, big Daddy! Natch," Melinda said, and ran off.

Melinda Hawthorn took her position as Entertainment Director very seriously at Tiki Island. It was a well known fact among the management and employees that although Eliot Hawthorn hired Rutger Bachman as General Manager, it was really his stepdaughter Melinda who was in charge. Hawthorn needed Bachman as a front man, an experienced hotel & hospitality industry heavy who had worked in every major hotel from New York City to London, and had a Masters Degree to back up his clout. But Hawthorn wanted to keep his dream Island in the family, and since he never had a son, Melinda was it.

Of course this caused some problems from time to time between Melinda

Hawthorn and Rutger Bachman, but generally they got along well enough for a civil working relationship.

Tuesday had been a disastrous day for Melinda. Bachman decided to take a second day off since the week was slow, and Melinda had no problem taking over control of the resort for a second day. Then the gardeners found that wicked skeleton in the garden, and all hell broke loose.

Then that charmer of a detective from the north kissed her, and her head damned-near flew off her shoulders. And to top everything off, Eliot began having the nightmares again, evil nightmares that made him sweat and scream and cower with terror at the headboard of his bed, curled in a ball like a small child trying to ward off the monster in the closet. When Wednesday came around Melinda was exhausted, depressed, and in the foulest mood since she could remember.

"Good morning, Melinda," Rutger Bachman said in an overly cheerful voice. "Did I miss anything interesting on the Island yesterday?"

He hadn't heard.

No one off-Island had. It had been hushed up pretty well.

"Come on Rutger, let's get some java and I'll tell you everything."

A half hour later, Bachman sat in the bamboo chair of the coffee shop splayed out in disbelief, an expression of true puzzlement plastered across his otherwise proud, somewhat snooty face. Melinda simply sat in a prim pose in her chair, stirring her coffee around and around.

"How can this be, Melinda? You've been here, what, more than twenty years! And no one ever knew?"

"She's buried four feet down, Rutger. We've never dug down that far before. Or in that spot."

"This is bad, very bad for the hotel. Once word gets out that there are dead bodies under the Tikis people won't come within fifty yards of this Island!"

She thought but managed not to say "No, Rutger, you idiot, wrong as usual," She did say "We can spin this. We can make it work to our advantage."

"Our advantage? But how? I can't imagine dead bodies in the garden ever working to a resort's advantage," he said with a seethingly sarcastic undercurrent, the exact kind of tone that made Melinda want to bury *him* in the garden.

"You don't know anything about public relations, Bachman. I do. Once we find out who she is, or at least why she's here, I'll spin this to make people want to come here even more."

"I can't see how."

"That's because you have no imagination," Melinda said, almost as sarcastically. "You just handle the bellhops and maids, Rutger. Leave the important stuff to me."

Melinda got up and left without giving Bachman a chance to retort. Her plans were already being put into production. She had an idea, and she was already weaving the words of the spin in her mind.

I nearly choked on the beer, and I think Jess damn-near did too.

"Uh, what exactly do you mean, Captain, that he figures *you* buried her?"

The old sea captain sat back in his chair, looking off to the wall behind me. The ancient chair creaked under his weight, and for a quick second I thought he'd collapse in a heap on the floor. The thought lightened the intensity of the moment, enough to let me get my act together and listen to his tale.

"The year was 1935," he began, as if reading from an old tome. "I was living here in Islamorada, working for Roosevelt's WPA during the summer months when Mr. Hawthorn spent most of his time in Miami. WPA - That was the Work Progress Administration, or the 'Wap' as me and my friends called it. Pretty much every man here on the key was a Wap worker, old World War One vets like myself, here to earn a living and try to survive through the depression. Florida was a might thick with evil things back then, mosquitoes the size of baseballs, palmetto bugs that would carry a man away in his sleep. Crocks and gators would wander down every now and then from the 'Glades and sun on your porch step. And the storms...aye, the storms were somethin' fierce.

We were building a road, out Card Sound way, parallel to the Overseas Railway. And we worked on the tracks too, iffin' they needed any mending. In fact, most of the men I worked with helped build parts of those bridges back in the day. Imagine that, 1910, building those bridges over miles of water with nothin' but their bare hands a few steam shovels. An amazin' task, and an amazin' accomplishment, iffin' ya ask me."

Once again he looked past our heads to the wall. I actually turned around and looked...just a wall.

"The summer of thirty-five as a hot one, hotter than most. Many a fella took sick with malaria, or sun stroke while workin' up on that road. When the rains came down from the 'Glades each day we rejoiced, sang and shouted to the rain to cool us off. You know, it'd last about five minutes or so, cool everything down for a spell, then be on its way. Such is the weather in the rainy season here."

"So I've heard," I said. This was a great story but I was eager for him to get to the meat of it.

"Then Labor Day Weekend drew near. Mr. Hawthorn rang me up and asked if I could cut out of the Wap work and come fix up the Island for a big party. I told him sure, I'd be happy to. Last week in August, we had the plans all set for one hundred and fifty people to come to Hawthorn Island for the biggest bash of the year, and that was saying a lot, I'd imagine."

"Wait, Labor Day Weekend, 1935 – that's the year of –"

"The Great Atlantic Hurricane," he finished for me, with much drama. "Yes, that was the year Hawthorn Island was destroyed. On Friday, just as the guests were supposed to come to the Island, the weather bureau sent out a telegram warnin' everyone in the Keys that a major storm was headin' our way. Most people just set up their storm shutters, stocked up on canned goods and planned to ride it out. Of course all the guests bowed out of the party, and Mr. Hawthorn was stuck with enough booze, food and cigarettes for a hundred and fifty souls twice over. He decided to hope for the best, to wait and see if the storm would pass up the coast or drift down to the Caribbean. Of course, it didn't."

He paused again to relight his pipe. I looked over at Jessica; she was ghost-white but seemed hung on every word.

"By Saturday it was pretty clear that the storm was going to hit the upper Keys. Mr. Hawthorn wired me and told me to come to the Island early Saturday, make sure the boat was running perfectly and gassed up, and told me to make for Key West where the storm was sure to miss. I did as he told me, and lived to tell the tale. Why he didn't take his own advice, I don't know. But for some reason he decided to head North, first here to Islamorada to catch the train. But the train was late, Mr. Riggins. No one dispatched it until late in the day."

"Yes, I've heard that too. By the time they sent the train down here to rescue the workers the storm was already in full force."

"That's right. And Hawthorn, along with his wife Vivian, weren't about to wait for it. So he decided to make for the mainland in his boat. He didn't make it. The boat was hit by a storm surge and deposited in the swamps up near Florida City. He was found lashed to the wheel. His wife wasn't so lucky. They never recovered her body."

Jessica coughed a little. For a second I though she'd lose it, but she held it together.

"Jess, you ok? Want another drink or something?" I asked as nice as I could.

"No, no I'm ok, just hard to hear this story, I've heard it so many times before. My family had friends that died in that storm."

"I'm sorry young Miss," the Captain said, "If the details bother ye. But it must be told in all, iff'n it's to be told right, I'd imagine."

"It's ok, go on Captain, tell Bill the rest."

"The rest is might bleak, Mr. Riggins. A thirty-foot high wall of black water, driving in from the Atlantic at more than forty miles per hour crashed into the east coast of Matecumbe Key, just on the other side of the road out there. It hit with so much force that it almost instantly crushed and mangled almost every building on this Key and the surrounding ones. It tore the railway tracks from the beds, ripped the bridges from their moors. And at around eight p.m., the ocean came across Islamorada and crashed right into that train full of men, over three hundred of them. It knocked that train clear off the tracks as if it were just an electric toy. Everything except the steam engine, since that was heavy enough to hold its ground. The rest of the cars were tossed and mangled like so many tin cans on a string. Not a single soul survived, Mr. Riggins. Over 400 people were officially reported dead or missing, but we knew that the real count was a lot higher."

"You were in Key West when the storm hit? Did you get any damage there?"

"Nearly none. Some street flooding, a few torn roofs. Not much else. But Hawthorn Island was completely destroyed." He got up then, retrieved three more beers from the icebox and returned to his chair, creaking it as he sat. "The next day they rounded up as many able-bodied men as could be found to help with the cleanup. Most of the bridges were washed out, so we took boats up through the islands. It was a horrible site, let me tell ye. Sections of the bridges had been torn to bits, twisted like scrap metal. Entire homes were floating out in the backwaters. And almost everywhere you looked, there were bodies. Men floating in the shallows. Women washed up on the beaches. Some had tried to endure the storm by lashing themselves to trees and buildings, only to be battered to death by the wind or drowned by the storm surge. But the worst was when we came to Islamorada. Bodies in the train cars, bodies lined up next to the tracks, bodies washing up on the shore. They had already been there overnight and through most of the day, and the sun had gone to work on them. By Wednesday most were unrecognizable as human. The heat, the flies, the crabs…the bodies swelled up from the heat, and – God help me – they burst, like red balloons full of ragged meat on the sand. A horrible site, that was. My lord, I can still hear the popping noises they made."

The Captain wiped his mouth with his sleeve and took a long pull of the beer. Jessica remained pale but steady.

"I was to help try to identify the victims, at first. But that proved impossible by Thursday. It was around then that the Army Corp of Engineers ordered the bodies to be placed in pine boxes, then stacked in a three-foot deep pit dug into the center of the Key and set ablaze. It was the most ethical thing to do, under the circumstances. For once the sun and the flies and the crabs had gotten to the bodies, there wasn't much left to even consider them as ever being people again.

The mosquitoes were laying eggs, and that meant the threat of more malaria. The flies were too, and that meant even more evil things. The smell...Son, even in the trenches of WW One, I'd never smelled anything so foul in my years. And 'til this day, I swear sometimes in the evenin's I can still catch a whiff of death, from back then." Another pause for a drink. His voice was getting hoarse. "We burned the bodies just up the road a piece from here. Afterward, the President had us erect a monument to the fallen. It still stands today. But it wasn't over then. As we began cleaning up the remnants of the Keys and the train, we came across more horrors. More bodies washed up on the beaches for days, even weeks after the storm. Once I lifted a piece of roof sheeting, and under it a little boy stared up at me with nothin' but holes for eyes. Never forget that. And of course the animals...all kinds, from rabbits to deers, drowned in the storm, turned into food for the crows and gulls. People's entire lives washed away, homes gone, cars, everything just, disappeared. But we pulled through. We cleaned her up and started to rebuild. Why, this here shack yer sittin' in is damn near a hundred years old. Found it floating a few feet out, somehow still intact, so me and a buddy reeled it in and set it back on the dock.

"You'd never know it," I lied.

"We salvaged whatever we could, and we rebuilt the bridges and laid down macadam for automobiles to ride on, and made the Overseas Railway into the Overseas Highway."

"You helped build the highway?" I asked, actually intrigued by his story.

"That's right. Right after I finished my business on Hawthorn Island," he said dramatically again, and it was all I could do to not say 'it's about time you got to the meat, buddy.'

"Two days after the storm was over, Eliot Hawthorn sent word down through the Sheriff's department to round up five good men, take a boat to the Island and survey the damage. I did, and found nothing but disaster. The mansion had been leveled, the gardens stripped bare. Most of the palms had been toppled too, and the beach had eroded so far in at one point that the water met the foundation of the house. The boathouse was gone too. All that remained was the limestone foundation and a few splintered boards. I wired back the damages to Hawthorn, and he sent word back to get a crew together, as many men as I needed, to plow the island clean, spread it over with four of five feet of good, heavy topsoil and plant as many trees, bushes and ferns as could fit. He planned to donate the Island to the government Parks and Recreation, to be saved as a sanctuary in the name of his wife."

"And what about the skeleton?" I asked, now more impatient than ever.

"Yes, the skeleton," he said, and relit his pipe...

On Friday the sixth of September, 1935 Reams got together a team of fourteen men, loaded a barge with tools and a diesel-powered frontend loader, and set out to Hawthorn Island. The men were hot, the men were exhausted, the men had seen so much death and destruction in the past few days that they were sick nearly to death themselves. But when Eliot Hawthorn was signing the checks, the checks were always fat, and they knew it. So the men traveled the hour-long ride from Islamorada to the Island, to carry out Eliot Hawthorn's requests. Their job description was simple: Clear the Island, remove every last piece of debris, fill in the mansion's foundation with gravel, and cover the entire Island with at least four feet of good topsoil. Then plant as many bushes, shrubs, trees, grass and flowers as could fit and leave the Island forever. Nothing was to be kept. Hawthorn made it very clear that he had taken everything of value (to him) with him when he left. Any salvage was to become the property of Reams, to be doled out or sold as he saw fit. Eliot wanted nothing to do with Island, or his past life again.

They began by picking through the wreckage, trying to get an idea of the scope of work ahead of them and looking for items that might be salvageable. Almost nothing was. Some cast iron cookware from the commercial-sized kitchen remained as it was too heavy to wash away, but the kitchen itself was gone, save for a twisted, stainless steel counter that got itself wrapped around one of the only surviving palm trunks. A water-logged steamer trunk held the soggy remnants of the Hawthorn's wedding tuxedo and dress. Among the hundreds of 78 RPM records that littered the gardens and beaches, most cracked or warped from the sun, Reams found a single playable Duke Ellington Columbia with The Mooch on one side. A few pieces of costume jewelry turned up here and there. And an Enfield rifle, wet but still in good condition. That was nearly the extent of the salvage. Hundreds of dishes, cups, glasses, and serving pieces were smashed and shattered as far as the eye could see. Faded clothes covered everything. Paintings, furniture, electric cords and books all twisted together into crumpled heaps. The water around the Island was littered with the same bits of junk, flotsam that hadn't made it to any shore as of yet.

But it wasn't until late afternoon that the worst of the 'detritus' had been found.

"Captain Reams, over here!" yelled one of the men from the North shore. He was waving his hands wildly in an attempt to get the Captain's attention. Reams dropped the broken framed photo of Vivian Hawthorn, and walked over to the man.

The afternoon sun was hotter than Reams ever remembered it. It beat down on him hard, burning his face and arms. Somehow the broiling heat of the sun was like an omen, a warning to stay away from the beachhead, to go back to the shade of the make-shift tent shelter. But he pressed on, almost knowing what he'd find before he got there.

"Four all togethah," the tall man who called him over said, wiping the sweat from his dark brow. "Least-ways that's all we done found so far. Ain't no recognizin' them either, Captain, they're too far gone from the heat."

Reams looked down at the body in front of him. It was a woman, that was evident by the vague shape of her body and the heeled shoes. She was laying on her face where the beach met the garden, wrapped in what was once her clothes. Four days in the sun hadn't been good to her. Neither had the crabs and maggots.

"Do we dare turn her over, Mr. Bryant?" Reams asked the man. The man just shook his head. "Can't be any worse than we've seen so far," he said to Bryant, and together they gently turned the body over.

They immediately wished they hadn't.

"Oh my Lord in heaven, have pity on her soul," Bryant said, then turned and vomited on the sand.

Reams felt the hot bile churn in his gut too, but managed to keep it down by looking away quickly. He found a piece of cloth and threw it over the woman's face without looking.

"My God, Bryant, her face. I've never seen…"

"I know it, Captain. Let's not dwell on the subject, if you catch my drift, 'k?"

"Yeah, I catch ya. Are the others this bad?"

"No suh, not nearly as bad. Two men, I think, they bloated up and burst days ago and are damn near nothing but bone now from the crabs and birds, over tangled up in them there bushes over there. Just bone, not so bad as this. One other, don't know if it be a man or a lady, floatin' out by the edge of the water there. That one's pretty bad, but still not so bad as this."

Reams took a deep breath. The smell of death came with it and before he could stop it he wrenched. He washed his mouth out with water from the surf, and standing up-wind inhaled big gulps of fresh, clean Gulf air. Then he turned to Bryant and said, "Get three or four of the men to line the bodies up about fifty yards from the shore, then cover them over with lye and sand."

"Don't you'all wanna bury them, Cap? Bad enough they's never going be claimed by their families. We should at least give them a Christian burial, I say."

"We will Mr. Bryant, we will. After all this is cleared away we'll be bringing in some good, heavy dirt and a load of plants and trees to cover over the Island. They'll be buried then, deal?"

"Yes suh, I suppose that's the best we can do, under the circumstances."

"Ain't no point in bringing them back to the Key," Reams said quietly, "ain't nobody going to be able to recognize them anyhow, I'd imagine. Just be giving false hope to some people already hurt too bad."

"I'm with you, Cap. I'll get the men."

"Good," Reams said, and as Bryant walked back to the camp, Reams said a little prayer, thanking God for saving him from such a horrible fate.

"So what did you do after that?" I asked the Captain as he paused to re-pack his pipe. "Did you ever tell anyone about the bodies?"

"Not a living soul," he said. A match ignited and the odor of cherry mixed with sulfur filled the small shack. "Not even my wife at the time. That is until a few years ago, when we were swappin' stories of the Great Storm at a tavern. We meaning myself, and a few of the boys that helped me on the Island, and ole Lem. That's how he knew to send you to me, I'd imagine."

I sat back on my own squeaky crate, satisfied the mystery was solved, but a little disappointed that it was that simple. Bodies washed up in the storm. The timeframe fit, the depth of Earth fit, even the heeled shoe he noticed was evidently the same heeled shoe that we found on the skeleton. Her face had probably been smashed up against a log or some coral. Case solved, class dismissed.

Jessica looked very sad, as if she'd known the victims herself. She'd sat quietly until then, and her soft voice seemed alien in the smoky, dank shack. "Captain Reams, tell me…why was the girl…her body, why was she so much worse than the others you found? You left that part out of your story."

"I did? Well now, to tell the truth I'd rather not say, young Miss. It was…well it was quite a gruesome sight, as you might imagine."

I was thinking about the skeleton, and the smashed skull. I didn't say a word.

Jessica said, "It's ok Captain, I think I can handle it. I've seen a few bad things in my day, and if your story hasn't made me sick yet, I don't think anything will."

I laughed a little at that, and so did the Captain. Jessica smiled. She was probably right; I'd seen some nasty things in my time, murders, car accidents, even a guy who fell into the subway and got fried on the third rail before the train hit him. But nothing quite like this.

"Alright Miss, but iff'n you have nightmares, don't blame old Reams, deal?"

Jessica suddenly turned very serious. Her eyes man, her eyes said it all, but I just didn't hear it. "It's a deal, Captain. Tell us."

Captain Reams sat back again, the familiar squeak of his chair setting the mood. He puffed on the pipe, looked up at the ceiling; then he closed his eyes and with what seemed like a lot of pain said the words that sealed it up tight.

"She'd been out on the beach, in the hot sun for four days. The heat does things to a body, here in the tropics. Skin does a sort of dance between drying up brown and getting all mushy and waterlogged. Critters go to work inside the corpse, flies lay eggs and eggs turn to maggots. They eat a body from the inside out, you see, and at first they release gasses that bloat up a body...sometimes to the point the skin bursts. Then the gasses escape, and the corpse rots fast in the hot sun. The smell attracts more pests, namely crabs and birds. They pick at it, claw at it, eat at it too. But sometimes a corpse is too gruesome even for the animals to chow on it. Such as it was with her. Her body had blown up, then collapsed back down. Ribs, bones could be seen through her skin in places, and in some places her fat had turned almost to goo. But it was her face...that was the worst of her, and even though I only saw for a second, I'll never forget that face." He took the pipe out of his mouth and finished off the rest of his beer before continuing. "The face was gone. Looked like it'd been caved in with a brick or something. Her eye sockets were just black holes, her nose was a gaping hole that met her mouth. Teeth just sort of hung in places, and her jaw was wrenched open, like she'd been caught in a death-scream. The skin was black as night, and puffed up like a balloon where it wasn't eaten away. And in that second I looked, something slithered out of her eye and made its way back into her mouth."

He shuddered at that. His face twisted, and he shook his head hard trying to lose the image. When he opened his eyes, they were red and tearful. To my left Jessica sat quietly, just listening. She showed no more emotion than sorrow for the horror of it all, but whether she wanted me to see it or not, she was trembling. Her face twitched, her hands shook slightly in her lap. Most people might not have caught it, but I was trained a long time to pick up on little things like that. I had no idea what it meant, but it was there.

"I guess that's all then." I said to the Captain. He let out a heavy sigh before answering.

"Not just quite," he said. "There's one more thing. As I said, we buried the bodies over with lye and sand, and a few days later when all the junk was cleared out and hauled back to the mainland, we came back with several barges full of sand, dirt and plants. We covered over the Island with the sand and dirt, and planted as much as we could. The whole project set Hawthorn back about twenty grand, but he was happy. I was happy too, because I made a cool two G's myself. And I was done with the Island. Or so I thought. Two years later I got a wire from Mr. Hawthorn. That's when he decided to come back, to make the Island into a hotel. My guts twisted up when I read that wire, Mr. Riggins. He wanted to come in with bulldozers and whatnot, and he wanted me to handle the excavation crew and direct the construction company on where the old foundation was. Now, you have to imagine the last thing I wanted was for anyone to find those bodies, so I had to be extra careful where I told them to dig. As it was, I left a marker on the site where we buried them, just in case something like that were ever to happen."

"What kind of marker?"

"Two trees, small palms criss-crossed. They were still there when I went back two years later. Far as I know they're still there today."

"They are," Jessica said, "Just on the edge of the northern garden."

"That's where we found the skeleton," I said, "right at the edge of the garden."

"And that would make sense, I'd imagine. I was very careful about avoidin' that spot, and convinced them to leave the trees since they'd grown so strangely. And they did. And all was good, and Mr. Hawthorn hired me on once again, this time as Captain of his fleet of boats and water taxis. It was a good time for me, I made good money and got to work on fine boats, until the summer of 1950. It was then that Mr. Hawthorn's new wife passed on. And the night she died, something very strange happened. I was doing my nightly walk-around of the Island, checking to make sure all the boats and rentals and all were back up on the beach, when I saw the oddest thing." He got that distant, staring into space look again in his eyes, and continued very softly. "That night I saw a woman, dressed in white and wearing a large summer hat walking in the garden near the two crossed trees. I began to walk towards her, as I seemed to feel she needed me for some reason. But as I drew up closer, she seemed to...to fade, become sort of clear-like. I kept walking towards her and when I got to be about five feet away she turned and faced me. I heard her voice speak, but her mouth didn't move. In fact, she didn't have much of a face at all. The voice came, and she...well she just sort of disappeared, dissolved into thin air."

Neither Jessica nor I said a thing. We just sat there waiting for him to talk. When he didn't I prodded him.

"Are you saying you saw a ghost, Captain?"

"Not really sure what it was I saw, Mr. Riggins. Don't much believe in ghosts. In fact, I firmly believe it was my mind playin' tricks on me, on account of what she said."

"What did she say," Jessica asked. Her voice cracked and gave her away.

"She said, 'Release me.' Then disappeared. I quit the next day. Haven't set foot on the Island since."

We said goodbye and thanks to Captain Reams, jumped in the Chevy and took off south down the Overseas Highway. The ride was quiet. Jessica watched the scenery go by, I watched the road ahead. A few minutes into the drive, I pulled over at a little roadside stand advertising orange juice for ten cents. What I really needed was to use the phone.

"You're stopping for orange juice?" Jessica asked, her voice sounding distant, dreamlike.

"You like orange juice, don't you? Besides, I have to make a couple of calls."

"Ok," she said, still sort of distant. "I'll get the juice while you make the calls."

She got out of the car in a sort of slow motion and started for the counter. I handed her a quarter without a word. She smiled, and continued up to the stand as I made my way over to the pay phone on the telephone pole.

When the first dime dropped, I asked for Melinda Hawthorn at Tiki Island Resort. She wasn't in her office, so I dropped another dime and asked for Sheriff Jackson, Monroe County. He was in and took my call.

"Hi ya'll doing, Detective Riggins?" came the husky voice over the wire. "Dig up anything?"

"Yeah, a bit," I said, and gave him the story.

"Not too surprised," he said dully, "Sort of figured that might be it. There's a lot of stories like that in the Keys. You say there are four buried there?"

"Yeah, that's what Reams said. One woman, three men. You still going to get the Tallahassee boys in on this?"

"Don't see much point. Probably best to just cover the remains over and put up a memorial. I think that's what Mr. Hawthorn would probably prefer. I'll talk to him tonight and see."

"Sounds good to me," I said, then without much pause added, "Sheriff, you ever have any trouble with Chief Roberts down in Key West?"

A loud laugh came over the line, and I smiled. "You mean old Lemon Head? Nah, he's mostly harmless. Sneaky, and he's got some muscle working for him but mostly harmless. Why, you cross his path?"

"He brained me with a sap, tied me in a chair and wanted to know why I was asking questions about Hawthorn. I'd say that's a little more than harmless."

"He did that?" the Sheriff asked sounding very surprised. "I guess he's knocking things up a notch down there. You ok?"

"I am now. I managed to bust out of the chair and teach him a lesson. I knocked him around pretty bad, until he gave up. I told him if he didn't stay away from me I'd get him indicted on corruption charges. I assume he is corrupt, correct?"

"He is. But I don't like it that he put the hurt on you. He must know you were working with me somehow. And he's always tryin' to buck me, from way back. You want me to give him a call, tell him to lay off?"

"Couldn't hurt. I plan on spending some time in Key West and don't want to have to look over my shoulder every five minutes," I said, meaning it. I was on vacation, dammit.

"I'll call him. You don't worry about a thing. He may be the local law there, but my boys are there too, plus we're in tight with the Navy base. By six p.m. everyone on the Island will know to steer clear of you. You sense trouble, you grab a sailor or deputy, got it?"

"I'm hip. Thanks Sheriff."

"No problem. Thanks again for your help, Detective. I'll make that call now." He hung up, I hung up, and dropped another dime. I called Tiki Island again, asking for Melinda. I watched Jessica as I waited, sitting at the little OJ stand. The place was so small it only had four stools. The whole thing was shaped like a giant orange. The hand-lettered sign read, "Fresh Squeezed Florida Organge Juice". 'Organge'. Florida was a weird place, I thought.

A voice came over the phone. It wasn't Melinda's.

"Hello, Tiki Island," the voice said. It sounded like a man in his fifties who'd been bred with the snootiest of demeanor.

"I'm trying to reach Melinda Hawthorn," I said, sounding official.

"I'm afraid Miss Hawthorn is unavailable. Perhaps I can be of service, this is Mr. Bachman, the resort Manager."

Oh ho! So it was Jerry's brother sounding snooty. Wow, what a difference from the Brooklyn boy his brother was. "Hello Mr. Bachman, this is Detective Bill Riggins, your brother's bud," I said as friendly as I could. After all, the man set me up with a suite and sweet deal.

"Ah, yes, hello Mr. Riggins! Nice to finally speak with you. Jerry's told me very much about you."

"Jerry's a great guy. And I really appreciate the room and all."

"Our pleasure, Mr. Riggins. What is it I can do for you?"

"Well, I had something I needed to speak to Melinda about. She's been very nice to me these last couple of days, by the way."

"I'm sure she has, she's a very pleasant person. She's out on the grounds getting things ready for tonight's luau. Shall I relay a message?"

"Just tell her I called," was all I said.

"Mr. Riggins, is this something to do with the skeleton found on the property, by any chance?" he asked, and I wondered if the guy had me tailed.

"Actually yes, it is. I got some info and wanted to let her know. I've already told the Sheriff."

"Would you mind telling me what it is you found?" he asked, the snootiness seeping through. I didn't really want to tell him anything. I promised Melinda I'd tell her if I found out anything, not this guy.

"I'd really rather tell her myself,"

"Mr. Riggins," he said snootily. Lot of snootiness flying around with this clown. "I *am* the General Manager of the Resort. I'd very much appreciate you communicating any knowledge of this to me."

I guess he was right, snooty or not he was picking up the tab for my vacation, the least I could do was give him the info.

"Oh, of course. She was a victim of the 1935 hurricane, buried on the Island by the workers who cleaned things up. There are three others buried with her. The Sheriff plans on discussing the matter with Mr. Hawthorn this evening. He's going to suggest you cover the body over and erect a memorial."

The line was quiet. I looked over and noticed Jessica was almost through her juice, and was getting impatient. The hot sun was dipping down into the gulf. It was getting late. "That's pretty much it," I said into the dead phone.

"Well, that's not so bad, I guess," Bachman said. "I suppose it's much better than a murder. Thank you Mr. Riggins. Will I see you tonight?"

"Yes, I'm heading down to Key West for a bit, then I'll be back to the Island."

"Very good. I should like to meet you, if you have time Mr. Riggins."

"I'll make time," I said.

"Marvelous. Good afternoon, Mr. Riggins. I'll see you this evening."

"Ciao," I said, and hung up.

Over at the Orange-shaped stand, Jessica was working on her second glass of juice. I walked over and joined her.

"'Bout time," she said as she handed me my drink.

"Business, doll."

"I thought you were on vacation?"

"Yeah, so did I."

We pulled into Key West around seven-fifteen. Surprisingly, it was still light out – the sun seemed to linger around forever in the evening here. In New York the sky would have been dark already, and the streets would be glowing with fluorescents and neon. There was a curious lack of neon here. I guess it never caught on so far detached from the rest of the world.

I parked the Chevy on Duval close to Jessica's apartment. Then we just sort of sat there for a minute.

"Listen kid," I finally said, "I don't want to be presumptuous...but the big luau is tonight on the Island, and since as it is I've never been to one, I'd like to hop on over...and I'd like you to come along." I made my intentions pretty clear, I thought, without coming off as a letch.

"I'll get my overnight bag, if that's ok with you," she said. Not much emotion in her voice, but she looked demure.

"That's A-OK with me, dollface. I'll wait here."

She smiled big, got out of the car and hoofed it up to her apartment. I lit up a smoke while I waited, scanning the street. Lots of people walking around, a few riding bikes. A couple of Vespas went by with screaming teenagers having a ball. Here and there a few old-timers strolled the sidewalks in sear-suckers and boaters, swinging bamboo canes. An occasional souped-up buggy or hot rod would tear down the strip, only to get hung up at the traffic light on the corner. Corny ragtime piano music seeped out of the bar next to where I was parked. Across the street, a couple of greasers in black T's and chinos were loading drums and electric guitars into another bar where a dozen motorcycles were parked. It was gonna be a rockin' night over there, that's for sure.

Less than five ticks slipped by when Jessica came down with her suitcase. It was an old brown leather job, well worn but still held together. It didn't have any of those port-of-call stickers on it like you see on most bags. She hadn't done much traveling, I guess.

"Toss it in the back," I said, "We've got to get moving or we're going to miss the seven-thirty boat." She tossed it, hopped up on the doorsill, swung her long legs around and slid into the seat.

"Let's motorvate," she said.

"I'm hip," I responded and dropped the hammer.

I parked the car just in time to get the boat before she shoved off. Handing the keys to the same old man I said, "Sheriff Roberts says no one is to go near that car except me and you. Anything happens to it, heads will roll."

"Don't you worry sonny," he replied with a wink. "I've got no love for ole' Lem either." So the word was out already. Good.

A few minutes later we were making the trip towards Tiki Island, just like we had a few days before. We ordered cocktails, both Mojitos, and sat along the edge of the aft deck.

"So you make this trip a lot?" I asked.

"A few times a month. When they need me."

"What exactly is it you do on the island?"

There was a slight pause before she answered, just long enough for one of those gears in my head to click, but I didn't notice.

"Mostly I hostess during private functions. You know, sit with people, tell them about the Resort and all it has to offer, stuff like that. Sometimes I help out in the back-of-the-house, or with banquet setup, that sort of thing. Easy work, not too exciting but it pays the bills. Got a smoke?"

"Sure," I said, and lit two. "You do the same in Key West?"

"My, aren't we inquisitive tonight?" She said, being funny, a little laugh in her voice.

"Just curious about you, that's all. I hardly know a thing about you."

"Not much to know. I was born here, raised here, live here, will probably always live here. I like rum and Bourbon, country-western music and rock 'n' roll. My favorite color is yellow and I've never owned a car. I believe in civil rights, and although I'm against communism I feel that people shouldn't be railroaded for going to a meeting. I was too young to remember much about the big war, but I'm deathly afraid of being incinerated by an Atom bomb. I had my first drink when I was twelve and kissed a boy for the first time when I was fourteen. Oh, and my favorite food is spaghetti and meatballs. That about cover it?"

I laughed and she did too. "That pretty much sums it up, huh? Will there be a quiz later?" I asked, and as I did her eyes met mine directly. Martin Denny's Hypnotique played over the boat's hi-fi. The Tiki torches danced to the rhythm.

"There may be," she said slowly, breathlessly, "So I hope you were listen..." Our lips met, that fire that burned so hot and bright two nights ago returning with a vengeance. We didn't care that anyone might be watching; it was our moment and we were in it, full blast. She wrapped her arms around my neck, and my hands found her back and I drew her in closer. The kiss intensified. It was like krazy, like wild. I'd never felt like that kissing a dame before. Oh sure, I got hot, I got pleasure, but not like this. Something was different, in a big way.

Somehow, somewhere along the line I'd started falling for this chick.

I knew it was bad news but I didn't care. Maybe after a week I'd never see her again. Maybe I would. Maybe I'd quit working in the City and get a job with Sheriff Jackson kicking Roberts' ass all over town. Maybe I'd...

She pulled away slightly and the kiss ended. She was smiling. The breeze brushed her golden blonde hair over her face, over her brilliant blue eyes. She was beautiful.

"One more smack like that and I might fall overboard," I joked like a goof. That was me, Mr. Smooth.

"If you did I'd jump in with you," she said coyly. "I need a refill. We still have twenty minutes before we get to the Island."

After the refills the conversation turned to me. I wasn't too happy about it since I'd lied to her about being a cop. I could have told her right then, but I didn't want anything to spoil the mood. Later, I'd fill her in. Then I'd tell her all about me *afterwards*.

"So were you born in New York?" she started with after the first sip of the second drink.

"No, Weehawken New Jersey, a city just across the Hudson. Lot of commercial shipping there."

"Why did you move to New York?"

I laughed. "If you saw New York in person, you'd know why."

"I don't think I'd like it much. Too big. I even think Miami is too big. I like a small town where you can walk everywhere you need to go."

"I walk all over the place," I said, "I don't even own a car."

"But what about that roadster?"

"It's rented. When I go home, it stays."

"Oh, I see. The way you pet that thing I thought it was all yours!"

"Pet it? Hey now hold on sister, I like the jalopy but I don't think I ever *pet* it." We were laughing again, and I stole another kiss. Just a small one this time, but still potent.

"So have you made any friends since you came to the Keys?" she asked, and the strangest thing happened. An image of Melinda flashed across my mind, of her in the white dress and white flower in her hair. Hadn't I felt strongly for her just a day ago? I started to think that switching from Bourbon to rum was playing tricks on my head. Melinda, beautiful Melinda. What was the last thing she said to me? 'I can't'.

"Bill, you OK?" came a sweet voice from in front of me.

"Oh yeah, I guess I was just drifting for a minute. This rum is crazy, it really sends me up."

"You get used to it after a while," she said somewhat sullenly, then quickly added, "Kind of a crazy story about that skeleton, huh?"

"Yeah, very crazy. And spooky too. Did you know that people claim they see the ghost of a young woman on Tiki Island?"

Suddenly Jessica's demeanor changed. The smile broke loose from her lips and I could detect a slight twitch in her face. She seemed very serious now.

"For real, Bill? I mean, for real people have said that or are you just makin' fun with me?"

"No, seriously, there have been claims. Even the woman who runs the Island says she's seen it."

"Melinda Hawthorn?" Jessica asked, as if she knew her.

"Yes, that's her. The Entertainment Director." Like, wow man, duhhh...of course she knew Melinda, she's worked for her.

"She never said anything like that around me. Then again, I guess it's not really the topic of general conversation."

"Hey now wait a minute, Jessica, you don't buy all this ghost and ghoul crapola, do you? I mean, come on!"

Jessica didn't seem amused. In fact, she seemed borderline angry.

"Listen Bill, just because you don't believe in something doesn't mean it's not true. There are plenty of things science can't explain. Just look around you. When this boat you're sitting in was built, Television didn't exist. The hotel room you're staying in was built before rockets or A-bombs were invented, and it's not even twenty years old. Hell, just over fifty years ago doctors didn't wash their hands in hospitals. We learn new stuff all the time, you know?"

"Ok, kid, don't get all defensive. I see your point. Just I've never seen a spook, and I tend to believe in things I can see, or touch, or at least measure somehow."

"Yeah, well..." She looked away. I put my hand on her arm; I could feel her shaking.

"Jess, baby, what is it?"

She looked at me. The fire in her eyes had turned to fear, simple, primal fear. "Jess?"

"I've seen it," she said in a voice that made me shiver. "I've seen it, more than once. I saw it a few weeks ago, then a few nights ago, and I came to Tiki Island to get away from it and clear my head. Then I saw it the morning after I stayed with you. That's why I left so fast. I saw it again last night, and I couldn't sleep. Now I'm coming here tonight, with you, and I hope it shows up again because if it does and you see it, it means I'm not crazy!"

She buried her face in my chest and sobbed quietly. I put my arms around her, squeezing her tight. "I don't think you're crazy," I said, "If you say you saw a ghost, that's good enough for me. If I see something tonight, all the better. After what happened here in '35, I wouldn't be all that surprised if this place was haunted."

She said very quietly, "Thank you, Bill."

Just then I looked up. "There's the Island. Look, you can see the Tiki Torches dancing," I told her. And once again, like Monday night, we were heading toward the entrance of Tiki Island.

"Take the lady's bag to my room," I told the porter as we exited the gangplank to the dock. "Jessica, do you think we'll have time to freshen up a little before we hit the luau?"

"Certainly," she answered, "The seatings start at eight-thirty but the entertainment won't go on until after nine."

"Good, I want to change this shirt."

"And I have a pretty Hawaiian dress I want to put on. It's *very* tight. Shows off my hips."

"I'm hip to your hips," I said as we headed up to the suite.

Drums. Krazy, kookie, wild Polynesian drums filled the night with sound as the flickering red and yellow glow of innumerable Tiki torches lit the darkness of the Island's South Beach. A hundred people or more were sitting around large wooden tables decorated with citrus candles, tropical plants and flower garlands. A grand buffet table, at least sixty feet long flanked the hotel side of the beach, framed by a black, lava rock backdrop fifteen feet high, complete with waterfalls. Chefs in pristine white jackets with teal cuffs and collars and tall hats carved fresh roast beef, turkey and pork. Two giant pigs were being roasted in pits adjacent to the buffet, and at the center of the long table a pile of tropical fruits, coconuts and pineapples made a six-foot high display surrounding a hand-carved Tiki totem. If I didn't know better, I'd think I was in Hawaii.

A small band of steel and slide guitars began to play along with the drums as a pretty waitress in a grass skirt and coconut bikini top led us to a table at the front of the stage. I had to really hold my tongue not to say 'nice coconuts' to her. But I couldn't resist saying it under my breath to Jessica after she walked away. I got an elbow in the ribs for my efforts. As we sat, another pretty girl in similar attire placed two very large, fresh pineapples on the table in front of us. Straws stuck out of the tops.

"Compliments of the house, Mr. Riggins," she said, "They are our specialty, Tonga Cocktails, served only during the luau." I smiled and said thank you. But I wasn't too happy. It's not that I wasn't grateful, it's just that the only way this doll could know me was if someone who knew me spotted me and told her. And the only one who knew me on sight was Melinda.

"What's in this drink?" Jessica asked, breaking my line of thought.

"Five different rums from the islands, fresh pineapple juice, Curacao, lime juice, and a few secret ingredients," the pretty hula girl replied. Yeah, secret ingredients like arsenic, or maybe cyanide…

Jessica said, "What's the matter, Bill, I thought you liked rum?"

I guess I wore my thoughts on my face. "Oh sure, I dig rum. Not so sure about five kinds all mixed together, but I guess there's only one way to find out!" I said, and took a sip. Good stuff. Strong, but good.

Five more Hula girls came out from behind the band and began to dance along with the music. They switched from the heavy drums to a more soothing, old-style Hawaiian repertoire as the native girls told their story in dance. A minute later they opened the buffet, and we got in line for our grub. Man, that food was fantabulous. Fresh-sliced pork roast and beef, egg rolls, Crab Rangoon, plus a mix of Chinese food and good old American dishes blended in such a way that it made sense and tasted great. These guys really had it down pat, I thought.

We got back to the table and settled in. The music was mellow, very romantic. Not sure if that had anything to do with it but Jessica started to open up to me, in a way that made me wonder if she was feeling the same things I was feeling about her.

"Someday I'd like to move away from here, maybe up to Palm Beach, where things aren't so crazy," she started with. "I know if I stay in the Keys they'll eventually kill me."

"Why do you say that, kitten?"

She paused a minute and looked over at the Hula girls before answering. "It's just too crazy down here, you know? Living in Key West is like having a party every night. The noise, the booze, the..." she trailed off, and I wondered what she was going to say next. "It's just a hectic lifestyle," she resumed. I had a feeling she just stopped herself from going too far.

"I guess there's a lot of trouble down here, behind the scenery they put up for the tourists, huh?"

"No, not a lot of trouble. We have our insanity just like any city, I guess. Sure, there's more problems with some things, like guys running drugs up from Cuba and all, and the occasional biker gang fight, but nothing much different than anywhere else."

"Listen doll, I work in New York City. Believe you-me, ain't nothing worse than that."

She saluted and pretended to smoke a pipe, and said in a funny voice a la Reams, "I'd imagine you're right about that, I'd imagine!" We both laughed at that, maybe a little harder than we should of because of the rum, but it sure as hell seemed funny at the time.

"What would you do in Palm Beach?" I asked, still laughing a little.

"I dunno, maybe get a job as a waitress while I look for a rich husband. Lots of wealthy men up that way, if you don't mind the grandfatherly type."

"Eek!" I said laughing again, and took another drink. Boy were these mangos strong. Eh, pineappleees, I mean.

It was then that a middle-aged man in a tan crepe suit walked over to our table. His hair was slicked back old-style, and he sported a moustache that would have been in high style around 1939. He was a tall, lanky egret with a thin cigar sticking out of his mouth. His tan buckskin dress loafers made it difficult for him to walk in the sand, but he hid it well.

"Mr. Riggins?" he asked, already knowing the answer.

"That's right." I instantly recognized the snootiness in his voice.

"It's a pleasure to meet you sir, I'm Rutger Bachman, Gerald's brother." Well, that explained the getup. The bird was on the clock, which accounted for the attire. I'm guessing he didn't come out to the luaus much, as they were Melinda's baby. "Mind if I join you a moment?"

"Not at all, Mr. Bachman, go ahead and park it."

"Please, call me Rutger."

"It's your dime," I said, and motioned over the waitress. "You a drinking man, Rutger?"

"Yes, normally but I am working at the moment, so just a club soda with lime for me, please."

"Kookie. We'll have two more of these pineapple concoctions," I said to the waitress, "And a club soda and lime for the boss." She bowed her head and slipped away. "Rutger, I'd like you to meet Ms. Jessica Rutledge. You two have a lot in common, your names both have "r-u-t" in them," I said, getting cornier as I got more inebriated.

The egret looked at Jessica with a smarmy half-smile that I didn't like so much. But the rum was clouding things up, so I wasn't sure what I didn't like about it.

"I already know Ms. Rutledge, she's worked for us on several occasions, helping greatly during our private events. Isn't that right, Miss Rutledge?"

Jessica looked the slightest bit unsure of what to say next.

"Yes, thank you Mr. Bachman," Jessica said, slightly embarrassed. Maybe more than slightly. Her cheeks flushed red, but it may have been the five rums.

Bachman turned back to me and spoke. "I trust you're finding your accommodations satisfactory?"

"Oh, yeah, sure," I said while swallowing a big chunk of meat. I guess this was talk time. The food would have to be put on the back burner for a while. "Yeah, the room is terrif. I can't believe the view. It's really swell of you kids to go all out for me like this, God knows I needed a real vacation."

"Well, Mr. Riggins, after what Gerald told us about you, it's our pleasure to have a hero staying at the resort."

"Ah, come on, I wouldn't go as far as to say that," I said humbly. The rum was really hitting me. I should have remembered how hard that stuff could pack a punch.

"Nonsense, imagine all the lives you saved by finding that murderer and bringing him to justice. Top notch police work, Detective."

"Oh, well thanks buddy. All in a day's wor..."

Jessica looked at me with eyes as big as pot pies. Her whole face lost its beauty in that second, replaced with a sort of combination of hate, anger, guilt and surprise. The rum had betrayed me. I wasn't thinking straight and now the cat was out of the bag.

"Will you both excuse me for a minute," she said, then quietly got up and left. I didn't know whether to follow her or what. Bachman kept on spieling.

"I'd like you to know that all of the Island's accommodations are at your disposal. Just ring the front desk, or my office for anything you need, and we'll be sure to satisfy you."

"Yeah, thanks," I said, trying to shake off the rum. "I'll do that."

"But I see you've already found some of our most...eh...*interesting* accommodations," he said with sly smile, the way you'd tell someone you just pick-pocketed some old rich guy.

"Uh, yeah, sure. Listen, I'd hate to cut you off but I think I should go after Jessica, she seemed a little..."

"Oh, come now Mr. Riggins, she'll be back, of course."

"It's just that I hadn't told her I was a cop, I think that kind of set her off a little."

"Ohhh! I see, how foolish of me, of course you wouldn't tell her. I'm very sorry to have said anything."

"Ah, don't mention it," I said.

Click.

"I'm sure she'll be back any second," he went on, "so before she does, I'd like you to know I've spoken with Mr. Hawthorn about the, eh, incident in the garden...and he's decided he needs to think things over before making any rash decisions. In the meantime, we'd appreciate your discretion with the matter. We'd really rather not have this made into a media event."

My head was clearing up a little now. "Isn't that Ms. Hawthorn's department? Public relations and all that? Not that I'm going to go blow a trumpet about your little graveyard, but shouldn't she be the one handling the press and all?"

It was then that I first started to really dislike Rutger Bachman. He sat up very straight in his chair, as if it gave him some sort of stature, and said, "Mr. Riggins, Melinda Hawthorn is the Entertainment Director of this Resort, nothing more. I happen to be the General Manager, and I report directly to Mr. Hawthorn. It is my responsibility to make sure the reputation of this establishment remains unmarred, and I will continue to do so as I see fit." His demeanor was so snide I damned near slapped him in the puss just to knock him down a peg. But a free room was a free room, and I didn't want to get bumped out because of a rum-soaked lack in judgment.

"Ok, Bachman, take a deep breath, no one's challenging your position." I took a short pull of the rum. "So take it easy. Your skeleton's safe with me. Besides, the last thing I want is to be involved with any police biz. I'm on vacation, you know."

He smiled, then laughed. "Vacation? Of course I know! Your vacation is costing me a mint!" he said, then got up and held out his hand. I took it and shook it. "Well I hope you have a marvelous stay, Mr. Riggins. Remember, anything you need, just give me a buzz. Anything. Although I think you have just about everything you need," he added, then winked and walked off. As he did, Jessica walked up behind me, and sat.

Click.

"Hey kid, have a smoke?" I asked, holding out the pack. She shook her head quietly. "You ok? What gives?"

She didn't answer at first. I just stared at her until she spoke.

"Why did you lie to me, Bill? About your job. Why did you lie about it?"

I stuck a butt in my mouth and lit it with the Zippo, blew a big puff of smoke out into the night. It hung between us for a second, pierced by the glow of the torches. She seemed a million miles away just then. "I didn't want anyone down here to know I was a cop. I'm on vacation and all I wanted to do was relax, maybe do some fishing, maybe meet a pretty girl...The only ones who knew were that guy Bachman and Melinda Hawthorn. I liked it that way. For a week I get to pretend I'm someone else, someone who doesn't care about crime, or drugs or any of it. But lucky me, the day after I arrive they find a twenty-year old stiff in the front yard. And it's a mystery who the stiff is, and like a big jerk I offer to help and sure enough the local law says 'oh sure, we can use the help' so I'm the guy who gets to flat-foot it all over the Florida Keys to find the answer. I pay for mileage on the rental car so I'm getting to pay a nice fat chunk of change for that, too. On top of everything else I got whacked in the head by a fat, corrupt cop for my troubles, and lost almost a whole day of my vacation. So yeah, I lied to you. I'm sorry about that, and I actually planned to tell you in the car on the way up to Islamorada but we were having such a gass I didn't want anything to goof it up. So the cat's out of the bag. I'm a cop. I'm a vice-squad detective with the New York City PD, and I bring down pimps and pushers and hookers and con artists and scumbags of all kinds every day, and I got in a heap of crap for knocking around some poor sap who probably didn't deserve it but was a wise guy and needed to learn a lesson about respect. Now that kat is holed-up in my apartment with a bunch of cops watching over him for his own protection, and I get to high-tail it out of town on a little vacation, courtesy of my buddy Jerry and his brother, Rutger Bachman. So am I sorry I didn't tell you? Yeah. Is it really a big deal? No. Everybody has secrets. You've got secrets, I'm sure. But who cares? I like you honey, you're a damn straight-on doll that's fun to be with and can hold a conversation that doesn't include pulling bubblegum. So unless you're a pimp, a hooker or a Horse peddler, you ain't got nothin' to worry about being around me. Ya dig?"

She seemed to shudder just a little with that last line, but remained quiet. Then she said, "What if I were a pusher, or a pimp? Which would be kind of funny, but just say I were...would you still like me then? Or would you send me up the river, like a good cop."

I didn't have to think twice. "Lady, I don't care if you murdered the mayor. I'm on vacation."

We'd somehow come closer during my little speech, close enough that I was looking straight into her eyes, into her soul.

If I hadn't fallen for her, I wouldn't have liked what I had seen.

Our lips met. The fire from the Tiki torches was nothing compared to what passed between us. The jungle drums beat a heavy cadence as fire-dancers jumped and twirled and twisted in front of us. We didn't notice.

Minutes later she was in my suite, first in my arms, then on the couch. I turned the lights down low and cued up Music for Lovers Only by the Jackie Gleason Orchestra. Then I fixed a couple of simple Cuba Libres at the bar, and brought them over to the thing of beauty displayed on my sofa. She never took her eyes off me. I stood in front of her and handed her the drink.

"Sit," she said as she stood up slowly. I sat. She slowly unzipped the dress, and with a fluid motion let it drop to the floor, exposing her young, naked body, shadowed in the glow of the soft lights. "Let's try something different," she said softly, turned and walked over to the Tiki Bar. She motioned for me to follow. I did. She drew me in close and kissed me, that fire burning hot as hell. Then she slowly turned around so her back was to me, took my hands and moved them up her body. She was warm, very warm, and quivered under my touch. Her breath got heavy when my hands reached her breasts. Breathlessly she said, *"Take me,"* and slowly bent over the bar. I obeyed.

Down at the luau, Melinda Hawthorn sunk back into the shadows from where she had been standing. She wasn't crying. She would be soon.

Thursday morning brought heavy clouds and a threat of rain with them. Jessica and I had breakfast on the lanai overlooking the Keys while pelicans dove into the sea for fish right in front of us. Quaker parrots flew from palm tree to palm tree, searching for snacks. By the time we knocked back breakfast, the clouds had moved on and the sun was shining clear and yellow in a cyan sky.

I looked up at Jessica over my java. She was gorgeous in the morning light. "So what should we do today, kitten?"

"I thought maybe we'd go back to Key West, let me show you around the island. There's a lot to explore. We'll go back there, and see how it goes."

"What do you mean, see how it goes?"

She took a long sip of her OJ, keeping her eyes on me. The glass made a solid clink as it settled on the table. It seemed like an eternity before she spoke, just looking at me with those big blues.

"I mean, no visions last night. No ghosts. Maybe you were right, maybe it was the heat or something. I won't know for sure until I go home."

"Then home it is, dollface. Anything in particular you want to do?"

"Oh, the usual Key West stuff. Shop. Drink. Go to the beach. Go to the sponge market. And one other thing."

"What's that?"

She dabbed her lips with her napkin in such a way that made me melt. "There's an old house at the end of the Key, been abandoned for years. They say it's haunted. I want to go check it out. If there really are ghosts, maybe they'll be there."

I thought before I spoke. I honestly thought this was all a load of bunk, but I sure as hell didn't want to say that to Jessica. Whatever was happening to her, whether it was in her head or something real, it wasn't my business to judge. "Ok, fine. We'll check out your little haunted house. Do you think bullets are any good against ghosts?"

"I doubt it," she laughed, and as she did she stood up and slipped the terrycloth bathrobe from her shoulders, once again baring that perfect chassis that could stop a steamroller in its tracks. "We don't have to leave right away, do we?" she asked, standing there in the morning sunlight, backed by the bamboo wall and Tiki gods. What a sight.

"No kid, we've got all the time in the world."

Sheriff Jackson came over on the ten a.m. boat from Sugarloaf Key. His shirt was already damp with humidity He met Melinda Hawthorn in the lobby, and said a silent prayer of thanks for air conditioning.

"Several sources confirm it, Miss Hawthorn, it's almost definitely a victim of the 1935 storm. Not too surprised, myself."

Melinda was glad to hear the news, though she had other, more pressing issues on her mind. There had been couple of complaints about last night's luau which she needed to address, and the morning's breakfast buffet had run out of grits already. Four of the room maids were sick with a cough, and one of the ice machines was broken. As Bachman was not much for coordinating day-to-day problems, the problems fell on Melinda to fix.

"Well Sheriff, if you're sure that's all it is than I guess that's great news. So what do we do now? Remove the remains or just cover them over?"

"I suppose that's up to Mr. Hawthorn and you. I'd say it's best to just recover the grave and leave a marker."

"And that's just what we'll do, Sheriff. Good morning, darling."

Melinda turned to see Eliot Hawthorn walking up behind her, dressed in cream silk pajamas and a red smoking jacket. He walked slowly, using a cane for support. As he walked up behind Melinda, Jessica and I walked up behind the Sheriff.

"And you must be Mr. Riggins, from New York. Melinda has told me much about you, sir."

His demeanor was old-school charm and aristocratic, more of a statesman than a hotel owner. His face wore his age well, and a full mane of white hair topped off the look. It was his eyes that got me, though, bright blue eyes with a look of youth behind them, not age. Yet the corners revealed a sadness; years of death and destruction had settled into the crow's feet that finished off the edges of the man named Eliot Hawthorn.

"Yes, Bill Riggins, a pleasure to meet you Mr. Hawthorn," I said shaking his hand.

"Oh please, call me Eliot, this is a vacation resort, not the state seat."

"Fine, then call me Bill. And this is Jessica Rutledge, of Key West."

Jessica held out her hand and blushed just a little.

"Oh, of course, I thought I recognized you, you've worked for us on some occasions, have you not?"

"Yes," she answered awkwardly, "In the banquet hall." Her voice trailed off, oddly. I cut in with,

"And hello to you Melinda, and Sheriff Jackson. How's everyone doing this morning?"

The Sheriff answered. "Hello Bill. We were just discussing the, eh, remains in the garden."

"A touchy subject," I said, "Have you come to a decision on what's to be done with them?"

All were silent for a moment. Eventually all eyes turned to Hawthorn. Hawthorn was looking straight at me.

"As a matter of fact, Mr. Riggins,"

"Bill," I interrupted.

"Yes, Bill, of course. As a matter of fact, that is the precise reason I've come down here today. I don't often come down from my loft during business hours these days; the light and the noise does not agree with me, as a condition of an ailment of age. But I felt this event warrants my complete attention. Therefore I have decided that I need to witness the remains myself, if you'll indulge me."

Again our little crowd was quiet, not knowing what to say next. I looked around, the others looked at Hawthorn, then me, as if they needed my consent or some krazy thing. I motioned to Hawthorn.

"After you."

He turned and headed for the door, Melinda on his arm. As she turned I could swear she gave me a dirty look, a sideways glance, daggers for eyes and all that jazz, as if I were to blame for the skeleton, Hawthorn's health, the weather, everything. Maybe I was seeing things.

The Sheriff followed Hawthorn and Jessica and I came up the rear. Hawthorn made his way through the large carved doors, down the steps and out to the right towards the garden. When we got to the gravesite, Hawthorn stopped and looked straight in. Again, silence.

He stood at the edge for nearly a minute, not uttering a sound, as if he were mourning someone he knew. I felt it, so did Jessica, so did Melinda. The Sheriff must have too; he removed his hat and bowed his head. Then softly, almost a whisper, Hawthorn spoke.

"This woman," he said shakily, "died in the storm that took my first wife from me. She was a victim of that terrible blow, just as Vivian was, just as many of my friends from the Keys and workers I knew. In fact, as Vivian's body was never found, this could very well be…her."

He faltered; Melinda steadied him. Tears welled up in his bright eyes, turning them to smoke.

"And there are others here, at least three men, one of which might be my best friend Gregor who was also lost in that horrible hurricane. These four -" His voice broke, and Melinda held him closer. "These four souls have been left here, unmarked for more than 20 years. It's time they are laid to rest properly. Sheriff, you're certain there is no way of knowing who these people are?"

"No, sir. There were too many lost in the storm. Could be any of hundreds of people."

"Then let us have a minister from Sugarloaf come to the Island and give them a proper send off. Then we'll cover this poor woman over, and I'll have a monument erected on the site so that no one will forget they are here, victims of the storm that changed everything for so many of us. Agreed?"

Melinda smiled at Hawthorn. Sheriff Jackson said, "Fine idea, sir. I'll arrange for the minister."

Hawthorn turned to me just then. "Any objections, Mr...eh, Bill?"

"No, not at all. I think that's a fine plan," I said, not really sure why he was asking me.

"Then it is settled. Sheriff, please arrange for the minister to say his piece tonight at sundown. I'll have the crew ready to cover the grave just after."

"Certainly, sir."

Hawthorn looked back down at the grave, this time squinting and leaning in just a little. He turned to me and said, "Young man, I'm certainly no authority on the human skeletal system, but it seems to me that skull isn't intact. Is that so?"

"Yes, she seems to have been...well I suppose during the storm, her body must have, eh, been..." I tried not to say knocked around like a cork in barrel. I didn't want to upset the old man anymore than he was. After all, like he said, that damned well may have been his old lady down there. "The waves were strong, Eliot, and there were a lot of coral rocks and such that she may have come in contact with."

"In contact with?"

The Sheriff came to the rescue. He laid it out flat. "What he's saying Mr. Hawthorn is that the body was probably forced up against a reef, or maybe the foundation of the house. A crushing blow came across her face at some point, no doubt after she had already died."

Just what I was trying not to say.

"Her face was crushed?" Hawthorn said, his tone and his body trembling.

"I'm afraid so," Sheriff Jackson said. Hawthorn stumbled again. This time I had to help Melinda to keep him from falling into the grave. We steadied him, and without further emotion he said, "Take me back upstairs Melinda. I've heard too much." They left, leaving the three of us at the gravesite.

"Well, that's that," Jackson said. "Thanks for your help, Bill. Saved me a lot of leg work."

"No problem Sheriff. I got to drive around the Keys and meet some interesting characters."

"You mean like Lem?"

"Ah, no. In fact I'd like to forget about him."

"Well, I don't think you need to worry too much about him. Like I said, he gives you any trouble, you just let me know."

"If he gives me any trouble he'll be looking down the business end of snub-nosed .38," I said, winking.

"Well let's hope it don't come to that. If y'all kill Lem it'll be a heap of paperwork I don't need to be doin'."

"I'll go easy on him," I said, and shook his hand.

"Goodbye, Detective. Thanks again for the help." He turned to Jessica and tipped his hat. "And you stay out of trouble, young lady." She smiled, he left.

"What was that all about?" I asked. Maybe it was the cop in me, but Jackson hadn't said two words to Jessica the whole time she was there. In fact, it was almost as if everyone had forgotten she was there, and she just melted into the background.

"Oh, I don't know," she said, "I suppose he knows me from around town. After all I did grow up down here, ya know? And I wasn't no angel when I was a kid."

"Well, you're an angel now and that's all that counts," I said, and kissed her in the garden next to the skeleton.

## 1950

The war had been over for nearly four years. People were working again, buying again, importing, exporting. Money was flowing. Vacationers from up and down the Eastern Seaboard and even other parts of the world were booking rooms at the Resort faster than the maids could clean them. The Tiki theme on which Eliot and Marietta had built their Island was becoming more popular than ever. Music – records like Mele Kelikimaka by Bing Crosby and the Andrews Sisters and Hawaiian War Chant by Tommy Dorsey had helped the movement along in the '40s, and the new Island sounds from Hawaii that included Asian and Polynesian influences were helping things along. Then the musical South Pacific hit theaters, and *everyone* wanted to visit Tiki Island. Melinda, now twenty, was doing a splendid job as Entertainment Director and Publicist. Life was good, until that day in March that Eliot got the news: Marietta was dying; a rare and fatal disease was eating away at her from the inside out.

For six months Eliot watched the second love of his life slowly die. For six months Melinda watched her mother slowly die. Then on a hot, wet day in September of 1950, almost fifteen years to the day Vivian Hawthorn was lost, Marietta Hawthorn's life slipped away while sitting on the beach looking out at the Gulf, Eliot by her side. She was buried in the Hawthorn family plot in Homestead, in the grave that had been intended for Vivian.

"We still have each other," young Melinda said to Eliot, hugging him tightly as she cried.

"Not quite the same, my dear," he answered through his own tears, "Not quite the same." He drew her in closer and held her tighter, and they wept together.

## 1956

Melinda and a bellhop helped Hawthorn back up to the suite at the top of the A-Frame, and laid him in his bed. She gave him a couple of nerve pills and a glass of brandy, which he took without any protest. Melinda left the room and he closed his eyes. Memories came flooding in, memories long suppressed, long buried on the back-roads of his mind. Waves. Rain. Lightning, thunder, dark purple clouds. Boats. Faces. Blood in the sand.

Vivian's face floated in front of him. He shot straight up and screamed.

"What is it?!" Melinda yelled as she bolted back in from the other room.

"Melinda! My god, it was Vivian, she was here, clear as day. I swear it!"

"Oh, Eliot," she said tearfully. She sat beside him and held him. "It was just your imagination. Vivian is not here." She almost believed it herself.

"I think she is. Look, past the mirror, tell me what you see." He was shaking. Melinda looked.

In the mirror at the far end of the room they could see their own reflections, the bed, the furniture, and something else. Something that didn't belong.

"Wait...what?" There was no denying this. There was a figure, pale and wispy, in the mirror. "I see it, Eliot. I don't...I don't know what it is."

"I think it's her. Good God, Melinda, what if..."

"Please don't say it," Melinda said shakily, holding him closer.

"What if that's Vivian down there, buried here, on Tiki Island!"

"Please Eliot, please stop!"

"Vivian? Is that you down there? Is that you in the mirror?"

"Don't!" Melinda screamed and covered her eyes, overcome by guilt and fear.

"Eliot *don't invite the dead* into our home!"

"Vivian, if that is you, please leave us, there's nothing we can do for you now!" He screamed.

Suddenly the mirror broke; hundreds of shards of glass shattered across the room. Melinda screamed and flung herself down on the floor. Eliot dove flat on his back in the bed, but was still hit by flying glass. He managed to just miss getting a large piece of mirror in his throat.

We hopped the afternoon boat back to Key West. They had a little buffet of tropical fruits, cheeses and crackers out. I took an orange. Jessica grabbed a banana.

"I don't think I've ever had a real Florida orange before," I said, digging in.

"That's not a Florida orange. That's a California orange."

"How can you tell?"

"They ship all the Florida oranges out of state. Use them for Orange Juice, mainly. They're not as pretty or orangy looking as Cali oranges, so for looks they bring in the ones from the West coast. You've probably drank a ton of Florida orange juice up in New York City. But if you ever ate an orange up there, it was probably from Los Angeles. Makes sense, huh?"

"Yeah, sense like drinking Scotch in Kentucky." Jessica laughed. I liked in when she laughed. "Where do you want to go first, kiddo?"

"My apartment, just to check on things. Then we can go to the sponge market."

"Sounds like a plan."

"You really have your gun on you?"

"Yeah, of course. Never go anywhere without one. Although I usually carry my Military-issue .45 automatic. But that sucker's too heavy to lug around on my belt, especially in this heat. So the .38 it is."

"Is it powerful?"

"Would you like to get shot with it?"

"I suppose not."

"Well there. Why do you ask, kid?"

"Just wondering. Just…in case."

"In case what? You expect us to get rolled or something."

"No, nothing like that," she said, and got that distant look in her eyes again. I hated the look, although I didn't know why. "It's just that pig Roberts."

"You've had trouble with him in the past, have you?"

"Everyone has. Everyone who isn't rich, or connected, or pays him to lay off, that is. Yeah, I had some trouble with him."

"What happened?"

"I'd rather…I'd rather not say, if you don't mind Bill. It's kind of personal, catch my drift? No offense, but I just don't want to talk about it."

"I understand," I lied. "But listen, if he did anything to hurt you I'll rip his head off, just say the word."

She smiled. "No, it was a long time ago. It's just that I don't trust him. I've never known him to give up on a fight, and what you told me about him laying off after that scuffle, that just doesn't fit the S.O.B. We should be careful, Billy. He might play it cool for a while, but I'd bet he has his goons waiting to pounce us somewhere. And if he already knows you're packing heat, they'll be ready for it."

"Don't worry sugar, I'm a fast draw and I always keep my wits about me. Besides, according to Jackson I've got half the navy looking out for us!"

"I hope so," she said, and looked out over the rail. That was the last we spoke until we got to town.

Lunch at a small but nice place on the water. A little shopping up and down Duval. A few drinks, dinner at an upscale seafood joint on the docks. A few hours later we were very happily half lit, throwing back Bourbon shots at a little place on Duval simply known as Rick's, a place sort of, but not quite, fashioned after Rick's Cafe Americain in Casablanca. The air was cool and the chicks hot. All around us girls in shorts and halter or tube tops sat with guys wearing bowling shirts or Hawaiian shirts and Bermuda shorts or rolled up jeans. Strictly casual here on Key West, not a sport coat in sight. Even though the bar was open-air, the air stunk with beer and smoke, and an occasional whiff of reefer.

At around eleven o'clock, Jessica had the bright idea to take a walk on the beach.

"What about the booze?" I asked with a sort of lilting slur.

"I think, William," she responded with an equally lilting slur, "I think that it will still be here when we get back."

"It'd better be," I said as I slid off the barstool onto a very uneven floor. Oh sure, I ain't gotta worry about goons, I keep my wits about me all time. That is except when I'm shooting whiskey with some kookie dame.

Jessica led me by the hand through the front of the lounge and into the street. Once again music bombarded my ears from every direction. Rock-a-Billie, Country/Western, even some four-part harmony by a barbershop quartet spilled out of the myriad clubs into the street like a river of musical mixed drinks. As we walked it occurred to me that there still might be some danger of retribution by Chief Fatso, so I tried to clear my head as best as I could, and felt for the butt of the .38 on my belt.

I did it just a second too late.

From behind I felt a big meaty hand grab me by the throat. At the same time I saw an equally meaty hand grab Jessica around the mouth and an arm around her waist. Before I could move both my arms were locked behind me and I was being dragged backwards into an alley, narrow, dark, between two tall buildings and full of trash and crates, but no people. Muffled screams came from my left and in the dim light I could see Roberts behind Jessica, his fat hand clamped over her mouth, the other trying to hold her by the pants. I don't think it was an accident that his hand slipped and cupped her square on her right breast, and that pissed me off royally. By that point I felt the punches come, fast and hard they hit me in the gut, then the face. The bastard rabbit-punched me in the kidney and that hurt the most; I doubled over and used it as an excuse to hit the ground. I hit it rolling, kicking off from the two mugs attacking me. I rolled twice and felt the warm liquid ooze flow from my mouth. I felt the stiffening of my right abdomen muscles as they tried to figure out just what the hell had rammed my ribs. And as I flipped I could see the whole picture: Roberts holding Jessica, and two goons about the size of a Buick poised and ready to start kicking me as soon as I stopped rolling. It was now or never, I knew. Either these guys were going to kill me or at least put me in the hospital. It was me or them and my mind was made up.

I guess Roberts didn't plan on me packing heat because when I came to my feet holding the .38 all I got back were blank stares of confusion. The two goons backed up with their hands up in front of them. I swung the gun towards Roberts and his hand slipped away from Jessica's mouth just long enough for her to let out a blood-curdling scream. Then everything happened so fast it was like a dark blur.

Roberts went for his gun. I was less than five feet away from him.

"Don't do it you lemon-headed sonuva bitch," I yelled, loud enough for him to hear over all the traffic and music. He heard me but he didn't stop; his service revolver was in his hand and coming up level. I didn't give him a chance. My little snub-nose was junk at long distances, but at short range I could take the cap off a beer bottle. I let him have it, one shot right into his hand. He squealed and his gun clattered to the bricks. The goons just looked at each other, trying to decide whether to run.

"Gat Dammit boy, you in a big fuckin' heap a trouble now, you som'bitch. Assaulting a po-lice officer! Attempted murder! I'll hang your ass personally from the tallest tree, city boy."

"You will like hell," I said and dragged Jessica away from his greasy, bloody hands.

Then he said to the two mugs, "Well don't jus' stand there lookin' stupid, get him!" The two goons didn't budge. They were evidently smarter than he was.

"Boy, you think you smart but you ain't. I got a felony on you now. You ain't gonna see the outside of cell block till yo' sixtieth birthday."

It was just at that point that the US Navy came to the rescue. Four sailors and an officer heard the shot and came running into the alley. At least one of them knew Jessica.

"Hey, what gives?" the officer said, then he saw the gun in my hand and the other on the floor. "Ginny, what you got yourself mixed up with now?" he asked Jessica.

"Hello Larry. This is my friend, Detective Riggins from New York. This fat pig of an excuse for a police chief tried to have him hauled over."

"You watch your tongue you tramp," Roberts got out, and in a quick step I backhanded him with my free hand.

"And you watch yours, clown," I said back. It sounded a lot tougher than it looks in print.

"Hey, now wait a sec," the officer said, "I heard about you through the grapevine. Heard old Lem here might try to cause you some trouble."

"Don't call me Lem, boy. That's Chief Roberts to you,"

"Yeah sure *Lem*. These two Mack trucks the ones who hauled you over?" the officer asked me, and as I nodded yes I could see the four sailors tensing up. Apparently Sheriff Jackson had a *hell* of a lot of friends in the Navy, and that friendship was about to pay off.

The officer spoke again. "Well Detective, I think this about does it. Old Lem here has been a thorn in this Key's side for a long time. Seems to me he's gone to far. Things will have to change."

"You have no authority over me, sailor boy. So you just back the hell up and be on your way before the five of you find yourselves in the lockup with a few new scars."

The four sailors laughed and officer grinned. "And who's gonna do that Lem, you?"

Roberts was boiling, his face a cooked lobster. He was finished and he didn't even know it. "My two deputies will see to it," he growled.

The officer, who I could now see by his stripe was an Ensign, snapped his fingers twice, low. The two larger sailors came forward and without a sound took down the two goons with three punches each. "What deputies?" the officer asked.

Roberts was heaving with short breaths and despair. His anger was so intense I'm pretty certain he had a mild stroke right there in the street. The blood was coming faster from his hand now, and he was beginning to sway.

"You som' bitch." Roberts' voice was low and breathy, growly like a mad bear. Sweat poured off his red face. "When the sun comes up I'm gonna issue warrants for every one of you. That includes you, Dee-tective, and your little whore too. I'll see every last one of you bastards hung for this."

"When the sun comes up," the officer said, "You'll be sitting in the Monroe County prison. Chief Roberts, you're under arrest for conspiracy to commit murder, assault with a deadly weapon, and unlawful abuse of office. Boys, put the cuffs on this asshole's hands, and make them tight. Real tight."

I don't know for certain how much authority the military has on civilian soil, but given the size of the Navy base on Key West, I'd have to believe it was a lot. Roberts couldn't move. He was shocked, but moreover he knew his goose was cooked. The reign of Chief Roberts was over, all on account of 'lil old me.

"What about this fucker?" he squealed. "That som' bitch done shot me!"

"Self defense," Jessica said. "And you can shove your threats up your ass, Roberts. I knew someday you'd pay," she said with a meanness I'd not seen in her before. "Happy pay day." She spit in his face. I noticed for the first time she was shaking all over. Beads of sweat ran down her face and mingled with the tears.

Roberts started to say something and I slapped him again, this time with hand that held the .38. I didn't know what he did to her, but whatever it was I was determined she'd have the last word.

"Are you ok?" the officer asked both of us. I said yes. Jessica just nodded. "Ok, then we're gonna take this *criminal* and his thugs up to the station and call Sheriff Jackson. Sorry we couldn't get to you sooner detective."

"That's fine, buddy, you got here in plenty of time."

"Well, pleasure to be of help. And a real pleasure to catch this scumbag in the act, finally. He won't be bothering no one anymore. Goodnight, Detective." He turned to Jessica. "Goodnight, Ginny. Sorry this had to happen to you."

"Goodnight, Larry." He tipped his hat and left with Roberts, who was wheezing heavily. I had a feeling they'd be taking him to the hospital, not the jail.

The four other sailors each turned back and said goodbye. Two of them said goodbye Ginger, and one said goodbye Ginny.

"Ginger?" I asked Jessica, still trying to catch my breath. "What's that all about?"

She sighed heavily and came into my arms. "It's a long story. Let's go down to the beach and I'll tell you about it there. I need the fresh air."

I nodded, and she led the way.

In a few minutes we were looking at the Atlantic Ocean. The moon, almost full, danced on the rippling waves as the breeze came off the water and played with Jessica's platinum blonde hair. We walked to the edge of the water, shoes in hand. The water was warm. Jessica was boiling up.

"The short of it is…that was my stage name."

"Stage name?"

"Yeah. I used to…dance."

Where I come from, there was only one kind of dancing where a dame's stage name would be Ginger.

"You're a stripper?" I asked coolly. Surprisingly, I somehow wasn't too surprised.

"Not exactly," she said, and the pain was clear in her eyes, pain of a thousand nights of acting a part she was never meant to play. "I don't actually strip...I...well, it's a private club." She bit her lip and spoke more softly, now looking out at the ocean, not at me. "I'm onstage...well, nude, usually with other women. The dancing it sort of...risqué."

All the Bourbon had cleared out of my head and I was sober as sin now. I kind of wish I hadn't been. That clicking that'd been bugging me since yesterday hit me again, this time loud and clear.

*Click,*

"Jessica....sex shows? You perform sex shows? Where in the hell are there sex shows in Key West?"

"I said, it's a private club. Mostly Navy men, some locals and a lot of out-of-towners. But it's not what you think Bill, please don't judge me." Now she was looking right at me and her eyes were pleading little melted balls of wax, sad and glistening in the moonlight. "It's just a show, nothing real happens. It's all just a show." She started to cry again.

"Calm down sugar," I said and held her close. "I'm a cop, not a judge. It's not my place to lay judgment on you. Although you've laid a pretty heavy load on me, baby. I wasn't really expecting that."

"I'm sorry Bill, I should have told you before, I know, but just like you didn't tell me you were a cop, everything was going so well I didn't want to foul it all up."

I held her closer, our lips almost touching. "I understand kid. That's why you looked so shook up when you found out I was the law. You thought I was going to put the pinch on you. I understand."

Her eyes twitched just the slightest then. "Yeah, that's why Bill. Do you hate me?"

"Nothing could be farther from the truth," I said and our lips connected, a new storm of fire ripping through our souls. I held her tight as we kissed, tighter than I ever held a woman before as if that would prove to her I didn't care, I didn't care if she was a stripper or a stag dancer or anything. I didn't care if every guy in the Navy saw her naked body swaying onstage, because it was I she chose to show off her best moves to, it was all for me. She'd given herself to me in a way that no one could ever dream of while eyeballing her on some dark, sleazy stage, and I had given myself back, all of me, maybe too damned much. In a few days I'd be back in New York, alone, and she'd be here in Key West with her choice of any of a thousand mugs to fill my shoes. But tonight she was mine, all mine, and I would take what was mine.

"I don't care what your name is, or what you do for bread. You can be Ginger tomorrow. Tonight you're Jessica, and you're all mine."

She moaned softly and we kissed again, and we found ourselves laying in the sand of the secluded beach, intertwined and heaving, our bodies becoming one and pulsing to the beat of the waves as they softly glided to the shore. My bruised ribs and scraped face didn't hurt anymore. The pleasure was too intense to let any other feelings come through.

In the moonlight Jessica arched her back one last time. The swell of her breasts shimmered, silhouetted against the darkness of the night sky, and we collapsed in the sand, the fury extinguished.

We fell asleep in each other's arms there in the sand, lulled by the sounds of the waves. It was close to one a.m. when I awoke, alone. I looked around and finally saw Jessica at the water's edge, outlined in the moonlight. She was talking to someone who was standing in the water.

Jessica awoke less than an hour after she had fallen asleep on the Key West beach. At first she was peaceful, laying there in the arms of the man who had finally freed her (she hoped) from Roberts' clutch, and maybe more. But soon her tranquility was cut short. The voices came, and she froze with terror.

In the surf a figure appeared, sickly and weak, walking in from the tide. It was just a shadow, but one Jessica knew well. The voice called to her, faint, distant, pleading. Without control she came to her feet and slowly walked to the water's edge. The figure met her there, same as before, same as always, with hideous countenance and sea creature-infested flesh.

"What do you want from me," Jessica spoke weakly, quietly, trying not to look the thing straight on.

*"Release me,"* the shadow said. Behind Jessica, Detective Bill Riggins was getting to his feet.

My eyes had sand in them, and rubbing them hurt and made them bleary. Through the darkness, lit up by the glow of the high moon I could see Jessica and the other person at the shoreline. Something seemed wrong. I was groggy but I could tell something just wasn't kosher. I got up and began to walk over toward them. I could hear Jessica speak now.

"Leave me alone, please, just stop torturing me. I can't help you! I don't know how!" she screamed as I came up behind her.

Everything got pretty trippy all of a sudden. I don't know if the alcohol settled in and had a relapse or what, but as I walked up behind Jessica the person she was talking to just...well, they just faded into the darkness. Gone.

"Jessica?" I said and put my hand on her shoulder. She about jumped out of her skin. She'd been crying, and her tear-streaked face wore an expression of fear, insanity and despair all balled into one. "Jesus, kid? What gives?"

"Bill! Bill!" she cried through hysterical tears. She was shaking hard. "Oh God Bill, you're here, oh God, did you see her? Did you *see* her Bill? Oh my God!" She was rambling on, kinda crazy.

"Who was it? And where did she go?" I asked, looking around for the shadowy woman in the ocean.

"Jesus Bill, you *did* see her! You did, didn't you, it's not just me, I'm not crazy!"

"Yeah, I saw someone, but she's gone. Tell me the story, will ya?"

"My God Bill, you don't know? That was *her!* That was the freaking ghost, Bill! That was the ghost I've been seeing all these nights! Now you've seen it too!" She was wild.

"Ok, calm down dollface, calm down. I saw someone, but I'm not so sure it was a ghost, it was just somebody walking down the beach, that's all."

"Are you fucking *kidding* me?" The language threw me, I'd not heard her utter words like that except when she was actually doing what she was talking about. But it sobered me up a little more, that's for sure.

"Jessica, there's no ghost here. We're alone."

"Exactly Bill...you saw her a minute ago, and now she's *gone*...where did she go?"

"I don't know...into the ocean for a swim?"

Her voice was hoarse, scratchy. "Into the *ocean?* She *disappeared*, Bill. She *dissolved* into the Goddamn ocean."

"Jessica, come on..."

"You saw her Bill. You saw her disappear. You just don't want to admit it because you can't understand it and that would piss you off to no end. Did you see her face?"

I didn't answer.

"Bill, did you see her *face?*"

"No," I lied. I had seen it. I thought I was still dreaming or something. And I sure as hell didn't want to admit I saw a black face with no eyes and crabs crawling over it.

"It was her Bill. Same as before. She won't stop coming to me."

"What does she want?" I asked, sort of like I was leaning toward believing her. I guess I was.

"God, I don't know. She tries to speak to me but it sounds like a hundred brakes screeching on a train. I think...I think she wants me to help her somehow, but I don't know how."

I held her again, tried to stop her from shivering. "Lets get out of here. We can go back to your place if you want."

"I, I don't have air conditioning. It's so hot in that damned room, and cramped. I don't want to go back there."

"We can get a room if you want."

"Yeah, that would be good. I know a few inexpensive places with air."

We began to walk back off the beach into town. Funny, it crossed my mind that it was funny she'd know which motels had air conditioning. She probably got so hot some nights she booked a room just to sleep in the air.

Click, click.

We walked up a side street to a motor inn with a vacancy sign lit up in neon letters hanging in the office window.

"I'll wait out here," she said, and lit up a smoke.

"Ok, I'll be right back." I went inside and rang the little copper bell on the counter. A tired man in a bathrobe came out from a door adjacent to the counter and said "Two bucks". I put the money on the counter and he got me a key. Just as he was about to hand it to me he stopped.

"Hey mack, you with her?" He pointed to Jessica.

"Yeah, what's it to you?"

He took the key back. "We don't run that kinda joint here. She can stay alone when she wants, fine, but no boyfriends. Sorry."

I scooped up the cash and said, "Great, a two-bit motel with morals. Thanks pal." He just turned and went back through the door. I went back outside to Jessica.

"Which room?"

"No can do, doll. He said you can stay here alone but no boyfriends."

She shuddered, and I mean all over. "Jackass. Fine, we'll go someplace else. This place is creepy anyway." We walked a little farther to another motor inn with another neon vacancy sign. This time we went in together. She rung the bell. The sounds of a radio filtered in from behind the desk. "Hey, Mel? Wake up," she said, and a paneled door that matched the wall slid back, revealing a rather voluptuous woman in her mid thirties, wearing a black negligee and an open housecoat.

"Oh, hello sweetie. Kinda late, ain't it?"

"I need air conditioning. This is my friend Bill. He needs air conditioning too."

"Don't we all," she said seductively and handed Jessica the key. "I'll put it on your tab, sweetie," she said, "and holler if you need any help with this one."

"All I need is some sleep, Mel," Jessica said and led me out the door.

"Night Ginger," I heard as we left.

"Let me guess…one of your old work buddies?"

"Something like that," she said and we walked up the sidewalk to room 102. Once inside we flipped on the lights and threw ourselves down on the bed. "I can use a drink," Jessica said, and rolled over on her back.

"Yeah, me too. Anyplace around here to get one?"

"Liquor store about a block from here, open till three a.m."

"I'll go," I said, "You settle in here."

I sure was on my guard as I walked to the liquor store. Not a soul in sight. When I got back a few minutes later, Jessica was sitting up in the bed, propped up on pillows with the radio on. Some modern jazz was playing, nothing I recognized but pretty good riffs.

"I found you a jazz station," she said as I rolled into bed with the bottle of hooch and the two motel glasses from the sideboard.

"Groovy," I said, and poured. We each took a belt, and she tilted her head back on the pillow.

"What am I going to do, Bill?" she asked, her eyes closed tight. "How can I make it stop?"

"I don't know kid, but we'll find a way,"

"What if we can't?"

"Then you come live with me up in the city. Ghosts are the least of your worries up there."

"That might be a nice change."

"Jessica, does everyone in Key West know you as Ginger?"

She sighed and took another drink. "Pretty much. I started using the name years ago, and it sort of stuck. Now even when I work at a hotel or serve drinks, I'm known as Ginger. It's ok, it gets me better tips. No one cares much for a 'Jessica'. But Ginger, that sounds like the name of a girl who's pants you can get into. So I get better tips."

"I can see the logic in that."

We drank some more and lit a couple of Camels. We didn't say much for a while, just listened to the music. An older tune by Miles Davis and Charlie Parker came on. "Damn, do I miss Charlie Parker. Bird, we used to call him."

"Who's Charlie Parker?"

I cringed a little. "Sax player, one of the best. Maybe *the* best. I used to watch him play in clubs when I was a kid."

"Where's he now?"

"Six feet under."

"Drag. What happened?"

I sighed. "My dad was a cop. Ran across him a few times in the city, strung out, high on H. He was an addict, bad. Said he could only play the way he did when he was juiced up. Finally, it killed him."

Jessica swallowed hard. "Overdose?"

"Heart attack, pretty much. The junk ripped his system to shreds."

"A heart attack? Oh so he was old."

"Nope, thirty-five. The doctor who found him thought he was 70."

"That's horrible."

"That's what riding the white horse does to you."

"It does, I know."

"Yeah."

Jessica leaned in close, snuggled against me.

"You know Riggins, it seems we've been through a whole lot in the last couple of days, yet I don't know much about you."

I took a sip of whiskey and said, "Not much to know, really. I'm twenty-eight but most people say I act a lot older."

"You do," she said to me. I guess I do.

"I was born in Weehawken, New Jersey but don't hold it against me."

She let out a little giggle. "I won't. Where's Weehawken?"

"Just across the river from New York City. I can see the skyline from the end of my block, where the wharfs are on the water." I continued on pretty flat, not much emotion in my voice as I remembered the years. I didn't like my past much. I certainly didn't like talking about it, so I gave her the short version. "My dad was a beat cop in the city and my mother took in sewing jobs on the side, so even during the Depression we did all right. My dad went into the big war as an MP, and when he came out in 1946 he was promoted to sergeant in the police department. I went to college in Boston, then off to Korea in '52 and when I got back a year later, decided to go into criminology. I had a knack for working cases and was on the fast-track to becoming a homicide detective. Then, in late 1953, a junkie high on Horse stabbed my father to death, leaving him to die in a back alley in Manhattan. That's when I decided to go into vice. A year later I made detective, and at 24 was one of the youngest ever promoted to the gig. A few weeks later my mother was run-over and killed by a guy who had a few too many at the local watering hole. Never had a steady girl, so that left me alone with my work, and I haven't stopped for a minute since, until I came down here."

"That's sad, that you lost so much just as you were succeeding in life."

"That's life," I said, and lit up a couple of smokes. I gave one to Jessica and blew a smoke ring with mine.

"So that's your history. What about now? What do you like to do when you're not catching criminals or digging up skeletons?"

"Oh, I don't know. After work I usually hit this little lounge across the street from my New York apartment. They have decent chow and a swingin' jazz combo that plays on weekends. I hang out with the musicians a lot, they're the beat type, way out there and a little screwy, so different from me it's fun to talk with them. Plus they're a good source of info on anything heavy going down in the city. They all smoke reefer but I don't bug them about it…and in turn they turn me onto people pushing the big stuff."

"More work."

"Work is my life."

"You don't do anything for fun?"

"Like what, golfing? I live in a city. When I want to do something fun I take in a show, or a movie. Sometimes I dig the museums. Sometimes I go to the burlesque shows, but I don't usually have any fun because I see all the crime associated with them, the dope, the graft, the prostitution."

"Yeah," she said somberly.

"I don't mean you, kid. I know you're not mixed up in all that. If you were you wouldn't be here with me, I'm guessing."

She didn't answer right away. "No, I try to stay away from all that," she finally said, and that little pause made that 'click' in my head go off again. Now I knew what that click was; I'd been ignoring it for hours, but all those little clicks were adding up and my brain wouldn't push them away anymore. Jessica simply wasn't being straight with me, just like I wasn't straight with her. She told me she was a hostess, which she is, but she held back that she was a stripper who performed live shows depicting steamy sexual acts between women at a private club in Key West. That's pretty big, as far as "holding back" goes. I knew plenty of dames that worked shows like that in the city, and there were very few who were straight. Most were damaged goods in one way or another. Some were junkies who did it for the money to get a fix. Some were just plain old-fashioned nymphos. Some were forced into it because they were weak-minded and fell in with the wrong kat. Some were hookers. Some were just plain, honest girls who found a way to make fast cash without doing a lot of work. I was hoping that Jessica was the later. Hoping, but not a hundred percent sure. *Click.*

"How did you get into that business anyway, kid? Were you that hard-up for cash?"

She shifted uncomfortably in the bed. Her head was swimming with the alcohol now, the great stuff that made her forget all the things she wished had never happened in her life. But it also screwed up her judgment, and she was afraid she'd tell me things she didn't want me to know, secrets of her past that needed to stay buried like the broken skeleton on Tiki Island.

"When I got back from Miami I was flat busted broke. I didn't have anywhere to stay, no money, nothing. So I went to a friend and asked for help. She told me she didn't have any waitressing jobs or anything available, but she could put me up for free for a couple of nights if I was willing to show my tits on stage and shake a little ass at this private club owned by a guy she knew. Believe me, I didn't want to do it, but then I figured what the hell, and that night Ginger was born."

"And it just snowballed from there?"

"Yeah, pretty much. After a couple of nights it didn't seem so bad, so I went to work full time. I got a free room and decent money. After the stage show I'd sit with the customers, talk to them, flirt with them, and they'd tip me, sometimes big. A few regulars got to liking me, and bought me gifts, nice things. Then I was told I had to do the sex show if I wanted to stay on."

"They rope you in with the money, then make you do the nasty stuff to keep it, seen it a million times," I said.

"Yeah. Something like that. Anyway the money was too good to pass up so I gave it a whirl. Turns out it wasn't so bad after all. The other girls were in the same boat so we were all nice to each other, and got along great. But I started to get a reputation in town. Jessica started to fade away. Ginger took over. And Ginger wasn't a nice girl."

"So how did you get out of it?"

"Out of it?" she laughed. "Oh, I'm not entirely out of it. Well, not until tonight."

"Why tonight?"

She sighed, and took a long swig of Bourbon before continuing. For the first time she slurred a little. "Roberts, Bill. Roberts runs the club. It was him who forced me to do the show." And some other things too, but she didn't tell me that.

### July, 1935
### Just over a month before the storm

Anger. Fear. More Anger. Anguish, confusion, sadness. *Extreme* anger. These were the emotions ripping through Eliot Hawthorn on that hot July day in 1935 as he docked his boat in his private Key West slip. Roberts was waiting at the dock along with two of his police buddies.

"Hello, Mistuh Hawthorn." Roberts yelled in his heavy southern drawl. "Got yo' message. What's on yo' mind, so urgent?"

"Just you, Roberts. The other two will have to go. This is something I need you to do alone."

"Ok, boys, you heard the man," he said and the two tipped their hats and walked off. "Anything I can do for you Mistuh Hawthorn, jus' name it."

"I need someone followed, Roberts. They can't know you're tailing them. And no one – and I mean no one can know you're doing this for me. Anything you find out, you tell me only. If a word of it gets out, I'll know who to come after, clear?"

"You knows there ain't no reason to worry 'bout me, suhr. My lips is sealed shut."

"Good. I'll give you the details on the way."

"On the way where?"

"We're going to that little den of yours on the east end. I need to find a girl."

"What girl?"

"Any girl as long as she's blonde, looks about thirty and is between five-foot-two and five-foot-four."

"Kind of sounds like yo' describin' Missus Hawthorn."

Eliot held back his emotions as he spoke. "That's not really any of your business now, is it Roberts? Just find me the girl."

"Ok, suhr. I'm sorry for askin'. Jus' strange, in all the years you been taken prostitutes to yo' parties, they all been from Havana. And I knows as a fact you ain't nevuh took none fo' yo'self, bein's yo' married an alls." Roberts was no fool. He could spot something funny from a mile away, and he knew something was funny now. He didn't really care what Hawthorn wanted a blonde hooker for; all he knew was there was probably a way for him to make an extra buck on it, if he could figure out the angle.

"Let's just say she's for a friend, Roberts, and leave it at that."

"Yessuh," Roberts said, but he was far from leaving anything at that.

### 1956

I woke up Friday morning a little confused. The Bourbon had knocked me out, and at first I didn't know where the hell I was. The room was bright; the fiberglass curtains did very little to keep the morning sun out. The whir of an air conditioner fan filled the room, and it was so cold I thought I was back in New York. I turned and for the first time saw Jessica sleeping, a beautiful girl even in slumber. She always seemed to get up before I did, but not today. She was sleeping like a babe.

I pulled my aching carcass out of the bed and assessed the evening's damage in the bath mirror. There was a nasty scrape on my left cheek, red but not bloody. There was a bruise below my mouth, and several on my gut. My right side ached where I got rabbit-punched, but the ribs where intact. One knee was skinned where I hit the bricks, and the knuckles of my left hand were red and swollen from back-handing Roberts. Now I wished I'd done more. I wished I'd shot the sonuvabitch through his fat gut, where it would hurt the most. But I knew he'd never use his right hand the right way again, and that made me happy.

"Jessica, wake up dollface, it's almost ten and I want to catch the ten-thirty back to Tiki Island."

"Let me sleep, honey. I have to work tonight. Just leave the cas..." she stirred a little and her eyes opened wider. "Just leave the air on high for me."

"You're not coming back to the Island?"

"I can't hun, I have a shift at La Concha, three to three, and I can't miss it. I need the dough, you know?"

I did. I was on vacation, but Jessica wasn't. She needed to work and it was selfish of me to keep bugging her to stay with me. In a few days I'd be gone, and she'd probably never see me again.

What a depressing thought.

"Ok, kid. But hey, wait a minute...you promised me a haunted house, if I remember right."

She opened her eyes again and sat up. "Ain't you seen enough?" she asked in a frightened tone.

I didn't really care about ghosts. I just wanted to spend more time with her.

"Nope. If there's really ghosts in the world, I want to see one close-up. You game?"

She rubbed the sleep from her eyes and yawned. "Ok, I'll show you the place. Shouldn't be too bad in the daylight, I guess. I need a shower first, though."

"Yeah, me too."

She got out of bed and slipped off her clothes, letting them drop to the floor. She was good at that. "Well come on, we can save some water if we do this together," she said with that breathy, sexy way she had of making every word sound like pure sex. I followed her into the bath. We didn't save any water.

An hour later we were driving the new Chevy to Old Town with the top dropped and the radio swinging. I cruised the Bel Air up Whitehead to Truman, then cut over to Frances that led us to the Key West Cemetery. Jessica pointed at a spot to pull over, right next to the fence and across from a street called Petronia.

"Creepy place," I said as I parked. "What's with all the cement boxes?"

"If you dig down five feet you hit water here. So the coffins are put in shallow graves lined with concrete, or above-ground cement caskets. Or Mausoleums. See?" She pointed at a large brick structure with an iron grate. Inside rested two caskets.

"Creepy," I repeated.

"Yeah...you should see it at night."

"Nix that. Now where's this spook joint?"

She waved for me to follow her up the street and across, where we stood in front of a big wooden house that had seen better days. The houses to the left and right didn't look much better but were obviously lived in. This one had all the earmarks of being abandoned. Weeds growing through the front steps, glass missing from windows, holes in the roof. A pair of dirty gray-white curtains billowed out of the second floor window, giving the effect of a phantom moving in and out of the room.

"Nice place. What's the rent go for?"

"Can't rent it out. Plumbing's shot. Come on, let's go inside."

We walked carefully up the creaking steps. Flecks of gray, peeling paint shifted under our feet and drifted down from the sagging overhang of the porch. Once close up, I took the whole place in.

Like most of the houses in Old Town, this one was a two-story, late Nineteenth Century job with clapboard construction and a tin roof. The house had been white once, but now sported a dirty gray luster reminiscent of old socks. The first floor windows were boarded up, and the front door hung partly open on rusted hinges. Paint was peeling off everywhere exposing dry, cracked hardwood bleached by the sun. A rotting rocking chair, legs broken on one side, leaned against the wall. The porch floor was a mockery of splintering wood and moldy, rotted black carpet. A piece of plywood had been placed in the middle for ingress through the front door.

"Doesn't look very safe, kiddo," I said testing the wood. "I'd hate to get an ankle stuck in the floor."

"Just stay on the plywood and you'll be all right. Same on the inside. The floors are all shot to hell from rain leakin' in. Lotta water damage. It's a real mess."

She wasn't kidding. As she opened the parched wooden screen door it broke apart in her hands and clattered to the floor with a bone-cracking sound. I winced. Then she pushed the heavy wood door open, and as it creaked on its ancient hinges I saw what she was talking about.

"Ya'll watch your step," she said, and her slight southern drawl instantly became thicker, more pronounced, as if she'd gone back in time to a period when she was a different Jessica.

We were in the living room, a large room that took up half the first floor of the house. Light seeped in through cracks in the walls, the ceiling, the boards over the windows, enough to cast a gray glow over everything. Chunks of plaster had fallen from the ceiling revealing broken lathe and rafters. Striped wallpaper, once blue and white, peeled from the walls from the top down in an eerie brown curl. Under it mold turned the plaster a mottled black and gray slime. Broken plaster and shards of glass littered the floor along with old newspapers, broken bits of furniture and beer bottles. To the right sat a small sitting room, brightened with more light as the boards from the window had been pried off. The ceiling had completely caved in and the room was impassable. To the left were the stairs heading to the second floor; they looked sturdy but I didn't trust them at all.

"The kitchen's in the back," Jessica whispered and led me through a door along the plywood path.

The kitchen was a disaster. A long porcelain sink and counter occupied the entire back wall. It had collapsed on one side under the weight of piles of iron pots, pans, and assorted junk. Most of it was covered with a wet rust, and stunk like old metal and decay. A 1930s icebox stood in pieces next to the heap, its doors ripped off and thrown on the floor. The kitchen table, large and made of hardwood, sat warped and cracked in the middle of the room, broken dishes and pie tins and booze bottles piled high. A single green metal lamp hung from the ceiling. An antique gas stove, rusted and decrepit, completed the look.

"Looks like someone was here having a party not too long ago, by the looks of the booze bottles," I said.

"Sometimes hobos would crash here, hang out during storms or cold nights.

Not anymore. They know better."

"To dangerous."

She laughed. "No, too scary. There's been a lotta stories about this place. Just last summer they found a man in here dead, a hobo that was tryin' to get outta the rain. When they found him, his face was froze-up in a kind of horror, eyes open wide, mouth in a scream, hands curled all up like he'd had the devil scared in him."

"I've seen bodies like that. All sorts of things happen to a body after it dies, you know."

"Believe what you want, detective. He wasn't the only one. Let's go up stairs."

"Is it safe?"

"Should oughtta be," she said and led me into the living room and up the steps. Someone had recently nailed boards across the worst ones, it seemed.

"How long has this place been abandoned?" I asked as we slowly climbed the embattled staircase.

"Let's see…Nineteen-forty…eight…nine…about seven years, give or take."

"What happened here?"

She didn't speak again until we reached the landing. A long, narrow hall to the right, filled with old bottles, pieces of junk, crates, and newspapers and covered in broken plaster and peeled paint stared back at us. On the left were four doors, on the right were two. An open window at the end of the hall let in plenty of stark, gray light. Everything was gray. Even Jessica looked gray in this place.

"To the left are the kid's bedrooms and the washroom. This first door on the right is a sewing room. Last door on the right is the large bedroom."

She opened the door to the sewing room. Something moved in front of us and I had the .38 out in a split second. It would have done no good against the billowing curtains, same ones I saw from the street.

"Jesus! Damned curtains."

"Damned everything in this house," Jess said. "This is the room where they found the man. It's also the room where two women were tortured and murdered back around 1948."

"That's why the place was abandoned," I muttered.

"Not entirely. It was vacant when the murder happened. For about a year, I think, the house was up for sale. But no one would buy it because of the noises."

"What noises?" I entered the room. A broken pedal-powered sewing machine leaned against the side wall, and a heap of moldy, wet clothes and sheets filled a corner. A large black stain filled the center of the floor. Smaller black stains splashed the walls and ceiling. "They were stabbed to death, weren't they."

"Throats cut, there in the middle."

"Blood stains on the walls and floor. Gaddamn."

"The guy who done it killed himself too. Slit his own throat out back in the yard," Jessica said with no feeling.

"So, what noises?"

"Moans. Whispers. Stuff like that. Voices in the night. Footsteps."

"Sounds like a Vincent Price flick."

"Vincent Price would run outta here screamin'," she said flatly and turned, moving back out to the hall. She passed two of the left doors and opened the third. A shiver went up my spine as we looked in. Jessica let out a little whimper.

In the middle of the room was a broken, twisted metal baby carriage, 1930s vintage. The canvas was rotted and ripped, the wheels bent. A child's desk and chair sat in the corner under a thick layer of dust. But what really gave us the creeps was the doll.

"She's still here. I can't believe after all these years, it's damned near impossible but she's still here."

"Who?"

"Rebecca."

"Who's Rebecca?"

"My doll," she said and stepped into the room.

The doll stood up against the wall under the open window. Time was not good to it. Its china face was cracked and flaking, its clothes rotted and faded. The china hands were broken and missing fingers, and the black hair was a tangled mess of cobwebs and dead bugs. But the eyes...piercing blue eyes, bright as the day they were manufactured. It was damned creepy. She seemed to be staring at us...following us with those eyes no matter where in the room we went.

Then it hit me. "Wait, *your* doll? What's your doll doing in this horrible place?"

She said sadly, "I used to live here," and turned to me. "This was my mama's house." Tears began to fill her eyes. "We lived here 'til I was three. Then she..."

Jessica broke down in tears, and fell into my arms. The doll watched.

"She went missing in the big storm of 1935. I never saw her again." She cried more.

"Shhh, ok baby, calm down."

"After she died, my grandparents took me in. They had some money to take care of me. But we couldn't stay here long. We just couldn't!" She was getting hysterical, and I didn't know why.

"Dollface, it's ok, come on, calm down. You want to get out of here?"

She calmed a little, but the tears still came. "No, not yet. One more room." She hesitated. Then she looked back at the doll and spoke. "At first everything was fine. Granny and Pop Pop treated me so well. I never knew my father, and Pop Pop was the best dad a girl could hope for. Everything was just great until I was around eight years old. It was then I started hearing the noises."

"*You* started hearing the noises? You mean you're the one who was haunted, when you were a kid?"

"I didn't think so then. I didn't know what was going on. At first, it was just footsteps in the night. Footsteps coming up the steps, down the hall. Then on some nights, as I lay on my bed trying to sleep, I'd hear the footsteps, then my door would crack open, but no one would be there."

"Just your imagination, don't you think?"

"No Bill. Not that at all. It only happened now and then. But when I was ten, there was someone at the door."

"Who?"

"I don't know, for certain," she said to the doll, then turned to me "But I saw her again last night."

"You mean...on the beach?"

"Yeah, Bill. And you saw her too." She was crying again. "So I ain't crazy. I ain't!" I held her again. She cried into my chest, and didn't let up for a couple of minutes. I kissed her forehead.

"Nobody thinks you're crazy, Jessica. We'll figure this thing out."

She looked up at me, then slowly looked toward the window. "Ok, detective, can you figure *that* out?"

I froze. I saw what she saw. There was no mistaking it, and no explanation. Sirens went off in my head and my heart beat red and hard. I'd been a cop for years, I'd seen death and cruelty and the strangest things from the streets of Manhattan to the jungles of Korea and I'd never seen anything like this. It was beyond reason, and that's what scared the hell out of me.

The doll was on the desk.

"Jesus H. Christ, Jessica! What's going on?"

"That's what I've been trying to tell you, Bill. Something's haunting me. Has been for years! First the noises, the footsteps. Then the woman with the black eyes. Then...then Rebecca...my little doll...she, she comes alive!" She said and buried her face in my chest again. I looked down at her, and looked back at the doll...it moved again, its head turning to stare directly at me. I *saw* it move. It was Gaddamned impossible but I saw it!

"Fuck!" I said, not being able to control my tongue.

"Don't tell me..."

"That sonuvabitch moved again!"

"She will, Bill. She'll keep moving until she's on top of you, her eyes staring straight into yours. She did it to me when I was a kid, more than once. I couldn't stand it anymore. When I was ten, I chopped her head off and buried her in the back yard."

"Buried?"

"She came back, Bill. She came *back*. I don't know how, or what's possessed her, or why. Thank God it seems she can't leave this house."

"That's why you moved out?"

"Yes. I kept pleading with my grandparents, but they didn't believe me. Finally, one night during a storm they heard me screaming and came in to find Rebecca on top of me. She was...she was *holding* me, I can't even explain it. That's when I broke off her fingers, to get her off of me. I threw her against the wall, and with my Granny and Pop Pop watching, she began...she began to crawl back to me, across the damned floor! They saw her, Bill! We buried her that night, in the rain. But two days later...Oh God, she came back, I don't even know how, but covered in black mud and wet and with her head barely on she crawled back in here and got in bed with me. That was it. We put the house up for sale, and left."

"Sonuvabitch," was all I could say. I looked over at the doll; it hadn't moved, but I swear it looked...sad.

"And it's still here," she continued, "after what, fourteen years and two other owners. No one was able to live in this house after we sold it. It wouldn't let them. They all said the same thing...noises in the night, footsteps, the door to this room opening and slamming shut, screaming, moaning...except no vision of a woman, just a shriek and nothing after that."

"You said there was one more room."

"Yeah," she said. "Just give me a sec." She walked over to the desk where the doll was. "Hello Rebecca. I think you've scared me enough for one day." The doll seemed completely inanimate now, just an old, broken doll. Jessica picked up the dirty thing and lovingly laid it in the baby carriage. "Goodbye."

I stood there looking confused. "I don't get it Jess."

"I guess I don't either. Rebecca was never...never *mean* to me, or evil or anything. She was just scary. She never hurt me. In fact, I think...this will sound screwy as hell...I think whatever's going on, she just wants to be, well, near me."

"That's crazy."

"I know. That's why we had to move. I couldn't take it anymore. Come on, there's that one last room."

She led me out of her bedroom and shut the door. Behind it we heard a thump; Jessica closed her eyes and melted a little, a grimace on her face. The doll had thrown itself out of the stroller and onto the floor. It was scratching at the door. "Oh god!" Jessica whined, and the crying began again but she held back the tears and pressed ahead of me to the last door on the right.

"This was my mother's room. When she died, my grandparents, they left it as it was. They slept in one of the smaller rooms. After we sold the place I guess no one came in here because even now, it's still the same as it was in 1935."

"That's pretty unusual," I said, not knowing what else to say.

"No more unusual than a possessed doll," she answered, and taking a skeleton key from above the doorsill, opened the rusty lock on the door. The door wouldn't open. "Seems to be stuck. You try it, Bill."

I cautiously put my hand on the white ceramic knob. The gray light that streamed in through the hall window seemed to get brighter, making everything glow with a strange whiteness over the gray. Details I hadn't noticed came out of the house, layers of different colored peeling paint on the door trim, remnants of a wool rug on the floor, exposed wires dangling from holes in the walls. I turned the knob.

The knob shook hard, as if someone on the other side were trying to open it too. I jumped back. "What the Sam-hell?"

"It shook, didn't it?"

"Yeah."

"It always does, been like that since my mom died. As if something's on the other side, trying to get out...or keep us out."

"You ever get in there?"

"Yes. And I can now. But I don't think you'll like what you see."

"Sure, play it up kid. What can be worse than that creepy doll?"

She stepped in front of me, and with a hard thrust turned the shaking knob and punched the door open. Then she screamed, and kept screaming as she stood in the doorway, shaking and twitching and screaming her head off. I looked passed her, and saw what she saw. I didn't really know what I was looking at, but she did. I came behind her and held her, pulled her out of the room and into the hallway shutting the door behind me. Her breaths were coming fast and hard and her heart was beating so hard I could feel the blood pumping through her veins.

"Oh God, oh my God, help me, help me dear lord," she kept saying over and over again as she gasped for air.

"Jess! JESS! Calm down, baby, calm down, I'm here, it's all right." She finally began to settle down, and breathe a little easier. "Jessica, listen, Jessica...who is that in there?"

"It's my *mother*," she said in a voice so foreign I almost dropped her.

What Jessica saw and what I saw were two different things, yet the same. She saw a vision, I saw what was real. When she opened the door, the acrid stench of death and decay hit us with both barrels. As she began to scream, I gave the room a once-over. The walls were covered with moss, mold, mildew, you name it, black and slimy and green and yellow. The floor was heaped with some kind of growth, vines or God knows what, and the ceiling had caved in exposing the rafters. In the center of the room was a four-poster bed, the posts festooned with cobwebs and more vines, dead brown things that strangled the wood. The mattress was rotted and black. But the worst was in the center of the bed; there lay a body on its back, wretched and decayed, the bedclothes blackened with mold like everything else, the feet mummified and gray, the hands skeletal and the face obliterated with time. I saw it for just a second before pulling her out. That is what Jessica saw, and what I could have sworn I saw.

"Why Jessica, why is she still here? Why did you come here? I don't understand."

"Look..look again Bill," she said through heaving sobs. "You saw her body, now look...again."

I didn't want to let go of her, but my curiosity got the better of me. I put my hand on the knob. Noises, banging, popping came from behind me. I turned; Jessica was standing perfectly still.

"The noises, you hear them now too."

"Yeah," I said, "What is it?"

"I don't know. But they're always here. Look at her Bill, tell me what you see."

I braced myself and turned the knob. I just couldn't understand why or how a dead woman's body could be kept in an abandoned house all these years. I opened the door, and had my answer.

"What do you see?"

I hesitated. The light was bright enough to see clearly. The room looked the same, black and moldy, but the smell was gone.

"Sheets," I said.

"Sheets," she agreed. She walked in behind me. "You saw her too Riggins, don't deny it. You saw a corpse on that bed not three minutes ago."

"I did," I said softly. I was truly shocked. "I did. And now –"

"Just sheets, see?" she said and walked over to the bed. Sheets balled up in the middle of the bed, moldy and black, in the vague shape of a person. She picked them up and threw them against the wall where they landed with a dull thud. "Just sheets."

"What is it about this place, Jessica? What happened here to cause this?"

"I don't know. At first I thought it was my mother's spirit, trying to reach me. But these things didn't start happening until around 1940, years after she went missing. But I know that was her body we saw just now, I know because I've seen it before, and it was wearing the same clothes she wears in the only photo of her I have."

I found myself in a strange way; I found myself not only believing in the paranormal, but trying to understand it. "We should get out of here," I said, "Unless there's more."

"Nope. That's the ten-cent tour. That's why the house has been abandoned."

"Where are your grandparents now?"

"They moved up to Tallahassee when I was sixteen." Jessica lied. "I stayed here in Key West."

"Who did you stay with when you were only sixteen?"

"A friend," she said, then quickly added, "You know, I tried to burn this place down when I was twelve. It won't burn."

"What do you mean it won't burn?"

"Try it. Go ahead, I could use a smoke anyway."

"That's crazy."

"Do it, trust me."

Fine I thought, I'd set a little fire in a piece of wood and stamp it back out just to make her happy. I lit two Camels and gave her one, then held the Zippo to a piece of wood on the doorjamb. I held it there for about thirty seconds. Nothing.

"See?"

"Hold on." I grabbed a piece of newspaper from the hall and lit that. It didn't catch. "Ok this is kookie. Maybe it's the mold or something."

"Yes, or something." Her emotions overwhelmed her and she broke down in heavy sobs, muttering indiscernible things of which I caught "...my whole life...", "...no wonder I'm so screwed up...", and "...should have stayed out when I had the chance." I held her close again, but it didn't help. The waterworks kept coming, for a good ten minutes.

Finally she cried herself out and got herself together.

"I'm sorry, baby. I don't know why I brought you here. I hate this place. But I just can't stay away. It's almost as if...as if my mother is still here, and this is the only way I can have anything to do with her, even if it's...it's..."

"Ok, kid, I understand. Look, can we scram now? I think I've had enough of Spooksville for one day."

"Yeah, let's get out of here. I don't think I'll ever be coming back." She wiped the last of her tears away. "I just wanted you to know I'm not a total nut case, Bill. I wanted you to believe me."

"I believe you sugar. I can't believe what I saw with my own eyes, but I believe you."

I dropped Jessica off at her place and drove the Chevy back to the dock where I parked it and handed the keys to the old man.

"Heard about ya'll and old Lem," he said, "Mighty fine police work, Detective. Law's been trying to nail that boy for years. But he's slippery like an eel, that one."

"I didn't really do anything except shoot him in the hand. The Navy boys got him."

"Thanks just the same. Was getting so a man couldn't make a decent buck without handin' over ten percent to that fat bastard."

"Tell me something, did he own a burlesque club? Someplace private?"

"You mean the whorehouse? Sure, he owns that one and one up in Marathon Key."

"Owns? As in still does?"

"Well, yeah, I reckon till yesterday. City'll probably shut them down now."

"Yeah. Hey, when you say whorehouse...you mean an actual *whore*house, or is that just what you call it because of the shows?"

He looked at me funny. "The place has rooms where you pay pretty girls for favors. What else would you call it?"

"Isn't there a stage with girly shows?"

"Sure, that's how the men decide which women they want to take upstairs." *Click.*

## 1935

Eliot Hawthorn had never been to a brothel in his life. The thought of paying for sex seemed both ridiculous and foreign to him. With his money and his youthful good looks, he'd managed to get pretty much any woman he ever wanted. Then he met Vivian, and decided she was the only one he'd ever need.

Roberts drove him down the island in the Ford Model A police car. The bumpy dirt road jiggled the car like a ragdoll, but Hawthorn wasn't concerned. He was on a mission and was focused on his goal. They pulled up at the Victorian manor, the place done up complete with heavy red velveteen curtains in the windows and two gas lamps burning out front, even though it was mid-day.

"This is it, Mistuh Hawthorn. Come on in, I'll show ya'll around."

"Stop calling me that, Roberts. Introduce me as Mr. Smith."

"Yessuh, Mistuh Smith."

Roberts led Hawthorn into the brothel, taking care to make sure no one who could spot Hawthorn was on the street. The inside of the house was dark and plush. Expensive but well-worn sofas and loveseats lined the wall, draped with over-stuffed pillows and velveteen throws. The colors were a mix of deep reds, purples and royal blues with gold accents, just the sort of sordid color scheme Hawthorn expected. The floors were carpeted thickly in deep red patterns. Low-lit electric lamps gave the place an atmosphere of constant night.

A tall, voluptuous woman met Roberts at the front desk. She was dressed in a corset and feather boa, just like in the movies, Hawthorn thought. Roberts said something to her and she smiled. She waved him up the stairs and said, "Room three."

Hawthorn followed Roberts up the stairs. The wall leading up was decorated with paintings of nude women, on the beach, on the sofas, on horseback. Hawthorn cringed as he recognized the setting for one of the paintings: The back porch of his own house in Key West.

"Roberts, who painted these?"

"Don't right know, suhr, they been up there for damn-near forty years, I'm sure."

"I want this one taken down and burned, today."

"But suhr, it's a part of the house's history!"

"Like you give a good damn about history. Take it down. I'll pay to replace it."

"Yessuh." Roberts wanted to ask why, but didn't care enough to get Hawthorn mad at him.

At the top of the steps they turned right and came to room three. Roberts knocked twice and the door came open.

"Yes?" A young woman opened the door. She fit Hawthorn's description to a 'T'. "Oh, Hello Officer Roberts," she said with fake enthusiasm. "What brings ya'll up here today?"

"I have a special customer for you. His name is..."

Hawthorn nearly smacked Roberts.

"...Mr. Smith, from Miami, down on business. He'd like some company."

"Well hello, Mr. Smith. Why don't ya'll come in?" She took Hawthorn by the hand, and led him into the room. "I'll take good care of him for you, Officer."

"You do that Miss Rose. I'll be seein' ya'll." Roberts left and Rose shut the door. Before she could say a word, Hawthorn spoke.

"Rose is it?"

"Yes."

"Listen, Rose, I don't want to sound rude, but I've never been with a hooker before."

"If you don't want to sound rude, please just say lady of the evenin', sugar."

"Fine. Sorry. Look, I'm...I'm a bit nervous about all this. It seems my wife...You know what, never mind all that. Just..." He took a deep breath and sat down. He looked at her fully; she was young and beautiful, blonde and curvy in all the right places. She could have been Vivian with a little work, he thought. "Please, remove your stockings," he said, "Slowly." If he was going to pay for a good time, he was going to have fun with it, and see how obedient she would be.

She obliged without hesitation. She sat on the edge of the bed and slowly unhooked her garter belt. Smoke from her cigarette curled around her face, shrouding her in a mysterious haze that seemed to intensify her sensuality. Then with a style only very few women can conjure, she slid each black silk stocking down her long, tan legs, and let them drop to the floor.

"What should I do next, sugar?" she said as she gently licked her fiery lips. Her eyes stabbed his and he shifted in his chair, realizing he actually was enjoying this.

"Stand up." She did. Her black negligee draped down around her body, revealing every curve, betraying every twitch of her taught muscles. "Slip off the negligee," he continued. She lifted it off her shoulders and let it pool on the floor. She was wearing nothing but a thin black slip now. It was see-through. Hawthorn's heart began to race with desire, desire for her body, lust for her soul, something he hadn't felt for another woman since marrying Vivian so many years before. He stood up. "Lose the slip," he said, and it to fell to the floor. She was naked now, a perfect specimen if ever he saw one. High, firm breasts the perfect size for her body, a lean, flat stomach and a swell to her hips that made him hard before he even touched her. "Come here," he said and she slowly walked to him until she was right in front of him. He looked at her closely, could smell the scent of her perfume and soap lilting up to him. "Do everything you know how to do," he said, "I'll make it worth your while."

Rose obliged.

## 1956

I was back in my suite on Tiki Island by one p.m. The maid service had cleaned up the room real nice, and a basket of fresh tropical fruits sat on the coffee table with a note that read, "Compliments of Eliot Hawthorn, enjoy your stay Mr. Riggins." Outside in the garden, a couple of workers were finishing the filling of the grave where the unknown woman was buried. It was Friday the twenty-sixth of October, and I wasn't due back to New York for over another week.

I took another shower to wash the heat and dust off of me from the abandoned house, and when I got out I realized I hadn't eaten a damned thing all day. I was about to call room service when I decided to have lunch in the mermaid bar. I threw on my clean white pants and floral shirt and headed down to the bar.

The lobby was abuzz with dozens of tourists checking in for the weekend. Families with tons of luggage, businessmen with a single suitcase, groups of women laughing, groups of teenagers already drinking. Two little kids were already running around with their Halloween masks on, one a vampire and the other Frankenstein. In the middle of the lobby Bachman was directing people to various desks and elevators. Melinda was nowhere to be seen.

I settled into a small booth near the back of the shipwreck bar where I could watch the mermaids swim. Only one was in there, swimming alone, doing her underwater acrobatics like a true pro. I ordered a double hamburger with French fried potatoes and a side of coleslaw, just the way I liked it. Too much of this vacation food was making me soft. The waiter brought me a Mai Tai without asking, and a dish of oyster crackers. I thanked him and took out my notepad for the first time on the trip.

I wrote down everything, from the minute I left the City until I stepped into the bar a few minutes before. I included everything about Roberts, Jackson, the skeleton, Jessica and her hauntings, Melinda and her unreachable beauty. I wrote notes about Captain Reams and the things he saw after the 1935 Hurricane, and I wrote about driving around in that midnight blue '57 Chevy convertible. Just as I finished writing, my burger showed up with a fresh Mai Tai. And a damned good burger it was.

I was just finishing up when Melinda walked into the bar. She saw me and stopped, and I think she almost turned around until she caught my eye. Then she smiled, a very professional smile, not the one that made me melt a few days ago. She made her way over to my table through the crowd.

"Hello Melinda! Care to join me for a drink?" She hesitated a little longer than I would have liked, then said, "Certainly," and sat down across from me. Today she wore a dark, almost black dress with vivid yellow and white flowers, a white floral lei and a white flower in her black hair. The combination was both striking and ominous. "How have you been, Mr. Riggins?"

"Oh, it's back to Mr. Riggins now, is it?"

She smiled again, the professional one. "It's best we keep things on a professional level, don't you agree?"

"Nope," I said, "I'm on vacation. Nothing professional about it. Mai Tai?"

"Yes please," she said and I motioned the waiter for two more cocktails. "I've really grown a taste for these drinks. I just can't drink too many of the krazy things or I get loopy."

"By loopy, do you mean you do, oh I don't know, crazy things? Things you'd regret when you're sober?"

I didn't like that question or the tone she pushed behind it. It was the first time I'd seen her be wicked, and I had a feeling she had a lot more where that came from.

"Maybe," I said cautiously. "Why, did I get drunk and stuff the towels down the toilet or something?"

"No," she said, "I just...well, it's not for me to say."

"Say it. Remember I'm here on your nickel. If I did something wrong, spill it."

"It's your friend, Ms. Rutledge."

So that was it. The little cat was jealous of the big cat. Damn. "What about her?"

"Well...she's a very nice person, and an excellent employee, but I'm afraid it's not such a good idea to have employees...eh...stay...with customers. It gives the hotel a bad name, if you know what I mean."

I didn't know what she meant. "I don't get it. Who's going to know if some doll spends the night in my room? You? Bachman? What's the big deal?"

She looked around the room, then down at her glass. "I think it would just be better if you were a little more...discrete."

So that was it. She didn't like seeing me with another dame. "Listen, dollface, I like you. I have since the minute I saw you. I thought we had some kind of connection and I really wanted things to work out, but you said the magic words."

"What magic words?"

" 'I can't'. When a girl says no, that means no. And it's a drag, because I think you're tops and we could have had some great fun and laughs together on this trip. And we still can, on a nice friendly level. But now I've met Jessica, and believe it or not she means a lot to me. I know I'm only here for another week, and chances are after that we'll never see each other again. But for right now I'm just trying to pack as much fun into this little fortnight as I can before I have to swing back to the urban jungle, ya dig?"

Melinda swallowed hard, took a second gulp and swallowed again. She looked straight at me, a touch of sadness in her eyes. Then she said, "I know how you felt Bill. I felt that way too, but I can't get mixed up with a client. Like you said you'll be gone in another week and I'll be here. I need something more permanent. That's why I can't make love to you, no matter how much I want to."

Damn it! And she hit me with that smile that made me melt all over again.

"As for Ms. Rutledge…Yes, I admit it. I am a little jealous of her. But that's not why I want you to be more discrete with her, Bill. You don't know anything about her."

"I know she worked as a stripper, if that's what you mean."

"That's part of it. She's got a certain reputation among people in Key West, and here. Do you know what I mean?"

"I can guess, and I can only say I don't care about that. I'm having a good time, the best I've had in years and in a week it will all be over and I'll be back to pounding the icy cold pavement looking for dead junkies and strung-out hookers in the snow. So please, Melinda," I said while taking her hands, "Just let me have my fun?"

She flashed her old smile again and I got butterflies. "Ok Bill, you can bring her here, but please, just be…"

"I know, discrete."

"Yes."

"Thank you. Now that that's out of the way, turns out she won't be joining me tonight. So if you're not busy, how about dinner on the beach? I promise, no funny stuff."

"I don't think so, Bill, we shouldn't…"

"Melinda, remember, I'm your VIP guest," I said smiling, "You wouldn't want me to complain to the owner, now would you? I'm a friend of his, you know."

"Oh, are you?" she laughed, and finally said, "Ok, eight o'clock, meet me in the lobby."

"Fantastico." She got up to leave. "See you then kiddo."

"See you tonight," she answered with another smile and left.

At quarter to eight, Jessica Rutledge walked the two blocks from her Duval Street apartment to La Concha hotel. She passed right by. A block down she came to another smaller hotel, one not quite as elegant or clean as the La Concha. In the lobby she met her contact, a man named Mateuse. He gave her the work assignment for the evening and directed her to the kitchen where she met up with another man named Appleton. He in turn brought her to the back of the house where she'd prepare for the evening's work.

"You look a little tired," Appleton said as she donned the uniform. "Need anything?"

"I slept all afternoon, but yeah, what have you got?"

"Here, take two of these, wake you right up," he said, "you can give me two bits for them when you have it."

"Just put it on my tab, Benny," she said. "Ok, how do I look?"

"Gorgeous. Go knock 'em dead, kid."

Ginger smiled and headed out to the ballroom.

Friday afternoon went slow and peaceful-like for me. I sat on the beach and read a magazine, swam in one of the pools (the big one surrounded by coconut palms and tropical flowers) and spent some time in the room watching the tube. I really wanted to head back to Key West and find Jessica but I knew she'd be working, and she told me not to try to contact her at work or she might risk losing her job. I wasn't about to screw things up for her so I just relaxed. I started thinking about dinner with Melinda, and spending Saturday with Jessica. Then it occurred to me that I'd been gone almost a week, and hadn't heard a word from LaRue on the Johnny Princeton situation. I grabbed the coconut-shaped phone on the bar and dialed the operator.

"Long distance please, New York city, Murry Hill 9734. Person to Person to Detective Frank LaRue."

The operater said one moment and a bunch of clicks a whirs later I had LaRue on the other end.

"LaRue."

"You sound tired."

"I am tired. Who's this?"

"It's the guy who's apartment you're stealing."

"Oh, hi Riggins. Thought you were out of town for another week."

"I'm in Florida, calling from a coconut."

"Sure you are. How's the holiday?"

"So far great. I got beat up twice, had to help solve a twenty year-ole skeleton story and shot a cop."

"Sounds like a blast. Bag any chicks?"

I had the feeling he didn't believe me. "Just one, but a real looker and more than once."

"Fabulous," he said, and I had the feeling he still didn't believe me.

"How's our houseboy?" I asked.

"Sitting pretty. All's quiet on the western front."

"Groovy. Make sure he doesn't steal my towels when he leaves."

"Sure. You hear from the Captain at all?"

"I haven't heard a word from anyone since I left," I said.

"Well, he's got everything smoothed over with that D.A. Turns out the D.A. has some dirty laundry he didn't want aired out on channel nine."

"Don't they all. Tell the Captain hello for me, will ya?"

"Will do Riggins. Oh, that chick was askin' for ya, your limo driver."

"Fast Freddie?" I hadn't given two thoughts to her since I left the state. What a heel I was.

"Yeah, that's the one. Says to give her a ring when you get the chance. I assume she meant a phone call."

"I'm sure she did," I said, then said goodbye and hung up. I picked the coconut off the cradle again and dialed the operator a second time. "Long distance, New York City, Francis O'Malley, Pennsylvania 6569, please."

The phone rang and rang, but no answer. I tried her office phone next, but got nothing. I'd try her again later in the evening.

My last call was to Jerry. I told him I met his brother and thanked him a million for setting me up so sweet. He asked if I scored any points with the chicks down here yet and told me I hit one out of the park. He whistled and called me a nasty name and we said so long and hung up. That was the only time I missed New York so far on the trip.

I mixed myself a V.O. Manhattan at the Tiki Bar and downed it in three gulps. It was almost seven, and I wanted to catch the mermaid show in the bar before I met up with Melinda, so I headed down once again.

The lobby was absolutely packed now, no less than a hundred people waiting to get up to their rooms. It was nice to see this place doing well, I thought. I wished them luck. I pushed my way through to the lobby bar and was lucky to get a seat at the bar itself, since the tables were all full. I ordered a Mai Tai (it seemed that's all I ordered in the bar) and turned to watch the mermaids. The crowd applauded as the three girls swam around each other, waved, did little flips and criss-crossed each other in a sort of underwater dance to the music of Les Baxter. They made it look easy, but I had a feeling they did a lot of practice to look that good. I was so entranced by the beauty of the Tiki Island Mermaids that I didn't even realize that Eliot Hawthorn had pulled up next to me at the bar.

"Good evening Mr. Riggins," he said as he raised his glass. "Hope you're enjoying your stay."

"Yes, very much so Mr. Hawthorn, I especially like watching the mermaids swim."

"As do I, as do I." We both looked over at the tank; the three ladies were swimming their tails off for the crowd. "I hear you are having dinner with my daughter tonight," he suddenly said in his gravelly, old man voice. I almost thought he was going to read me a sermon on the chastity of young women in the Florida Keys. Instead he said, "She is a very special person, Bill. Very special. She is wise beyond her years and will someday inherit and run all of this herself." He turned away from the mermaids and smiled at me. "But you know, she doesn't need to do it herself, Bill. If you catch my meaning."

That kind of threw me. What was this, a sales pitch?

"I don't follow you, sir."

"Bill, do you understand just how much she admires you, how much she feels for you? I don't think she's felt that way for a man in a very long time. My health is failing. I won't be around forever. She needs someone to help her, to look after her when I'm gone, someone to protect her from the horrors of the world."

I interrupted, "Mr. Hawthorn, if you're asking me to consider staying here on Tiki Island...if you're talking about marrying her," I had to laugh a little, "I've only known her a few days, and I have a life in New York. I don't think I could just drop everything and leave it, just as she couldn't leave this place."

"Well," he said sounding somewhat deflated, "At least consider your feelings, and hers. Tiki Island's not so bad a place to spend the rest of your years, believe me. It's...paradise. As long as you're with the one you love."

In my head, I still kept hearing his voice say 'how much she admires you, how much she feels for you'.

"I'll remember that," I said.

"Good. Then I shall take my leave. Have a good evening, my good sir."

"Good night, Mr. Hawthorn." The old man left slowly, cane in hand. He was met at the door by one of the porters who helped him away. When I turned back around, the mermaids had already finished their show.

At a few minutes to eight I found Melinda in the lobby. She was wearing a new dress, a green one with orange and yellow flowers. "How many of those dresses do you have?" I asked as I walked up to her, grinning like a goofy prom date.

"Thirty Five," she answered, "Plus several sun dresses and a mini skirt." She gave a little laugh and suddenly spending the rest of my life on Tiki Island didn't sound so bad after all. I don't know what kind of Tiki voodoo this chick could cast, but it was some strong stuff.

"Come on, Bill. I have a private table waiting for us on the south beach."

She turned and I followed. It seemed that every time I set my peepers on this chick I saw something new, something wonderful. This time it was the way her hips swayed from side to side as she walked, sexy but not sleazy, alluring but not trashy. Tropical flowers swaying in the ocean breeze. Long, tan, sensuous legs proudly striding at just the right speed. The perfect walk from the perfect girl. She was so different from any of the other women I'd ever known, sophisticated and down-to-Earth all at the same time. So different from Jessica who was worldly only within the confines of the world of the Florida Keys, not sophisticated but no bubble-headed blonde either. I never planned on falling for a dame down here on vacation. I was in danger of falling for two.

Not good, kid.

The hostess sat Melinda and me at a table far off from the others. We ordered Mai Tais and a Crab Rangoon appetizer, and I settled in with a smoke.

"Cigarette?" I offered.

"No thanks, I don't smoke."

"Really? Huh. I thought everybody did."

"I've tried it. It dulls my senses. I want to taste everything, enjoy the aromas of flowers and foods. Cigarettes just don't do it for me."

"I'm hip," I said, and crushed out the butt in the sand.

She started right in with, "I heard what happened with you and Chief Roberts last night."

"Already?"

"News travels fast in the Keys. I'll bet you didn't know Chief Roberts and my father used to be friends."

That seemed queer at first, but then I remembered Hawthorn's parties and his imports to go with them. "I wouldn't have guessed he was friends with Mr. Hawthorn. He seems like a pretty dirty guy."

"Maybe 'friends' is too strong a word. Roberts did jobs for my father, years ago."

"Like importing party favors from Havana?"

"That's a nice way of putting it." She took a drink of her Mai Tai, never taking her eyes off me. She was back-dropped by the ocean, a palm tree and a Tiki torch. If I had a camera I could have shot one of those advertisements for a mystical island get-away. "He brought in the liquor, the drugs… did you know he owns a brothel in Key West?"

"I heard a rumor. I also heard it's a private club, not a brothel."

"Oh, it's a brothel," she said with disgust. "They have nude shows there, and afterwards the members get to pick which performer they want to bring upstairs."

"You've been there, have you?" I said playfully.

She scowled. "No, of course not. But I have had to…" she sighed and looked down. "I shouldn't be telling you this, as you're a police officer and now that Roberts is out of the picture there's nothing stopping you from doing something about it."

"About what?"

"This is a Resort, Bill, and we try to cater to everyone's wishes." She left it at that. I wasn't exactly sure what she meant.

"So you send people to Key West when they want a little action, is that it?"

"Yes," she said and looked down at her drink again. She made little swirling motions with the swizzle stick. "And sometimes, we bring them…here."

I got a lump in my throat that made it hard to swallow anything just then. I tried to take a shot of the cocktail but Mai Tais are for sipping and it didn't go down so smooth. Hookers at a hotel wasn't anything new. I just didn't even think about it at such a class place as this. I shouldn't have been surprised…you couldn't spit without hitting a call girl in the lobby of the Plaza hotel on a Saturday night, but I was a little surprised anyway…and surprised she was telling me.

"You're right, you shouldn't be telling me all this. Why are you?"

"I wanted you to know now that Roberts is out of the picture, I'm confident we'll be able to discontinue these services. You see, Roberts knew something about my father that he nor dad would ever tell me. Something from his past, from before he met my mother. It must have been something devastating because Roberts was able to lord it over my father for years. Whatever it was, as long as we continued to supply clients for Roberts' businesses, he swore never to tell his story. Those places will no doubt be shut down soon, and the arrangement will come to an end."

"Florida politics, just like in the dime novels," I muttered. "If Roberts thinks it will get him off the hook, he'll squeal his head off, you know that, right?"

"Dad says there's nothing to worry about, so I'm not worried." The appetizer showed up with a second round of drinks and we ordered dinner. She got the surf and turf, I ordered Chicken Teriyaki. I actually had enough steak for one week.

"Melinda, how much about me have you told your old man?"

"Oh, I don't know, a few things. Why?"

"He found me in the lobby bar earlier. Talked with me a bit."

"Really?" She seemed excited. "Well, it's nice to see he's getting out a little."

"He thinks we should get hitched." Melinda's eyes widened so big they looked like a couple of saucers with a dollop of coffee in the middle. Then she bust out laughing, and so did I.

She said, "And what, I should move to New York City and spend the rest of my life working at a Manhattan Tiki Bar while you're out arresting criminals?"

"No, actually he wants me to move down here and help you run Tiki Island."

She got a little serious then. "I don't need any help running Tiki Island."

"I don't think he meant you did. He's just looking out for you, kiddo."

"Well, I suppose he doesn't realize that you're already involved with someone else."

"Involved?" What a Gaddamned heel I am, really. "I'm not involved with…oh, you mean Ms. Rutledge." Damn, I'd forgotten all about Jessica that fast.

"Yes."

"I don't know what…I'm not sure as to what extent I'm involved with Jessica," I said honestly. "I mean, I'm on vacation. She knows it. She knows that I leave in a week and there's very little chance I'll ever see her again."

"I'm sure she doesn't mind," Melinda said, and I wasn't sure how to take that. I didn't want to get into it with her so I just shut my trap. The fastest way to ruining a good time with a chick is to challenge her opinion of a chick she's probably jealous of.

"I just want to have a little fun," I said. "Like you said, next week I'll be back to walking the icy-cold streets of the city, chasing down pushers and pimps, finding junkies frozen to death in back alleys, sitting in my dreary, brown office banging away at a twenty-year-old typewriter without a palm tree in sight. I just want to make the best of things while I'm here."

Melinda was getting a little tipsy, the first time I'd seen her that way. "And that's what we're here for, Bill. That's why Tiki Island exists. It's a fantasy world, a little slice of paradise at the end of the Earth. Staying here for two weeks is great. Living here forever isn't perfect, but it beats the rum out of what you just described."

"Yeah," I said under my breath, realizing Melinda was making a sort of half-baked pitch for me staying. "But it would only be worth staying here if I had the right woman to stay with," I added, playing along.

"And what do you consider the right woman?" she asked, leaning in. If we weren't a table apart I'd have kissed her right then.

"Oh, I don't know, someone interesting, tall, tan, young and lovely, with big brown eyes and a beautiful face. Someone with a great smile that makes me melt every time she flashes it. Someone with brains and wit and a fantastic frame to go with it."

Melinda slowly rose from the chair with the jungle movements of a hungry tiger. She walked up beside me and looked down at me with an evil grin.

"Are you making a play for me, Mr. Riggins?" she said coyly. I got up from my chair with much less grace.

"Maybe," I said, and as I brought my hands around her back I drew her in and kissed her, harder and more passionately than I ever kissed a woman before, even Jessica...

And Jessica's face floated on my mind, her bright smile, her flowing blond hair, her crystal blue eyes, and I as I pulled away from Melinda's burning lips I said to my own surprise, "I can't." And I walked off the beach, leaving her there alone.

I paced the room like a madman, drinking Bourbon and trying to figure out what the hell to do. I got myself in a real mess. Two gorgeous dolls, and I wanted them both. But I couldn't have either without turning my whole life upside-down. I was a cop, I'd always been a cop and the idea of spending my days counting guest towels and checking room receipts sounded as ridiculous as leaving the city to live in the Keys. Maybe my life as a cop was dreary and cold, maybe I came across the dregs of the Earth every day but dammit, that's who I was and I liked it.

Didn't I?

Could I live in this place for the rest of my days, happily making love to Melinda and drinking rum and eating fine food like I was on vacation every day? Or could I take Jessica away from this place, away from her torments and bring her to live in my world? Would she survive in the city, or would it kill her?

I flipped it over so many times I forgot I was supposed to be enjoying myself. I took another shot of Jack and made up my mind. I'd go see Jessica, tonight, damn her work, I had to see her, had to see if she felt the same way I did. I had to know if she'd come back to New York with me.

I called down to the concierge and ordered a private boat to bring me to Key West. I was there by midnight. I jumped in the Chevy and roared down Truman to Duval. The La Concha was close and I parked.

I flashed my badge at the front desk. "I'm looking for one of your employees, Jessica Rutledge. She's not in any trouble but it's important."

"I don't know anyone here by that name," the girl answered, "just a minute sir." She picked up the phone and said something I couldn't hear. I man in a tan suit walked up behind me.

"Can I be of some service, sir?"

"I'm looking for Jessica Rutledge, she's working a banquet tonight."

"I'm afraid we don't have anyone on staff by that name."

"Are you the manager?"

"Yes. I would know."

"Look, she's about twenty-five, five-foot-six, slim build, busty, blonde hair, blue eyes."

"I'm sorry sir but you just described half of our staff."

Of course. "Are you having any banquets tonight?"

"We're having a private affair in the ballroom."

"Let me have a look, maybe I can spot her," I said, and began to walk towards the ballroom. The manager, a pretty big guy, gently held me back.

"Sir, please, I'm afraid I can't allow you to disturb the guests. It's a private party, and they are a very secretive organization who demands total privacy. You can understand, can't you?"

Damn! This guy was good. I could have flashed my badge again but he'd see it was NYPD and would know I had no jurisdiction here. "What time does the party let out?"

"The room is booked until one a.m." he said. You're welcome to wait in the lobby, and see if your friend comes out."

"Thanks," I said, "I think I'll just come back." I left the lobby and sat in the car. A million images flew through my brain, from Melinda to Jessica to ghosts to skeletons. Then one stuck: the image of Jessica onstage in a stag show with other women, and suddenly I wanted to see what kind of place Roberts really had been running. If it was still open tonight, that is.

I turned the car around and headed down to the other end of town. It wasn't too hard finding the place; private club or not it still looked like a sex house. Blacked-out windows, cars parked behind a fence, faint sound of burlesque music coming from within.

I parked the car and walked up to the font door. Just for fun I knocked three times like the old days. The door opened with a gorilla of a bouncer behind it.

"This is a private club," he said in a gruff, growling voice.

"I'm a friend of Chief Roberts. They sent me over from Tiki Island."

"Who sent you?"

I thought fast…it wouldn't be Melinda, no she wouldn't have her name associated with this place. Not Hawthorn, he hardly saw anyone. "Rutger Bachman," I said, and he opened the door full

"Any friend of Roberts is a friend of mine. What's your label, Mister?"

"LaRue," I lied. First name I thought of.

"Come on inside, Mr. LaRue. The show's about to start."

The gorilla-like goon in the faded tux led me through the lobby of a Victorian-era parlor complete with antique sofas, loveseats and armoires. Everything looked to be recently upholstered with red and purple velvet and gold trim. I could hear the band playing clearly now, not too loud but strong jazz from a bari sax, piano and drums. At the end of the parlor was a heavy door. He swung it open and pushed me through. Smoke hung thick in the air and the smell of it mixed with perfume and stale liquor almost made me heave. The place was packed with about thirty men, half of which had luscious-looking dames sitting with them, flirting, teasing. The other half looked either drunk or mean, or both. The band consisted of three cats that looked like they stepped out of the '30s, complete with wide-brim fedoras and suspenders. They rattled out "Love for Sale" and I got a bad feeling in my gut. A fat guy sitting with a hot young redhead laughed hard and got up from his table. He kissed her square on the lips and she laughed too, and the two of them headed out through the heavy door.

They were right. This was a brothel.

The music stopped and a long, lanky guy in a monkey suit took center stage. He adjusted a mic and cleared his throat. Then in a deep voice made for radio he said, "Welcome gentleman to the Low Key Club. Is everyone having a good time?" Plenty of greasy hoots and hollers came from the crowd.

"Good. Then get ready for the night's main event, our world famous Femina Exotica!" He led the applause and got off the stage. The band struck up with something dark and low, ominous sounding and exotic. The stage went dark except for a pinlight center. The show began.

The pinlight grew to about a two-foot spot, and as the music swayed movement could be seen in the light…movement of women, first an arm, then an ankle, then a thigh; this went on for a few minutes so that the crowd could realize there were at least seven different women crowded onto the stage. The music swelled slightly and the big tease turned more erotic as breasts began appearing in the spot. Then the spot began to grow, and we could see more of the ladies, touching, caressing each other, kissing passionately. The crowd which was at first quiet was now gasping, clapping, shouting. The spotlight grew to encompass the stage, and the tease was over. Seven women intertwined, kissing, licking, devouring each other in a sensual orgy that had the crowd going wild with excitement. Moans and groans from the stage added to the fantasy.

The fantasy. Jessica said it was all a show.

She lied.

This was no show. This was showing off.

The women on stage weren't just acting the part. They were showing off their skills to the crowd, vying for the attention of the wealthiest clients picked from hotels all over the Keys. Their actions were real, as real as would be in the rooms upstairs. Tongues against soft flesh. Lips caressing. Fingers sliding into places that had the room boiling. The moans, groans, the shrieks may have been elaborated, but the causes were real.

I shut down places like this three times in the last four years in New York. Not because I'm a prude. This kind of thing might disgust some people but not me. I don't care one way or another how people get their kicks behind closed doors. It's everything else that goes with it that I can't stand. Behind the show are girls down on the their luck, or strung out and hungry for a fix. There are pimps that control the girls with a heavy hand across the mouth and the threat of more. There are crooked cops, like Roberts, and politicians backing them, all to make a buck. And in some cases there are girls who are kidnapped and forced into the business. Very few women work in joints like this and stay clean. Most wind up dead of an overdose or killed by their pimps before they hit thirty.

The writhing bodies on the stage had the men so worked up that some were already leaving with the girls they had. The music came to a head, and with a cymbal-crash the lights went dark and the crowd erupted with applause that shook the walls and rattled glasses on the bar. The houselights came up dim, and the band started in with the slow, soft sounds they were shooting before. This time it was a dragging, sultry version of Night Train as the girls from the stage came into the room one by one, wearing shear robes and leaving little to the imagination. I was near the back and liked it that way, as I was in no mood to have to turn down a dame.

I finished my highball and settled up with the waiter. I saw all I needed to see. So I thought.

All seven girls came out into the reddish dull light, sitting with men who waved them over. In the low light they all looked the same; blondes looked like redheads, brunettes looked like redheads, redheads looked like darker redheads. They were all built, all curvy in the right places and it showed through the robes. Almost immediately three went off through the heavy door with men.

I got up and was about to leave. I threw a buck down on the table for the waiter and as I did, my back was turned to the door. It was then I heard the voice, the voice that made me almost crumble back down in the chair. The voice was behind me, going through the door.

"Come on sugar," the voice said, "My name is Ginger, but you can call me Ginny."

*Click.*

### 1935

Eliot Hawthorn was disgusted with himself, but felt incredibly free and pleasured at the same time. He'd never actually *cheated* on Vivian, not once, not by his definition, not even when young drunken girls presented themselves to him in the late hours of his Island parties. He always stayed true to her (in his way) until now, and now he wondered why he ever bothered.

This was the fourth time he had seen Rose since he met her in July. Now in late August, he began to set a new plan into motion.

"I'm not who you think I am, Rose. My name is Eliot Hawthorn, and I live on a private Island just off Sugarloaf key. I'm married, but I don't care about that anymore."

"Why ya'll telling me this? I don't need to know yo' business, sugar."

"Because I want you to come to the Island with me. I want to make love to you right under my wife's nose."

"Why ya'll wanna do that?"

"I have my reasons. I'll pay you double what you normally make in a day to come with me tonight, and stay in my boathouse. You're not to come out, and you are especially not to come up to the mansion. You'll stay there and I'll come for you when I want you. I'll have a boat take you back tomorrow night. Do this and I will reward you handsomely. But don't breathe a word of it to anyone, especially my name, or the repercussions will be deadly. Do you understand?"

Rose did understand and was frightened. She was frightened for herself, that she might accidentally say something to the wrong person, as she was known to have a big mouth. And she was frightened for her daughter, that if anything should happen to her, her daughter would have no one to turn to.

"I'm not so sure I'm the right gal for this," she said, "I have a daughter and I can't leave her alone overnight."

"Where is she now?"

"With family, being watched."

"I'll give your family a hundred dollars to watch her overnight. Will that suffice?"

"My, I suppose it will. Let me just call them and tell them – "

"Don't tell them where you're going!" Hawthorn warned.

"No, no of course not. I' just goin' to tell them I'll be away overnight."

"Fine. I'll be downstairs. Meet me in five minutes. Pack lightly."

Hawthorn's yacht was decidedly small enough for him to motor himself without a crew. He enjoyed being the captain, but now found his hobby more convenient then he ever could have thought necessary. He navigated the small yacht from Key West up to Hawthorn Island and slipped it into the boathouse.

"There's a loft upstairs," he said to Rose as he helped her out of the boat. "Very nicely kept with a bed and a hotplate, and running water. Make yourself at home. There's a radio you're welcome to use if you keep the volume low. Try not to make any noise that might attract attention. If you're hungry, there are some cans in the pantry and fresh bread and fruit. I'll be back for you around ten."

"Is there anything in particular you'd like me to do while you're gone, sugar?"

"Yes. Get naked by ten." Without a goodbye he turned and left Rose in the boathouse and made his way up to the mansion.

"Vivian! I'm home," he called to the large house. Vivian Hawthorn rose from her armoire with a magazine and said, "Well dear, it's about time. It's almost eight."

"My business with Roberts took longer than expected. But we should have everything we need for the Labor Day party next week."

"Good. Oh, Gregor was here earlier, he said to tell you hello."

"Was he. Any reason in particular?"

"No, he just had the boat out and wanted to say hello."

"How is my boat," Eliot asked somewhat sarcastically.

"Oh, Eliot, don't be that way. You agreed to lend him the money, it's not his fault the depression hit him a little harder than us. If you're going to be generous you can't take it back."

"No, I suppose not," Eliot replied, holding his temper. "What's for supper?"

"Cajun Gumbo, I believe. Dora has been cooking all day."

"Fine. I'm starved."

When supper was over, Eliot and Vivian retired to the sitting room for coffee. Vivian went back to her magazine, Eliot took up the morning newspaper. At five minutes to ten Eliot said, "I'm going out for a walk. Too stuffy in here."

"All right Eliot. I'm going to bed."

"Goodnight," he said emotionlessly and headed for the boathouse.

## 1956

My head screamed. I grabbed the back of the chair for support as the blood rushed to my brain and almost knocked me out. My heart pounded hard in my chest and for a minute I though I'd lose my cool, but I got it under control and turned around just in time to see the back of a blonde head move through the door with a guy in a blue pin-striped suit. I followed, not sure what I was going to do. In my mind the phrase, "It's not her, it's another Ginger," echoed over and over. I kept following them through the lobby and when they turned to walk up the steps I stopped and took out a Camel. They climbed the landing, then the first few steps and were facing me now as I lit the wrong end of the cigarette.

Jessica.

*It was her.*

My heart sank so low it hit my stomach and I got that feeling like I was going to vomit everything I ever ate in my life, but I somehow kept it down. She didn't see me; her attention was focused on the mook she was leading up the stairs, up to his own little bought-and-paid-for paradise. She looked amazing, I might add…done up like a Hollywood starlet, not a small town hooker.

A hooker!

How could I have missed it? How could I have ignored all the signs, all the little clicks that had been nagging me for days? Sure, she was a hooker. Melinda practically told me so. So did Bachman. So did a hundred little hints Jessica herself left, but I was too damned blind to see them. Too blind or too….

Her heels clicked up the steps past my head, and I decided to follow. I don't know why, I didn't have a plan. I guess I was hoping she'd drop the guy off and come back downstairs to sell cigarettes or something. Gad*dammit!* How could I not realize what everyone was trying to tell me! Roberts even *called* her a whore, and he meant it! It all started to make sense now. She stayed with a 'friend' when she was sixteen. Sure, I'll bet you dimes to donuts that friend was Roberts, or one of his lackeys. Took her in, gave her a place to stay, and in return talked her into turning tricks. It's not so bad, they'd told her, just a few minutes work for so much money. Sure, she'd probably hated it at first, but after a while she wouldn't care, it was just a job. Then it got so she couldn't live without the money, and so she kept on going. But why now? And why lie to me about it? Doesn't she know I wouldn't care about all that? Everyone gets a bad break. Who am I to judge?

But the lying. That, I just couldn't dig.

They reached the top of the steps and turned right. I hid my face with my Panama and just caught them stopping at room three. She said something and they both laughed. A great time they were having. She opened the door and they went in. When I got to the top of the stairs, they shut the door.

I stood in front of room three smoking a Camel down to the butt. A million thoughts swam through my head, thoughts of how I met her, how I got here. For a minute I thought it was even possible that Bachman had set her up to meet me on Monday night, so I'd have a good time on my stay. Then I realized even Bachman wasn't so stupid as to hire a call girl for a vice cop. No, everything Jessica had told me had been the truth, with two exceptions: She was still working at the Low Key Club, and she was a Gaddamned prostitute.

I wanted to go into the room. I didn't dare go into the room. Other couples came up the stairs, others went down. The place was pretty busy. I didn't notice. I finished the butt and twisted it out on the rug. Then I knocked, three times.

Clattering and muffled voices came from within. Then Jessica's voice.

"Who is it?"

I changed my voice. On a crazy hunch I said, "Rutger Bachman." The door opened and Jessica was already speaking.

"Oh, hello Mr. Bachman, is something –" She stopped dead in her tracks as she looked up at me. Her see-through black negligee must not have left anything to the imagination, but I didn't notice. The expression on her face was one I'd never seen on a woman before; surprise, fear, betrayal, embarrassment and sadness all rolled up into one.

"Hello Ginger," I said with a tint of melancholy.

"Oh," she said, the rest of the words stuck in her throat. "Oh, it's…you."

"Yeah. It's me."

The guy was sitting on the bed, taking off his shoes. "Is there a problem, Ginger?" he asked pretty nicely. She turned to him and said, "I'm sorry, Johnny, you'll have to go. This is…my parole officer. I'm afraid I'm in a little trouble at the moment."

"Aw hell," the guy said. "Look buddy, I don't want any trouble. We were just talking, see?"

"No trouble as long as you get out of here on the count of ten. One, Five, Seven…"

"I'm out!" he said and pushed past Jessica out the door.

"Come in Bill," she said quietly. I did. She shut the door.

The room was what I'd expect in a whorehouse. Red drapes hung from every wall, plush red carpet, soft double bed with purple bed-sheets and throw. A single chair next to a small table with liquor and a setup. An electric fan blew cool air in from a vent. The lighting was low, as was a radio in the corner playing classical music.

"Why didn't you tell me?" I asked calmly.

She swallowed hard, gave a half smile and said shakily, "Why didn't you tell me you were a cop?"

"Because I was on vacation."

"Same here," she said. "Remember, I went to Tiki Island to get my mind off of work."

"What about later, what about all this week?"

She gave out a fake laugh and threw herself into the chair. "Oh, sure. I find out you're a vice cop, and you want me to tell you I'm a call girl? Right." She held back tears as best as she could, but they defied her. "You couldn't leave well enough alone. You couldn't just enjoy our time together. You had to play detective and screw everything up." The tears flowed more freely.

"Jessica, I came here tonight looking for you, but not here. I went to La Concha. I asked around and nobody ever heard of you. I only came here because I was curious about the show. I never expected in a million years you'd be here!"

"How did you get in?" she asked through sobs.

"I dropped Bachman's name."

"How did you know?"

"I didn't. I guessed. I put two and two together and came up with Bachman arranging hookers for VIPs at Tiki Island."

"Please don't use that word."

"Sorry, call girls. When you work at Tiki Island as a hostess, that pretty much means you work as a call girl, doesn't it."

"Yes," she said, and the sobs began again.

"Jessica, listen to me. I don't care." I knelt down beside her grabbed her by the arms. "I don't care what you do. Your business is your business. It doesn't change the way I feel about you."

"Yes it does. How could it not? You spend your life locking up people like me."

"Not like you. In your line of work, yeah, but not like you. You're different."

"How do you know? You hardly know me."

"Gimme a chance. I've only been in your life for a few days, after all."

"I know, I know you have. That's why it's so unfair. In a few days you get to go home and leave all this. I can't. I tried to get out but I just can't. I can't get a job anywhere in the keys because Roberts put out the word that anyone hires me, they get big trouble. Now he's out of the picture and it's only a matter of time before someone else fills his shoes. I'm trapped. You get to go home to your job and your life and your Manhattan apartment. I get to stay here and do…*this!*"

The tears came full force now, and I was worried a bouncer might hear and bust in on us. I didn't want any extra trouble at this point.

"Calm down kid, here," I said and handed her a drink from the table. She took it and swallowed the whole thing in one gulp. "I can help. I can get Jackson to undo the damage Roberts did. You can get a regular job somewhere and leave all this behind."

"Jackson? The Sheriff? What would *he* care. He has his own problems."

"He owes me one. I can probably even get you a job at Tiki Island if you want it." She laughed hard at that one.

"Are you that naive, Billy? Don't you know that Roberts worked for Eliot Hawthorn? Hawthorn has his hands in everything Roberts did, including this place. Who do you think backed Roberts when he needed cash?"

"Hawthorn."

"Of course. And who do you think does his dirty work, now that he's too old and frail?"

It made sense. "Bachman."

"Right. Rutger, your buddy's brother. Hawthorn didn't need him to run the Island. He needed him to run the stuff he doesn't want his daughter getting into!"

I flipped that over a minute. It fit. Melinda could run Tiki Island with her eyes closed. Then, without thinking any further, I let it out. "You could come back to New York with me. I know plenty of places you could get a job, get a fresh start. No one would have to know about your past. You could leave all this behind you, finished and done with."

Her big blue eyes, rimmed in red, looked up at me with such sadness I almost bawled myself. "Don't you understand, *I can't leave Key West,"* she whispered, and as she did a knock came at the door.

"Ginger, you OK in there?" came the voice of the bouncer.

"Yes, I'm fine."

"Johnny Miller said someone threw him out. What gives? Open up!"

"Everything's fine, Chuck, I'll be done in a minute and Johnny can come back up."

I said, "Johnny's not coming anywhere. You're coming with me. I'm getting you out of here before something really bad happens."

"No Bill, I can't go with you," she said, wiping the tears from her face. She turned to a little mirror on the wall and fixed her makeup. "It wouldn't be fair to you, or me. This is who I am, Billy. It's already too late." She was calm now, and cold as if talking to a brush salesman. "You better go now. Show Chuck your badge and he'll back off. Please go."

I was speechless. I stood up but didn't go.

"Ginger!" came along with more knocking from Chuck.

"Jessica, I..."

"It's Ginger, sugar. It's always been Ginger. Go now. It was a fun week but it's over."

I took a deep breath and let it out slow. She just stood there, waiting, cold. I took out my badge and gun, and opened the door.

"Back off sonny, if you know what's good for you." The goon backed up with his hands up low. "I guess she's all yours," I said, and pitching a last glance at Jessica, I left.

1935

Eliot Hawthorn laid next to his mistress Rose on the soft bed in the loft of the boathouse, smoking a cigar and watching the water reflect moonlight through the window. Rose lie breathless, sweating and in need of something cold.

"I'm taking a beer from the icebox, sugar. Ya'll want one too?"

"Sure," he said, and puffed away.

"That sure was…uh…mighty intense, sugar. You ain't never been like that before."

"I guess it's the thrill of knowing my wife is less than a hundred yards away. I get great satisfaction knowing while I'm balling you, she's sitting in our bed reading a magazine just up the path."

"You must loathe that woman, sugar. Why on Earth would you feel that way?"

"I have my reasons," he said. "Listen, we absolutely must do this again sometime. Maybe next weekend?"

"But next weekend's Labor Day weekend. Ain't you got a big party or something going on?"

"Oh, that's right. Ok then, the weekend next. But I'll still come see you on the Big Key in between time, OK?"

"Sure sugar, anytime you want!" she said handing him the beer. Then she laid on top of him, laughing, and the beer got hot real fast.

## 1956

I never felt so low. Even when my father was killed by a junkie, even when my mother was killed by a drunk, I never felt as low as I did just then. I made my way out of the house and down to the parking lot, and slid behind the wheel of the Chevy. I really liked that car, and thought about maybe buying one when I got home. Sure, I'd only drive it now and then, and the garage fees would be through the roof, but I really did like it. Thinking about it got my mind off Jessica.

I started her up. The big V8 came to life under me and roared. The whole car twisted with torque when I gunned the gas, something you never get to feel when you ride in cabs everywhere. I shifted the selector into drive and motored out of the spot, heading down town.

As the night flew by I thought about the last thing she said. "Don't you understand, I can't leave Key West." I didn't really know what she meant by that. I thought maybe she meant her roots were here, and she didn't want to leave. Then I thought maybe it had something to do with that crazy house she brought me to this afternoon. Then, I thought maybe she owed some people money. That was probably it.

I swung the car down Duval Street and ended up at Sloppy Joe's. There was no place to park so I had to circle the block twice before I found something. I parked it and walked into the old watering hole.

I took a small table near the back, far from the other people and the stage. A piano, bass and drums were banging out some old-time boogie-woogie and the crowd was eating it up. I ordered a double Bourbon on the rocks. It was too hot to drink it straight.

Two hours and six double Bourbons later I didn't remember who Ginger was or Jessica was, and didn't care. It was after two, and the place was closing up so I ordered one last double and drank it straight down. When I got up, I almost didn't make it. The room spun a little and I realized too late I was drunk as hell. I didn't care. I threw a ten-spot on the table for the waiter, picked up my panama and headed out into the street.

It was quieter now, but still lively. A different crowd was out at this hour, weirdoes, bikers, sailors. A brawl broke out at the joint across the way and spilled out into the street. It was over as fast as it started when one of the mugs went down flat with a lucky left hook. Someone got him to his feet and the guy who slugged him offered to buy him a drink. Laughs, a pat on the back, best friends.

I walked down to the waterfront where the big ships were parked. A cruise ship loomed up in front of me so tall that I almost got vertigo. Two kids smooched on a bench to my left. On the right, cars parked by the dock hid lovers maximizing the space in their backseats. I thought of Jessica. I thought of Melinda. For some odd reason I thought of Fast Freddie, and wondered if she ever saw a show like the one I saw tonight, and what she'd think of it. I turned around and walked back up Duval.

I walked around for I don't know how long. I passed President Truman's place...a hell of a house, a real beauty. I walked down a side street and passed the Audubon House, another museum I planned to hit before leaving this vacation. I found the Aquarium I'd heard so much about, and promised myself I'd see that too before heading north again.

Then I found myself in front of Jessica's place. What a poor sap I was. Here I was fooling myself into thinking we had a connection, when she was just making nice for the Tiki Island 'VIP'. Oh sure, maybe Bachman didn't give her the order, but it occurred to me she'd have hell to pay if she didn't make *any* VIP happy.

I looked up towards her floor. Her room was in the back.

I climbed the outside staircase to the second floor.

Light came through the bottom of Jessica's door. She was home.

The liquor helped me work up the nerve I needed. I knocked, three times.

Nothing.

I knocked again.

Still nothing.

I tried the door.

It was locked.

I heard a stirring inside, then the sound of something falling and hitting the floor.

"Jessica, let me in," I said a little too loudly.

Nothing.

For the second time, I slid down in front of her door and sat on the dirty boards.

It was two-thirty when John Miller finally finished with Ginger. He was in rare form tonight, she thought, stronger and more hungry than most nights. He made her do everything, even the stuff she hated, the stuff that hurt. But it was his nickel and she needed it. When he was finished he tipped her a C-note and left with a smile on his face.

She packed her small bag, slipped on some jeans and a pink pullover top and headed out down the back stairs. At the bottom she cashed out, giving the house their thirty percent and taking her cut in small bills. She managed to keep over three hundred for herself tonight, a damned good haul, all things considered.

Then she found Chuck.

"Call me a cab, sugar?" she said, and he knew what that meant. From a little box in his jacket pocket he produced a wax paper package about six inches long and an inch in diameter. "Thanks sugar. Here's a ten for your trouble. Now really,

I need that cab," Jessica/Ginger said, and like a good soldier Chuck picked up the phone and called for a Checker to meet her out back.

Ginger sat on the back fence and waited, stuffing the little package down deep into her purse. When the cab showed up she directed him to her apartment, and in a few minutes was home.

She showered off first, then took a half a ham sandwich from the Fridgidaire and ate it with a bottle of Coke. A decent breeze came through her window tonight, and she knew she'd sleep well. When the sandwich was finished, she took out the little wax paper package and slowly opened it on her table. Then she took the black zippered case from under the clothes in the second drawer of her bureau, and opened that next to it.

A few minutes later any memories she had of ghosts or Johns or Bills or anything were lost in a cloudy dream.

I woke up about three-thirty a.m. in front of Jessica's door. My head was a lot clearer now and I knew she was in there. I needed to see her.

I pounded on the door. "Jessica, let me in. It's Riggins."

I heard a stirring, then a faint, "Go away."

"I ain't going away. I'll pound this door until the neighbors call the cops," I yelled, and a light came on in the next apartment. Then I remembered how flimsy her lock was. I didn't want to break the door down, but it was a cinch I could pick the lock with nothing but a hairpin.

If only I had a hairpin.

Then I remembered her lock used a skeleton key. I looked under her mat, then on top of the doorjamb. Sure enough, she left an extra latchkey over the door.

I opened the lock and opened the door.

Damn.

Sometimes I should just quit while I'm ahead, but I don't. If I did, I'd be telling you the story of how I met this smokin' hot chick on vacation, who I found out later turned out to be a call girl. End of story. Kind of crazy, a little funny, but not so bad.

But I had to push it.

A pushed the door open slow. A small bulb glowed on the nightstand, giving the room a quiet, dead feel with strange shadows clawing at the walls. Jessica was laid out on her bed naked, one leg off the side and one arm over her face, shielding her eyes against the dull light. She didn't move when I came in. On the table sat a piece of wax paper with white powder on it, a spoon, a candle, and a syringe.

I didn't have to look twice to know what I was looking at.

H.

Horse.

The White Ghost.

*Heroin.*

"Jesus H. Christ, Jessica!" I yelled as I ran to her. I looked at her arms. No tracks. Of course not, she needed to look good to keep her clients. I spread her toes. Sure enough, there were enough pinpricks to make a connect-the-dots picture.

I shook her. "Jessica, wake up. Jessica!"

She muttered very low, "I'm…Ginger."

"Gaddammit, I don't care if you're Vera Lynn, wake the hell up!" Then it hit me. I checked her pulse. It was racing but weak. Her breathing was shallow. Her pupils were dilated like hell.

The dumb broad over-dosed herself!

I picked up the phone and asked the operator for the nearest doctor to her address. She rang me through to a Dr. Watson (yeah, really, how about that?) who sounded groggy but concerned. I told him I was a Detective and he said he'd be over in five minutes. Four minutes later he knocked on the door.

He checked her vitals and gave her a shot of something. Then he turned to me.

"She'll be fine. She didn't take a lethal dose. Is she a friend of yours?"

"Just met her this week. Just found out tonight she on the junk."

"Do everything you can to get her off of it, Mr. Riggins. She keeps this up she won't last past her thirty-fifth birthday."

"Just like Bird," I muttered.

"Yes, just like him. Such a waste." He closed up his bag and gave me some pills. "Give her two of these when she wakes up. It will help with the pain that she's going to have in her head. Two every four hours after that. Good luck, Mr. Riggins," he said and left.

I wasn't going to wait until she woke up. I shook her hard and she woke up on my schedule.

"Jessica, get up."

"Wha, what do you want?"

"It's me, Riggins. I want to know what the hell this is all about."

She shook off the sleepiness enough to answer me. "It's all about me, Bill, it's about me. This is how I live with myself. This is how I can do what I do, and forget. This is how I get the voices to stop. This is how I get the ghosts to leave me alone."

I was yelling. "Jessica, this stuff will *kill* you, don't you understand that?"

The groggy answer came, "I don't care."

"How could you not care! I've seen what this stuff does to people!"

"I need it."

"You're a *Gaddamned junkie!*" I screamed, not realizing how loud I'd been. A dog barked downstairs. Someone pounded on the ceiling above. "Jesus, Jessica," was all I could say. I was losing it, losing my cool. I could put up with her being a stripper. I could put up with her being a sex dancer, and even a Gaddamned prostitute, although that was really pushing my sense of morality. I could even forgive her for lying about everything. But the one thing I couldn't forgive was a junkie.

Then the final gear clicked into place, and the motor ran smooth and quiet. Click.

"That's why you can't leave Key West," I finally said. "Because you've got your whole system set up here. You make big money fast turning tricks, then you spill it all week on H. That's why you live in a six-by-twelve apartment, that's why you wanted me to stay away today. No wonder you see freakin' ghosts, you probably hallucinate half your life away!"

"The ghosts are *real!*" she yelled, jumping from the bed. Suddenly she was full of life, full of energy. "They're real, you saw them yourself, Riggins. Don't you dare tell me you didn't. I *need* this stuff just to get through the nights. Thank God I found something that can help me through, or I'd be dead already!"

"Bullshit!" I retorted. "What you need is a good shot in the head to set you straight. Heroin doesn't help anything. It makes it worse. So you've been seeing strange things for a few days. Cope with it."

"A few days?" she said quietly. "You dumb sunofabitch, haven't you been listening to anything I've been saying? Haven't you paid attention to what I've shown you? It hasn't been a few days. It's been my *whole fuckin' life!*"

She broke down in tears again and it seemed the only time I saw her now was when she was crying.

That had to change.

I had to try to help her. I knew it was crazy, but I had to try. Maybe it was just the cop in me, or maybe I felt something for her that I never should have started feeling in the first place, but it was out there, and there was no suppressing it, no denying it.

"Jessica, look at me." She looked up and I realized at some point she had come into my arms, and she was still naked. I held her close and talked softly. "No matter what you think, I can help you. I know doctors who can help you get off the Horse without going cold turkey. Come with me to New York, and leave all this behind. Leave your past, leave your ghosts. Start over again. Let me help you."

She gave a short laugh. "Why?"

"Why what?"

"Why do you want to help me?" she asked through drug-soaked sobs.

"I…I just do. I want to."

"Is it because you love me, Billy?"

"I…" I didn't' know how to answer.

"*Do* you love me Bill? *Can* you love me?" She put her arms around me and kissed me. Something didn't seem right. She looked into my eyes. Hers were glistening with tears. "Can you still kiss me knowing where my mouth was earlier tonight?"

Something grabbed the back of my mind and threw it against a rock wall. Disgust, hatred, loathing all balled up in my gut and I pushed Jessica off of me onto the bed. She just laughed. I spit, wiped my mouth with my arm.

"You don't love me, Billy. You just want a project. You just want someone you can take care of, because you miss taking care of the pushers and hookers and lowlifes you work with. Admit it, Riggins, once you go back home you'll forget all about me and you won't care whether I live or die."

She laughed again. She was a monster, not her real self, not Jessica but Ginger, the strung-out, naked whore with needle tracks under her toes and a heart as cold as ice. The Bourbon spun my brain and I had to get out of there. I left her there laughing on the bed as I ripped the door open and shot down the stairs.

I found my car and fired it up. An hour on the boat was too long to get back to the Island, so I floored it and raced through town, then raced up US 1 as fast as the road would let me to Sugarloaf Key. The road was a dark, winding snake that stunk of marsh and rose with treacherous bridges barely wide enough to let the car through. My high beams cut through the night; shadows leapt from the sides of the road and threatened to turn me over but I held her steady at almost ninety for most of the way. I was in Sugarloaf in what seemed like minutes, and I parked at the edge of the dock that said, "Hawthorn Industries." No one was around, but a motorboat with Tiki Island painted on the side sat ready. I jumped in, cranked it up and took off for the Island. It wasn't far off but the boat barely pushed twenty, and it seemed like it took forever to run the half mile stretch. When I finally got to the Island I just beached the boat near the front, and tied it to a Tiki pole.

A minute later I was in my room, in the shower, washing off the grime of the night. I brushed my teeth twice and looked at myself in the mirror. I swear I aged ten years.

Shaking, I poured myself a Wild Turkey neat from the Tiki bar and sat in one of the big chairs. It all rushed in.

*Jessica was a hooker.*

And she was an addict. Not just a reefer smoker or a cocaine party girl, but a certified heroin junkie complete with her own do-it-yourself juice kit.

And she was wrong.

I *was* falling in love with her.

How could I be so stupid? How could I let this happen, me, Detective William Riggins, the smartest cop on the force, the youngest to be made Detective in thirty years? I swallowed the belt and threw the glass against the wall. It shattered into a thousand tiny pieces and spread across the room. That just made me madder.

I was going crazy. I didn't know what to do. I left the suite, and at four-thirty in the morning I found myself in the one place I should never have gone.

I knocked.

It took a minute, but Melinda opened the door to her room and stood there sleepily, yet beautiful. It was like in a movie when a doll goes to bed looking like a million bucks and wakes up the next day with perfect hair and makeup. She was gorgeous through and through, wearing nothing but a flimsy silk housecoat.

"Bill?" she asked. She seemed surprised. I didn't say a word. I pushed the door open and pushed my way in. I took her by surprise so fast that the she let the silk robe slip a little and I could see she wasn't wearing a damned thing underneath. I kicked the door shut. We were alone.

"Bill, I…"

I didn't let her finish. I took her by the arms and pulled her up to me, pressing my lips against hers. The fire broke out and sparks flew all over the room, chasing away any thoughts I had of Jessica or Ginger or whoever the hell she was. Melinda kissed back. She wrapped her arms around my neck and gave in completely. We'd both dreamed about this minute for days and now it was here and there was no stopping it.

The kiss ended and she stepped back, her breasts heaving with passion, her mouth open with desire. She untied the robe and in one soft move it floated to the floor, exposing that tan, lithe body I'd dreamed so much about. "Take me," she said softly, and I moved in slowly and kissed her again, the passion roaring up inside us like an atom bomb loosed on the world. I picked her up and laid her on the bed. I ripped my shirt off and buttons flew everywhere. I didn't care. "Take me," she said again.

She didn't have to ask twice.

I woke up late Saturday morning. It was around eleven and the taste of Bourbon and Melinda still lingered. A crazy thought occurred to me then, that they should make a cocktail and name it the Bourbon Melinda. Then I realized any drink named after her would have to be made with rum, so the name didn't make sense. Then I realized I must still be a little drunk if I was thinking thoughts like that.

Melinda was nowhere to be found, but she left me a note on the bathroom mirror:

"Dear Bill, I hope you had as wonderful a night as I did. I figured you'd want to sleep so I didn't wake you. I had to coordinate a breakfast for a group this morning and won't be available until after eleven. I've left word with the front desk to send up a package of clothing for you; it should be waiting outside my door. I'll see you soon, love, Melinda."

Oh boy. 'love, Melinda'.

I splashed some water on my face to wake up and grabbed the clothes from outside the door. A nice pair of pleated tan pants, tan socks, and white shirt with red and orange flowers and a pair of boxers, all the right size. This hotel was first class, all the way. I dressed fast and went back to my room where I showered and shaved before showing my mug in public again.

I sat on the balcony and looked out over the Gulf to Key West. What a night. What a day and night. A haunted house, a brothel, a sex show, finding out Jessica was a call girl and a junkie, all that booze and ending up with most beautiful, most sensual girl I'd ever known. I might have thought Jessica knew a few tricks, but honestly she could have taken lessons from Melinda. Where that girl learned her techniques I didn't know…and come to think of it, I really didn't want to know.

As I stretched out on the lounge chair I thought of my life, how it was going, where it was going. I was a cop, no doubt about it. But could I really be happy here, on this Island, with Melinda? Could I fall for her, and make it stick? I'd still have to be a cop…not a doubt that Sheriff Jackson could find something for me to do, maybe even get a gig with the state cops. I don't know if I could wear the southern-style uniforms though, I'd feel pretty silly wearing a cowboy hat while talkin' wit my Joisey accint. Of course if I moved here, I'd have more use for a pretty blue 1957 Chevrolet Bel Air convertible. That's a thought.

The autumn sun rose high in the Florida sky, and a cool breeze came off the Gulf into my room. It occurred to me that it was probably cloudy and in the low forties in New York today. It didn't seem fair that the greatest city on Earth had to be cold and dreary nine months out of the year. Then again, if it didn't get cold there, New York chicks wouldn't wear tight pullover sweaters and black boots.

I had enough of the view and decided to look for Melinda. I didn't know what last night had meant to her, and I wanted to get things straight before I put my foot in my mouth. I was at a point where dropping everything and moving to Tiki Island didn't sound too bad, but still sounded crazy and unrealistic.

I went down to the lobby and asked the concierge if they knew where she was. They didn't so I tried the lobby bar and the restaurant. Nothing. I decided to try back at her room, just for the hell of it.

She left me a key so I let myself in. She wasn't there either, but I decided to stay a while. Detective mode had kicked in, and as such I couldn't help but do a little snooping. Now don't get sore, I wasn't going to invade her privacy, wasn't going to sniff her panty drawer or anything like that. I just wanted to give her apartment the once over, see what books she liked to read, what TV shows she had circled in the guide, what photos she had sitting out.

Her place was converted hotel rooms so it was set up in such a way that you walked into the bedroom first, then went down a short hall to a living room space. A bookshelf in her bedroom held a couple dozen hardbacks, every one of them out of place with each other. There was a book of Hawaiian history and culture next to a Mike Hammer novel (she's got good taste, I noted). Next to that was a book on shipwrecks of the Florida Keys, then Frankenstein, then a couple of romance novels, then another Mike Hammer and a book of poetry. Her tastes were all over the map when it came to books. I liked that. I left the books and wandered down the hall, a short but interesting passage lined with thatch mats and hung with black velvet paintings of tropical beaches and topless native women.

Her joint was on the exact opposite of the hotel from mine, so her view was of the North, mainly of the next few Keys and the Gulf. Her living room was smaller than mine, and instead of a corner Tiki bar she had a set-up on a sideboard. But the décor was pure Polynesian. Tiki totems and masks covered the walls, which were laminated in thin strips of bamboo. The floor was bamboo too, with oriental rugs strategically placed among the rattan furniture. Instead of dark leather, her furniture was covered in bright tropical floral patterns with green leaves and a sky blue background. One wall was all lava rock, and featured a built-in waterfall that ended in a small pool near the floor. Fish, what kind I couldn't tell you, swam in the pool.

To the left was another room. It was more of a closet, filled with the thirty-five dresses she boasted about, plus evening gowns, skirts and bathing suits. She must have had ten pairs of shoes, a lot less then most New York women I knew. To the right was another door. This one had a key in the lock, and was locked. I tossed it over in my mind whether to go in, then figured what the hell, and unlocked the door.

It opened on the strangest room I'd seen since I got to Florida, and that included the haunted room of Jessica's mother...except the ghosts of this room were not ghosts at all, but photos.

The room was covered from top to bottom with shelves, and the shelves were filled with old photos. Most of the photos on the left side of the room were of a young Eliot Hawthorn, and presumably his first wife, Vivian. There were enlarged photos of a giant white mansion with the name "Hawthorn" etched into the frames, and pictures of Eliot playing golf, Eliot on his boat, and Eliot in the garden always with Vivian by his side. The photos on the right were of Eliot with his second wife and stepdaughter, Melinda. The oldest was from 1936, and showed a very young Melinda playing croquet on an unknown lawn. The remainder showed the family through the years, ending in 1950. Melinda was twenty.

An ornate desk at the far end of the room included blueprints for the Tiki Island Hotel, an old typewriter, and a journal. I flipped the journal over and was creeped out to the utmost. Page after page was written with the same thing, in an old man's cursive: *"I am not cursed, I am not cursed"*. I turned to the last page, and in a different script, very scratchy it read, *"Yes you are."* I closed it up quick and just tried to forget about it.

Continuing around the room, the photos changed from family to the Islands. An overhead shot of Key West from 1922 hung above the desk. Photos of men building the Overseas Railway, plus framed tickets from the inaugural trip flanked the Key West photo. Further down, photos of the destruction of the 1935 Hurricane lined the wall, including pictures of the overturned train, the collapsed bridges, and the damage on Hawthorn Island. Melinda was right; the Island had been completely destroyed, leaving nothing but piles of sticks and ruined beaches in the hurricane's path.

I heard a slight noise and saw a glimpse of movement out of the corner of my right eye. I turned, expecting to see Melinda. No one was there. That was my cue to get scarce, and I locked the door behind me just the way I found it.

It was already after twelve and my guts were rumbling for some chow, so I made my way back down to the restaurant. The hostess said that Melinda had left word for me to meet her on the second floor Tiki deck, which I didn't even know existed. The hostess directed me to the deck, and I left.

Hostess. I had to wonder if she was a hooker too. Suddenly I looked at every girl that worked there as a potential prostitute, from the flirty cocktail waitress on the Tiki Express to the bartenders to the Hula girls. Impossible, I knew. Just my beat-up mind playing tricks with me.

I found the deck and boy was I surprised. I don't know how I missed this one. This was much different than the rest of the hotel. For one thing it was very bright and lively. The deck flooring was made of polished teak, so shiny you could comb your hair in it. It was enclosed by giant glass windows, floor to ceiling, twenty-feet high and looking out in a sort of semi-circle over Sugarloaf Key and the Atlantic Ocean. The air conditioning was pumping so cool it felt like home. Giant waterfalls graced the sides of the rock-wall entrance, and the tables were all bamboo and rattan with matching chairs upholstered in bright floral prints. The aromas of charbroiled meats and fresh fruits mingled into a tango of culinary splendor. A steel guitar band softly played Hawaiian songs on a small stage and a single Hula girl swayed with the tunes. The Tiki Deck was really more Modern Art than Tiki...a kind of a Polynesian theme meets William F. Cody.

Man, what a joint.

Melinda spotted me from a window-side booth and waved me over. I walked up to the table and leaned in to kiss her cheek. She turned so I planted one on her lips.

"Good morning," I said cheerfully.

"Good afternoon," she said and waved for me to sit down. Her eyes were big and bright, her smile real. "Did you have a nice time last night?" she asked rather coyly.

"One of the best of my life."

"Only *one* of? I must be slipping," she said, and took a sip of her cocktail.

"It probably was the best. I'll let you know when I wake up from this dream," I said with a wink.

"I've ordered lunch for us. Another surprise I think you'll like."

"Wait, how did you know I was coming?"

"Oh, I have my ways," she giggled. "Honestly, Deena called me from the Hukilau room."

"Ah, yes of course, the hostess."

"That's right." The food arrived quickly, along with an orange concoction as a drink.

"I think you'll like this, William. Filet mignon tips sautéed with Maui onions and green peppers over a toasted fresh hardroll, topped with a special blend of cheeses and spicy peppers."

I looked at my plate. "A cheesesteak! You got me a cheesesteak!"

"A Tiki Island special cheesesteak, of course!"

"Fantastic!" Was this girl a keeper or what? "What's in the glass?"

"An excellent lunch cocktail, not as potent as a Mai Tai. It's orange juice, pineapple juice, dark rum, coconut milk and a dash of bitters. Try it, it's heavenly."

I took a sip. She was right, it was good stuff and not too strong. "This is great. What do you call it?"

She laughed. "A Melinda Lindy," she said with a giant smile. "The bartender named it after me. He created it especially for my eighteenth birthday."

Well I'll be damned.

"Well, here's to the Melinda Lindy, to you, to me, to Tiki Island and a great weekend." We clinked glasses and dove into the chow. The cheesesteak was the best I had in a long time, so good we hardly spoke during the meal. The silence wasn't awkward at all, but fantastic.

I almost lit up a smoke after I finished, then remembered Melinda didn't dig coffin nails. No big deal. But it would have been nice to have a prop when I started laying on the trip about last night. The Melinda Lindy just didn't cut it.

"So, sweetheart, about last night." I waited for her to say something. She didn't. She just looked at me with those big, happy eyes. "I uh…" There I went again, Mr. Smoothy.

"Didn't you have fun?" She asked, slightly hurt.

"No, I mean yes, of course I did, it was…" I took a breath and quit the nervous schoolboy routine. "It was fantastic, start to finish. I'm just not sure where to go from here," I said as lightly as possible.

"Oh, not a problem. I've already reserved the ballroom for next month. That should be enough time for you to get a guest list together."

"Guest list?"

"Oh course. Don't worry, Eliot will arrange for your friends and family to come down and stay for free. Then of course we'll take care of the catering. But I don't know what religion you are, so you should decide on a priest or minister…or rabbi?"

She threw me. "Priest? Rabbi? What are you talking about?"

"Well, of the wedding, of course. I mean, you do realize that in Hawaiian culture once you sleep with a woman, you're practically married."

"Married! Married? Melinda, come on, I can't make a decision like that over breakfast!"

"Lunch."

"What…whatever!" She started to laugh and I realized she was giving me the business. "Oh, very funny doll, very funny. Give a guy a heart attack why don't ya."

"I'm sorry William, I couldn't resist. You just seemed so…nervous."

"Yeah, I get like that around beautiful, crazy women. And what's with the 'William' bit all of a sudden?"

"Everyone calls you Bill. I want to be different. Don't you like it?"

"I don't mind it. Just seems a little strange to my ears."

"If you don't like it, I'll stop, William."

"No sweat. Now listen, seriously, about last night."

"Well, what did it mean to you?" she asked while buttering a cracker.

"I can't honestly answer that, not yet. I know I like you. I know I've wanted you from the minute I laid my lazy brown eyes on you. And I wanted you more than anything last night."

"Why last night? Why so suddenly?"

"I think you know why," I said looking her straight in the eye.

"You found out about Jessica Rutledge, didn't you," she said sadly. "You found out what she is, and came to me because you needed to feel better about yourself." The smile died away.

"No, not like that. Yeah, I found out about her. But I also realized I was falling for two women at the same time. At first I thought you were the one. Then you flat out told me no."

"When did I do that?"

"The first night we kissed. Your words were, 'I can't'." She looked down at her hands.

"Oh."

"So I backed off. Then Jessica came into the picture clearer and I thought she was the one. But I found out last night she's not."

"Because of her profession?"

"No believe it or not. Because she's a heroin addict."

Melinda's eyes grew wide with surprise, and she actually gasped. "I...I didn't know."

"Few do. She hides it well. I came to you because my whole world got turned upside-down and I just wanted to see a friendly face. I had no intention of putting the moves on you, you have to believe me. It's just whenever I'm around you I melt. I don't know what it is. It's like you're everything I love in a woman and more. Much more." I took her hands and held them in mine. The smile came back and I melted a little more. "I don't know what's next kid. I just know that last night and every time I've seen you has been fantastic, even now sitting here with you...there's no place I'd rather be."

"And what about tomorrow?"

I shook my head. "Not a clue. But if it's with you, I know it will be tops." She was silent but her smile seemed to say it all. It wasn't a one-night fling for her either. There were sparks and we both knew it. "So what about you, kid? What's your take on it all?"

She didn't answer right away. She took a sip of her cocktail with her eyes on mine, and I remembered that move from the other night. She was blunt. "It's been wonderful, but I think come Friday you'll check out of the hotel, and I'll never see you again."

She was probably right.

"Well it's true that I've got a life in Manhattan just like you've got a life here in the Keys. You make people's lives better, and so do I. Your life may be more glamorous but mine means something too. I'm good at what I do and I think I should stick with it. But then I look into your eyes and suddenly I want to forget it all and move to the tropics."

She laughed and her whole face lit up. "Well, William. We've got six days to see what happens. I think we should just play it by ear. What do you say?"

"I never did learn how to read music," I said, and leaned over and kissed her over the table.

It never occurred to me to ask her why on Tuesday she said, *"I can't"*, and last night she changed her tune so completely.

She tried to cry herself to sleep. When that didn't work, she downed two shots of cheap gin. It didn't make her sleepy but it mixed with the Horse galloping through her veins and made her feel the full force of her fix. The room closed in around her and she had to get out.

Throwing on a bathing suit and a sarong, she grabbed a blanket and headed out to her favorite spot. When she reached the beach she dropped the blanket and walked right up to the water's edge.

The shadow moved. It started far off and slowly floated on the surf up to the beach. Jessica stood her ground, stood firm in the wet sand while the cool water swirled around her ankles. The shadow came up to her, right in front of her.

These were the only times she could stand it. These were the only times her mind could comprehend what was happening without driving her insane. Only with the aid of the juice could she face the apparition that had called on her so many times over the years.

"What do you want?" she said to the black being. The face was puffy and oozing. The eyes were black holes with something festering inside. It answered something garbled and wet. She couldn't understand.

"What do you want?!" she screamed. The morbid thing opened its mouth and black mud and small crabs flowed out. Jessica was ready. She had seen it all before.

"Wash your damned mouth out and tell me what you want, woman!" Jessica screamed to the apparition.

The apparition shrieked, "*HAWWWWWTHORN*," spitting muck and seaweed on Jessica. Jessica winced, choked, and the phantom dissolved into the ocean once more.

Jessica swayed.

"Oh God, what the hell have I done."

The deep morning breeze blew purple and black. It did nothing to calm her. She passed out on the beach, just near the water's edge.

# CHAPTER THREE

Eliot Hawthorn was a disparaged man. His first wife Vivian was only twenty-nine when he lost her to the sea, and his second wife Marietta hadn't yet reached her fortieth birthday when death came calling. His whole "new life" revolved around Marietta, Melinda and Tiki Island; when Marietta died, his spirit died with her. He lost all interest in running the Resort, and within a year of Marietta's death… 1951… he had completely stopped managing Tiki Island. If not for Melinda, Tiki Island would have folded. And Eliot Hawthorn would have folded with it.

Overseas Highway over Pigeon Key to Key West, Florida

It was Melinda who took control in late 1950, only a few months after her mother passed away. Still in shock and grieving, M e l i n d a took up the reins and brought Tiki Island Resort back from the brink of financial collapse by marketing heavily to vacationers from the North-East and once again using the war, this time Korea, to her advantage. Giving all active and retired servicemen free accommodations for three extra days when they paid for four was an idea that forever put Tiki Island on the map as a favorite vacation spot for anyone in the armed forces.

But even in mourning Hawthorn knew he couldn't allow Melinda – a young woman – to have total control of the Resort. There were just certain things that he didn't want Melinda involved in – or even aware of when it came to entertaining important guests. Besides, in the eyes of the world, a five-star Resort like Tiki Island needed a five-star general at the helm. If Tiki Island were to remain on par with resort hotels in Miami, Atlantic City, San Francisco and Aspen, it simply couldn't be run by a girl. In 1953, over Melinda's protests, Hawthorn hired Rutger Bachman, a well-respected man in the hospitality trade to run the Resort.

Now at age sixty, Hawthorn was a hermit, secluded and frail, tormented nearly to the point of madness. His past was destroying his present, and each day brought him closer to complete insanity - over the demons of his past, which promised to bring on his demise. That he lasted all these years was a testament to Melinda; it was only she who kept him from putting the barrel of a revolver to his temple. Without Melinda, the first few years after Marietta's death would have been unlivable. The nightmares, the visions, the constant torture would have been too much for him to bear on his own. Even with the daily doses of prescription pills, even with the almost constant flow of fine brandy, it would just be too much to bear.

So Hawthorn lived in his self-imposed pseudo-exile, up on the top floor of the world's most luxurious and beautiful Polynesian-themed Resort overlooking the Florida Keys and the Gulf of Mexico, with the heavy drapes constantly pulled shut and his door locked with two deadbolts and a chain. He still had his hand in running the Hotel, though only through Melinda and Bachman, never directly with guests. Which is why it was so amazing, so extraordinary that he came out of hiding last Wednesday to address Sheriff Jackson and meet the nice young Detective that helped solve the mystery of the skeleton in the garden.

Yes, extraordinary it was, but Hawthorn had his reasons. For one thing, any skeletons found on his Island required the most delicate of handling with the police. A lot happened on his Island in the past, and he didn't need any of it returning to haunt him. He already had his fill of that.

For another thing, he very much wanted to meet Detective Riggins of whom Melinda had spoken so excitedly about. Hawthorn knew he wasn't getting any younger. In fact he didn't expect to live much longer, and the idea of Melinda being alone without a man to take care of her (and help her take care of Tiki Island) made him both sad and distraught. He wanted Melinda to be secure before he passed on, and he was ready to do whatever needed to be done to ensure that. He imagined that in his physical state there wasn't much he *could* do, but Hawthorn was wealthy, and he was prepared to sign over his considerable fortune to Melinda and the man who would make her happy.

Melinda, on the other hand, had very little interest in marriage. She had her own ideas about her life and her future, and they didn't necessarily include monogamy.

At first Hawthorn had hoped that Melinda would take a liking to Bachman. Nothing could be farther from the truth. Bachman had proven himself to be a smarmy playboy, chasing cocktail waitresses and hula dancers until there were none left to chase. Then he started on the guests. No, Bachman simply wasn't good enough for his daughter.

Then there was a very nice Food and Beverage Manager who came around in 1954. He and Melinda hit it off very nicely, but Hawthorn knew the relationship was doomed to mere friendship when he discovered the manager taking more of an interest in the men who worked the loading docks than Melinda. Que sera sera.

But this young Detective looked promising. He was smart, good looking, and all man from his broad shoulders to the way he wore his hat. Here was a man who could take care of Melinda (and the Resort). He just needed a little convincing.

Hawthorn knew he had to act fast. He saw the signs; his health was failing, both mentally and physically, and the visions…he just knew that the day would come soon that he'd leave Tiki Island forever. That's why he drummed up the courage to face the world outside his door, that's why he put on his nicest yet most comfortable clothes and made that giant leap from his threshold into the public area of the hotel. That's why he braved the lobby bar and even went as far as to speak with Riggins, to plant the seeds that would hopefully take root and secure Melinda's future. Melinda would just have to see it his way, no matter what she may have felt. She would just have to let go.

Finally, he convinced her. And over tearful embraces she ultimately agreed that Hawthorn was right, and that she should think about her future and what she really wanted out of life.

That was Wednesday.

Now it was Saturday, and Hawthorn knew Melinda had given herself to Riggins.

He should have been happy.

He realized he was not.

Que sera sera.

### Saturday

Melinda had a full day of hitting the grindstone ahead of her, so after lunch I kissed her goodbye and told her I'd meet up with her later at the shipwreck bar. She told me I should try snorkeling so I did. I was a pretty good swimmer, always liked it but had never been snorkeling. A pontoon boat took me and eleven other people out to a coral reef on the Atlantic side of Bahia Honda. The crew gave us the lowdown on the gear, and in twenty minutes we were checking out beautiful, colorful reefs with the craziest kinds of fish and creepy-crawlies I ever saw. A barracuda slipped between me and a pretty redhead, and that was enough for the Captain to call it a day. It was still early so the Captain asked if we wanted to head down to Key West for a tour of the Turtle Kralls and the Aquarium. Everyone agreed, and we headed down. The sea turtles were amazing...giant creatures, relics from the age of dinosaurs. They said some of those suckers were over a hundred years old. Imagine that, turtles that had been around during the Civil War. Seemed a shame to kill them just for soup, but I guess that's all in the circle of life. The Aquarium was small but nice, with lots of colorful fish with names I'll never remember. Even the ride back was nice...with a great view of a half-dozen half-naked chicks sunning themselves on the front deck of the boat.

I was back in my room by five-thirty, showered, shaved and all nice and presentable. I fixed myself a Manhattan and checked out some of the albums on the hi-fi. Everything was Jazz and Exotica….Arthur Lyman, Martin Denny, 101 Stings, Les Baxter, all the stuff you'd hear in some swanky bachelor's pad on the Upper East Side. I tossed a Les Baxter platter on the hi-fi and let it roll. What a sound, let me tell you. It sent me right off into Tikiville. I ditched the Manhattan and cobbled together a Mai Tai as best I could. It was decent. One of those quickie Florida five-minute rainstorms came through, throwing just enough thunder around to set the mood perfectly. I sat on the balcony (correction: In Florida, I was told, it is called a lanai) and watched the storm drift off down the keys and out to the ocean with the lilting music in the background. What a scene.

I was hooked and I didn't even know it.

Around seven o'clock I made my way down to the lobby shipwreck bar. For the first time I noticed the entrance itself looked like the back of a sunken ship. Wooden letters spelled out "Tahitian Queen" across the top, and I wondered how much else I'd missed since I got here. Some detective.

I was lucky to get a seat at the bar. It was more crowded than I'd ever seen it, and the mermaids were in full show, five altogether. I was in the mood for something strong so I ordered a Zombie.

Bachman walked in and it was only a few seconds before he spotted me. He zeroed in and I was stuck.

"Good evening, Mr. Riggins, enjoying your stay?"

"Immensely," I answered.

"Where is Ms. Rutledge tonight?" he said looking around the bar. He had to ask.

"Working, I'd guess," I said. I wanted to say, "you tell me, jackass" but I held my tongue. Didn't want to upset the cart, not with things going well with Melinda and all.

"Oh, I thought she'd be spending her time here during your stay," he said, somewhat cautiously. "Did you not, eh, get along? She's a wonderful person once you get to know her."

I honestly couldn't tell if he was being nice or checking up on his employees. I was having a good day and really didn't want to get into it with him, so I said, "We had our fun. Time to move on...life's pretty damned short, and this vacation is even shorter. Right?" I smiled when I said it, but it wasn't easy.

He smiled too. "Of course, of course, I understand completely. Variety is the spice of life, yes?"

"Yeah," I said, hoping to end the conversation. I don't think he had any idea I knew he was pimping out girls to his guests, but at the same time he seemed to be treating me like a 'client'. Kookie.

"Well, Mr. Riggins, I'm sure another companion will turn up, if you're interested." He gave me a wink and turned to leave. "Remember, anything you need, just ask," he added and left the bar.

I could swear one of the mermaids flipped him the bird. Nahhh, couldn't be.

Not three minutes went by when a long-legged doll in a red evening dress pushed her way up to the bar beside me. She spoke with a southern accent not unlike Jessica's.

"Mighty crowded in here tonight, ain't it? Mistuh, mind if I squeeze in here? This lady needs a drink."

"Go right ahead," I said and moved over a little to let her in. She waved down the bartender (another pretty Polynesian chick in a sarong) and ordered a Jim Beam on the rocks. Instead of taking her drink away, she stayed squeezed in standing at the bar.

"Thank you mistuh, much obliged."

"Don't mention it."

She paused only a second, then went to work. "My name's Penelope. I'm only here for the weekend, on my way to the Bahamas. How about you?"

"Pleased to meet you Penelope," I said and held up my drink. She clinked it and we drank. "The name's Riggins, but most people call me Bill. Here through the week on vacation."

"Just you? Or are you here with your family, or a group?"

As if she didn't already know. "Just me."

She turned slightly more towards me and leaned down the slightest bit, just enough for her v-crossed dress to open an inch or two and allow her cleavage to spill out the perfect amount…not too much, not too little, just enough for a tease.

"Got a cigarette?" she asked and licked her lips. She took another drink without taking her eyes off me. I unloaded two sticks from the deck and lit them both. I offered her one and she took a deep drag, then let the smoke out slow. "Thanks."

"De nada." I took another belt of the Zombie.

"Well, Bill, it would seem we're both here alone this weekend. Now is that any way to spend a holiday?" Her movements were a symphony of sex. The way she slowly brushed her long, chestnut hair away from her face, how she teased the rim of the glass with her index finger. The way her cool brown eyes stayed wide and focused, and how her lips parted ever so slightly, suggestively. She was a pro, no doubt about it. She was sent by Bachman as a party favor, a part of the VIP treatment. I guess he didn't know I wasn't in the market. But I decided to play along, just to see the pitch.

I didn't make a move, just spoke. "No, that would be a shame now wouldn't it. So what did you have in mind, doll?"

"Oh, I don't know," she said coyly, "Maybe dinner?"

"How about we skip dinner?" I said low. She didn't flinch, just gave me a sort of naughty look.

"You work fast," she said.

"You said yourself you're not here long," I answered and took a sip of my cocktail, this time not taking my eyes off of her. I could play the game too, ya know.

"Your room?" she asked quietly, smiling just a little.

"No dice, I have a suite and made some friends here, and too many of them think they can walk in anytime. Have to be yours, kitten."

"All right," she said, "Shall we?"

"Can't right this minute. Meeting someone here in a few. Slip me your key and I'll meet you at eight."

"Al'right sugar," she said, got up from the bar, smiled and left. Her key was next to her drink.

"Sugar," I said to myself. I was beginning to hate the term.

A half a Zombie later Melinda floated in on a cloud. She looked spectacular, more than before. Tonight she wore a stunning black dress with red tropical flowers intertwined with dark green vines. Her hair was held back by a nearly-black orchid, and her smile was so bright it lit up the room. Every eye in the place turned to her when she walked through the door…even the mermaids'.

I left the bar and met her near the entrance. "Hello kitten," I said as she gave me a somewhat friendly, professional kiss on the cheek. She was still at work after all. I could dig it.

"Hello William. Shall we have a drink? I could use one."

"Not here, it's too crowded. Don't you have a less sardine-like place we can go?"

"Oh, certainly. There's a quiet deck bar out on the North Beach, near the garden. Not usually crowded. Let's go there." She led and I followed. We walked through the garden, which had taken on a mystical quality in the late twilight. Twilight seemed to last forever down here, I thought. It was past seven-thirty and the sky was still purple and blue. The Tiki torches were already lit around the

Island and the effect was pure magic.

We walked by the gravesite. It was the first I'd seen of it since Wednesday, and it looked much different. The grave had been filled in and grass sod placed over it. Small tropical plants and a stone bench were placed off to the side, and just over it a waist-high bamboo monument was built, set with a bronze plaque that read, *"In memory of the hundreds of souls who perished in the Great Atlantic Hurricane of 1935, you can never be forgotten."*

"Eliot do that?" I asked Melinda as we strode by.

"Yes, he felt it was the right thing."

"Last line is a little odd."

"Why do you say that?"

"'You can never be forgotten.' Seems 'You *will* never be forgotten' would sound better, no?"

She shrugged. "Maybe the signmaker got it wrong. It was a rush job. Eliot insisted it be up as soon as possible. I think he just wanted the whole thing over with. He had them pour the concrete and shovel over the dirt as soon as –"

"Pour the *concrete?*" I interrupted, and that cop alarm in my head started to buzz. "What concrete?"

"Over the body…he had the workers seal the bones in a foot of concrete, I guess so they'd be preserved. Is that unusual?"

I didn't want to cause any unnecessary suspicion so I said, "No, not really. A little overkill I guess, but it's done often enough." I lied. It was *very* unusual, downright oddball, and it wasn't done often at all. Then again, she said he was cracking up a little at a time, so maybe it was just that. Maybe.

We wandered down the flagstone path to the North Beach, and there out on the surf was a small thatched hut built on pilings, set about forty feet into the water. A gangplank led up from the beach, and as we entered the bar the only male bartender I saw on the Island greeted us with a big smile and "Aloha, Ms. Hawthorn, Aloha, friend."

The bar was open-air and dark. Everything was made of coconut logs, bamboo and thatch, all stained a rich, dark brown and inlaid with hand-carved designs. The floor was wood planks spaced a half-inch apart. You could see and hear the ocean underneath.

There were only a few people sitting around, but we took a small booth in the back corner anyway. Without asking, the bartender built two cocktails and brought them over. He made the drop, smiled, bowed and walked off. I checked my watch. It was quarter to eight.

I started in with, "Nice shack. This joint's full of surprises."

"Yes it is. Here are two now." She held up her drink and said, "Navy Grog. Something you haven't tried yet."

I picked up my drink and toasted. "Here's to surprises."

"Mahalos," Melinda said sweetly and held up her drink. For the second time tonight I clinked glasses with a pretty girl. This time I meant it.

"So what's the plan for tonight?" I asked.

"No plan. Dinner I suppose," she said rather nonchalantly. "Of course there is this great band playing in the Hukilau dining room tonight."

"Anyone I'd know?"

"Maybe. If you've ever heard of Martin Denny."

"Holy cats! *The* Martin Denny? From Hawaii?"

"The one and only," she answered smiling brightly.

I was a jazz & swing man at heart, but I was a sucker for Bossa Nova and

Exotica. "Yeah, I'd dig that."

"I thought you might. They go on at nine."

"Perfect," I said, remembering the chestnut-haired doll waiting in room...what was it? I pulled out the key and threw it on the table.

"By the way, Melinda, is there anything special about room 322?"

Melinda looked down at the key, a somewhat irritated expression glazing her perfect face.

"Where did you get that?" she asked without looking up.

"A chestnut brunette in a red dress and peekaboo cleavage handed it over to me in the bar."

"Let me guess," she added, "You talked to Bachman today."

She knew the score. How much she knew, I knew not.

"About three ticks before the dame showed up. She came on hot and heavy. Didn't blink when I said I should meet her back at her room."

"It's not her room. It's one of several rooms Rutger keeps on reserve in case a VIP customer calls for a last-minute stay. He says that's done in all the major hotels. I suspect those rooms don't stay vacant very long."

"How much do you know about Bachman's...eh...VIPs? And how he treats them?"

She took a long pull of the cocktail and finally looked up. "I'm not supposed to know anything. But I do. I'm not an idiot, although he and Eliot sometimes think so. Sometimes our guests have special requests. The staff is instructed to direct them to Key Largo or Key West when they ask for things like girls or...well anything illegal, really. But Bachman has his own way of doing things. I know he...*arranges* things for people. But I can't do a damned thing about it because Eliot has the same philosophy. And as long as he's still the owner of Tiki Island, I can't change it."

"So Bachman is running hookers through here. I pretty much figured it. Jessica Rutledge works for him."

"Yes," she said, "I wasn't sure if you knew that. I wasn't going to be the one to tell you. You had to find out for yourself."

"You know you're talking to a vice cop, right?" I said with a half-smile.

She smiled too. "You're a little out of your jurisdiction, aren't you Detective?"

"Maybe. I could call the Sheriff."

"But you won't," she said teasingly.

"No," I said, "I won't." She was right. It made me sick, but it wasn't my business.

Unless I made it my business.

"Just out of curiosity, dollface, what if old man Hawthorn's wildest dreams came true, and we got all nice and hitched and I left the police racket and became your partner in running this joint. What would happen then?"

Her answer was very serious. "Then Eliot would sign over the entire estate to me, and the first thing I'd do is fire Rutger and end the little side-business he's running."

I finished my Navy Grog...helluva strong drink, by the way...and held up the key to room 322. "You can start putting a dent in things tonight, if you're up for it."

She smiled.

Melinda and I stood in front of the door to room 322 at three minutes to eight. We went over the plan one more time (it was a simple plan) and got ready. Melinda moved a few feet away and I knocked.

Penelope opened the door wearing a silk robe and slippers. Her makeup was fresh and a little gaudy. A radio played softly in a corner, generic Rockabilly. "Come on in, sugar," she said with that southern lilt. I walked in and shut the door. "Have a drink?" she asked and poured herself a Jim Beam, neat.

"Same as you're having is fine," I said and sat on a chair by the bed. The room was small, much smaller than my suite, but still decorated with plenty of bamboo and rattan. A black velvet painting of a nude woman laying on a tropical beach in the moonlight hung over the headboard. Imagine that.

Penelope turned and handed me the drink. Her belt slipped, and the robe opened slightly leaving her secrets exposed. "Here sugar," she said and leaned down to hand me the drink. I got an eyeful.

"You're coming undone," I said.

"Oh dear, I am," she said and let the robe slide to the floor.

She stood their naked with one hand on her hip and the other holding her lowball. Her cream-white skin reminded me more of New York chicks than the tan variety found here in the Keys, but she was a taught-bodied beauty nonetheless. I didn't say a word. I just waited for the knock.

It didn't come.

Penelope took a long belt of her drink, put it on the table and came over to me in the chair. She sat on my lap, straddling the chair with her long, strong legs and hooking her hands around the back of my neck. She closed her eyes and began to twist her hips, swaying with the music from the radio. She leaned down to kiss me and found my lips. Hers were burning hot. Mine were cold. Funny, but all I could think of was Melinda, and why she hadn't knocked yet.

Penelope slid forward, pressing her breasts against my face. Normally I'd be all over the chick, but not tonight, not like this, not with Melinda on my mind.

I gently pushed her away and said, "Hand me my drink, will you sweetheart?" She did, and finally the knock came at the door. "Expecting company?" I asked. She got a very concerned expression on her face and said, "No, you?"

"Maybe," I said.

She jumped off and threw the robe back on as the second knock came. "Just a minute," she said and tying the belt, opened the door.

Melinda stood there smiling. "Is Mr. Riggins here?" she asked cheerfully.

"Uh," Penelope said and looked at me. I nodded. "Yes, he's here. Won't y'all come in?" Melinda entered the room and sat on the bed. "Hello William," she said.

"Hello dollface. Do you know Penelope?"

"I don't believe we've met," she said and held out her hand. "Hello Penelope. I'm Melinda Hawthorn. I own this place."

Penelope looked confused and a little afraid. The freshness had left her face. "I don't understand. I...I'm a guest. I was just..."

"Can it doll," I said flipping my badge. I was far enough away that she couldn't see it was a New York badge. "We know you work for Rutger Bachman."

"Oh. Oh, my," she said and sunk to the bed. "I...I don't know what to say."

"Don't say anything, kid. Just play along and you won't get into any trouble."

She looked at me, then Melinda, then back at me. "Play along? Well all right mistuh, but I don't do no girl-girl shows, at least I ain't yet, so it may not be so good…"

Melinda let out a yelp, then she started laughing. "Oh, dear, you think that I…that we…oh, no dear, no it's nothing like that." I laughed too, although the thought didn't sound all that bad to me. Oh well.

Penelope looked even more confused. "Oh, my mistake. Then what do you want?"

I picked the telephone off the nightstand and handed it to her on the bed. The wire just reached. "Call Bachman. Tell him Mr. Riggins needs to see him here in your room right away. Tell him to bring another bottle of Jim Beam, too."

Reluctantly Penelope dialed the front desk and asked to have Bachman paged. We waited a few minutes and he called up. She told him what I said to, and hung up. "He'll be here in a few minutes," she said, and finished off her drink. "Mind if I have another?"

"Go right ahead," I said. She did.

A few minutes later there was a knock at the door. I answered. "Hello, Bachman," I said with a big smile. "Thanks for coming up." He stood there with a bottle of Bourbon in his hand, looking uncharacteristically nervous. I held the door so he couldn't see Melinda.

"Hello Mr. Riggins. Is there a problem? Something you need?"

"Small problem," I said and let the door swing open. He saw Melinda sitting there with an angered look on her face. He said nothing, but his face wore surprise and regret.

"Come on in, let's chat," I said, and he did.

"Getting crowded in here," Penelope said while pouring herself another drink. She was nervous.

"Don't worry," Melinda said, "We won't be long. Bachman, you're exposed."

"I don't know what you're talking about," he said with a half laugh. "Is this some kind of prank? If it is, I don't get it."

"No prank, Jack. You do realize I'm a cop, right?"

"Yes, a homicide Detective."

"See, that's where you got your facts all jumbled. I'm a vice cop. Catching that murderer was a favor. Generally I nail pushers, hookers, conmen, gambling rings, *pimps*…stuff like that. Ya dig?"

"I don't understand."

"What's to understand? We know Ms. Penelope here is a prostitute." Penelope cringed and sucked down her drink in one shot. "We know you run hookers here from Largo and Key West. I know you're tied to the Low Key club down there, and the prostitution that goes on. And I know Jessica Rutledge works for you."

Bachman was silent a moment, then said, "You can't prove any of that. You can't prove…."

"I'm not interested in having you arrested, Rutger," Melinda said. "But I don't have to prove anything to fire you,"

Bachman turned to her and with his smarmiest voice said, "Mr. Hawthorn is aware of these activities and has given his approval."

"Mr. Hawthorn feels he is no longer capable of making intelligent decisions concerning the Resort, and has relinquished control of Tiki Island to his sole heir, yours truly." She gave her chest a little tap as she said it, one of those "I'm the big cheese" gestures. "So if you want to keep your position, I suggest you close up shop on your little side business tonight, and stick to running the housekeeping and gardening staffs." She rose from the bed and I did too. "Good night, Ms. –"

"Oh, uh Smith. Penelope Smith."

"Right," she said, "Good night Ms. Smith. Please have your things packed and be ready to leave tonight on the nine o'clock boat to Key West." She turned to Bachman. "Bachman, if you have any other ladies here in your employ, tell them to do the same. And please return the keys to rooms three-twenty to three-twenty-five to my office, tonight. That's all. Please leave."

Bachman said nothing. He remained haughty and left without closing the door. Penelope got her suitcase out from the closet; it was already mostly packed. "I'm very sorry, y'all," she said as she packed. "I'm just a workin' girl trying to earn a livin'. I had no idea someone else ran the place. He told me he was the owner."

"I'll bet he told you a lot of things that turned out to be lies, didn't he," I said more than asking. "I'll bet the first time he bedded you he told you that you were special, didn't he. Then he asked you to do a favor for a friend, and gave you a couple of bucks for it, didn't he."

"Somethin' like that," she said sadly.

"Kid, there's more to life than this. Try to stay away from the Bachmans of the world and you just might be all right." I took Melinda by the arm and we left, shutting the door behind us. Melinda was shaking.

Heading to the elevator I asked, "Was that true, what you said about Hawthorn giving over the hotel to you?"

"Yes, it was."

"How did you swing that?"

"I made a deal with him."

"What kind of a deal?"

She paused to hit the Lobby floor on the elevator buttons. "I told him I'd marry you," she said. I don't know if the knot in my gut was from the elevator or Melinda.

Bachman was no idiot. He left room 322 and went straight for Hawthorn's apartment on the other side of the hotel. He was steaming, but by the time he knocked on Hawthorn's door he had regained his regal composure.

He knocked, waited, knocked again...The special knock that Hawthorn had taught him so he'd know it was Bachman.

He waited longer. Finally he heard the deadbolts thrown back, the chain unchained. The door opened to an eerily dark room with a dim light cast by a single candle. Bachman entered and the door shut behind him, along with the three locks. From the darkness near the door came a tired voice.

"Sit down Rutger," Hawthorn said. Bachman did as he said, sitting on a carved-wood seat next to a giant stone fireplace. His eyes adjusted to the darkness as Hawthorn emerged from the shadows. "What brings you to my loft at so late an hour, my friend?"

"It's Melinda, sir. She and that Detective from New York. They've discovered our...network."

"Oh dear," Hawthorn said and sat across from Bachman in a large bamboo rocker. He sipped hot tea and brandy from a vintage mug. "How did this happen?"

"I don't know. That's not very important. What is important is that your *daughter*," he put such loathing into the word that Hawthorn flinched, "has taken it upon herself to disband the operation, and has told me we are no longer to have ladies entertain our guests."

"Did she"? Hawthorn whispered to himself.

"And furthermore, sir, I believe she has completely out-stepped her authority. She told me that you have given her total control over the Resort, because you are too incompetent to run it yourself," Bachman added with even more disgust. "Can you imagine the nerve?"

"Well, yes, I can." Hawthorn finished his tea and poured himself another brandy. He offered none to Bachman. "I must say I am a little surprised."

"Surprised? What an understatement. You should be furious, sir."

"Furious? No, not at all. Jubilant if anything."

"Jubilant? Are you…I mean, wait, what *do* you mean?"

"I mean Rutger that I *have* given her that authority, on a single condition: That she marry that fine Detective from New York and settle in here to run the Island together. I suppose she must have made her decision. I should be very happy for her."

"Good God, man, what did you do that for?" Rutger was beside himself. The outrage he felt earlier was nothing compared to what was happening to his boiling blood now. "Don't you realize what that means?"

"I suppose it means you'll be out of a job if you don't listen to Melinda from now on. Come Monday I'm announcing her as Executive Director of Operations, and you'll be working for her, directly."

Bachman rose and helped himself to a brandy without asking. He drank it down fast and almost missed the table with the bottle in the darkness. "Listen to me, Mr. Hawthorn. If you allow this to happen you'll have undone years of work setting just the right people and events in motion to run things the right way. And if we lose that, the hotel will lose its most prominent clients, and a lot of the things we get away with will become impossible to do. Do you understand me?"

"Perhaps it is time for some changes, Rutger. The world is changing around us. Rhythm and Blues music is replacing traditional standards. Television is replacing radio. People want faster cars and longer vacations. Perhaps those Very Important People you cater to aren't all that important anymore."

"You're talking insanely, with all due respect, sir. The world is the same. Men still want to have a good time when they're here and that includes not only the finest food and drinks but the finest women to sleep with and the finest narcotics to help them sleep. Take that away and we're just another hotel on the water."

Hawthorn suddenly grew angry. He rose from his chair and smacked his cane against the floor. "You hold your tongue, Bachman. Tiki Island will *never* be just another Hotel." His words were shaky but stern. The anger showed on his face, even in the low candlelight. "No matter what you think, no one comes here for the hookers and drugs. Certainly they have in the past, and that's how things were before the Resort was here. But I say this place is a wonderland, a place of mystery and beauty. We may have needed the girls to get things going, but today Tiki Island can stand on her own. And if you can't see that, Rutger, perhaps it is time for us to part." He sat back down, breathless.

Bachman rose once again and straightened his tie. "Sir, I have no intention of leaving this place or dissolving our relationship. In fact, I think you should reconsider Melinda's appointment as Executive Director before you announce it. I think you should consider me for the appointment, and I think you know why."

Hawthorn stopped cold. "Are you *blackmailing* me, Bachman?"

"Just pointing out that I know a few things about you that you'd not like the public to know. A few small things, old things but nevertheless important things.

Things from your past you thought would remain buried, if you know what I mean."

"Get out, Bachman," Hawthorn said. "Leave my room now."

"Certainly sir. I'll be back tomorrow for your answer. I think I know what it is already." Bachman gave a short bow and unlocking the door himself, left. Hawthorn quickly set the locks behind him, went back to his chair, and poured another brandy.

In the dark the voices came, then the apparitions, and he ended his torment for one more night with the little yellow pill prescribed by his doctor.

### Saturday Night

Melinda and I took a private reserved table in the Hukilau dining room at around eight-thirty. A guitarist and bongo player along with low, colored lighting set the pre-show mood. Melinda had phoned our orders ahead, so appetizers of shrimp cocktail, chicken satay and crab Rangoon were already waiting for us when we sat.

"You really know how to set up an evening," I said to Melinda as we sat. "Nice touch."

"I was in a much better mood an hour ago when I set this up," she said sulkily.

"Oh, come on kid, don't be that way. Things are gonna change now, you'll see. With or without me, they'll change." I raised my glass to her. "Here's to the future, with you at the helm."

She raised her glass back, and said, "And here's lookin' at you, kid," which made me smile.

We didn't talk much about Bachman or room 322 or even about the Resort. Somehow the conversation turned away from those unpleasantries and settled on each other. I told her all about my home in Weehawken and my apartment in the city, about Fast Freddie and Jerry, about the dive bars and hash joints I called home. She told me about her early days in California, about being schooled right here on the Island, and about how easy it was for her to learn four languages but how algebra left her flat. We laughed and ate a dinner that would have impressed the greatest chefs of the world.

Then precisely at nine, the stage lights dimmed and an announcer called out, "And now ladies and gentlemen, for your entertainment pleasure, direct from Hawaii, Martin Denny." The applause shook the house as the stage lights came up. "Black Orchid" rang out of the vibes, and for the second time I felt that I was actually in Hawaii.

"This is better than Hawaii," Melinda said as if reading my mind. "You only have to go a hundred miles to hit the mainland here."

"And Hawaii doesn't have *you*, kitten." She actually blushed a little.

We finished our dinner just as the band finished their first set. For dessert we had a sort of Crème Brule with tropical fruits, and Melinda introduced me to the exotic coffee drinks on the menu. I settled on something with chocolate liqueur and rum; it came flaming and almost scared me to death. Melinda laughed and we stayed on through the second set of Martin Denny's incredible, mysterious Exotica music.

After the second set was finished we decided to take a walk around the Island. I led the way through the tables holding Melinda's hand. It was nice.

"I love the beach at night," she said. "There's magic in the moonlight.

Sometimes I even see the essences of old frigates and pirate ships out in the Gulf."

"Essences? You mean like ghost ships?"

"Yes!" she said laughing. "Of course it helps if you've been drinking a lot of rum."

"I'm sure it does." We found ourselves on the North Beach again, in a fairly secluded spot away from the lights of the Hotel. A few couples were sitting on blankets looking out over the surf.

"Sit with me," she said softly.

"We haven't got a blanket."

"Sure we have, wait here" she said, and made her way over to a little cabana. She returned with a giant beach blanket decorated with palm trees. "I have a key to everything," she said.

"Including my heart, it would seem." We spread the blanket out on the shore and looked out at the Gulf. Lights from ships twinkled in the distance. A cool summer breeze kept things perfect.

"So, William, what do you think of all this, really?"

I took a deep breath and looked over at her. She was perfect in the moonlight. "I think it's paradise."

"So do I," she replied and leaned against my side. We just stayed like that for a while, then she kissed me out of the blue. It was a nice kiss, a very loving kiss, not filled with fire like the night before but with plenty of emotion. At least that's how I felt it.

I opened my eyes and was surprised to see someone walking very close behind her, so surprised I jumped back.

"What's wrong?"

"Nothing, that woman just startled me, that's all."

"What woman?"

I turned and looked all around. No one was to be found within thirty yards of us. "I swear, I just saw…aw, that's just crazy."

"No, nothing's crazy on Tiki Island, William. I told you before I've seen some strange things myself."

So had I, but I wasn't about to spill the Key West haunted house story to her just yet.

"Probably just too much rum. That stuff knocks me on my ass."

"William!" she laughed and kissed me again. This time the fire was back. I was getting antsy.

"Listen, why don't we move on, maybe find somewhere without any ghosts?"

"You mean like my room?" she said flirtingly.

"Am I that obvious?" I said.

"Don't be coy." She got up and I did too. "I'm just as anxious as you are," she said and gave me another passionate kiss, one that had me going wild. "Let's go. Leave the blanket."

With that, we headed up to her room.

The phone rang at one a.m. We were both exhausted and could barely move, but she managed to pick it off the receiver before the second ring.

"Hello? Yes, of course…no, it's all right Eliot, calm down, I'll be there in a minute." She said nothing to me as she rose from the bed, her naked body silhouetted against the open window for just a few seconds before she threw the silk robe over her back. She grabbed a brush from her vanity and ran it through her hair.

"Eliot needs me, William. He's having nightmares again. I'm afraid I'll need to stay with him until he falls asleep again, which could be a while. You're welcome to stay here, or go back to your own suite if you want." She turned to me. "I'm sorry, darling, but you must understand…"

"I do," I said. "Go on, do what you have to do for your old man. I'll catch you tomorrow."

"Breakfast at nine?" she asked.

"Make it ten. I'm on vacation."

She smiled, leaned over and kissed me again with the fire that brought me up here. "Breakfast in your room at eleven," she said. "*I'll* be there at ten."

"You're on." She blew me a kiss and left through the hall, presumably through the connecting room with all the photos. I threw my clothes on and wandered back to my room where I almost immediately fell back asleep.

I got a loud banging in my head around nine-thirty Sunday morning. I'd been dreaming of walking down Broadway at night, dodging bullets from gangsters with Tommy guns. The machine gun fire turned into knocking at my door, and when I realized I wasn't full of holes, I got up and opened it.

"Your nine-thirty wakeup call, Mr. Riggins, as requested. And this is for you." The porter handed me a small package wrapped in green tissue paper. I handed him a buck and said, "Thanks kid."

Nine-thirty wake up call. That was Melinda's idea, of course. She wanted me to be awake when she got here at ten. I turned the box over to open it only to find a little card that said, "Not until I get here, M". I tossed the box on couch and headed for the shower.

I was shaved and ready at three minutes to ten. Melinda showed up one minute later.

"Hello kitten," I said as she walked into the room. She was wearing a yellow sundress with an open back. I closed the door. She turned to me and in one quick move the dress was on the floor.

"Now, where were we?" she said, and came to me.

"Right here, I think."

Exactly an hour later room service showed up with the biggest breakfast I'd ever seen in my life. They served it to us in bed, no less. Even the coffee was fantastic.

"It's from the Isle of Kona, in Hawaii," Melinda told me. "The richest in the world."

"It's good Java, this Kona," I said and for some reason she laughed.

"What time do you have to be back at work?" I asked, looking at the clock. It was after eleven.

"I don't," she said, "Today I'm all yours."

"Groovy. What's the plan?"

She jumped out of the bed and took a bite out of an apple. "I thought we'd spend the day in Miami."

"That could be fun. Except my car is all the way the hell down in Key West."

She threw me the apple. "No problem. I have a car on Sugarloaf. You drive. I'm taking a shower. You next."

"Me next nothing," I said, "That shower is big enough for two."

We left a lot later than we intended.

We took the launch to Sugarloaf Key, and walked down the dock to a building that wasn't quite a warehouse, but was too large to be a garage. The building was old but well cared for. On the side a sign read, "Hawthorn Industries. Private."

"In here," Melinda said. She used a key to open a box next to a large garage door, and pushed a big red button inside. The garage door opened on an automatic motor.

"*That's* your car?"

Staring me in the face was the reddest Cadillac convertible I ever saw. It was a 1939 model in new condition with more chrome on the grill than most cars had all around.

"Yep. It was Eliot's. He gave it to me for my birthday a few years back. Do you like it?"

"It's swell," I said. "A real class job."

"I had the attendant gas it up, clean it up and put the top down for us. Here," she said, and handed me the keys on a custom Cadillac leather key fob. "It's a Hydromatic. Very easy to drive. And if the sun gets too hot, it's air conditioned."

"Sweet ride," I said and started her up. The big V8 engine purred under the hood. I dropped the selector into drive, let go of the brake and the car eased out of the garage like the queen she was.

"I wouldn't take her over eighty on the Overseas Highway, William. The road's too narrow. Wait until we get to Homestead to really open her up."

Which I did.

## Sunday Afternoon

Rutger Bachman hung up the phone in his office. His man in Miami had his orders, and that should take care of things without much further problems. He hated doing things like this, but was ever mindful of how important they were. He made his orders clear: Melinda was to remain unharmed, but frightened. Riggins was to be dealt with separately.

He leaned back in his red leather chair, the only piece like it in the otherwise tropical-themed Resort. Bachman's entire office was out of sync with Tiki Island; modern walnut bookshelves, striped carpet and an Eames desk clashed with each other and with the décor of the Resort, but Bachman didn't want any of the bamboo and rattan 'junk' that filled the Island. It was a matter of pure fact that Bachman hated tropical décor. He tolerated it because the climate agreed with him, and it was the only five-star resort in the area. He had made himself a small fortune at Tiki Island and wasn't about to stop collecting his easy money now.

Bachman was a confident man. With Riggins out of the way and Melinda frightened into submission, he could go back to Hawthorn and demand that Executive Director title. If Hawthorn refused, he still had the ace in the hole…his knowledge of Hawthorn's past, and the things he'd done. Bachman didn't really care what Hawthorn did so many years ago, but he did know that Eliot Hawthorn's name still meant a great deal in South Florida and the Keys, and he knew Hawthorn would do anything to protect that name. He had him cold. And to think, it was just a simple error that led him to find out the truth, an error that anyone could have made but never did.

A hot breeze blew through Bachman's window. He didn't mind. He liked the heat.

He was about to bring some heat on himself.

Melinda directed me to park in front of an art deco-style hotel on A-1-A in Miami Beach.

"This is one of our hotels. We own it but we don't run it. It's leased out to an entrepreneur. They have an excellent restaurant and live music at lunch."

"We just finished breakfast!" I said.

"Don't worry, they serve lunch until four. Let's spend some time on the beach."

We spent about an hour on the sand, then had lunch in the little hotel. She was right, the food was tops. After lunch we drove off the beach to a place called Parrot Jungle. It was a cool tropical jungle with plenty of real parrots, hence the name. It really was a happening place, filled with tourists taking snapshots and trying to talk to the birds. Later we drove over to a very crazy place called The Coral Castle. The whole joint was carved out of coral rock and built by some cat who had nothing but a hand saw and a couple of homemade leverage tools. Yet it was amazing, with some of the rocks weighing tons.

"He built this to show his love for a woman who never loved him back," Melinda said. "I met him a few times. A nice man, but a little strange. He used to charge ten cents to see the castle. Now it's a quarter."

"Sounds like a kook to me."

"A kook? Maybe. But a romantic one."

The sun was getting low in the sky. The coral sculptures cast long shadows across the courtyard, giving the place an eerie, mythical atmosphere. Honestly, I'd had enough of eerie for one trip.

"How about we get back to the beach. I hear Miami has some swingin' big bands."

"Yes they do. As a matter of fact, Benny Goodman is playing tonight."

"Goodman!? Where?"

"At the Jackie Gleason Theater. See!" She opened the little green package and held up two tickets, front row of course.

"You are such a doll," I said and gave her a big kiss. Maybe the Coral Castle was romantic, after all.

Goodman started swinging with "Let's Dance" at five after eight. The concert was fantastic. Harry James and Hellen O'Connel appeared as guests and it was just like the old days when they played New York and Atlantic City. Even Melinda got into the swing of things and was be-bopping along with the tunes. Afterwards we had drinks in the lobby and we got to shake Goodman's hand. A nice guy, that Benny. A real hep cat.

We were flying high on cloud nine until we left the theater. I didn't valet the car as I didn't trust the kid with such a classic, and we had to park around the back. As we walked through to the back lot, I realized we weren't alone.

Out of the shadows two goons appeared. One had his hand in his jacket pocket. It was obviously on a gun.

"Stop right there, Riggins," the goon with the gun said. "We've got business."

"If you work for Roberts, forget it. That guy's going up the river for a long time."

"Not Roberts. This is a message from Mr. Bachman."

Melinda said, "Bachman?" and before she could take another breath the goon without the gun grabbed her and held her mouth closed. I went for him but goon-one took the gun out of his pocket. It had a silencer. He gave me the "no no no" signal with his gloved left hand, then let that hand fly. It hit me square in the jaw and knocked me on my ass.

I went into cop mode so fast I took myself by surprise. As I went down, I formed a plan. I had the .38 on my side but there was no way I'd reach it before he got a shot off. So when I hit the deck I rolled right into Melinda and the mug holding her. They tumbled on top of me and that gave me just the time I needed to pull my piece. I kept it hidden and got them off of me, but got an elbow in the side from the goon on the ground before I could make a move. It hurt hard. I could feel my muscles turn to ice on that side. But it gave me focus. The guy with the gun was only five feet away and his attention was on Melinda as she tried to run off. He didn't shoot. Instead goon-two made a grab for her and missed. That was my chance. I pulled the rod and let one rip. It hit goon-one like a bulldozer in the middle of his chest. He went down and didn't get up.

The other guy saw what was happening and a giant chop slammed down on my hand, knocking the rod away. He came back swinging and caught me under the chin. It almost flattened me, but adrenaline was pumping through my blood faster than a Blue Comet. I went with the punch and rolled again, and when I stopped I was able to land my heel right in the guy's face. Twice. He stumbled and fell backwards; I pounced on him like a tiger and brought my elbow down into his chest. I could hear the ribs crack as his eyes bulged with the stinging pain that punctured his lungs. He gasped and I came down on him again. Just like they taught me in Korea, no prisoners.

When it was over, Melinda was out of sight. I picked up my piece from the ground and checked goon-one. He was gone. They both were.

I'd have a lot of explaining to do to the Miami police.

Bachman went to Eliot's apartment at four in the afternoon. Eliot talked to him through the door.

"Go away, Rutger. I have no business with you."

"Have you considered my offer?"

"Not in the least."

"You'll feel differently tomorrow," Bachman said with a touch of evil. "Believe me."

I found Melinda sitting in the car shaking. She'd been crying and her makeup was a smeared mess. "There's nothing to worry about, dollface. Those goons won't be hurting anyone ever again."

"William, they…they work for *Rutger*. They were going to kill us."

"Not kill us, I think, just bust us up a little. Send a message."

"What message?"

"To leave him alone, of course. Let him run things his way. Funny, I pegged him as a slime ball, but not the type to use muscle. He'll get his, kitten, don't you worry. In the meantime I'm afraid we've got to report this to the Miami cops."

"Oh, no William!" she screamed, "Please no, let's just go. They'll never know it was us."

"Sorry kid, it doesn't work that way. Cops aren't dumb, you know. They'll know we were here. The tickets were bought in your name. They'll know I carry a .38 and that I'd been attacked once already on this trip. Wouldn't take much for them to figure things out."

"Then can we…can we at least leave Bachman out, for now? Can we keep the Island out of it? You know what a scandal there would be if the newspapers got a hold of this. We're talking international, William. Please?"

I thought it over. Our testifying that they *said* they worked for Bachman wouldn't stick much. "OK, we don't say they mentioned Bachman. I'll say I suspect they worked for Roberts, which is true. OK?"

"Yes," she said. "Thank you."

"Don't mention it."

An hour and a half later we were released from the Miami police department. We gave our statements three times to six different officers. They wanted to make sure we were telling the truth, and besides leaving out the name Bachman, we were. There would be a lot of complicated paperwork and some explaining to do back in the City, but for now we were free without charges, acting in self-defense.

"Some crazy vacation," I said to Melinda as we headed out of the station. "I've been beat up twice, been hustled by hookers more times than I can imagine, shot a cop and killed two goons."

Melinda shuddered. "You talk as if you kill people all the time. Those men may have been criminals, but did they really deserve to die?"

She was still shaking. I think this was the first time she'd ever been exposed to anything so bad, so evil. I turned her to face me. Tears hung in her eyes. "No one deserves to but everybody does. Some people just bring it on themselves faster. In a situation like that, it was them or us. I'll pick us anytime."

"But did you have to…*kill* them?"

"No kid, but that's the way it played out. They had a gun, I had a gun. Bullets fly. Sometimes they miss. Sometimes they hit solid. That's that.""Aren't you even the least bit sorry?"

I looked at her funny. "No, I'm not. Not the least."

"How –"

"They wanted to hurt you, and I'd kill or be killed myself to keep that from happening." She melted into my arms, sobbing softly. I held her tight, brought her in so close that she almost became part of me. I never held a woman that close in my life, never wanted to.

She didn't want to let go, but I finally eased her off and said, "Let's get out of here, dollface."

"Let's go home," she said timidly, and we left Miami. By one a.m. we were back on Tiki Island, safe and sound in my suite.

## Sunday Night

The call came at three-thirty a.m. We'd barely fallen asleep when the incessant ringing belted our ears and shook us out of bed. Melinda, afraid it was Eliot, nearly jumped out of her skin. I took the call on the fifth ring and answered in as annoyed a voice as possible.

It was the doctor from Key West.

"Mr. Riggins? Dr. Watson here. I'm with Ms. Rutledge."

"Ms. Rutledge and I have parted ways, doctor."

"Well, she was asking for you. Mr. Riggins, she almost died tonight. Heroin overdose. Someone found her on the beach with the needle still in her arm."

*In her arm!*

I was silent. Why should I care? Just another juiced up hooker gone too far. Right? Then why did I care?

"What do you want me to do about it?" I asked the doctor in a not-so-nice way. Melinda was beside me now, trying to hear what was going on.

"Mr. Riggins, you helped her once, I thought you might try to help her again. I don't think...I don't believe this was an accident."

I thought about that. Suicide. Sure, why not? The voices, the hauntings, the all-around wreck her life had become. She thought she loved me and threw it away for China Red and the life around it. It made sense, in a way.

And I was a cop. Sworn to protect the public. Vacation or not, if I didn't do something to help this chick then I'd be a bigger hypocrite than the jackasses I always put down, the ones that ran for office and abused their power, the ones who complained about crime and the justice system but didn't do a thing to change it. I wasn't bound by law to help her, but I was bound by a code. My code.

"Where is she now, doctor?"

"She's at my office."

"I can be there in around an hour," I said, and Melinda looked shocked. He gave me the address and I hung up.

"What's going on?" Melinda asked somewhat fearfully.

"This may not make any sense to you, but it's Jessica. She's overdosed on Horse. The doctor said she almost bit it."

"My God, that's terrible! So you're going to see her?"

"Yeah."

"Can I ask why?" There was no jealousy in her voice, only question and concern.

"The doc said she asked for me. I don't know, maybe I can help her. Maybe I can put her on the right track and talk her out of this goofed-up life she created for herself. Maybe I..."

"You have feelings for her, don't you," she said, again not jealously, just a little hurt. I turned to her and looked her straight in the eye. "Melinda, I'd be lying if I said I didn't feel *something* for her. But I feel something much stronger for you. Her, I just want to help. I *have* to help her. I'd be the biggest heel on the planet and a lousy cop too if I didn't at least try to set the girl right. But it ends there, kiddo. No matter how things play out between you and me, anything I had with Jessica Rutledge is finished. Over and out. Class dismissed. All that's left now is, can you trust me?"

She thought a minute, didn't answer right away. There was a lot of truth and a touch of sadness in her voice when she spoke. "I don't know William, like you said before, we've only known each other a couple of days. On Friday you'll check out, and unless you decide to turn your whole life upside-down you'll go back to New York and be a cop and I'll stay here and run Tiki Island. Can I trust you? I think so. Does our relationship warrant trust? I think probably not."

Man, she was a sharp cookie. Melinda had to be the only dame I ever met who put reason before her emotions. "Good point, kid. And very true. This is all for fun right now, right?" She nodded a quiet yes. "Neither of us really knows what's going to happen at the end of the week, do we?"

She put her head on my chest and I held her gently.

"I'll tell you what. Why don't you come with me?"

Melinda looked up. She certainly seemed surprised. "Come with you? To Key West?"

"Yeah, to Key West. You know Jessica too. She's worked for you and if your opinion of her hasn't changed she'll probably work for you again. No reason on Earth why you shouldn't come along. She might listen to you more than me anyway."

"No, William, I can't. It's already after three and I have a full day of work ahead of me tomorrow."

"Let Bachman do it."

"It's his day off."

"Frig him, call him in. You're the boss now."

"Sure, that sounds fine when you say it. I can guarantee he's already off-island. No, I'll have to stay here and take care of things on this end. But I'll tell you what I will do for Ms. Rutledge, as a friend of yours and as a good employee she's been for us. If she needs to get away from Key West for a while, she can stay here, in one of the rooms that Bachman had reserved. It's the least I can do."

"Thanks kid. That's a nice thing to do."

"Just make sure she's OK, William," she said and nearly choked up. "Then come home to me." Melinda kissed me again with that fire that burned through my heart and soul and made me wish I never heard of the cop business or New York or any of it. Then she softly slid away and said, "I'll wake up the Captain and have a fast boat waiting for you at the dock in ten minutes. She quietly dressed and left.

"Here we go, Mr. Reeggins. Got here mighty mighty fast, it's only four-thirty." This Captain was different from the one on the Tiki Express. He was rougher, older, very dark skinned and talked with a strange island accent and yes, he actually had a hook for a left hand. A chrome one, a double that he could open and shut. Every time he clicked it I shuddered. "Should I wait here for ya or are you comin' back on the Express?"

"I'm not sure how long I'll be, but I'd really rather take the private boat back with you. I can give you a couple of bucks for a room."

"No bother, Mr. Reeggins. I have plenty friends in Key West where I can stow my carcass for a night."

"Groovy. How about we meet back here at ten?"

"Aye, that works for me, Mr. Reeggins. Ten o'clock, that be fine."

The shack with the keys to my car was closed up, but unlocked. I fished through the keys until I found the one with the Hertz U-Drive key fob and was off to the doctor's house. The doc lived in an 1890s-vintage three-story, not unlike Jessica's old place, but much nicer. Verandas held up by white columns adorned the front of the house, and the railings had interesting decorations carved into the posts. When I got a little closer, I saw they were carved in the shape of stethoscopes. Nice.

I knocked lightly on the door. A minute later an older woman in a maid's uniform answered. She directed me to the back room where Jessica was laying on a single bed.

She looked horrible and beautiful and the same time, if you can picture it.

Her skin was pasty-white and there were dark rings around her eyes, but seeing her, alive, made me want to get on my knees and thank God someone got to her before it was too late. That stirring inside me started again. Melinda was right. I still felt something for her. Dammit.

The doctor came in behind me. "Don't wake her yet, Mr. Riggins. I finally got her stabilized and the rest is good for her right now."

"When can she be moved?"

"A few hours, I think. What did you have in mind?"

"I can take her back to the Resort, if she'll come. She's worked there before and the owner's daughter knows her. She said she'd put her up there as long as it takes to get her clean."

"That's nice of her. Although I don't really think she's a junkie. More of an occasional user, does it when she gets it."

"I don't know about that, doc. I've seen a lot of people in my day who said they could take it or leave it, but they always took it as much as they could. Horse is a mean drug. It screws with people's heads, makes them believe life is better when they use it. Nothing could be farther from the truth."

"I know. And I agree. But I also know this town, and most of the people in it. I know her supplier."

"Seriously?"

"Yes. And no, I won't give you that information because he's a patient. If you want his name you'll have to go through legal channels."

"I'm on vacation," I said, disgusted.

"Good. Then I can tell you I phoned him and asked him point blank, and he told me she only shoots up a few times now and then. He said he hadn't sold her anything for weeks, until Friday night."

"Friday night. Figures," I said. "So what you're saying is that if she's not a junkie, she's just stupid."

"Maybe not in those words…"

"She needs someone to believe in, doc. She needs to know she can have a different life if she wants it."

"That would certainly help her."

"Yeah," I said, knowing that was a long-term commitment. One I was in no position to make. Maybe a few days ago when things were different. I dunno.

In the middle of my thoughts the doc said to me, "Did she mention anything to you about visions, or voices, Mr. Riggins?"

No kidding, I thought. "Yeah, she did. She sees things. Apparitions. Ghosts. They tell her things but she can't understand them, usually. Why do you ask?"

"She believes these things as true. I tried to tell her they were probably brought on by the drug. She told me they were not."

"And what do you think, doc?"

"I don't know what to think. Jessica told me she drinks and takes drugs to silence the voices, stop the apparitions from coming. She says when her senses are dull, only then can she not see or hear them."

"So that makes her sort of crazy in the head, doesn't it."

"Not necessarily."

I wished the doctor would get to the point. So what the hell, I said, "Get to the point, doc."

"There are a lot of things we as scientists don't yet understand. I believe Ms. Rutledge *is* seeing ghosts."

Well, that was easy. "Seriously? And what do you base this on, as a scientist."

"I've seen things with my very own eyes, Mr. Riggins. Strange things. Inexplicable things. And I think you have too."

"Let's leave me out of this for the time being. What have you seen, doc?"

"I have a patient down on Eaton Street. When he was just a boy, his five-year-old brother died of consumption. To help with his grieving, the Haitian housekeeper sewed a doll for him and told him his brother's spirit lived on in the doll. As the boy grew into a man, he kept the doll, telling everyone he knew that his brother's spirit did indeed inhabit the doll. He married but had no children. The doll, however, remained an integral part of his life. He furnished the entire third floor of his home with doll-sized furniture and posed the doll in different rooms doing different things. His wife came to me one day and told me she was worried, not for her husband's sanity, but because she was quite certain the doll had moved on its own. Over the next few years I visited that house, and saw that doll many times. It never moved when you were looking at it, but if you turned your back for just a second, Mr. Riggins, it would certainly move. I witnessed this myself on several occasions."

"You saw the doll move."

"No, I saw it placed on a chair in a corner of the room; we locked the room and had supper, everyone accounted for. Afterwards we unlocked the room. The doll was standing against the window, looking out on the opposite side of the room."

What is it about dolls and Key West? I thought. "Sounds creepy."

"Quite. I also have been to the Rutledge house in Old Town, Mr. Riggins."

"You have, huh?"

"Yes. And I believe you have too."

"I have. The place is nuts."

"So you saw…things…too?"

"Yeah. Things I don't understand. What do you make of it?"

"Well, Ms. Rutledge's mother was swept out to sea in the Great Atlantic Hurricane, as you know. I believe she's trying to contact her daughter."

"Assuming that's possible, why would she do it?"

"You're the detective. I was hoping maybe you could find out."

"But I'm on *vacation*."

As Riggins left for Key West, Melinda Hawthorn stealthily made her way back to her apartment. She wasn't surprised to find Eliot awake, waiting for her in his room.

"Thank you for coming again, my dear. It was the visions again. Vivian, I'm sure of it, and that other creature, the one with…"

"Please don't, Eliot. I don't need nightmares too."

"I'm sorry, my dear. Could you give me a snifter of brandy, please?" Eliot pulled the covers up close to his face as Melinda poured the Courvoisier. "I'm afraid things are getting worse, my dear. I can feel it. My past is catching up to me."

A pang of guilt echoed through Melinda's soul. "Oh, Eliot, you've been saying that for years now. And yet you never say what it is that's "catching up" to you."

"No, no I daren't. It's long forgotten and should stay as such."

Melinda tried to remain calm and talked to Eliot as nicely as she could, but it was very difficult under the circumstances. She knew Eliot was right; the doctor warned her that his condition…though not fully understood…was slowly killing him, eating away at his sanity and body.

"If it's forgotten," she said sweetly, "why do you keep repeating it?"

"Forgotten by some, not by others. Not by...*them*."

"Eliot, these things are all in your mind," she lied. "That's why they go away with pills and brandy."

"If only that were true my dear," he answered. "Melinda? Where were you earlier? I tried knocking until almost two."

Melinda blushed but in the dim light of Eliot's room, it couldn't be seen. She thought quickly and said, "I was in Miami with William. We didn't get back until very late."

"The boat came up at one," he said.

"We had a nightcap in the lobby bar," she lied again. She didn't want Eliot to know she'd slept with Riggins. She didn't know how he'd react to that, and didn't want to find out. It was her business anyway, but she felt that the man she had been closest to most of her life might not feel that way, and she certainly didn't want to hurt him.

"Ah, youth. I remember nights like that. A few drinks early in the blackness of night, sitting on the beach in the moonlight, walking along the eastern shore as the sun rose in a pink and black sky."

"We didn't get quite that far, Eliot," she said smiling.

"My dear, I hate to ask, but would you please stay with me tonight? I'm very...very concerned. I think something terrible may happen if you're not here with me."

Melinda moved over to the bed and laid down next to Hawthorn. "Ok, Eliot. I'll stay with you." She put her arm around him and closed her eyes, drifting off to sleep well before sunrise.

The doc offered me a guestroom to crash for a few hours before taking Jessica back to the Resort. I set the alarm on the nightstand for nine-thirty, and when it rang with that incessant clanging of steal on brass I nearly threw the damned thing through the window. Good thing I remembered it wasn't mine.

The doc was up, and had Jessica awake and alert. Her eyes got huge when they saw me. Then she smiled.

"Billy! You came!"

"Yeah kid, the doc telephoned me. How ya feeling?"

"Probably not as bad as I look."

"Hello doc. How is she, really?"

The doctor turned and said, "She can leave at any time. I believe the poison is out of her system now."

Poison. Yeah.

"Good deal." The doctor nodded and left the room. I leaned in close to Jessica and whispered, "Hey kid, what gives? I mean, what were you thinking, huh?"

"Bill, please don't. I just...I couldn't stand it anymore. You, the Low Key Club, Bachman, Roberts, and...*her*."

"You saw her again, on the beach?"

"Yes. She talked to me. I understood her this time."

That was a shocker. "Really...so what did she say?"

"One word, Billy. *Hawthorn*."

"Hawthorn? What do you think he's got to do with you?"

"I...I don't really understand any of this. I never have. I just know you saw her too, so I know I'm not kookie in the head. It's my *mother*, Bill. I'm sure of it. She's trying to tell me something but I don't want to know what it is!" She started to get a little weepy and I calmed her down.

"Look, kid, I want you to come back to the Island with me."

She lit up like a Christmas tree. "With you? You mean it Billy?"

"Yeah, I mean it. Melinda's going to let you stay in one of the rooms as long as you want."

"Melinda?"

"Yeah, she said she'll even find full-time work for you at the Resort if you want it. Roberts is out of the picture for good, and believe me when I tell you Bachman is next. You don't have to stay in the life. You can get out while you're still alive."

"A room at the Resort? Don't you want me to stay with you?" Her eyes were confused, pleading. I couldn't help but push back just a little, far away enough that I didn't have to answer. "Bill, I thought...I thought you came for me because...because you loved me. I thought you wanted me to be with *you*."

I froze. Maybe I did love her. She was sweet and beautiful and flawed. Or maybe I loved Melinda. She was sweet and beautiful and perfect. Or maybe I was crazy and didn't love anybody, and this whole thing would pop like a big balloon when I got back to my real life in New York. "Sweetheart, Jessica, things have changed a little now. Things are a little more complicated."

Tears started to well up in those beautiful blue eyes of hers. She spoke softly. "They've changed. You've changed. It's because I'm not the same person I was a few days ago, isn't it? It's because in your eyes I'm just a junkie and whore, a mistake you made along the way, isn't it?"

"No, Jessica. Things are different because you lied to me, and I could never trust you. But it doesn't mean I don't still have feelings for you. I still want to help you. We can be friends, but nothing more."

She sunk back down into the bed, her hands over her face. She kept repeating, "I'm sorry, I'm sorry."

"Don't be that way dollface. It wouldn't have mattered, in a week I'd be gone and you'd be here and that would be that anyway."

"I suppose," she said through her hands.

"Come with me to Tiki Island. Let me help you start over. It's the least I can do for a girl who was such a big part of my life, if only for a few days."

## Monday Morning

Jessica and I met Captain Rango on the dock at ten (I found out his name when he introduced himself to Jessica, taking her hand and kissing it like a gentleman. Oh, yeah, he took it with his good hand, not the hook. Thank God.) We got on the boat with her suitcase and a couple of cups of Java from a stand and headed to Tiki Island. It was Monday and unseasonably overcast. There was a coolness in the air that I didn't feel since a month ago up North. Out over the Atlantic the sky was dark and gloomy.

"Big storm headin' up our way, folks," Rango said. "Hella bad one, tossed two ships under already, way out in the waters."

"A hurricane?" I asked, noticeably worried. After those stories of 1935 I didn't want to be within a hundred miles of one of those babies.

"Not yet, Tropical storm. Very late in the season. Should veer off and go up de coast, I hope."

"Yeah, me too."

We motored ahead and the Island was in sight. It was close to eleven when we pulled up at the dock. To my surprise, Sheriff Jackson and two deputies were standing there. Apparently they were waiting for me.

"Mornin' Detective. Got a moment?"

This couldn't be good.

"Is it so important I can't even get out of the boat first."

"Yessir. That important. Come with us." They led Jessica and me up the dock and through the main entrance of the Resort without saying a word.

"What gives, Sheriff? Is it about last night?"

Everyone stopped. The Sheriff spun on his heels and looked me dead in the eye. "Don't say another word, Detective. Not until we're inside."

This was bad, I could feel it. Something was wrong, more than the two goons I offed last night. Something worse. Something…*bad*.

We went into the Hotel and into one of the small meeting and banquet rooms on the right. The room was divided in two with a door in the movable wall. One of the deputies took Jessica through he door. The other stayed with me and Jackson.

"All right, Sheriff, mind telling me what this is all about?"

"You packin'?" He asked. Again, not a good sign.

"Of course, I have my .38 on my belt."

"Would you please let me have it?"

"Sure," I said, and slowly took it off my belt and handed it to him, grips-out. He tucked it in his belt.

"Sit down, Bill. We've got a big problem." I sat. This was his territory, and if there was a problem I was going to respect his position. "Where were you last night?"

"What time?"

"Between midnight and four a.m."

I thought a minute. "I hadn't actually been clockwatching last night, so let me piece it together. Melinda and I left the Miami Police Station around eleven-thirty, I think. We were back on the Island by one a.m."

"I know about what happened in Miami, by the way. Go on."

"Well, I went back to my suite when we got back, fell asleep around two, two-thirty."

"Alone?"

I didn't answer.

"This is no time to be coy, Bill. We've already talked to Ms. Hawthorn."

"Then you know she was with me."

"I had to hear it from you."

"Am I being charged with something?"

"Not yet. Just answer the questions, OK?"

"Fine," I said, getting a little hot under the collar. "We fell asleep around two or so. Then I got a call at three-thirty from a doctor in Key West. He phoned to say Ms. Rutledge had taken ill and wanted to speak to me. Melinda left and I hopped on a boat before four. I was in Key West by four-thirty and drove my car to the doc's place on White Street. I was there until around nine-thirty, drove back to the dock, got the boat around ten and here I am now."

The Sheriff wrote everything down as I said it. He checked his notes and said, "So between the time that Ms. Hawthorn left and the time you got on the boat, that was less than a half an hour?"

"Yeah, I guess so. You could check with Captain Rango to see when he logged the time."

"I already checked. You shoved off at three-forty-seven."

"Again, you know the answers better than I do. Now tell me what's going on."

Jackson took off his hat and ran a handkerchief over his bald head. He put the hat back on and sighed. "Seems we've got a murder on our hands, Bill."

"The skeleton? I thought that was all settled."

"No, not the skeleton. This time a full-skinned corpse, upstairs in one of the rooms."

Oh, Jesus.

"Which room?"

"The one that belongs to Rutger Bachman, Bill. Someone killed him in his sleep."

Jesus! Bachman? A thousand thoughts and images scrambled across the front of my mind. Jerry, and how would I tell him. Hawthorn losing his long-time manager. Melinda...could she? *Would* she?

"Bachman? Why? How?"

"Why, we don't know yet. How...he was suffocated in a most unusual way. His windpipe was crushed with a pipe."

"Holy hell," I said while my mind raced with the events of the last few days. "The same night I get attacked by two of Roberts' goons, and Roberts and Bachman were in Kahootz. No wonder I'm a suspect."

"Those weren't Roberts' men, Bill, they were Bachman's. They were his muscle to keep his prostitutes in line, and they ran drugs up from Cuba. But maybe you knew that."

"I didn't," I said, "Although I had my suspicions."

"So you see the spot I'm in Bill," Jackson said mournfully.

"Sure. I get mixed up with a chick that I later find out turns tricks for Bachman. I get roughed up by Roberts twice. I almost get killed by two guys that work for Bachman, and kill them in self-defense. Last night I come back here, and have all the reason in the world to want to put Bachman out of commission for good. Except I've got an alibi...minus twenty minutes.

"And it doesn't take twenty minutes to get from your room to the dock, Bill."

"It does of you wash up and put on clean clothes first."

"Maybe."

I took out my Camels and shook one out of the deck. It was the first butt I'd had in two days, since Melinda didn't like smoke. I lit it with the Zippo and let the smoke float high before I said another word. "Well, Sheriff, it wasn't me. Plain and simple. Am I being charged?"

"Not yet," Jackson said to me with a touch of sadness. He knew if I was guilty, in Florida I'd get the chair. "But you are a suspect, so you know the deal...don't leave town and all that there stuff."

"I'm not planning on going anywhere. I'm on vacation."

"So you keep sayin'. Funny how most people just come down here and fish."

"Yeah, funny."

I wasn't laughing.

In the next room they were interrogating Jessica with the same questions. She honestly didn't remember much, so there wasn't much to tell. I told Jackson about her almost overdosing, and that I'd volunteered to help her clean up. He agreed not to press charges on her (he didn't have any proof but he still could have made her life hell) if I kept an eye on her.

"Sheriff, honestly, do you think I did this?"

He looked down at the ground, then at his belt. He took my revolver out and handed it back to me. "Honestly Bill, I don't know what to think. I've got no motive other than Bachman was into some bad stuff. But no, personally, I don't really think you did it. First of all, you wouldn't have been so foolish as to make yourself look like a suspect. Second, I don't think bashing a man's throat in with a pipe is your style. I just hope I'm right."

"You're right, Sheriff. That's not my style. I'd have gotten the goods on him and turned him over to you."

"Yeah, well, try to stay out of trouble for the rest of your trip, Detective. I'm still here if you need me, or if anything turns up."

"Thanks Sheriff. I'll keep my ear to the ground."

"I will be watching y'all, just so you know."

"I'd be disappointed if you didn't."

I brought Jessica down to the lobby restaurant and had the waiter page Melinda. We had coffee and a couple of plates of good old fashioned ham and eggs – with fried potatoes, not grits thank you very much – while we waited. An hour went by and Melinda didn't show.

"I'll take you back to my suite for now, Jessica, and go find Melinda so we can get you a place to stay."

Jessica looked at me funny, and said, "Billy, I don't understand. Why is Ms. Hawthorn taking an interest in me? I hardly know her."

"Because you're a friend of mine, kid, that's why."

"Is she this nice to all her customers?" She knew. She must have sensed it with that special radar they dish out to girls when they're born. She knew about me and Melinda but didn't want to come right out with it. She wanted me to tell her. Or she expected me to lie.

I wasn't much of a liar so I said, "Since you and I had our, eh, run-in, Melinda and I have gotten…sorta close."

"Close? As in you're seeing her?"

"Yeah, at least while I'm on vacation."

"I see. Now I know why you didn't want me to stay with you," she said, and I was afraid the waterworks were going to start back up. Happily for me they didn't. "I understand now. She's nice, Bill. Pretty."

"Let's not go into that, kid. All I'm thinking about right now is getting you a new start, right?"

"Sure Bill," she said, and we headed back to my suite.

I set Jessica up with a Seagram's Seven highball and went looking for Melinda. Funny thing hit me as I left the suite: I didn't get those knots in my gut, those impulses to take Jessica right there on the couch. I wasn't sure why. Maybe it was because I realized she was just a pretty doll that I was lucky enough to have a little fling with. Maybe it was because all along my feelings for Melinda were stronger.

Nuts. It was because I was scared silly that I was about to get a murder wrap hung around my neck when I didn't even see the guy last night.

I headed over to Melinda's apartment and knocked. No answer. I tried Hawthorn's next.

Bingo.

Melinda, teary–eyed and shaking, opened the door. Like an omen, a far-off rumble of thunder preceded her words.

"It couldn't have been you," she said shaking her head. "It just couldn't have. I was with you the whole night, and you couldn't have had time…"

"Can I come in?" I asked quietly.

"Of course," she said and opened the door wide.

The place was dark except for a few candles. Hawthorn sat in a large, bamboo rocker smoking a pipe. The thick, dark air was drenched with the heavy smell of cherry tobacco.

"Sit down, William, anywhere is fine," Melinda said and poured three glasses of brandy. She took hers down in one swallow, gave one to Hawthorn and one to me. "What did you tell the Sheriff?"

"Same thing you did apparently, or we'd both be in the hopper."

"William, please, tell me…you didn't have anything to do with this, right?"

"No kitten, I didn't kill Bachman. I had a plan to set up some juicy evidence and hand him over to Jackson. That's all. I don't kill for sport, kid."

"I knew so. I just needed to hear it from you." She wrapped her arms around me and held me for a moment, then let go. No kiss.

"How's your old man?" I asked softly.

"He's in shock. So am I really. Neither of us ever expected something like this, here. Plus the scandal…dear God, William, once this gets out to the newspapers people will avoid this place like the plague."

"You can spin it, can't you?" I knew it was a long-shot.

"I can try. Once the facts are in maybe I can make it look like he was tied to the last of the old-time gangsters or something. Still, the security issue alone…"

"Don't worry about that now, kid. There'll be time to fix the Island's reputation later. For now we've got to try to figure out who did this and why."

Hawthorn looked up from his chair for the first time. "Mr. Riggins, isn't that what the police are for?"

"Certainly, Mr. Hawthorn," I said looking his way. The candlelight danced on his ancient face, playing tricks. He looked like a ghost. "But I'm afraid at the moment the police think *I* did it, and that's what they're going on. I need to get the jump on them so I don't wind up in the clink myself."

Hawthorn stared at me, sort of funny-like. "Mr. Riggins, you seem to be overlooking one very important fact."

"What's that?"

"That whomever killed Rutger may be after Melinda or myself next."

Melinda and I looked at each other as another thunder roll came in at just the right time. "I hadn't thought of that," she said, the slightest bit of fear in her voice. "Do you think that's a possibility?"

I thought about it a minute. "Sure, I guess it's possible, but knowing what Bachman was into, I think it's much more likely it was someone from the underworld that rubbed him out."

"Such a crass way of putting it, Mr. Riggins. Rutger may have had his faults, but he was still my friend, as it were."

I guess I was being sort of cold. I get that way when people try to kill me. "I'm sorry, Mr. Hawthorn. That was insensitive of me."

"No harm," he said, and went back to his brandy, Melinda just frowned. I nodded my head toward the door and she got the idea.

"Eliot," she said softly," William and I are going down to the dining room. Would you like anything sent up?"

Hawthorn just shook his head. We headed down to the restaurant and talked along the way.

"I came looking for you because Jessica's in my room. I didn't know what else to do with her."

There was only a slight twitch in her step, and a half-second pause before she answered, "We can put her in 320. But I need to eat something first or I'm going to be sick."

I said "Ok," tentatively. I really wanted to get Jessica taken care of. "Well, how about we stop at the front desk, you get me the key and I get her squared away then meet you down here?"

Melinda sighed, a sort of angry bull type of sigh. "I'd really rather not, William. We have some things to talk about and she's honestly the last thing on my mind."

I stopped us just shy of the elevator. "What things?"

"What things? Well, for one, both Eliot and I are being considered suspects by Sheriff Jackson."

I went cold. The Sheriff was no dummy. It occurred to me that if he had them on his list of suspects, he had more of a reason than just the plain fact that they worked together. What was in his head? What knowledge did he have that I didn't? Did he know all about Bachman's pimping? I tried like hell not to let the questions show on my face. I cleared my throat and said, "Really?" with a little more surprise than I actually felt. "I mean, I can't imagine either of you having the bal…the inclination to do something so horrible." I shifted a little and if Melinda were in the detective racket she'd have known I was hiding something because I just wasn't a good enough actor to pull it off. Lucky, she didn't catch on. I changed the subject fast. "Did he seal off the Island?"

"Yes. No one comes or goes without his knowing. He's got twelve deputies on the Island, too. They're interviewing everyone, starting with us, then the staff, then you, and now they're starting on the guests. It's a nightmare, if I ever saw one."

The elevator came up and we got in, alone. The air inside seemed stuffy, hot. Close. Uncomfortable. "So, you have any idea who might have done this?" I asked, not looking at Melinda. She slowly turned to me and said, "Only every girl on the Island. He was a snake and put the moves on anything with heels. And of course, their boyfriends would be suspects too."

"Can you narrow it down at all?"

"Not much," she said as we exited the elevator. "Maybe down to the prettiest girls. I know he had something going with Kaliki."

"The mermaid? How did a guy like him manage to get his paws on a doll like her?"

"I don't know, money? Position? Blackmail? Who knows."

We entered the dining room and took a booth near the back under a giant palm plant. Melinda ordered a Tiki version of a Waldorf Salad (it had orange slices in it) and I ordered chicken lo mien and a Jack and Ginger.

"No Mai Tai today, William?" Melinda asked in a flirty yet tired way.

"Not today kid. Today is too much like work to pretend I'm on vacation. Now what else do you want to talk about?"

"Funny you should mention work," she said. "I was going to ask...and please don't feel you have to say yes...but I was hoping maybe you would do some investigating of your own, to try to find out who killed Rutger."

"Ohhh, so it's Rutger now?"

"William, I may have loathed the man, but I never wished him dead."

"Well, somebody did. And yeah, I'd be happy to find out who it is. You're not the only one with your head on the block. The answer just might save my neck." I drank down half the hi-ball in one shot. A boom of thunder much louder than the others shook the hall.

"Aren't you worried at all about that storm?"

"No," she said. "We get storms all the time. The staff has already made preparations, tied the boats down, taken in the beach furniture. We'll be ok."

I was almost convinced, then something horrible crept into my mind, one of those thoughts that starts out slow then hits you over the head with a ball-peen hammer. "Oh, Christ," I said a little too loudly.

"What is it? Is the Bourbon watered down? I'll give that bartender the boot if she..."

"No, the booze is fine. I'm not. I just realized something."

"What?"

"Bachman is dead. Somebody's got to tell his brother, Jerry."

Melinda was silent. So was I.

It was well after two p.m. when Melinda got me the key to room 320 and we parted ways, her to run the hotel and me to get Jessica out of my room. She wasn't too happy about getting stuck alone for almost an hour, and I noticed a bottle of gin was a lot lighter than it was that morning. I told her I had some work to take care of and set her up in room 320. I ordered her a platter from room service and got out before she had a chance to try to make me stay.

Back in my suite I stared at the coconut phone for a good ten minutes before dialing the operator. The scene through the picture window was bad...dark clouds to the south and east, gray and swirling to the west. The sun, for the first time since I got to the Sunshine State, was nowhere to be found.

A low rumble shook the room. Very suddenly the sound of large, flat raindrops banged against the glass here and there, then stopped. I picked up the receiver and spun the dial with my finger in the "O".

A few clicks, a few whirs and some static later I had Jerry on the other end.

"Hey pally, how's the south treating you?" He sounded like he was in a swell mood.

"Well kid, everything's been great up 'til now."

"Why? What happen, you spend the night alone for once?"

"This is serious, Jerry. You better sit down."

I heard a glass clink on the other end. "You're scarin' me, pally. What's so important I gotta sit down?"

"It's about your brother, Rutger."

"I'm listening," he said with a quiver in his voice. He already knew at that point.

"Jerry, I'm afraid he's been murdered. Sometime during the night. No one knows who or why, yet. I'm sorry."

The line was silent for a few seconds, then I heard a glass smash on the floor. "Jerry? You all right kid?"

"Riggins, you were just supposed...you were supposed to be on *vacation*, for

Christ's sake. How could you?"

"Me? Now listen Jer, I had nothing to do with it! I actually only met him a couple of times because he was so busy. It wasn't me who put him on ice, but I'm gonna do everything I can to find out who the killer is, that you can take to the bank." I could hear the sobs coming on the other end. Then I could hear them in his voice.

"He...he was supposed to come visit me this Christmas. I ain't seen the guy in three years, ya know? Aw, goddammit, Bill, what the hell happened?"

"You really wanna know?"

"Yeah, give it to me straight."

"Someone killed him in his sleep. Smashed his windpipe with a lead pipe, or something like it. Probably quick."

"Why?"

"Don't know. Jerry, you may not know this, but your brother was mixed up in some crazy stuff."

"I know, Bill. That's why I thought...look, I knew he had some side businesses going with girls and party favors. I didn't want to tell you because...well really, it ain't any of my business. Besides, I didn't think you'd take the vacation if..." His voice trailed off in to soft sobs. It broke my heart.

"Listen buddy, don't worry about any of that now. I'm not on vacation anymore. I'm gonna find the creep who did this and bring him in, and don't worry 'cause I'll make it stick. The trouble is I got a little mixed up with one of his girls...I didn't know it at the time...so people are pointing fingers at me. They figure I got a motive on account of this chick."

"That's crazy, you're a cop."

"They have a different way of looking at things down here, kid."

"Yeah, true." I heard the sound of glass tinkling on glass, then the muted gulp of a long swallow. "Listen, Jerry, if you have any idea who I should start with...maybe your brother mentioned a name, someone he was having trouble with?"

"He didn't talk about work much, Bill. I think he was afraid someone was listening in."

"Well if you think of anyone..."

"There was one guy, Bill. I think his name was like, Robbins. He mentioned him a few times, that he wished the mug would get lost. Someone he did business with."

"Roberts," I said, and my heart sped up just a little bit as my fingers curled around the phone and pulled so tight I thought it'd break in my hand.

"Yeah, that's it. Roberts. Didn' like the guy one bit. Said he was stupid, and was gonna mess up the whole operation he had going. That help?"

"It might." Yeah, it just might.

"Good. Listen, Bill, let me go. I wanna be alone for a while, all right?"

"Yeah, I'm hip. Sorry I had to be the one to give you the news but I thought it was better than a call from some jerk deputy who don't even know you."

"Yeah, thanks Bill. It is better coming from you. I'll catch you later," he said and hung up before I could answer. A loud static charge busted my ear as another clap of thunder rattled the house.

Sometimes I hated this vacation.

I looked all over the lobby for a familiar face and found none. Now the rain was coming down hard so all the guests were scrambling in here, making it hard to spot anyone through the thick sea of tanned hides. The front desk girl said Melinda was somewhere out on the grounds dealing with a private party that was supposed to happen that afternoon and got moved. She had no idea where the Sheriff was.

It was really Jackson I wanted to talk to. He wasn't in the interrogation room, and by now he'd have interviewed all the staff but not all of the guests. He was either taking a break, gave up or moved rooms. I really wanted his sheet on suspects. I had a few of my own that needed to be added. I decided wandering around the whole place was pointless, so I checked the restaurant, the bar, the deck restaurant and all the meeting rooms and gave up.

I walked into the lobby lounge where the mermaids swam. There were no mermaids in the tank, but there was one at the bar who was well on her way to getting tanked. She sat alone. I sat beside her.

"Hey, there, aren't you one of the mermaids?" I asked politely. She gave me the once over with a sort of annoyed look.

"Yes, I am," she said quietly and went back to her drink, something brownish in a rocks glass. Whiskey, straight. She finished it in one gulp. This doll could put it away.

"My name's Bill. Saw you swimming earlier. Can I buy you another one of those?"

I got the same annoyed look, then in a breathy, low voice she said, "Please, don't put the moves on me pal. It's been a long day and whatever you're sellin', I ain't buyin'." Her voice wasn't only low and breathy, it was tinged with a little agony and a side of slur.

She had a distinct Brooklyn accent, kind of like Bugs Bunny but blonde. I could see she wasn't in the mood for a pickup, and frankly neither was I.

"Sorry kid, I didn't mean to come off that way. Just looking to make some friends while on vacation, that's all. If you want I'll leave you alone, but the offer still stands on the drink."

She looked up from the glass and stared straight ahead at the back of the bar, eyeing up the bottles stacked on glass shelves, lit from behind with a soft blue glow.

"Ok, one drink. But don't think it gives you the right to flip my fins, got it?"

"I'm hip," I said, "Order away."

"Another double Johnny Black on a glacier, Linda. This one's on this guy here," she said to the bartender who was already pouring. "Thanks mister. Today I need all I can get."

"Forgive my nosiness, but what troubles can a mermaid who lives in a Tiki bar possibly have?"

"What else?" she said. "Man troubles. Every guy I meet turns out to be a slime." She took a long drink of Scotch and continued. "I was supposed to be in Miami tonight. Little vacation. Me and this...jackass I've been going around with. Should have known better. He's skipped without me. Won't answer his phone, nothin'. So I get to go back to work for a week instead of playin' it up in the city. And I really thought he was the one, ya know? Jerk. At least he can't fire me."

"Fire you? Who is this guy?"

She looked at me sideways. "Who do you think? The hotel manager." She finished the Scotch in a final slug, fast.

"Bachmann?"

"Yeah, that's him."

Oh Christ, she hadn't heard yet.

"I'm sure he'll turn up," I said, and finished my drink too. I didn't want to have to tell another person that Bachman was dead. I didn't need anyone else's miseries piling up on top of mine. I had enough of my own, piled up like a house of cards, ready to come down any minute in a gust of wind from that damned storm brewing outside. I decided to make a run for it, quick. Like pulling off a bandaid I said,

"Well, sorry to hear that doll. Thanks for the company. I gotta run."

"Wait a minute, mister," she said, pulling lightly at my shirt. "You mean…Well, you didn't even try."

"Try what?"

"To flip my fins. You didn't even make a pass."

"You told me not to."

"I tell everyone not to. They always do anyway."

"Well then there's still hope."

"Hope for what?"

"Still hope that not all men are slime," I said, and made my exit. She watched me leave the bar, and ordered another drink.

I went back to the lobby and got a newspaper, sat down on a big bench carved out of a tree and buried my face behind the print. The paper was the Sunday evening edition. No Monday paper. Jackson had sealed off the Island before they delivered the paper. I wondered what time he got called in…something I neglected to ask. If Bachman was killed in the early morning hours, and his body was discovered before the paper got delivered that meant there was only a very small window for the murderer to leave the island. I walked over to the front desk again and got the attention of the older yet very pretty girl working it. She smiled as she came over, a sort of half 'work' smile and half 'I really am this pleasant all the time' smile.

"Yes Mr. Riggins?"

"Can you tell me what time the morning edition gets delivered to the Island?"

"Certainly, it' always here by five-thirty. A boat comes every morning with fresh fruits and other supplies for the restaurants, and the newspapers come with it. We have a special driver that starts in Fort Lauderdale with the Sentinel, gets them just as they come off the presses at midnight, then runs down to Miami for the Herald, and down to Largo for the Ledger. He usually makes it to the dock just as the boat is ready to shove off."

"He always make it?"

"Hasn't missed a boat in fifteen years."

"So there's no paper today because –"

"Because that Sheriff wouldn't let the boat leave Sugarloaf Key."

"Any idea what time the Sheriff got here?"

"Yes, Mr. Riggins. Around ten-thirty."

I was confused. "Ten-thirty? That's impossible, he was already here when I got here this morning."

"No, Mr. Riggins, not ten-thirty this morning. Ten-thirty last night. Sheriff Jackson was here overnight, as a guest of Mr. Hawthorn."

Damn.

It was around four in the afternoon when Melinda confronted Sheriff Jackson and insisted he allow the boat carrying the daily food and supplies to dock and unload. He was adamant not to, but she was more adamant to run her Resort. She allowed complete supervision by his deputies, and when she made it a point that he'd no longer get free meals and rooms he finally obliged.

But no one was leaving Tiki Island.

Jackson and his deputies did a room-to-room search and interrogation of every person on the Island. Being a Monday, the Hotel was only at seventy percent capacity, which made things a little easier, but it was still slow going. He finally wrapped things up around five, and that's when I found him strolling across the lobby from the elevator to the dining room.

"Hey Sheriff, having dinner?"

"Yessuh, famished. Care to join me?"

"Don't mind if I do."

The storm was in full swing now but besides the rattle of occasional thunder we'd never know it. The Hukilau dining room had no windows. It was a darkened cavern in the traditional style of the American Polynesian Pop Tiki Bar, a mysteriously-concocted thatch and bamboo village within a building, shadowed by dark, woven palms, lit by candles and blowfish hanging lamps. Just as the architect intended, we were cut off from the outside world.

We sat at a small round table with a view of the kitchen. I guess I'd gotten so used to the VIP treatment I almost complained, but Jackson was hungry and didn't mind where we sat. He ordered without looking at the menu. Fried chicken and sides of mashed potatoes and collard greens. I don't even know what a collard green is, and once I saw them I was even less interested in knowing. I ordered a plank steak medium rare and a Jack and Ginger. The Sheriff drank coffee.

"That booze will mess with your head, son," he said as I spun the Tiki Island swizzle stick in the glass.

"My head would be more messed up without it. Besides, I'm on vacation."

"So ya'll keeps sayin'."

"Yeah well maybe today is turning out to be a work day. Who's on your list of suspects?"

Jackson looked up from his chicken and said, "Now why should I tell you that?"

"Well you want me to help you, don't you?"

"In case you forgot, Mr. Riggins, *you're* still on my list."

"No kidding. But I *know* I didn't do it, so let me give you a hand. I may have a name or two to add to your list."

"You think so?"

"Maybe. You give me yours and I'll give you mine."

He put down the chicken and carefully wiped his hands on his napkin before taking out his little brown notebook. I took out my little black notebook and between the two of us we looked like a couple of guys comparing notes on the dinner. Nobody would have suspected we were comparing notes on a murder.

He flipped a few pages and squinted, then took a pair of wire-rimmed glasses out of his pocket and began to read.

"Ok, Bill, here's my list in no particular order. You, Mr. Hawthorn, Ms.

Hawthorn, Ms. Rutledge, Jason Trembol, and Dustin Marlin."

"Who? Wait…Jessica was in Key West when Bachman got iced."

"Still, she's connected to you and the Island and him, and she showed up this morning. She could have had someone do it for her."

"Someone like me."

"Maybe."

"Thanks, pal."

"Just business, Bill."

"Who are these other two goons?"

"Jason Trembol works on the loading dock. He also was a sort of gofer for Bachman. They had a falling out a week or so ago, and Bachman cut him off. He'd been making serious green bringing in illegal narcotics and cigarettes without tax stamps for Bachman."

"And the other?"

"His replacement."

A crack of thunder shook the hotel and the lights flickered. They came up and after the momentary interruption I looked over at the Sheriff with disappointment. "That's it, huh? Interrogated everyone in the joint, and all you got is a frail old man, a petite young woman, an out of town cop, a hooker who was an hour away and two guys that worked penny-ante for 'em."

Jackson looked hurt. "Well, yeah Bill. What did you expect?"

"You don't get a lot of murders down here, do you?"

Now he looked a little embarrassed. He flipped his book shut and said, "Well honestly when we do, it's pretty obvious who's behind it. Drunks in fights, drug pushers tearin' into each other, cheating spouses. That sort of thing. Never anything too mysterious."

I looked down at my Jack and Ginger. The ice was already starting to melt. "Open your book, I've got some names for you."

I told him all about Penelope first. He checked a list and found out she was still on the Island. She never left last night because after we left her room, Bachman returned and told her to stay put. She said he threatened to fire her if she listened to us, and she stayed in her room all night. No one to back up the story though. Next I told him about Roberts, and how Jerry mentioned Bachman was having problems with the fat man from Key West.

"Roberts is behind bars, Bill. You know that. You put him there."

"Are you sure about that? You sure he didn't get sprung on bail?"

"Pretty sure."

"Well we should check."

"Ok, fine. I'll give the prison a call when we're through."

"Find out if he had any visitors or made any calls. He might have had someone do it for him. Someone with connections."

"Maybe," he said, "Although I don't know why."

"Who knows. Revenge maybe. Or to get Bachman out of the way so that one of Roberts' own men could move up to the number one spot."

"That's not a half bad idea, Bill."

"Yeah, well that's why I make the big lettuce."

I gave him the mermaid last. "Her name is Kaliki. I don't know how deep she was in with Bachman, but she seemed pretty busted up when I saw her at the lounge. And according to Melinda, he chased every skirt on the payroll, so you might want to see if he was getting dirty with any of the girls, and if they had jealous boyfriends."

"No one said anything in the interviews."

"You thought they would?" I asked, and was honestly getting a little annoyed at the Investigation-101 course I was teaching the Sheriff. "Jackson, you don't ask a chick if she's been getting the business from a guy who wound up murdered. You ask her if she knows *someone else* who's been getting business, dig?"

Jackson was getting a little angry now. "Ok, *detective*, I may not have had the fancy schoolin' you did, but I know how to interrogate suspects."

I was getting hot and sounding condescending. You know, me with my degree in criminal investigation, two years in the military, six years as a cop, three of which were as the youngest detective in New York history... "I'm sorry pal, I didn't mean it to come out that way. I'm just saying I'll bet you dimes to donuts that snake was spending more time with the bedding than the maid staff, and there's gotta be a couple of girls here who would love to dish the dirt on people they don't like."

"Well look Bill, as the law I've gone about as far as I can go. While you're here, you're not a cop. You're in another state on leave, and that gives you the same rights as any citizen...meaning you can do some asking around yourself without worrying about it being on the books. Y'all come up with a good lead and my boys will run it down. As for me, my list of suspects stands, along with the hooker and the mermaid as people of interest. As for Roberts...we'll see where that leads us after that phone call."

I finished off the last of my highball and said, "When do I get to see the crime scene?"

Jackson looked surprised. "Who said you are?"

"Well either you can show me or I can get old man Hawthorn to give me the key to Bachman's suite. Either way."

"That's a crime scene, you can't just go bargin' in there like a fox in the henhouse –"

"Then let's go for a walk," I said and got up. The Sheriff huffed and puffed and got up too.

I found in Bachman's apartment the usual stuff you'd find in a usual hotel room. No Tiki or Hawaiian décor here. His living room was ultra-modern with fancy black acrylic chairs that looked like you couldn't possibly sit on them, a sofa made of leather-upholstered black and white circles, and a striped rug that almost gave me vertigo. A glass coffee table with a selection of Playboy and Esquire mags centered the room. The art that hung on the plain white walls was minimalist-modern, made of geometric shapes or colored lines. A few non-tropical indoor plants accented the black and white theme. A hi-fi with a built-in television set lined the wall opposite the windows. The vertical blinds were drawn. No photographs, knick-knacks or anything else that might lend a touch of personality to the place was present.

Here on the third floor the storm felt the worse. Even with the blinds shut you could tell it was storming from the thick gray light that oozed around the edges of the windows. The rain bashed itself hard against the roof and windows, and when the thunder hit, it sounded like it was cracking right over our heads.

"Sheriff, should we be worried about this storm? I'd hate to be up here when the roof blows off."

"Roof? Aw, don't be a chicken, Bill. This is only a tropical storm. Never hurt anyone. You just don't want to be outside in it, that's all."

"Sure," I said. I wasn't sure at all.

Jackson led me through to the bedroom where the body'd been found. Besides the obvious signs of a police investigation, the room seemed neat, orderly, untouched. Bachman died in his king-sized bed under black satin sheets. There were no blood stains. The white walls of his bedroom were accented only by a few more geometric paintings, plus one large aerial photo of the The Keys over his headboard. A minibar sat next to his bed and doubled as a nightstand. An electric clock, modernist lamp and ashtray shaped like a kidney were the only extras in the stark room.

"So this is where he got it," I said, not asking.

"Yeah, this is where Bachman took his last breath."

All the rum on this trip had made me soft. I looked around again, then went back to the front door, then back to the bedroom. "Sheriff, there's no sign of forced entry. No sign of a struggle, nothing."

"Nope, not at all. Whoever killed Bachman waltzed right in here while he was sleeping, took his time to aim perfectly with a heavy pipe, and came down right on his throat crushing his windpipe. They did it a couple of more times, or held it down on him hard just to make sure the job was done right."

"I'm guessing Bachman didn't sleep with his door unlocked, did he?"

"Nope. Whoever did this had a key, or access to a key."

"Like someone who works in the hotel."

"More specifically, like someone who works in the hotel who can easily get a key, or already has one."

"Like Hawthorn."

"Yes, or his daughter, or you, Bill."

"Now I see your line of thinking."

"So you see why my list is so short."

"And why you added the hooker and the mermaid so fast."

"Exactly."

"Or, maybe...they were a guest of Bachman...staying the night, waited for him to go to sleep, than whacked him and took off."

"Possible, but there were no signs of a second person here. No extra glass in the sink, the pillow next to his wasn't touched..."

"No used rubbers in the trash."

"Yeah, that too. No, I think whoever killed Rutger Bachman, Bill, did it last night sometime between one a.m. and four-thirty a.m., had a key, and took the murder weapon with them."

"Murder weapon could be in the middle of the Gulf by now."

"Yep, tossed off the side of a boat on the way to Key West, maybe."

He had a point. He was wrong, but he had a point. Dammit.

"And now I see why I'm really a suspect."

"I thought you would."

"But we both know I didn't do it."

"Do we, Bill?"

"Well let me ask you this, Sheriff. Where were *you* last night, at the time of the murder?"

Jackson stepped back a little, not expecting that question. He hesitated only slightly. "I was here, on Tiki Island, with Mr. Hawthorn part of the evening, then asleep in one of the rooms on the third floor. But I suppose you already knew that piece of information."

"I did. And why were you here?"

"Mr. Hawthorn asked me to come here. He…wait, I ain't got to tell you any of this, bub."

"You don't have to but it may help."

"Help what? You're trying to make it look like *I'm* a suspect, you crazy Yankee."

"You were here because Hawthorn said he had a feeling he was in trouble, that something bad was going to happen. He wanted you here for protection. Maybe you protected him against Bachman, and went a little too far."

Jackson laughed, hard. "Oh man, you are one crazy som'bitch. Ok, sure Bill, I did come here because Hawthorn was afraid. But it was ghosts he said he was afraid of, as usual. The poor man's brain is dying off, Bill. He sees things. But he didn't mention nothin' about being a'scared of old Bachman. No, you can rest your mind it wasn't me."

"Just as you can rest your mind it wasn't me. I check out on Friday, and unless cupid comes down and shoots a V2 rocket at me and I fall head-over-heals for Ms. Hawthorn, there's nothing stopping me from going back to my twelve-hour a day cop gig in the big City. I've got no reason to stick my neck out for anyone here, no dame, no old man, no coconut-bikini'd hula dancer, nobody. I've got an alibi that's not perfect and that makes it more believable than if I'd been in Miami all night. And moreover, I've got no reason to kill Bachman at all. He gave me two weeks free hotel and meals, and his brother is my best friend. I'd have to be some kind of nut to pull the rug out from under the guy, and the faster you catch on to that the faster we can both start looking for the real killer."

Jackson didn't say a word. He lit a cigar and puffed, looking at the glowing tip. Finally he said, "Bill, I think you've been square with me from when we first met. And I'm inclined to believe you. But you've got to see it my way. You're mixed up, in whatever way, with two very fiery young women who both had a deep hatred for Bachman, and a lot to gain by his death. I've seen plenty of strong, smart men take the bait and off a man they didn't even know for the touch of a woman. The movies are full of it, and the movies get it from real life. Sure, I think you're a fine man, and a fine cop. And I'm inclined to believe you. But if I find out down the line that you've played me for the fool, so help me Detective Riggins, I'll personally see to it you never breath fresh air again. Deal?"

I smiled and held out my hand. He shook it, strong and hard. "Deal," I said. "Now let's make that call on Roberts."

Jackson called the prison where Roberts was being held from the front desk telephone. Sure enough the rat was still in his cage. A few minutes on the line and Jackson found out he had no visitors and made only two calls, one to a relative and one to a lawyer. The lawyer hadn't shown up yet.

After that we parted ways and I headed back to my suite for a break. It was almost seven. The day had flown by, and all I could think was another day of my vacation gone, wasted. I didn't want to screw around with trying to figure out a murder of a guy I didn't even know. I wanted to go to Key West and see the sights, have lunch in an outdoor café in Bahama Village, check out the museums or watch the sailors bring in the giant sea turtles. I wanted to do more diving along the reefs and maybe rent a powerboat for the day. I'd even settle for a few hours in and by the pool. Anything but this.

My room seemed dark. The blinds were open but the sky was so strange and alien that it cast a dull, charcoal light over everything. The sun had been lost long ago somewhere over the Gulf, far beyond the swirling overcast clouds that broke loose with tons of heavy drops on our little Island. The roof of the lanai kept the rain from pelting the glass of the windows, but the roar of the wind and now almost constant thunder reminded me this was no joke.

There was a note taped to my door ordering all guests to keep their windows closed under possibility of injury or death. Twice a porter came and knocked to make sure I (and the other guests) were adhering to this rule. Hell, you'd have to be a brain-dead moron to open the sliding glass doors in this mess. You couldn't see ten feet out anyway…just a fuzzy gray wall of water and fog.

Made me think. Made me wonder about some things. Made me wonder about Hawthorn, twenty-one years ago, driving his boat through weather like this toward Islamorada, braving the rain and wind and waves to get away from this very Island. Made me wonder what he was thinking when he decided to abandon the train and continue up the coast in his boat. It was the right decision, but it must have been a friggin' nightmare.

I wondered why he waited to the last minute.

Then I wondered why I was wondering all this. What did I care? That was long ago and far away. Another storm, another time.

## Saturday, September 28, 1935

The storm was an inevitability. It would come, and nothing but God or Poseidon could change that. How strong and when were not certain, but Eliot knew one thing: He'd have to go to Key West tonight. He needed her. He needed Rose, needed her back on the Island when the storm came, needed here more than anything. Without her he'd never be able to make it through the storm. He knew that, and he knew it was the only way. On Saturday evening he cranked up the Chris-Craft Double Stateroom Cruiser and made his way to Key West.

The waters were calmer than he expected, the visibility much clearer. It was still early evening when he docked at his private slip, but no one was around. Most of the vessels had already left the Island for cover up on Florida's west coast, past Everglades City, up in Venice Beach. He even had trouble finding a taxi on the Key.

But he found one.

He motored up to Roberts' place, and told the cabby to wait.

Inside he found Rose sitting on a settee in the parlor. She was shocked to see him.

"Well hello, sugar! What brings y'all down here this weekend? I hear the weather's gonna be just nasty."

"It is. And I don't want you to stay here. I need you to come with me, back to the Island."

"But sugar, I —"

"Don't argue. It's not…safe, here. I want you to come with me where you'll be safe. I…I don't want anything happening to you."

"Aw, sugar, that's sweet but I've got to stay here and work. Roberts' orders."

"Fuck Roberts."

"I'd rather not," she said with her southern charm, and Eliot suddenly felt horrible, then sick, then hardened.

"I'll deal with Roberts. Get your things. You have five minutes. I'll wait here."

Rose got up from the settee, her long legs unfolding like a spider. She sashayed her way over to Eliot and put her arms around him. She kissed him, not like she kissed her customers, but like a woman hot for a strong man. "I'll be back in four, sugar," she whispered, and ran up the steps.

The taxi sped them back to the marina. A light rain had started and the sun was gone.

Before Rose got into the boat she asked, "You sure it's ok, with the storm comin' and all? It seems a might dark out."

"I've got a spotlight," Eliot said, "and a compass. We'll be fine. Just get in and make yourself comfortable, baby."

"Mighty fine yacht, Mr. Hawthorn."

"Yes, she's a fine vessel. Now shut up and get in the cabin."

They took off from the dock quietly and slipped out into the Gulf unnoticed. The taxi driver didn't recognize Eliot. No one saw them on the dock.

An hour and a half later Rose was on her back in the boathouse and Eliot forced his way deeper and deeper inside her, taking every ounce of pleasure from her he could derive. Then he left her, with the usual instructions not to come to the house or turn on the lights.

"But what if...what if the storm kicks up?"

"If it does I'll come and get you. We have a safe room that can withstand any storm."

"And you're wife?"

"I'll tell her you're one of the new maids. She's always so drunk she won't know the difference."

## Monday Night, October 29, 1956

The sun was gone and the wind was whipping black fury against the thin glass that separated me in the safety of my room from the certain watery death waiting outside. I'd never been through a storm like this before. Sure, we had Nor'Easters that could tear your head off, but this was different...I wasn't in a steel and concrete building in the City or anchored in my old brick row-home in Weehawken; No this time I was sitting in an overblown Tiki hut with the Atlantic Ocean knocking on one door and the Gulf of Mexico banging on the other, and if the two decided to rendezvous I'd be caught in the middle with no goulashes.

I tried ringing Melinda twice, but got no answer at her apartment. The front desk said she hadn't been around for hours; she'd had her hands full organizing the storm preparations. Then I remembered Jessica, and wondered how she was doing. I decided sitting alone in my room wasn't going to do anyone any good so I threw on a clean white shirt and my beige summer sport jacket and made my way up to Jessica's room.

"Man, am I glad to see you, chum. This storm is giving me the heebie-jeebies." Jessica lit a cigarette as I entered her room and shut the door. She waved one my way and I accepted. "Have a drink?" she asked, pointing at a bottle of Jim Beam on the dresser.

"Sure. Ice, soda if you've got it."

"I do," she said and poured us a couple of highballs. She was acting very relaxed, as if nothing had happened, as if we were still pals like we were a few days ago. She was sober. I was surprised. "You look good kid, I guess a little rest is all it took."

"Usually does. And I always rest better here, for some reason. Here on the Island. Like I...I don't know, it's silly I guess, but I always feel like I belong here, like this is home."

"Whatever it takes, kid. Cheers." We raised glasses and I took a generous sip. Then I put the drink down and sat on the edge of the bed. "So, you have time to think about your future?"

Jessica took a long drink and set hers down next to mine. She looked around the room, then parted the curtains and took a peak out into the darkness. The rain fell so hard and the thunder came so often now I'd almost gotten used to it. Almost.

"The storms are when *they're* at their worst, you know," she said quietly.

"How's that?"

"The spirits…when it storms, they come out in full force. At least they do in Key West. Never seen them here during a storm." She turned and looked at me with big, blue, sad eyes. "Glad I'm here now, with you."

"Jessica," I said in a sort of tired way, "Ok, I've seen some crazy stuff since I met you. But I still find it hard to swallow that you've got ghosts tormenting you all the time. Don't you think a lot of it can be the booze and monkey juice?"

She laughed at me, and shaking her head said, "Billy, I told you. That stuff doesn't cause the visions. That stuff makes them go away."

"And what if you went far away, maybe all the way across the country. Would they follow you?"

"Maybe. I don't know."

"Look," I said standing up. I was close to her now, too close for my own good. Everything was topsy-turvy now, and I wasn't playing it smart. I knew Jessica was a bad seed but I couldn't help how I felt. I didn't want to fall for her. I didn't want to fall for Melinda. Dammit, maybe it was the rum, or something in the limestone under this crazy place but I just couldn't help it, couldn't control myself the way I had with other women.

I took a step closer to her and said, "I want to help you, Jessica. I want to help you get away from these – things, whatever they are. I want to help you get cleaned up and find a decent way to make a living, far away from the Roberts and Bachmans of the world. I want –" I couldn't finish the sentence. She moved in so fast I didn't know she'd done it until her lips were on mine and her arms were wrapped around me. I gave in and kissed her back hard, holding her head in my one hand, her waist in the other. I pulled her in close and kissed her and didn't stop until I couldn't breath anymore. Then I let the oxygen flow back to my brain and I got wise and gently pushed her away.

"Bill," she said, pleading, begging. "Bill, I…I love you." Her eyes were watery and a little red. I stared down at her, not knowing what to do or say. Her lips quivered just a little. A tear made a path down her soft, pale cheek. "Bill, please, say something."

I stood there like a mute jerk, without even an expression of love or hate or anything in between on my poker face. I was still holding her arms. I could feel her tremble under my fingers. I gently let go.

I said low and quiet, "I can't," and left her there in the room, crying.

I hightailed it down the hall as fast as I could without making a racket and found myself at the entrance of the back deck dining room. The room was full of people eating and drinking and looking out at the foggy, rainy mess through he picture windows. I asked the girl if Melinda was in there. She was not.

I walked some more. I walked down the newer wing, built for the economy class. I just walked and walked and tried to clear my head as best I could. What was it about that dame that cast a spell over me whenever she was near? Dammit, if I was going to complicate my life, I could do it with Melinda – smart, beautiful, rich, living in paradise. Why was my head playing tricks on me, trying to get me to fall for the equally as beautiful and smart but oh-so-screwed-up Jessica?

How could I possibly have any feelings for a junkie, even if she was just a *borderline* junkie?

I walked and walked and found myself in a strange place, a back-of-the-house storeroom. It had a padlock that'd been jimmied open with a crowbar. My old gumshoe senses kicked in and with a heavy dose of caution I went inside. Strange shadows jumped out at me from all kinds of crazy stuff piled up in the dark, illuminated only by the light from the open door. I found a light switch and flipped it up, and a bank of dim fluorescents cast an eerie light over the stock.

What a weird place, I thought.

Lined up against a wall were giant carved Tiki Gods, none smaller than five feet high. To the left were dozens of round wooden tables, folded up and ready to be deployed for a banquet. All sorts of decorative props filled in the space in between, from plastic palm plants to wood columns. Boxes of gold chains and seashells created a pile near the door. Next to them sat a very old looking desk, fitted with a green banker's lamp not unlike mine in New York. Curiosity got me and I pushed the black "on" button on the lamp.

I don't know what led me to that room, but what I found on that desk answered some big questions and raised a lot more.

The wind and rain bashed itself against Jessica's window so hard she thought any minute the glass would shatter and the gale-force wind would drive thousands of crystalline shards into her shivering body. She'd already drank a little too much and didn't dare drink more; if Bill should come back and find her drunk he'd really have nothing to do with her.

But she was scared, oh so afraid of what might come out of that storm. For it was on nights like this with the wind howling and the raindrops beating and the thunder crashing through her skull that the phantoms came out in full force, not just one but dozens, sometimes hundreds of souls appearing from nowhere, forming first as dark, wispy mists then growing clearer and more horrifying with each flash of silver-white lightning. It was on nights like this that Jessica would sit curled up and shivering in her Key West apartment, terrified at what she had done, as her walls disappeared and the beach came to her doorstep, and wave upon wave of the dead would slowly emerge from the surf, black and rotted and covered in barnacles, dark green seaweed crawling with myriad unknown sea creatures dangling from their bloated skin. Their eyeless faces would direct themselves toward her, and from mud-filled mouths they would call out her name; evil, gurgling sounds from hell with the underlying tone of *"Jessica"*.

It was nights like this that turned the sweet, young girl into a vacant shell of a woman filled with alcohol and despair. It was nights like this that first made Jessica turn to pills when the alcohol didn't work, and finally heroin when the pills lost their effect.

Tonight she had nothing but a fifth of booze and the sliver of hope that Bill Riggins would change his mind, that he would love her the way she wanted, needed to be loved, be her knight in shining armor and save her from the hideous fate that either the monsters from the sea or the monster in the hypodermic needle had intended for her.

The loudest crack of thunder yet crashed against the room and sent rivets of pain through Jessica's head. She held her hands to her ears. She should have shielded her eyes.

The visions began.

The wind ripped the wall away from her room, exposing her to the rain and the wind and the night. Lit by the bolts of energy from the sky, she could clearly see the beachhead before her, and the churning of the Gulf as the monsoon spun its mischief. Even though the shoreline was hundreds of yards from her eyes Jessica could see it as if it were right in her room with her; every wave, every line of foam, every bit of flotsam was as clear as the bed next to her. She tried to look away but as always could not. She was locked in her gaze as only can happen in a nightmare.

She gazed on.

Something appeared in the water, just off the shoreline.

From one end of the beach to the other, as far as she could see, figures started forming out of the raging surf. Black, hideous phantoms, they were the walking dead rising from their watery graves, coming ashore like an army of the of damned with only a single objective: *Get Jessica*.

She stumbled and fell against the bureau. The bottle of Bourbon fell to the floor with a thud but didn't shatter. She grabbed it, popped the cork and took a long shot straight from the bottle.

The apparitions moved forward.

She screamed. She took another long pull and screamed again.

The apparitions grew larger, closer. She could hear them faintly call her name through the wind and rain.

She struggled to get up against the wind. Now standing, she looked on to the wretched sight before her. Thirty or more phantoms seemed to float up from the beach and into her room. They were there with her now, in the dark, lit only by the glow of the clock radio. Another crack of thunder and lightning, and she saw them clearly.

Black and green bloated faces stared at her. Crabs crawled over the bodies and feasted. In the center was Jessica's mother, her arms stretched out in a pleading gesture. Jessica knocked back another long jolt from the bottle. It didn't do a thing.

Finally, desperately she screamed. "WHAT DO YOU WANT FROM ME!"

*"Hawwwthorn,"* her mother's ghost groaned.

"I don't have him!" Jessica screamed as loud as should could, and threw the bottle straight at the apparition.

The bottle smashed against the wall, just missing the window by a few inches. Glass and liquor flew everywhere, and Jessica melted against her bed, weeping, heaving.

The vision was over, the apparitions gone, for the moment.

It was nearly seven before Melinda finally had all the Resort's storm preparations under control. Normally these things would have been done hours before the storm arrived, but with Bachman's murder and the Sheriff complicating things, she was lucky to get the last of the storm shutters up before the winds made it impossible.

Now the first-floor windows were covered, the small boats were all pulled up on the beach and tied to the building's foundation, the outdoor furniture stored in the sheds and the big boats triple-tied in the loading harbor at the back of the Island. All guests were brought indoors and given battery-operated flashlights and oil-burning lamps in the event of an electrical blackout. Men were stationed at every exit to make sure no curiosity seekers tried to go outside in the gale. To make everyone relax, she ordered the bars, restaurants and room service to offer free well drinks and chips through nine p.m.

She'd been through many storms on the Island, tropical storms and hurricanes, but never in those years had she gotten used to them. On the outside she was a pillar of strength, but on the inside she shook with terror like a delicate autumn leaf, remembering Eliot's account of September, 1935.

A storm as bad as the Great Atlantic Hurricane hadn't occurred since.

To her, that just meant it was a matter of time.

Storms meant a lot more to Eliot. In the years following the Great Atlantic Hurricane he had simply laughed at storms, saying that if he could live through 1935 he could live through anything. But that cocky young boasting gave way to guarded concern and eventually drop-dead fear as he reached his sixtieth year. And with this being the worst storm of the year so far, and so late in the season, Eliot found himself more frightened than he had been in a very, very long time.

It wasn't the rain or the wind or the lightning that frightened him.

It was what came in with the tide.

For Eliot Hawthorn, storm-drenched nights meant one thing: The ghosts of his past would come visiting soon, and in record numbers.

He tried to calm himself with brandy and sleeping pills, but tonight they seemed to have little effect. He paced the candlelit study, mumbling inaudible speeches to the Tiki statues and fish carvings. With every jump of the candle a new shadow leapt, and with it Eliot froze with fear until he realized his fears were, for the present, unfounded.

More brandy.

Another pill.

Eliot's mind whirled. He steadied himself on the back of a chair and slowly found his way to the seat. The drugs were taking effect finally; finally he could drop his guard and get some sleep, hopefully sleep through this God-forsaken storm and awaken with a new dawn fresh and bright. He started to slip away…

A harsh and sudden crash of thunder and a searing white light invaded the room and shook Eliot to his core. Only the slightest sound passed his quivering lips but if he had the strength to scream, he would have. For at the end of the room near the doorway leading to his bedroom stood a most hideous apparition, one he had seen only a few times before on the worst of stormy nights, a horrible mockery of a human devoid of soul or features that would lend any semblance to a living creature. It stood motionless, a muddy, bloated, black mass, hovering just a few inches from the floor. Swamp grass wrapped itself around the thing, dark green and black and rotten. The head was an oversized globe fitted for a monster, crawling with small crabs and sea serpents, eels and God knows what else. Where the eyes should have been were two deep holes oozing with black muck and water.

Eliot froze stiff where he stood. He could feel his heart thud violently in his chest. He closed his eyes trying to believe the apparition was nothing more than a hallucination brought on by the liquor and pills, but when he opened them the creature was even closer, even more disturbing than before. It moved toward him, grotesque arms outstretched in a horrifying reach. Eliot fell back into the chair, his arm trying to shield his eyes from the fate that grew nearer.

"What do you want from me?!" he cried, and again, "What? I can't do anything for you now!"

All at once the phantom flew straight at Eliot so fast he hadn't time to scream. It was on him now. He sat face to face with the loathsome entity, and just as he did before he looked at its bloated, blackened face and he recognized it, and with that realization he screamed, screamed louder than he ever had before.

The phantom screamed too, a high, shrill, ear-piercing howl muffled by the gurgling of mud and slime as it flowed from the thing's mouth.

Eliot was mortified. Black mud and sand crabs dropped onto his lap as the thing tried to speak. It raised its wispy arms and began to wrap its hands around Eliot's throat. Panic and fear ripped through his body as he clamored to get out of the chair and away from the entity. He kicked his way up from the cushion and fell across the side-table and onto the floor, taking a carved Tiki and a shattering glass ashtray with him. He spun onto his back and looked up. The phantom was directly above him now, and seemed to be gathering strength, and form, becoming more...*solid*. With one last gasp Eliot screamed as loudly as he could...

He heard the locks click and the door open, then a bright yellow light filled the room. The phantom was gone.

Melinda screamed, "Eliot!" as she raced through the door. With the lights on she could see him sprawled on the floor surrounded by broken glass, shivering, staring into nowhere. "My God, Eliot, what happened? Are you hurt?"

"Melinda, my precious darling," he said breathlessly, "Oh Melinda yes, I'm fine now, I'm fine now."

Melinda helped him into the chair. She held him tightly while the tears flowed from her eyes. "Eliot, what happened? And where did all this mud and water come from?"

Only the desk had been searched, the rest of the room was cluttered but orderly. Whoever had searched that desk was looking for something specific, and something that belonged to Rutger Bachman. This was his desk according to the black and white engraved metal sign screwed to the side, not his regular office desk by the lobby but a secondary desk used for convenience, one with blank copies of bills of lading, accident reports, stock forms, junk like that. There was an old, well-worn blotter, a twenty year old typewriter and a few pens and pencils in a white coffee cup. Strictly bare-bones, functional.

The locked drawers had been jimmied open, then removed and turned over on the floor. The file drawer was open and the files mostly gone. A few empty folders remained, but not many. The rest had been turned to ashes in a metal trashcan by the loading door. The pile on the floor was small and held the usual desk stuff, pencils, pink eraser, sharpener, stationary, scissors, letter opener, a broken stapler, clips, a few dollars in change and a blotting pad.

So someone broke in here, went through Bachman's secondary desk and burned a bunch of files that should have added up to no more than a few receipts and reports. Why? What was the connection? Did his killer do this, or was it someone else who had something to hide, who didn't want it found when Bachman turned up dead?

Then I realized three things. First, if someone broke in here it meant they probably didn't have a key. Second, they must have done it after Jackson's boys finished their snooping. Third, they found what they were looking for because they finished the job right there at the desk. They didn't take the whole place apart. I looked at my watch; it was just before seven. I decided to do a little snooping myself before reporting this to Jackson.

Using a rag I lifted the desk blotter and flipped it over. I got lucky on the first shot. Numbers, like a date or a combination to a lock. 07-19-53. I wrote that down on a piece of paper and kept looking. I felt under the desk, all around. Nothing. I found a flashlight and got up under the desk, checking for more hidden type. Nothing. I pulled the file drawer...it wouldn't come out. So I ripped it out. Bingo. Taped to the bottom of the drawer was a key, the type that opened padlocks or lockers, or small safes. I took the key and threw the drawer down with the rest of the junk.

A key and some numbers. A safe? Maybe. But where?

I wiped the prints off the flash and turned out the lights, taking the key and the paper with the numbers with me.

A few minutes later I was in front of Bachman's apartment. The crime scene tape was still up but the door was unlocked. I went in.

Inside I searched everywhere for a safe. The walls, behind paintings, the floor, under furniture, under the bed, even in the bathroom. I even checked to see if the hi-fi was a dummy. Nothing. If he had a safe on Tiki Island, it wasn't in his room.

I quietly stepped back into the hall and headed for his office on the first floor. It was after seven now, and the storm was really taking off. The lights flickered a few times and every time they did I could hear the entire lobby and dining room gasp, then explode with laughter. A bellhop caught me on the way down and told me they were serving free drinks in the lounge. I told him thanks, but I had more important things on my mind.

The girl at the front desk let me back, but Bachman's office door was locked. She said she didn't have a key, that Jackson had taken it and locked the office himself. I thanked her and headed up to Melinda's room. I was hoping she'd be finished for the day and resting, but somehow I didn't think she would be. When I got to her room I knocked and waited. Nothing. I knocked again. I heard some muffled noises, and it occurred to me she'd probably be with Eliot so I went down the hall to his apartment and knocked there.

Melinda opened the door.

The scene was very different now. Eliot wasn't in the parlor room and the overheads were on and shining bright. The rug was soaking wet and there were globs of mud on the floor and chair. Melinda was pale, too pale for a tan-skinned Hawaiian. Her eyes were wide and red. She looked at me but didn't say a word.

A knot started up in my stomach. My heart started pounding faster than it should have and I got that feeling a cop gets when he knows something's bad and all hell's about to come raining down on him. A clap of thunder struck directly overhead shaking the whole hotel just then, and that didn't help matters in the least.

"You Ok, kid?" I said to Melinda. She just stared at me, not blinking. It was eerie. I grabbed her by the arms and gave her a little shake. "Melinda? Answer me. What gives?"

The shake did it. She came out of her strange trance and looked up at my eyes with hers.

"Oh, William!" she cried, and grabbed hold of me tight. I put my arms around her and held her in the doorway while she wept.

"What happened?" I asked quietly.

She looked back up and said, "Oh, you wouldn't believe me if I told you. It's too...too insane."

"Try me."

She pointed to the mud and the wet floor. "Eliot...had a *visitor*." She emphasized 'visitor' as if it were Hitler coming to discuss train schedules.

"Who?"

She hesitated. "We don't know for certain who. But we know *what* it was, William. It was..." She took a deep breath and continued very quietly. "It was one of *them*, one of the entities that have been torturing Eliot all these years. It...*materialized*."

She was right, that was pretty hard to swallow, even after the things I'd seen. "You mean, Eliot saw a ghost and he thinks it became real?"

"No William. It was real. It was here, and it left proof." She pointed to the mud and water. Suddenly an image of Jessica's vision popped into my mind, the woman with the mud and water gurgling out of her mouth as she tried to speak. I shook it off. "You sure there wasn't just an employee up here who got caught in the rain?"

Melinda almost screamed with frustration. "No! Dammit, no employees. Eliot wouldn't have let them in. He was in here alone until I came in about fifteen minutes ago. I heard him scream just as I was opening the door. I threw the light switch and saw him on the floor...William, there was something *over* him, hovering, something black and smoky, and it had..." She choked up a little, then went on. "It had its hands...if you could call them that...around his throat. But as soon as the light came on, it turned to me, then disappeared, dissolving into thin air!" She began to cry again, and I held her close once again. "It was dripping, William, dripping with water and Eliot said the mud came from its mouth and –"

"Shhhh," I said and stroked her hair. "Don't think about it. I'm here now, no spooks can hurt you, or Eliot." I was strong for her, but inside my guts were twisting.

Because I believed her.

I believed every word she said and that scared me more than any ghost ever could. "Where's Eliot now?"

"Sleeping. I gave him a sedative. He was hysterical, William, as you can imagine."

"Yeah," I said, but I couldn't, not really. "Listen, doll, are you all right? There's something I need your help with, if you can leave Eliot alone."

"I...I don't think he's going to wake up for a while, even with this storm. What is it you need?"

"Do you know, did Bachman keep a safe somewhere? Maybe something private that was supposed to be a secret?"

A crazy, loud knock rattled the apartment door before she could answer.

The storm raged on, both outside and in Jessica's head. She'd reached her breaking point. If she had her juice, she'd have shot up every cc to make the hurt go away, but she had none, and her liquor was soaking into the rug, and her nerves were shot and her mind burning with the visions that had tormented her to the point of insanity. Before now she could almost tolerate them, with the help of the monkey juice and the booze and the company of strangers. But not this time. This time they had gone too far, too damned far. Even after all she'd been through, her mother's apparition in the old house, her possessed doll, the visits in the night, this was just too much for her to handle. A fuse blew out in her head, she could feel it, a little pain that shot down her spine and changed her forever. It was subtle, but it was there.

She got to her feet and made her way into the bathroom. The light seemed dull as she pondered her reflection in the mirror. Her eyes were weak, red. Her skin flushed. She washed her face and mechanically applied some makeup to look more presentable, then left her room.

Jessica tried Riggins' room first, but he wasn't there. She asked for him at the front desk, the lounge, the dining room. No one knew where he was. Finally, sadly, she tried Melinda's room. She was both disappointed yet at the same time relieved he wasn't there. Then she thought of Hawthorn's room, and walked toward it.

I streak of lightning ripped through the hotel. Thunder crashed all around, rumbling through like a locomotive gone haywire. Then the lights died, and in the sudden darkness Jessica slumped to the floor crazed with terror, afraid of what she might see when the lights came up.

The lightning flashed again.

They were there.

The rotting dead, all around her, moving through the hall, hovering over the balconies. Her mind twisted with blood-red winds and black rain. She tried to scream but her throat closed up and wouldn't allow it. All that came out was a hoarse shriek of air, a broken teakettle in the dark. The lightning flashed again and the entities were practically on top of her, in her face, their vacant eye sockets dripping, their rotten lips mimicking her name, *"Jessica"*.

Her heart must have stopped, at least for a second. A pain tore through her chest like a red hot knife piercing her soul. She squirmed and closed her eyes, and when she reopened them the lights had come up and she was alone in the hall. She jumped up and ran to Hawthorn's suite and pounded on the door like a madwoman fearing for her life.

Melinda and I looked at each other as the barrage of knocks continued on the door. Without a word I stepped over and opened it. It was Jessica, her eyes crazy and her knuckles red and swollen from knocking. She screamed my name and spilled into the room, grasping at the rug as she pulled herself along the floor towards Melinda. Then she felt the water, and saw the mud, and started screaming her head off as if the floor were soaked with acid.

I slammed the door shut and ran to her, at the same time Melinda reached her. Jessica was in hysterics, screaming, kicking, trying to wipe the mud away from her hands. We both grabbed her and pulled her away from the watery rug.

"Jessica, calm down, JESSICA! Look at me kid, you're with me now, you're safe!"

She didn't believe me. She kept kicking and screaming and gave Melinda a good shot in the leg that was going to leave a bruise. "Melinda, you got any more of that sedative?"

"Yeah, I'll get it," she said and was gone in a flash, back in an instant with a needle. She half-filled it with a clear liquid and stuck it in Jessica's arm while I held her down. Within seconds Jessica was settled down, breathing hard in the chair but the screaming had stopped and she wasn't kicking anymore.

"Strong stuff. What did you give her?"

"Phenobarbital with a dash of Demerol."

"Jesus. That should keep her calm for a while."

Jessica said quietly, slowly, "Calmmmm. Maybeee, on the outside; my head is...racing. I think...I think I'm going to have a heart attack. Hmm."

"What happened dollface?" I asked, kneeling in front of her. Melinda crossed her arms.

"They...they came again," she said weakly.

"Who? Who came, kid?"

She looked at me, then at Melinda, then back at me. "You *know* who, Billy. She knows too. Them."

"You mean the apparitions?" I asked. Melinda looked nervous.

She rose up and said "YES!" very loudly, then sunk back into the chair. "They were in my room...and the hall...and oh God, they were here too! You saw them, didn't you! The mud...the mud from their eyes!"

She covered her face and cried. Melinda froze, her eyes staring wildly at Jessica. She was trembling.

I asked Melinda, "Do you know what she's talking about? Give."

"Yes, I think I do," she said softly, hesitantly. "I can't believe it's possible, but do you think...do you think she's seen the same things as Eliot?"

Under her breath Jessica said, *"You know I did."*

I got up and ran my hand through my hair. I was about to believe anything at this point.

"What exactly did Eliot see?"

Jessica answered. "The dead, from the ocean. Walking in on the waves. Bloated, black bodies that had been dead in the water for days or weeks or years. Covered in seaweed and creepy little white crabs. Their eyes are always gone, hollow, their heads filled with nothing but mud and seawater. And it spills out, slimy and wet, out of their eyes and down their faces and out of their black mouths over their black swollen tongues and, oh God! Why are they torturing *me?!"*

Melinda was shaking more visibly now. She looked at me and said, "Yes, that's what Eliot describes. That's why he drinks, and needs the sedatives. That's why he's..." She didn't finish; she just twisted her face holding back the agony and tears.

I went to her and held her. I wanted to hold Jessica too. I wanted to save them both from whatever was tormenting them, make them happy again. I couldn't believe such a beautiful place could be so cruel to such undeserving people. Whatever these things were, whatever it was they wanted had something to do with this Island, and they were trying to get what they wanted through Hawthorn, and Jessica, and Melinda – and now me.

*Me.* Why *me?* Why now, after all these years of haunting Jessica and Hawthorn, why was this happening *with me here*... insanity all around me... while I'm only here for a couple of weeks? Was it coincidence? Could something as simple as coincidence really have brought me and Jessica and Melinda and Hawthorn together on this crazy stormy night? Or was it something more..intentional? Something (or some beings?) more *sinister* at work?

The thunder crashed and a moan came from Eliot's room. Melinda broke from my arms and ran to him.

"Come on kid," I said to Jessica, "I'm not sure what's going down but I think it's a bad idea to be separated just now." I hoisted her up and grabbed her around the waist to hold her up. She smiled at me. "Into the bedroom," I said.

"Sure thing, Billy," she said groggily yet seductively. I rolled my eyes and helped her into the bedroom.

Melinda was sitting on the bed next to Eliot. I sat Jessica down on the big reclining chair in the corner.

"What's this?" she asked, the drug taking its full effect. "Listen, I don't do," she paused and seemed to count us, then herself in a very drunk-like manner, "...foursomes. The chick can stay," she paused again, "But the old guy's gotta go." She then tilted her head to the side and passed out. I couldn't help but laugh.

"Oh, you think that's funny, do you?" Melinda asked, half serious and half joking.

"Well at least she picked you over Eliot."

"Uh huh."

"How is he?"

"He was already back asleep when I walked in. Nightmares now. Only nightmares."

I walked over and sat next to her on the bed. It was as hard as a rock, and I wondered how the old man got any sleep at all.

"Melinda, we've got to talk. If there really is something...abnormal..."

"Paranormal, it's called."

"Ok, whatever it is...if something really is going on here, and Bachman was murdered..." I trailed off. I couldn't bring myself to say it.

Melinda said it for me. "You think these apparitions have something to do with Bachman's death?"

It sounded crazy. It *was* crazy. I tried to think of a way to make it sound less crazy but there weren't any. I tried anyway. "All I'm saying is that Bachman was a real person who was really murdered. What's happening to Eliot and Jessica, no court in the world would believe a word of it. If word gets out that either of them...or you for that matter...are seeing ghosts, Sheriff Jackson will probably consider that a sign of insanity. He could have Eliot put away for that. It won't look good for you, either."

"Or for Jessica," she said, and for the first time a little jealousy crept into her tone. There was no smile, either.

"Jessica's got bigger fish to fry. To be honest, a chick like her shooting dope and boozing it up all the time, I'd be surprised if she *didn't* see things. And Eliot, you said it yourself, his mind is slipping. He's been a recluse for years and he's putting away a good amount of brandy and barbiturates himself. Again, any jury would say he's hallucinating."

"Are we hallucinating the mud and water on the floor?"

"No, of course not. But again, any employee who was working outside could have brought in mud and water."

"But they didn't."

"I know," I said, getting irritated. "That's not the point. The point is, no one is going to believe that Hawthorn is being visited by real ghosts. Period."

"What about her?" she asked, pointing to Jessica. "Is it just a coincidence that they're seeing the same things?"

"Kiddo, you don't have to convince me. I've seen enough crazy stuff on this trip that I'm not dismissing anything anymore. It's the rest of the world you'd have to convince. Jessica works here. You're putting her up while she dries out. Obviously you two and Eliot here could have cooked up this whole ghost story thing to throw the cops off the trail."

"Off the trail of what?"

I took out my Camels and shook one out of the deck. I didn't care anymore that she didn't like it. Hawthorn smoked cigars and this was his pad. I needed one and that was that. I lit it and blew the smoke away from Melinda. She didn't say a word.

"Off the trail of a murderer, kid."

She thought a moment. I watched her, noticed how her big brown eyes seemed to reflect every bit of low light from the room, how her dark hair shined, how her breathing seemed to get more intense.

"So you're saying you think Eliot or I killed Bachman, is that it?"

That surprised me.

"Hell no, I don't think *you* did it anymore than I did it. But Jackson might see it that way, and he can make things very difficult for you if he wanted to."

Melinda rolled her eyes and got up from the bed with an annoyed groan. She walked over to the mini-bar set up near the window and poured two whiskeys. "Detective Riggins, I'm starting to lose faith in your powers of deduction." She handed me the juice and drank hers down in one shot. I sipped mine.

"What gives?" I asked.

"Don't you get it? Of course Eliot and I are the prime suspects on this murder, as are you. In fact, it would make plain sense that I wanted Bachman out of the way so I could run the Resort the way I want, and used you as the muscle."

"Sure, that's an angle. Not the best one but it fits."

"And why do you think any of us are still free, and not locked up at the county jail?"

I thought a minute. It hadn't occurred to me until she said it. Sure, we were trapped on an Island but there was enough circumstantial evidence to at least put me in the hold. There was only one reason why Jackson hadn't taken any of us back to jail. "Hawthorn's paying off Jackson, isn't he," I said flatly.

"Of course he is, William. How do you think Bachman's been able to get away with bringing girls in here? How do you think that little house in Key West is still operating? Money. Eliot's been throwing his money around since the 1920s. People have just come to expect it. He used to pay off Roberts too…and only recently decided that Roberts was a liability. If not, no matter what Roberts did to you, he'd be out on the street again in a week. The only reason Jackson is able to make the charges stick now is that Eliot told him to, understand?"

Damn.

"I hadn't pegged Jackson for a crooked cop," I said, deflated. "Not him."

"Crooked? He's not crooked at all. He's as upstanding as they come. But he knows his place. He knows what he can get away with. Eliot's money is a formality. An insurance policy. If Jackson didn't take it, he'd be run out of the Keys and Eliot would find someone to take his place. Instead he plays ball on a couple insignificant issues and gets to serve and protect the way a real Sheriff should."

It was hard to swallow, but with what little I'd learned about Florida politics it seemed to fit. Jackson wasn't running the house or the girls or the other party favors. He turned his back when he had too, and kept them all in line when he had to, but he didn't have anything to do with the business. Strange politics, I guess, but really none of my business. Like I said, I'm on Va...

A crack of lightning lit up the room like a summer day, then died. The lights flickered again but held. The storm raged on.

"Well kid, somebody killed Bachman. And somebody is going to take the fall for it. I can guarantee it won't be me. I'd sure as hell hate for it to be either of you." I finished the Scotch and handed her the glass. "Now, if you'll answer my previous question. Did Bachman have a safe somewhere?"

She thought a moment before answering, then shook her head. "No, not that I know of."

"Can you give me the keys to his office then? I need to search for one."

"Jackson doesn't want anyone going in there, he said."

I took a long drag on the cigarette and blew the smoke out slow. "I'm not worried about Jackson. He's on the payroll."

Melinda stayed with Hawthorn and Jessica while I went down to check out Bachman's office. The lobby was full of people, mostly drunk, many singing along with a guitarist that was strumming standards. The front desk girl let me back and I opened the lock with Melinda's key.

Inside the office had been picked clean by Jackson's crew. Fingerprint powder was everywhere. Every drawer had been opened and every piece of furniture moved.

I started moving things myself.

I checked under the chairs, the couch, the desk. I moved every book off of the bookshelves and checked for loose carpeting everywhere. Again, nothing. Nothing in the walls, nothing in the floor. If Bachman had a safe, it wasn't in his office or his room.

I did find something I didn't expect, though.

On his desk was a notepad, and on the notepad was written: Hawthorn, 4pm Sunday. I also found his personnel file, left out on the desk no doubt by one of the deputies. I sat on the corner of the desk and thumbed through it. The usual stuff was there, home address, age, copy of his resume, copy of his degree from college. But one thing really stood out from the others: his date of employment.

It was July, 1953.

07-19-53.

A date, and no doubt in my mind now a combination to a safe.

I put everything back the way I found it and left.

## Sunday, August 30, 1935

She slept late in the summer heat, cooled only by a small electric fan and a single open window. She dared not open the other window, the one facing the mansion and the grounds. Hawthorn wouldn't like that.

Rose stretched and yawned, naked in the late morning light. A soft breeze lightly rustled the palms, and the only other sounds she heard were of the water gently lapping at the yacht in the boathouse and the far off cry of a pelican. She peaked out the window. The Gulf was smooth and placid.

"Hard to believe a big storm is comin'," she said to herself. Rose tossed on a light robe and got herself an apple and bottle of orange juice from the icebox, then settled in at the little booth by the window and gazed out over the Gulf as she ate. Boredom quickly overcame her.

She decided to explore the yacht. That took all of about fifteen minutes. Then she dropped down into the cool water of the boathouse. It was refreshing but felt oily. She toweled off and found some books on a shelf. One was The Great Gatsby, a book she'd heard about but never read. "Now's a good a time as any, I suppose," she said to herself again and settled into the bed with the book and a second apple.

It was around two o'clock when she heard the roar of boat engines. They started, gunned, then drifted away. She lost interest and went back to her book. She had gotten as far as page twenty-seven when Eliot showed up at the boathouse.

"Hey sugar! I sure am glad to see you, I'm goin' out of my cotton-pickin' mind 'round here."

"Well, your worries are over. My wife has left the Island. We are alone."

Rose jumped up from the bed, elated. "Really? Does that mean that…"

"It means you can come up to the mansion, like a proper guest. It means a proper luncheon and a bath, too."

Rose was so excited she almost didn't notice the subtle change in Eliot. But she did notice; he seemed quieter somehow, with an almost imperceptible sadness about him.

"You sure everything's ok, shug? I mean, you sure no one will know?"

"I'm sure," he said, that twinge of sullenness still there. She decided it was nothing, just the stress of dealing with the upcoming storm, and canceling the big party.

"Well all right then! Let's go!"

Eliot opened the door for Rose and she got the first look at Hawthorn Island in the daylight. It was beautiful. A pristine white plantation home with a shiny metal roof and long, tapered columns running up the front. The gardens were beautiful too, with giant, colorful flowers, the likes of which she had never seen before in her life. But once inside the house her heart melted. She had always dreamed of living in a house with a double-circular staircase in the center of the entranceway. This house had just that, white-painted oak with red accents spiraling up to an indoor veranda that overlooked the magnificent marble and stucco room.

"This is absolutely fabulous!" Rose exclaimed as she whirled through the rooms.

"Go have a bath, sweetheart. You must be all sticky from the heat."

"Hey, wait a sec," she said, "Am I crazy? Or is this place…cool?"

"It is quite cool," Eliot said smiling. "An invention of an old friend. They call it air conditioning. I have it in my Packard, too."

"My, my," she said. "I think I adore air conditioning!"

Don't get too used to it, Eliot thought but didn't say. "Go on up and take a nice, long bath. I'll have some roast chicken and tangerines ready for you when you're finished."

Rose hugged Eliot around the neck. "Thank you sugar. This is a fine way to spend a Sunday!" she said, and ran up the stairs.

"It's on the left," Eliot yelled up, "Try not to get lost."

A half an hour later they were dining on meats and hors d'oeuvres prepared for the party, French wine and imported chocolates. Rose forgot all about the gray, windy death lingering a hundred miles off-coast in the Atlantic. Almost.

"Eliot, sugar, if you don't mind my askin', why did your Mrs. leave the island if you have a safe room here?"

"Because she's a fool," he answered, patting his hands on his napkin. "She doesn't trust it here. Fine with me. Gives us time to have some fun together."

Rose got up from the table. "And fun's what it's all about, ain't it sugar?" She let the robe slide to the floor, revealing her curves wrapped up in a midnight blue negligee that pushed things just the right way, in just the right places. A pair of black silk stockings and black heels finished off the ensemble.

"Black. Nice, but it's not after Labor Day yet," Eliot quipped. Rose slowly made her way to him, walking deliberately in such a way that every part of her moved in harmony, like a wild cat on the prowl.

"Well," she said, "Maybe I can find a way to get you to forgive me."

"Maybe," Eliot said as she kneeled in front of him. "Maybe you will."

He enjoyed every minute, but his mind was in another place.

## 1956

Melinda let me back into Hawthorn's room.

"Eliot is fast asleep in bed," she whispered as I walked into the darkened parlor. "Jessica is knocked out on the sofa in his bedroom" A crash of thunder shook the walls. The sounds of rain splashing against the side of the Hotel and wind whipping through the halls made it difficult to hear her whispers.

"How can they sleep with all this noise, kid?"

"The sedative is pretty potent. They'll probably be comatose for hours."

"Do you think we can leave them alone long enough to grab some chow? I'm starved."

Melinda seemed apprehensive. "I suppose we could have room service bring something up here."

"Nix that idea," I said. "I can't stand it cooped up in here with this crazy storm shaking the place. I need to be around people, kid."

Melinda looked around at the room, not sure what she was looking for. Then she looked back at me. Her big browns shined in the candlelight, just the way they had at our first dinner. I hadn't realized how close she was to me until then. Before I knew it I found her arms around me, and I drew her in close. Our lips met softly, in one of those moments when the world slips away and you forget what it was you were talking about, and all that matters is you and her and the touch of her lips against yours. I closed my eyes and for a second I could feel myself wanting to be with her, forever, here, in this flawed but still beautiful paradise.

A burst of lightning shot through the cracks around the shuttered windows and broke the spell. A split second later the thunder crash came, searing and loud and hot.

"It's almost on top of us now," Melinda said. "This will be the worst of it. Now."

I was still holding her close. "How long do you think it will last?"

"Hard to say," she answered, still whispering. "Probably long into the night. The storms slow down when they hit the keys, then pick up speed and usually head west or north when they move into the Gulf.

"These things make me nervous," I said. I wasn't used to being on an island in a tropical storm, was all.

"Don't worry, this place was built to withstand one-hundred-thirty-mile-per-hour winds, and a twenty-five-foot tidal wave."

"How big was the wave that hit in thirty-five, again?"

"Twenty feet," she said, smiling.

"I feel better already. What about that chow now, huh?"

She blew out a deep sigh. "Sure, I think the kids will be ok if we leave them alone for a little while. *I think*."

Melinda called ahead to the Tiki Deck on the second floor and had them set up a table and prepare dinner for us.

"We might as well have some sort of view," she said as we walked in. The windows were all uncovered, exposed to the elements.

"Isn't that sort of dangerous? What if something comes flying through that glass?"

"Settle down, scardy-cat!" she joked. "It's bullet-proof. Four-inch thick glass. Eliot had it made especially for this room. You could hit it with a truck at forty miles-per-hour and not go through it."

"You guys thought of everything, didn't you?"

Melinda suddenly turned very serious, in a way I hadn't really seen before. It spooked me a little. "Eliot lost his wife and his best friend in that storm, William. And he believes it was his own fault. So yes, before allowing a single soul to spend the night on this Island, he thought of everything. There's even a Safe Room below the building, carved into the limestone and sealed against the water."

That got my attention. "A Safe Room? Like a basement?"

"Exactly. We can hold over two hundred people in there. There's a supply of canned food, fresh water, toilets, everything needed to survive for weeks even if the Island is totally submerged."

"Like a bomb shelter," I said as I settled into my plank steak.

"Sort of, except not meant for any real long-term living. Just a place to ride out a storm, if necessary. Luckily we've never needed to use it."

"Let's hope you never do, especially tonight." The waiter brought two Mai Tais. "Buddy, can you do me a favor?" I asked him. "Give my Mai Tai to the lady and bring me a double Bourbon on the rocks?"

"Certainly sir," he said.

"Make it a Wild Turkey. I need something stiff."

"Right away sir," he answered and ran off.

"Bourbon?" Melinda asked.

"Yeah. This ain't a night for no foo-foo drinks, doll." Melinda laughed. I just smiled.

### Sunday, August 30, 1935

It was about four in the afternoon when Eliot heard the loud engine of the Deputy's boat.

"Who is that?" Rose asked as she lay in Eliot's bed, in the place where Vivian had lain for years.

"Not sure, probably Roberts. You wait here. I don't want him knowing you're here."

"Ok sugar," she said, and slid back down onto the pillows.

Eliot dressed quickly and made his way down to the rear loading dock. There Roberts and two of his men were docking. Roberts came up on the landing, waving.

"Just checkin' to see everything's all right, Mistuh Hawthorn," Roberts yelled from the dock.

"Fine, fine. Everything's buttoned up and ready for whatever hits us."

"Ya'll know, suh, they's sayin' this storm's brewin' up to bein' one of the worst ever to hit us. You sure ya'll want ta stay here on the Island? Might be better to head up aways to Miami, don't ya think?"

An annoying man, Roberts was, Eliot thought to himself. "I'm sure we'll be fine, Roberts. This house has stood for over forty years. I don't think a little wind is going to blow it away."

"Suit yo'self, suh. Just wanted to make sure ya'll was ok. How's the missus?"

Eliot twitched slightly, not enough for Roberts to see. "She's trying to get some rest up in our room. She's quite deflated that our Labor Day party plans have fallen through. She put a lot of work into this affair, you know."

"Oh, I'm sure. Well suh, you should know they's warnin' people all up and down the middle Keys to evacuate. I won't be able to come on out here again before the storm hits, so if ya'll need anything, I guess you're on your own."

"Well thanks for stopping by, Roberts. Everything is Ok here. Say, what time do they expect the storm to hit us?"

Roberts took off his hat and wiped his hair with a grayish rag. "Well, the people outta Miami been sayin' they figure we oughta start feelin' some wind by morning, tomorrow. Waves should start kickin' up around mid-afternoon. But they ain't sure. Say the storm could veer off, run up the coast and not even touch us. Ya'll know how it is."

"Yeah. Well, thanks again. I'll see you after the storm, I suppose."

"Yessuh," Roberts said somewhat gloomily, "I'll come by after to make sure ya'll are ok. Say hello to the missus for me, kay?"

"Will do. Thank you Roberts."

Roberts let out a heavy breath. "Yessuh."

Eliot turned to leave the Deputy behind, and started back toward the house. A stiff, short breeze hit his back. It was starting already, he thought. Then he felt a tap on his back. Roberts was right behind him.

"Just one mo' thing, suh."

"What is it, Roberts?"

"I didn't want to say in earshot of the other boys. That whore you been seein'…"

"Rose?" Eliot asked, even more annoyed.

"Yeah, that one. You ain't seen her as of late, have you?"

"Not since last weekend, why?"

"She's gone missing since last evening. They said she left in a cab with a man, but no one saw jus' who it was. All she said was she didn't want to ride out the storm in the Keys, and was heading somewhere safe."

Eliot thought a minute, then said, "Well, that's not really missing, is it? I imagine she went up to Miami then. Maybe further. I'm sure she has plenty of clients who would oblige."

"I'm sure," Roberts said rubbing his chin. "Well, ok then. Good luck Mistuh Hawthorn. I'll see you after the storm."

"Good luck to you to, Roberts."

Eliot stood and watched Roberts walk back to the boat, get in, and leave. When the boat was out of sight, he took a walk through the garden where he'd left so many memories, where the grass grew thick and the flowers bloomed year-round. He paused just for a minute, reflecting on his actions and their possible consequences, and in that moment he knew he'd made the right choice, and that no matter how horrific today and tomorrow might be, in the end everything would be all right.

## 1956

The food and booze went down easy with Melinda as company. Even the heavy downpour being whipped sideways into the giant glass windows didn't seem to bother us. Of course when the lightning struck, that was another thing altogether. The searing white light lit up the entire coast of Sugarloaf Key, revealing a pretty disturbing scene: Palm trees that seemed to bend almost in half, boats bobbing like apples in a swimming pool full of kids, and a bay that seemed way too high for anyone's comfort. The rear loading dock was situated at an angle and in such a way that you couldn't see it from the restaurant, but just by looking at the bay you could tell that dock was under water.

"Those palm trees make it look like the end of the world," I said to Melinda.

She laughed. "Palm trees are so phony. You get a fifteen mile an hour gust and they look like it's a typhoon. Don't let them worry you."

"I won't," I said. And I wouldn't, but something was gnawing at me the whole time, something I couldn't put my finger on.

"Is there any possibility of the Island getting flooded?" I asked Melinda as we got up to go. She frowned. It was sad.

"Three times in my lifetime, the entire Island was under water. But none of the buildings. The only damage was that some of the plants couldn't survive the salt water. But the buildings were always fine. It's as if Eliot knew just how high to put them."

I was confused. "The buildings are attached to the ground, ain't they? I mean, the front entrance has some steps but the back end and the side wing open onto ground level, don't they?

Melinda laughed. "They don't. They just appear to. It's a sort of illusion. All the buildings are built up on steel pilings anchored into the limestone. Not one building is less than six feet above sea level. And even in the worst floods, we've only recorded about four feet."

"Krazy. How do you pull it off?"

"Well, in some places its just the rolling, hilly nature of the Island, capitalized on by some very ingenious engineers."

"If the buildings are built up, what's under them?"

"Fill. Mostly rock and sand. Everything's been filled in and built up. Except for the Safe Room."

There it was again, that crazy safe room, and that same gnawing that had been bugging me all night. That was it. That's what my fuzzy, liquor-fogged mind was trying to tell me. There was something not right with that safe room.

"Melinda, where is that room?" I asked as we walked toward Eliot's suite.

"Right below us. It takes up most of the main building area."

"No, I mean the way in."

"Oh, well there's one in the back of the house, next to the kitchen in the Hukilau dining room. The other is in the front of the building."

"Where?"

She thought what I was thinking before I even had a chance to think it. I think. Her eyes lit up wide.

"In the hallway next to the General Manager's office."

"So you're saying the entrance to the Safe Room is next to Bachman's office."

"Yes," she said, smiling, "And a set of keys are kept in his desk."

Bingo.

We checked in on the sleeping beauties before venturing down to the Safe Room. They were both out cold. Apparently apparitions didn't like barbiturates.

The minute we stepped off the elevator Melinda was berated with questions by several very tired, very worried-looking employees. One was afraid they were going to run out of hors d'oeuvres and didn't know what to do. Another said the guests were drinking faster than they could wash glasses. Melinda put one hand up and everyone clammed up quick. There was no doubt about it now. She was in charge.

"Ginny is the M.O.D. She can handle anything you need."

"Ginny's up to her ears in trouble," one of the boys said.

Melinda responded with, "Then Ginny needs to delegate. She's got twenty-five years in hotel management in the Keys. Believe me, she can handle anything you throw at her. I have more important issues to take care of right now. But for now, since you already asked, have housekeeping bring two racks of room glasses down here to cover the guests. At this point I don't think they care if they get their liquor in a fancy glass. And as for the hors d'oeuvres, have the kitchen whip up some Swedish Meatballs and cheese-filled puffs. We've got enough of the ingredients for those to last a week."

The boys thanked her and ran off.

"I'm impressed, Hawthorn, you really know your stuff."

Melinda gave a little laugh. "I picked it up along the way."

"What's a MOD?"

"Not a mod, an M.O.D. Manager on Duty. You think I work twenty-four hours?"

I smiled back a mischievous smile. "I happen to know for a fact you don't, kitten."

"Rrrrrraaaarrrrr," she said back as we headed to Bachman's office.

We found the keys quickly and headed down a short hall to a fire exit and a door with a sign that read "No Access, Authorized Personnel Only, Alarm Will Sound If Opened." Next to the door was a big red bell that looked like something from the last century.

"Fire alarm?" I asked.

"Nope, security. If you open this door without the proper keys, it rings so loud you'll wish you were dead."

"Good thing I know the chick with the keys," I said. She just shook her head and opened the door.

Thunder clapped loud. It seemed to be all around us, penetrating us. I actually felt it in my chest. "I'm starting to have second thoughts about heading underground during this storm."

"William," she said, "It's the Safe Room. The *Safe* Room. We don't call it that because of the pool tables."

"Gotcha," I said. Sometimes I could be pretty silly.

The door opened on a gray-painted hallway with a water-tight door at the end, one that looked like it belonged on a submarine. She opened it to a strange, wide, dark staircase that smelled like wet concrete. She found a switch and a dozen fluorescents came to life, buzzing and flickering before giving us their full attention. The steps, walls and ceiling were solid concrete. The steps were painted white. They showed almost no sign of action.

Melinda said, "No one hardly ever comes down here anymore. I used to play down here on rainy days when I was a kid. I myself haven't been down here in years. We send a cleaning crew in once a month to make sure the place is tidy and the food is still in date." At the bottom of the steps was a small landing and another door. An old clipboard hung on the wall. She picked it up and checked the last page. "Last inspection was on October first. Everything A-OK."

"So no one's been down here in a month?"

She opened another large, steel, watertight door to the Safe Room. "No one who signed the sheet." Automatic lights flickered and came up exposing the room's expanse. It was nothing like I expected.

The room was decorated in the same fashion as the hotel but richer, with bamboo furniture and rattan walls, carved wood ceiling fans, blowfish hanging lamps and hand-painted murals of underwater scenes including mermaids and shipwrecks. There actually were pool tables, or rather billiards tables at one end of the enormous room. A bandstand with a drum-set and amplifier system sat at the opposite end. A carved mahogany and ebony bar ran along the entire expanse of the far wall. It was fully stocked with what looked like hundreds of bottles. A couple of dozen bar stools appeared to be carved from single pieces of tree trunks and upholstered in some exotic leather, perhaps ostrich. Behind the bar were doors that appeared to lead to a kitchen or pantry.

"This is a Safe Room? It looks like a ballroom! No wonder you used to play in here."

"What were you expecting?" Melinda asked curiously, a laugh in her voice.

"I dunno, something like a bunker, you know, like an atom bomb shelter. Concrete walls, metal-spring mattresses, first-aid kits. Stuff like that. Not *this*," I said as I spread out my arms dramatically.

"William, this is *Tiki Island*. It's owned by one of the wealthiest men in the south. Nothing here is utilitarian."

"Isn't it kind of crazy that he'd spend all this lettuce on a room that never gets used?"

Melinda laughed again, that beautiful, joyful laugh that made me think bad thoughts. "Well, I wouldn't exactly say it never got any use. You have to remember, Eliot was a socialite. He loved to entertain his friends, so much so that his former home was known for it's great parties. Things didn't change with Eliot when he built Tiki Island. For years he still had his parties, just like he did when this was known as Hawthorn Island." We walked over to the bar. Melinda sat on top, swung around and landed behind it. She opened a bottle of Jack and poured as she spoke. "This was his private party room. This is where he and my mother and their friends lived it up, secretly, away from the eyes and ears of the regular guests. This is where he continued his traditions of wild, crazy parties with gambling tables, dancing girls from Cuba and guests from all over the world."

That kind of threw me. "I thought that all ended when he lost his first wife?"

"No, not entirely. Oh, some things changed…he no longer imported prostitutes or illegal drugs from Cuba. No, my mother wouldn't allow that at all." Melinda's tone changed to something more mischievous, more playful. "But from what I hear, most of the girls he brought in as entertainment were 'loose'. They weren't prostitutes in the traditional sense. They just got paid an awful lot for dancing around wearing next to nothing, and had a habit of not spending their nights alone."

"There it is again. Tell me, is the seaside resort business really built on vice?"

Melinda smiled. "This one was. But not all." She handed me a glass of Jack. "Sorry, no ice."

"That'll do."

"Eliot was...unique. He was the proverbial child trapped in a grown man's body. When he was younger he wasn't happy unless there was music and laughs and dancing and...well, you know."

"Sex?"

"Yes. And lots of it." She leaned closer and talked in a loud whisper, as if what she was saying was so naughty even the booze bottle shouldn't hear it. "I've heard that the men would bring their wives and trade them off to other men, then rate them on performance!"

"No way," I said, feigning innocence. "Come on, that's stuff made up for the pulps."

"No, really! Of course Eliot and my mother never involved themselves in that action, but I've heard from people who worked here that they'd trade two or three times a night! And sometimes they'd even get one of the dancing girls to join them."

"Yeah, right," I said and took a long sip of my drink. "I've been a vice cop for five years and I've never come across anything like that for real."

"Then you've never come in contact with the idle rich, my friend," she said, and knocked back her Jack. She winced, and poured another.

"And they used to do that down here, huh?" I asked, looking around.

"Well, no, I guess they went up to their rooms. Although I bet if they had the chance they would have made each other right up here on the bar." She set her drink down, turned around and jumped up on the bar again, then spun around slinging one leg over my head and back down so she was sitting in front of me, her long, silky legs wrapped loosely around my waist. "Don't you think so, William?"

My head was spinning just a little from the liquor. Dull, muffled thuds pounded through the walls; thunder, shut out by the rock surrounding the Safe Room. Melinda slid off the bar in front of me.

"You're a bad girl for thinking such thoughts, kitten," I said as her lips brushed against mine. "You better stop."

She tilted her head up so that her eyes were looking up into mine. Her arms found their way around me and she leaned in close. One of her thighs pressed up against me in just the right way. Those big, hungry browns bored into my soul. She wet her lips gently with her tongue in a way that made me glad God made me a man.

"Make me," she said softly.

"Yes mam," I said. Then I did.

The room didn't shake with the thunder but it sure felt like it did. We ravaged each other, more ravenously than ever, harder, faster, stronger. She was a tigress, I was a lion; together we brought down the jungle around us with a heat that could have melted the balls off a brass monkey. Her bare breasts quivered under my touch, and she moaned with more pleasure than I ever heard a woman moan before. She made a quick move and was on top of me like the tigress on her prey, and with taut muscles and beads of sweat she devoured her prey with a ritualistic jungle fever that carried me to places I never thought ever existed. My whole body shuddered with ecstasy, and with that final explosion we slumped to the floor and lay there panting in the heat.

I fished the pack of Camels out of my pants, then decided against it. I turned to Melinda and asked breathlessly, "What the hell did you play down here when you were a kid?"

She returned with that fantastic laugh, the one that brightened up the room and made me think of leaving my old life forever. "I used to play billiards. But I've always wanted to do *that* down here." She was still smiling when I asked,

"Why didn't you?"

"Never met anyone I wanted to bring down here. Not until now."

"Excuse me, but didn't we come down here to look for a safe?"

"Well, *you* did," she said teasingly, and rolled over onto her stomach.

"I did," I said.

"Are you complaining?"

"Nope."

"Good," she said looking back along her body. "Then I'm ready for round two whenever you are."

This girl was going to kill me yet.


It was after ten when we finally had enough 'go' in us to get dressed. It was great and it was fun, but I still had that safe on my mind. "Where should we start looking?"

"I don't know," Melinda said, "You're the Detective."

"Keep reminding me. I keep forgetting."

"Why don't we start with the obvious places, like behind the bar?"

"Ok," I said. We walked to the end of the bar and went behind, checking every sliding door, nook, and possible hiding place along the way. I said, "Do you think Bachman had enough character to hide a safe in the Safe Room?"

"I think it would be more of a coincidence that the one room of the hotel that hardly gets any use, where it would make the best place for him to hide something like a safe would also be called the Safe Room."

"Good point," I said. "Which brings us to another point." I stopped Melinda from looking through a cabinet and we both stood up straight. "If he'd go all through the trouble of hiding it down here, away from areas of high use, he wouldn't hide it behind the bar."

"No, I suppose not. So where do we look?"

"Maybe you can tell me. You used to play down here, so I'm guessing you did some exploring. Any out-of-the-way nooks or closets?"

She thought a minute, then said, "Oh, of course! The storage room!"

"There's a store room down here too?"

"Yes, where all the emergency supplies are kept. You know, in case we get stuck down here for a couple of days… stuff like metal-spring mattresses, first-aid kits, stuff like that."

"I'm hip. Where is it?"

"Behind the bandstand. Those doors on either side lead to it."

"Well let's go," I said, and we made tracks to the storeroom. The door was locked but Melinda had the key.

She slid the thin strip of brass with the serrated edge into the slot in the lock, and twisted it clockwise. Metal slipped against metal, tumblers fell into place and the small machine worked its only purpose. The door opened.

We peered inside the dark, musty room. Shadows jumped as we moved, backlit by the main room's overhead lamps. Melinda found the light switch, but it didn't work.

"Figures," she said.

"Maybe intentional. Seems unusual the lights would have gone on the blink since October first."

"True. You have a flashlight with you, William?"

"No. Do you?"

"No."

"Look around near the door, there might be one hidden if these lights were blacked out on the know."

"Ok," she said, and felt around by the floor. Something tumbled over with a big racket and Melinda let out a little scream.

"What happened?"

"I thought I saw something move. Just a trick of the light I guess. But look, here's a spotlight."

She brought up one of those big commercial jobs with the can battery and focused lens. She snapped it on. It lit up bright.

"Detective work. Exciting stuff when you're right, ain't it?"

"Yeah. Here Dick Tracy, you hold the light. It's heavy."

"Sure thing doll." I took the light and spread it around the room. Creepy place, even creepier than the storeroom full of Tikis. This one was stacked with surplus army cots, tables, wooden crates labeled canned meats, K-rations, candles, first-aid supplies and canned juice. There were also bed linens, towels and cases of toilet paper. Everything was clean as a whistle, no dust, no cobwebs. The Tiki Island cleaning crew was the best in the biz.

"You ever play in here?"

"I didn't really play, but I've gone through the boxes a few times. The cots are from the big war. Before them we had feather mattresses. Eliot said they were terrible because they soaked up every bit of dampness down here and were always wet."

"Seem dry now."

"That's science at work. He installed dehumidifiers in the late forties. The K-rations and the first-aid supplies are Korean War surplus. Those have a ten-year expiration. Before these he had stuff from 1944. He gave it all out to the employees in '52."

"Fascinating history lesson doll, but that doesn't help us find the safe."

"Well, it may. You see, Rutger was in charge of maintaining this level. He would have managed how to arrange the storage. Now when I was a kid, the mattresses were stacked up against the back wall, there." She pointed to the far corner. "Then when we bought the cots, we stacked them in the same place."

"But now there are shelves with towels there," I said as I shined the flash on them. "And the cots are on the other end of the room."

"Right. So he moved them. Maybe he moved them for a reason."

She was a sharp cookie, this one.

"Maybe because it's easier to move towels than it is to move army cots."

"Yes, my thought exactly, William."

"Let's check that theory out, shall we?"

We walked to the back of the room where the towels were neatly stacked on racks. I shined the light around, and found that the shelves were free-standing, not secured to the wall. Melinda and I each grabbed an end and pulled the shelves out.

Behind the shelves at floor level was a crack in the wall, almost imperceptible but there. I shined the flash right on it and realized the crack was really the outline of a square panel. I pushed it, tapped, then pushed the top corner inward. The bottom swung out and the whole thing fell on the floor revealing a very old, very dusty iron safe mounted into the wall with a combination lock and a key.

"Well I'll be a Humuhumunukunukuapuaa's uncle!" Melinda screamed.

"A whatsahumuwhosit?"

"It's a fish."

"Right. Just hold the flash, will ya?" I gave her the light and she shined it on the knob. I took the paper out of my pocket with the combination on it. "Seven, nineteen, fifty-three," I recited as I spun the knob. Then I slid the key in the lock and turned it, and held my breath as I twisted the old brass handle.

Clunk. Nothing.

"It didn't open," Melinda said.

"Thanks, kid. I wasn't so sure."

"Ok, smart ass, why don't you try the key first, then the combination."

"Yeah, let me try that." I did it. Still nothing. I spun the knob a few times past zero and tried again. Zilch. "What the hell? We finally find the hidden safe and the combination doesn't work!"

"Well, the key works, right?" Melinda asked.

"Yeah, it turns all the way. It wouldn't do that if it weren't the right key."

"So then this must be Rutger's safe, right?"

"Yeah, makes sense. This was his key, from his desk. So, yeah."

"Then that must not be the combination. Maybe he changed it." I thought about that for a minute. Maybe he did. But then again, this note was fresh, written on his desk pad recently. "Maybe it's backwards or something. He was pretty shifty."

"Ok William, try it backwards."

I tried it backwards. Then I tried it front-wards again. Then I mixed the numbers up and tried it again. Still nothing. "Gad-friggin-dammit to hell! No dice, kiddo. He must have changed it recently, or that was never the combo to begin with."

"Damn, William. I really wanted to see what was in there."

"So did I. But if that combination died with Bachman, the only way we'll get into this safe is with a really big drill or dynamite."

"I don't think dynamite's a good idea, William."

"Why not?"

"The Gulf of Mexico is on the other side of that wall."

## Sunday Night, August 30, 1935

The evening turned cool and breezy. Rose sat on the balcony outside of Eliot's bedroom sipping an iced Coca-Cola and enjoying the view of the Gulf and lower Keys. She was in heaven. She'd never known such luxury, such opulence. Eliot's bed was the softest and finest she'd ever laid on, and the quality of the food and liquor was so far beyond anything Rose had ever tasted that she wished this day would never end.

She snapped on the little radio and waited for it to warm up as she gazed toward the setting sun. A single bird flew overhead, heading north. The radio came to life in the middle of a storm update.

"...and rough seas expected starting tonight and lasting through Tuesday evening. Marine advisory in effect for all of the Florida Keys. Storm now eighty miles off-shore due East of Matecumbe Key. Heading East-North East at twelve miles per hour. All Keys residents advised to evacuate to the north..."

Rose turned the dial and tried to find some music, but every station was the same: storm warnings. She snapped the radio off and went downstairs to look for Eliot.

"Oh, there you are sugar." Rose found Eliot in the study, smoking a Cuban cigar and drinking brandy, reading a large book with a blue leather cover. "Sorry I fell asleep up there, you certainly know how to wear a girl out." She looked around the room. It was covered in bookshelves, floor to ceiling, and each shelf was packed with books. There were two red and gold, overstuffed wing-backed chairs on an Oriental carpet. Eliot sat in one of the chairs.

Eliot looked up from his book and smiled. "Go on back to sleep, Rose. I'm quite content to catch up on some reading here in the study. After all, once this storm is over, I may not have a study left in which to read."

"Oh, shug' don't go talkin' like that. I'm sure this house will be fine in that lil' ole storm."

"I wish I could share your optimism, but I'm afraid the power of this hurricane is stronger than anyone first suspected. It's a small storm, yes, but very strong. Very strong." Eliot's voice trailed off and he went back to his book. Rose remained standing in the doorway.

"Well, if it's that strong, don't you think maybe we should go?"

"Go where?"

"I don't know, maybe Homestead? Or Miami?"

"Homestead? Miami? What makes you think it will be any safer there? All that storm has to do is change its course at the last minute and head north. Miami will be just a memory."

Rose was nervous but she tried not to show it. "But are you sure we're safe here?"

Eliot closed his book and smiled. "Yes, completely. I told you, I have a Safe Room."

"Well, where is this Safe Room?"

"In the basement."

Rose's eyes widened and she gasped. "The *basement!* But that's...that's impossible, isn't it? I mean, you dig two feet down here and you start to hit water!"

"Four feet. And not everywhere. The core of the Island is pure, solid limestone. Part of an ancient reef, I'd imagine. The Safe Room is dug into the limestone."

"But what if there's a flood? We'd drown for sure!"

"Got that taken care of too. There's a sixty-foot air vent that runs up the side of the chimney. Even the most treacherous winds and strongest waves couldn't topple that piece of iron and masonry. And there's never been a tidal wave higher than forty feet recorded here. It's quite safe.

Rose thought a moment, wondering. "Can I see it?" she finally asked, her curiosity getting the better of her. "Just for fun."

"Well," Eliot said cautiously, "It won't be much fun if we have to spend the day in there." He considered it some more, and realized he had no reason not to show her the secret chamber. "All right, come on!" he said and jumped from his chair. Rose lit up and clapped with excitement.

"Oh goody!" she almost screamed. Eliot thought she seemed rather childish, but at this point didn't care one way or another. He led her through the entrance room and into a small corridor behind the staircase. This hallway led to the servants' quarters with a storage room at the end. He unlocked the storeroom and flipped on the light. Stacks of linens, glasses, cases of liquor, cooking fuel and dozens of other strange culinary items lined the walls. In the center of the room was a trap door, padlocked. He unlocked it and opened the door. A short staircase led down into the hole.

Eliot flipped another switch and the staircase lit up. He brought Rose down to the bottom landing where a door that looked like it belonged on a submarine stood in silence. Eliot turned the giant wheel that unsealed it, and opened it up. He stepped through and Rose followed.

"This is it," he said, fanning his arm dramatically around the space. "It's thirty feet long by twenty wide, a good size to ride out a storm. There's canned food down here, fresh water, ice, liquor, and a radio. All the comforts of home."

Rose didn't much agree with that statement. The room stood in stark contrast to Eliot's mansion. It was fashioned entirely of dark gray concrete, and had a damp smell. The floor was cold beneath her bare feet. There was a wooden bar with plenty of liquor, but it was very utilitarian, not at all inviting. The only furniture in the room were three well-padded chairs, a large metal cabinet and a full-sized bed. The cabinet had a padlock on it like the one on the trap door. Everything was dusty. Cobwebs clung to the corners of the ceiling. But the thing that really disturbed Rose, and she didn't really know why, were the strange, large, dark stains on the floor.

"You come down here often?" she asked with a slight tremor in her voice.

"Not too. Now and then to make sure everything is in order. Occasionally I'll sneak down here to escape a particularly boring party, or, more often, my wife. It's the one room in the house that's all mine."

Rose didn't seem to listen. "What are those awful stains on the floor?"

Eliot shifted his weight and answered slowly. "Oh, those. They're…grenadine. I keep it on hand for Singapore Slings. Dropped several bottles one night while drunk. The stuff never goes away."

"You might try covering those spots with a rug," Rose said quietly. Just like a woman, Eliot thought, you show her a secret room and all she wants to do is clean it. "What's in the cabinet?"

"More liquor."

"Why do you keep it locked up?"

Eliot was getting irritated. "Why do you ask so many questions?" He came up behind her and wrapped his arms around her body, sliding his hands up to her breasts. "Enough questions. I think we should just go over to the bed now."

Rose, for no reason she could consider rational, did not want to go anywhere near that bed. She didn't even want to be in the room. "Not here, sugar, it's much too damp. I'm afraid I don't breath so well in the damp. Mild asthma, had it for years."

"Oh, nonsense! Come on," Eliot growled as he forced her to the bed. Rose fought him.

"No, really Eliot, I don't want to!"

He spun her around so that she was facing him now. "May I remind you who is the employee and who is in charge here?" He pushed her away, and she fell on the bed, stunned.

"Sugar?" Her voice was sad, hurt. "Is that all I am to you?" Tears revealed themselves in her tired eyes.

Eliot took a deep breath. She was right, this was no way to treat her, not now.

"I'm sorry, baby." He reached out a hand and pulled her up. "Come on, we'll go upstairs." She dried her tears on the robe's sleeve as Eliot lead her back up the steps and out of the Safe Room.

## 1956

After being in that muffled anti-chamber every little noise seemed louder and shriller. The next crash of thunder was so loud it made me jump like a kid. Melinda thought that was pretty funny. Smart ass.

We tried Bachman's office once more to look for another combination. We found none.

"We could try his apartment again," she said to me.

"Forget it. I took that place apart once already. I didn't find anything like that."

"So now what?"

"Let's go check on the children. Make sure they're still snug in their rugs. Then we can sit down and think this through."

The lobby was thinning out, people were returning to their rooms. Even the lobby bar was half empty. At the height of the storm people were hitting the hay to sleep it off.

We rode the elevator up with four very sloshed people who weren't sure what floor they were getting off. We convinced them to get off at two. We got off at three. Melinda was just opening the first lock when we heard the screams.

We only looked at each other for a split second but it was enough to see the terror in her eyes. She fumbled with the keys, and through her shaking was finally able to get the three locks undone. She threw open the door and ran for Eliot's bedroom. I was right behind her.

The screams came from both Eliot and Jessica. Not your average 'I just had a nightmare' kind of screams, but the kind of screams you only hear when someone is really, truly terrorized, afraid of living, afraid of dying. We flew into the bedroom and found Eliot and Jessica in the bed, pushed up against the headboard, holding each other as tightly as their limbs would allow, their faces stark white, steeped in fear and horror, their eyes fixed hard on something at the far end of the room. Melinda ran towards them. I stayed put and swung to the right, to the direction of their object of terror. What I saw was more *puzzling* than horrible.

Hanging all over the paintings and Tiki masks and shelves of oddities on the bedroom walls were several strands of what appeared to be seaweed. Wet seaweed. Wet, glistening, slimy seaweed. I walked over to the wall as Melinda calmed Eliot and Jessica down.

"Don't touch it!" Jessica screamed at full voice as I reached out to take a piece of the wet vegetation. "Don't, for God's sake Bill, don't!"

"What happened here?" I asked, not touching the seaweed. It's not that I was afraid of it, you know, it's just that I didn't want to upset Jessica any more. "How did this get here?"

They were both silent, too frightened to speak. Jessica's eyes were bleary and red, wide as saucers. She was shaking. Eliot just sat silently, staring at the wall.

"Hey, kid, snap out of it…tell me, how did this get here? Come on, it's OK now, I'm here." Finally Jessica started to move her mouth, but no sounds came out at first except a raspy moan. Then,

"They were here, again Bill. We were both sleeping. I woke up when Mr. Hawthorn started screaming. He saw them before I did. They were…They were *coming through the wall."*

Melinda's eyes widened too now, and she seemed more apprehensive than before. It was then I realized she was hiding something from me. She knew more – or saw more – than she let on. "Did you see them too, Jessica?"

"Yes. Just for a second. I awoke and saw them coming…I threw myself off the sofa and landed in the bed. I remember crawling up to Mr. Hawthorn as fast as possible. When I turned back around –" Her voice trailed off into a sob and she hid her face with her hands. Melinda put her hand on Jessica's shoulder. The roar of the wind and thunder made an ominous backdrop.

"It's ok. Tell us what happened next."

"They…they were right there, at the end of the bed, moving closer like before. Then a noise came from the door…you, opening the locks. They…I think they heard it, Bill. They stopped, and just *dissolved*. Then you came running in."

Melinda turned pale. "You mean, they were just here? *Now?"*

"Yes!"

With a slight shock of realization, I turned directly to Melinda. "*You've* seen them *too*, haven't you!" She looked at me with a half-frightened, half-embarrassed look. "*You* know what *she's* talking about."

"Melinda?" Jessica uttered turning to her. "Tell him."

Melinda took a deep breath and let it out slow. She ran her hand through her thick, dark hair in such a way that any other time would make me melt, but not under these circumstances. "I have," she said very quietly, tearfully. "Just glimpses in the night, when with Eliot. They come to him. But they don't want me to see, I don't think. They always disappear just as I show up. Sometimes not fast enough.

I walked over to her side. "I had a feeling there was more to this. Tell me, did these…*beings*…ever leave solid seaweed behind before?"

"No," Melinda said holding Hawthorn closer. "Never."

"How about you, Jess?"

"No Bill. Not like this. They've always been more like…like dreams, surreal. Visions that go away and everything is back to normal. But not tonight. Tonight they were more –"

"Real," Hawthorn said, not taking his eyes off the wall. "Tonight they were real."

Melinda began to cry quietly. "Eliot," she said softly.

Quietly, I asked, "Mr. Hawthorn, why were they here?"

His answer came in an eerie voice, one that will forever stay locked in my mind:

*"Bitter brine upon our tongues, the brackish water fills our lungs."*

"Mr. Hawthorn? Who are they?"

*"With darkened woes our life lines slip, our bodies bare, our organs rip."*

"Eliot?" Melinda said again, very softly.

*"And while we die, the others live. Our fate to those we soon shall give."*

"Mr. Hawthorn?"

*"Wrought with the storm, your last night's breath, we carry you now to your wretched death."*

"Mr. Hawthorn," I said more forcefully, "Tell us what they want."

He looked up from his blank gaze and his eyes, black as coal and rimmed in red pierced mine to my soul. "They want *me*, Mr. Riggins. And they won't rest until they've taken me under with them."

## Labor Day Monday, 1935: The Day of the Storm

Eliot Hawthorne rose early on Labor Day Monday. He made a sweep of the grounds to make sure everything was secure, and placed a call to Roberts on Sugarloaf Key.

"Mr. Hawthorn, suh, it ain't no use ya'll stayin' on that Island," Roberts told him. "Navy's already lost two boats out there. Winds are blowing up to two-hundred knots. We've lost, suh. Mother Nature's done cast her dice an' come up boxcars. The whole of the Florida Keys will be under water by mid-afternoon."

"I thought Key West was in the clear," Hawthorn said into the telephone.

"And it ought to be, but there ain't no way to get to it 'cept by boat. And the seas are already six to ten feet in the open water. Your boat won't make it."

"What about the train?"

"Only one train comin' down far as Matecumbe. Then it's backing back up to Homestead as fas' as she can."

"What time?"

"Callin' for five."

"Fine. Dammit! Ok, I give up. I'll take the boat and run it up to Islamorada. We'll get the train there."

"Ya'll better leave soon, suh. Seas are getting' rougher by the minute."

"I'll leave soon enough. Will you be there?"

"No suh, we're evacuating on a Navy cutter in an hour."

"All right Roberts. I'll see you on the other side of the storm."

"Yessuh, I hope so suh."

Hawthorn set the receiver back on the cradle. He realized it would probably be the last time he ever used that telephone again.

Eliot woke Rose from a worried sleep. "Wake up darling. The storm's gotten a lot worse than expected. Get dressed. Fast." He said no more and left her. Rose shook, although she was warmed by the fact that Eliot called her 'darling'. She grabbed the first thing she saw in Vivian's closet, a yellow sundress, and slipped it on. Eliot was back in minutes. He stopped to look at her, almost alarmed, Rose thought.

"What's wrong, sugar?"

"That was Vivian's favorite dress."

"Well she can have it back, I just picked the first thing that looked like it would fit."

"No, it's fine, Rose. Here," he said, and reaching into his pocket pulled out a string of beautiful pearls, Vivian's pearls. "Put these on too. They're hers, but she won't need them right now, will she?"

"Oh, Eliot, they're beautiful!"

"Just for now, darling. I'll have to give them back. But I promise to buy you a string just as beautiful someday." Rose smiled and slipped the pearls around her neck. "Come on, no time to waste."

Eliot led her down the steps to the ground floor, and continued out the door.

"Wait, sugar, what about the Safe Room?"

"It's not as safe as I thought," he said as he dragged her across the lawn to the boathouse. Rose could tell the storm was getting very close now; the sky was a strange shade of pinkish gray to the west, dark gray to the east. Clouds in the sky moved fast, forming strange, circular bands. The winds were picking up hard and the Gulf was churning.

"Let's go back to Key West, Eliot. Key West never gets hurricanes. They always miss it."

"No way, too late for that now."

"Then where on Earth are we goin'?"

"We'll have to make a run for Islamorada," Eliot said to the very frightened woman as he helped her onto the boat. "I'm sure our yacht will cut through the rough waters without hesitation, but it will be a bit bumpy, I'm afraid."

"Islamorada? But that's…that's insane! That's runnin' right into the path of the hurricane!"

"The train isn't coming any farther south than that. We have to go there or else we'll be stranded here."

"We should have gone back to Key West," she replied, shaking.

"I told you that's no good," Eliot screamed above the rising sounds of the wind and the roar of the Gulf. "Waters are too open, we can capsize too easily. Too late for that. We'll stick close to the islands and make it up to Islamorada in less than two hours, tops."

"Let's just get this over with," Rose said, this time more disgusted than afraid, and slipped into the cabin. Eliot took a last look at his home, his mansion. A last look at everything, knowing very well it would probably be the last time he ever saw any of it again. He untied the rope from the stern, started the engines, and ran them up to full power heading towards Matecumbe Key.

It was a long, hard, sickening two hours. Rose's stomach couldn't take the swells and three times she was sick into the Chris-Craft's head. Eliot got his sea legs quickly but had to lash himself to the helm to avoid being washed over. Even between the islands the waves were getting fierce. Four-foot swells crashed over the mahogany bow of the yacht. The twin engines whined with stress as they tried to compensate for the ripping currents. Rain began tearing down in heavy sheets, reducing visibility to less than thirty yards. The smaller islands were already flooding over, making it difficult to keep the boat from bottoming out. But Eliot persevered. He ran the boat under the train bridge around to the marina by the station, and managed to moor it on the Atlantic side without crashing against the pier.

"Come on Rose, let's get our tickets and get the hell off this Island."

"What about all this stuff in the boat?"

"Don't worry about it. It's lost. The boat's lost. Everything's lost. Just be happy we're alive." He felt like a heel but couldn't think about that now. The plan was working. They were in Islamorada.

They ran up the dock and up to the station. It was filled with WPA workers and locals waiting to get the evacuation train from Miami. "Listen darling, one thing, and it's important. Anyone asks, you're my wife, Vivian, got it?"

"Ok, Eliot, whatever you say."

"Good. Now lets get those tickets." They walked into the station and right up to the ticket window. A tired-looking man in a dirty gray uniform came up.

"Passage for two, and if you've got room for luggage we've got plenty," Eliot shouted to the man behind the ticket window. "One for me, and one for my wife, Vivian. I'm Eliot Hawthorn," he added, as if his name meant anything.

"We've got room for people and one bag you can carry yourself, no more."

"That's fine. How much are tickets?" he asked, pulling his wallet from his drenched jacket.

"No fee today, mister. This is an evacuation, not a vacation."

"Ok, ok. Just let me know when the train is leaving."

"Leaving?" the man said disgustedly, "It ain't even *got* here yet. Wired Homestead yesterday we needed a train here pronto. The dumb suckers didn't have one ready! Had to bring it down from Palm Beach to Miami. Just left Miami this morning, and with this weather...aw, hell, sure as hell ain't gonna be here before five, maybe six o'clock!"

"Six o'clock!" Eliot screamed, "You realize the storm will likely be here by six," he said mournfully.

"Yessir," the man said, his face showing fear thick and real. His eye twitched just a little. "Yessir, we are well aware of that." With that he turned and left the ticket window.

"Rose, we can't stay here. That train might get in too late. I'm not sitting here leaving anything to chance."

"What are we going to do?"

"We'll take the boat and head up the gulf coast. Everglades City. We'll be safe there."

"Everglades City? That's hours away!"

"We've got plenty of fuel and I've got the nerve. Let's go."

A man standing by heard the conversation and moved over next to Eliot. "Mister, you say you got a boat?"

"Yes, what's it to you?"

"Take me with you. Me and my family. I've got my wife here and two kids. We won't take up much room. I can pay you."

"No, no," Hawthorn said sternly. "I can't take on any more weight. The boat is laden down."

"Take me too, mister," a voice came from behind him. Eliot spun and saw an old man and young girl. "Take me and my granddaughter. At least take her, please. She's only thirteen."

"I can't, no passengers. The boat's not big enough –"

"Please buddy, I seen your boat, it's a fifty-footer at least. You can hold a good thirty people in there if we pack in tight!"

The voices grew thicker and more desperate as Hawthorn pulled himself and Rose through the crowd toward the door. They clung to him, pleaded with him, but he couldn't afford this latest twist, couldn't allow anything to impede his plan.

"I can't, I'm sorry. The train will be here. The train will take you to safety," he yelled over the crowd. He was almost at the door when a large man grabbed him by the shirt.

"You'll take us and you'll like it, you rich bastard," the man said with a menacing voice that shook Hawthorn's shoes. But Hawthorn was no dummy. He was prepared for the worst.

"Back off!" he screamed as he pulled his Smithfield revolver out from under his shirt. He fired a single shot at the man's foot and just clipped it as the bullet traveled through the wooden floor. The man screamed and fell to the floor grasping his injured foot. The entire station fell silent, save the howl of the wind and the beating of the rain. "Next guy who tries a stunt like that gets a gut full of lead," he said waving the gun around the room like a movie gangster. "My boat is heavy with fuel and supplies and I'm not taking a chance on capsizing with people and kids. Now you people just hang on here and wait for the train. Have some faith in your government for Christ's sake."

"Just like you, mister rich man," came a small voice from the rear.

"I'll take my chances with myself and my wife," he said, and Rose looked over to him with a sort of stunned and angered look. "Not with any of you. Good luck to you." He pushed open the door. The wind came in, damp and fast. "Come on," he said to his stand-in wife, and pulled her out of the station and back into the rain and wind.

"What gives?" she exclaimed as the wind nearly pulled the door off the hinges. "What are you doing? You know those people will all die if that train doesn't come!"

"Overloading the yacht is a sure way to get us all killed. There's nothing I can do about them. Let Roosevelt save them."

"You're a cruel, evil man Eliot Hawthorn. I never saw the real you until now."

"Fine, whore!" he yelled to Rose as he got on the boat. Rose shuddered. "Fine. Think what you want. Would you like to stay here and take your chances with the storm or come with me and live?"

Rose's heart sank so low she thought she'd drown in a puddle. She never detested anyone with all of her being as she did Hawthorn that day. "I'll go with you, but this will be the last time," she said.

"Yes, yes I do believe it will," Hawthorn replied, and helped her onto the deck. Rose didn't understand the irony. Then she stopped, froze. A horrible feeling came over her with that last remark. "What exactly do you mean by that?"

"I mean just what you said. It's time for Plan B," Eliot responded. In another minute he had the twin diesel engines pushing the boat hard, heading North along the Gulf side of the Keys.

### 1956

It was too much to take. The crying, the screaming, the secret room with the hidden safe and the combination not working, Hawthorn's constant muttering of ghosts coming to get him and the incessant thunder was creating its own swirling hurricane in my head, blowing cold, wet, wild wind through my skull and tearing my thoughts apart. I closed my eyes hard and ran my hand roughly through my hair and over my face, my nearly numb face that needed some blood flowing back through it, some blood and oxygen passing through to my brain.

On the bed, Melinda tried to comfort Hawthorn, holding him as he rocked back and forth mumbling his crazy poem over and over again. Jessica had moved to the sofa and sat there sprawled, somewhat catatonic. She was oblivious now to Hawthorn's rantings. She just stared at the back wall of the bedroom, waiting for more ghosts to come.

A severely loud crack jolted the entire room as it filled with a white-hot light for just a split second. Sheets of rain pounded against the shuttered windows. The storm was intensifying.

"Melinda," I said quietly, "Can I talk with you in the next room a sec?"

"I don't want to leave Eliot alone," she said almost tearfully.

"Just outside the door. We can leave it open."

She got up and walked over to me. She stood in front of me for only a second, looked at me with a sad look, then walked out of the room. I followed.

"What is it, William."

"Why does Eliot think ghosts are out to get him, kid? What did he do to bring that kind of crazy jazz down on him?"

She looked down at the floor and sighed lightly. "I don't know, William. He's never told me why. Only that he's done some 'bad things' in his life."

I tried to look in Melinda's eyes. I couldn't, as she was looking down when she spoke. For the first time I began to believe she wasn't being one hundred percent truthful with me.

"Bad things?"

"I can only guess," she continued now looking up. "Remember I told you he talks in his sleep?"

"Yeah."

"I've heard him say some things. Once he said something about 'leaving all those people to die.' Another time he talked about 'that poor girl'. Then another time, it was, 'all those girls, all those girls, all those people'. He was sleep-talking, just dreaming, but somehow it seemed…it seemed like he was reliving something, something from his past."

I pulled a stick out of my deck of Camels and rolled it between my fingers. Somehow feeling the solidly packed tobacco helped me to remember that this was real, this was really happening, now. "That's it, huh?"

"Yes. No idea what he was referring to. I tried asking him a few times. All he'd say is that he'd done some bad things in his life, in his *previous* life…before he met my mother."

"Let's ask him again, right now doll. I don't know what he saw, and I still don't believe in ghosts. But that wet seaweed didn't put itself on the wall, and the apartment was locked from the inside. Which means another thing happened that we can't explain. And if Eliot thinks ghosts are coming to get him, we pretty-damned well better do something about it before he dies of a heart attack…or something really does come. Either way, I can't protect him if I don't know what to protect him against."

"What about Jessica?"

I looked around the room. The sound of her name coming from Melinda sounded strange…almost, dirty. "I think I already know what's tormenting that kid. It's one of two things. Either she's hallucinating because of the drugs…"

"She's not hallucinating seaweed," Melinda interrupted.

"No, she's not. And if she's not, it's got to be her mother trying to reach her. I don't know why yet, but I think her old lady has been trying to get to her for years."

"Her mother? If that's so, then why is she and Eliot having the same visions at the same time?"

"Isn't it obvious?" Melinda just looked up at me with those doey brown eyes. "Her mother died in the big storm. If Eliot is saying things in his sleep like 'that poor girl' and they're both seeing her mother's ghost…"

Melinda's face twisted as she strained to hold back the tears. She lost the battle and the waterworks came, heavy and sad. I closed her in my arms and held her tight until she cried it out.

"Let's ask Eliot now," I said, and with a sad face she agreed. She walked into the room and sat beside Hawthorn.

"Eliot, darling, William is here. He thinks he can help you."

Hawthorn turned to me and laughed. He was eerily calm and sober now. "Help me? Oh, Mr. Riggins, I'm quite sure your revolver and police training are no match for the fate that awaits me."

"Tell us why they're after you, Eliot," Melinda said. "No reason to hide things now. Let us help."

Hawthorn looked over at Jessica, then at me. "Well, Mr. Riggins, let's just say I've done some bad things. Evil, heartless things."

"Not good enough, Mr. Hawthorn. Come on, spill it."

Hawthorn started to tremor. He lifted and dropped his hands in a strange way, as if he were going to start talking and suddenly couldn't speak. Then, finally, as tears began to choke him he blurted out all at once, "Thirty people!" and clasped his hand over his mouth.

Melinda held him. "It's ok, Eliot. It's ok."

"Thirty people," he repeated more quietly. Jessica broke her gaze from the wall and looked his way. "I had room on my boat to hold thirty people. I could have saved them. I could have saved thirty of them. I didn't. Instead I went with just Vivian. I was afraid they'd capsize the boat. I could have taken the children. All of them. I could have taken all the children and some of the parents. I didn't. I left Islamorada in the middle of that damned storm knowing very well those people were all doomed. Vivian couldn't stop me. I forced her back into the boat and we rode up to the north, until a giant wave tossed her over the side!" His voice cracked. He began to cry hard, heavy tears. Melinda held him closer. Jessica's mouth opened, but no words came out, at first.

"I could have saved them!" he shouted. "I could have saved some of them at least!"

Thunder struck again, loud and close. But it wasn't nearly as horrific as Jessica's words. "You MONSTER! You sonovabitch! My *Mother* died in that storm! Now I know why she wants your ass tanned! You could have saved her and you didn't!"

Hawthorn looked up from his tears. "I...I didn't know your mother, young lady."

"Of course not. She was just another blank face in the crowd waiting for the storm to wash her away, wasn't she! You *BASTARD!*" she screamed, and lunged off the couch like a lion, landing on the bed just inches from Hawthorn. Melinda jumped back and hit her head on the headboard, knocking her senseless. Jessica scurried up the bed and grabbed Hawthorn by the throat.

"I'll kill you myself you fucking bastard!" she screamed as she pressed her thumbs into Hawthorn's neck. "I'll kill you myself!" It all happened so fast I barely had time to react. By the time I got to the bed Jessica had full-fisted punched Hawthorn at least three times in the face, and was choking him again. I came up behind her and tried to pull her away, but she was wild, wild like a crazed woman hell-bent on getting her revenge. Her arms flailed, and as she broke from me she punched Hawthorn again. He screamed with agony as her boney fists landed over again on his nose and mouth. Finally I gave up on restraining her and grabbing her by the ankles pulled her off the bed and onto the floor. She kicked and screamed and tried to scratch my eyes out but I was too quick for her. I flipped her over onto her stomach and pinned her down with a knee in her back. I gave her a medium punch between her shoulder blades that froze her up in pain, and grabbed both her arms in my left hand and pushed forward. The resulting pain made her spit out a shriek that could have awakened the dead, again. With my other hand I pulled off my belt and tied it tight around her wrists.

"Stop it, Jessica!" I yelled, "Knock it off right now or I'm going to knock you out with a lamp over the head, do you understand?"

She was crying hard, heaving, shaking. Through it she kept repeating, "Let me kill him, he let my mother die, let me kill him..."

"No, Jessica. No." I said, and let her cry it out. I looked up at Hawthorn. Melinda came back to her senses and was trying to stop his nose from bleeding. Blood flowed out of his mouth and a split in his cheek, too. Jessica really did a job on him.

"Melinda, you better get some more of that sleeper juice for this one."

"Yeah," she said disgustedly. She got up fast and got another kit out of one of Hawthorn's drawers, filled up a needle and came over. Without a word she sadistically stuck the needle in Jessica's leg and pressed the plunger. Jessica screamed and struggled for only a few seconds, then passed out.

It was 'round midnight when I finally got Jessica into her own room, snug as a bug in bed. Melinda dosed up Hawthorn and stayed with him until I got back. The storm was worse than ever, but there was no sign of anything from the watery afterlife for hours.

Melinda retired to Hawthorn's study. She poured us both a double brandy and we sat quietly in the big wing-backed chairs, just listening to the rain and the thunder. The storm seemed to be going on forever. Close thunder. Far-off thunder. Thunder that sounded like it was inside the damned hotel with us. The rain threw itself against the building like buckets at a car wash. The howl of the wind was both scary and surreal. As I sat, I reflected on the long, crazy day, the longest I'd had in a long time. It seemed ridiculous to think that just this morning, a little more than twelve hours ago, I'd found out that Bachman was dead and I was a suspect, Jessica and Hawthorn were both being... haunted? by the same entities, and I was shown a secret party room in the basement of this kooky Island. Shovel on top of that this tropical storm, Jessica's come on, Jessica's ghosts, and making love to Melinda twice and that adds up to at least a week of Tiki insanity floating around in the lagoon of a single day.

"It's only Monday," I said groggily into the room.

"Technically it's now Tuesday. It's almost one a.m." Melinda answered in a monotone tone. "I suppose we should try to get some sleep."

"I assume you don't want to leave your father alone."

Melinda closed her eyes, and sort of twitched. "No, I shouldn't leave Eliot alone. God knows what will happen if he wakes up and no one is around. I'll sleep in there with him. You're welcome to take my bed, unless you want to go back to your room."

"What I want is to take your bed, with you in it," I said smiling. No reaction. "But I guess I'll go back to my suite. I need a shower anyway." I got up and walked over to Melinda. She opened her eyes and I reached down and kissed her, gently. She smiled up at me with that old smile that made me melt, the one that I seemed to have first seen years ago in another lifetime. "I'm a phone call away if you need me kid," I said, and left.

Back in my suite the storm seemed louder and the water stronger as it slammed against my shuttered glass doors. Hawthorn's place didn't have the big sliding glass doors that this suite had. Big difference. I took a long hot shower and poured myself a Jack on the rocks. I tried the TV and couldn't get any reception. I tried the radio and got nothing but static and storm warnings. One announcement said the storm's center had passed over the keys and was heading into the gulf. They estimated the worst was over, winds down to less than forty-five miles per hour. It was expected to be gone by four a.m.

I gave up on the radio and slipped a Les Baxter album onto the Hi-Fi. The jungle sounds fit in perfectly with the noise of the rain, thunder and wind. I sat back in the big leather couch and put my feet up. The Jack was only half done when I finally fell into a deep, black, thunder-less sleep.

Melinda removed the remainder of the seaweed from Eliot's room and sent it down the garbage disposal unit. She wiped up as much of the standing water and sand as she could, and finally called it a night. She slipped into the bed next to Eliot, who was sleeping soundly, and turned out the light. A few seconds later she turned the light back on, got out of bed, turned on a smaller lamp across the room, and went back to bed turning off the large light. Not sleeping in the dark tonight, she thought to herself.

Her tired mind wandered over the events of the day. She was concerned about the rooms at the back of the hotel where the wind seemed to be the worst. She was ever mindful of the tide, knowing high tide would come at around five a.m. and the possibility of flooding with it. She had plenty of staff keeping watch, but basically if a flood came there wasn't much she could do about it. The salt water would kill a lot of the flowers, and would probably ruin the grass, but that wasn't so bad. The Island would have to flood over six feet to damage any buildings, and that hadn't happened in her lifetime.

She also thought about Eliot. About his dreams, and what he said aloud. She thought about the years they spent together after her mother passed away, how happy they were at first, but how things started going downhill when he started having the visions. She thought about Riggins too. About how she hadn't felt the way she did with him in years, and she wondered if she was falling in love, or if she'd just gotten caught up in the newness of it all, the excitement of the relationship.

She wondered what Riggins thought of her.

Did he have any real intention of staying, giving up his old life for her? Or was he just enjoying his vacation as much as he could? The fact that she couldn't honestly answer that question disturbed her. She liked him. She wanted him. She believed she could love him.

She *needed* him.

A crack of lightning split the night. White light filled the room for a brief second, then flickered out. No apparitions appeared. Melinda took a deep breath and let it out slow, and closing her eyes began to finally relax. William would have to wait for tomorrow. Tonight she needed to sleep. The last embers of her awakened fire died out, and sleep took hold of her deeply.

In the garden below, just outside Hawthorn's window, a glowing white figure of a woman in a summer hat hovered in the night above the recently sealed grave.

# CHAPTER FOUR

Tuesday Morning, October 30, 1956

The noise crashed against my skull like a brick. I thought I'd slept through the thunder, but the noise hit me again, hard. I jumped and fell off the couch. When I opened my eyes, a harsh white light infiltrated my head and the pain started immediately, running down the back of my neck. The noise came again and I screamed "Shut up!" but it didn't help.

Then my mind started to come together, bits of brain waking up and realizing what was going on.

It was morning. The light wasn't from lightning, but from the sun coming in full blast through my un-shuttered glass doors. The noise wasn't thunder, it was the phone.

I picked up the coconut-shaped contraption and yelled into it.

"WHAT."

"Well good morning to you, Mr. Sunshine. Sleep Ok?"

The voice was Melinda's, bright and pert and awake. I hated her.

"What time is it?"

"Almost eight. I've been up since six. It's a beautiful day. Storm is gone, out over the Gulf. No flooding. Very little damage. We were lucky."

"Eight...in the morning? Didn't anyone tell you I was on vacation?"

"Come on sleepy head. I can use some help."

"Help?"

"Yes, help. Today is my first day as General Manager, and I've got a lot on my plate. Also, Sheriff Jackson would like to see you at some point."

Great, just what I need. "Wake me up at eleven," I said and hung up the receiver. A few minutes later I was in bed with the shades drawn, falling asleep.

It didn't last. At nine I heard the door open and woke up. Standing in front of me was Melinda. She was wearing a peach and white dress covered with tropical flowers, and a peach-colored flower in her hair. I got up and squinted. She was smiling.

"Nice uniform," I said. "Why are you here?"

"To take you to breakfast. I have some good news."

Twenty minutes later we were dining in the big room with the windows on the second floor. I think Melinda must have shot-up with some speed, because she was talking a mile a minute and was more awake than I'd seen her all week. She told me all about how the Island survived the storm, how only one small boat broke loose but was recovered, and how Jackson lifted the no coming and going order. In her spiel was something about fresh fruit, new flowers, and great fishing. I caught about half of it over three cups of coffee and a muffin.

"How is Eliot?" I finally asked.

"Up and about and in good spirits," she answered. "Strangely, I think last night must have been very liberating for him. He seems more like his old self now."

"What about Jessica? Anyone check on her yet?"

"No," she said, and changed the subject. "Tomorrow is Halloween. We've got a boatload of decorations coming in today. I'm going to have the staff decorate the entire Hotel. Plus we'll have lots of candy for the kids. I thought maybe you'd help with organizing the decorating."

"Decorating? Me? I don't know the first thing about decorating."

"Well, I don't mean actually putting up streamers and pumpkins. I mean organizing the crew. There will be thirteen people working on it. I thought that was an appropriate number."

"So you want me to manage thirteen people for the afternoon, is that it?"

"Yes. See how you like it."

I didn't say a word and my silence gave away my thoughts.

"Of course, you don't have to if you don't want to, William. I just thought it would be a nice way to see how you like...you know..."

"The hotel biz," I said and smiled. "Sure, I'll try it on for size."

She lit up. "Good! Meet me at the aft docks at eleven. I've got to go see to some other things now."

"Eleven? Hey, *you* got me up early. What am I supposed to do until eleven?"

"Go check on Jessica, I suppose. If she's up to it, put her to work on the decorating crew. Least she could do for putting her up for free," she added, then winked and took off.

As I left the dining room a strange feeling came over me, the kind of feeling you get when you go into a haunted house ride on the Wildwood Boardwalk, just before some big, paper maché spider jumps out at you and makes you scream like a little kid. It wasn't a feeling of fear. It was a feeling of dread. The sort of dread that makes people quit in the middle of the night and take off to another town for a crack at another life.

I shouldn't have felt like that. There was no reason to.

I decided to take Melinda's idea and check on Jessica. As I passed the second floor rooms I thought about the people staying in them. Families. Couples. A few singles. Some retirees. And in at least one room stayed a murderer.

I shivered a little, even though it was well into the seventies.

I reached the glass elevator and took it up to the third floor, looking down at the people in the lobby. From up here everything looked like a big piece of carved bamboo with a bunch of heads floating around on top of it. One of those heads might be a killer.

I just couldn't get that out of my mind. A man was murdered just a day ago, and I'm going to be hanging orange crepe streamers and helping carve Jack O'Lanterns. Something just didn't jive.

Before I knew it I had reached Jessica's room and was ready to knock. That oddball feeling came over me again, and I hesitated. My brain started running circles with all sorts of crazy ideas. What if I found her drunk? Or worse, stoned?

Or worse…

I shook it off and knocked. Nothing. I knocked again and still no stirring from within. I decided I was being a fool; it wasn't even ten yet and no doubt Jessica was still sleeping off the sedative. I took out the passkey that Melinda had slid me at breakfast and opened the door.

Jessica was gone.

The bed was unmade, and her suitcase lay open on the floor. It just looked like she got up and went for breakfast. "Well, she's a big girl. I'm sure wherever she is, she's fine," I said to the room and shut the door. Then I got that weird feeling again, and shook it off.

I didn't feel like tracking her down so figured I'd kill an hour sitting on the beach, or at least at the beach bar. I wandered out to the South Side of the Island, ordered an orange juice and took up a chair next to the cabana, facing Key West. The morning sun was warm but not too hot, and an easy breeze sashayed across the beach like a burlesque dancer. I closed my eyes and started to think, think about the events of the last few days, about the craziness of the seaweed in Hawthorn's room, about the oddball things I'd seen. My mind wandered to the Safe Room, and then to the safe.

And finally, after being in vacationland for a week, my brain woke up and snapped into cop mode.

"It's the wrong safe!" I said out loud, and a couple of kids walking by stopped and looked at me like I was a goofball. "Not you, kid," I said, and got up from the chair.

I damn near jogged back to Melinda's office hoping to find her there. She wasn't. I telephoned her apartment, then Hawthorn's. Nothing.

But while I had old man Hawthorn on the horn, I asked him the one question I should have asked yesterday. "By the way, Mr. Hawthorn, do you have a private safe somewhere on the Island, someplace you might keep valuable papers?"

"Why yes, as a matter of fact I do. It's will hidden in the depths of the building."

Bingo.

"You wouldn't happen to know if Mr. Bachman also had a safe somewhere, would you?"

Hawthorn was quiet as a mouse. All I could hear was labored breathing. After a few seconds he said, "Not to my knowledge, but then again Mr. Bachman may have installed one without my knowing."

"Thanks Mr. Hawthorn," I said and hung up. Without a word he told me more than he thought. So that was that. The safe we found in the Safe Room was Hawthorn's safe. No wonder the combination didn't work. And Bachman had his own set-up, God knows where on the Island, if it even was *on* the Island.

The wheels were turning. It was twenty minutes to eleven and the last thing I wanted to do was play babysitter for a bunch of goofs hanging paper skeletons and crepe witches. The cop department in my mind was working at full tilt and I wanted to search for answers. I had the clues…the combination, where I found it, the fact that Bachman probably had the safe installed without Hawthorn's knowing. That meant it had to be someplace where Hawthorn would never go. That pretty much ruled out the Safe Room, or his office or apartment. So what was left?

Back of the house.

The storeroom where I first found the combination. That was my best guess. I checked it once but that was with little light and no idea what I was doing. Now would be different.

I looked at my watch. Ten 'til eleven. I didn't want to let Melinda down but I sure as hell wanted to search that room. Then I got an idea.

I headed back to the loading dock where Melinda said to meet her. She was there already with her thirteen workers, all ready to decorate. She made the introductions and gave me the general plan of the décor and candy stations. She wished me luck and took off for a brunch she had booked, and I was alone with six women and seven men.

"Ok, you six ladies and five of you men," I pointed to each of the men I wanted, "Take this plan, load up the boxes you need on dollies and start at the back of the lobby and move forward. You two, come with me."

"Where are you going, Señor?" One of he women asked in a heavy Cuban accent.

"To get some Tikis out of storage. I'll meet you kids in the lobby. And don't screw around or no bonus."

"Bonus?" she yelled smiling, "Aye!"

We reached the storeroom and I opened it up. Ah, cheap labor. Maybe I could get used to this.

"I need those two big Tikis moved out. Just get them out into the hallway, and if they're too heavy to lift you can go get a dolly," I said to the two big men. Without a word they obeyed. The Tikis were heavy, but no match for these two goons. They had them both out in the hallway in a few minutes.

"Ok guys, carry them up to the lobby please. I'd like them in the front entrance."

"That's not on the plan, Señor," one said. The other hit him in the arm.

"It's ok guys, I want to have a little fun with the decorating too. Go ahead and bring them up for me, ok?"

They nodded and hefted the larger of the two, and were off. As soon as they were out of sight I zipped back into the room and checked the floor below where the Tikis stood.

Dammit. Nothing.

I took the room apart. I moved every box, every piece of furniture. I even tapped the walls looking for hollow spots. Not a damned thing.

It occurred to me I had gotten no further than I had before, and that I now had the added task of decorating two rather large and heavy Moai with Halloween garb. Dammit.

I made my way down to the lobby and found that the decorating had progressed very nicely. The two Tikis where placed perfectly in the front, just in front of a small fountain. I instructed the ladies to decorate them with black crepe and skull masks, then used the house phone to call Jessica's room. No answer. I tried Melinda's office and got no answer there too. Finally I decided to let the workers finish the decorating job on their own, and went looking for Jessica.

Forty-five minutes later I'd circled the entire Island and found hide nor hair of her. I told security to be on the lookout for her, and they in turn alerted the staff. It was after one o'clock, and for the first time I started to worry a little about Jessica.

Ok, worry a lot.

More than I should have.

Just as I was ready to start the search all over again, a security guard came up to me in the lobby. He was sweating and out of breath.

"Mr. Riggins, we've found her," he said. Dark eyes twitched in his pale face, just a little as he spoke.

Dammit.

### Melinda

As if nothing ever happened. That's the phrase that floated over Melinda's mind as she went through her daily checklist. Fresh foods arrived on time. Check. All bars fully stocked. Check. Lifeguards on duty. Check. Housekeeping running at full capacity. Check.

As if nothing ever happened.

No one said a word to her about their (previous) boss, the late Rutger Bachman, the man who had run the Resort in the fashion of a five-star European Hotel for more than three years, the man responsible for bringing in some of the most well-to-do and influential people to visit the Island, the man murdered in his sleep in his second-floor apartment not more than 48 hours earlier.

Melinda sank to a stone bench in the garden and put her face in her hands, trying hard to hold back the tears. She failed, and the tears came freely.

"Why?" she asked softly to the birds and the trees. "Why?"

She gently wiped the tears from her streaked face, remembering the good times with Bachman as people do when they're confronted with a sudden death. For Melinda never hated Bachman; sure, she disliked him most off the time, and was appalled by his lack of character when it came to women. And she certainly detested the way he ran the 'underground' operations of the Resort. But there were good times too, and she remembered those now that he was gone. There was the first year he worked at the Resort, when he treated Melinda more like a sister than an employee. There was the time he organized a giant surprise birthday party for her, bringing in friends she hadn't seen since high school. And there were the times when he dropped the egotistical façade of the uppity General Manager and actually taught Melinda some of the tricks of the trade, management skills he'd learned in the top schools and at the top hotels around the world.

Yes, she thought as she sat there in the late October sun, there was a lot of good in Bachman. He was just too focused on making Tiki Island his own.

Melinda left the bench and strolled the garden, her clipboard and checklist in hand. She smelled the sweetness of the hibiscus and ran her hand along the trunk of a twenty-year old palm tree, one she watched grow from a few feet to over thirty. The sounds of a live steel drum band came across the warm morning breeze. The sun glistened on the Gulf of Mexico and the waves exploded into a million tiny diamonds. Children ran along the beach and laughed. Legionnaires in red fezzes swallowed aspirin and drank Bloody Marys at the beach bar as they swapped stories about the girls they talked into going back to their rooms the night before. The Resort went on, the guests went on, life went on.

As if nothing ever happened.

## Jessica

The last thing she remembered was the cool water washing over her face. It was dark; the moon had been obliterated by the remaining clouds and that side of the Island was never lit at night. Sand, darkness, water, nothing.

By the time I got to her the Island's doctor already had her cleaned up and resting under crisp, white linen sheets on a cot in the infirmary. More white linen billowed from the windows as the afternoon breeze came in cool and sweet. A small, gray metal radio in the corner played orchestral music. The doctor sat on a black swivel-stool smoking cherry tobacco from a worn-out old pipe.

"What happened to her?" I asked as I walked into the small room. He swiveled around and took the pipe out of his mouth.

"Nearly drowned. They found her washing around in the surf early this morning. We had no idea who she was until the porter came in with the news a girl was missing."

I was a little confused and a little sad and a little angry but managed to hold it all in without popping a cork. Jessica was a wreck. Her eyes were puffy and a purple bruise took up most of her left cheek. Her lip was split and there were bandages on her neck and shoulder. The sheet covered most of her but it was thin, and I could tell there were more bandages up and down her body. My heart thumped hard. I hated seeing her like this.

"Why didn't you report this to management or something?"

"I did," the doctor said. "I left a message with Ms. Hawthorn's secretary. Apparently she's been MIA all day."

True, I thought.

"Who did this to her?"

"Oh, I don't think it was a who, so much as a what. I think she got herself a little tipsy, then went for an early morning stroll after the storm, and zonked out on the beach. Tied came in, tossed her around a little, maybe hit some of the rocks out there, but she was lucky enough to keep her head above water. She only swallowed a small amount of seawater."

"So how is she? She's just sleeping, right?"

"Not sure," the doctor said, "I don't think she's in a coma or anything like that. I think she's…well, I think she had a little help getting to sleep, if you know what I mean."

"You mean drugs," I said straight out.

"Possibly. Possibly dosed up with something, possibly a sedative or maybe something a little stronger."

"Like heroin?"

"Possibly. Or morphine."

"Can you wake her up?"

"I'd rather not."

"Doc, do you know who I am?"

"No sir, can't say I do. I imagine you're a friend of hers, or perhaps a boyfriend," he said without malice.

"I'm a cop," I said and flashed my badge. "Jessica's been a naughty girl. She's got a problem with heroin and she's been put under my supervision until we can get her to a rehabilitation hospital on the mainland. If she shot up, I need to know."

"I could do a blood test if you like, officer."

"Not necessary. She's a user but not a liar. When she wakes up, make sure you call me, please. I'm in the Kona Kai suite. If I'm not there leave word with Ms. Hawthorn's office. And don't let her leave here."

"Will do officer."

I left that disgustingly ugly white room with it's Gaddamned billowy curtains and crisp sheets with the beat up body of Jessica resting in it, and knew I couldn't kid myself about my feelings for that chick another second. Seeing her like that brought all the stomach-wrenching, head-spinning, heart-pumping feelings from last week back to me, and I was caught again in the middle between two of the most incredible, beautiful women I'd ever laid eyes on. I came down here to get away from the drama, to get some R-and-R, and I let myself get trapped between a smart, rich, beautiful charmer who wanted me to turn my life upside-down to go into the Hotel business and a sexy, intriguingly brain-damaged prostitute who made me feel more like a man than any other dame I'd ever known. Between the two of them I wind up killing two thugs, sending a crooked cop to the clink and getting myself mixed up as a murder suspect. I was dressing funny, hadn't seen a live jazz band or a beatnik in so long I almost forgot how to talk jive and couldn't remember the last time I strapped my .45 automatic under my shoulder.

October thirtieth. In New York, right now, the weather is cold and rainy, that bone-chilling cold that gets down into your muscles and freezes you from the inside-out. The sun probably hasn't come out in a week, and everything is gray and wet. Kids are getting ready for Halloween, making masks, decorating their windows with paper pumpkins and cornstalks and stuff like that. Junkies are shooting up in alleys, staying warm under piles of old newspapers. Hookers are swinging it on the side streets. Dock workers are huffing in the cold air, trying to make a buck. Fast Freddy is motoring that hotrod cab of hers down Park Avenue and Captain Waters is reading the riot act to someone else for a change. And here I am, sitting on a bench made of coral rock and bamboo under a hot sun on an eighty-five degree Florida day, wearing a blue and white flower-print shirt with white linen pants and the soft-soled shoes Melinda gave me, sporting no hardware except my snub-nosed .38 tucked neatly away, and sipping a fruity tropical drink.

Tropical drink? Where the hell did this come from? Aw, Christ. Now I'm losing my memory.

It was at that point I made up my mind.

It was time to leave Tiki Island, for good.

Screw Melinda, screw Jessica, screw old man Hawthorn and his plans of snagging someone to watch over his daughter, screw their ghost stories and their hidden rooms and their vintage Cadillacs and their murders and their damned tropical foo-foo drinks. I needed to get home. I needed to feel the cold concrete under the soles of my cop shoes again, feel the bite of the hammer of my .45 as it digs into my ribs, feel the heat a shot of Jack Daniels can give, feel the pain of the city and hear the screams of the night as I move around the shadows. That was me, a city boy, a night owl. A diner-burger eatin' Village bar-drinkin' jazz-lovin' city gumshoe with a thing for shady friends and a knack for finding the dregs of the dark and throwing the book at them, with hopes that a couple might turn themselves around and end up a little better off in the end. *That* was me. Not the guy with the white pants and Panama hat. That was just a costume, a Halloween costume at that, a fun make-believe outfit for vacation time and with the help of a couple of hot chicks I started to fall for my own joke. But my head was on straight now. I was far enough away from both dames that I could think with my brain instead of my driller for once and my head was telling me to get the hell out of Dodge.

There was only one catch.

Jackson.

The Sheriff would never let me skip town while he still had a murder tab on my head. If I was gonna fly, I'd have to take care of this pesky Bachman murder first. It was time to get back to my old self. It was time to shed the comic clothes and get back to work. No more fantasy time.

I took the Panama off my head and sailed it over the palm plants and into the Ocean.

A few minutes later I was walking along the beach on the Gulf side of the Island, trying to sort my thoughts, put the few facts I had into the little filing cabinets of my mind. The breeze coming off the water was stiff and a little cold, unexpected on this hot October day. The sun was shining over Tiki Island, but out to the west I could see the remains of the tropical storm that hit us the night before. Thick, dark clouds clung together in a tight nest just above the horizon; white swirls grew from the center and even from this far away I could see shocks of lightning arc across the clouds and down to the sea. It was as eerie a sight as I had ever seen. But to the east the sky was clear; the sun shined brightly and ricocheted off the whitecaps with a blinding silver light. People swam in the surf and lounged on the beach, kids built sandcastles and cabana boys shuttled drinks between the beach bars and the guests.

As if nothing happened, I thought. As if a man hadn't been brutally murdered a couple of days ago, and the murderer is still running around free, very probably an employee of the Hotel, maybe someone they've worked with for years, maybe their best friend.

Very probably an employee of the Hotel.

Why did my mind go there? What had I missed in this convoluted mystery? What important fact was sliding away from me while I soaked my brain in rum and lime juice?

I ran down what I knew again, as best as I could without taking notes. Bachman ran Tiki Island. He also ran hookers and drugs to Tiki Island for VIP guests. Hawthorn knew this. Melinda suspected but stayed out of it. She didn't like the idea but didn't do anything about it. Jessica worked for Bachman. And Roberts. Roberts ran the whorehouse that supplied the hookers, along with Bachman. Roberts got nabbed and the house got shut down. Roberts puts out a hit on me that fails.

Melinda was with me when they tried to ice me.

Next day Bachman shows up dead.

What if they weren't after me? What if it was Melinda they really wanted? What if Roberts had sent word to clean house? Anyone involved with the cathouse in Key West that could implicate him...Bachman, Melinda, maybe even

Hawthorn? And what about Jessica? She got her goods from one of Roberts' boys. Maybe he gave her a hot dose to put her out of the picture too?

Was Roberts really that powerful, and that brutal? I didn't know the answer to that. But I knew it fit, mostly. If Roberts gave the order from jail to kill Bachman, why not give the order to finish the job with me, Jessica, Melinda and Hawthorn? Plus it didn't hand me the strong man. That could be anyone on the whole damned Island.

I rounded the Island and found myself on the South Side, under my suite's window. I could see clear down to Key West now. Yet to my right the sky was dark as night. As I walked I thought about Roberts. The only way he would order anyone killed was if he knew they could put him away longer than he expected to get for corruption and running hookers. Did Bachman know something more?

Was that what was in the elusive safe?

"Dammit!" I yelled and kicked a bunch of sand up in the air. The breeze carried it away from me and luckily there was no one close to get blasted. But as I watched the grains fly away on the wind a thought hit me. A crazy, far out thought.

Maybe it was the other way around.

Maybe whoever killed Bachman was going to kill Roberts too.

Maybe they both knew some things that could do some damage. If that were true, it meant whoever killed Bachman would go after Roberts next. And there were only a handful of people who had the chance to murder Bachman and would have a reason to off Roberts, and I didn't like any of the answers to that one.

At two-thirty I phoned Sheriff Jackson and told him what I planned to do. He agreed and told me to come any time before seven. Next I phoned the front desk and asked them to get a message to Melinda to meet me in her office at three. They said they'd track her down and let her know. I hung up and made one last call…to my apartment. I gave the pre-agreed ring pattern and waited. No answer. I tried it again and still nothing. LaRue was gone, Princeton was gone. I hung up and dialed the precinct. I got LaRue on the line and asked him if everything was kosher. He said it was, Princeton was all wrapped up, the DA dropped any charges he was conjuring for me and I was actually missed around the office. Turns out what I did made a difference after all. He asked how the vacation was going and I lied that it was great and hung up. Next I dialed Jerry's bar. Jerry answered.

"Hey bud," I said. "How's the hammer hangin'?"

"Low and to the left. What's the word on my brother?"

"Nothing yet," I said, "Still working it. Got some ideas but nothing concrete."

"Then why'dya call me?"

"No reason. Just checking in," I said as I lit a Camel. "Oh, there is one thing, Jerry."

"Lay it on me Riggins, I ain't got all day."

"Rutger ever mention a safe to you? Something with a combination?"

"No, not that I remember."

"How about any dirt he might have had on anyone?"

There was a pause, then Jerry said, "Once or twice he mentioned something about having "a little insurance policy for a rainy day". He never elaborated but I figured he meant he had something to pin on someone. Why?"

"Just a hunch. If it plays out I'll give you the whole thing."

"Ok Riggins, whatever you say. When ya coming home?"

"Soon buddy, very soon. Later."

He mumbled something and hung up. I looked at the star clock on the wall: Two forty-five. I had to get ready.

I brought my dark suit out of the closet and laid it out on the bed. I got a crisp white dress shirt from my suitcase and put that on first, then tugged the dark blue pants on and buckled the belt. I slipped into my black Endicott-Johnsons and laced them up tight. A dark red and blue tie finished off the look. Then I slipped on my old shoulder holster, the speed rig I had specially made for my frame. I snapped it up and picked up my .45 from the suitcase. It felt strangely heavy. I ejected the magazine and spit the chambered bullet out. I checked the mag…six bullets. I reloaded the last one and slid the mag back into the butt of the .45, then pulled the slide back to chamber the first round. I let the hammer down easy and shoved the gun into the holster. It felt odd there, bulky and heavy, but familiar. I threw my jacket on, stood up straight and tall. Now everything felt right, felt *real*. I slid the .38 into my belt holster and buttoned the jacket. All I needed was one last thing to bring me all the way back…from the top shelf of the closet I lifted my dark gray fedora and hung it on my head, cocking it to the right like I'd done for so many years.

Now I was back. Back in my element. No longer wearing the costume of a man on vacation. Now I was *me* again, top to bottom.

And I was going to work.

Melinda was waiting at the front desk when I hit the lobby at five of three. She took one look at me and her eyes went wide.

"What are you all dressed up for?" she asked with a smirk. "Halloween's not 'til tomorrow."

"The flowery shirt was the costume, baby. This is the real me. And I'm on a case."

"Case? You mean Rutger?"

"That's right. I've got a theory and I need to run it down. I'll need a boat to Sugarloaf. And if you don't mind too much, I'd like to borrow your car."

She hesitated, then said, "I suppose it's ok. No one but Eliot and myself have ever driven it though. Have you ever driven a Cadillac?"

"No, my chauffeur always drove for me. Gimme the keys."

She motioned for me to follow her into her office. Once inside she shut the door behind us. "You know, detective, you look quite manly in that get up."

"That's what they all say." She moved closer and put her arms around me, pulling me in. I stood like a rock. She reached up and kissed me and the rock turned to butter.

"We haven't been together in over a day," she said seductively, then jumped up and sat on the edge of her desk, her long, shapely legs dangling playfully, an evil smile on her lips.

"I can't kitten, I gotta bolt."

"Not even time," she said with that breathy, sensual voice as she let her dress fall off her shoulders, "for a quick one?" She slid off the table and the dress slid to the floor. She was wearing nothing but the flower in her hair.

"Well, maybe just a quick one," I said and wrapped my arms around her. Her lips and body pressed against mine and the fire blazed up again, but it was different this time. This time she felt the cold steel of the .45 against her breast, and it burned into her soul and made her feel things she never felt before. Her primitive spirit took her hard, and she was an animal, forcing her lips against mine, clawing at my clothes. Before I knew what was happening my zipper came undone and she climbed on me, a jungle cat taking her mate with an intensity that was rare in the human species. She buried her face in my chest to muffle her hungry cries as we both exploded with untamed pleasure.

Breathless and hot, we collapsed onto her couch. Five minutes later I was on a launch to Sugarloaf Key with the keys to her garage and the big red Cadillac.

### Jessica, 4pm, Tuesday

She began to stir and moan, and the doctor came to her side.

"Miss Rutledge?" he said softly, gently rocking her, "Miss Rutledge, can you hear me?"

She slowly opened her eyes, squinting at the afternoon light. "Where am I?" she asked quietly.

"Tiki Island Resort, in the infirmary. I'm Doctor Finch. You nearly drowned."

She adjusted herself so she was on her elbows and opened her eyes a little wider. "What day is it?"

"Tuesday. It's about four in the afternoon. We found you early this morning."

"The storm," she said to no one in particular. "They were calling me."

"Who was calling you?"

"The..." she stopped and looked at the doctor in a very suspicious way. "No one. I was dreaming. Sleepwalking. I do it a lot. I usually wake up on the beach."

"The tide came in early this morning. You must have gotten caught up in it. You have some bruises. Were you accosted by anyone?"

"No," she said flatly, remembering the night. "Just sleepwalking." The images raged through her mind now, images of those hideous creatures reaching out to her in her room, in Hawthorn's room, seaweed hanging from their faces, crabs eating through their bodies. Then of *the one*, the single apparition who came to her so often, the one she imagined to be her mother calling from beyond her watery grave. She wondered if they would ever get what they wanted, or if she would just die in the process. "Can I go to my room now? I want to see my friends."

"I think it best if you just stay here, Ms. Rutledge. I'll call Mr. Riggins and ask him to come down here."

"Ok, I guess." She slipped back down to the bunk, too weak to argue, and closed her eyes.

"By the way, Ms. Rutledge, were you using any narcotics or drinking alcohol last night?"

She opened eyes and looked at him squarely. "Plenty of alcohol. No junk."

"All right. Rest now. I'll tell you when Mr. Riggins comes down."

But the doctor's call to the suite would end with no answer. I was already on my way to Islamorada.

The launch landed on Sugarloaf Key at three thirty. The bay was rough and made me a little queasy, but I shook it off. Once on dry land I watched the small boat head back toward Tiki Island, perched a few hundred yards off in the distance. The resort seemed to gleam like steel in the mid-day sun, nearly blinding me against the slate-gray backdrop of the western sky. Tendrils of lightning slithered down to the sea along the horizon and split the slate gray with a piercing white strobe for just an instant. For certain, last evening's tropical storm hadn't lost an ounce of vigor on it's way across the gulf. If anything, it picked up strength.

I was glad it was heading away from me.

I made my way up the dock to the warehouse-garage where Melinda kept her Cadillac. Using her key I opened the electric door, exposing that bloated, red beast. She was shiny, but the slightest film of dust could be seen on her fenders. No time for the mechanic to wipe her down today, I guess.

As I was about to climb into the driver's seat something caught my eye. Just a quick movement at the back of the stall, but enough to get my haunches up. I pulled the .45 from my side, clicked the hammer back and snapped the safety on, then peered around the back of the car for whatever it was that made that move.

"Who's there?" I asked softly, almost as if I didn't want an answer. I moved around the back of the Cadillac and surveyed the room. It wasn't a very big area, only large enough to hold the car and a steel workbench that ran the length of the left and back walls. Neatly stacked on and under the table were boxes of parts, tools and assorted lubricants. A hydraulic jack sat in one corner, and in the other were stacked eight brand new white-wall tires wrapped in cellophane. The right side wall was covered with hanging fan belts, hoses and wires. A pneumatic grease gun hung from the ceiling. Otherwise the stall was empty.

"Got the frickin' heebee geebees, that's all," I said and stashed the rod. Then I climbed into the driver's side of the car, turned the key to 'ON', pulled out the choke, pumped the gas twice like Melinda did and stepped on the starter. The engine roared to life like a pissed-off lion awakened from a long nap, and balancing the clutch carefully I pulled out of the garage. There must have been some type of electric trigger or sensor on door, because as soon as I was clear the electric door lowered itself down.

Melinda wasn't kidding when she told me the Caddy had it's own ride. Man, that car floated down the Overseas Highway like a duck on a pond. That Chevy was a sweet ride, but this baby was one fine 'chine. I sat back and let the engine slowly wind up to seventy as I crossed the big bridge, and thought to myself, I could get used to this.

I pulled up to the prison around four-thirty. A few clouds were rolling in from the east so I decided to put the top up. I had to struggle with it for a few minutes before I realized it wouldn't budge. Then I remembered...Cadillac...hydraulic top. I found the button and the top came up by itself. Another button put up all the windows. Tight seal.

The building surprised the hell out of me. It looked more like a hotel than a jail, sand-colored stucco with coral pink trim, a terra-cotta roof and a pair of curved palm trees at the entrance. The parking lot was crushed seashells and there wasn't a weed in sight. Inside a skinny guy in a gray uniform and cowboy hat had me sign the guestbook and took me back to the cell where Roberts was held.

The skinny guy said, "He gives ya'll any trouble, jus' come git me, I'll put him in his place."

I thanked the officer and sat on a chair outside the bars of Roberts' new home.

"Hello, Roberts," I said and lit a Camel. "Smoke?"

Roberts was sitting on his bunk with his face down. He turned lazily when he heard my voice. "What ya'll want, city boy?"

"Just to talk."

"Ain't got nothin' to say to you, boy."

"There's a pack of Camels in it for you."

He shifted, then sat up. "Well, maybe we can converse a little." I handed him a smoke. He spoke softly, slowly, sadly. "What's on your mind, Yankee? Had enough of your whore and looking for another?"

My face was iron. "Now now, redneck, let's keep this civil. I think you've got some information I need. Give it up and I can make things nice and soft for you, get you a sweet deal with the D.A. here."

"Horse shit, Yankee. The D.A.'s my brother-in-law."

Well, that backfired.

"Look Roberts, the truth is in three days I'm leaving this one-horse gaggle of islands and the chances of me coming back are slim to none. New York is my home and that's where I'm headed. So you and your D.A. brother-in-law and all your kissin' cousins can do whatever the hell you want and not worry about me giving you trouble. But before I leave I'm going to find out who murdered my friend's brother, with or without your help. I'm thinking if there's any validity at all to that badge you carried around for twenty years, you'd want to help. Help me and I'll find a way to make it sweet for you. Don't help me…well, your loss pal. Take or leave it."

Roberts got up from the cot and walked over to the bars. He held his hand out for another butt and I gave him the one I lit. "What'chu mean, your friend's brother?"

"I mean Rutger Bachman. The reason I came down here is because his brother is my best pal up in the city. He arranged the whole vacation for me. Now I get to be a pallbearer at his funeral."

"So then you knew about Bachman's side business before you ever got here."

"No," I said, "I only found out through you. And that's what I want to ask you about. Namely, did Bachman have a safe that you know of? Maybe someplace he'd keep some dirt on some people as a little insurance policy."

Roberts eyes got real big and his whole face lit up. He smiled so wide he nearly dropped the cigarette out of his mouth. Then, as if it were molten lava boiling up and blowing from a volcano, he let out the loudest, heartiest, most menacing laugh I'd ever heard in my life. He laughed and laughed at me so hard his face turned red; he smacked his hands on his legs and did the whole routine like a cartoon character.

"What the hell's so funny? You gone batty or something?"

Through his guffaws he managed to shout, "Boy! You are somethin' else! Did he have dirt? Oh hell, that Yankee had dirt on every man or woman of any worth from Mallory Square to Hialeah! Dirt! Ha HA!" he went on, laughing and hooting like a kid. Finally I had enough. I reached through the bars and got his shirt with both hands, and pulled him hard against the iron. His faced smacked up against the cold bars and he stopped laughing real quick, his smile replaced by a look of terror and fear.

"Now you listen to me, fat man, if you don't come clean I'll smack your face against this iron until it's nothing but a bloody pulp, and don't think for a second that scarecrow out there will come to your aid. So quit being smart and tell me what you know. Got it?"

Tears were forming in his fat little eyes. With his lips pressed sideways against a bar he said "Yefs."

"Good." I eased up a little, just enough for him to breath. "Now, Did Bachman have a safe?"

"Yeah, yeah he did. But I don't know where he hid it. He mentioned goin' to put stuff in the safe. That's how I know."

"Did he give you any clue where it might be? Come on, give!" I said and pulled him up tighter.

"No, no never…just that once, he said he had to put something in, and he left the Island. So I figure it ain't on the Island."

"Is it in the whorehouse?"

"No, no I know every inch of that place, it ain't there."

"You said he's got dirt on everyone. Anyone you know of who might have wanted to kill him over it on Tiki Island?"

"Aw, hell, I don't know…My first guess would be old man Hawthorn, if he wasn't so feeble. Him or that crazy girl of his."

"Crazy girl?"

"Yeah, his daughter, you know her, she practically ran the place when Bachman was out doing the dirty work. He kept them both in line with the dirt he had on them. That's why they never got rid of him."

"You mean all that stuff about wild parties back in the twenties? Who would care about that now?"

"Twenties?" he laughed, "Hell no boy, I mean about the rackets they been pushing for years. The whores, the drugs, the gambling, Bachman had evidence that would take both of them down if they ever cut him loose."

"Wait, dirt on both of them? What are you talking about? Bachman was the one running the hookers and party favors through Tiki Island."

Again he let loose such a sincere laugh that I had to let him go. He fell back and laughed and laughed, so hard he could hardly talk.

"Come on clown, knock it off and tell me what you're talking about."

He finally calmed down and managed to squeak out, "You really don't know? Bachman didn't run nothin', boy. He was the front man. Old man Hawthorn ran the show until he started going batshit crazy, then his daughter took over. Melinda Hawthorn is the brains behind the show at Tiki Island. Bachman was doin' her dirty work, just like I used to do Hawthorn's dirty work back in the old days. Ha HA! That chick's dirtier than that whore you been runnin' around with. Oh, an by the way city boy, that little girl Jessica has been on Melinda Hawthorn's payroll for a long time, in more ways than one if you know what I mean."

I didn't know what he meant. I didn't want to know. My blood was boiling, my head getting hot. "You're lying, you fat bastard. You're a dirty, rotten two-bit liar."

"You…don't tell me you…Well I'll be damned, you been dippin' you're ladle in that honey pot too? Hot damn, boy, you get around! Well say, have you had them two together yet? I hear they make a great double-team."

Without thinking I ripped the .45 out of my holster and pointed it straight at Roberts' head. "Shut your trap Roberts or I'll make pudding out of your skull."

"Oh Jesus Christ, man," he said hysterically, crawling backwards away from me. "Put that thing away, boy, don't go losin' yo' head!"

"You're about to lose yours, you Gaddamn sonofabitch," I said and cocked the gun. Roberts started screaming his fool head off for help, and I stashed the rod just before Ickabod rounded the corner.

"What's the trouble, Officer Riggins?" he asked, his hand on the butt of his revolver.

"Nothing buddy, I was just finishing up with him. Roberts," I said to the puddle of puss on the floor, "I'll be seeing you again before I leave. Next time I won't be so pleasant."

The V8 roared as I stomped on the gas and headed back south. The Caddy ground up the macadam like sausage and in what seemed like no time I was sitting in front of a familiar little gray shack on the edge of the Gulf. It was only a little after five but the sun had sunk into the distant clouds, giving everything an eerie pink sort of dull glow. Even the gray shack looked pinkish in the late afternoon haze.

I sat in the car with the windows down and the top up, letting the words Roberts spewed gnaw at my guts. Melinda? Running the vice operation? It was impossible. It didn't fit. I saw how she reacted when she caught that hooker waiting for me, how disgusted she looked when she talked about Bachman. And Jessica in on it too? And what was that bastard insinuating, that Jessica and Melinda were…no, it was too crazy, just didn't make any sense.

Then Fast Freddie's face popped into my head, and what she said about 'girls like her' in Key West, and an image of her pressing herself intimately close to Jessica floated by my mind and all of a sudden things didn't seem so crazy after all. Could it be? Was any of it true, or did Roberts just say those things because he knew they'd get my goat?

There was only one person who I could trust. One guy who didn't give a damned what anyone knew, or what they thought, and had nothing to lose by giving me the truth, and that was Captain Reams.

I rolled up the windows and headed for the little Bait and Tackle shop on the dock.

The decorations for the Halloween festivities were up and looking spookily grand, but Melinda couldn't take any pleasure from them. Although Halloween had always been her favorite holiday for as long as she could remember, she knew this one was going to bad, very bad. Too many indicators were pointing toward catastrophe. Eliot had taken a sudden downturn late in the afternoon, going into a strange sort of catatonic trance, emerging for only a few seconds at a time to blurt out insane prophesies of his own demise. Jessica was still in the infirmary, trying to fight back from near-death herself. William had left on his wild trek to find the truth behind Bachman's death, a truth Melinda wasn't so sure she wanted anyone, including herself, to face. And at five p.m. the teletype came over from the weather service: The tropical storm had strengthened into a force two hurricane, and was hovering over the Gulf gaining even more strength. What was worse, its pattern and direction were completely random. It could go north and hit the panhandle of Florida, it could go south-west and run into Mexico, or – and this was extremely rare and improbable yet still possible – it could hook around, backtrack and run smack into the central Florida Keys again, this time attacking from the west. If it did, it would hit Tiki Island dead-on, something that had never happened in Melinda's time on the Island.

Melinda knew the main buildings could withstand winds up to one hundred and twenty miles per hour. Anything more would threaten the glass and roof. At one hundred and forty, the roof would be ripped from the anchors and interiors would be destroyed by wind and rain. Anything over one hundred and fifty sustained for over an hour would flatten the buildings.

The teletype estimated winds at one hundred and ten miles per hour and gaining.

She couldn't take the chance. She had to take action before it was too late. She sent the word out to the Island's staff to meet at six-thirty in the Bali Hai Ballroom on the third floor for instructions. Then she went to the infirmary to see Jessica.

"My God, you look…" She cut herself off from saying 'horrible' as she realized she was saying it out loud. She fought to hold back the hot tears as she gently held Jessica's hand. "What happened?"

"They came again," Jessica said weakly. "This time they were pretty mad. They…" She closed her eyes and swallowed hard, feeling that heavy lump in her throat that came from nearly drowning. "They want him, Melinda. They want him bad. Even my Mother couldn't hold them off this time from getting to me. They tried…they tried to get me to join them, in the water. To help them. I fought them off. I don't know how I survived. I don't think I could do it again."

Melinda couldn't hold back a minute longer. She broke down and the tears came, gushing all at once like a fountain. "I can't lose him, Jessica, I can't."

"Then I think you've got to get him off the Island. It's the only way."

"He'll never leave."

"Force him. Knock him out with the juice and take him to Miami. Or farther."

"I can't do that to him, he'll hate me for the rest of his life."

"Well, sugar, then he'll have to meet his fate, won't he," Jessica said and let out a moan of pain.

"Where's it hurt, Jess?" Melinda asked tenderly,

"Everywhere. I'm all beat up."

Melinda squeezed her hand a little harder, then reached down and gently kissed her on the forehead. She looked around the room. They were alone. "Would you like me to give you something…you know, for the pain?"

Jessica took in a deep breath and let it out slow. "No. I don't want it. I'm done with the stuff. I'm staying clean now."

"For William?"

"Yeah, and for me."

I banged on the door four times and yelled Reams' name five before I heard stirring inside the shack. I heard a loud bang and a lot of clanging followed up by some expletives, and the door creaked open on its rusty, antique hinges.

"Detective! Aye, what brings you to me humble abode on this dreary eve?"

He sounded more like a pirate than a Floridian now, and the bottle of Meyer's Rum in his hand gave away the reason.

"I wanted to talk to you some more, if that's ok."

"Sure, sure, come in an' take a load off. Have a drink. Where's your lady friend?"

"Not with me. I think maybe there were a few things you may not have wanted to say in front of her."

He squinted one eye and twisted up his face as in deep thought. The crags and caverns of the face could have told a thousand stories. "Aye, you're a sharp tack, I suppose. There be a few things I may have left out. Come inside, we'll talk."

I walked in and sat at the familiar spool table. Reams finished off his bottle and pulled a new one from the shelf, then poured two cups, one for me, one for him. "What is it you want to be knowin', Detective?"

"Well for one, I'm pretty sure you know Ms. Rutledge, even though you didn't let on."

He dropped his eyes to the table. "Do you know how I know her, Mr. Riggins?"

I paused only a second before saying, "From a brothel in Key West, I'd imagine."

With his eyes still to the table he said, "Yes sir, I'd imagine that's true. I'd been...*with* her...on a couple of occasions. A fine woman, she is."

"Yeah." My guts twisted just a little. "She also works over at Tiki Island Resort. You know anything about that?"

"No, not beyond the obvious. She entertained clients."

"She ever entertain Hawthorn?"

He took a long gulp of rum and refilled his glass. "Oh, I don't know that for certain. Mr. Hawthorn always had a soft spot for the blondes. I suppose it's possible, especially after his second wife passed on. She was a brunette, you know. He never had much of liking for brunettes. Back in the old days, back in the twenties and thirties before he turned the Island into a hotel, he'd have his wild parties, and bring up girls from Havana, as I said before. Mr. Riggins, you asked me plain out last time you was here, had I ever heard tales of rape or murder at those parties. I laughed it off and said no. But it was because I didn't want to say anything in front of the young lady."

My guts twisted some more, and I took a long swig of the strong rum myself. "What did you hear, Captain?"

"Some of those girls them brought up from Cuba. Some of them had some nasty things done to them. On a few occasions I ran the boats down to get them, and the day after the party I brought them back. A few had been banged up pretty bad, Mr. Riggins. Bruises on their faces. Rope burns on their wrists. Occasionally, deep cuts or broken limbs. They were given fine medical care and an extra hundred dollars to shut them up. A hundred dollars was a lot of dinners and clothes in Cuba in those days, I'd imagine."

"A hundred bucks is a lot today."

"Yeah. Well, on a few of those boat trips, a girl or two less ended up on the return trip."

My guts were twisting pretty good now. "What do you think happened to them?"

"Oh, I don't know," he said and looked out a cruddy window toward the Gulf. The sun was almost gone now, and the sky was a strange purplish gold, like something in a bible painting. "But I hear rumors."

"Spill it."

"Some say those girls went off to be sold to white slavers across the country, over in Portland and Seattle. Some say they left the Island and made their way up to Miami, to stay in America. And then others said –" Before he could finish a gust of wind came up out of nowhere and shook the shack. The windows and doors rattled and the plank floor rumbled under my chair. I jumped in surprise.

Reams just sat there and took another drink.

"What the hell was that?" I asked in a much squeakier voice than I would have liked.

"The sea is angry, Mr. Riggins. I'm afraid we haven't seen the last of that storm."

"Great. You can't imagine how much I love tropical storms."

He smiled and said, "Wait 'till you experience a hurricane for yer very first time." Then he laughed and finished off his rum. He refilled his dented tin cup and offered me some more. I accepted.

"Finish what you were about to say, Captain. Others said what?"

He sighed heavy and tilted his head back, closing his eyes as if to remember. He ran his large, battered hand through his wavy salt and pepper hair, and wiped his face. "Some say they were killed, Mr. Riggins. Killed for sport, used as sex slaves for deviants in private rooms at the parties, tortured and beaten and congressed until the life spilt out of them. But they were just stories, just rambling and rumors started by the rabble Keys folk who were jealous they couldn't attend the parties. There was never a dust of proof on any of it, but it was certain that some of those girls never made it back to Cuba on my boat."

My brain was swirling like the storm out on the horizon. Deviant sex parties? Murdered hookers? "Captain, who did they say did the killing?"

"Well," he said with a smirk, "As I said they was just rumors."

"Who, Captain?"

He looked me in the eye, and I knew that he believed the story he was telling me, not as a rumor, but as an absolute truth. "Mr. Hawthorn, I'd imagine."

"And how did you hear this?"

Another deep sigh. "I heard from a very drunk, very anguished young man named Roberts, a very long time ago."

### Eliot, early afternoon

His mind was filled with the decaying, black memories of his past, memories that eroded his sanity and predicted the grim fate that he knew awaited him, soon. Eliot sat on the veranda of his top-floor suite, staring out at the Gulf as he had so many times in his life. But this time the tranquility of the crystalline waves gave him no solace, the cool, gentle breeze gave him no peace. Although the early afternoon sun shown intensely from behind the Resort and lit up the ocean like a floor of diamonds, far across the horizon to the west he saw the darkness, the absolute storm that blotted out the western sky and sent black tendrils of death swirling from its center, like an ink-stained octopus gathering its strength for an attack. In that darkness he saw death, the death of hundreds of others, and his own.

A shiver ran down the old man's spine as he contemplated his fate. "A pistol," he said quietly to the wind, "in the garden. But then Melinda would find me so," he muttered, "No, that won't do."

A gust of wind came up, nearly taking his hat. A gull screamed as it glided by. "Pills, that might work," he whispered. "Anything but *them*. I can't let them take me. I can't face that torture."

A woman's voice came softly, eerily from behind him. *"But you will,"* she said. But no one was there.

Eliot cried.

### Jessica, late afternoon

The thunder was miles away, but she could hear the low rumble as clearly as if it were the low tones of a bassist thumping out a jazz rhythm on the room's small radio. The doctor was gone, evacuated with the last of the guests and crew. She was alone in the bright white infirmary, just her, the white sheets, and the thunder. Melinda had tried to make her leave the Island but she insisted on staying, insisted on riding out the storm where she felt safest – with Melinda, and Riggins.

Jessica knew what was coming.

And she knew there was no escape from it this time.

She carefully rose and walked slowly to the window. It opened on the east side of the Island and gave her no view of the Gulf. To the east the sky was bright, with only a few puffy white clouds hanging on the light blue canvas. But the Island was deserted. No one swam in the warm waters, no children played on the beach. No sounds of exotic music floated up from the bar. The Island seemed almost…dead.

Funny, she thought, that she'd used the word, 'Dead'.

Jessica took a deep breath and gingerly made her away out of the room and down the short corridor to the west side of the infirmary. There the windows had already been boarded up. "Great," she said to the windows, and continued down the hall to the exit. When she opened the door, her heart sank.

It was much closer than she expected. A swirling black mass hung over the gulf, not on the horizon but nearer, so near she felt she could touch it if she stood on her toes. Bright flashes of light quickened over the clouds, shooting thousands of volts of electricity across the sky and gathering energy with every strike. A line divided the Gulf where the sun met the storm; twinkling whitecaps played in the sunlight until they crashed against black breakers beneath the behemoth of wind and power. That wind was already reaching the Island, weak but sure. A gust came up and bent a palm tree in a grotesque dance.

"God help us," she said under her breath, but she didn't expect any help from God tonight.

"I'm afraid I'm gonna have to cut our time short, Mr. Riggins. That storm's turned itself around, a highly unusual thing for a storm to do but that's what it's done, and it's not going to wait any longer before it starts bearing down on us, I'd imagine. Got to get my tub to calmer waters." Captain Reams got up from his squeaky chair and gave his back a stretch, one that made his bones crack and my nerves crawl. He took a last drink of the rum and held out his hand. "Sorry you got yerself mixed up in all this, Detective. But things in the Keys have a strange way o' workin' themselves out."

"I hope you're right, Captain," I said and shook his hand. It was trembling just a little, and not from the booze. "You Ok, Cap?"

He let out a sigh. "Not exactly, sonny. That boat's taken a few shelackin's over the years, but I'm fearin' it may not take it much longer. I should have left hours ago."

"Cap, I'm sorry if I held ya up…"

"No, Detective, it's not yer fault. I just been puttin' it off. Somethin' was tellin' me to hang about fer a while today. Now I know what it was. Somethin' wanted me to wait fer you."

"Well, Cap, I'm glad I caught you. Is there anything I can do for you?"

"Sure, Detective, one thing."

"Name it."

He took a set of keys off a rusty hook, turned and looked at me and said, "Say a prayer."

Captain Reams started up his twin diesels at the same time I cranked over the Caddy. A stiff breeze had picked up and I could feel little droplets of mist mixed in with it. I watched as he shoved off and headed north, then I shoved off and headed south.

The traffic going north was heavy. A string of cars, trucks and police cruisers slowly made its way along the Overseas Highway, heading towards Miami. It got me wondering just how bad this storm really was. By the time I got to Sugarloaf, the traffic was gone.

I parked the Caddy in Melinda's garage and locked it up tight. Then I went to the payphone and called the Island for a boat. I got no answer. From the edge of the Key I could see Tiki Island clearly, now looking dull and lifeless under the late afternoon sun, a sun that was obscured by thick gray clouds. The sky was still clear and blue to the east, but to the west…deadly dark.

When I still didn't get through on the third try, I decided to go down to the dock and see if there was already a boat or a message. I got both. A small speedboat with a giant sign that said "Riggins" on it sat tied to the dock. It bobbed around like a toy in the choppy surf, but I managed to climb aboard without flipping myself overboard. A note taped to the wheel read, "Tiki Island evacuated except key employees, myself, Eliot and Jessica. Take this boat to the aft dock and tie it down tight. I'll have the crew bring it up to stow it. Use the key to start it – push the key in to set the auto choke and turn to start. Then put the gear lever full forward and hang on. See you soon. Be careful, Melinda."

So she thinks I don't know how to run a boat, huh? Well…yeah, ok, she's right. I followed her instructions and got it started on the second try. Then I untied the bowline and the line on the stern (see, I know something about boats!) sat in the captain's seat and put her at full throttle. The front of the boat tipped way up and I thought it was going to flip over, but then planed off and started skipping along the tops of the whitecaps with ease. I pointed the boat toward Tiki Island, heading into the dark west at a fast clip.

The ride only took a few minutes, but it was enough to let me collect my thoughts. I had gone over everything Reams told me as I drove the Caddy back from his dock. Now I had those thoughts all organized, catalogued, and cross-referenced in my head as sure as if they were on paper. I knew the right questions to ask to get the right answers. And I was going to get my answers tonight, come hell or high water.

Bad analogy, I thought as I gunned down the engine and motored the speedboat into the slip at the ass end of Tiki Island.

By six o'clock every window of the Resort had been covered with the special hurricane-proof shutters that Eliot invested in twenty years ago. The doors were reinforced with heavy wood barricades, and the only way in and out of the building was through the rear loading dock. The small boats had been drug ashore and stowed in the boathouse. Every piece of lawn furniture, every Tiki torch, every bottle of booze and pack of matches had been removed from the outdoor bars and beaches and stored in the watertight storerooms. Tiki Island was sealed up as tight as possible against the oncoming rage.

At six-fifteen, Melinda said goodbye to the last of the crew. The twenty men shoved off in the launch, heading for Sugarloaf Key and the safety of Florida City. The Island was mostly vacant, except for herself, Jessica, Eliot, and of course, me.

The four of us sat in the Shipwreck Lounge, quietly drinking brandy. Melinda suggested the brandy, and we somberly took up residence at the table nearest the water tank. Even the fish seemed depressed and worried, sensing the oncoming fate.

We'd been there for over an hour, but hadn't said more than a dozen words to each other. Melinda was too busy battening down the hatches, Hawthorn was mute and Jessica was in a half-sleep. Finally, around seven thirty, Melinda came back and sat down with a new glass of Courvoisier.

"I'm exhausted," Melinda said quietly as she stared down at her drink.

"Yeah," Jessica restated, also looking down. She shot a quick glance my way. Then her eyes filled with terror and shot back down to her drink. I guess the look on my face wasn't so pleasant.

Distant thunder rolled along the background of our minds. Then a closer, louder but still well-off boom carried its way into the room. There was no flash of light, as the Resort was sealed shut.

"Storm's getting closer," Hawthorn said with a strange, breathy tone. His eyes never left the fish tank.

"Yes, Eliot, it'll make landfall in a few hours. But I'm sure we'll be safe here," Melinda said softly, putting a loving hand on his shoulder.

"Like Hell," I said, having enough. "If that storm's anywhere near as strong as everyone says it is, we should cut and run now. If we leave now, we can take the Caddy up to Miami before the storm gets anywhere near here."

"Eliot won't leave the Island," Melinda said softly yet sternly.

We'd been through that already. That was the dozen words we had. I said, let's shut the joint up, take the launch back to the car and head for the hills. Melinda said Eliot wouldn't leave the Island, under any circumstances. I said she was nuts. She said I could leave if I wanted to, alone. I really didn't want to stay on that damned Island, not with the storm crawling up our guts. But I couldn't leave her, and Jessica, alone.

"You want me to get Eliot to leave the Island? One whack with the butt of my .45 in the back of his head and he won't have any say in what we do," I said strongly.

"Sugar," Jessica muttered, finally forcing her eyes to meet mine, "Don't, Bill, it's too late to leave now. The Overseas Highway will already be flooded by the time we hit Key Largo."

I looked at Melinda. "It's true," she said, "Even if we left now, we'd get stuck in the Keys. We're safest here, in the Safe Room."

I ground my teeth and took a long swig of the brandy. I hate brandy. "Fine. Nice work. We stay. God help us." I rose from my chair, knocking it away, and got a bottle of twelve year old Scotch from behind the bar. I filled a highball glass with ice, and brought it along with the bottle back to the table. "But if I'm gonna be stuck in here all night with you three kooks in a storm that might very well take us out, I'm drinkin' the good stuff."

"I'll take one of those too," Jessica said a little louder.

"Go get some more ice from the bar, kiddo. You set 'em up, I'll pour."

We sat in silence, drinking and staring, for what seemed like hours. In fact it had only been ten minutes. I talked big about the Scotch but really I had no intention of getting drunk. I paced myself real nice, milking the highball for all I could. The last thing I wanted was to not have my wits about me if a big wave came crashing across the Island. Then I thought about that, and wondered if getting drunk was the thing to do. Then, out of nowhere, Melinda perked up.

"Hey, this is crazy you guys. We're all acting like this is the end of the world. Why? The building can resist a force-three hurricane, and the Safe Room is almost completely storm proof. It would take a forty-five-foot seawall, hanging over the Island for twenty minutes to flood it. That's so close to impossible it might as well be a fairy tale. We'll be fine. And if there's any damage to the Resort, the insurance will cover it. The important thing is that we got all the guests and crew off the Island long before they were in any danger. Now all we have to do is relax, have a few drinks, have a few laughs, maybe a nice meal, and get through the night without hating each other." She was all smiles. Miss Tiki Island, 1956. That somehow made me feel a little better, believe it or not.

The feeling wore off fast as an extremely muted, far-off thunder roll sounded eerily like the pounding of drums; rhythmic, intentional. Just my imagination, no doubt, but creepy nonetheless.

"It's coming," Hawthorn said as eerily as before. "No stopping it now."

With Hawthorn's weather report, the gloom resumed over our little quartet. I took a quick drink of my Scotch, and said, "When do we go downstairs?"

"Not until much later," Melinda said. "The storm hasn't even reached us yet. We can keep an eye on it from Eliot's apartment for now. There's a viewing window built into his storm shutters, and it looks straight across the gulf. I'd expect the first of the strong winds to start reaching us within the half-hour. By eight-thirty, the tide should swell enough to engulf most of the beaches, up to the garden. Remember, the gardens and the buildings are elevated, so if there's any flooding, it won't come until the storm is in full force."

I asked, "When will that be?"

"Around midnight," Melinda replied.

"Great," Jessica said, "The Witching Hour on Halloween."

In all the commotion I'd forgotten tomorrow was Halloween. Not that I'm a superstitious guy, but after the weird stuff I'd seen this week, it seemed pretty damned ominous.

"I think ghosts and zombies are the least of our worries tonight, kiddo," I said to Jessica.

"Yeah," she said into her drink, noting the irony. She took a deep breath. "Yeah."

Melinda looked at each of us, and took a sip of her brandy. I wondered how much she'd had that day. It was my experience that she could hold her liquor like a sailor. Right now, she was wavering just a little.

"I think we should have dinner. I haven't had a bite since noon, and for one am famished. I can whip something up in the dining room kitchen. What do you say?"

"That sounds good to me, doll. Maybe a couple of plank steaks will take the edge off the evening," I said. "I can give you a hand if you want."

"No bother," she said getting up. "You stay here. I'm going to bring Eliot back up to his room to rest for now, then I'll go fire up the steaks. I'll bring everything back here when it's done."

Melinda released the handbrake on Hawthorn's wicker wheelchair and without another word wheeled him out of the lounge and off to his room. Jessica and I watched as they left, until they were out of sight.

"You and me have some talking to do, kiddo," I said as I lit two Camels and offered her one.

"I knew this conversation was coming," she said, blowing the smoke high into the air and letting her eyes settle on mine. "So did Melinda. That's why she left us alone. Where should I start?"

I took a long pull of the cigarette and blew the smoke out slowly, letting it curl up around the two of us. "Start with you, Melinda, and Hawthorn together."

"You get right to the point, don't you detective."

"Yeah," I said. "Now give."

"Melinda," Eliot said, "Not here, by the window. I want to see it coming."

"There's not much to see, Eliot, it's too dark."

"I'll catch a glimpse with each bolt of lightning. I want to face my fate."

Melinda sighed. "Why do you keep talking like that, Eliot? You're acting as if we're all going to succumb to the storm tonight."

"Not all of us, my dear, just I. Just I."

"Nonsense," she said, walking him to the window. The shutters were sealed, but a two-foot square, three-inch thick glass window, set in the center just at sitting height, gave them a view of the Gulf. All that could be seen was darkness. Then lightning flashed, and thunder shook the room. The lightning lit up the whitecaps long enough to show them that the sea was indeed angry, and indeed creeping up to the garden.

"No my dear, it's true. Tonight's the night. Tonight I pay for my sins. There's no escaping it. I've been told."

"You're talking gibberish," she said, not wanting to believe him, but fearing the truth. "Nothing's going to harm you, Eliot, I'll make sure of it. No one – *nothing* can get into the safe room. And we'll be down there long before midnight."

"You think concrete and steel can stop them, Melinda? You're wrong. They're coming. They're coming for me, for what I've done. There's no escape."

Melinda's eyes turned red with tears. "I won't let them!" she choked, and threw her arms around him, kissing him, letting the tears flow freely. "I won't let you go!"

Eliot held her tightly, remembering the warmth, the love they shared. "You must," he whispered to her, "I deserve this. You don't know the things I've done, before you and your mother came into my life."

"What things? What could you have possibly done to deserve this?"

"No, my dear, that I'll never tell. I want you to remember me for the man I've been these last twenty years, not the monster I was before then."

"What have you heard?" Jessica asked as coyly as a child.

"I've heard a lot. Some of it sounds believable. Some of it sounds like a tall tale."

"The stuff that sounds believable is probably all lies."

"And the stuff that sounds crazy?"

She took a puff. "Lies too."

She was playing, trying to weasel out of getting to the point. "Come on Jessica, come clean."

"Come clean? I don't even know what it is you think you know, and I sure as hell don't know why you care."

That kind of steamed me. "Why? Because the two of you have been playing me for a pawnshop fiddle and I don't dig it, ya dig?"

"I don't know what you mean, Bill."

"You're lying. You've been lying since I first met you on the boat coming over here. A hostess? Yeah, fancy name for a –"

"Please don't Bill, don't say it." She held back tears and I felt like a heel. I was mad, sure, but I wasn't being myself. Putting down dames wasn't my style, no matter what their profession. Still, I didn't apologize.

"Ok, tell me this. Did Melinda hire you to play up to me? As a kind of a favor to the "hero cop" VIP coming to the Resort?"

She waited a few seconds before answering. Her eyes were turning red. "No. She had nothing to do with it. When I met you, I had no idea who you were. That first night we spent together, that was real."

"And after that?"

"Bachman…*encouraged* me to see you again. But I didn't do it because he told me to. I did it because I wanted to."

"Sure," I said and poured another Scotch. The next question was a hard one.

"Did you ever work directly for Melinda? Did she ever run the girls through here or what?"

"Well," she said softly, "Not exactly. Things were…different, a few years ago."

"Different how?"

She looked away, almost as if she were ashamed of something. I went for the jugular. "You and Melinda were lovers, weren't you, kid."

She shot a glance at me that damn near tore my head off. "No, *not* lovers. But we did…"

"Sleep together?"

"Yes," she said quietly. A rumble of thunder, closer than ever rattled the fixtures.

My gut twisted in a strange way. I'm no prude, but somehow I couldn't take it, these two women that I'd been so intimate with, had experienced so much pleasure with, had been *together*. It was just weird to me. I'd never been with a doll that was into other chicks, let alone two that had been into each other. Sure, I was close to Fast Freddie but I never bedded her. She was strictly chicks only, true to the core. But these two…

"Does knowing that bother you, detective?" she finally asked, now looking more sadistic than ashamed.

"A little. I mean, how do you even…How?"

"You want details?" she asked, a little shocked.

"No."

"It was just in fun, Bill. We were young…this was years ago. Melinda would come down to Key West with her college friends and hang out at the same places I did when I wasn't on duty. One night we sat next to each other at Captain Tony's and got to talking. A few drinks later and we were on the beach, me, her, and a half dozen of her friends. They were all paired up, boy-girl and making out on the beach. So it was just me and her, and joking around I said we should make out too. She laughed and said we should. Well, hell, I'd done plenty on stage with chicks so I kissed her. It was…nice. The beach, the booze, this pretty girl with soft lips. We made out for hours. A week later she came back to Key West and looked me up. That night we went all the way, and it was fun. So we did it from time to time, ya know, just as a lark. We became good friends."

"You never let on to me that you were friends."

"We weren't sure how to play it. Things took off pretty fast, you gotta admit, sugar."

"And you weren't lovers."

"We were never in *love*. Never lovers."

"Why not?" I asked, lighting my fourth Camel.

"She was in love with someone else."

"Oh, great. And banging you on the side."

She took a deep breath, and a long drink. "It wasn't quite like that," she said, and finished the Scotch. She poured herself another, silently.

"So, what *was* it like?" I asked, already knowing the answer.

"I think that's something you should ask Melinda, not me," she replied, and drank down the double Scotch in a single throw.

A crack of thunder and bolt of white lightning struck at almost the same time, jerking Melinda out of Eliot's arms and jolting them both out the chair. "It's on top of us," Eliot said dramatically, throwing his arms in the air. Melinda looked out the little window at the beachfront. With the next lightning strike she could see the Gulf…and no beach.

"The beach is completely flooded, Eliot. We've got to move down to the Safe Room."

"What's the point, my dear? There's no *point*."

She pulled him up from the lounge chair, bringing him shakily to his feet. "You're coming down to the Safe Room with me, now Eliot. No negotiation." Being stronger than he, Melinda easily forced him to obey. A few minutes later they were at the doorway to the Shipwreck Bar where Jessica and I sat, smoking, drinking, and going out of our minds.

Melinda said from the doorway, "The beach and gardens are completely flooded. There's no doubt now, the sea will reach the doorway to the Resort within the hour. We must go down to the Safe Room now."

"Jesus H. Tapdancin' Christ!" I shouted, the Scotch getting the better of me. "Already? I thought –"

"Whatever you thought, you thought wrong. Let's move, now!" Melinda bellowed. "The building is wind resistant, but not waterproof."

"And going twenty feet below sea level is a good idea to you?"

Eliot said in a quivering voice, "The Safe Room is sealed against the sea, Detective Riggins. It's basically a sealed tank, with an excellent air vent – "

"I know, I know, forty feet above sea level, I get it. I just don't want to go swimming in that tank."

"I'm sure you'll all be safe there," he said, and cast his eyes down to the carpet.

"Come on," Melinda cried, "Let's get going!"

Jessica and I followed Melinda and Hawthorn down the familiar back-of-the-house hallway to the Safe Room's entrance. Once inside, Melinda shut and locked the two sealed doorways.

"How will we know when it's safe to come out?" I asked genuinely.

"There's a viewing hole built into the outer door. If we look out and see water, we don't open it. Also, there's a radio down here. We can call for help in the morning. These storms almost always last only a few hours, and the waters usually recede within a day."

"If we make it through the night," Jessica said, "The sun will be out tomorrow."

We were silent after that. Hawthorn rested on a couch as the two girls and I made our way to the bar. Melinda poured us each a glass of Scotch, eighteen-year-old single-malt with a name I never heard of, better than the stuff we had upstairs.

"What, no Mai Tais or Zombies tonight, barkeep?" I asked jokingly, you know, to lighten the mood.

"No. Not tonight," Melinda said solemnly, and I could swear I heard her say under her breath, 'there better not be.'

We sat in awkward silence for a few minutes, drinking. Hawthorn seemed to have fallen asleep on the couch. Jessica got up from her stool.

"I've got to use the lavatory. Be back."

The minute she was out of sight, Melinda asked, "Did she...tell you, what you wanted to know?"

"Some," I said, playing it cool. Melinda looked sad, exhausted and deflated all at once. "Not everything."

"What did she tell you?"

"She told me that Bachman encouraged her to pursue me. She told me how you and her were and item."

Melinda's eyes got wide for an instant, then her face settled back into that expression of distraught melancholy. "She told you about that, huh?"

"Yeah."

"Are you...angry?"

"Just that you both lied. And that neither of you told me a thing about it. I mean, not that it would be any of my business, normally, but this trip has been anything but normal."

The room shook slightly, tinkling glasses and vibrating the bar stools. I looked around, startled.

"It's just the waves, or the thunder. You can't hear thunder much down here, not until it strikes very close."

"Yeah, the thunder doesn't bother me. It's those waves you mentioned. But let's get back to the subject. Why didn't you tell me you knew Jessica so...intimately?"

"I don't know. I guess I didn't think you'd understand. Or worse."

"Worse?"

"That you'd be...I don't know, morally appalled by it all."

"Me? Moral?" I laughed. If only she knew some of the things I'd done, the beatings I'd given to cons to get a confession, the borderline evidence planting to get a conviction, all in the name of morality. "No kid, two chicks going at it doesn't turn me off. But *you* two…that's a little hard to take, after what we've been through."

Another tremor rattled across the room, and I could swear it felt like the whole building moved. "That normal?"

"I don't know for certain," Melinda said. "I've never been down here during a full-on hurricane before."

"Great."

I took another long drink of my Scotch. I wanted to keep my head, but it wasn't playing out that way. My head was saying no, but my nerves were saying, "Drink up!"

"Melinda, there're some things I need to know, besides what you've told me."

"Like what? Just ask, William." She looked down mournfully. "I've got nothing to hide now."

"Did you run the girls and drugs here on the Island?" I just asked her flat. No use beating around the bush.

"I…Some," she said hesitantly. "For a short time. Rutger…when I was twenty, he tried to bring me into it. He didn't want me to make him…and Eliot…stop bringing in the girls, and the narcotics, because they were making so much extra money with it, and because it was keeping the Island in the black. I tried…I so wanted to please Eliot…but I just couldn't bring myself to do it."

"You supplied Jessica with her heroin, didn't you. You turned her on to it."

Tears started in her eyes and she made a sour face. "Where did you hear that?"

"First from a guy I didn't trust. Then from a guy I do. Is it true?"

"No. I didn't give her her first dose." She got up and paced around, holding herself with her arms folded around each other in a very worried, sad fashion. "But I re-introduced it to her. We were kids, teenagers. We were in Key West, having fun. She was already a – call girl, when I met her. She was already taking pills and occasionally cocaine. Friends I was with had heroin. I never used it, but for some reason I offered it to her. I know now what a mistake that was."

"Yeah, a big mistake."

"It's part of what eventually ended our friendship," Melinda said, tears now rolling down her beautiful, tan cheeks. I took a napkin from the bar and blotted them dry, lovingly, although I didn't know why. "That put an end to…everything. The drugs replaced me as her companionship."

"But you still had someone else to go to, didn't you," I said with no contempt in my voice or manner.

Her eyes flashed wide and bright, a scared little girl caught doing something naughty. She trembled visibly for a second, and pulled her arms in tight. I just stared straight into her big, brown eyes.

"How…how did you find out?" she asked, shaking.

"Roberts told me. I didn't believe him. It seemed too…too far out there. So I asked a local I met on the trip, a guy who used to work for Eliot. He verified the story. How long were you sleeping with Eliot, Melinda?"

She was very quiet, very still. "From around the time my Mother passed away, when I was seventeen," she answered, and the loudest crash of thunder I'd heard yet ripped through the room, shaking glasses and causing the ceiling to shake, raining dust and bits of paint down over the whole place. Hawthorn jumped from his chair in terror and screamed a fantastic noise. Melinda threw her arms around me and buried her head in my chest, and the patter of running feet from across the room brought Jessica up behind me. She threw her arms around me too, and I stood there mute, the two girls cowering and crying, locking me in a stranglehold, Hawthorn screaming his fool head off, and the thunder reverberating through the cavern like a train in the night, the unexpected noise of wind rushing through the resort as if the roof had torn off, the roar of a hundred thousand tons of angry ocean crashing against the Island.

Then the lights went dead, and my whole world went black.

## Late Labor Day Monday, 1935

Eliot was no master Captain, but he knew how to motor his own yacht in the waters of the Florida Keys. Adding hurricane-force winds on that stormy Labor Day Monday gave him a challenge, but he still knew what he was doing. His passenger, however, wasn't buying it.

"Eliot please!" Rose screamed as the black waves crashed over the bow. The sea was so angry that when they slipped into the valley of the waves they were engulfed by dark water, peaks high enough to obliterate the waning sunlight. It was like being entombed in water, she thought, and shivered at the idea. "Can't we get on dry land? I'm fucking terrified!"

Eliot winced at her choice of words, even though he knew it was her uneducated attempt at conveying substantial fear. He cared not. He carefully maneuvered the craft through the undulating waves, taking every precaution against turning over. The storm hadn't yet made landfall, and the rain was coming in sudden bursts with moments of lull. Visibility was poor, but still clear enough that he could see the Keys to his right and the marshy land ahead.

"Eliot! Answer me!"

Finally Hawthorn turned and looked at his stand-in wife. He said simply, "I'm done with you now. I no longer have any use for your services," and without another word he swung the lead pipe he had kept next to the helm for just this moment, and winced only slightly as it crashed against the side of Rose's skull. Somehow, it didn't take her down, and she stood there on the back of the boat, her eyes crazed with terror and shock, blood pouring down her cheek and neck, just starring. He swung the heavy pipe again, this time backhanded, and crushed the right side of her brain, knocking her senseless. She dropped to her knees. Bits of skull and brain and hair clung to the pipe. She was still alive.

"Why won't you die?!" Hawthorn screamed, and lifted the pipe high in the air. Through the wind and rain and crash of waves he heard Rose's soft but angry voice say, "I'll get you, Hawthorn," and he brought the pipe crashing down in the middle of her skull, bashing in her brains and killing her, finally, as he intended. A sick feeling came over him, but it only took him a second to regain his composure. He threw the pipe overboard, then, without any emotion at all, threw Rose's body over after it.

The rain washed the blood from the deck as Hawthorn gunned the throttle and made way for the marshes. He ran the boat for almost an hour, finding calmer waters and clearer visibility, and when he thought he was safe, he ran the boat right up into the marsh where it hung up on a patch of thick sawgrass. This is where he rode out the rest of the storm, waiting to be "rescued" early the next day.

In the cabin of his boat, as the tide roared against the hull, Hawthorn thought about the last words Rose said, about the people he left on Islamorada, about the countless women he…

He thought and thought, and a bottle of good brandy got him through the night, and he vowed that his old life was over. He vowed to move far, far away, someplace where the temptations of the Keys and Cuba and Hawthorn Island would be forever wiped away, a distant memory. He vowed to never take another human life again.

He would earnestly try to keep that vow, but it wouldn't save him from his fate.

In all my years I had never seen darkness so absolute, so all-encompassing as the giant black rag that stuffed itself into the Safe Room. My sense of space was completely out of whack. I felt the two girls holding me, shivering; I felt their hands but had no idea whose they were; I felt hot, scared breath on my neck but didn't know whose breath it was.

For a moment, all was quiet. Then the thunder came, but it was no thunder. Drums.

Deep, lurid, jungle drums, quiet at first, muffled, then louder, pounding harder as they came closer to the Island. We stood there stunned in the darkness, horrified, shivering. The pounding pounded faster, louder, penetrating our souls to the point of madness.

Hawthorn was the first to give way. He began screaming at the top of his lungs, "They're here! They've come for me, Oh dear God, they've come for me!" Melinda, I think, began crying hysterically in front of me. I was pretty sure it was Jessica who was holding me from behind, cowering, whimpering. They had my arms locked down in their hold, and that was making me nervous. Finally, I said, "All right, girls, give me some space, I've got to find a flashlight or something," and broke free of their grip. I pulled my Zippo out and gave it a flick. In the dim light from the lighter I could see Melinda's face in front of me, streaked with tears. I turned to see Jessica…but she wasn't there. As my eyes adjusted I could see her outline as she sat on the floor up against the bar, her knees tucked up under her neck, shaking back and forth. My mind swirled a minute, and I asked her, "Jess, how long have you been sitting there?"

"From before the lights went out. I'm scared as hell, Bill."

"Then who the hell was holding me from behind?" I said to myself. Melinda of course heard me, and she started to shiver even more, her eyes widening and her throat making funny sounds. "Alright, doll, calm down. You'll be ok." I said, knowing she wasn't.

"The drums," she croaked out, "I...I know what they are..."

"Forget that now. Where can I find a flashlight?"

"Lights," she managed, "Emergency lights, behind the bar, lead me there with your lighter."

I did, and after stumbling around a minute the whole place was suddenly illuminated with a dull red glow, like something you'd see on a submarine. "Is this it?" I asked.

"No, it's not supposed to look like this. Something is wrong."

Yeah, something was wrong all right. And we were all about to find out just how wrong.

The drums grew louder, louder and closer, now in the room with us....and stopped.

Then a strange, black shadow grew, hovering over the doorway, twisting and forming like a serpent. We didn't notice it at first, not until our eyes adjusted to this new, reddish hue. Jessica was the first to see it, announcing it with a simple, *"What's that?"*

Melinda and I looked where she was pointing, seeing only that the area in front of the doorway was in shadows, enough to darken the glow from the polished brass fittings. Then it *moved*, morphed sort of, getting larger and more distinct. It split and separated into two dark, swirling shadows, then three, then more and more until the entire wall was lined with human-shaped dark masses, evil figures hovering a foot or so off the teakwood floor... even in the dim, red light it was obvious that the floor was now wet beneath these shadows, as if the shadows were dripping seawater rudely onto it.

Between us and the wall of shadows sat Hawthorn, glued to his chair, his back to the shadows but his face showing extreme fear and panic.

"What is it, what do you see?" he managed to force out in a strange whisper.

Melinda said softly, "Eliot, no," and ran to him, grabbing his arms and ripping him out of the chair. "Eliot, they got in!" she said to him almost hysterically, and I realized that she knew everything, knew what he'd been yammering about, knew what was happening all around us. She knew what happened in his room, and knew what was coming to get him. "We've got to get into the closet, it's our last hope!" she cried, but Hawthorn resisted.

"It's over, my dear, I'm through," he said dejectedly. "I've not a choice. I've gotten away with my crimes for more than twenty years. Now I must atone for my sins."

"Sins? *What sins?* What did you do that you could possibly deserve *this?!*" she screamed, but he didn't answer. The shadows were upon them.

## 1935

It was early on the morning of Tuesday, September 3$^{rd}$ when the coast guard vessel found Hawthorn's yacht. They sounded their horn and called out, but got no answer. It was only that Hawthorn was passed out, sleeping off his bottle of brandy that he didn't hear...but the third blast jolted him, and with a stammer he cried out to the boatmen for help. An hour later he was in Homestead nursing a hot coffee along side dozens of others who had survived the Great Atlantic Hurricane.

It was then he got a visitor.

"Roberts? I wasn't expecting to see you here," Hawthorn said, looking up from his java. Roberts was a wreck; his face was black and blue, blood stained his tan sheriff shirt and his arm was in a sling.

"I barely made it out of Largo, Mr. Hawthorn. Was runnin' a truck fulla people up here, wiped out on the long stretch at Card Sound. I got a broke arm. A few others wasn't so lucky."

"Good to see you made it ok, Roberts. Sit with me, have some coffee."

"Don't mind if I do, suhr. See'n as I have a little somethin' I'm needin' to discuss with y'all."

"Oh? What is it?"

Roberts situated himself painfully on the wooden bench next to Hawthorn and leaned in close. "Suhr, you an' me, we been workin' together for many a year now. I've always turned a blind eye to...well, some of the goin's on concernin' y'all."

"And you've been paid well for it. What are you getting at, Roberts?"

"Well suhr, it's like this. I know you had that young lady from Key West with y'all on the Island last night."

Hawthorn froze. His mind spun. How could that be? He'd been so careful, so specifically cautious every step of the way. "I'm not sure I know what you mean, Roberts."

"Well now, let's just say, for the sake of argument, that ya do." Roberts took out a cigarette and lit it. He didn't offer one to Hawthorn. "Let's just say I know a lot of things about what y'all been doin' up on that island, Mr. Hawthorn, more than I let on I knew on account'a y'all bein' as powerful as y'all are. See, I ain't no dummy. I may sound like a redneck, but I been around the block a few times, and I know the score, see what I mean?"

"No."

Roberts took a long drag of his cigarette and blew the smoke out away from Hawthorn. "I mean, Mr. Hawthorn, that I know why you took that girl along with you."

Hawthorn didn't move a muscle, didn't blink, didn't breathe. "What do you want, Roberts?"

He didn't answer right away. He looked around the room at the moaning, aching survivors, the nurses in their bright white uniforms, the locals wet and dirty. He looked at the cots of bloody people, the children, the old men. The smell of sweat, urine and blood was getting to him. "Take a look around, Mr. Hawthorn. These people...they's my friends, my family. Now, I don't care none what y'all do with some two-bit whores from Cuba. But Rose...she was one of us. Whore or not, she was part of the Keys, and part of our little community. My family...they known her family for fifty years, Mr. Hawthorn." He took another drag of the butt and put it out on the floor. "You know she had a daughter?"

"No," Hawthorn said cautiously, "I wasn't aware."

"She did. A darlin' lil girl. No daddy. Gone long ago. That little girl's mommy is gone too, now, Mr. Hawthorn. I 'spect her grandparents are gonna have to bring her up now. A real hardship though. They ain't exactly flush with money. Catch my meanin', sir?"

"I think so."

Roberts turned deadly serious and looked at Hawthorn with such contempt that Eliot was actually afraid. "Now, y'all listen to what I'm tellin' ya," Roberts said in a low, dark voice. "You may be powerful an' all that, but I'm still the law around here. Now, I know there ain't no way I could ever pin Rose's disappearance on ya. But I know it was you. And I know why. So here's what y'all are gonna do. Yo gonna put a nice bundle of money in the bank for that child. Enough to get her and her remainin' family through the next twelve years or so, see? I figure that will just about be the least y'all can do for her. You'll do it anonymously, of course, to save face. Then yo gonna pack up and leave F-L-A for a while, I think."

"Am I?"

"Yessuh, y'all are. I'd say, at least a year or two. Let things settle down a bit. An' when ya'll come back, there won't be no mo' parties, no mo' hookers from Cuba, no mo' cocaine and heroin 'less I give the say so, OK?"

"So you're running the show now, is that it Roberts?"

"Yessuh. That's about it. An' they won't be no mo' killin', no Cuban whores or nuthin', clear? Otherwise I'll see to it that you become right intimate with a couple of rounds from a thurty-eight."

Hawthorn squirmed in his chair. His coffee grew cold. "So you're judge and jury, ruling on something that you can't even prove."

Roberts laughed quietly. "Oh, suhr, I said I can't nail you on that po' girl's death. I ain't never said I didn't have no proof of your other...*endeavors*. Matter of fact, I've got a few nice little photographs, some of which you took yo' self. Mighty nasty stuff, suhr. Twisted, sick. Even in black and white, *very* nasty stuff. Now, ya'll wouldn't want any of that getting around, would ya suhr?"

Hawthorn ground his teeth together in disgust and hatred. How could he be so foolish? How could he let this...this peon get the better of him? "I suppose I have no choice," he finally said.

"I suppose not."

"Well, Roberts, it just so happens I was planning to leave for the west coast after all this. Can't you see I'm in mourning? My wife is dead, lost in the storm. The last place I want to be is the Keys."

Roberts shuddered. "Sounds like a good enough story to me, suh."

Hawthorn shook. He held back real tears, and swallowed hard. "To be honest with you, Roberts, these deviations have caught up with me. I'm through." He couldn't hold back the emotion then, as if confessing to Roberts had released the pent-up anguish he had hidden for so long.

"Good to hear, suhr. Good to hear." Roberts gazed across the room at a little girl clutching her mother's hand, and he nearly came to tears himself. "Ya know, your island is gone."

Surprised, Hawthorn exclaimed, "Gone?"

"Well, the limestone is still there, and a few tree trunks. But the house is destroyed. Leveled."

"Any bodies found there?"

"Not as yet. No one's been out to survey there yet. But I expect they'll find at least one, or two."

"Two," Hawthorn said, hanging his head low. "And another in the sawgrass, probably."

Roberts excused himself. He left Hawthorn sitting there, alone, and walked through the makeshift hospital, past the broken souls, the crying children, the people who had lost everything and had no home to return to. He continued walking out through the rear doors to a path in the woods and kept going for a hundred yards or so. Then he found the largest branch he could find on the ground, and beat it against a large tree over and over again, smashing it, pulverizing it, screaming and crying and beating the tree until his hands were bloody and his muscles sore, allowing his anger and disgust and hatred to flow out of him until he had none left.

Thunder crashed so loudly we thought the roof had been torn off the Safe Room. Those dark, hideous shadows grew in size and began to encircle us, trap us. Hawthorn stopped screaming and began muttering something...maybe prayers, maybe nonsense. The four of us huddled together, having no idea what to do. I was tempted to reach for my .38, but what good would bullets do against shadows?

In the eerie light of the Safe Room, the shadows began to take on the shapes of men, and women...and even a few children. It was sickening. As their features became clearer, it was evident they'd been dead for a very long time, entombed in the deep, cold waters of the Gulf and the Atlantic, rotting away slowly, painfully. Melinda screamed at the sight. Jessica just looked on in terror. Then, slowly, one rotting figure of a women came right up to us. Her flesh sloughed off the bone as she moved. Small green crabs darted across her skeletal face. I damn near lost it, especially when she spoke.

With a voice like a hundred nails tearing across a chalkboard in hell, the phantom growled, *"Eliot, you bastard!"* The phantom twisted and choked as greenish mud slopped from its decaying lips. With an ear-splitting screech it screamed, *"I told you, you would pay!"*

Hawthorn shuddered in fear. "I know, Rose," he answered faintly. He looked at Melinda, who was white with fear. "I have to go now," he said to her. "Goodbye, my darling."

*"Not yet, Eliot,"* the entity screeched with an unearthly fury, *"First, they must see what you really are."*

"Oh, no! God no, please!" He screamed, "Don't! You mustn't! I'll go with you, take me to your ocean grave but please don't retell my secrets!"

"What the hell is going on?" I said quietly, to no one in particular.

Jessica answered, "It's my mother." Her voice was strange, her eyes glazed over, staring at the rotting thing in front of us. "And I think I know why she's been coming to see me all these years now."

*"You must tell them, Eliot,"* the thing said again with that hideous sound that conjured images of a thousand violins screeching against each other, *"You must Pay For Your Sins."*

Then, as if that were their cue, the other entities began chanting *"pay for your sins"* in similarly disturbing voices, filling the room with their tortuous sounds. Some came forward...a woman, or the remains of one, with no hands or feet, another with her head split in two. Another with rope burns on her wrists and neck. A man with his head caved in. Then, from the back, the woman with the large hat, the one I'd seen in the garden by the unmarked grave. She wasn't like the others...she was all in white, and floated a little higher than the rest. She came up to Hawthorn and he gasped.

*"Hello, Eliot,"* she said almost lovingly. *"It's time. Confess your sins, and come with us where you belong."*

"I can't bear it, I tell you! I just can't!"

*"TELL THEM!"*

"No, I've changed, for twenty years I've been a *changed man.*"

Suddenly the woman in white grew dark and hideous, a rotted corpse with the tattered remains of a dress clinging to her bones, her face smashed in. *"Then we'll tell your story for you!"* she screeched, and the room swirled with red and black light, and the phantoms swirled with it, and we were transported in time and space to Hawthorn's past.

## April, 1931

The party had been in full swing for hours when Senator Grady approached Eliot in a somewhat inebriated, buoyant state. "Hawthorn, old boy!" he shouted, clapping a meaty hand on Eliot's back. "What a fantst..fastasss...what great party you're havin'. I can only think of one thing to make it better."

Hawthorn knew immediately what he wanted. "A young lady, would that do?"

Grady shook with laughter. "Yes, my boy. One of those cute little Latinas from down south." He smiled, then his demeanor changed; he grew more serious, darker, quieter. "I think tonight I'd like something a little...different."

"Different how? Would you like two women to escort you upstairs?" Eliot asked innocently.

Grady leaned his two-hundred-eighty pounds in close to Eliot. "No, Hawthorn. I need something...*different*. I hear some of these girls...they have no families, no one to care if they...uh...go missing."

Eliot thought a moment, the alcohol confusing him, clouding his mind just enough to let him know something wasn't right, but he wasn't sure just what that something was. "I don't follow you."

"Roberts. He confided in me that some of these women are...*expendable*."

"He did?"

"Yes, he did."

"I know nothing of it, Senator. These ladies are all hired for the evening's entertainment. Tomorrow they all go on a boat back to Havana."

"Hmm...maybe not...quite...all."

Grady looked around the room until he spotted a tanned-skinned girl in a pink dress. "Her, the one with the dark hair and the pink outfit. Roberts said I could have her, to do with what I please."

Hawthorn still wasn't sure what the Senator was implying. His head swam with expensive Gin and Vermouth. "Ok, I suppose Senator, if Mr. Roberts said so."

"Is there a place where she and I can be alone, Hawthorn? And I don't mean upstairs...I mean, alone...where no one can hear or interrupt us. Someplace secluded...someplace that, you know, can be maintenanced easily?"

Hawthorn was so confused now all he could think of was trying to accommodate the Senator, a very important guest that he needed to help close a deal on a land grab in the panhandle. "I, uh...There's the boat house."

"Too public. Anyone could come by."

Eliot thought. "The basement."

"You have a basement on this island?"

"Yes, it's cut into the limestone. It's a Safe Room in the event of a storm. Water tight, sound proof. Somewhat small and not very comfortable, I'm afraid, but there is a cot."

"Take me there, Hawthorn. Let's grab that hot little firecracker whore on the way."

"Whatever you say, Senator."

They picked up the girl and Eliot led them out of the ballroom to the rear of the mansion where they came upon a locked door. The whole way Grady and the girl were laughing, joking, stopping now and then to kiss or grope. "Down here," Hawthorn said as he unlocked the heavy door. A pull-string lit a bulb that cast a sickly yellow glow over a set of wooden steps. "Go ahead down, Senator, it's all yours."

"You come too, Hawthorn, let's make it a real party."

"I'm afraid not Senator, my wife wouldn't approve."

"Don't be a goddamned prude, Hawthorn. If you want that land deal to go through you'll come down and have a drink with us."

Eliot pondered the request; he needed that deal to come to pass, so he said, "One drink."

"That's the spirit!" Grady shouted, and they all descended the stairwell to the Safe Room. Once there Grady pulled out a bottle of Sherry, poured three glasses, handed two to his guests and said, "Cheers!" The three drank the toast, then Grady smashed the bottle across the face of the no longer pretty Latina from Havana.

"Please, stop!" Eliot screamed as the phantoms whipped around the room. Melinda tried to shield him, but to her horror was ripped away from his side and thrown to the floor. "No more, I'll go with you, please just don't show her…"

"Jesus Christ Grady, what are you doing?" Eliot shouted over the screams of the poor girl. "Are you out of you mind?"

"I told you, Hawthorn, she's expendable. Roberts says so. She's bought and paid for. She's mine," he continued as he ripped the bloody dress from her shaking body. "Help me get her up on the cot!"

"I'll do no such thing!" Eliot shouted, backing toward the stairs.

"You'll do it and you'll shut up about it Hawthorn, or I'll ruin you, understand me? I have plenty of friends in the Treasury that would shut down your operation and put you in the poorhouse with a single phone call. Now help me."

Dazed, Eliot lifted the girl's feet as the Senator lifted her arms to the cot. Grady finished stripping her naked while the girl's screams and strength weakened. "You want a turn, Hawthorn?"

"No, not at all."

Grady unbuttoned his trousers and forced his way into the girl as Eliot stood aghast, too drunk to stop him, too frightened to leave. The girl moaned and cried. Grady punched her full on in the face, bloodying her further. He grabbed and twisted her breasts demonically as drool spilled out of his mouth into her eyes. With every plunge the girl seemed to become weaker; Grady seemed to grow darker. His breaths came faster and as they did he picked up the neck of the broken bottle and thrust it into the girl's body, twisting it and tearing it out with chunks of flesh and rivulets of blood. The girl screamed in agony as he came inside her, and with his final thrust he ripped her throat open with the jagged glass, drenching himself in her blood. With horrible, disgusting gurgling sounds, she clawed at her throat and took her final breath.

Eliot, dumbfounded, slid down the wall to the floor, staring at the horrific mass of blood and dead flesh that once was a vibrant young woman, his mouth gaped open in a caricature of horror, his heart pounding so hard it hurt.

Grady dismounted with a grunt, and buttoning his fly said, "Tell Roberts to clean this up. Whew!" He wiped the girl's blood off his face with a linen handkerchief. "Excellent party, Hawthorn. That land is yours. I'll be back for next month's party. Tell Roberts I want a blonde this time." He took a deep breath, and ascended the stairs.

Eliot screamed as loud as he could, "Melinda, my darling, please don't watch, they're lies, all lies!" Eliot screamed, but the phantoms muffled his plea.

*"Not lies, the truth!"* the ghostly woman screeched as the phantoms swirled. *"The truth! THE TRUTH!"*

## July 4, 1932

It was after two in the morning when Eliot's wife finally passed out from too much gin. The guests had either paired off and gone to their rooms, or had gathered in the music room for a rather decadent preoccupation. Eliot made his way to the music room, finding no less than twelve men and twenty women on the floor, undressed and indulging in every deviant sexual act possible. Eliot, once very shy but now very accustomed to this custom, joined the array where two young women seemed to be not working hard enough for their pay. He spent a great deal of time with them both, enjoying them as much as biology would allow, but grew bored of the ritual, bored of the decadence that had become so ordinary. He yearned for something more, though he knew not what it was.

He stood as the two ladies knelt in front of him, orally pleasing him. He was in arm's reach of a bottle of full-strength Canadian whiskey, and took a long shot from the bottle. Neither the alcohol nor the women gave him much satisfaction. Then, from nowhere, an idea invaded his mind, an idea that he desperately tried to suppress, an idea that had started a year before. He looked down at the two heads bobbing before him, and realized one of the girls was from Robert's house in the keys, while the other was a Cuban girl, one who had been to his parties before. She was a runaway, a girl with no past…and no future. Harshly, impulsively, he stopped the two girls and dismissed the blonde. "You, vamos," he said to the Cuban, and led her to the Safe Room.

"Eliot, NO!" Melinda yelled, over and over until her voice cracked. "How could you!?"

"Please, for God's sake, stop showing her! You evil beings, I've paid for my crimes for twenty years, and will surely pay in the afterlife, *please* leave my love out of this!"

But the phantoms didn't care.

"We haff good time, no?" the young hooker said as she slid her dress to the floor. The Safe Room was chilly and dank, but she didn't care. She was about to lay the owner of Hawthorn Island himself, and that made her very happy, for she knew there would be a truckload of money in it for her down the line.

"Oh, yes, I think we'll have lots of fun."

She didn't notice the dark red stains on the floor or the walls. She didn't notice the pieces of rope tied to the cot, or the chains anchored to the wall. She simply climbed on the bed in a sultry fashion, and spread her tanned legs open just slightly, suggestively, not in the typically whorish way as she'd been taught to in Cuba.

"Do you like wha you see, señor?"

Eliot let out a mischievous laugh. "Yes, indeed." He slowly opened a metal cabinet across from the cot and removed a blindfold. "Put this on, I would like that," he said in a low, breathy voice full of anticipation.

"Oh ho ho!" she said shaking her finger at Eliot, "a naughty one! Sí, I put it on." She slid the blindfold over her eyes and lay flat on the cot. Moving quickly, Eliot tied her hands, then her ankles, to the bed frame.

"Oh, my, Señor Hawthor', you are so keenkee!"

"You ain't seen nothin' yet, sister," he said under his breath, and taking a small axe in hand, mounted her.

"Enough!" Melinda cried, tears streaking her haggard face. "Enough, I don't want to see any more."

Hawthorn had given up trying to stop the phantoms. He simply slumped in the chair, his head hung low and sorrowful. Jessica, to my right, seemed to be in some sort of trance, her eyes fixed on the ghostly woman next to Hawthorn. Me? I didn't know what the hell was going on. Things were so far out, I couldn't be sure I was really seeing them or if one of the chicks slipped me a mickey. Either way, things got even heavier as the show went on.

Eliot knelt in a pool of blood and other bodily fluids as they soaked into the cot. Before him lay the ruins of a girl, not yet eighteen, dead and bloody beyond recognition. Her hands were severed from her arms. Her once beautiful, full breasts were a mound of torn flesh and chopped, broken ribs. The axe was still imbedded in her heart, the final blow that ended her torment. Eliot was covered in blood, was soaked with it. And finally, he was sated. At least for a while.

The images swirled around my head like strawberries in a blender. Was this insanity really true? Eliot Hawthorn, a murderer? And a crazy fucking psychopath at that? It was too much. I knew I was just an unlucky observer in someone else's nightmare, but I couldn't hold back any longer.

"How many, Hawthorn?" I yelled over the sounds of the phantoms, in a much angrier voice than I intended. "How many, you sonofabitch?"

"Twelve!" he shouted at the top of his ancient lungs as if his volume would acquit him.

Strangely, everything went quiet. "Twelve, plus three," he finished softly.

It was on the "plus three" that all hell really broke loose.

**Sunday, August 30, 1935**

Sunday was as calm and non-threatening as Saturday had been, with the exception of that evil, eerie darkness lingering in the east and an occasional gust of wind blowing through the tops of the palms. There was no doubt now; the weather service issued a hurricane warning for all of the Florida Keys.

Eliot sat on the veranda of his elegant island home, sipping bourbon and ginger ale from a tall glass. The island was now deserted except for his wife Vivian, his best friend Gregor, and Rose. Rose was tucked safely away in the boathouse where no one would find her. Gregor was stowing the last of the luggage on his boat. From Eliot's position he could see Gregor, the boat, and the Gulf of Mexico.

Strange images floated over Eliot's mind as he made his way down to the dock, lazily twirling a nine-iron. It had been months since he learned of his friend's secret, but the memory still burned in his mind as if it were still happening. Gregor had no idea that Eliot knew. But he soon would.

"Ahoy there, captain!" Eliot hollered to Gregor as he approached the dock. "All set?"

"Ah, just about, Eliot. What's with the golf club?"

"Oh this?" Eliot asked, looking at the club as he raised it to eye level. "This is for you." Without hesitation he whipped the club around and landed it squarely against Gregor's temple, a whack hard enough to knock Gregor to the ground. He squirmed in pain, holding his hand against his bleeding, broken skull.

"My God, Eliot? What on earth did you…why?"

"I know about you and Vivian, old chum."

Gregor rolled with pain. "Jes…Jesus, Eli..Whatever you think…"

"I saw you with my own eyes, old chum. Two months ago, in the cloakroom. I suppose you thought I'd retired for the night. I hadn't."

"Eli-Eliot, wait, I can explain, the parties, everyone was partaking…"

"Not Vivian. She has a strict rule about not sleeping with anyone at the sex parties. Which can mean only one thing, old chum. She was having an affair, with you."

"It's not…OW!" Gregor screamed as Eliot smashed his left kneecap with the club. "Christ, Eliot! Please, I swear it was only an indiscretion. Eliot… we've been best friends for fifteen years!"

"Yes," Eliot said sadly, "Fifteen years. And no longer." With that, Eliot lifted the heavy club high into the air and brought it down fast and hard, dead-center on Gregor's forehead. Gregor barely had time moan before he passed out. Eliot repeated the action twenty-four times, counting each time, until Gregor's lifeless body was completely unrecognizable. "Sorry, old chum," he said to the bloody mass that was once Gregor's face. "It seems I've gone over par."

Black and gray clouds formed inside the Safe Room, growing from nothing and covering the ceiling. Real lightning struck from them to the floor and furniture; the thunderous cracks shattered our eardrums and brought us all to our knees. The hurricane wind began to blow around us, and I knew that the storm had reached its solitary victim.

Eliot walked along the beach, the bloody club dripping by his side. He had no remorse for murdering his friend. It was all part of the plan, all part of his final solution to ending his old life and starting anew. Everything was falling into place...even Mother Nature was cooperating fully, holding off the hurricane until the following day. In a little more than twenty-four hours he would be completely free, and would never need to return to Hawthorn Island with all its horrors again.

Up ahead, walking in the surf was Vivian, her shoes in hand, her white dress and hat flowing in the breeze. He gained on her steadily but softly, twirling the club in that nonchalant way that was so unnervingly disturbing. In a moment, he was upon her.

"Going golfing, Eliot?" she asked sweetly, not noticing the dark red essence of her former lover dripping from the metal.

Eliot got right to the point. "Vivian, I know about you and Gregor."

"I know," she answered, looking out over the Gulf. "I could tell by your demeanor these last weeks."

"Why?" Eliot asked, almost childishly. He hated himself for that.

"Why indeed," she said looking down. "Things have gone much too far, Eliot. You've changed. Our whole world has changed. I pretend to look away, but I know about the...the women. The women who...disappear. I can't stand idly by as you continue this travesty, Eliot. And so...And so I'm leaving you, this weekend. I'll shove off with Gregor, and we shan't have to see each other again. Our lawyers can hash out the details. You can keep the Island for yourself. I don't want anything to do with it ever again."

Eliot was as cold as ice on steel in the dead of January. "No, Vivian. That won't do."

"It will have to. My mind is set." She looked out at the Gulf, as if she knew it would be the last time. "I'm leaving Hawthorn Island forever."

"On the contrary," Eliot said as he cocked back the club, "You're going to spend eternity right here, with your dead lover." And before she even had a chance to cry out, with nothing but a look of shock and a short gasp from her throat, Eliot Hawthorn swung the iron golf club with as much force as he could muster and drove it into the middle of Vivian's face, shattering it instantly, driving the bones deep into her brain.

My mind was so screwed over that I couldn't tell reality from hallucination. Had the storm somehow entered the Safe Room, or did it rip the building down and expose us to the elements? Heavy rain pelted us, lightning surrounded us. The black wall of phantoms seemed to stretch on forever. Then with a mighty crack, the walls exploded, allowing the dark waters of the Gulf to come pouring in around us.

It was then the horrid specter of Jessica's mother seemed to grow ten times her size, and swirling around the room like a whirlpool I could hear her harsh voice spatter, *"It's time, it's time."* In the center of it all, Hawthorn's screaming body was carried up by the ragged ghosts, twisting him, tossing him. Water circled around my legs and pulled me down, but I managed to grab onto a table for support. It was too dark to see Melinda or Jessica now; only during the flashes of lightning could I see the phantoms tormenting Hawthorn.

"For God's sake, Riggins, do something!" I heard his scream over the cacophony of wind and rain. "Help me!" He wasn't ready to meet his fate after all. But there wasn't a damned thing I could...or would for that matter...do to help the bastard. "HELP ME!"

"Help me!" Vivian cried as she tumbled to the sand. Her vibrant, crimson blood gushed from the hole in her face and splashed across her white dress. Her hands involuntarily clawed at her smashed face, trying to find her eyes, her nose. Her breath was labored. With a gurgling sound she said, "I never...thought...you would...kill me."

"You were exceptionally incorrect," Eliot said, and swung the club as if aiming for the eighteenth hole. Vivian Hawthorn was dead within seconds.

Eliot dragged her limp body up from the beach, through the thicket of palms to the garden, and laid her body next to Gregor's. He removed the support of a nearby cement bench, and dropped it on her face to make sure identification was impossible. When he did the same to Gregor, his skull collapsed entirely, leaving a surreal, flattened mass where his head once was. Eliot then tossed the cement support a few feet away, went inside his mansion, poured another bourbon, and took a shower. Soon, he would bring his whore into the house, ravage her in his and Vivian's bedroom, desecrating their marital bed. One last spike through his unfaithful wife's heart before finalizing his plan.

The next day Eliot made sure there was a length of heavy, lead pipe on the boat. The golf club just wasn't heavy enough to quickly and efficiently finish the job he intended for Rose.

"*MURDERER!*" Screamed the phantoms as they pulled on Hawthorn, twirling him around like a ragdoll. "*PERVERT! WRETCH*"

The ocean was pouring in at a quick rate, so quick that I figured it would be less than five minutes before we suffered a freezing, drowning death. As my eyes adjusted to the light I could see Jessica, shivering, clinging to the bar. Melinda, on the other hand, had somehow managed to conjure the courage to insinuate herself among the phantoms, trying desperately to free Hawthorn from their grip. Her efforts failed.

The water was at waist-level now. All I could think of was getting to higher ground, maybe finding something to float on. Tables and chairs floated by, crashing against each other. To my left was Jessica at the bar, to my right Melinda and Hawthorn among the spirits. The doorway to the stairwell was blocked.

I slowly sloshed my way over to Jessica. She looked at me with such a combination of sorrow and terror, I didn't know whether to hold her or put a bullet in her head to relieve her misery. Then I realized, for the first time, what her torment was actually like. Her dead mother coming to her for so many years. The phantoms in the night. The torment, the terror. No wonder she shot up with heroin. Most people would have just jumped off the highest bridge they could find. "Jessica, do you..."

I didn't get a chance to finish asking if she knew another way out. Before I could she screamed at the top of her lungs, "JUST GET IT OVER WITH AND LEAVE US ALONE!"

They say a mother's love for her daughter lives on forever, even after the body dies. I believe that to be true. As Jessica screamed, Rose emerged from the bramble of spirits and came to us. As she did, the wind and rain died away, the lightning and thunder inside the room subsided. The water calmed. A light grew from above, and stayed lit.

"You got what you came for," Jessica cried. She was still shaking, cold and wet. Sadly she muttered to her mother's spirit, "You've got him, finally, after all these years you've got your revenge. Can you just leave us alone now?"

As the phantom of Rose hovered in front of us, the hideous countenance changed subtly; the small crabs and mud disappeared, and the true face of Rose shined through, smiling. *"My precious daughter,"* the phantom said, *"Yes, now that you know, now that you know everything, we can leave in peace."*

A rumbling noise came from behind the bar, and the room shook hard. Glasses fell off the shelves and shattered. The mirror cracked and fell to pieces, and the entire wall gave way, exposing the night outside, the beach, and the angry Gulf. *"We can leave now. Goodbye, my daughter."*

Jessica wept quietly. *"We're leaving,"* the ghost said again. Rose's face turned black and skeletal as she shrieked the words. *"And we're taking HIM with us!"*

And with that the drums began to beat again, louder and heavier and more menacing than before, and the entire roomful of phantoms began shrieking and screaming, ripping through the air like jets, carrying Hawthorn away on their misty backs. Hawthorn screamed over and over again with a horrified yell as the phantoms carried him out through the broken wall, over the beach and into the raging surf. The struggling, screaming man, mad with horror, crazed with the knowledge of his fate screamed again and again until his screams were finally drowned in the Gulf. Melinda tried desperately to follow him, to save him, but the wall sealed itself up before she could reach it. Hawthorn was gone, tied to his fate, murdered in the ocean by those he had murdered in the past.

And as if that were the final curtain on a horrifying play, the storm clouds retreated from the room. The water drained away, leaving a soggy, mucky mess. The emergency lights came back up dull and white. All was quiet, except for the distant, muffled sounds of the storm topside.

Jessica sat on the bar, crying. Melinda dropped to her knees and cried too, wailing with such sorrow I though she would die right there of a broken heart. As for me? I walked over to the bar, opened a new bottle of eighteen year old Scotch, and poured myself a triple. Raising the glass, I said quietly to myself, "Happy Halloween," and downed the drink in one shot.

The hours after Hawthorn was…*taken away*, were very surreal, like walking through whipped cream with a bad headache. Melinda sat in a heap on the floor sobbing. Jessica sat in a captain's chair, staring at the wall through which the apparitions departed. The sloshing water was gone, leaving only a clinging wetness that dampened the room. The roar of the storm outside had let up too.

I found a door at the very end of the room, next to the bar; a heavy carved teak door, inlaid with mother of pearl and depicting a Hawaiian sunset. I figured behind it was Hawthorn's private office or room.

I was right, although it was more of an anti-chamber than an office. There was a desk, but I believed it to be purely ornamental as there were no papers or even a pen on it, just an electric clock and brass lamp. There were several sofas and over-stuffed chairs, and the walls were lined with lawyers' bookshelves, the kind with the glass doors covering them. There were books, mostly standard classics, along with some knick-knacks and very expensive-looking bottles of booze behind the glass. But I found what I was looking for in the bottom desk drawer.

The leather case held a hypodermic needle, two vials of liquid, and two vials of pills. One of the vials was marked Valium. I took it and returned the case to the drawer.

"Take these," I said softly to Jessica. "Two will knock you out for a few hours."

I hated giving a junkie drugs, but under the circumstances it was a necessity. With lifeless obedience she swallowed the pills.

"Melinda," I said, "Take these pills. They'll get you through the night." With the same silent, limp manner she swallowed the pills down with a whiskey chaser.

"Now let's go into the other room. There's sofas in there where we can crash 'til this storm flies over."

"Storm's over," Jessica said in a raspy, weak voice. "It got what it came for."

I didn't want to think about that just yet. The Jello I was wading through was becoming thicker, the whipped cream sloppier. I knew my mind and my body couldn't take much more before I'd collapse for a week, and I needed to get the kids to bed before they passed out on the floor.

"Let's go in here anyway. Sleepy time down south, girls. Let's vamoose."

Like zombies the two women followed me into the anti-chamber. I laid Melinda down on the big couch, and Jessica on a smaller love seat. The pills were working fast, and I'm pretty sure Jessica was out before I sat in the big chair.

"Good night, kids," I said, took two of the pills myself and turned off the light.

The hideous, ear-splitting screams drove icy shivers down my spine and made me jump so hard my head and neck seized up in fear, sending shots of purple pain through my skull and back.

"TURN IT ON!" she screamed over and over, with insane wailing and screeching in between. It was Jessica, going mad. "THE LIGHT! TURN IT ON! *TURN IT ON!*"

I obeyed, turning the gaddamned thing on as fast as I could. Jessica was shivering, cowering into the corner of the loveseat, her eyes opened as wide as her skin would allow, peering at the closed door. Melinda was curled up in a ball, shaking and rocking on the sofa, crying loudly. I jumped up and ran to Jessica, calming her. "It's on, for Christ's sake the light is on, dollface!"

I don't know how long it took to finally get them calmed down. It seemed like hours in the soupy slosh my brain was in, but it was probably only minutes as the Valium worked its magic on the three of us. As I started to drift off, I could hear the wind rattling against the building, the waves crashing on the beachhead outside. The storm was letting up, certainly. The worst was over.

The worst was over.

All over.

Tomorrow, I would leave Tiki Island, and the worst... would... be... overrrr...

# CHAPTER FIVE

Wednesday Morning, October 31, 1956
*Halloween*

It was the bone-chilling silence that woke me the next morning. No wind, no waves, no thunder crashing. Just silence, except for the far-off hum of the Island's generator, still running and keeping the lights going all night. A quick look at my watch told me it was eight thirty. I was hoping to be out of it until at least noon, but I guess the Valium didn't do such a good job on me as it had on the girls...they were out cold. I was wide awake.

As the fog lifted from my brain I wondered what was left of the Island. Had the hurricane been so bad after all? Or was it just... a smokescreen, a convenient cloak for...for what? You were about to say for some gaddamned ghosts to come along and murder Hawthorn, weren't you Riggins? That was crazy, and I knew it. But gaddamn it, it happened, sure as hell it happened. I *know* it did.

I got up from the chair and made my way out to the bar. The place was in shambles, chairs knocked around, seaweed everywhere.

Yea, it happened. Sure as hell.

I found the men's room and splashed some cold water on my face. The whipped cream I had wandered through last night was melting away, and reality was setting in, way too fast for my style. I knew I had to go topside to check out the damage. I was afraid of what I'd find.

When I stepped out of the men's room, Melinda was standing there. I almost jumped out of my already goose-bumped skin

"Oh, eh, sorry doll, I didn't meant to wake you." There was something that just didn't seem quite right about her. Her eyes were wide but tired. There was a twitch in her face. She hardly blinked. Poor kid.

She said in an alien voice, "You didn't. I just woke up, no reason. I need to see the damage."

"Yeah, I was just about to go topside myself," I said, taking her hand. "What about Jessica?"

"Out like a light. She took an extra pill and washed it down with a glass of whiskey."

I nodded. "Listen, Melinda, about last night…"

"No, don't William," she interrupted softly, on the verge of tears. "Not yet. I can't bear it." She looked around the shattered room and shook her head. "One catastrophe at a time."

The door to the stairs opened with a wet creak. Some water poured in, but not enough to make us nervous, at least not yet. The stairwell was dim but not dark, lit by an emergency light at the top landing. The little window was obscured by the darkness. I unlocked the heavy, watertight door at the top, held my breath, and opened it. A little water came through, but nothing more.

Without a word Melinda and I walked up the gray hallway to her office. The door was closed, the way we left it the night before. I turned the handle and gave it a budge. "It's stuck," I said.

"Probably warped from the water," Melinda answered mechanically. I turned the knob and gave it a good shove. On the third try it busted open. "Jesus," was all I said. Melinda said nothing.

Her office was a disaster. Furniture was tossed around, bookcases toppled over. Everything was wet, dripping with seaweed or covered in salt and sand. Soaked papers littered the floor and stuck to the walls. The desk, on which I made love to her less than a day ago, was broken and wedged up against the back wall.

We picked our way through in the dim, wet office to the front door, the one that opened out to the front desk and the lobby. I put my hand on the knob and looked at Melinda. Her eyes were moist, and I could tell she was choking back a lot of tears.

"Are you ready?" I said softly.

She tenderly let the word "Yes," escape from her quivering, joyless lips.

I opened the door.

At first it didn't seem too bad. Bright sunshine filled the lobby, giving the wood walls a clean, fresh look. The front desk was intact, and showed no signs of damage. But once we moved around the desk to the lobby itself, we saw what the storm had done.

"Flood," Melinda said quietly, "My worst fear, for the island." We carefully picked our way over some debris, planks of wood, a chair, a mound of sand, so that we were standing in the center of the lobby. It was, in a word, disastrous. "Completely flooded, William. Destroyed."

The two giant, mahogany front doors had been ripped from their hinges. One was splintered, rammed into the base of the toppled Tiki that I had installed the day before. The other was wedged up against the front desk. Every chair, table, ashtray, everything had been tossed around by the angry sea and re-deposited in a place it was never meant to be. Pieces of driftwood, palms, seaweed and other assorted detritus festooned the floors and walls. The glass of the elevator was shattered. Piles of wet sand coated every surface. Several shafts of sunlight pierced the air through holes blown out of the roof by the winds.

"Look here, William," Melinda said in a stronger yet still surreal voice. "Here's the waterline where the tide was at its highest. About four feet, I'd say."

"Four feet above sea level?" I asked innocently. Melinda laughed, not a happy laugh but an annoyed, horrid laugh.

"No, no. Don't be so foolish, Riggins. Remember what I told you about the building."

I shook my head and it came to me. "The main building is built up ten feet above the ocean, right?"

"That's right."

"That means that last night...we were sitting in that room with more than twenty feet of water over our heads?" The thought scared the carp out of me, to say the least.

"Eliot didn't call it a Safe Room for nothing," she responded, and that was the last straw. She couldn't hold it together any longer and the water works started running full force. "Eliot!" She let out a wail that could wake the dead, and collapsed to her knees on the wet, sandy floor of her beloved Resort. She cried and screamed and cursed God and the Tiki Gods and pounded her fists on the sand, her face and soul twisted in pain. All I could do was stand there, and when she couldn't scream any more I held her and let her cry it out.

I don't know how many minutes or hours went by as I knelt on the cold sand holding this beautiful, broken women in my arms. I wanted to tell her everything would be all right, but I couldn't. We both knew it wouldn't...nothing would ever be all right for Melinda ever again, not after this, and all of my lies and kisses couldn't change that one bit.

Finally she let up, and got to her feet. "I have...I have to check on the fish, William," she said as she tried to pull herself together.

"Fish? What fish?"

"In the tank. In the Shipwreck bar. I have to see if they survived." I followed her to the aquarium in the lobby bar. The bar was dark, but throwing the switch turned on another emergency light. It wasn't a pretty sight. The chairs and tables were mostly thrown up against the glass of the tank, put there as the tide went out and the water receded. But the glass was intact. "Oh God, thank you," she said quietly as she realized her forty or so aquatic pets were ok. She turned to me again, her eyes red and swollen with tears. She took me by the arms and stared her big browns directly up at mine.

"William, I...I'm so afraid, William. And so...sad, oh God, I don't even know how to express it. Eliot was...he was *everything* to me, and this place...I know to you it's just a hotel, but it's my *home*, it's all I've ever known, and it's...it's *destroyed*, William. My whole life, everything I've ever loved is gone...except you...and you'll be gone soon, too...I...I don't know what to do..."

I swallowed hard. I knew what was coming next.

"Please, William," she pleaded with a desperate heart, "Please, tell me you'll stay, here, with me, tell me you'll help me rebuild the Resort for the two of us! Tell me everything's going to be ok!" She broke down in tears once again, burying her face in my arm. I wanted to tell her to forget it. I wanted to be cold and tell her she was on her own, and that she was a big girl and would be just fine on her own, without me. But I couldn't.

"Everything will be ok," I lied, and held her closer. "This is all just stuff, Melinda. It can all be replaced. Get a good crew in here and throw around a few bucks, and this place'll be Spic 'n' Span in a few months. No sweat."

"But nothing can bring Eliot back, William. He's gone. Gone forever." She wept quietly this time.

I looked down at her and said, "Eliot knew this was coming. He knew for a long time and he tried to prepare you as best as he could. You know that, don't you?"

"I do."

"That man may have done some screwed up things in his life, but it seems to me that you and your mother turned him around. Remember him for the man he was to you, not the man those...*things*...made you see."

"I know," she said softly, "And I will. But...it doesn't make it any easier, William. I loved him, I loved him." Her voice trailed off as the crying went on.

I took a deep breath. "Let's go check out the damage to the outside of the Island. I'll bet it's not so bad out there. Probably make you feel much better."

Man, I couldn't be more wrong.

As soon as we walked out the front doors, we saw the real devastation. The Island had been eviscerated of almost all of its plant life. Once lush gardens were flattened dunes of mud and seaweed. Giant palm trees were turned into poles, stripped of their fronds. The beach had eroded so badly that two of the Tiki bars had washed out to sea. From dead fish to broken chunks of boat hulls, debris littered every inch of the Island. Some of the hurricane panels had been ripped from the windows, and the glass was shattered. The dock and thatched beach entrance, along with the Tikis and other décor, were simply gone, ripped up and carried away by the wrath of the storm.

"Destroyed," Melinda said to herself.

"Time and money," I said, "And it'll be as good as new. You're insured, right?"

"Yes, of course."

"Then you're golden."

We walked along the beach, being careful not to step on any wood or debris in fear of nails or other nasty things. The Gulf was very calm. The sun was shining brightly in the early morning sky. Only a few clouds hung with it. It was a cool seventy degrees, with a light tropical breeze. The day was, weather-wise, perfect.

Other-wise, it was one of the worst days in Melinda's...and consequently my...life. And it was about to get worse.

She woke up alone in the unfamiliar, dimly lit room. Her mind was still groggy from the pills, she knew that much. She focused on the desk across from the couch, and recognized it right away. It was Eliot Hawthorn's desk, the desk on which she had let him do things to her while Bachman secretly filmed it with his eight millimeter camera. The couch she lay on was the one on which she first made love to Melinda, years ago. She wasn't sure why she was in that room, but the memory of the night before began to seep back into her mind, and she shook.

We had come upon the ruins of the front boat landing of Tiki Island when I saw the heap in the distance. I saw it, because I was trained to see such things. Thankfully, Melinda was not.

"Wait," I said, "There's something up ahead. You wait here."

"Why?"

"Because...I think it might be a body, and you don't need to see that." She obeyed, and sat on what was left of a stone bench, one which had a missing cement leg. I walked on ahead.

As the heap came closer into view, I got that twisted feeling in the pit of my stomach, that feeling that in the city would tell me to stop and wait before going into that dark alley, to make sure my rod was loaded and in my hand, to look behind me before taking another step. I wasn't sure what it meant here, but I knew it couldn't be good.

I approached the mound of clothes, and realized I was correct…it was in fact a body. But not just any body.

It was Eliot Hawthorn.

Jessica called out for Bill, then for Melinda. When she got no answer she got up and, shakily, investigated the room. She was alone, but the door to the stairwell was wide open. She surmised they had awakened early and decided to check out the damage, so she followed in their steps. She was amazed at the damage she found in Melinda's office, the office where the two girls had spent so many stolen moments doing naughty things to each other while the customers waited at the desk out front, the office where Melinda had handed her hundreds of dollars in cash for entertaining certain guests, the office where Melinda had first suggested they both visit Hawthorn together in his bed.

She walked through the office and out the lobby, where she found even more wreckage. Footprints in the sand led to the bar, and back out through the front door, all the way to the beach. She gasped in dread at the condition of the gardens, the beachfront. Then she followed the prints down to the water's edge, where she found Riggins standing over what appeared to be a pile of rags, and Melinda kneeling in the sand, screaming at the sky, her fists raised in anger towards the heavens.

Why do broads never listen? I told Melinda to stay put, but she had to do things her way. My back was to her as I turned Hawthorn's waterlogged body over. She came up behind me just as I did, and saw the horrible sight I didn't want her to see. Just like he had done to his wife and friend, his face had been smashed in beyond recognition. Small crabs crawled over his features and devoured his flesh. The only way I knew it was him for sure was by the custom-made heavy silk robe in which his mangled body was entangled. Melinda took one look at his face and started screaming her head off again. She dropped to the sand and once again cursed every God she could think of, from Zeus to Poseidon to some Hawaiian kats I never heard of, and screamed until her screamer broke and all she could do was cry a raspy, gurgling wail. I quickly turned Hawthorn's body back over to hide the grotesque cavern that was once his face, and got up to calm Melinda down. Again, I held her. I tried everything I could to soothe her. Time. It took time, and finally she calmed down. It was right about the time she stopped crying that Jessica showed up.

I saw her walking up the beach and jumped to my feet. The last thing I wanted was for her to see the body too.

"What's goin' on?" she asked as she approached.

Quietly, I replied, "Hawthorn's body washed up on the beach. It's not good."

"Jesus," she said low, looking over at Hawthorn. "No wonder Melinda's having a cow."

"Yeah. Listen, we've got to get off this gaddamned Island. Do you know where they stow the boats?"

"There's a drydock where the loading docks are out back. Might be one there, if it's still in one piece."

"Can you please take Melinda to the boats and see if you can get one going? I'm going to move Mr. Hawthorn off the beach so the birds don't get to him."

"Jesus, Bill, can you spare the details?"

"Sorry kid. I forgot you were…"

"It's ok. I'll take Melinda to the boat. Ya'll, just don't take too long, ok?"

I realized she seemed surprisingly coherent and unemotional to me. "Yeah. Listen, are you ok? I mean, last night was pretty…"

"Last night was nothing," she said very darkly. "Last night was a walk in the park, and if I'm lucky that was the end of it." She looked over at Melinda and squinted in the bright sunlight. "It's a lot tougher for her, she lost Eliot. Me?...well, let's just say I'm not too broken up that my murdered mother got her revenge." Jessica then went to her, got her up, and helped her walk along the surf toward the rear-end of Tiki Island.

When they were far enough away for comfort, I grabbed Hawthorn by the shoes and pulled the body, gaping face up, all the way up to the building. There was a small storage shed there where they kept beach chairs. It somehow survived the flood, so I removed the chairs and stowed the bloating corpse inside, hopeful that it would keep from exploding in the hot sun the way Reams told me bodies tended to do. Once he was put away, I washed my hands in the surf and headed for the docks. When I got there, Melinda and Jessica were already in a boat with the motor running. We left Tiki Island at nine-twenty a.m. on October thirty-first, Nineteen fifty-six.

The girls were quite. When I pulled the boat up to the virtually undamaged dock on Sugarloaf Key, they said nothing. They said nothing as we walked up the path to Melinda's garage-warehouse, which was completely intact. Besides some palm fronds and a few pieces of roof shingles littering the lot, you'd never know a major hurricane had just come through.

I used Melinda's keys to open the garage. The Cadillac car was there, top down as I left it, without a scratch or any sign of flood damage. Dry as a bone. The girls climbed into the back seat and I motored the car up the clamshell driveway to the Overseas Highway. Again, almost no sign of any significant damage. I turned the Caddy right and headed towards Key West. As soon as I got on the road, Melinda, out of the clear blue, finally snapped and let go the water works. Jessica did her best to comfort her, but it was a long, painful drive down to the big Key.

Somehow Key West seemed more beautiful, more alive than it did the first time I drove in. Maybe because living through the storm gave me a different perspective on what life down here was like. Sure, there were crazy sheriffs, junky hookers and men like Hawthorn, but you had that everywhere. But only in the Florida Keys could you drive across the sky where the Atlantic Ocean meets the Gulf of Mexico. Only in the Keys could you snorkel a coral reef, dive for lobster, go deep sea fishing and have a drink where Ernest Hemmingway hangs out. Key West had been the richest city in the country, and the poorest city in the country. It was home to pirates and presidents and was full of history dating back long before the Europeans ever knew it existed. It may have had its ghosts and demons, but it sure had its share of coolness too.

Apparently the Key West locals didn't even bother to evacuate, because the town was in full swing. We pulled up to La Concha Hotel at around one-thirty. A boy took the car for us and we headed into the lobby. Melinda had pulled herself together, and was taking charge.

She walked up to the front desk and announced, "I'm Melinda Hawthorn, owner of Tiki Island Resort. Our Hotel was damaged in the storm and we need three rooms for tonight."

"Damaged? Really?" the front desk girl asked with a southern accent full of amazement.

"Yes, major flood and wind damage. Luckily we evacuated the guests. Do you have any rooms available?"

"Oh, oh yes Miss Hawthorn, we have several available. Most of our guests evac'd when they heard the foul weather was a'comin' too. All for nothin', as y'all can see."

For the first time Melinda noticed that nothing else had been damaged. It was pretty clear to me, that storm was meant for Tiki Island, for Eliot Hawthorn in particular. Crazy, man.

"Well it's a good thing we evacuated *our* clients," Melinda said a little snootier than the front desk chick deserved, "It's in ruins. Small twister tore right across the Island. You…you Conchs got lucky."

"I suppose we did," the girl said as she took three room keys off the rack. "Rooms 41, 42 and 43. All three are connecting."

"That'll do fine," Melinda said, "I don't have any cash on me so I'm signing for these."

"That's fine, Miss Hawthorn. Do you have any luggage?"

"Didn't have time to pack," she replied somewhat dazedly. "Just raced out of there."

"I can have someone bring up some bedclothes if you'd like."

"Yes," Melinda said, again on the verge of tears. "I'll send for someone in an hour with sizes. Please have the porter bring up some ice and a set-up, and a couple of bottles of liquor…bourbon, vodka, mixers…the good stuff, none of that rotgut you give to the tourists," she said with a wink.

"Yes ma'am."

"And a lunch menu, please."

"Right away ma'am. Call down if ya'll need anything else."

Melinda took the keys, looked at me mournfully, and headed to the elevators. Jessica and I followed, and in a few minutes we were each taking nice hot showers in our own, air-conditioned rooms.

Jackson motored the small boat to the rear of Tiki Island. Even from the shore he could see the place was in shambles. Felled palm trees, stripped docks, holes in the roof of the hotel…he found it hard to believe it could have gotten so damned messed up when the storm petered-out and did nothing but dump a few buckets of rain on the Keys. Then again, he knew the Island had a strange history…and as he thought about it more, it didn't seem all that strange to him after all.

He searched the whole Island, searched the Hotel's lobby and bar. He found no one. Completely bare. "Riggins! Mr. Hawthorn! Anyone!" he cried out, but got only muffled echoes of gulls in return. He had never seen Tiki Island dark and deserted before. It kind of gave him the creeps. "Riggins!" Still nothing. "I don't know what happened here," he said half out-loud, "But Riggins, you better be around somewhere or I'm gonna throw your butt in jail for a good long time."

When he returned to Sugarloaf Key, he found the garage open and Melinda's car gone.

Lunch was fantastic. Grilled tuna caught that morning over fresh vegetables, a California salad and fruit. They really knew how to cook in the Keys.

Melinda was finally coming around, starting to deal with the unbelievable tragedy that had happened only a few hours before. Jessica was also starting to lighten up as the realization that she was finally free of her Mother's hauntings began to settle in. The case of booze the management sent up on the house was certainly helping us all along, I might add.

Eventually, Melinda started talking about what happened.

Honestly, I didn't want to hear it.

"I can't believe he's gone," Melinda said as she stared down at her third Bourbon and Coke. "But somehow, I knew this was coming. I mean, he warned me so many times, and I'd seen the signs…But it's just so…unreal, *surreal*, it's as if it was only a dream."

"A nightmare," Jessica added over her fourth Vodka Collins. "A nightmare that's over, Lin." I'd never heard Jessica call Melinda 'Lin' before.

"Yeah, over," I said over my fourth Scotch rocks. "I'm so sorry Melinda, for your loss, kid. But as you said, Eliot knew…this was a long time comin'."

"Those things he did…what they showed us…I never knew."

I cut her off. "Forget all that. It's moot. That's not the Eliot you knew, dollface. That's not the Eliot you…fell in love with (it was hard to get that out), it was a different person, one who changed. People can change."

"You really believe that?" Jessica asked.

"I have to. Otherwise everything I do is for nothing." I poured Jessica another Vodka Collins and Melinda another Wild Turkey and Coke.

"So if he changed, William," Melinda began, "Then why did he…why did he deserve…*that?*" She was starting to falter again, and I thought Jessica might start in so I cut her off fast. "Try not to think about that now, kid. Think about the future. About rebuilding the Island."

"Ha!" she laughed groggily. "Maybe. Maybe not. Takes time, money."

"You have plenty of money."

"Not really. Not liquid. The insurance company could take weeks or even months to settle a claim. And it will take months to get the Island back in shape for guests, and by then the season will have ended. That's a big hit to take."

"Can't you do something to speed up the insurance?"

"Sure, there's things you can do…lawyers, politicians. But not enough, never enough. They'll weasel out of paying most of it through some loophole. I'll have my lawyers on it, but their fee will eat up half the award."

Jessica asked, "So you're just giving up? Gonna shut the Island down?"

Melinda sighed and took a long drink. "No, I suppose not. We'll rebuild, and it will be splendorous once again!" she said lyrically as she toasted the air with her glass. The booze was affecting her, strongly. "As long as I have my friend, my best friend Jessica beside me, and my love, my William there to help. With you, I will have the courage to rebuild. With you!" She yelled that last part and nearly slid off the chair. Jessica laughed. I did not.

The afternoon was spent mostly the same way, drinking, laughing, dozing, eating, drinking some more. At six, a delivery came with fresh clothes, and we changed out of the bathrobes and into some khakis for me and light dresses for the girls. A floral-print shirt, slightly tight, and a pair of boat shoes finished me off. We decided to go down to Duval Street for some air and more booze.

The evening found us at Sloppy Joe's. The bar was only a short walk from the hotel, so I didn't mind getting hammered. A band played rip-offs of Elvis tunes and everything Bill Haley ever did, but did it pretty well so it wasn't half bad. At least I don't think it was. After the fourth double Scotch, I didn't seem to care much.

Melinda and Jessica were pretty sullen at first, but the music and the booze soon lightened them up, and before the sun went down they were the life of the party, dancing, drinking, blowing kisses. It wasn't until Jessica started to do a strip-tease on top of the bar that things started to get a little out of hand, and the manager very nicely asked us to take a powder. I wasn't in a fightin' mood, so I let it go, and the three of us stumbled lightly out of the bar.

"Food!" Jessica said much louder than it seemed. "Need some vittles, kids!" She was without doubt the farthest gone of our little trio, being held up in the middle by me and Melinda.

"How about that cart over there, they have sausage and peppers," I said, steering in the direction of the street cart. "I could go for some sausage."

"*I* could go for some sausage," she shot back with a mischievous smile, "Some New Yorfssssausage!" she slurred. "How's 'bout you, Lyn?"

Melinda, sort of moving in slow motion, answered, "Sure."

Without propagating the innuendo I managed to get us to the food cart, and ordered up a couple of sandwiches. I was too stoned to see the little numbers on my dough, so I handed the guy a bill and asked if it would cover it. He said yeah, and gave us the heroes. I think I slipped him a twenty. My fault for getting sloshed.

We walked and ate, as hard as it was, passing the different bars on the way back to La Concha. Hot west-coast jazz simmered out of a double-decker joint on the corner. I stopped for a minute and listened…it felt like home for a minute, and I realized through my ethylene haze how much I missed home, how much I missed the city. That dirty, soot-soaked, rat-infested island I called home.

The girls weren't digging the tenor sax the way I was, and pulled me away. Further up the block we passed a place that was jumpin' with Irish folk music. A bunch of people inside were doing a jig from the old country, giant mugs of beer in hand. A couple of doors down a Cuban band played a meringue for some tanned dancers in white suits and red dresses. For certain, you could find any kind of entertainment you wanted in this town.

We pulled up to the hotel at a quarter past nine. The bellman was nice enough (for a buck) to help us find the right rooms. The girls insisted it was too early to turn in, so we all wound up in Melinda's suite, the largest of the rooms.

"Put on the radio, Lyn," Jessica said as she poured us each another round of Jack Daniels. "Find something slow and easy." Melinda found a station playing standards. Sinatra's voice filled the room, softly.

I lifted my glass. "Well ladies, here's to one hell of a vacation," I said, and they toasted without a word.

"It ain't over yet, Billy," Jessica said with a drunken southern lilt.

"No, but it's almost. I'm leaving tomorrow. I have to get back home."

"Why?" Melinda said, seeming genuinely surprised, and hurt. "You can stay here. You'll have everything you'll ever need, ever want right here." She moved closer to me, very close. Right next to me.

"I'm still a cop, kid," was all I could think to say under the influence of the booze. "My place is in the city."

"Your place," Jessica said as she moved in very close too, "is here, with us."

This was weird.

The two dames were so close to me, to each other, that I couldn't focus on them. I was sitting on the edge of the bed, Melinda to my right, Jessica to my left. They were both leaning in, their faces almost touching mine, almost touching each other's.

"I…This ain't real, it's just a…a surreal dream, a crazy vacation that went all wacky. None of it is real. It couldn't possibly be," I said, trying to convince myself more than them. Melinda touched a finger to my cheek, and gently turned my face towards hers.

"This is real," she said seductively, her eyes soft, her lips open just slightly. She leaned in and kissed me, the fire rising once again, the passion we'd felt returning full force. I felt her hand run up my back as she pulled me in a little closer, kissing harder. All the torment, all the sorrow and death was forgotten in the fog of liquor and adrenaline.

Her lips finally pulled away from mine. My head swam; I sat there like a goofy kid who had just had his first kiss. Then I felt another warm hand on my face, turning me the other way. It was Jessica, more radiant and vivacious than she had been in what seemed like forever. Her eyes were open wide, a bad-girl smile graced her lips. Before I realized what was happening, she leaned in and kissed me too, with as much fire and heat as Melinda, maybe more, certainly more than she had ever kissed me with before on this insane trip.

I was caught up in the moment. My mind was gone, but as she kissed harder I realized that Melinda was still there next to me. I released her, slowly, expecting to find Melinda in tears, or enraged. I found neither. She was smiling, a thin, almost evil smile that both confused and aroused me.

"You…you're ok with this?" was all I could say, the innocent idiot too dumb to realize what was happening.

Melinda didn't answer. She leaned over close to my face again, and just as I thought she was about to kiss me, her lips brushed by mine, slowly, and met Jessica's in a passionate lock that rivaled our own.

Holy Hell! I thought to myself. What's going on here? I don't…I never…I mean, I'm a *vice* cop, for Christ's sake. Stuff like this is supposed to *disgust* me.

Somehow, it did not. Maybe it was the booze, maybe it just seemed natural in this unusual land under the palms. Either way, I let my mind go, and before I knew it the three of us were undressing each other, kissing, caressing, exploring. The two women laid me down on the bed, and did things to me that were both incredible and probably illegal. As Melinda kissed me, Jessica made her way down my body. Then Melinda joined her, and I felt things I never thought imaginable. My heart started racing and the booze went into overdrive, turning everything into an orgasmic blur. Minutes, hours, days went by…I don't even know…and when we finally collapsed, completely worn out, it was a sure bet that everyone had a taste of everything.

Breathless, Melinda said, "Are you sure you won't stay?"

I fell asleep cold before I could answer.

"Coffee, toast, scrambled eggs, maybe some bacon, for three," I whispered into the phone. "And a bottle of aspirin," I added to the room service girl. "And be quiet about it." I hung up the receiver as gently as possible, and laid back down on the bed. The wall clock told a grumpy story of one p.m.; a sliver of white light from under the window shade said it was a bright and sunny day, this Thursday, November the first of 1956.

My head felt like it had been split open with a sledgehammer. I tried to remember how much I had to drink, and gave up after six doubles. The night was foggy, but I remembered everything.

Man, did I remember everything.

The girls were still asleep, passed out on the king-sized bed. I splashed some water on my face to wake up. When I looked in the mirror, a beat-up kid looked back at me. It was times like this that my own reflection would sort of spook me. Inside, I felt much older than the twenty-eight year old kid in the mirror. I felt at least thirty-five, maybe even forty at times. This morning I felt about fifty-six, born in nineteen hundred and boozin' every day since. Yet although my countenance looked tired, it still looked young, healthy and strong. But tired. *Very* tired.

When room service arrived I took a handful of aspirin and washed them down with a full cup of java. It was hot but tasted great, like only fancy hotel or restaurant coffee can, that special kind of coffee flavor that said, "yes, I am very expensive and exquisite, drink me, mere mortal." That kind.

At one thirty I woke up the girls. They fought me on it but I eventually won out.

"Rise and shine, kids. We can't spend our lives in bed."

"Why not?" Jessica whined. "Sounds like a plan to me."

"The sun is shining, it's a beautiful day, and I've got a murder to solve."

"Murder?" Melinda asked, blinking the sleep off.

"That's right."

I could see her fight off the tears. The booze had worn off. Reality was slipping back in.

"William, no one will believe what happened to Eliot...we have to just say it was an accident, the storm…"

"No sweetheart, not Eliot." She and Jessica looked puzzled. Short memories. "You're forgetting all about Bachman, ladies. I'm still on the hook for that guy."

"Oh, God," Melinda said, "I…I'd forgotten, with everything that's happened."

Jessica said, "Does anyone really think you killed him, Billy? I mean, why would you?"

"No, probably not. But Jackson is the law, and he told me to stay put until things are cleared up. Out of respect, I won't leave until the case is settled. At least not until my name is cleared."

Melinda pouted. "So then…you're not staying? I thought we'd convinced you it would be a good thing for you to stay, last night," She said timidly.

I just shook my head. "Doll, I don't have any idea *what* the hell I'm doing." I looked at Jessica, who was sitting up, her blonde hair tossed, looking stunning as usual. I looked back at Melinda, the tanned, dark-haired Island girl who couldn't lose an ounce of beauty even after crying her eyes out. "You…you're both wonderful, incredible girls…and honestly, I don't know what the future's gonna bring for any of us. But either way, I've got to head home at some point. Even if I somehow get roped into living in sin with you two chicks here in the Keys." I smiled as I said it, and got a little chuckle out of both of them. "One way or the other, I've got to clear some things up with Jackson. And Roberts. And my old pal, Captain Reams."

We finished breakfast without another word of Bachman's murder, ghosts, Eliot or the destruction of Tiki Island. Afterwards they turned on the tube, getting nothing but soaps, and I took a long, hot shower and shaved. I climbed into the new clothes Melinda had sent up, and for the first time since leaving the Island I realized I didn't have my hardware. The .45 was still in my room on the third floor, and my .38 was probably in the Safe Room. It felt strange.

"I'm taking the car, kid," I said to Melinda as she entered the shower. "Probably be back before it gets dark."

"That's fine," she replied as she let the robe slip to the floor. "Everything I need to do, I can do on the phone…from bed." She winked, and I had a feeling it was going to be another crazy night.

As I said goodbye to Jessica she said, "Do you want some company, along for the ride?"

"Not today, dollface. I've got to do this my own way…alone, as usual. Catch you later," I added, tipped my new hat and left with a wink.

I called Jackson from the payphone in the lobby. He had already sent a boat to Tiki Island to search for us, and found nothing. Not even Hawthorn's body. I told him what happened…that Hawthorn went bat-assed crazy during the storm and ran out to the beach, causing the wind to come into the building causing so much damage. I said we tried to follow him but the hurricane carried him into the surf before I could get anywhere near him. I told Jackson we found the body on the beach the next morning, as we did, and told him where to find it. Then I said I needed to see him in person, but not until early evening. He agreed, and with the top down on the Caddy, I motored North toward Islamorada.

The sun was hot, hotter than I ever imagined it could be in November. The temperature reached the high eighties by mid-afternoon, and the cloudless sky seemed to intensify the tropic sun. It felt good, but it just seemed *wrong*…November should be cold, snowy, rainy, cloudy. Dark. *Sinister*, in a way. Not bright and sunny and warm as hell. Driving around in a convertible the day after Halloween just didn't seem *real*.

I motored the car all the way up to Islamorada. You'd never know a 'cane came through here that damn-near destroyed Tiki Island. Not a palm tree out of place. Not a roof without a shingle. It's as if the storm was meant for the Island alone.

I believed it was.

No one else would.

It was close to three when I stopped the car on the side of the road. I wasn't sure what I was doing there. I wasn't even sure how I knew where to find it, but there it was in front of me…the memorial, the monument erected over the mass grave of over three hundred souls who lost their lives in the Great Atlantic Hurricane of 1935. It was a large limestone marker, a tribute to the men and women who never had a chance as the late-running evac train was washed off the tracks by a tidal wave. My heart felt heavy then, as if I knew these people personally. In my heart, I knew I had at least seen a few of them, the night they exacted their revenge on Eliot Hawthorn.

I walked up to the monument, mindful that I was standing over the graves of the storm's victims, and read the plaque, weathered but legible:

DEDICATED
TO THE MEMORY OF THE
CIVILIANS AND WAR VETERANS
WHOSE LIVES WERE LOST
IN THE HURRICANE OF
SEPTEMBER SECOND, 1935

It seemed so…simple. Just a single sentence. Twenty-one words. That was all that was left of over three hundred lives, three hundred living, breathing, working, playing people who were cut down by the rage of the sea and force of the winds. It had been over twenty years since that storm, and this is all there was to remember it, remember the *people*.

Over twenty years, and still nothing in the United States had come even close to its power.

Well, not counting Tuesday night's storm, confined to a small, sandy island off the coast of Sugarloaf Key.

I read the plaque again, and then did something I hadn't done in a very long time. I hung my head, and said a prayer. I quietly asked God to grant these people peace, if he already hadn't. I don't know exactly why I did that. It just seemed that someone, anyone, should. I prayed for their peace, and I made a little vow that I would somehow, someday make sure their story was told, so the world would never forget.

When I turned to go back to the car, I got a shock that to this day still sends shivers down my spine. I wasn't alone.

Behind me a group had gathered. Dozens, maybe hundreds of people, quietly standing behind me. Through them I could see the car, the road, the palm trees. I could see because they were transparent, transparent because they were phantoms, the same dripping, black, wet, morbid, smoky wraiths that had come to drag Hawthorn away for their revenge. Hundreds of them, seaweed dangling from their black cloak-like bodies, sea creatures crawling over and through them. They were all...*staring*, without eyes, staring at me, hovering, silent. Then, as if with one collective mind, they shed the black cloaks, shed the seaweed and crabs and rotted flesh and other horrors and revealed the bright, glowing souls of their former selves, souls of real people, not morbid, hideous corpses but images of living men and women, smiling in the afternoon sun. Many looked to the sky, others kept looking at me with renewed eyes that seemed alive and joyous.

I stood amazed, not daring to move. A full five seconds ticked by, seeming like an hour. Finally, one spirit moved forward, and hovered to me.

She looked into my eyes. I saw her soul.

*"I am Rose, Jessica's Mother. Thank you,"* she said softly, *"Take care of my girl."* She floated off to my right and another spirit came up to me, a man in workman's clothes. *"I'm Jim Butler, I worked on the railway. Thank you,"* he said, and floated away. Another spirit, a woman with a young boy, came up and said, *"I'm Gretchen Bergen, this is my daughter Anna, my husband survived, we weren't so lucky. Thank you."*

One after another after another came up to me the same way, introduced themselves as if they wanted to...needed to tell one last person who they were in life, and thanked me. And as I watched, dumbfounded, the host of entities began to rise upward into the heavens, dissipating as they left this plane of existence forever, rising higher and higher into the great, blue sky until they were nothing but a memory.

It took me about twenty minutes of just sitting in the front seat of the Caddy before I stopped shaking. I guess these 'entities' didn't really get under my skin before, because for one thing I just sort of made believe everything was an alcohol-induced dream, and for another, they...whatever they were...never really aimed their attention at me. It was always Jessica, or Hawthorn, or even Melinda. But not me. This time was different, and it spooked the hell out of me.

I pulled myself together and headed over to the now-familiar bait and tackle shop owned by Captain Reams. The storm hadn't touched the place. Its slate-gray weathered boards still clung to piling beams with rusty nails, the walls held together more with rusted tin advertising signs than anything else. A barrel filled with useless fishing poles guarded the door. The only thing that was missing was his boat, which I regarded as a sign he hadn't come back from the north just yet.

In any case I decided to see if he or anyone was in. I was prepared to wait an hour or so if needed, so I lit a smoke and rapped on the old door. From inside I heard a stirring, and what sounded like someone sobbing, quietly.

"Captain Reams? You in there? It's Riggins, from the City."

No answer. Just more sobbing. I tried the door…it was unlocked, so I slowly opened it. It creaked and moaned, but it opened. "Reams?"

"Who's there?" Reams yelled from a darkened corner. I heard the click of a pistol's hammer being cocked and threw myself to one side. "Take it easy Reams, it's Riggins. The detective."

"Riggins," he said mournfully, his voice choked with wetness. "Don't come in, son."

"Reams, what's wrong? You need help?" I didn't move. Through the little bit of light coming in through the door, I could see the heap of a man leaning against his spool table, the silhouette of an antique gun in his hand, pointed at the wall about ten feet from where I stood. There were two bottles of rum on the table, one empty and laying askew, the other sitting with his ancient hand wrapped around it. "Put that thing down, Captain, it's me, Riggins."

"Riggins," he said again more tiredly. He took a long pull from the bottle. "What you want here, boy?"

"Hawthorn is dead. Tiki Island was destroyed in the storm."

"Not the least bit surprised," he said, and took another gulp of rum. "How about the girl?"

"Jessica?"

"No, the other one…Hawthorn's girl?"

"She's fine. They're both fine."

"Huh," he said, and finally put the gun down. "Take a seat by the door, Riggins. Don't come no closer to me."

"What's the matter?" I asked, taking a folding chair and sitting in the light of the doorway.

"I…It's time for me to atone for my sins, Riggins. They've made that very clear, I'd imagine."

"They?" I asked, knowing damned-well what he was talking about. "You mean…" I couldn't come out and say it.

"The dead, son. The floating dead, up from their watery graves to exact vengeance on those who fouled them. They dragged Hawthorn into the sea, didn't they?"

"Yes. We found him on the beach in the morning."

"They took my boat," he said sadly, "I never made it past Largo. A giant wave, as God is my witness shaped like a giant hand came down and smashed her to bits. I floated ashore on a piece of the transom. But they weren't finished with me."

"What…why you, Reams? What could you have possibly done?"

"Well," the old man said, sounding tired, drunk, feeble. "I…I sometimes *watched*."

A chill ran through my shaking bones as I knew exactly what he meant. "You watched…Hawthorn?"

He sobbed. "Ye..ess. I watched him, stood by as he had his way with those poor Cuban girls, then hacked them to bits. I helped him…remove…the parts, destroy the evidence. I just stood there, and watched."

He choked, and drank down a good part of the bottle of rum. "I just fucking *watched*."

The ringing started in my head again, that siren from some horror flick, the kind you'd hear just as something horrific was about to happen. That, on top of that queasy feeling I got in my gut when I knew something really bad was going down in real life, something so bad I'd have to use all my cop training and cop knowledge to get through.

"Reams...what did they do to you?" I asked, and immediately wished I hadn't. He threw his chair back as he got up from the table, knocking empty booze bottles scattering across the floor.

As he stepped into the dull afternoon light he said, "They took my Goddamned eyes, Riggins! They took my eyes!" And the horrific sight the ringing and the queasiness forewarned me of came into full view, as Reams stood there, shivering; empty, lidless, bloody sockets where his eyes had once been, ochre red blotches marring his face and beard. "They...took...my...eyes," he cried, but no tears fell.

I stumbled, nearly falling as I jumped from the chair. "Get out, Riggins, get out now while you can. Take your car and drive, drive north until you hit home and never come back to this God forsaken string of islands again, GO!"

"Calm down Reams, I'll get you some help, I'll bring back a doctor."

He laughed a low, menacing chuckle as he receded back into the shadows. "Sure, son, you do that. You do that, Detective Riggins. Go on. Go now. I'll be here, one way or another."

I wasn't sure what he meant, but I had no intention of spending another minute in that damp, tomb-like place. I tripped over the chair on my way out and slammed the door shut hard.

When I got halfway to the Cadillac, I heard the single gunshot come from within the old shack, and I knew that was the end of Captain Reams.

Still shaking, I motored the Caddy up to the jailhouse. I needed to talk to someone sane, someone whom I could trust to not be covered in blood or seaweed or any other crazy-assed thing. When I pulled up to the jail, I found Jackson sitting on a bench outside, smoking a cigar. It was the most natural scene I'd seen in three days.

"Good afternoon, Sheriff," I said cordially, hiding my anxiety like a pro. "Any damage from the storm?"

He looked at me the a way lion looks at a slab of meat. "Just your place," he said, and took a long puff on the cigar.

"You mean Tiki Island?"

"Yeah, that's what I mean."

"You been there? It got tore up pretty bad."

He sat back and said, "Yep, I been there. Found Hawthorn's body in a shed."

"Like I told you on the phone, I put him in there," I said. "Found him on the beach in the morning."

"So I've heard. Ms. Melinda told me the same. Said he went for a walk and got caught in the wind."

That wasn't the story we were supposed to stick to, so I didn't say a word. "What brings ya'll up this way, Detective?" he asked, enjoying his smoke.

"Well, there's still a little matter of a murder to solve. I'm due to go back to the City this weekend, but you've asked me to stick around until you're satisfied it wasn't me."

"Satisfied?" he laughed, "Well, hell son, you're not only implicated as a suspect in Bachman's murder...but now we might add on Eliot Hawthorn's on top of that! And maybe even a third."

"What? Hawthorn? You know I had nothing to do with that!" I snapped, losing my cool. That took the cake. "He drowned in a gaddamned storm, how do you get off trying to make me the sap?"

"Oh, come off it Riggins. Ya'll and I both know that man done hardly ever left his room, let alone takin' long walks on the beach in the middle of a 'cane. I have a hard time believin' that man wasn't somehow dragged out and dumped in the sea!"

Son of a bitch, I thought, could he have known? "Maybe he was. But it wasn't me," I said. "I ain't got no motive. No reason at all."

"Take over that Island and all its riches."

"Balls. I could have had that anyway. Melinda Hawthorn is practically writing up wedding invitations. Her old man was no trouble. He wanted us hitched up."

"He wanted you hitched up," Jackson said, "Because he knew he was checkin' out soon. Otherwise he'd never have given up that little honey pot. No, he knew his time was a'tickin', and so did you. Maybe you just made it easier for him, faster."

I was steaming up like a lobster. "Up yours, clown. You know damned right well I didn't kill anyone on this trip except those two goons Roberts sent after me. Hawthorn died for the gaddamned horrible fucking crimes he committed, a lot of them under your own crooked nose!"

Jackson jumped to his feet and went for his baton. I damned near went for my piece, until I remembered it was still on the Island.

"Boy, you remember ya'll are talkin' to the law here. This ain't New York City, and I'd just as soon beat you upside the head with this here billy club as hear ya'll talk to me like that!"

My heart was racing. My fists were clenched and I was ready to take a hit to the arm or shoulder with that big piece of oak to burry my fist in his gut. My body was planning the attack as my mind realized there was no reason for it. I backed up a step and put my hands forward, low. Jackson took his hand away from the billy.

"That's more like it boy. Now answer me a few questions and maybe we'll be all right. All right?"

"Yeah, shoot em."

"Where were you last night?"

"Sloppy Joe's til around one, I think, then back to La Concha."

"You got witnesses?"

"Melinda, Jessica. Bartender at Joe's. Bellhop at the hotel."

"What about this morning?"

"Slept late, drove up here about two."

"Where you stop at?"

"The Hurricane Monument. I wanted to see it."

"Any place else?"

"Yeah. Captain Reams' joint over on the Gulf side."

"Reams?"

"Yeah. Roberts turned me on to him, he used to work for Hawthorn."

"What did you see him for?"

"I dunno, I was in the area so I thought I'd stop in. He was drunk as a skunk. Said he lost his boat in the storm."

"That all?"

"Pretty much, why?"

"He say anything about Roberts?"

"No."

"Nothin' at all?"

I was getting annoyed. "No. I said no, didn't I? What the hell?"

"I'll *tell* you whut the hell, Riggins." He stomped out the cigar in the sand and let out the last puff of smoke. "Roberts is dead as a doornail. Found him this morning, drowned to death, seawater in his lungs."

"Drowned? How the hell did he get out?"

"He didn't."

"I don't follow you."

"We found him locked in the cage. He done drowned *inside* the cell, in seawater." He paused to light a cigarette. Chain smoking, this afternoon. "He drowned inside the cell. But the cell was dry as a fuwkin' bone."

Jackson and I took his patrol car a few miles north to a roadside tavern that looked more like something from the mountains of West Virginia than a bar in the touristy Florida Keys. The place wasn't much more than a wooden shack held together by old license plates and fishnets, but the drinks were strong and the pretzels were free. We spent about an hour talking about Hawthorn, Tiki Island, Jessica, Melinda, and Roberts when he finally came out with the sixty-four dollar question.

"So tell me, Riggins. And shoot straight with me. What happened to Eliot Hawthorn?"

His demeanor was so frank, so serious, that I could only answer him with complete honesty, as ridiculous as it may have sounded. I regretted it the minute I said it, but I said it, and there it was.

I took a drink first, then sighed, then said flatly, "He was hauled off by a gang of very pissed-off phantoms that wanted revenge for their deaths."

I expected a big laugh. Instead, Jackson said, "Did it happen durin' that freak-assed storm?"

"You believe me?"

"I believe what you're saying is a possible scenario."

"It did. At the height of it. Probably around one a.m. Once he was gone, it was all over. The girls were hysterical so I gave them some Valium and we all slept it off until the next afternoon."

"Then you found the body?"

"That's right. I moved it into that shed so it wouldn't turn to mush in the sun. Then we went down to Key West."

Jackson finished his bourbon and lit another cigarette, the last in his pack. "You'all know, a more reasonable explanation would be that you murdered him so that Melinda would inherit all his wealth, taking you along for the ride."

"Sure," I said, staring straight into his eyes. "But getting the place to look like it was hit by a force-three hurricane would have been a real bitcher."

A smile started to form on Jackson's lips. He didn't believe I killed Hawthorn anymore than I did. "Well, Detective Riggins, what about Melinda? She's also a prime suspect. Killed the old man off for his money. Hell, she may have even killed Bachman to get him out of the way."

I laughed hard. "You're killin' me, Sheriff! Next you'll be saying Jessica did it to get revenge for her mother."

"I know all about Miss Jessica's mother, Riggins. I done known for many years that Hawthorn murdered her."

"What?" That threw me. "How? Why didn't you do something about it?"

"Do something? Like what? Arrest him for a twenty-year-old murder without any evidence? No, Riggins. I knew because Roberts told me in a drunken stupor one night–"

Apparently Roberts had a very big mouth when he was hitting the bottle, I thought to myself.

"–But there wasn't a damned thing I was ever able to do about it."

"Well old man, you didn't have to. Jessica's mother did it herself."

"How's that?"

"She was leading the pack that dragged Hawthorn into the sea. One seriously enraged ghost, if you can believe it."

Jackson ordered a shot of Jack and knocked it back. "I can believe it, Mr. Riggins."

"Seriously?"

"Oh, yessir. You see, I been down to Miss Jessica's house down in Key West. I seen the things she seen. Have you?"

I'd almost forgotten about Jessica's place. "Yeah, I have. Freaky place."

"To say the least."

"So that's why you believe me?"

"That's why," he said, taking his last puff on his last cigarette. "I believe the ghosts of Tiki Island have done cleaned house."

I finished my second cocktail and refused a third. "That still leaves Bachman," I said, getting up to leave. He got up too.

"That it does. Any ideas?"

"A few. I'll know for sure by tomorrow, latest. What will you do about Hawthorn?"

"Official cause of death was drowning. Official report will read he ran out into the storm, a little dazed and crazy. You tried to bring him in but the wind took him. Can your lady friends corroborate?"

"I'm sure they will."

"Good, 'cuz they ain't no one but you, me and them girls that's ever gonna believe the truth."

"I'm hip," I said to myself as we left the bar.

There are times in a man's life when he's got all his ducks in a row, when he knows exactly what's around every corner and is in total control of his surroundings. The last two weeks were not anything like that for lil' ole me. But that was about to change.

I motored the Cadillac fast down The Overseas Highway, high-tailing it south back to Sugarloaf Key. There were some men on the dock, and several boats were in transit moving back and forth between the Key and Tiki Island. I managed to catch a boat that was leaving the dock, and with a fin convinced the workers to let me ride over.

It was a strange ride. From the dock the Island looked fine, beautiful, peaceful, but once we landed on a makeshift dock that listed dangerously to one side, I once again saw the destruction, the chaos, made even more morbid in the eerie twilight.

Dozens...maybe hundreds of men and women were there, cleaning, organizing, upending fallen palms, making repairs to the roof. Melinda hadn't wasted any time. She couldn't afford to.

I made my way through droves of workers, carefully stepping around broken glass and chunks of nail-pierced wood until I made it inside the building. They had the generators going and the electricity was working pretty well, considering the place had been under water two nights ago. Giant fans blew air everywhere, attempting to dry the watersoaked carpets, furniture and walls. Already all the sand and seaweed had been removed from the lobby. Even the front doors, although busted and cockeyed, were re-hung.

The elevator was working so I headed straight for the third floor. I didn't have my key, so I had to bust the door in. I didn't think it made much of a difference at this point. I found I'd been lucky...the storm shutters held, and my room had been spared the onslaught of the storm. I snapped on the lights and got to work packing my stuff.

It was so good to see my old Colt .45 automatic again. I thought I'd lost her, thought some of the workers might have given the place the once-over and clipped it. But there she was, ole Suzie, right where I'd left her. I dragged that gun through the Korean war and all over New York City. I was pretty happy I didn't lose her for good.

She felt good strapped there under my arm in that custom-made leather speed rig. I slipped the jacket on over it, and as usual, you'd never know I was sporting a piece. I buckled up the suitcase, slipped the lid on my head and said goodbye to Tiki Island.

Once back on Sugarloaf, I threw the bag in the trunk of the car and was ready to leave for Key West when my curiosity got the better of me. Melinda's keys had one that fit the side door to the main building, so I decided to do a little snooping. Funny enough, with all the commotion down at the Island, there was no one in the warehouse. I flipped a switch and the whole place lit up, exposing some pretty generic and thoroughly uninteresting crates and boxes, mostly non-perishables, linens, glasses, mattresses and general kitchen supplies. The place was big but not so big that I couldn't take it all in at single glance. Just dull boxes.

And a staircase.

A staircase leading to what appeared to be an office loft, taking up just one end of the warehouse, not very big. Something drew me towards it though, maybe cop instinct, maybe something else. Something just didn't seem right. I took the stairs carefully, as they seemed kind of old, but they were solid. The office was locked, and none of Melinda's keys worked which I found very strange. Looking around I found an open toolbox with a big screwdriver. I laughed at the odds and jimmied the door open.

Inside it was just an office, a metal desk with inventory reports and ledgers, a cheap lamp, a phone. A few old, wooden filing cabinets held more generic paperwork. The desk seemed pretty generic too; it didn't seem to belong to any one person, it was more like a desk that was used by several managers on different shifts. I pulled the drawers and found nothing interesting. The only thing that gave the place any personality at all was a pin-up calendar showing October, 1956 with a very nicely done photo of Marilyn Monroe naked on red satin. I recognized the photo...it was the one she did a few years back, the one that made it into that Playboy nudie mag that was supposed to take the sleaze out of the sleaze industry. "Yeah, good luck with that, probably be out of business in another year," I said out-loud. Once a vice cop, always a vice cop I guess.

I was about to call it a day when I noticed the closet door had a big padlock on it. Seemed a little odd, I thought, to padlock a closet. It was a big old iron job, probably from the turn of the century, pretty much un-pickable. But the door was light wood and my friend the screwdriver, along with a little friendly persuasion had it open in a few seconds.

Some closet, I thought.

I flipped on the light exposing the biggest surprise of the day…bigger than Roberts drowning in a dry cell, bigger than Tiki Island crawling with laborers so fast. This closet wasn't a closet at all. It was a bachelor pad.

The place had Rutger Bachman written all over it. The Ultra-Modern furniture, including a leather couch, two Eames chairs and a king bed, along with a stylish bar and a hi-fi were so close to his Tiki Island apartment that the two could have been interchangeable. The only difference was this was a single room, along with a bath, and this one was set up for entertaining, period. Black satin sheets, nudes painted on black velvet, and giant mirrors over, behind and in front of the bed gave that away. Bachman was a real swinger, all right. He probably took his pick of the hookers from the cathouse, and probably even scored a few lonely broads that came to the Island for some R and R. Sleaze.

I started poking around the room. Expensive liquor on the bar. Jazz and swing albums. Nothing corny, strictly legitimate swing and New York Jazz. He had good taste, that was certain. Beyond that, I wasn't really sure if finding this place meant anything. So he had a sex pad off-Island. No big deal. Was it?

My brain was cranking overtime. Something wasn't right, wasn't *ordinary*. What was it? What was I seeing with my senses, but missing with my eyes? I took a deep breath and closed my eyes, imaging the whole room in my mind, letting my brain let me see what it wanted me to see. And I got it. When I opened my eyes, I looked at the door leading back to the office. I stepped through. Then I stepped back.

It was simple. The office was a few feet deeper than the bedroom.

There was a filing cabinet against the wall next to the door. I looked at the floor, and sure enough there were scuffmarks in a semi-circle, faint but there. I put my weight against the cabinet and shoved…and it moved fairly easy, exposing another door with another lock. Mr. Screwdriver did his thing, and I found myself in a small nook behind the bed, behind a two-way mirror. Damn! So that was Bachman's gig! Behind the mirror was a thirty-five millimeter camera, a good one on a tripod, and a sixteen millimeter movie camera. The cameras were pointed at the bed. A small ladder led up to an area over the bed with another camera setup pointing down. Both cameras had a timing device that seemed to be set for thirty-second intervals. There was even a reel-to-reel tape machine with a microphone built into the end table next to the bed.

What a sweet setup. And with this little bit of unexpected information, all the pieces fell into place, and I knew finally, for certain, who killed Rutger Bachman.

All I needed was the proof.

I put everything back as best I could and wiped the warehouse clean of prints before I left. Nothing was taken, so for all anyone would know a worker, or even Bachman could have lost the keys and busted into the place himself. I left in Melinda's Cadillac, not even bothering to close the garage door. Then I remembered it closed itself. Ah, the rich.

An hour later I pulled up to my rented Chevrolet in its roost by the dock. The crazy old man was there, so I got the keys and loaded my bags into the trunk. I gave him a twenty and told him I was keeping the keys. He nodded and that was that.

I didn't go back to the hotel right away. Those two sirens were in there, waiting to steal my soul and turn it into a hotel manager, and I wasn't quite strong enough yet to resist that kind of temptation. So I parked the Caddy in front of Sloppy Joe's and slipped inside.

My old pal Fernando was there, and greeted me like a life-long friend. "Aye, señor! Good to see you again so soon! You no longer look like you are on vacation, my friend."

"A cop's threads, buddy. Vacation is just about over." I bought him a drink; he asked about the trip.

"So, señor, do you have any thing eenteristing to tell me? You find a Fantasma on the Island?"

"You wouldn't believe me, buddy."

"Aye, try me my friend."

I ordered us a couple more drinks and started giving him the highlights. I told him about the storm, about Hawthorn predicting his own death. I told him *Hawthorn* thought he saw ghosts...and ran out into the storm to escape them, only to be washed away by the hurricane. I told him the girls saw some things too, but I never said I had any personal experiences. I was no dummy, after all.

"My friend, I think you leef a few things out, no?"

"I told you the good parts," I said with a wink, then I went into cop mode. "I've told you my story. Now I need some info from you, buddy."

"Of course, anything I can do for you."

"Rutger Bachman," I said, "He ran the cathouse on the other end of the Key. Know him?"

"Ah, I know of heem, but don't know heem personally. Ladies of the evening are not, wha you say, my cup of tea, no? Why, señor?"

"He got himself murdered, and I'm on the case."

"Aye, no! Tha's terrible."

"Yeah, bad scene all around. You know if he had a place on the Key?"

"No, no I do not, but de bartendah, he know," he said and called the bartender. "Hey, Reg-ggee! *Ven aquí!*" He whispered to him, in Spanish, then sent him off. He wrote down an address on a napkin and handed it to me. "Here, señor, a fair trade for the drinks. I thin you go now, no?"

"Yeah, I think I will. Thanks buddy."

"You never tell me...did you see dee Fantasma?"

I just looked at him and smiled.

"Ah, ha ha," he laughed, "You come say goodbye before you leef, no?"

"I will...tomorrow or Saturday, for sure." I tipped my hat and left the bar, heading down Greene Street to Simonton.

Bachman had a two-story house with a nice little sun porch and a garden filled with palms and roses. It was very homey, and looked more like a place that had a woman's touch than a bachelor pad...at least on the outside. Inside it was totally dark...no lights on at all. The front door was locked so I tried the back. It was locked too, but I found a key under the mat and let myself in.

A light switch on the wall flooded the room with a white glow. I was in the kitchen, a very modern, sleekly styled kitchen that didn't fit the quaintness of the house's exterior. A brand new Fridgidare, an electric oven, and one of those automatic dish-washing machines that I'd only seen in magazines, all turquoise blue and shining in the glow of the recessed light contrasted perfectly with the snow-white cabinets and countertops. The place reeked of dough. The spendable kind, not the cookie-making kind.

The next room was a dining area with an Eames table and chairs, hardwood floors and a flagstone fireplace. Cubist paintings hung on the pure white walls. Beyond that was the living room, decked out in more Eames furniture (the real stuff, not the cheap Sears knock-offs) and a black rug. A corner bar held bottles of the most expensive imported booze. The largest console hi-fi-television combo I ever saw took up one whole wall. The screen on that tube must have been damned-near twenty-seven inches, if that's even possible.

I helped myself to a glass of Chivas-Regal and sat in Bachman's Eames chair as I looked around the room, thinking. A very expensive-looking electric starburst clock told a story of eight-thirty. The girls would be wondering when I was coming back for more of their charms. I tried not to think about it.

I finished the Scotch and got to work taking each room apart, very carefully, making sure to put everything back where I found it. I wasn't worried about prints because I had snooping rights care of Sheriff Jackson. I went over the entire living room, dining room, kitchen, and first floor bath. Nothing. Not even a deck of cards where they shouldn't have been. When I was satisfied, I moved up to the second floor.

I half expected to see a ghost up there. I don't know why. I guess that was just the way things had gone on this trip. Instead I found that the entire second floor had been customized into a single bedroom, larger than my entire apartment in the city. The bed was one of those king-sized jobs with black satin sheets and a mirror overhead, Bachman's M.O. There was another bar, and another big TV set. The hi-fi still had a Miles Davis album on it, collecting some dust.

I began my search.

And very quickly I found what I was looking for in the back of Bachman's clothes closet, set into the wall. I took a tattered piece of paper from my pocket, read the numbers off as I dialed, slid in the key and opened Bachman's safe.

Bingo.

A half-hour flew by. I sat on the bed, dazed, surrounded by the contents of a dozen or so manila envelopes I got from the safe. Each was marked with a half-assed code. One with an "M". One with an "H". Another "Misc". There was an "R", a "J" and even an "SJ". The envelopes held photos, photos of Melinda, Hawthorn, miscellaneous business men and women whom I didn't recognize, Sheriff Roberts, Jessica, and Sheriff Jackson. There were photos of prostitutes, some alive, others hacked to death in Hawthorn's Safe Room many years ago. There were eight and sixteen millimeter films, sex films from his hidden cameras. There was audio tape too, and although I didn't see a tape machine handy to play them, I could pretty much guess what sounds were recorded on them.

Blackmail, extortion, protection…whatever the reason Bachman had all this stuff, in the end it didn't help him one damned bit.

The safe held more, more cans of movies, more photos, a few ledgers and not surprisingly a few stacks of hundred dollar bills, non-sequential and well worn. Pocket money for a man like Bachman, dirty money made on the backs of teenage hookers, several of which probably never made it home after Hawthorn's parties, and dope pushers, and hop heads, and thugs and God only knows who the hell else. It was dirty alright, dirty cash stained with innocent blood, and that was the dirtiest of all.

There was about twelve grand sitting there, not taking up much space. The temptation to pocket it flashed through my mind, but I quickly tossed that thought away. I knew if I left it here, it would eventually be found by the cops, and one of the crooked sons-of-bitches would just pocket it himself. I knew only one man who could rightfully claim any of this dough, and that was my pal Jerry, Bachman's brother. So I looked around the house and found a box and some packing tape, put the money in the box along with a little note that said, "This money is from your brother. He wanted you to have it. If it stayed here it just would have gotten pinched, so take it. Just don't tell no one." I thought a minute, and decided to count out five one hundred dollar bills for myself. I was, after all, on a case now, and I had wracked up a few bills in the process. I would no doubt have to come back down in a few weeks to settle up in court on the two goons I iced back in Miami, too. So I took just enough to cover expenses. Then I signed the letter "–R", sealed up the box and wrote Jerry's bar address on it. Then I shut the safe, took up all the envelopes, wiped the place down for prints anyway and left.

I threw everything on the front seat of the Caddy and drove back to my Chevy. The trunk of the Bel Air was nice; it had a new, clean rug and fancy cardboard inserts hiding the fenders and back seat. I carefully removed the cardboard and hid the box between it and the seat, and locked the car up. Then I left the Caddy there, along with another ten-spot with the old man, and drove the Chevy back to the Hotel.

It was pretty late now, around ten. I grabbed the envelopes and headed up to our room, not really sure what I was going to do next. It occurred to me I could just set fire to the whole bunch, take the Chevy and leave. Jackson wouldn't bother coming after me as he didn't have a damned thing on me. Melinda would be up to her tits in trouble with the Island, and Jessica would just go back to her old life, working at the brothel. Status quo. I wondered if the cathouse was still open for business. I wondered who might have slunk in as head pimp. As I got off the elevator, I wondered why I cared.

Really, I didn't. Not a damned bit.

I wish I could tell you this story had a happy ending. I wish I could say I took a leave of absence, as well as a leave of my senses and shacked up in a life of sin with two hot dolls on a tropical island for a few years. Looking back, sometimes I wish I had done just that, but it wouldn't have stuck. I was a cop to the core, a hardened, twisted being with a moral code that teetered somewhere between good and just plain evil. Either way, my future was laid out ahead of me, and it didn't include any palm trees.

Melinda was in the room when I opened the door. She was on the phone, so I parked it in the big chair and threw my hat on the bed. She smiled and ended her conversation.

"I was wondering if you hijacked my Cadillac and drove back to New York," she said, leaning over with a kiss.

"Not yet. I don't have to be back to work until Monday."

"If you go back to that job," she said with a wink.

"Where's Jessica?" I asked.

"She went back to her apartment to pick up a few things. Said she'll be back later tonight."

I sighed, and said, "Pull up a seat dollface. We gotta talk."

She sat on the edge of the bed, a worried look taking over her face. She looked tired all of a sudden, absolutely exhausted. "Something the matter?"

"Yeah," I said. "I know who killed Bachman." I stood up and threw a manila envelope on the bed next to her. Her eyes followed it as it landed in slow motion, taking what seemed like days to finally hit the mattress.

"What's that?" she asked innocently.

"Photos. Tapes. Film. Found it all in Bachman's safe. Turns out he has a joint here on Key West. That's where the safe is, the safe that matches the combo I found on Tiki Island. There's about twenty envelopes like that, each put together for a specific purpose."

"A purpose? What on earth…"

"Blackmail, baby. Plain and simple. Blackmail and extortion. All the little dirty little things that people do, but don't want anyone to know about are documented in that safe. There are sixteen millimeter films of deputies nailing hookers in a special bed he had set up in the company warehouse. Tapes of Sheriff Jackson giving the OK to narcotics and bootleg liquor coming over the docks from Cuba. Photos of politicians going upstairs at that brothel on the other end of town. Photos…of your father, Eliot Hawthorn, doing things I won't say out loud, things we both saw the night those…*entities*, came for him. Photos taken by Roberts, back when he was just a deputy working for your old man. Bachman got a hold of all of it, and he was using it to run Tiki Island his own way. And he was murdered for it."

I leaned against the wall and lit a Camel. The smoke trailed up to the ceiling fan and out the window. The night was hot and sticky and all I wanted to do was get this over with and get the hell out, out of this state, out this climate, out of this insanity.

Melinda's eyes started to turn glassy. "So…who do you think…did it?"

I frowned in surprise. "Isn't is obvious?" I asked, and took a long draw on the cigarette. "All the evidence points to one person, and one person only."

"Eliot."

"That's right. Eliot. As frail as he seemed, he had enough juice running through him to smash Bachman's windpipe with his walking stick while Bachman slept, then pressed down on it with his weight until the life ran out of him. It would have been an easy job, even for an old man like Hawthorn. And he had a damned good motive, too. He knew he was dying, or would die soon. He knew Bachman had the goods on him, and would use that against you to take over the Resort once he was gone. Hawthorn couldn't let that happen. He needed to protect you. And he needed someone to protect you once he was gone. With Bachman out of the way, and me on the scene, he could rest easy. That's why he killed Bachman. That's why he pushed you into getting with me."

"He didn't have to push me," she said weakly.

"And you knew he was right. That's why you played along. That's why you tried to get me to stay, even going as far as getting Jessica to play along too."

"No, William, it's not like that," she continued. "Eliot never pushed me toward you. And I never asked Jessica to come on to you. That…we both just fell for you, on our own. You can see that, can't you?"

"But you did know that Eliot killed Bachman, didn't you, Melinda." The tears, real ones, came flowing.

"I did."

"Tell me."

"He…Eliot told me, days ago. I couldn't tell you. I just couldn't! He knew they were coming for him…the wraiths…they'd been coming to him for years, taunting, warning, but for some reason they grew more powerful in the last few weeks. He knew he would be taken. And he wanted my future to be free of any of the wrongdoing he did. That's why he killed Rutger. He knew the police would eventually figure out it was him, but by then it would be too late. He would be gone, and that would be the end of it."

"Just like that?"

She wiped the tears from her face and stood up. She came to me, putting her arms around my waist and pulling in close. "Just like that. It's over. You've proven it. Now we can get on with our lives. Stay with me, William," she said breathlessly, her lips seconds from mine.

Again, one last time, she almost had me convinced.

One last time.

"Open that envelope on the bed, kiddo."

She drew back with a strange look. "I don't need…"

"You do," I said. "Take a look, for me."

She slowly turned to the bed. The clock on the wall struck eleven. Outside, the sounds of happy people and cars lilted their way up to our window. Somewhere, people were happy. Not here. Melinda opened the envelope.

She took out the photos, her back to me. She shivered. She started going through the photos, slowly at first, then more quickly. Her whole body shook with her tears as she realized what they were.

"Hawthorn didn't kill Bachman, Melinda." The crying came harder now. She threw the photos on the floor and stomped on them.

"NO NO NO NO NO!" She screamed through her tears as she fell to her knees, tearing at the photos. "No, it can't be," she cried, now softer, "That bastard," she said very quietly. She was surrounded by shredded photos now. Not photos of Hawthorn murdering young women. Not photos of prostitutes or drug dealers. Photos of Melinda, much younger. Photos of Melinda in a large, modern-style bed, taken from above and from the headboard. Photos of Melinda and Bachman, in bed together, with dates and times. Photos of Melinda at the brothel, arranging clients with women. Photos of Melinda directing prostitutes on Tiki Island, leading them to clients' rooms, handing off narcotics. There was film of her having sex with Bachman and two other women, too, with audio of her discussing dope deals with Bachman and a pusher.

She still had her back to me as she knelt on the floor in a heap of tears.

"That's why Bachman was able to get away with anything he wanted at Tiki Island. That's why you never did anything to stop him. And that's why, when you knew you could rely on Roberts to take over the dirty side of the business, you knew you could get rid of Bachman. So you waited until the time was right, and murdered him, making it look like Hawthorn did it. You knew Hawthorn would be dead within days, and that he would be the obvious mark. But your plan could only succeed if you could seduce me too, get my head so full of mush I'd never think like a cop again. That might have worked on an ordinary cat. But not on this one, kid. You just don't know me. You don't know what kind of ground beef and pulverized guts I'm made of. You don't know how I learned to kill without remorse fighting in Korea, learned to dispense justice on the streets of the city when no one was looking. You don't know that I can detach myself from my work, my friends, even my women and be the cold, hard sonuvabitch I need to be to keep my streets just a little tiny bit safer. A man like that doesn't change, Melinda. A man like that breathes and eats and drinks down the city with all the crime and grime and cancer and disease and spits it back out without caring one bit. That's who I am Melinda, and that's why I know you murdered Bachman."

She didn't say a word. She just wept, quietly. I poured myself a Bourbon from the setup and drank it down straight. I poured another and handed it to her. She took it, and sipped.

In a whispered hush she said, "That's not the whole story, you know."

"It never is," I said back, quietly.

"He forced me into it, Rutger did. There was a time...when...I was very young, I thought I was in love with him. That's what Eliot wanted, and I wanted to do anything Eliot wanted, even if it meant sleeping with another man. Eliot knew we could never be together, not in public. The scandal would have destroyed us, destroyed Tiki Island. So he wanted me to have a secure future. I wasn't supposed to be part of the drugs, the prostitution. I knew about it but was supposed to be left out. Rutger pulled me in. He did it very sneakily, making deals in front of me, asking me to help with small favors. Eventually he told me I was all in. When I tried to resist, he told me about the photos, and the films he'd taken of us. He threatened to pass the photos and films out around the Keys, "leaked" accidently. I couldn't chance it. I couldn't stand it! So I did what I was told. It was only after I grew older that I had the strength to break away from him, but Eliot insisted on keeping him to run the Island. I knew he was right...I didn't have the stomach for the dirty work."

She got up and faced me. Her hair was a mess, a black, stringy mop matted to her cheeks with myriad tears. Her eyes were wide, but red.

"And you thought maybe I did?"

"No," she said honestly. "You had it right, I was relying on Roberts to do that. He's good at it."

"Not anymore he isn't."

"He'll be out of jail soon. You don't know how Florida politics work."

"I don't care how Florida politics work. He's stone-cold dead."

Melinda gasped in shock. "What? How? When?"

"Wednesday night. He drowned to death in his cell."

"Oh my God, Islamorada flooded?"

"Nope. His cell was dry. I suspect he had a few visitors."

Melinda shook some more, and new tears formed. "My God, William. Why?"

"Because he helped your old man with those girls so long ago. I guess ghosts have a good memory."

She suddenly grew cold, hard. "He deserved it. They all did. Even Eliot, he knew he deserved it for what he did. Roberts deserved to die a long time ago. You know it was him that turned Jessica onto the junk, don't you."

"I suspected."

"She was never like that. She was a good-hearted soul. He did that to her. Now he's dead. And I'm glad." The tears were gone; an unfamiliar rage was taking their place. "And Bachman deserved to die a long time ago too, William. Believe what you want, arrest me if you want. He was an evil, conniving man with no conscience. If you knew how many young girls he corrupted, practically forced into selling themselves..."

"You never stopped it," I said. She glared at me with a look I will never forget.

"Oh, I sure as hell did, William, I sure as hell *did*. Just not soon enough." Melinda stood in front of me, shaking hard, her nerves raw and her sinew taught with anger, rage, disgust. She stabbed me with her eyes, never blinking, staring up at me through squinted, swollen lids. And as she did, two things happened.

First, I realized that she and I were not nearly as different as she had led me to believe. The sweet, bubbly, innocent girl that took me for a two-week spin had a dark, old soul, and a sense of right and wrong very much like mine. I saw that now. I saw who she really was, not a scared little girl, not just a young career woman trying to make her mark. She was also an avenging angel, a woman strong enough to know when enough was enough and take matters into her own hands. She was right; I didn't know Florida politics, but I knew enough to be certain that Bachman (and Hawthorn) would have had every cop, judge and politician possible in their pockets. There's no way Bachman would have been sent up on any charges, his little stash of photo albums would have seen to that. And Melinda knew it. She saw a chance to rid the world of one more piece of vermin, and took it.

But it was my job to uphold the law. Even though some of the things I did were outside the laws of our great country, everything I did, I did backed by a badge, and I did it in the best interest of the people. At least that's what I told myself to get to sleep at night. While I pondered this, the second thing happened right in front of me, but behind Melinda.

A mist was forming. At first I thought it was a cigarette, but neither of us were smoking. Then I realized the mist was taking a shape. A human shape. Arms, a chest, a head, a face.

As Melinda stared at me, Hawthorn's spirit rose behind her. It only took seconds, and I only looked past her for a second, but I clearly saw the old man's face. He mouthed a single word.

*"Please,"* he said. Melinda didn't see him. She turned to look at where I was looking and he was gone in an instant. But I knew what he meant.

"What is it, William?"

"Nothing, just thought I saw something. Still a little spooked from the other night, I guess."

"I think that's all over now," she said. "It's the living we have to worry about from now on." She sat back down on the bed, picked up her Bourbon and finished it. "So, Detective Riggins, what now?"

What now, indeedy.

Jessica didn't go back to her apartment right away. At around nine she left the hotel and wandered down to the beach, back to the same place she had spent so many sleepless nights haunted by the phantom of her long-dead mother. She sat in the sand at the water's edge, looking out over the glassy Gulf into the moonlight. She sat for minutes, then hours. She expected someone to come by. No one did.

At around two a.m. Jessica got up from the sand and walked back to her small apartment on the third floor of the rooming house on Duval. A slip of paper under the door reminded her that her rent was due, as it was already November First. She crumpled it up and threw it down the stairs. Once inside her little room, she opened the window, turned on the radio, and poured herself a shot of gin. She knocked it back, and for the first time in a very, very long time felt very, very lonely.

A few minutes later she walked down the mostly deserted street until she came upon her old house. She went inside, lighting a candle to see her way through. Up the steps she crept, wondering which apparition would greet her first. None did. She opened her old room's door, only to find it empty. The doll was gone, the stroller gone. She paused, then opened the door to her mother's old room. It was just a room, with a dilapidated bed and rotting mattress, but nothing more.

She almost went back to the hotel, but decided against it. She knew Bill had no intention of staying around the Keys. Even if he did, it was obvious he was in love with Melinda, she thought, and would eventually have nothing to do with herself. She hated goodbyes, and thought it best to just go home. And so she did, and she poured herself another shot of gin, and then another, and when the memories still didn't dissolve and the voices still didn't cease and the loneliness still didn't fade, she opened the drawer and took out the leatherette case which held her closest friend.

Melinda and I made love one last time that night. It was different than any of the other times, maybe because we knew it would be our last, maybe because we finally knew who each other really was. It was tender yet rough, loving yet sadistic. We saw past the smeared mascara and bruises, past the facades we'd put up to impress each other and ourselves. I was a cold, hard, bastard of a cop. She was a calculating bitch with the acting skills of Bette Davis. It was all out in the open now, and we understood each other.

She seemed surprised when I told her that as far as I knew, to anyone who asked, Eliot Hawthorn murdered Rutger Bachman in cold blood, and probably intended on killing himself the night of the storm. I never told her about Hawthorn's ghost, reaching back to our reality from the afterlife, still trying to protect the girl he loved in a twisted way as both a daughter and a lover. She didn't need to know that. We burned what was left of the photos and film that had anything to do with her, and I gave her Bachman's address and the combo to his safe. I also told her about the bachelor pad in her warehouse, along with the photography gimmicks he had set up. She never knew the cameras even existed.

Jessica never came back to the room. I waited until around ten the next morning, in case she wanted to come by. She knew I had to leave on Friday…so I pretty much figured she just had enough.

At ten, I said goodbye to Melinda.

"William," she said, once again holding back the tears. "I want to make sure you know it was real, all real. The only time I ever lied to you was about Rutger, and the sordid business he dragged me into."

"I know kid, I know." Yeah, that was a big lie, too, I wanted to say, but I held my tongue.

"I…I do love you, William. And I…Please, just consider it once more, to stay here, with me, on Tiki Island or here on Key West. Anything you want. I've got more money then both of us will ever need. I can run the hotel while you fish all day, or even go into police work here. Please, consider it. For me."

"I have considered it kiddo, very hard. Sure, it all seems like a bunch of roses now, you're in the clear, the Island will be fixed up. But one day one of us will wake up and realize it's all a lie, all just a pile of empty coconuts holding up forgotten fantasy. I'll miss the city and resent you for it. You'll miss Hawthorn and resent *me* for it. The world'll keep spinning but for us it'll be a make-believe world, the world we *thought* we wanted, but really just wanted to *believe* in. By then we'll realize we wasted a lot of years for nothing, and we'll hate each other for that too. So that's that, kiddo. I'm goin' home to my dirty, cold, crime-ridden city that I love. You go home to your warm, charming, joyful Tiki Bar. And maybe once a year you'll think of me, on Halloween, and remember the good times."

I kissed her one last time, a long, burning, sorrowful kiss. I'd fallen in love with her. And I'd fallen in love with Jessica too. How the hell could I let that happen? But it happened, and my heart was breaking that I was leaving Melinda, and was breaking even more that Jessica didn't even come to say goodbye. At least Melinda had a dream, made one last pitch. Jessica gave up before I did. Damn.

I put the top down on the Chevy and pulled off the curb without looking back. Somehow I knew Melinda was watching through the window. I was afraid if I saw her I'd slam on the brakes and spend the rest of my life making cocktails in a Hawaiian shirt.

Three hours later I was in Miami, pulling up to the hotel. I was sure sad to see that car go. The valet gave me the fish eye when I took apart the trunk to get to the package of dough, but a fin closed his eyes up quick. I gave the package to the man at the concierge desk and asked him to mail it for me, had my bags taken up to my room and spent the rest of the day sitting by the pool in the hot Miami sun, listening to Cuban jazz and drinking Cuba Libres like the locals. I caught a picture at eight, just something to get my mind off the girls. It was a Hitchcock movie, "The Wrong Man" with Henry Fonda. I should have gone for the comedy that was playing, "Around the World in Eighty Days". That sucker was over three hours long.

I hit the sack hard around eleven. I was taking a non-stop flight back to the city the next morning, and just wanted to get it all over with. Fourteen hours later, I was back in my icy-cold, dirty, smelly, Gaddamned wonderful New York.

# CHAPTER SIX

Friday Morning, November 2, 1956

Melinda didn't cry. Even as she watched William Riggins drive away in the shiny blue convertible, her eyes stayed dry. Any tears she had for him were shed the night before. Now he was gone, and she knew somehow that she would never see the strong, caring man again. "His loss," she said to herself, but she didn't mean it.

It was after ten and Jessica still hadn't returned. She didn't want to alarm Riggins, so she didn't say what she felt, but her gut feeling was that Jessica couldn't handle Riggins' leaving and went off the wagon. So she got dressed, put on a pair of sunglasses and left the hotel to find Jessica's apartment.

She'd only been there a few times, and after ten minutes of searching began asking around for the address. She finally found herself in front of Jessica's door at eleven.

"Jess? Jess, it's me, Melinda. Open up." She knocked on the door softly, then a little harder when she heard someone moving around inside. "Come on, Jess. Let me in." More muffled sounds came from inside, and with a click the door opened. Jessica was on the floor, naked and half conscious, dried blood on her face and hands. She was barely able to open the door in her condition.

"Jesus Christ, Jessica! What happened to you?" Melinda yelled as she pushed her way through the door.

"Fell, I think," Jessica answered weakly. "Hit my ndoze."

Melinda got her cleaned up and a little more sober. She put on a pot of java and got Jessica to drink most of a cup. "You shot up last night, didn't you."

"No."

"Don't lie to me, Jessica."

"I'm dot lying," she said, the bandage on her nose affecting her speech.

"Jessica, you're Goddamned needle is on the floor. There's a bruise on you arm and a red hole. Don't tell me you didn't shoot up."

"Ok, fine. So I did. Big whoop. Who'all cares about me an-dy way."

"I do, Jess. You know I do."

"Sure. Where's Billy?"

Melinda looked down at the floor. "Gone. Home."

Jessica screwed up her face, holding back the rain. "I knew it," Jessica said. "I knew he wouldn't stay once he figured things out. I was a damned fool to think...well, just a fool."

"To think he loved you? You're not a fool, Jess. He did love you. *Does* love you."

"Oh, sure. No, Lyn, I was just a vacation fling to him, just like you were."

"You're wrong," Melinda said quietly. "I tried to get him to fall for me. I almost thought he did. But when it came down to it, it was you he wanted. I was just fun for him, a rich girl with her own island, someone who could give him a fantasy life. You...were different. No matter what I offered him, I couldn't give him what you could. I could see it every time he looked at you. He never looked at me that way. Never."

"You're batty."

"No, it's true. But it doesn't matter now. He left and never looked back."

"'Course he didn't. He couldn't. Would you, if you were a cop and he was a murderer?"

Melinda dried a tear, and said, "It wasn't that, Jess. Not that at all. Believe when I tell you, William wouldn't care if the both us were serial killers. He's just...he's not *like* us, he doesn't belong *here*, in the south, in the Keys. He's a city boy, and that's that. And he's a cop, through and through, and being a cop runs in his blood. It has nothing to do with us, or with...*that*."

"But he did figure it out, didn't he?" Jessica answered.

"Yes...well, mostly. Not...*everything*."

"What do you mean, not everything?"

Melinda turned to Jessica with a look of such deep seriousness that the girl knew what Melinda meant.

"Melinda, what exactly did Billy say when he found out who killed Bachman?"

Melinda gave a half smile. "He's telling the Sheriff that Eliot killed him. Plain and simple."

"Eliot? Then he..."

"He didn't figure out the whole story, Jess. Our secret is still safe."

"You mean, he doesn't know..."

"Our secret is safe. Leave it at that."

Jessica sat and contemplated that thought a moment, silently. "I would have thought he'd figure the whole thing out. He's a smart guy."

"Certainly, and with the evidence he found, he made a smart decision. You know that bastard Bachman had dirty photos of me and him together, and films too? And tapes. William found them in his safe." Melinda got up and leaned against the door. "William put the pieces together the way he wanted to. So now it's all over."

"No cops, nothing?"

"Nothing. Eliot murdered Rutger, and Eliot is dead. End of story." Melinda's voice broke on those last words, and she had to choke back a new set of tears. "Look, Jessica, I want you to listen to me," she continued in a quiet, serious manner. "I want you to pay attention, because what I have to say is very important and I want to make sure you understand me."

"Ok, Lyn...what?"

"You can't ever, and I mean ever, talk to anyone about what happened Wednesday night on Tiki Island. You can't tell anyone what happened to Eliot, and you *absolutely* can't tell a soul what really happened to Rutger. Do you understand?"

"Sure, Lyn. Sure."

"I mean it. If you say *anything* about any of this, neither of us will be safe. For certain, I'll be arrested, and you'll end up in an asylum. Do you understand?"

"Yes, Lyn, come on, I understand, don't get so heavy."

Melinda took a deep breath. "I don't want you living here anymore, in this little apartment. I don't want you working in...in that *place*, anymore. You don't have to. I know I've said it before but now you know you have no one to answer to, your life is your own. I want you to come move in with me, to Tiki Island, for as long as you want."

Jessica laughed. "Move in with you? Really? Oh come on Melinda, why all of a sudden? So you can keep an eye on me?"

"Actually in some ways yes. And it's not all of a sudden. I told you long ago you could have your own apartment on the Island, rent-free. You insisted on being on your own."

"Nothing's *free*, Lyn."

"You could work there."

"As your concubine?" Jessica answered, rather sarcastically.

"No, don't be stupid. At the front desk, or in the restaurant, anywhere you want. Food and Beverage Manager. Frigging Director of Maraschino Cherries. Anything."

"Funny," Jessica said, still a little high, "You never *really* wanted me to stay on the Island before. Now...now that Eliot is gone, and Bachman is gone, Riggins is gone...you've got no one. You're alone for the first time in your life. So now you want me?"

Melinda took it with a grain of salt. "I'm going to assume that's the junk speaking, Jessica. I've invited you to stay on the Island a hundred times. Your Goddamned ego always made you say no, like I was giving you a handout or something. This is no handout. I want you to come live with me."

"As your sex toy?"

"No, Goddammit!" Melinda yelled.

Jessica said more seriously, "As your lover?"

"As my *friend*," Melinda said, and put her arm around Jessica. "You're right, a little. I'll be awful lonely in that big hotel without my best friend."

Jessica started to cry a little. She said, "If I'm your best friend, why did you let all those things happen to me? Why did you let Bachman...do..." She broke down in complete tears.

"Shh, calm down, Jess. I tried to stop him. Really, I did. You know that. And you know I couldn't stop him. I tried. There was nothing I could do once you were hooked on the junk."

"I need it, Lyn," she cried, "I really do."

"For what, Jess? Really, what the hell do you need it for?"

"To get through the days. And nights. To escape…you know, my life. My job…and my mama."

"And have you seen her since Wednesday?"

Jessica thought. "No. Not here, or at the beach, or even the house."

"And with Bachman out of the picture, you don't have to work in that horrid place any longer, right?"

"I suppose not."

"Then it's over, isn't it?"

"I…I guess so."

"Then you don't need that crap any more, do you?"

"No, I guess not."

"Come live with me on Tiki Island, Jessica. You'll have anything you want; money, cars, clothes, anything. I owe you that much."

"Maybe. I don't know. I can't think straight. I need to think it through."

"What's there to think about?"

Jessica tilted her head back and closed her eyes. "Oh, little Melinda. Not *all* the memories of that place are good ones, are they?"

"No, not all." Melinda got up and went to the window. The morning was clear and bright, the temperature already in the seventies. It annoyed her that Jessica's flat didn't have air conditioning. "I have some business to take care of today. You should stay at the hotel today, it's cooler than this place. Get some food, relax by the pool. I'll be back around six. Promise me you'll think about it, ok?"

"Ok, Lyn, I promise."

Melinda walked toward the door. "Really, stay at the hotel. This place is…depressing."

"Lyn?" Jessica called as Melinda was leaving.

"Yes?"

"Did Billy say anything about me before he left?"

"He waited until ten. He thought you didn't want to see him."

"I didn't really. Not when I thought he knew the truth."

"He wouldn't have cared, Jess. The way he feels about you, he wouldn't have cared."

Jessica stood up, shakily, and hugged Melinda. "Thank you baby," she said, holding her tight. "I *will* come with you to Tiki Island. I will," she said through shallow breaths and smoky tears.

### Saturday, December 22, 1956

It was another long week full of junked-up hookers and hop-head mechanics, high-schoolers on reefer and a half a dozen related murders. Crime always picked up in Manhattan around the holidays. It was just something I'd grown to expect.

I finally got a Saturday off. I'd been asking for a whole weekend off since I got back from the Keys, but I guess the Captain thought two weeks in Florida was enough time off to last me the year. I finally got on his good side, nabbing a half-baked kid who liked to set fires in abandoned row-homes. So here I was, home on a Saturday, with Sunday off too. And I had no idea what the hell I was gonna do.

It snowed overnight so I decided to stay at the apartment in the city. It was too early to go to Jerry's and too late to have breakfast, so I threw on my overcoat and hat and walked down to the diner on the corner. The ice-cold air felt good, like an old friend. That crazy summertime weather in October stuff was just not my style. Florida could keep it.

Funny, I thought as I looked over the menu. I said I didn't miss Tiki Island, but every day since I got back, I seemed to find something to compare it to. The weather, the fashions, even the food. The fact that this diner didn't serve surf and turf for breakfast, or have Mai Tais on the drink menu seemed odd. I found myself looking around, pointing out areas of the grill area that could use some bamboo and reeds. I also found myself imagining pretty girls in sarongs replacing the old, dumpy waitress that had worked there since the Dark Ages. And I imagined, just for a moment, a beautiful blonde and an equally beautiful brunette sitting across from me, smiling that mischievous smile of which only I knew the real meaning.

Some kid, who should have been in school threw a couple of nickels in the juke box, and Elvis Presley's Return to Sender began to play. I ordered a plate of ham and eggs over easy and borrowed a newspaper. I somehow managed to get through all the news and into the classifieds before the eggs were done. And there, looking right at me, was an ad for a brand new, 1957 Chevrolet Bel-Air Convertible, complete with radio and heater, for $2499. The dealer was only four blocks away.

I finished the eggs and another coffee and said, "What the hell," and took a walk.

Three hours later I was driving a brand new blue convertible back to Weehawken in the snow. Crazy, man.

I drove around most of the afternoon, with the top down, the radio on and the heater going full blast. Going slow was ok, but going over twenty-five was a bitch. Twice I nearly lost my hat. I wondered how the hell they managed to always keep their hats on in convertibles in the movies. And they never looked cold. Even with the heat blasting, sure my feet were on fire but the top half of me was a block of ice. I didn't care; I was having a ball in the first car I ever bought.

I pulled up near Jerry's place mid-afternoon. He was wiping down tables after the lunch crowd. A pianist I didn't recognize played mellow west coast jazz on the bandstand, the kind of easy stuff that floats around on clouds of cigarette smoke and settles into the top of your rocks glass. I grabbed a stool at the bar and waited for Jerry to finish his busywork.

"Hey old man," he said to me. "Coming in a little late for lunch, aren't you?"

"I was toolin' around town. Lost track of time."

"Toolin'? With who? Fast Freddie was in here not more than a half-hour ago."

"On my own, Jack. Bought a set of wheels."

"What? When?"

"This morning. Got an itch I had to scratch."

"No kiddin'? What kind of jalopy did you fetch?"

"No jalopy, kiddo. A real hot rod. Wanna look?"

"Natch. Where's she parked?"

"A couple of spots up the street. Come on." Jerry grabbed a jacket and we went out into the bright day. Funny how fast your eyes adjust to a darkened lounge. The snow killed us. Squinting, I said, "Right up here. The blue one."

"Holy hell, Riggins! Is that a Roadster?"

"Sure is. A brand new 1957 Chevrolet Bel-Air, with a clock, a radio and a heater. Oh, and Hydromatic transmission. Two-eighty-three V-8 engine, power top, even has a gimmick that turns the headlights on when it gets dark, just like a

Caddy."

"Nice ride, buddy. Freddie's sure gonna be sore. What put the bee in your bonnet?"

"Remember I told you this was the car I rented when I went down to the Keys?"

"Oh yeah."

"That's it. Decided the best part of that trip was the car."

We were both quiet for a minute. I was remembering a certain blonde, and a certain brunette. Jerry was remembering his brother. "I can't tell you how sorry I am about Rutger," I said quietly.

"Hey, at least you found out who his killer was, and the sonuvabitch is dead."

"Yeah, he's dead," I repeated awkwardly. It's not easy to lie to your best friend, even if it's to save a dame's hide. That's something I'd have to live with, I guess. "Come on, let's get back to the bar. I'm starved."

"Yeah, congrats on the car, Riggins. Try not to let it get stolen."

I laughed. "In this city? Forget it. It'll be gone in a week. I know it for a fact, the cops here stink."

I hauled the rod up to my house in Weehawken at a quarter to four, and parked right out front. A couple of neighbors saw it and came out to gab about "the fine 'chine." After a while they drifted away, and I finally got inside my nice, warm house.

Gaddamned phone was ringing as I walked through the door. On what seemed to be the fourth ring, I grabbed the receiver.

"Yeah?"

"William Riggins?" the operator asked. Weren't many people who called me William.

"Yes?"

"Person to person call from a Miss Melinda Hawthorne, long distance from Florida. Will you accept the call?"

Gaddammit. I didn't want to accept the call.

"Yes, I'll accept the call." *Dammit.*

"Just a moment sir." There were some clicks and whirs, and Melinda's voice came streaming through sixteen hundred miles of copper wire and into my head.

"William?"

"Hello Melinda. How's the weather?"

"Weather is fine. Jessica is not. There's a plane ticket waiting for you at the airport, six o'clock flight to Miami. There's a private plane there waiting to take you to Key West."

"Melinda, if you think I can just…"

"Please William, it's…it's very important that you come."

I thought a minute. I hadn't heard a peep from either of them in nearly two months, and I liked it that way. Now this. "I can't just pick up and run, kid. I've got a job…"

"She's dying, Will. I don't know how long she can hold on."

"I'll be on the plane," I said sadly, and hung up. *Dammit!*

The jet was delayed an hour because of the snow. I didn't get into Miami until well after nine, and the puddle-jumper that took me to Marathon took another twenty minutes. Melinda's driver met me at the airport with a Packard limousine. He drove me to the dock where a speedboat was waiting. The speedboat made it to Tiki Island in under ten minutes. Melinda met me at the newly rebuilt dock.

"William," she said softy, and hugged me tight. "I'm…I'm really happy you came. It means a lot to Jessica."

I almost didn't hear what she said. I took in the Island in one long gaze, amazed at what I was seeing. As if nothing ever happened, Tiki Island was back to its old, paradise self, holding me in that crazy, tropical magical trance that it had so easily caught me in before. The Tiki torches flaming against the twilight sky, the Islander girls in their Hawaiian garb, the lazy steel guitar and ukulele music floating on the warm air. All back, all perfect. All fake.

I forced myself from the spell and asked, "How is she?"

"Resting," Melinda replied with a mournful note.

"What happened?"

Melinda took my arm and started walking me toward the main entrance of the Tiki Island Hotel. "One guess."

"She OD'd, didn't she."

"Not quite." We reached the doors, perfectly restored, and she led me inside. She didn't say another word until we were seated in the Shipwreck Bar. Three beautiful Mermaids swam their water ballet as Arthur Lyman's Quiet Village played in the background.

"Come on kid, give."

"Her body is dying. It's her liver, mostly. And her heart."

"The drugs."

"Yes," Melinda said flatly, lighting a cigarette. I guess she took up smoking.

"Fuck," I said without thinking, the blood boiling in my brain and cooking away any morals I had left. "Sorry kid."

"No need," she said, blowing a little smoke ring into the air. Her eyes began to glisten. "That's exactly what I said when the doctor told me."

Something changed in Melinda since I saw her last. Not just the smoking, but her entire being was just a little askew. She seemed a little older, maybe a little wiser. Definitely a lot less innocent. Running Tiki Island, losing Hawthorn, and now losing Jessica was making her grow up fast.

A waitress brought over a couple of drinks. Mine was a Bourbon on the rocks. Melinda's was something clear, neat. I took a slug and said, "The junk. Always the junk. I've seen so many kids dead one way or another from the stuff, it kills me a little every time I see. Ain't there nothin' the doctors can do?"

"No," Melinda answered, the tears finally creeping through and rolling slowly down her bronzed cheeks. "It's too late. She's too far gone, they say. Her liver…it's diseased, beyond hope. Even if they were to fix it, her heart…it just wouldn't take it."

"Jesus. How did this happen? I figured she'd be ok now, after everything was over. Didn't she come to live with you?"

"She did. But it wasn't over, William. It's not over. I fear…"

The waterworks came again. She tried to cover it up but her own tears betrayed her.

"What kid? Tell."

"It won't be over until Jessica is dead," she said through the tears, and buried her face in her hands. I reached across the table and put my hand on her head, running my fingers through her soft, dark hair. "Anything, anything at all that I can do kiddo, just name it. I'm here now."

She looked up. Her eyes were brown discs floating in reddened pools. "She needs to see you, William. She needs to talk to you."

"Ok," I said. Seemed like a simple request.

"She needs you to…to hear the truth."

Now that's a late change in the starting lineup. "Truth? What truth are we talking about?"

"*Her* truth. And you need to hear it from her. You need to listen to her, and most importantly, you need to end what Jessica started."

I finished my drink and sat the glass down gently on the bamboo table. I thought for just a second as the exotic music filled my mind. I thought how the atmosphere in the lounge was just perfect; dark and mysterious, a wrecked boat sunken in an ocean of tropical fish and mermaids, no light except for a few candles and some strange red and blue glows emanating from hanging blowfish lamps. The scent of fruit, coconut oil and tobacco, mingling into a strange, foreign air. Even Melinda herself, wearing an untypically dark blue dress with dark flowers, and a black orchid in her hair. Everything, every sight, every sound, every smell told me something wicked was about to unfold, to get the hell out of there and never come back to this evil, haunted, maniacal place again.

"Whatever she needs," I said, "I'll do it, for her, and for you."

*Dammit!!!*

🌴 🌴 🌴

We took the elevator to the third floor, a ride that seemed familiar yet strange, like something remembered from a far off dream. I wasn't surprised at all when we stopped in front of Eliot's door.

"During reconstruction I had them turn both apartments into one, with a bedroom each for myself and Jessica," Melinda said as she unlocked the three separate locks on the new door. She swung it wide and hit the light. I *was* surprised to find most of Hawthorne's room had remained intact, including his wing-backed chair and Oriental rug.

"Still looks the same," I commented.

"Just this room. I always liked this room. Jessica's in the back." She led me down a long hallway flanked with Tiki-style art, black velvet paintings and carved-wood masks to a locked door. "She's in here. Here's the key."

"You're not coming in?"

"No William," Melinda said softly, "This is between you and Jessica." She hesitated, then said, "She still loves you, you know."

I didn't want to hear it. "Sure."

"I mean it, William. She loves you more than anything, even herself. Even more than me. And I know you still love her, William, so don't play mister tough guy and try to pretend you don't."

"There was a time," I said without thinking, "That I thought I may have loved you."

"No," she answered, "You never did. You were enamored with me because I did everything in my power to make you feel that way. You loved the idea of loving me. But you never really fell in love with me, Melinda, the person. It was Jessica you loved. It's always been Jessica. And it's Jessica you still love now."

I didn't say a word. Melinda turned and walked away, her sandals clapping softly on the hardwood floor. In a second, she was gone. I sighed, then slipped the ancient skeleton key into the antique lock, and turned. It clicked. I pushed on the latch and opened the door.

What I saw next will be burned into my mind for the rest of my life.

Jessica was sitting up in bed, her face white as a sheet, her eyes puffy and red. Here flowing blonde hair was a nest of turmoil, matted and frayed. She was crying, saying something inaudible…to a dark, misty shadow hovering over her bed. As I looked on, she turned to me, startled, and the shadow dispersed into thin air.

"Billy," she said breathlessly.

"Hello Jessica," was all I could say. She began to cry a little harder, and coughed. I closed the door and sat beside her.

"Billy." She threw her arms around me and held onto me for dear life. "Billy, I'm dying," she said.

"I know."

"I screwed up," she said with a cough.

"It's ok Baby," I said, holding her.

"No, Billy. It's pretty fuwkin' far from Ok, pardon my French."

I gave a little laugh. I couldn't help it. "How long, kid?"

Jessica sniffed, thinking. "Maybe a few days. Maybe...tonight."

"Jesus," was all I could say. It didn't seem possible. It didn't seem real. "There something you want to tell me, kid?"

"Yes," she said shakily. "Yeah." She let go and took a drink from a cup on her nightstand. "I got a lot to tell you. I just hope I make it through long enough to tell you it all."

"Don't say that Jess."

"It's true, sugar. The doctor said days. That was days ago. I truly think I'm down to hours, buddy." She took another drink. I could tell from the smell it was whiskey. I guess it didn't matter now.

"I'll stay here with you, baby," I said, holding back some tears of my own. Melinda was right; Somehow I had fallen head over heals for this charming, sweet, broken, screwed-up, beautiful junky prostitute. How the hell it happened, I'll never know. No wonder I was conflicted about running the Island with Melinda. I *never* loved Melinda. I *should* have loved Melinda, but sometimes fate slams a rock over your head and next thing you know you're a vice cop falling for a hooker. "I'll stay with you…however long it takes. What is it you want to tell me, kid?"

"The truth, Billy. From the beginning. The whole truth. And I think maybe then ya'll will understand me a little better, understand why I had to do what I did. Understand why…Why I asked you to come here, at the end."

I looked down at my watch. It was eight-thirty. I poured myself a drink from the bottle on the nightstand. "I got all night, baby. Lay it on me."

"You're not going to like it, Billy. Not one bit of it."

"I'm sure I've heard worse."

"No," Jessica said in a very serious tone. "I don't think you ever have. Better make that drink a double. You're gonna need it, sugar."

## Jessica's Story

Baby Jessica was only three years old when she went to live in the nineteenth-century house in Key West. Her mother, Rose, had gone missing in the Great Atlantic Hurricane of 1935, an occurrence that many friends and family found strange, as she had packed up and gone off-island for the weekend without telling anyone why or with whom she was going. She simply dropped baby Jessica off at her grandparents, said she had some business out of town, and would be back in a few days. That was the last Rose's parents ever saw of her, and though they knew she'd been lost to the storm, they never learned the truth behind Rose's death...or more accurately, her murder at the hands of Eliot Hawthorne.

Though it was the last her parents ever saw of Rose, it certainly wasn't the last that Jessica would ever see of her.

"I still remember," Jessica said as she gazed past Riggins into some distant space and time, "The night she died. Even before my Grandmama knew, before the Sheriff came to say she'd been gone missing, that night she came to me, while I laid down in my crib. She was beautiful...shining, glowing like an angel. She hovered over me, and touched her hand to my cheek, but I don't recall feeling it. Then she just...disappeared, sort of turned invisible as I watched. It's as if she came to say goodbye on last time. I don't remember much of my childhood, but I sure as hell remember that."

Yet that wasn't the last time Rose came to Jessica's side. Through the years, as Jessica grew from a baby to a child, from a child to a teen, on hot summer nights when the moon was low a shimmery shadow would float into Jessica's room at her grandparent's home. Sometimes she would see it, sometimes it was just a feeling, but she knew it was her mother, coming to check on her, visiting to make sure Jessica was doing well. Jessica welcomed these visits...and although anyone she tried to tell simply said she was crazy, fantasizing and dreaming, she knew that the visitations in the night were real, very, very real.

"Then when I was fifteen, I met Ricardo," she continued, taking a short swig of Bourbon. "Ricardo, the boy who convinced me he was in love with me, who wanted me to go to Miami with him."

Jessica was smitten. She had never had a boy tell her she was beautiful, or that he loved her. He plied her with flowers and cheap booze along with talk just as cheap, and finally, one cool night on a dark beach at the north end of the Key, he convinced her to let him touch her, to feel her, to let his hands wander over her young body as no other hands had before. With the help of some gin laced with a few pills, Ricardo took her virginity that night on the beach, though Jessica barely remembered it.

Once he had her convinced that they were in love and would someday be married, he introduced her to something a little stronger than alcohol: Reefer. It took some convincing for her to try it, but she finally caved in. And she enjoyed it...with him...so much so that when he suggested trying some pills, she didn't object. It was while high on pills that he first convinced her to have sex with another girl while he watched, and then joined in. Again, she was barely aware what she was doing...blinded by her love for him and the mind-bending drugs. When it was over, Ricardo convinced her that it was something they should do again.

"Oh, he was good, that one." Jessica continued. "He knew just how to manipulate young girls, get them to fall for his good looks and charm then get them hooked on pills or horse or whatever he could get them into. With me, he hit the jackpot. On a dull, hot, sticky summer night my grandparents were killed in an auto accident while driving home from Duck Key, and my world shattered. Ricardo was there for me, comforting me, telling me everything would be a-ok."

Then to soothe her soul, he proposed they try something new together...and at the age of sixteen, Jessica had her first injection of heroin, a special cocktail that Ricardo mixed himself. She got high, and he pretended to get high, and she loved it. She loved that this twenty-two year old man loved her, loved her enough to share such incredible things with her. She loved it so much that when he suggested they do it again the next night, she cheerfully obliged. And the next night. And the night after that.

And just when she was hooked, just when going without the junk for a few hours started to hurt and she needed a fix, that's when Ricardo told her she had to start paying for her own supplies, and it wasn't cheap. Jessica's grandparents had arranged for their life insurance to pay off the taxes on the house through 1960, to make sure she always had a place to live. But after the funeral expenses there wasn't much left for a sixteen year old girl to live on, so, as Ricardo had hoped, she had to go to work.

He got his friend (boss), a man named Roberts, to give her a job as a bar waitress at a sleazy place on the edge of town, a burlesque house that "entertained" gentlemen upstairs. Jessica was made to do every menial job from serving drinks to stripping the dirty, wet linens off the beds. She was disgusted by what she saw, but knew it was necessary...Ricardo took all her money, and gave her a fix whenever she needed it, plus bought her groceries and clothes. She didn't see as much of him now, as he often had to go to Miami on business (a business she still wasn't sure what it was), but when he was out of town there were several other 'connections' she could rely on for her daily bread.

"It wasn't long before things began to change, of course. Prices went up. It got more difficult to find Ricardo, or any of his 'friends'. That bastard Roberts cut my hours down and demanded more work from me when I was there. It seemed pretty damned unfair to me, and it was...it was because it was a completely calculated plan, one that had worked on dozens of girls over the years...get them hooked on the junk, introduce them to the life, and slowly pull them into where the real money was."

One night, after Jessica had been dry for two days and had the shakes something terrible, she begged and pleaded with Roberts to give her a fix...but her money was spent.

"There's one job left ya'll ain't yet done," he said to her, "I could put you up on the stage. I recon a pretty, well-built babe like you dancin' nekked would bring in some big bucks. Can you do it?" Jessica nearly vomited at the thought...no one but Ricardo had ever seen her naked, and she liked it that way. But the monkey was a strong one, and he was pulling on her back so hard she couldn't stand it.

"Will you give me the fix first, Roberts?"

"Sure baby, you just let me have a look at the goods first, make sure ya'll as pretty under them clothes as ya promise to be," he said to the girl, licking his lips like a disgusting hyena.

"Here? Now?"

"Yea, darlin'," he said, taking a needle kit out of his back pocket. "I've got ever'thin' ya'll need right here. Don't be shy. Let's see whatcha got." And knowing that it was the only way to shut the monkey up, Jessica let her clothes slide to the floor, keeping her eyes closed the entire time.

An hour later she was onstage, dancing in a dreamlike state, the horse running through her veins like it was on fire. She peeled the clothes off one piece at a time, somewhat in rhythm to the heavy drums and throaty sax. She could hear the crowd go wild as the g-string fell to the ground, and she realized she was doing the same moves she'd seen the other girls do, the moves that made her embarrassed to watch. But she realized that it wasn't so bad, having all those men admiring her, applauding her, throwing crisp five and ten dollar bills at her. The song ended and she scooped up the tips...and when she was sober enough to count them, her total for the night was over one hundred dollars...more than anyone she knew made in a week. Yet no matter how much she made, it never seemed to be enough...the prices were always rising, the house fees were getting higher too, and it wasn't long before a man named Bachman came to her with a proposition.

"I have a client," he told her, "That is very important. And this particular man just happens to have an appetite for very young girls, such as yourself." Still a teenager and looking very young, she was the perfect fit for Bachman's out of town client, a wealthy European who stayed at Tiki Island Resort up in the middle Keys a few times a year. "I can offer you five hundred dollars to spend the night with him," he said without a run-around. "Plus I can guarantee you no house fees here for your dancing for one month, and, as an added bonus...the price of your...*medication*...will be reduced by twenty percent."

Jessica's mind whirled. She really needed the money, and the lower price on the H would really be helpful...but to sleep with a man...a stranger...for money...

"This is a one-time offer," Bachman told her. "You can leave with me now, for Tiki Island, or stay here for nothing. Did you get your fix?"

"Not yet, not today."

"I can give it to you, on the Island. Come with me, Jessica. You won't regret it."

"That's how I met Bachman," Jessica told me as she rearranged the pillows behind her frail head. It was depressing to see her like this, the pale, parchment-like skin, the yellowish eyes, the shaking. I did everything I could to act like I didn't notice, but the poor chick looked like hell. Gaddamned monkey.

"How long ago was that?"

"About six years ago, I guess. I dunno, really, time sort of means nothing to me anymore. Anyway, I had already known Melinda, and it wasn't long before Melinda and I became close friends, then, over a jug of wine on the beach, we became more than friends...we became lovers in the most taboo sense of the word. But Melinda was all over the place. She'd been having an affair with Eliot, then with Bachman. She slept with cute men who would come here on vacation, she would have quickies with the kitchen help on a dare. She talked me into sleeping with her and Eliot together, and eventually together with you, although that didn't take much convincing."

I just smiled. I really didn't want to hear any of this. I had no idea why she was telling me any of this, either. I just wanted it to be over so she could have her peace and I could go back to New York. That may sound insensitive, but you have no idea what this poor kid looked like. Besides, this haunted freaking Island gave me the creeps.

She continued, "It was Bachman who made me a prostitute, although I suppose Roberts had a lot to do with it too. And myself, of course. I just couldn't get the monkey off my back. I hated him for that, I think you can understand."

"Losing your mother, then your grandparents so young...no one to take care of you...I can see how you got mixed up in that life, kid."

Jessica laughed. "Oh, Billy, it wasn't that. I could handle my grandparents dying in that crash. I could even handle Ricardo leaving me. No, there was something else that happened at the same time, something that at first I thought was wonderful, then realized too late how horrible it was. Something...something so horrific, it changed me, and it made me change my life, and by the time I realized what was happening, it was too late to do anything about it."

"What happened?"

"I found out that my mama had been murdered, that's what happened, and everything went to hell after that."

# CHAPTER SEVEN

April, 1951

It was late on a hot, wet day when Jessica awoke in her small apartment above the bar in Key West. The clock ticked away as she lie in her bed, thinking about what she needed to do in a few hours: work. Stripping, baring her young body for a bunch of sleazy, sex-crazed lowlifes so they could get it up to give it to the hookers that were waiting to take them upstairs at the club. It was a disgusting way to make a living, she thought, but it was a quick way to make easy money... money she needed to feed the monkey, the one that made life feel so good, even when things were so screwed up.

It was already past five, and she needed to be onstage at the The Low Key Club by eight. She jumped in the shower, threw on her clothes, grabbed her work suitcase and headed out.

She arrived early and got herself set up in the dressing room. With an hour to spare, she decided to head out for a bite to eat before taking her shift. There was a little sandwich shop a block away, perfect for something light before her shift.

The minute she walked in she wished she'd made something at home. There was Sheriff Roberts, that fat som'bitch that kept her on a leash, calling her over to sit with him. It was too late to turn around and leave, so she obliged.

"Eve'nin, Sheriff," she said politely. She detested him, but in general he was good to her, giving her a fix whenever she wanted it, making sure she got time off when she wanted it, supplying her with pretty much anything else she needed.

"Hey, ya'll lil' darlin'," he said, obviously drunk. She sat and ordered a ham and cheese sandwich and a ginger ale. Roberts started talking, and wouldn't shut up. She missed half of what he said, as his speech was so slurred it was impossible to catch it all, but when she heard the word, "Mother," that got her attention.

"Wait, Sheriff, what did ya'll jus' say?"

"Your mother. I known your mama. She was as sweet a child as you can imagine, an' a real looker, too. Jus' like you."

"Wow!" she exclaimed feeling kind of silly afterwards, but it wasn't every day she talked to someone who knew her mother. "Well tell me more, how did you know her? What was she like?"

"Well hell, she done worked for me, darlin'! Thought ya'll knew that!"

"Worked for you...you mean, she worked for the Sheriff's department?"

Roberts let out a huge laugh, the kind only large men can conjure. "Oh, hell no, baby! She was a workin' girl, jus' like you!"

Jessica reeled. "What? You mean she was a stripper?"

"A *stripper?* No, no, darlin', she was...well, ya'll know...a lady of the evenin', in fact she worked in that same house that ya'll are workin' in tonight!" He laughed again as Jessica began to tremble. She stood up and smacked Roberts hard across the face.

"You take that back you som'bitch," she said. Everyone stopped and stared. The diner was so quiet you could hear a pin drop.

Roberts rubbed his face. He wasn't expecting that, but when he thought about it he realized he deserved it. Then he said very seriously, "Girly, I thought ya'll known about that, and I'm truly sorry that I'd been the one to tell you." He motioned for her to sit down, and she did. "Yo' Mama was a fine, decent and wonderful women, Miss Jessica. She was the sweetest, most darlin' girl you'd ever meet. But she was what she was, and that was a lady of the evenin', workin' in that there cathouse where you shake yo' ass currently. That don't make her any mo' or any less of a good person, ya'll remember that, girly. Jus' like it don't make you no better or worse."

He got up, left a five on the table and left. Jessica broke down in tears, crying for her mother for the first time in over fifteen years.

A few hours later, a man named Rutger Bachman would offer her a chance to make $500 to sleep with one of his VIP clients, and Jessica would say yes.

**Late October, 1952**

Jessica and Melinda were comfortably spread out next to each other on towels on the beach near Jessica's apartment in Key West. The sun was hot, and they soaked up the rays, 'going native' on the secluded beach for that no-tan-line look. At five, they decided to head back to Duval for a quick dinner before going back to Tiki Island.

They ended up at a little out-of-the-way place that served Caribbean dishes. The last person they ever expected to see there was Sheriff Roberts.

"Oh, Jesus, this guy's like horse manure, he's everywhere and he stinks," Jessica whispered to Melinda and they had a good laugh. They took a table far away from the bar, but it didn't help. The inebriated man stumbled over to the two girls.

"Good even'n ladies, mind if I join ya'll?"

"Well actually –"

"Thank ya, don't mind if I do." He pulled up a chair and sat on it backwards, something Melinda detested. Then, as usual, Roberts started shooting off at the mouth the way he was known to do when he had a few too many mint juleps. He talked about the weather, about the citrus trees, about a secretary in the police station who got knocked up by a night janitor.

"Roberts," Jessica finally interrupted, "Did you follow us down here? Seems like a kind of an odd place for ya'll to be drinkin'.'"

"Well, lil' darlin', matter of fact, maybe...maybe I did."

"Why?"

"Uh..." he searched around for a good reason. He had none.

"Jus' checkin' up on ya'll."

Melinda said, "Well, we're fine. And we'd like a little privacy, if you don't mind Sheriff."

Roberts got slightly indignant. "Well, ok then, ya stuck-up hussy, you and your little whore can be all alone! God damned lezzies." He tried to get up, but for the second time Jessica let loose a full-handed slap that nearly knocked him off the chair.

"Some day, you som'bitch, ya'll are gonna go too far, and I ain't jus' gonna slap yo' fat face, boy," Jessica said, trembling. Melinda tried to calm her down but it was no use.

Roberts knew he'd done it again, he'd stuck his fat foot in his fat mouth. He didn't mean to be such a prick, it was just that he so much wanted to get close to Jessica, Rose's daughter, and he didn't have a half a brain in his head to know how to do it right.

"Miss Jessica," Roberts said, humbled, "I am sorry. I don't know what come over me. It's jus..."

He stopped talking. Jessica hovered over him, Melinda remained seated. "Well, what is it?"

"It's jus' that this time a' year always reminds me of yo' Mama, that's all," he said, almost in tears.

"What? What the hell do you care about my Mama? She died almost seventeen years ago."

"I knowed it."

"So what you care?"

"I...I jus..."

"You jus' what?"

"I...I wish I coulda saved her, that's all."

"You? What in hell could you have done against that storm? They ain't nobody that coulda saved her from that 'cane, and ya'll know it!"

"Cane!" Roberts said, "Aw, fuwk that 'cane. Ain't no hurricane done killed yo' mama, she was murdered, sure as shit she was murdered and that 'cane was just a way to cover it...aw, shit," he continued, then hung his head down low. Under his breath he whispered, "Ya done fuwked up this time, boy."

Jessica was in shock. "Murdered?" she asked quietly, her heart beating fast, her whole life turned upside down with the single word. "Who? How?"

Roberts looked up at the girl, the spitting image of her beautiful mother, the only woman Maynard Roberts ever loved, ever considered loving, but would never dare confess. Certainly he had paid for Rose's services a few times, but that was as close as he ever dared to get to the blonde angel that he dreamed about, the woman he thought about day and night...the woman that was murdered by that evil som'bitch Hawthorn, in cold blood, just to cover his own ass. The woman who was used as a changeling, murdered by the man he continued to work for all these years. Murdered by the man that Rose's beautiful, precious daughter Jessica and that lowlife slut Melinda Hawthorn were both taking to town every night. It killed him to imagine it, twisted his guts to think of Jessica bedding that disgusting man after he murdered her mother. Roberts couldn't stand it any longer. He'd held Hawthorn's secrets for seventeen years, but he couldn't hold them a minute longer. He had to tell her. He had only found out a year or so ago that Jessica Rutledge was in fact Rose Divine's daughter, as he had never known Rose's real last name. But now that he knew, now things were different. He couldn't allow her to go on the way she was. He had to stop it.

Funny, he thought, how he found out by chance that Rose's daughter was now *working* for him, at The Low Key Club, as a prostitute. Funny, that she was conceived around the same time that Roberts first took Rose to bed upstairs at the Low Key Club...And he couldn't stand it any more, couldn't stand what Rose's daughter had become, couldn't stand that he allowed Rose's murder to go unknown for so many years.

He took a swallow of his booze and said very shakily, "She was murdered, Miss Jessica, beat to death with a lead pipe and thrown over the side of a boat during that horrific storm. The storm was just a way to cover it up, cover many things up," he said flatly, using every ounce of courage he had to spit it out.

"But who? Who would do such a thing?" Jessica asked, now letting the tears fall to the table.

Roberts said, "It was..." and he stopped short, not able, even now, to admit to the world who and what Eliot Hawthorn really was. He wasn't sure why he couldn't allow the words to leave his lips. Maybe he was afraid. Maybe he couldn't really believe it himself. Maybe, it was just too heartbreaking to say it out loud. "It was never solved," he said, "I'm sorry." He got up from the chair, tipped his hat, and stumbled away leaving Jessica and Melinda with that Earth-shattering news to hang around their necks.

### December, 1952

Her rage consumed her. She found Roberts and asked him time and time again about her mother's murder but he insisted that he only had circumstantial evidence that it was even really a murder, and had no idea who the 'mysterious' man who took her away from Key West in a boat that fateful weekend had been.

Finally, Jessica couldn't stand it anymore. She knew a lot of people in the Keys, some good, some bad, many helpful. She called Melinda and told her what she wanted to do.

"Are you sure about this?" Melinda asked over the phone. "Being half Hawaiian, I take these things very, very seriously. I've heard some very disturbing stories about people who have tried this, and things went seriously wrong."

"It's the only way I know of," Jessica answered. "And I have to know. I've tried others...Gypsies, a VooDoo priestess...no one could help me. You're my last hope. Will you help me or not?"

"I will," Melinda sighed, "Come to Tiki Island tonight. I'll have everything prepared."

Jessica arrived on the Island at eight p.m. A storm was brewing in the Gulf, somewhat unusual for this time of year, but appropriate, she thought. Melinda met her at the dock.

"Do you want a drink first, or some supper?" she asked shakily. Always the good hostess, Jessica thought.

"Nah, Lin, I just want to get this started. Where is she?"

"The Tiki Hut on the north side of the Island. I have everything set. We can go right now if you'd like."

"Yeah, let's get crackin', shug'. I'm anxious as hell."

Melinda could tell by Jessica's demeanor that she'd had a little help getting to the Island. Speed, she thought, possibly cocaine. She was concerned about Jessica using the stuff. She was young, but had already seen what it could do to people...and wished she'd never gotten mixed up in the business of it to begin with. But that was between her and Rutger Bachman, and she'd take that cause up at a later time.

She led Jessica around the Island path, through the gardens where the criss-crossed palm trees grew, past the Tiki beach bar where the Hawaiian band played, past the 'cheap' rooms and to the secluded thatch and bamboo hut built over the water, reserved for private parties and currently empty...except for one soul.

"She's in here. Now remember, she is very old and very strange, but very wise. Don't say anything that might upset her."

"Upset her? It's *my* mother who was murdered!"

"See," Melinda said, "That's exactly what I mean."

"Ok, fine, I'll be calm. Does she know why I'm here?" Jessica asked as they opened the door.

"Jessica Rutledge," the old woman said in a strange, gruff voice, the accent of which was difficult to discern. She was surrounded by small clay jars and bowls, feathers, open coconuts, fresh palm fronds, colored rocks and a few other items that seemed strangely out of place. "Yes, I know why you are here. Sit down. This will take some time."

Thunder rolled in from the Gulf. Jessica and Melinda watched as the old woman said some strange things in Hawaiian, rattled some sticks, stirred some ingredients into the coconut bowls and made several unusual signs with her hands. To Jessica, it seemed like something out of a carnival sideshow. To Melinda, this was a very serious, very ancient ritual, one very seldom discussed let alone seen in person.

The woman chanted something three times and beat a small drum four times. Unearthly blue and green lights seemed to grow from behind the woman. She chanted again and beat the drum. The lights intensified and a dark, ominous shadow began to form behind the woman, taking the form of a winged creature as she spoke.

"Tell now," she said to Jessica, "Tell the Goddesses of the Earth what it is you want to know!"

Suddenly Jessica started taking things very seriously.

She grabbed Melinda's hand and held it so tightly Melinda thought it might break. She looked into her friend's eyes, gaining strength from her, assurance. She looked to the old woman. The woman's eyes were completely black. Thunder crashed so loudly she thought the roof would cave in. "I want to know who murdered my mother, Rosey Rutledge, and I want to know why!" she screamed over the thunder and crashing waves beneath the dock.

"*Kapo'ulakina'u,*" the woman shouted, "Bring us this night our answer, show us the soul who would bring this injustice against a child of the Earth!" She added a pinch of purple dust to a pan and it flashed with a brilliant blue light... and at that exact instance, against the carefully rehearsed plan she had made with Melinda to find the name of her mother's killer, Jessica screamed, "And take *revenge* on him!"

"JESSICA!" Melinda screamed and pulled away from Jessica in shock, her eyes wild with fear and regret. The old woman's eyes bulged too, and she shouted as loud as she could, "Pele, Goddess of Fire, protector of women, listen to our plea, and avenge this woman's death!"

"NOOO!" Melinda tried to stop her; she kicked away the brews and drums and began shouting things in Hawaiian but it was too late. With a final crack of thunder, a piercing bolt of lightning tore through the roof of the hut and connected with the old woman's staff, pulling energy from the Earth, the universe, from all things living and all things in the afterlife into the room. And as the brilliant light burned, the black winged shadow grew larger and larger, finally reaching the roof and morphing into the full figure of a woman, her face smashed in, her skin rotted and gray, black mud dripping from her vacant eyes and gaping mouth. The wraith screamed, and thousands of creatures erupted from her throat, crabs and eels and innumerable horrors, roaring forth and spinning around the room in a black typhoon. And as suddenly as it appeared, with a final scream the phantom ripped through the roof of the hut and hurled itself into the night.

Melinda moaned deeply and hung her head down low.

"Our fate is sealed," she said hoarsely. "The Gods are awakened."

The old woman closed her eyes and mumbled something in Hawaiian. Jessica sat wide-eyed, in shock, not understanding what had just happened. Melinda, however, knew exactly what had just happened.

"So what the hell does that all mean?" Jessica asked innocently. "Who's the murderer?"

Gaping in horror at Jessica, Melinda said in a scratchy, hoarse voice, "Jessica, have you any idea what you have done?"

"Well...no...I mean, well..."

Melinda shivered, and swallowed hard. "You don't know what power you've just released. You have no idea what you've just awakened."

Jessica got up and wiped a few tears from her face. "Well, I rightly don't give a God damn, Lin," she said, holding back more tears. "Whoever killed my mama," she said quietly, "Deserves to die too, and die in a most horrible way. Don't ya'll agree?"

Melinda was silent.

"Thank ya'll, Ma'm, for ya'lls help," she said to the old woman, and left the hut.

Melinda looked at the old woman, her teacher, Haukea.

Haukea said softly, "That girl, she will not like the outcome of this, I fear."

"Neither will I," Melinda said.

"No," Haukea said, "I'm afraid, my dear, you shall not."

"I didn't see Lin for a long time after that. She wouldn't return my calls, wouldn't see me if I had a job on the Island. She'd been pretty much carryin' me along, moneywise, so when I didn't see her no more I had to go back to work at the club." She finished off her drink, then motioned for me to pour her another.

"Where is it?

"In the dresser."

I found the bottle and poured her a full glass.

"That was when everything started, Bill, that night with that crazy Hawaiian Voo-Doo women. That's when we...that's when *I* released the phantoms, or demons, or Gods, or whatever you want to call them. I released the evil side of my mother's spirit, and those of Hawthorn's wife, and the women he killed. I don't know how it's even possible, but it happened. That's when Eliot started seeing things, too. He started seeing things because he was the murderer."

I hung my head low. Three months ago if anyone had told me that story, I'd say they were bats. But not now. "Jesus kid, so you knew the whole time it was Eliot who murdered your mother?"

"No," she said, "Not at all. In fact, it wasn't until the weekend before he was taken away that the ghost of my mother came to me, and finally was able to...to talk to me, to tell me who it was that was responsible for her murder. That was the night I..." she trailed off, closed her eyes and held back more tears.

"That was the night you tried to kill yourself," I said, finishing her thought.

"Yeah. I realized then and there that I'd signed Eliot's death warrant. That's why they were haunting him, ya know what I mean? They were gaining strength, strength from every storm, every turn of the tide, getting stronger and stronger until they were strong enough to..."

Her voice trailed off again and she took a long pull of her booze. It didn't seem to be affecting her much. "We didn't realize it was Eliot who they wanted, because he's always been such a sweet man to Melinda and me. We just figured they'all were trying to get to any of us they could, like they was comin' to me, just to get more energy or make contact or somethin'."

I sat on the small chair next to Jessica's bed, just shaking my head.

"Ya'll don't believe me?"

"This is all pretty hard to take, kiddo," I said. I didn't know what the hell else to say. "But it's all over now, right? I mean, they got what they wanted, so it's over."

"Not exactly," she said to me and coughed. There was blood in it. "They wanted Roberts too, for his part in all of it."

"And they got him, no doubt about it."

"Yes, and they wanted Captain Reams, for his part," she said quietly.

"The got him too, Jessica. He's dead."

She frowned. "I though as much. And there was one other they wanted."

I thought a minute. Who was left? "Bachman?"

"That's right," she said, "But they didn't get him."

"I know they didn't kid. I know who did."

"No Billy, I don't think you do."

I was a little puzzled. I wasn't sure if Melinda told her the truth or not, that she had killed Bachman but that I told everyone it was Hawthorn who murdered him. "Er, who do you *think* I think it was?"

"I know you told everyone it was Eliot," she said.

"Right."

"But I know that you found out that it was Melinda who killed him, because of what he'd done to her."

"So she told you."

"Yes."

"Then what's the big secret?"

Jessica took a deep breath, then took another swig of her whiskey. "Melinda didn't kill Bachman, Billy. She was ready to take the fall for me."

"For you?" I asked, not understanding what the hell she was talking about. "You. Why would you kill Bachman? And how could you, considering you were in Key West all night?"

"Not *all* night, Billy."

Drums.

This was new, Jessica thought as she lay on her hot, sticky, sweat-drenched bed. Drums, far off and ominous, meant for her ears only. The drums *summoned* her, called her down to the beach where she'd gone so many nights before. In her half-dreamlike state she obeyed, strolling right up to the water's edge.

The drums grew louder, louder, then stopped. Like so many waves ebbing against the shore, the apparition whom she had come to know so well began to grow from the depths of the Gulf, looming up in front of her, a dark mass of death filling her soul with dread. But this time she wasn't alone. Behind her, black and evil and full of hate were four hundred souls, some drowned, others hacked to pieces, others simply smashed beyond recognition, drifting up with the tide and obliterating the horizon.

"What do you want from me!" Jessica screamed. "I can't help you!"

Like the searing screech of a thousand steel bows ripping over thousands of rusted violin strings, the creature's voice groaned with disgust, *"Hawwwwthorn"*.

"Oh my God," she whispered. "No, no it can't be! Not Eliot! He's a good man!" she screamed, "He's a good man!!!"

*"Not a good man,"* the entity exclaimed, *"An evil, murdering man!"*

And the others screamed, *"Murderer! Pervert! Monnnster!"*

And Jessica knew, as her mind filled with images of swirling waters, hurricane winds and dark, painful death, that the phantoms were speaking the truth.

She dropped to her knees, bursting with tears and mournful wails. Finally when she was able to speak again, she simply asked, "When?"

*"Threee days,"* the phantoms replied in unison, an evil, gruesome sound that tore at her ears and shot like a bullet through her brain. *"Look for the storm, it is then that we shall exact our revenge."* With their message sent, the phantoms slowly, quietly dissolved into the sea.

"Oh, dear God," Jessica cried to the Gulf, "I'm so sorry Melinda. *I'm so sorry.*"

"Why are you telling me all this?" I asked Jessica, the images swirling around in my head like phantoms in the night. "How does murdering Bachman fit in?"

"You don't see it?" Jessica asked wearily. "I thought it would be obvious."

I thought for a second, letting all the little pieces of the giant puzzle fit into place. Then, those cop smarts that got me the title of Detective younger than anyone else in the history of the New York City Police Department kicked in, and

I had it.

"You did it for Melinda."

"Yes, detective. I did if for Melinda." Jessica looked down at her thin hands, crossed on her lap, shaking slightly, uncontrollably. "And I believe you know why."

Of course I did. It was all plain as day now. "You really had no idea that Eliot Hawthorn was your mother's killer when you had that old woman cast the curse, did you?"

"No, not even a little" she responded hoarsely, "As a matter of fact, I suspected it was Roberts who done it."

"So when you found out that it was Hawthorn..."

"I was devastated. I knew Melinda would just die if she found out, and I knew there was no way to keep it from happening. I'd screwed things up so much, I knew the only way to try to make it up to her was to...I dunno, make things *easier* for her, somehow. I knew she hated Bachman as much as I did. I knew without Eliot to protect her, Bachman would push Melinda out of the Island and take it over for himself."

"So you devised a plan, a fast, sneaky, smart, evil plan to kill Bachman, right under my and everyone else's noses."

Jessica laughed. "Always the cop, ain't ya, Billy? That's right. Right there, on the beach, it was like I came up with the whole thing in my mind, in minutes."

"And it would seem you pulled it off. It's the part about getting to the Island and getting back to Key West that's a Duessy."

"Think you know how I did it?" she asked with the first smile I'd seen all day.

"I think I have a pretty good idea," I bantered back.

"Would you like to lay out your theory for me, Mr. Detective?"

I smiled. "Don't mind if I do," I said, and got up from the chair. "Shall I do it like the movie detectives?" I asked with a smile.

"Oh yes, please do...I ain't been to the cinema in months!" she laughed. It was nice to see her laugh.

I paced a few times across the room, just for effect, and started in.

"Sunday, October Twenty-Seventh. It's late evening, and you hear the drums calling you to the beach. You follow them, scared and weary but you follow, and the phantoms come...and that's when you learn that Eliot Hawthorn, a man whom you've been intimate with, the man who is your best friend's closest...eh...father, lover, whatever the hell he is...is the man who murdered your mother in cold blood all those years ago. You know too that these...*entities*...will take their revenge on him, in three days' time. You know because they told you so. And there ain't a damned thing you can do to stop it. You're feeling guilty because it was you who brought this down on Hawthorn, you who set these creatures free to do their will. You also realize that Melinda will be completely devastated by Hawthorn's death. So you decide you need to do something, *anything*, to ease the pain of this impending horror. Is that the gist of it so far?"

"Yes, so far you are on target, detective."

"Groovy. Ok, so you can't *tell* Melinda what's going to happen. You'll try to warn her to take Eliot away, but you know he'll insist on staying in his home, and won't leave the Island. So, keeping in mind that Eliot will be gone in three days, you decide to kill a couple of birds with one stone...the first bird Rutger Bachman, making it look like Hawthorn did it."

"Rutger Bachman," she said softly, "If anyone deserved to die..."

I interrupted, "Yeah, Bachman, the man you hated, the evil bastard who ran the

Low Key Club and pulled the strings to rope you in, the sonovabitch who was really behind your drug addiction, the man who got you into prostitution, then exploited you, filmed you, used you...even to extort Melinda, the one true friend you've ever had."

The look on Jessica's face could stop a train. "Yes, Bachman," she answered in an eerie tone that made my skin crawl.

"You'd thought about killing him before, didn't you? You'd thought about it but knew you'd never get away with it, and even if you did you'd still have Roberts to contend with. But now thanks to me Roberts was out of the picture, and you had the perfect opportunity to do Bachman in, without anyone ever knowing it was you. You could strangle him, murder him in his sleep, slip out the backdoor of Tiki Island and back to Key West, making it look like Eliot Hawthorn...or hell, that even *I* was the murderer."

"I never meant for it to look like it was you," she said.

"Damn near got me put behind bars, kid."

"I'm sorry Billy. Truly."

"Forget about it. Now, we know why you did it...and where you did it..."

"Now you have to figure out *how* I did it."

"Let me take a whack at it," I said, and took a sip of the whiskey straight from the bottle. It was strong stuff, just what I needed. "Sunday night, you called Bachman."

"So far, so good."

"I'm guessing you told him you needed something to get you through the night...something *special*, something that only he had, something that you'd be willing to come all the way to the Island to get it."

"That's right. He always kept a very special stash of the best...*medicine*, here on the Island. I called him and told him I needed a special fix."

"And that you'd spend the night with him as a thank you, no doubt."

"Well," she said, seeming embarrassed. "Yes, it was the only way."

"So he arranged for a boat to pick you up on Key West. You knew that since this was a covert, illegal operation, that he would pay someone not to ask questions, and not to ever talk. In fact, he probably hired a non-hotel employee from Key West to shuttle you here."

"He didn't have to. I just took a random boat, taking a dozen people up to Islamorada. Dropped me off here at the Island without saying a word. I told the man to come back at one a.m., and to keep his mouth shut about it. A hundred dollar bill sealed that deal. A red wig and glasses made sure he'd recognize me again."

"So you came up to Bachman's suite, say, around ten o'clock?"

"Yes, around then."

"You got your fix, and bedded him in return, insuring he'd be knocked out and sound asleep when you were ready to do him in."

"A girl's gotta do what a girl's gotta do," she said, looking down again.

"So after he fell asleep, you quietly made your way to Hawthorn's suite. I'm guessing you have a key to Melinda's room, and got in through the connecting doors?"

"I do, and I did."

"You grabbed Hawthorn's walking stick while he was sleeping, crept back to Bachman's room, and, not knowing exactly how to bash his skull in, you decided it would be easier just to crush his big old Adam's apple with that heavy hunk of wood. One well-placed blow would have smashed his windpipe well enough to keep him from having much fight in him. Whack!" I said, bringing my fist down in my hand.

Jessica jumped. "It wasn't so easy, Bill. It took me almost a half hour to get up the nerve. Turns out, funny enough, killing people isn't my thing."

"You get used to it," I said under my breath. She pretended not to hear. Her voice was ice cold when she began to talk again.

"The first strike smashed his throat up pretty good, but it woke him up, in a lot of pain, too...he started clawing at his throat, and tried to scream, but he couldn't get any air out. He couldn't get off the bed. He struggled for a minute then started to turn blue. I beat his hands away from his throat with the stick, then laid it across his neck and pushed down as hard as I could. His eyes bulged, his tongue stuck out of his mouth and he gasped but nothing came out. I was...I was sickened, almost ready to throw up it was so horrible. Then I remembered all the horrible things he'd done, and I pushed down harder. He was too weak to push me off. He just laid there, dying under me. The last thing he heard was my voice."

I was having a lot of trouble believing what she was telling me. She sounded like a hardened murderer, someone who took pleasure in taking another man's life. But then, she probably *did* take pleasure in killing Bachman. My angel, my sweet Jessica. An executioner for justice. Not so much different than someone else I knew...

"What exactly did you say to him?" I asked quietly, almost afraid of the answer.

Coldly, she replied, *"I'm really enjoying this, Bachman. I'm really enjoying watching you die by my own hands you rotten som'bitch."*

I looked straight into her eyes. She stared back at me, emotionless. "And then he died?"

"Not right away," she said. "Just for fun, I backed off, just to let him think for a minute he might live. Was that an evil thing to do, Billy?"

"Yeah, that was pretty heavy, kid."

"He coughed, wheezed, tried to breath. His eyes were begging me to let him go. He reached out to me, pleading. I smashed his hands with the cane again, then I put the cane back on his throat, pressed down hard, and laughed as the life ran out of him."

"Jesus, kid," was all I could say yet again. I'd heard the coldest, most horrifying confessions of some of the most evil bastards to ever walk the Earth, but I'd never heard anything so horrific come out of a girl so sweet. "Once Bachman was dead, you returned the walking stick to Hawthorn's suite, collected up your things, and took that one a.m. boat back to Key West."

"That's right."

"Like nothing ever happened."

"Yep. Like nothing ever happened."

"You would have been back before two. I got the call at three that you'd tried to kill yourself."

"I stole all the juice that Bachman had on him. By the time I got back to my apartment, I realized what I had done, and it hit me pretty hard. I took a dose to escape reality. It didn't work exactly the way I'd hoped it would. I felt worse, to the point I didn't think I could live with myself. I knew you would hate me when you found out. I knew Melinda would hate me, or at least think I was crazy enough to never want anything to do with me again. Ending it all...it seemed like the right thing to do. I don't suppose it ever occurred to you ask that doctor how he found me that night, did it?"

"No, actually. How did he find you?"

"My mother brought him to me," she said. "She wanted me to live."

Jessica had taken more than forty-five minutes to tell her tale, forty-five minutes of my life I wish I'd never lived. I'd have been very happy thinking Melinda killed Bachman, and that Jessica was nothing more than an innocent victim, rescued too late from a fate brought on by a tough life, bad people and too much of a bad thing. But that bridge was washed out, lost forever. I thought I was at the center of my little world. It turned out Jessica was at the center of everything that happened to me in that two weeks in Florida, and was the center of everything that happened to Melinda, Hawthorn, Roberts, Bachman, and even Reams and the phantoms of four hundred souls, including her mother's. It was Jessica who started the ball rolling, and she who made it come to an abrupt stop.

"She's going back to sleep," I said to Melinda as I shut Jessica's door. "That confession knocked her out."

"So she told you everything?" Melinda asked.

"I guess so. She told me she killed Bachman. She told me about the old Hawaiian War Chant lady."

"Don't make light of that, William. She is a powerful woman, as you have seen."

"Sorry kid. What exactly...what did you three conjure up, anyway?"

Melinda sat on the sofa and lit a smoke. I couldn't really get used to that. "In Hawaiian culture, there are many legends, many stories of Gods and Goddesses. Some are just stories. Some, however, are based on real events, real..."

"Tiki Gods?"

She smiled. "Something like that. There is a legend, involving the Goddess *Kapo'ulakina'u*. She is said to be able to call upon the dead. That is who Haukea..."

"What's that?"

"My teacher's name...the old woman, she was my Hawaiian teacher here on the Island...still works here as a story teller. Her name is Haukea, it means...well, it means "snow white"."

"Kookie. Go on."

"Anyway, the spirit of *Kapo'ulakina'u* is who Haukea invoked. According to legend, she would indicate who killed Jessica's mother...not by becoming mortal and telling us straight-out, mind you, but by leaving signs, or clues over the next few weeks. But when Jessica interrupted and demanded revenge, Haukea invoked *Pele*, the Goddess of the Volcano, of fire, and of the female power of destruction."

"Seriously," I said, my head spinning.

"Very seriously. Whether you believe me or not has no bearing on what's happened, William. Jessica asked a very powerful priestess to call on ancient Earthly powers to call on the dead and to take revenge on the living. And that is *exactly* what happened. The invocation tore a hole through our plane of existence into the plane of the dead, allowing the souls of Jessica's mother, Vivian Hawthorn and all those women that Eliot..." she paused, unable to say it. She choked something back and continued, "...those *other* women, and the victims of the Great Atlantic Hurricane to spill through, forcing them to be trapped between worlds. It was then that Eliot's hauntings started, as the entities tried to get their revenge on him as their powers grew. But they were weak, much too weak to do anything to harm him at first. So they waited, gaining strength with every storm, every bolt of lightning, every crash of thunder that cracked over Tiki Island, until..."

"Until they got strong enough to act," I said, and lit myself a Camel. "They came in with the tropical storm, and when it turned into a hurricane they finally had enough juice to make themselves infinitely powerful, am I right?"

"That's exactly right. It was then...in the early hours of Wednesday, October the Thirty-First, that they rode the storm, gaining enough strength to become...destructive."

"Was it just a coincidence that it happened on Halloween?"

"Probably. Then again, it is a holiday that was observed by ancient cultures."

"What about the drums?" I asked, intrigued by the idea that the dead could reach into the world of the living. "What were they all about?"

Melinda sighed a heavy sigh, then said, "In Hawaii, there are spirits that roam the Islands each night. They're believed to be the souls of ancient warriors, looking for new battles, or perhaps looking to re-enact old battles they won or try to win battles they lost. They march through the night to the beat of deep, ominous jungle drums. On the Islands they are known as Night Marchers. I believe that here, on Tiki Island, the souls of the dead who came for Eliot came as the ancient Hawaiian Night Marchers have for centuries." Melinda lost it on that last line and the tears began to fall. I got up and sat next to her, holding her. It felt strange.

Night Marchers. Ancient curses. Hawaiian Goddesses. All kookiness. I never believed in any of it, not even in ghosts until I saw one for myself. Now I was to believe that Jessica and Melinda conjured up these *things*, these phantoms, these Night Marchers to take revenge on a killer? It was hard to take. Then again after all I'd seen in the Florida Keys, it didn't seem all that insane after all.

"When will it all be over, Melinda?"

She looked over at me, her eyes red. "When Jessica is dead."

"Why her?"

"Because there is a price to pay," she said through the tears, "for asking the Goddesses for such revenge." The tears came faster now.

"You mean to tell me, she's dying because those...those *things* are killing her?"

"Not exactly. Oh, William, she would have died soon anyway. Her liver is gone. Her heart is failing. It's her own fault, and mine too. But they're coming for her. Nothing can stop them now." She came up close to my face and spoke in a hushed whisper. "Her mother...her mother's spirit...*is here almost all the time!*"

That's what I saw when I first entered Jessica's room. That dark mass hanging over her bed...it was the phantom of Jessica's mother, plying her, trying to get her to let go of her life and succumb to the sea. "When, Melinda?"

"Tonight," she said solemnly. "They're taking my Jessica tonight!"

There was no fanfare, no big storm, no swirling phantoms. At ten minutes to two in the morning, as Melinda and I each sat beside Jessica as she lay in her bed, the phantoms came. Her mother, glowing beautifully white, along with several others materialized right in front of us. Jessica looked over to Melinda and said goodbye, then she looked at me and said, "Thank you for believing in me, Billy, and for the best two weeks of my life. I love you." I couldn't help myself. I mouthed the words, "I love you too," and she smiled. Then she said, "I'm ready. Take me, Mama. Take me away from here forever." And very quietly she lay back down on her pillows, closed her eyes, and took her last breath. Melinda and I watched as a white, misty figure rose from Jessica's body; it hovered for only a moment, then slipped away with the other phantoms through the picture window, disappearing into the Gulf. Melinda moaned and cried bitter tears and I held her; there was no point in being cruel now. We covered Jessica's body with a clean white linen and left her in her room. A few minutes later with the help of some Valium, Melinda fell asleep in my arms one last time.

The next day was as depressing as they come. Melinda dressed all in black, the first time I'd ever seen her that way. She arranged for Jessica's ashes to be spread across the beach as the tide came in, just as she had requested. I made arrangements to stay on Tiki Island through Tuesday, to make sure Melinda was all right, and to be there for Jessica's ceremony. It was beautiful, with thousands of exotic flowers covering the beach, and dozens of people there to pay their respects. As for me, my heart cracked in half. I'd gone down to Florida for a nice little vacation, an escape, and ended up falling in love with a fallen angel. 'Til this day I still think of Jessica every time I see a young girl shooting up, or walking the streets, and it kills me a little, twists my guts so hard I can't stand it. Maybe that's why I'm such a sonovabitch when it comes to dispensing my own kind of justice to pushers and pimps. Maybe that's why I stayed a vice detective all these years...maybe.

"Melinda and I stayed in separate rooms of the suite. It wasn't easy staying away from her, but I knew it was for the best. Tiki Island was her home. New York was mine. We said goodbye on a rainy Tuesday afternoon in December, I believe, and that was the last time I ever saw Melinda Hawthorn or Tiki Island."

Juan snapped off the little cassette tape recorder and wrote a few notes in his book. Remembering all those crazy things from so many years ago had really got my mind going. "I have a few other stories if you want to hear them, kiddo," I said. "Might take a while to remember the details. I ain't a kid no more, you know."

"Aye, I would love to hear dee stories, Beel," he said with that dark voice and heavy Mexican accent of his, "But I thin, I have enough to keep me...what you say...occupado for a while, no?"

"I'd say you do! After you write the book, are you going to publish it or what?" I asked, knowing damned well that Juan was just doing this as an exercise to learn better English.

"Who know," he said thickly. "Maybe so, maybe no. But I try."

"Well, if you do, make sure I get a signed copy. And leave my name out of it."

Juan laughed. After all we'd been through with Heather's place and that damned Jack Slate, it was nice to see *anyone* laugh, especially one of the old gang. I thought he was crazy when he asked me if I had any *other* paranormal experiences in my life, before the whole business with Heather's closet. But after thinking about it I remembered Tiki Island, all those memories from damned near thirty years ago that I'd pushed to the back of my head a long time ago, locked away with a lot of other things I'd rather not remember.

Funny, I thought, how different things were back then. I was only twenty-eight when I stayed on Tiki Island. Pushing sixty now, I really didn't *feel* so much different...except maybe for a few bullet holes that hurt like hell now and then. There were no fax machines or car phones back then, no little computers you sat on your desk to write books with or draw pretty pictures. No pushbutton phones, Hell, no color TV! The '57 Chevy was long gone, run up to a hundred and ninety thousand miles before it blew up. Captain Waters and La Rue were long gone. Johnny Princeton was long gone, changed his name and lived out his life as a rancher in Colorado. Tiki Island was long gone too, finally closed up in the mid-seventies and turned into condos like everything else that was cool or interesting. But some things are still the same...I still have my home in Weehawken, and I still have old Suzie, my .45 automatic that's been with me to hell and back (literally, but that's another story). I still like Tiki bars, and would order a Mai Tai over a Cuba Libre any day. And I still have my memories.

I never went back to Tiki Island. I did take a few more great vacations down to the Florida Keys...very relaxing, completely uneventful and amazingly ghost-free vacations, I might add, filled with fishing, boating, drinking and sightseeing. But nothing as crazy, nothing as so incredibly unbelievable as those two weeks in 1956 ever happened to me down there again.

"I go now, Beel. Please say hello to dee Meeses for me, no?"

"I will kid. Careful driving out there, it's still snowing."

Juan left, and I stared at the picture postcard that I had in my hand for most of the talk. It was of the main building on Tiki Island, post-dated December 22$^{nd}$, 1973. It was just three lines, from the manager of the hotel. "Dear Mr. Riggins, thought you would like to know, Ms. Hawthorn passed away in her sleep this morning, apparently of a heart attack". December twenty-second. Same day that Jessica was taken away by her mother.

For just a moment, I wondered if there was a connection.

Then I put the postcard away in my old desk drawer where it had sat for ten years, and finally closed the book on that part of my life, and Tiki Island, forever.

THE END

APRIL 19, 2011

# AUTHOR'S NOTE

Detective Riggins is a recurring character in a series of pulp-noir novels I've been working on for years. He was first introduced to the public as a much older character in Murder Behind the Closet Door. Murder on Tiki Island is the second in the series, a prequel introducing Riggins as an already hardened detective at the age of twenty-eight. Juan, at the end of the story, is a character that Riggins meets in Murder Behind the Closet Door. If you don't know what the hell it is they're talking about at the end of the story, you'll just have to buy MBTCD for yourself to catch up!

*-Mahalos, Tiki Chris P.*

# ABOUT THE AUTHOR, CHRISTOPHER "TIKI CHRIS" PINTO

Christopher Pinto is the author/editor of Tiki Lounge Talk (TikiLoungeTalk.com), a web-lounge dedicated to remembering and celebrating the kool stuff from the Atomic Age and beyond, from big band music to cocktails at the Tiki Bar, and curator of The Retro Tiki Lounge Facebook page. He's been writing for over 25 years, has had several plays produced, and has won awards for his creative efforts. During the 1990s he was producer/director of a highly successful traveling mystery theater company in the Atlantic City area, StarDust Productions.

Pinto currently lives in South Florida with his wife Colleen, four birds, two cats, a miracle dog, a '53 Chevy hot rod and a Tiki Bar. Pinto moved to Fort Lauderdale, Florida in June of 2000, only one week after marrying his wife, Colleen. It was these major changes in his life that led to an avalanche of memories from his youth, including many happy days and nights spent on the Wildwood and Ocean City Boardwalks. He decided to write these memories down... and those notes became the basis for his first full-length novel, Murder Behind The Closet Door. (wildwoodmurdermystery.com). It was after moving to South Florida and becoming a regular visitor to the Florida Keys that he was inspired to write a tale set in the unique, mysterious, magical string of tropical islands.

Pinto was no newcomer to writing when he began penning MBTCD. He began writing at an early age and won several awards, including a creative writing award from the Philadelphia Bulletin at age twelve. In 1985 he wrote a full-length musical entitled "SwingTime", including the score, which was adapted for production in his senior year at Egg Harbor Township High School, NJ. After college, he began acting in shows at Elaine's Famous Dinner Theater in Cape May, NJ, where he starred in several shows over two years. His time in Cape May (and the adjacent Wildwoods) piqued his interest in the history, architecture and people of the area. Later he would use what he learned and experienced while writing Murder Behind the Closet Door and Murder on Tiki Island.

Pinto started his own traveling theater troupe in 1989, with its first show produced being "A Christmas Carolette", a spoof of the time-honored *A Christmas Carol*. This lead to the forming of StarDust Production, Southern New Jersey's premier traveling dinner theater company through 2000. Pinto wrote all the scripts for the shows performed, including "Wildwood Memories", which was put into production for a run at Neil's Oyster House in Wildwood…but was unfortunately never performed, due management changes at the restaurant (soon to be a novel, maybe?). Pinto's shows for StarDust Productions always maintained a retro/noir theme. From jazz music and vocal standards to shows set in the 1930s, '40s and '50s, every show transported the audience through space and time to a kooler, kookier and more swingin' age.

In addition to writing fiction and plays, Pinto has also written for the Atlantic City Press as well as several blogs and flash fiction websites, and is also an award-winning graphic designer and advertising Creative Director. He is an accomplished jazz and swing clarinetist and saxophone player and an avid collector of 20th century pop culture junk. In his spare time he restores and customizes vintage cars, including his own custom 1953 Chevy Bel-Air hot rod (named StarDust), digs swingin' standard tunes on the tenor horn, and of course, enjoys growing and sharing his collection of vintage memorabilia.

For more, visit StarDustMysteries.com or facebook.com/RetroTikiLounge.

Aloha From Tiki Island

Enjoy a delicious & mysterious Exotic Cocktail,
prepared from the original, secret recipes from
the famous resorts of Hawai'i

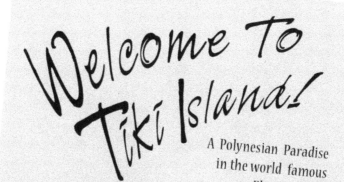

# Welcome To Tiki Island!

A Polynesian Paradise
in the world famous
Florida Keys.

Opening for the 1956 Season
September 1

Join us opening week-end for our exclusive

## Labor Day Luau

Hawaiian Music • Fresh Fruits • Hula Girls
Carved Roast Pork • Fire Dancers
Mysterious Exotic Cocktails

Tiki Island Hotel
& Polynesian Resort
#1 Tiki Island, FLA
Phone: Tiki-68

CPSIA information can be obtained
at www.ICGtesting.com
Printed in the USA
LVHW041728071118
596308LV00001B/172/P